Courtesy of Sven Nielson, painting from the Café de la regence

The Chess Players

Paul Morphy

FRANCES PARKINSON KEYES

The Chess Players

FARRAR, STRAUS AND CUDAHY

New York

Printed in the United States of America

Contents

PART ONE

"The Queen is the Strongest Piece on the Board"

January, 1825–February, 1829

"Early in 1726, Father de Beaubois set out [from New Orleans] for France, in order to recruit laborers for his own missions, and acquit himself of the important commission confided to him by the Governor of Louisiana. . . . On New Year's Day, 1727, the Ursulines, destined for Louisiana, assembled to offer their filial homage to Mother Mary of St. Augustine, whose nomination to the responsible charge of Superioress, had already been approved by Bishop St. Vallier, in a letter addressed to Father de Beaubois. . . . On the 22nd of February, the Ursulines . . . embarked on a ship named the GIRONDE . . . and, after five months of perilous navigation, reached the mouth of the Mississippi on the 23rd of July, 1727. . . . The first party reached New Orleans on the 6th of August. . . . Father de Beaubois conducted the Ursulines to the home assigned for their abode until the completion of the Convent. . . . On the evening of July 17, 1734, the Ursulines removed to the monastery, for which, we are told, they sighed as ardently as the Israelites of old, for the Promised Land. . . . On New Year's Day, 1821, the Ursulines, with the approbation of their ever kind father and devoted friend, the Rt. Reverend Bishop Du Bourg, decided to have another convent built on a plantation, purchased, on November 26th, 1818, in one of the most salubrious parts of the suburbs. The principle cause of this decision was the opening of streets through the Convent enclosure, for it was feared that they would prove an obstacle to the strict observance of the cloister rules. *On this occasion, the community was obliged to sell a good deal of real estate, in order to pay for the newly acquired property and to be able to defray the expenses of the building. The main edifice was finished in 1824.*"

The Ursulines in New Orleans, 1727–1925. Anonymous.
(P. J. Kenedy and Sons, New York.)

1.

"Reverend Mother, M. Le Carpentier has arrived to keep the appointment which you were good enough to grant him."

Mother St. Joseph de Laclotte, Superior of the Ursuline Convent of New Orleans, glanced at the time; the French clock facing her serviceable desk was just striking three. She smiled at the novice who had made the announcement and who now stood before her in an attitude of respectful attention.

"M. Le Carpentier is certainly on time to the minute. We must be equally punctilious. You may bring him here at once."

The novice bowed and, turning, noiselessly opened the door which she had closed with care behind her when she entered the small bare office a minute earlier. This time, she left it ajar and stood aside, bowing again, to admit the expected visitor.

The contrast between the Superior and her caller was striking. Although her bearing was one of great dignity, she was short and slight and her fine countenance was completely devoid of color. The sorrows and privations she had endured in the course of the French Revolution had left their mark even before she had embraced the cloistral life; and she had observed its fasts and mortifications to the letter. While she did not disdain the feasts of the Church, they had no special appeal for her. M. Le Carpentier, on the other hand, gave the immediate effect of a bon vivant. He was a large man, tall and well proportioned to such a degree that his portliness became him, making his figure seem impressive, rather than heavy. In like measure, the ruddiness of his face in no way detracted from the firmness of his features: a strong square chin, lips not over full, clear gray eyes beneath heavy black brows, a prominent, though shapely, nose. He was elegantly dressed, but this elegance did not take the form of flamboyance; the colors of his coat and breeches were rich, rather than bright, and only his flowered waistcoat betrayed a taste for finery which, if not crushed, was at least curbed. Everything about him bespoke prosperity, self-confidence and authority; if, despite all this, he still looked the bourgeois, rather than the aristocrat, the reason eluded the Superior, while she recognized the fact; and it was not often that she was puzzled, even momentarily. Slightly to her annoyance, the man roused her curiosity at the same time that he compelled her reluctant admiration. She inclined her head and spoke with courtesy tinged by a certain aloofness.

"M. Le Carpentier? Unless I am mistaken, this is the first time we have had the pleasure of welcoming you at our Convent."

"You are not mistaken, Reverend Mother. It is my impression that you make very few mistakes." The visitor also spoke with complete courtesy, but in his manner there was no aloofness; indeed, there was almost a hint of audacity. Nevertheless, the Superior did not find either his words or his manner of uttering them displeasing and, after a barely perceptible pause, he continued, "I have not wished to trespass upon your valuable time, when a call from me would have been merely an imposition—an honor for me, but all the same a purposeless intrusion."

"And this time, I take it, Monsieur, your visit has a purpose."

"Exactly, Reverend Mother. Have I your permission to tell you what it is, without preamble?"

"Pray do. Would you care to be seated?"

He thanked her, taking the chair she indicated, and placing his tall hat, spotless gloves and slender walking stick on a small nearby table. She noticed that he did all this without awkwardness or embarrassment; his manner had all the accustomed ease of a Creole gentleman. Yet, her first impression persisted: this was a man of the people whose acquired polish was superficial. Ambition, rather than instinct, was responsible for the fine showing he made.

"I believe it is no longer a secret," he said, without waiting for her to address him again, "that, with the approbation of the Bishop, your Community has been giving careful consideration to a change of headquarters—in short, that you are building a new convent on the tract of land on Jordan Avenue, near the levee, which you purchased several years ago, believing you would be assured of more privacy in the suburbs than is possible in the heart of the city."

"You are correctly informed, Monsieur. There is nothing in the least secret about our plans, which are already past a point of mere consideration. They form a definite project."

"Ah . . . then, perhaps, it's not indiscreet to say there is also a rumor to the effect that you might be induced to sell part of your present property, which, obviously, you will no longer require, and which will not be needed by the Bishop who, I understand, is to take possession of this noble building for his residence when you leave it."

"Again, you are correctly informed, Monsieur. The expense of erecting a suitable convent and school on our suburban property will be heavy. We must take the proper steps to meet it. Not that I wish to give the impression such an undertaking is a burden we are unwilling or unable to assume. We are confident, with God's help, that we can achieve our ends. Nevertheless—"

"Nevertheless, the prospect of a purchaser for a substantial portion of your present holdings would not be unwelcome, would it, Reverend Mother?"

The interruption had displeased the Superior. A gentleman would not have broken in upon her speech as Le Carpentier had done, and her feeling, previously vague, that for all his fine clothes and easy manners, the man was an upstart, took more substantial form. As this happened, the curiosity which had been tinged by admiration, began to subside. She was not curious any more; she saw him for what he was, and it was a type she did not in the least admire. But she was a practical woman and a wise administrator. She could not allow personal prejudice to stand in the way of a possible transaction which might be of advantage to the Community and its charges —those young girls whom it was her duty and mission to educate as Christian gentlewomen. It was on their account that she had consented to the move. As far as she was personally concerned—and she knew this was true in the case of many of her other nuns—it would be a wrench to leave the convent which the Community had built to replace their first temporary headquarters and which they had now occupied for nearly ninety years. With this as their center, they had seen the population in panic over Indian massacres; they had nursed the citizens during the epidemics which threatened destruction to the colony; they had welcomed the peasants and orphans from France, guaranteed virtuous by their parish priests, who had been sent over as wives for the colonists by order of the Duke of Orléans— maidens who had become known as the Casket Girls, because each had carried a small box strapped to her shoulders, containing her dowry from the king and consisting of sheets and a blanket, stockings, headdresses and a pelisse. The nuns had also watched O'Reilly's fleet, as it sailed up the river, when Louisiana was ceded to Spain from France and, later, the reversal of this process, when the Spanish flag was lowered before the French tricolor. And finally, they had seen the tricolor replaced by the Stars and Stripes after the so-called Louisiana Purchase; and, during the Battle of Chalmette, they had prayed to Our Lady of Prompt Succor that it should not fall before the Union Jack—a prayer most gloriously answered. Every window, every stone on the place was permeated with history. Moreover, the convent was one of the few important structures, typically French in character, which had survived two disastrous fires in the city, thanks to its protected location, with the river on one side of it and a great garden on the other. The new city, which was now taking shape, was Spanish in form, as well as in feeling and direction; and, like most Frenchwomen, Mother St. Joseph had no natural love for anything or anyone Spanish, though she had stood by her post, instead of returning to her homeland, as many of her spiritual sisters and daughters had done. The place was unspeakably dear to her: the pantry, the linen room and the infirmary, to only a slight degree less than the sacristy and the chapel; the cemetery was sacred ground. She recognized that the ordinance, providing for a new street which would go straight through the convent enclosure, would prove an obstacle to the strict adherence to the cloistral rules which must be observed at all costs; but the realization brought her no solace. She sighed and then started a little, conscious that her reflections had delayed her answer and that her visitor was waiting for this. She forced herself to speak, without giving any sign of offense, though her words were weighted with caution.

"That would depend, of course, Monsieur, upon the circumstances. If these were favorable. . . ."

He interrupted her a second time. "I believe you would consider them so. The prospective purchaser would not haggle as to price and he would pay cash. The portion of the property in which he is interested is that directly across the street from your present convent. He would require a large corner lot—sufficiently spacious for a garden and an orchard, as well as a commodious residence—and slave quarters in the rear. In fact, he has already selected an architect to draw the plans for him—provided, of course, that no impediment is placed in the way of the sale."

"May I say, Monsieur, that you seem very well informed concerning the prospective purchaser to whom you refer? It is necessary that he should remain anonymous?"

"No, Reverend Mother. As I think you have already guessed, he and your present visitor are one and the same. I trust the fact that I am an auctioneer would not prejudice you against the transaction?"

An auctioneer! Of course! Why had she not instantly realized that this was the celebrated slave dealer known as the "double-tongued," not only because he was bilingual, but because he could shift as quickly and easily from one side of an argument, or one aspect of a bargain, to another? Le Carpentier was by no means an uncommon name, or Joseph, either; there were probably half a dozen Joseph Le Carpentiers in New Orleans at the time; it had never once entered her head that the writer of a note, asking for an appointment about "an urgent matter," was the trader, whose traffic in human flesh had been carried on in such a way as to give him a bad name. What could a slave dealer of this type want with the Superior of the Ursuline Convent? Moreover, there had been rumors, a few years past, that he had aided and abetted Spanish piracy through connections with Beluche, the notorious lieutenant of the still more notorious Lafitte. For a moment, she almost forgot that she was a nun; she was still the French aristocrat, one of the *haute noblesse,* most of whom, including every member of her family, except herself, had been guillotined. Though she had succeeded in detaching herself completely from worldly goods and pleasures, she had never changed her ideas as to what constituted good breeding and good manners . . . and she had not forgotten that Spaniards, even those who had newly declared their independence from the mother country, were the traditional enemies of France. . . .

"I see that I should have identified myself more promptly," the visitor was saying. "I was mistaken in believing myself so well known that it would be unnecessary."

There was more than assurance in his voice now; a certain arrogance had crept into it. He was not apologizing for his nefarious trade; he was bragging about its réclame. Mother St. Joseph tried to suppress the mounting antagonism which his attitude aroused.

"I must ask you to excuse my failure to place you at once," she said quietly. "You are, of course, a famous figure. But, since it is rather an infrequent occurrence—at least, in my experience—for a cloistered nun to number an auctioneer among her acquaintances, perhaps you will overlook my lack of perceptivity. . . . You wish to acquire this property as the site of your personal residence, Monsieur?"

"As a residence for myself and my family, Reverend Mother."

"And your family consists of—"

"My wife, nee Modeste Blache—the daughter of Don Luis Carlos Blache and Marie de Tournade—and our four children: Amenaïde and Charles, who are still in the nursery; Amélie, who is sixteen and who, I am sorry to say, is rather sickly and shy, and our eldest, Louise Thérèse Félicité Telcide. We call her Telcide and it is especially about her that I wish to speak with you. She has just celebrated her eighteenth birthday and we think she is very lovely. So, apparently, do many others. She is also very talented—she plays the piano and the harp and has a pleasing mezzo-soprano voice. Moreover, she speaks Italian almost as well as she does French and English. We have already had several requests for her hand. Nothing is, as yet, decided; but among the aspirants is a young gentleman of fine family, whom we are inclined to regard very highly. We know, my wife and I, that our daughter's background does not compare favorably with his, that my line of work does not recommend itself to social recognition—any more than it recommended itself to you, Reverend Mother. But we believe that, with Telcide's natural intelligence and beauty and with the advantages we are prepared to give her, she could prove herself worthy of a loftier station. We are striving to see that she has it." He paused and, for the first time, spoke hesitantly, almost humbly. "Perhaps, you will consider these personal details superfluous, Reverend Mother. I mention them only so that you may understand that the happiness and welfare of a beloved daughter are of great importance to me."

Involuntarily, the Superior realized that her antagonism to the man before her was abating. True, Le Carpentier was ambitious. But the ambition was not, after all, for himself; it was for his child, and its basis was one of parental pride and parental tenderness.

"I do not think that these personal details are superfluous," she said, with a gentleness which surprised herself as well as her caller. "I think they have a distinct bearing on your wish to acquire the property. Moreover, your attitude toward your daughter does you credit. Of course, you are aware that the decision concerning a sale would not rest with me alone. I must confer with the Bishop first of all and then with other advisors, besides consulting the Community. And I must give the matter thought and prayer. But I may say this much: unless something which has not been mentioned arises to change my feelings, I shall recommend that your request be given proper consideration."

Joseph Le Carpentier strode from the Superior's office without a glance at the beautiful staircase, curving upward from the spacious entrance hall, or in the direction of the two handsome parlors which opened from it. Then, oblivious both of its fragrance and of its beauty, he walked quickly through the walled herb garden which separated the Ursuline Convent from Chartres Street. But, when he reached the banquette, he stopped and gazed fixedly in front of him for some moments. Actually, there was nothing arresting to look at—green grass, a few shrubs and trees, on land otherwise empty. But, in his mind's eye, he already saw the house he intended to build there, which would outdo in elegance and luxury any belonging to the families of his acquaintance. And this house, as he visualized it, was not empty; in it, he saw Telcide, encircled with suitable admirers, while he and his wife hovered hospitably and benevolently in the background. He could hear light laughter, pleasant music, the tinkling sound of refreshing drinks; he could smell the scent of flowers and savory foods. And later, there would be other sights and other sounds to delight him—a happy young couple, toddling grandchildren, baby voices, lullabies. . . .

His first approach to the Superior had been inept; he should never have assumed she would not be prejudiced against him because he was an auctioneer. Of course she was prejudiced—that was only natural. Slave trading was legal enough, as he handled it; there was nothing secret about his auction rooms on the corner of Chartres and St. Louis streets or what went on there; he did not, like the Lafittes, use a blacksmith's shop for a front, and traffic illicitly in "black ivory," seizing Negroes from Spanish slave ships and selling them for a dollar a pound, instead of for a fair price—which could easily run to a thousand dollars. But he had dealt with Lafitte, both directly and through the latter's intermediary, Beluche, in matters advantageous to them all, though these were mostly unconnected with "black ivory"; and he drew much of his stock from the notorious "slave farm" in the swamps near New Orleans, where the savage imports from Africa were confined until they were either cowed or killed. When the wretched survivors had learned the rudiments of civilization, so that they could wield an ax or plow a field, they were brought into the city and sold to Le Carpentier and other traders—McCoy, Dutillet and Mossey, for instance.

Nevertheless, however careful he had been to observe the letter of the law, the slave farm had given him and its other patrons a bad name—perhaps even a worse one than those pirates who accommodated the aristocracy with stolen wares at a nominal price. Auctioneers were considered as belonging to a low stratum of society. Le Carpentier's appointment to the committee, formed to improve the deplorable state of the mail service in New Orleans, showed that he was more highly regarded than many others; but probably the news of this appointment had not penetrated the solid walls of the Ursuline Convent, even though rumors of a less favorable nature might well have done so. However, he felt reasonably sure that the disclosure of his wife's maiden name had made a favorable impression; the Blaches were undoubtedly a cut above the Le Carpentiers in the world. And, at the end, he had won the Superior over by his talk about Telcide and Telcide's future. At heart, they were much alike, these nuns, he told himself comfortably, shrugging his shoulders slightly; they had no pleasures and pastimes, no love life of their own; hence, their vicarious enjoyment in the love life of others was always deeper, tinged though it might be by jealousy. Fortunately, the Superior had not interpreted his concern to mean that his daughter was merely a pawn in the game he was playing. . . .

In the gathering dusk, he walked slowly toward the house on Bourbon Street, which differed so greatly from the mansion of his dreams. This present home of his was only a story and a half high, and constructed of *briques entre poteaux*—plastered brick supported by solid beams, not unlike the half-timbered houses of Normandy; and it contained only four rooms, besides the *cabinets* which led, by narrow interior staircases, from the two large bedrooms back of the two parlors. Until lately, it had seemed to suffice: one of the large bedrooms was, of course, the conjugal chamber; Amenaïde and Charles shared the other with their nurse; Telcide and Amélie slept in the *cabinets*. But this left the family without a guest room—a *chambre à donner* —even though Charles, when he was older, would occupy the *garconnière* which faced the slave quarters in the grass plot at the rear, and was its twin in size and shape. The terrace which "gave" on this grass plot served as a dining room in all but the coldest weather; it was conveniently near the quarters where the cooking was done, and food arrived hot to the table. During the rare periods of severe weather, one of the two parlors made do for dining and no one minded. But now Le Carpentier was through with such cramping and such makeshifts for both sleeping and dining. . . .

As he opened the door which led directly from the street into one of the small square parlors, Telcide, who had been seated at the piano, rose quickly and ran toward him. It was seldom that she broke off in this way and the abruptness of the action surprised her father. At the same time, he realized that he had never seen her look lovelier. Her dark hair was bound with a narrow blue ribbon and, beneath this, her curls cascaded over her shoulders. Her highwaisted white dress was belted in the same pale blue, just below her budding breasts, and her neck and arms were bare. She was wreathed in smiles. Obviously, something had made her very happy.

"Alonzo has been here again," she said. "He brought me all those flowers." She indicated the overflowing vases on either side of the piano. "He wanted very much to see you, too, Papa, but he could not wait, because of some legal appointment. But it does not matter. We had a nice visit, anyway, and he said he would return later and that then his father would come with him. It seems that you and Don Diego are to play chess together this evening."

"Yes, yes. So we are. I am glad you reminded me, *chère*. I have been thinking of so many other things that, actually, I had quite forgotten about that game. Will you set up the board while I return to my office for a few minutes? There are some papers I need to put in order, preparatory to important transactions which I have just learned may come up as soon as tomorrow morning."

Telcide nodded, happily, and began taking the chessmen of lemonwood and ebony from the box in which they were kept. The sight of his daughter, the fresh realization of her innocent love, had roused new fears in Le Carpentier's breast. He must make sure that nothing would come to light which would confirm certain suspicions that he was afraid the Superior still entertained—not that he thought Lafitte or Beluche had ever been responsible for a "leak" about his dealings with them; it would be detrimental to their interests, as well as his own, to risk any disclosures; and he himself had always been circumspect. Still. . . .

As he strode rapidly along toward his auction rooms, now closed for the day, he found himself dwelling, inescapably, on the cause for the Superior's possible suspicions: some years earlier, a vessel called *La Caridad*, which belonged to Christobal Juando, a Spanish merchant with headquarters in Santiago de Cuba, was on her way back to her home port from New Haven, where she had gone with a cargo of provisions. She had almost reached her destination when she was attacked by two vessels which, at first, displayed the American ensign and then raised the flag of the newly established Republic of Cartagena. After a gallant but futile show of resistance, *La Caridad* surrendered. Her crew was set on shore and the cargo ship was towed away and lost to sight.

A few months later, an imposing vessel appeared for the first time in the harbor of Cartagena. Two cannon thrust their noses from her portholes and she carried a crew of ninety men, heavily armed with guns, pistols, swords and daggers. She had a commission signed by the president and the war secretary of Cartagena and the lettering on her side proclaimed her to be the *General Bolívar*. Nevertheless, not a few persons recognized her as *La Caridad* in a state of transformation. She was authorized to "take all ships and property of the Spanish nation and its dependencies," which she promptly proceeded to do. In the course of the next few months, however, she somewhat mysteriously changed hands. Her new owner, José Guerra y Poseda, was not an officer, but a merchant of Cartagena; her commission was signed by Beluche, the lieutenant of Lafitte; her captain was one Joseph Clements. He was given a letter which plainly revealed that much of the time unaccounted for, after the disappearance of *La Caridad*, had been spent somewhere in Lafitte's Barataria hideout. Clements carried with him a letter which, in due course, he presented with a flourish to Le Carpentier.

"I give you the command of the *General Bolívar*, because you have my entire confidence. May the wind permit you to raise anchor and make sail for New Orleans. The corsair, *Independence*, of Cartagena, with the blessing of the Pope, will convoy you until you are in Spanish waters. On board you will observe the strictest discipline, and conform with the laws of the government. Do not, for any motive whatsoever, operate alone, and do not invite pursuit. You will protect neutral ships, which you will be bound to restore, according to the laws of the sea. If, in the course of your voyage, you capture any Spanish vessel (the value of which cannot be identified), send the booty to Cartagena and burn the vessel; such is the will of the president. As soon as you arrive in New Orleans, you will call upon M. Le Carpentier, who will advance you the money necessary to repair your privateer, which work you will hasten with all possible diligence, and put back to sea, and speed to Cartagena.

"I salute you in friendship.

Beluche."

"If for any reason you cannot have the ship repaired, let M. Le Carpentier dispose of it, but remember the vessel belongs to the government and, therefore, sell it to the best advantage."

Presumably, Clements had a copy of that letter and so did Lafitte and Poseda. This could not be helped; it could only be hoped that neither of these, nor the subsequent activities of the *General Bolívar*, with which Le Carpentier was connected, would come to light—at least, not until after Telcide and Alonzo were safely married. For the moment, all Joseph could do was to destroy his own copy of the letter. That was what he was now hurrying off to do.

He unlocked the door of his private office, then the secretary where he kept his papers and, lastly, slid aside the panels which hid a secret compartment. Only then did he breathe a sigh of relief. The letter from Beluche was where he had put it, safe from prying eyes. He read it through, to make sure it was still intact, and then he tore it into tiny pieces. Still unsatisfied, he gathered up the scraps and made a neat little pile of them in the fireplace, where he watched them burn. Not until the last spark had faded from the ashes did he look away, relock the secretary and his office and return to his home.

Again Telcide greeted him with effusive affection. The chessboard was set up, everything was in readiness for the game. Don Diego and Alonzo would be there at any minute now and Joseph Le Carpentier was prepared for them.

THE MORPHY COAT-OF-ARMS.

Morphy, alias Murphy. Quarterly argent and gules; four lions rampant interchanged; over all on a Fesse Sable three garbs or, Crest; a lion rampant holding a garb. (No Motto.)

"I, Don Joseph de Jaudenes, Commissionary of the Royal Forces of His Catholic Majesty and His Chargé d'Affaires in the United States of America, etc., etc.

"Inasmuch as the King our Sovereign (whom God preserve) has deigned to authorize me to appoint the Consuls whom I shall consider necessary to protect the Commerce of Spain with the United States.

"Therefore, and having confidence, in the love and zeal of Your Honour, Don Diego Morphy, towards his Majesty, and ability to execute these matters with full integrity and precision, do purpose to appoint and by these presents do appoint you, in the name of the King, our Sovereign, Consul of Spain for the States of North and South Carolina and Georgia with headquarters in the City of Charleston; and by these presents I further pray and command all good Spaniards who reside or may reside hereafter, or pass through or hereafter may pass through the said States, or who may disembark at any port therein, to pay Your Honour all the submission and respect which the Laws of Spain and the pleasure of His Majesty may decree, to the end, that they may deserve the protection which the King affords to His Royal vassals through you, acting as his Consul where to Your Honour will give the most immediate attention; and at the same time I beseech in the name of the King, my Sovereign, that all the Magistrates and other officials of the United States, and especially of the States of North and South Carolina and Georgia, shall forthwith upon the recognition of Your Honour as Consul of Spain for the aforesaid States by the President of the United States, extend to you all the protection, hospitality and attention which are in effect between all civilized nations.

"Granted at Philadelphia and signed by my hand and sealed under my patent, and recorded by the Secretary of His Majesty, this thirty-first day of January, 1795."

(Signed)   Joseph de Jaudenes.

Translation, from the Spanish, of Don Diego Morphy's Commission as Spanish Consul.

(Courtesy of the Good Companion Chess Problem Club of Philadelphia.)

2.

Don Diego Omorfu—as he would still have preferred to designate himself, though, through force of circumstances, Omorfu had become Morphy—was, by birth, a *Madrileño* or a *Malagueño*—some said one, some said the other; and if, in Spain, his forebears had been *caballeros*, rather than grandees, he still managed, after years of exile, to give the impression that it was to the latter group that they really belonged. This impression was intensified by the fact that he was formal of manner, slender and graceful of build and austere of countenance; and that he always dressed in elegant old-style black, with knee breeches, lace ruffles at the wrists and silver shoe buckles, instead of wearing the flowered waistcoats, the richly colored coats and the pantaloons strapped under the boots which had become the current fashion. Just why he had emigrated to San Domingo, and there married an Irish girl named Molly Creagh, he never told anyone in New Orleans and no one ever had the effrontery to ask. It was known, however, that during a Negro uprising he had skillfully maneuvered the escape of his wife and infant child by sending Molly, with a basket over her arm, to an English vessel anchored in the harbor. The basket allegedly held vegetables, and the announced purpose of the trip was to sell these to the captain of the man-of-war, who was short of provender for his crew.

"To be sure, there *were* vegetables in the basket," Alonzo Morphy, Don Diego's son, had told Telcide Le Carpentier when she listened, wide-eyed with excitement, to this tale. "At least, there was a thin layer of them on top of it. Underneath them was a baby, and the captain conveyed this baby and his mother safely to Philadelphia."

"And you were the baby?" Telcide asked breathlessly.

"No, no, the baby was my elder brother, or rather my half-brother. I have two half-brothers, Diego and Ernesto, and two half-sisters, Matilde and Elena. Several months after this thrilling escape I have told you about, my father managed to slip away from Cap Français and join his family. Later on, they moved to Charleston, which was selected for his headquarters when he was appointed Consul of Spain for the State of Georgia and both Carolinas, and which he still claims is the peer of New Orleans in charm and culture."

"Surely you do not agree with him in that, Alonzo!"

"I can just barely remember Charleston. You see, I was very young—only five—when the family left there. But my father is seldom wrong about anything."

"Then he must have been right to move to New Orleans! And he must have done so because he thought it surpassed Charleston in every way. Otherwise, he would not have stayed, even if he came to look it over!"

"He did not come to look it over. He came because he was appointed Spanish Consul here, which was considered a promotion. But he left with regret. And some time before that he had lost his first wife—the young Irish lady who carried the vegetable basket with such happy results—and had married my mother. Her maiden name was Louisa Peire and she belonged to a prominent Huguenot family. My three own sisters and I are her children."

"A Huguenot family?" Telcide said doubtfully. "But Huguenots are heretics, aren't they?"

"My mother's family would not thank you for referring to it in that way; and I assure you it is among the most aristocratic in Charleston."

Momentarily, Alonzo spoke arrogantly, as his father was in the habit of doing, and Telcide felt a swift pang of jealousy. The Le Carpentiers, as had often been brought home to her, were not among the greatest aristocrats of New Orleans. In fact, they were not aristocrats at all.

"Be that as it may, we are all good Catholics in this generation," Alonzo said more mildly. "You are not going to let the fact that my mother was once a Huguenot make any difference, are you, *chère?*"

Telcide shook her head. She knew that nothing was going to make any difference, as far as Alonzo was concerned, if she could only have him. She had lost her heart to him the first time she had laid eyes on him; and she thought—though of this she could not be sure—that he had not remained unmoved, either. But, so far, he had not said anything to commit himself. She did not know, for sure, whether this was because he did not want to himself, or because Don Diego did not want him to. . . .

For Don Diego, as has been said, was still very much the Spanish grandee in manners and viewpoint. He would have never visited the Le Carpentiers had it not been for the fact that Joseph Le Carpentier, like himself, was an avid and accomplished chess player. True, his eldest son, Ernesto, also excelled in the game; but Don Diego wanted to play chess every evening and Ernesto, very much the young man about town, was not always available. Consequently, when Ernesto was out with other gay blades, Don Diego visited the Le Carpentiers. He had been doing this for a time before he realized that his younger son, Alonzo who—as boys went—was becoming a good chess player, too, and who often accompanied him, had an ulterior purpose in doing so.

He had, however, begun to realize it only too well when he went for his customary game on the same evening that Joseph Le Carpentier made his offer for the property opposite the Ursuline Convent. Don Diego also realized, as he took his seat before the black and tan board, where the chessmen of ebony and lemonwood were already set up, that his host, always inclined to conviviality, seemed to be in unusually high spirits, even for him; likewise, that Telcide, the *jeune fille de la maison*, though perfectly respectful, seemed less overawed than usual by the guest's presence. Was it possible that Alonzo had so far forgotten himself as to speak to her father—or even to address her personally—without full parental authority? Don Diego found it hard to believe that such a lapse from filial duty would have occurred, for practical as well as sentimental reasons. True, Alonzo had been graduated from the College of Orleans with high honors, had done equally well in his legal studies and had been admitted to practice by the Supreme Court of Louisiana. But his independent means were limited. He still drew an allowance from his father and this, with his earnings, barely sufficed to meet his expenses, for his tastes and habits called for lavish living. Unless he were prepared to make sacrifices, which Don Diego hoped there was reason to doubt, Alonzo could hardly afford a wife, even if she brought with her a very substantial dowry as a bride. And, though Le Carpentier appeared to be prosperous, he could hardly be wealthy, or he would be living in a more elegant establishment than this pleasant, but small and unpretentious, half-timbered house on Bourbon Street.

The usual amenities had been observed before the two men took their places on either side of the chessboard: inquiries as to the respective health of their families—fortunately good; remarks on the weather—unusually mild; the offer and acceptance of a friendly glass of good French wine and an excellent Havana cigar. Then the two experts were ready for the real business at hand.

Le Carpentier picked up two Pawns, put them behind his back and, bringing his closed hands forward, invited Morphy to choose which he should open. Morphy, after a moment of apparently intense deliberation, chose the right, which proved to contain the white Pawn, thereby giving him the privilege of first move. He advanced the King's Pawn two squares and Le Carpentier, playing with the black pieces, made a like move. Having thereby gained the same advantage as his adversary, he leaned back to await the next play and spoke genially.

"I came very near to being late for our game this evening. I had an appointment with the Superior of the Ursuline Convent. You know her, of course?"

"Reverend Mother St. Joseph? Certainly. My younger daughters have all attended her school," Morphy replied, moving his King's Knight to the King's Bishop's third square. He was too polite to *say* that he was surprised Le Carpentier's daughter had not been similarly educated, but this was evident from his manner. Le Carpentier pretended not to notice and asked,

"But you have had no occasion to approach her on a matter of business?"

"No, never," Morphy answered, his manner indicating that he thought it strange Le Carpentier should have done so. He knew perfectly well that the servants at the convent were not selected from the slave farm in the swamps from which Le Carpentier drew most of his stock in trade. The host, however, showed no signs of embarrassment as he replied with Knight to the Queen's Bishop's third.

"I found the Superior's manner somewhat haughty and aloof at first," he went on conversationally. "Possibly, this was my own fault. I am not accustomed to convents and I did not approach her as tactfully as I should have. But gradually she softened. I could see that the proposal I made to her had a certain appeal, when I succeeded in explaining its purpose to her."

Without inquiry into the nature of the purpose, Morphy moved his Bishop to the Bishop's fourth square and, for the next few moments, there was silence while Le Carpentier replied with his Bishop to the Bishop's fourth square. Morphy castled on the King's side and Le Carpentier moved his Knight to the Bishop's third.

Then Le Carpentier spoke again. "I knew that the Ursulines were preparing to move their establishment to a different site and that they needed money to build and equip their new plant. Also, that the Bishop, who is soon to take possession of the present convent, would not require all the land that goes with it." While his host was speaking, Morphy moved his Pawn to the Queen's third square, and Le Carpentier replied with the same move, as he went on talking. "The two circumstances combined to make me feel the moment propitious for suggesting a transaction which would be mutually advantageous: the Ursulines might sell some of their Chartres Street property in order to finance their suburban property. I might secure a lot of land for a residence more suited to my needs than this one."

At this point, Morphy was not able to restrain his curiosity and played somewhat hastily, moving his Bishop to the King's Knight's fifth, as he remarked, "So you feel this pleasant little house doesn't meet them?"

"I have felt so for some time," Le Carpentier replied, advancing the Pawn to the King's Rook's third. "But I have not previously been able to find anything that did. Now, I believe I have. My offer was for a large corner lot, and I stated plainly that I would pay cash, without haggling over the price. I have reason to believe the offer will be accepted."

"And then?" Morphy inquired, playing the Bishop to the Rook's fourth.

"And then, of course, I shall engage an architect to draw plans and a builder to carry them out. I propose to do everything on a spacious scale. We must begin to consider my elder daughter's marriage as an eventuality that will not be far in the future. Naturally, we shall follow our Creole custom of having her spend her honeymoon in her parents' house. It is her mother's desire and mine that her bridal apartment shall be in every way worthy of so lovely a being." He paused and moved the Pawn to the King's Knight's fourth. "I trust Your Excellency will forgive a fond father for referring to a beloved child in this way?"

"It is natural and fitting that he should. Am I anticipating overmuch when I ask if you are considering this house you hope to build not only as the residence of Mme Le Carpentier and yourself and as the proper setting of your daughter's honeymoon, but also as the more or less permanent residence of the charming Telcide and her fortunate husband?"

"You have sized up the situation most accurately. Telcide is still young. Though her mother and I would not oppose an early marriage—providing, of course, the applicant for her hand were acceptable to us—we would wish to keep her under our wing for some time to come. It is also better, in our opinion, that there should not be too much disparity between the ages of husband and wife. Therefore, if Telcide married in the near future, her bridegroom would also be young and, however promising in his chosen career, probably not yet a man of substantial means. Though, with Telcide's dowry—which will, of course, be a handsome one—it is doubtful that they could maintain an independent establishment on the scale that I desire for my daughter. Therefore, I shall insist that she remain under my roof."

Without replying, Morphy, obviously deep in thoughts not wholly confined to chess, moved the Bishop to the Knight's third.

"Naturally, the family of Telcide's husband will be made welcome at all times," Le Carpentier went on, moving the Pawn to the King's Rook's fourth. "I am thinking not only of a beautiful bridal chamber and the corresponding apartments, including *cabinets*. I visualize, also a *salle de compagnie* and a dining room of ample proportions. Likewise, quarters for an adequate number of slaves to provide efficient service—slaves who will, of course, be selected from those already trained in our best families—a coachman, cook and butler, scullery maids, parlormaids and chambermaids, personal body servants and, in due time, I hope, nurses."

He had become so absorbed in this rosy vision that he was caught unawares when Morphy captured the Knight's Pawn with his Knight. The reluctant recognition of this was accompanied by silence, which Morphy made no attempt to break. There was a perceptible but pregnant pause, in both conversation and action; then Morphy said, rather hesitantly, that he had not realized Le Carpentier's plans took such definite and elaborate form.

"Yes, indeed," Le Carpentier assured his guest, playing Pawn to Rook's fifth. "If I understand the Superior correctly, I shall have her answer within a few days. And I am willing to wager with any odds you choose, that it will be favorable."

"I will not wager with you about this, my friend. I am convinced that

I should lose on that basis, though I do not seem to be doing so now," Morphy answered, capturing the Pawn with his Knight. "And, having secured the property, I assume you will start building operations promptly?"

"I certainly shall," Le Carpentier retorted, casually disregarding his temporary setback and, in his turn, scoring an advantage by removing the Bishop with his Pawn. "And, as soon as these are completed, we will have a housewarming that I hope will take the form of a wedding. What could be more appropriate?"

"Nothing," conceded Morphy, taking the Queen with his Knight, "provided, of course, that there has been an appropriate betrothal in the meantime."

"That I am taking for granted. I may tell you, in confidence, that Telcide has only to make her choice—subject to parental approval, of course." He moved the Bishop to the King's Knight's fifth square. "And she has, at present, no less than four suitors, any one of whom would meet the requirements of her mother and myself."

"So many?" inquired Morphy, moving his Queen to the Queen's second square.

"I assure you I am not exaggerating. But, naturally, many things must be taken into consideration—a suitor's family background, which must be good; his personality, which must be pleasing; his character, which must be above reproach; his ability, which must be outstanding." Le Carpentier paused to move his Knight to Queen's fifth. "And then, of course, Telcide's own preferences, if these seem to have a basis of sound sense and not mere infatuation. . . . Yes, my dear, what is it?"

It was tacitly understood that the chess games should not be interrupted; it had never happened before. Yet, here was Telcide, who had come noiselessly into the room and was now standing behind her father's chair, looking across at Don Diego with an expression at one and the same time beguiling and disarming. He had not remembered that she was so beautiful and, for all her innocence, so provocative. He was not only surprised; he was startled. He played Knight to Bishop's third and Le Carpentier moved Knight to Bishop's sixth, with the triumphant exclamation of "Check!" In a desperate effort to extricate himself from certain defeat, Morphy took the Knight with his Pawn; but Le Carpentier promptly retaliated by taking the Pawn with Queen's Bishop. Morphy gazed, almost unbelievingly, first at the board and, secondly, at his smiling opponent. Then he spoke, slowly but firmly.

"I see it is useless to continue this struggle, my friend," he said. "You will win, whatever position I take—either here at this table or in our general relation to each other. *Le jeux est fait.* Shall we ask Alonzo to join us?"

DEED OF SALE OF LAND

by Joseph Le Carpentier and his wife to Joseph St. Cyr.

June 26th, 1827, appeared before Joseph Arnaud, Notary Public at New Orleans in the State of Louisiana, in the presence of the witnesses hereafter named and whose signatures are affixed:

M. Joseph Le Carpentier and the Lady Modeste Blache, his wife, who live together in this city; the said Lady assisted and authorized by her aforementioned spouse to the effect of what follows: these persons each for that which concerns himself, have by these presents jointly and separately sold, ceded and transported against all disorders, transfers, mortgages, evictions and other obstacles of every kind, to M. Joseph St. Cyr, also living in this city, here present and accepting for himself, his heirs and others having legal rights:

A plot of land, situated in this city, on Bourbon Street between Dumaine and St. Philip, measuring forty-two feet, nine or ten inches in width, French measure, and a hundred feet in depth; bordered on one side by the property of Mr. Stephen Corderiola and others, and on the other side by that of the widowed Lady Fleytas, and in the rear by that of Mme Auxere, together with the half-timbered house, roofed with shingles, and all the other appendages and outbuildings on the property. . . .

The present sale is made for the price and sum of five thousand five hundred piasters. . . .

Condensed translation of the original French document on file in the office of Custodian of Notarial Records, Parish of Orleans, State of Louisiana.

3.

Joseph Le Carpentier was right in believing he would have the Superior's answer within a few days and that it would be favorable; the main building of the new plant on Jordan Avenue was already finished and Mère St. Joseph was eager to take possession of it as speedily as possible. Le Carpentier's prompt and liberal payment for part of the Ursulines' original property greatly facilitated her arrangements, and she was able to close her consciousness, both to regret at leaving the convent which had so many and such precious associations for her, and to her repugnance toward her benefactor's trade. However, occasions for delay arose from unexpected quarters.

In the first place, there were disagreements which took a long time to iron out, regarding the style and placement of the new house. Le Carpentier had visualized a two story brick residence with kitchen and slave quarters, also two stories high and also made of brick, in the rear; these three buildings he proposed to locate in the center of his lot, with a yard forty feet wide on either side. The residence was to have a front gallery extending the full width of the house, and the steps were to ascend within the porch, as they did in many plantation houses at that period. The central hall was not to reach all the way to the front, nor was there to be a central entrance; instead, two large rooms with a double fireplace between them were to open upon the gallery. Le Carpentier was wholly satisfied with the drawings for this plan and made arrangements with four presumably reliable firms to do the work: Thomas Roe and Alonzo West contracted for the carpentry and millwork; Peter Ogier and Justin Williams for the masonry. But when Diego Morphy was shown the architectural drawings he objected to them violently.

"That is not in the least the sort of house I thought you had in mind when you talked to me about your project!" he exclaimed, disdainfully pushing the plans to one side.

"Why, what is the matter with it?" There was amazement no less than indignation in Le Carpentier's voice as he answered.

Morphy drew the drawings nearer again and placed an accusing finger on the portion which showed the two front rooms. "Have you not lived long enough in a house where every Tom, Dick and Harry can enter your parlor directly from the street, if they wish to do so?" he inquired. "What kind of proper privacy is possible without a central entrance and a central hall? With those, a knock at the door can be answered, as it should be, by a servant, and an unwelcome visitor can be sent away, or left cooling his heels in the corridor, instead of being perforce received immediately into the bosom of the family. Telcide may be approaching the most melodious bars of some musical masterpiece; Mme Le Carpentier may be embroidering a beautiful shift for her daughter's trousseau, with just time to finish her stitchery before dark; worst of all, you and I may be at the most critical point of a chess game and—clop! clop! here is a tiresome gossip or an importunate tradesman or even a filthy beggar, clamoring for admittance. The melody becomes a jangle of inharmonious sounds; twilight descends and the wedding garment remains unfinished; and your Bishop takes my Pawn, exactly as this happened the evening I was hurried into a rash agreement because of Telcide's entrance! After such interruptions it is impossible to proceed as before, whether with music or needlework or chess. No, no, my friend, I cannot agree that such a house as you have in mind would be a suitable residence for my son. As you must know, he is already a representative to the state legislature and there is now every prospect that he may be the next attorney general of Louisiana. Do you want him at the beck and call of every drunken vagrant in need of legal advice?"

A hot retort rose to Le Carpentier's lips, but, fortunately, failed to pass them; he could not afford to offend Don Diego, either for Telcide's sake or his own. It was still possible that his connection with the profits of the *General Bolívar* might come to light. But her name had been changed again, this time to the *Atalanta;* it was the custom of the Baratarians to employ different names for their merchant ships, in order to complicate investigation of their illegal actions, and even to throw dust in the eyes of their sponsors, the Cartagenians. Apparently, their actions had also blinded most residents of New Orleans, Don Diego among them, for if he had ever heard of Le Carpentier's connection with the vessel, which had had so many aliases, he would certainly have brought the matter up. And the poor ship had finally been seized, when Patterson raided Barataria, and brought to New Orleans as booty of war. It had been sold at auction to a highly respected citizen, Captain Thomas Reynaud, and Reynaud had never confronted Le Carpentier with questions about her past. If he did not, it was improbable that Don Diego would ever do so, either. At all events, this was not the moment to worry about it. Le Carpentier tried to say that, of course, Alonzo's clients would seek him only at his office, that tradesmen would naturally go to the rear, and that other importunate visitors were rare. Don Diego refused to listen and, as a matter of fact, Le Carpentier's soothing words failed to carry conviction. Moreover, when he later brought up the subject with his wife and daughter, hoping for support from these quarters, he was doomed to disappointment. Mme Le Carpentier agreed completely with Don Diego; she had had enough—more than enough—of finding herself face to face, in her present house, with visitors she did not want to see; if she were to be no better off in the new one, what would be the use of moving? Besides, her husband should not need to be told that the current trend was away from the outmoded French style. They were building for the future, were they not? Very well then, a Spanish type house was what they wanted, with a garden at one side, if he insisted, but certainly with a *galeria* and a patio in the rear. Telcide was equally emphatic; her father did not seem to realize how important a figure Alonzo was becoming; but she did. The dignity of his exalted position must be maintained at all costs. . . .

Le Carpentier strove to temporize, but he realized almost from the beginning that his was a hopeless battle—one of the few he had ever lost. Fortunately for his pride, the presumably reliable builders already engaged were unable to furnish a proper surety for fulfilling their nine thousand dollar contract, and it was cancelled without loss of face to the ambitious auctioneer. Nevertheless, he felt that he had been snubbed and his feelings toward Don Diego underwent a change; he was tempted to seek another alliance for Telcide, one in which he would be master of the situation. But though he had not exaggerated in saying that suitors were numerous, none of the others had the background or the standing of Alonzo Morphy; besides, Telcide was in love with the prospective attorney general. She would not listen to covert suggestions that the betrothal was not yet official, that she could withdraw from it if she chose. Instead of listening, she wept; and her father could not endure the sight of her tears. At last, reluctantly, he said he would try to find other contractors, men who would carry out plans that were generally acceptable; though, for his part, he could not see there was anything the matter with those originally made.

Again, Don Diego took charge of the situation. What Le Carpentier needed, he said loftily, was not primarily a contractor; it was an architect, and he knew exactly the right one—that superior craftsman, Francisco Correjolles. He gave the name its proper pronunciation and Le Carpentier did not instantly recognize it.

"Cor-re-hol-yes?" he said questioningly. "Oh, you call it Corejoal, as if it were French," Don Diego said condescendingly. Le Carpentier was finding it more and more difficult to bite back sharp rejoinders. "Yes, I call it Corejoal, and so would anyone of true Creole ancestry," he said rather shortly. "You are referring, I suppose, to this newcomer recently arrived from Baltimore?" . . . "Baltimore was merely a way station for him," Don Diego replied. "He is a Spaniard like myself and, though the best influence that Maryland provides is evident in some of his work, I assure you that he will worthily carry on Castilian customs, in both architecture and manners, no matter how much he is impeded by provincial hybrids."

This time, Le Carpentier rose abruptly and left the drawing room. Telcide, who had been sitting on the other side of it, strumming lightly on her harp, excused herself with gentle sweetness to Don Diego, apologizing because she had not brought him his sherry more promptly; after following her father from the room, she returned to it, bringing not only the visitor's favorite Amontillado, but some little cakes of which he was especially fond, and sat conversing amiably with him while he consumed these delicacies. The next day, when Francisco Correjolles called, he was civilly received.

His first drawings were rather crude. They showed a front portico with four columns, but the latter were irregularly placed; and a curving stairway, rising from the high basement to the main floor, was indicated only on one side of the exterior. Moreover, this was designed to be of wood, with turned balusters, instead of the beautiful ironwork, which eventually replaced the single staircase, together with its graceful twin. The fine central doorway—the feature on which Don Diego had dwelt with such insistence —was not even shown. Nevertheless, the eventual results revealed amazing perfection of detail; the contractor, James Lambert, worked closely with Correjolles, who supplied more finished drawings whenever these were required, and the building progressed rapidly.

The new plans called for an entirely different type of house from that which Le Carpentier had first visualized and Don Diego expressed himself as entirely satisfied this time. On one side of the wide central hall were three large bedchambers, with a smaller *cabinet* at the rear; on the other, was a square *salle de compagnie*, or parlor, in front of an immense rectangular apartment, its length equivalent to that of the two bedrooms it faced; this could be used either as a ballroom or as a banqueting hall, and was also provided with a *cabinet* behind it, and this, unlike the one on the other side of the house, was flanked by a steep narrow staircase, which led to an upper half-story with five dormer windows. Once reached, this half-story offered great possibilities, although the approach to it was inconvenient and unprepossessing; it could easily provide two extra rooms and these would accommodate the sons of a future family, until they were old enough to follow the Creole custom of living in the *garconnière* on the grounds of the main house, but apart from it. For the present, the space might remain an unadorned attic; but the plaster work in all the rooms on the *rez-de-chaussée* was exceptionally elaborate. The decorated cornices at the ceiling lines were "run" and the rosettes, or "center flowers," from the middle of which the chandeliers were hung, had all been modeled before being applied. This was really the work of a sculptor and the results were superb. Three elliptical fanlight transoms surmounted the French doors of the rear gallery and the center door of this, as well as the front entrance, which was elaborately paneled. The doors connecting the bedrooms were all surmounted with rectangular glass transoms divided into patterns by delicate muntins; and the classic doorway with Ionic pilasters, between the *salle de compagnie* and the ballroom, was a magnificent example of the Greek Revival style. The marble mantels were shipped down from New York, already made, and installed in their entirety, so that, though there was considerable delay in transportation, the actual installation did not require anything like the amount of skill and time represented by the plaster work and the woodwork. The rear gallery, enclosed by the two *cabinets,* would serve, under most circumstances, for a dining room, as in the case of the house where the Le Carpentiers were still living. The kitchen, though in a separate building, was conveniently near by, and the *cabinet* back of the banqueting hall could do double duty as a warming pantry. The slave quarters and stables were well removed from the rest of the imposing structure. Don Diego's complacence increased as the building advanced and, as it neared completion, he began to talk, after chess games which he won, about the desirability of fixing a day for celebrating the official betrothal.

Before this could be done, however, it was, of course, necessary to agree on the terms of the marriage contract, so that no unseemly last-minute argument could possibly mar the harmony of such a joyous occasion. Le Carpentier had been quite sincere in telling Don Diego that he proposed to give Telcide a handsome dowry; it had honestly never occurred to him that he and Don Diego would not see eye to eye when it came to interpreting exactly what this meant. Therefore, when rather importantly, he mentioned the sum of three thousand piasters as the one he had in mind, his dismay was comparable only to his astonishment when Don Diego, who had just scored a very signal victory after a long drawn-out game of chess, and therefore should have been in the most favorable of moods, held up his hands with a sudden gesture of indignation.

"Three thousand piasters!" he exclaimed, his voice as agitated as the lace ruffles at his wrists. "Surely you are jesting, my friend! And, if you will permit me to say so, the dowry of a beautiful young gentlewoman is not a proper subject for pleasantry. It is a matter of serious concern."

"I have so regarded it. Do you mean to tell me that three thousand piasters—"

"Is a paltry sum unworthy to be mentioned in connection with Telcide?" Don Diego interrupted, his usual calm voice rising higher and higher. "Yes, M. Le Carpentier, that is exactly what I mean to tell you! No such sum, I assure you, has ever been mentioned in connection with the dowry of the young ladies in *my* family!"

Nothing he could have said would have been better calculated to emphasize the alleged superiority of a Morphy over the Le Carpentiers. Joseph, portly and prosperous as he was, recoiled from the arrogance of his shriveled but powerful antagonist.

"What sum is mentioned in their connection?" he heard himself asking, almost humbly.

"I—" Don Diego had not been prepared for so abrupt and definite a question. "I do not have the exact figures in mind. I should have to look them up, but I will do so and let you know. I confess, at the moment, I am not prepared to answer your question accurately. You see, when you told me you intended to give your dear daughter a handsome dowry, I dismissed the whole matter from my mind. You have now taken me completely by surprise in mentioning three thousand piasters."

Joseph Le Carpentier realized that, for the first time in the course of this unwelcome discussion, he had the advantage of his wily antagonist. Whatever any devious aristocrat might say to the contrary, sometimes it paid to be blunt; and it did not embarrass him to talk of money in specific terms; as an auctioneer, he was used to doing so.

"Suppose we do not wait for you to consult your records," he said with rising self-confidence. "After all, we have lost considerable time in waiting to get a house built that would suit you. Let us not waste any more in arriving at a marriage contract that will suit you. I will leave you free to decide what settlement your son shall make on my daughter; and if you will tell me, here and now, that the sum of four thousand piasters would be agreeable to you for her dowry, we can consider this discussion at an end and fix a day for the betrothal. Otherwise, perhaps I had better consider the qualifications of some suitor other than Alonzo."

Confronted with such an ultimatum, not to mention terms far more liberal than he had ever dared to visualize, Don Diego quickly capitulated. The day was fixed, the party planned. And then, before the celebration could take place, with a suddenness unbecoming his deliberate and dignified habits, Don Diego was stricken with mortal illness, and died so quickly that Alonzo and his elder brother, Ernesto, could scarcely believe that their bereavement was an actuality.

They rallied sufficiently to give him a magnificent funeral. The hearse was drawn by four black horses, richly caparisoned in sable and silver, and great black plumes surmounted both hearse and horses. The Funeral Mass took place in St. Louis Cathedral, with the Bishop of New Orleans officiating, numerous monsignori assisting, and a full vested choir singing the dirges. Every dignitary of the city was present at the ceremony. The cortege, which slowly wound its way to St. Louis Cemetery with Diego, Jr. and his wife in the first carriage, Ernesto and Alonzo in the second, their sisters in the third and various members of the Le Carpentier family in the fourth and fifth, was one of the longest ever seen in New Orleans. The gentlemen not only wore black suits, black ties, black gloves and black shoes and carried handkerchiefs with black borders an inch wide; bands of crepe encircled their tall silk hats and their broadcloth sleeves. The ladies' equally sombre dresses were trimmed with crepe and their faces were covered with crepe veils. But when the last of the obsequies were over and Telcide was alone with her parents, they realized, with alarm, that the tears she was shedding were not all with grief because Don Diego had died, but with bitter disappointment because the fulfillment of her own plans had been hopelessly thwarted.

"You know what this means, of course?" she said, between sobs, mopping her pretty eyes with her black-bordered handkerchief.

"I am afraid I do not quite understand, *chère*," Modeste Le Carpentier said soothingly, if mendaciously. "Just what do *you* mean?"

"I mean that Alonzo will be in full mourning for two years and in half-mourning for a year after that. We can't even celebrate our betrothal officially, much less get married."

M. and Mme Le Carpentier exchanged glances. "Of course not, my dear child," Modeste said, still soothingly. "But the time will pass very quickly. After all, a great deal of preparation is necessary, and that will occupy us. Why, we have not even moved into our new house yet! And, though a sale for this one now seems assured, it is probably wiser to remain here until that is actually consummated. And, meanwhile, we shall be selecting furniture and working on your trousseau. I want you to have the most beautiful *lit à ciel* that Seignouret ever designed and, of course, it should be made to order. The fluted blue lining to the canopy must be arranged as a sunburst and the lace draperies caught up with figurines of cherubs. All this requires careful workmanship and selections which cannot be made hastily. Then it will take me months to embroider your wedding nightdress alone, not to mention all the other nightdresses and the chemises there are to make. You have not been of much help to me so far, if I may say so, darling. But now that you will necessarily be seeing less of dear Alonzo for a little while—he is, of course, too prostrated with grief to think of paying visits, even to his fiancée—perhaps you will be more industrious. And when the first shock is over, he will come quietly to play chess with your father and—"

"He and Ernesto can play chess together at home. He won't even have that as an excuse for coming here. And when he does begin to go out, it will be to his office. He cares more about law than he does about me."

"*Chère*, you are very unjust. Alonzo adores you."

"Well, Ernesto does not. And now that Don Diego is dead, he will have enormous influence with Alonzo. As far as that goes, you know very well that Don Diego was not nearly as enthusiastic about the match as you were, Papa," she said, turning toward her father. "You practically had to bribe him into giving his consent; and even after he had given it, he tried to withdraw on the pretext that he did not like the house you wanted to build."

"You did not like it, either, Telcide."

"Yes, I did. That is, I liked it well enough. But I could see it was better to agree with Don Diego."

She refused to be cheered or even comforted and, after a few weeks had passed, during the course of which she received several mournful notes, but no calls from Alonzo, her parents began to feel that she had cause for complaint and that they had cause for concern on that score, though, on another, Joseph could not suppress a very real sense of relief. Obviously, Don Diego had never got wind of the auctioneer's dealings with the pirates of Barataria. If he had, he would have possessed more than a pretext for delaying his son's marriage to Telcide; he would have had a valid reason for hesitating to countenance an alliance with the Le Carpentier family. Now, all danger in that direction was past. With inward satisfaction, but well-simulated sympathy, Joseph promptly made the indicated *visite de condoléance* on the bereaved brothers; and he had found them, not sitting amidst darkened surroundings in stunned silence, but playing chess together in a well-lighted room. He did not dare tell his daughter how prophetically she had spoken; and though, in due time, her suitor began to call again, his conversation did not take an amorous turn. He spoke, with solemn satisfaction, of the fact that his half-brother, Diego, Jr., had been appointed to succeed his father as Spanish Consul, and that, of course, the former would do his best to follow the illustrious example that had been set him. For the rest, Alonzo talked about his own career, which had passed the point of promise and was definitely now one of success. After he left, Telcide looked at her father significantly and he winced; she had been right on that point, also.

Nevertheless, the transactions leading up to the sale of the house on Bourbon Street were proceeding in a satisfactory manner, and the elder Le Carpentiers were both deeply interested in the purchase of furnishings and decorations for the new one and sparing no expense in making their selections. The two outstanding cabinetmakers of the time and place, Seignouret and Mallard, were both given commissions; brocades for draperies and upholstery were chosen with care, as were crystal chandeliers and Aubusson rugs; so were the ornaments especially dear to Creole hearts—girondoles, *garnitures de cheminée,* and the *miniatures* to supply étagères. Silver, porcelain and crystal the Le Carpentiers had in abundance already, but they bought more—épergnes, candelabra, sets of egg cups with little dangling spoons, immense platters covered with sliding silver domes. Mme Le Carpentier would have liked to make a trip to France, as had several of their acquaintances, on purpose to do such buying—they even knew one family who had chartered a whole ship in which to travel and bring home their magnificent household goods. But Joseph could not leave his auction rooms long enough for a voyage, and regretfully his wife resigned herself to the fact that it would not be seemly for Telcide and her to go without him, helpful as the distraction would have been for the girl. So, while she was not out shopping, Mme Le Carpentier went patiently and skillfully on with her fine needlework. There must be a dozen dozen of everything, all of the finest linen, all initialed, all embroidered. She spread the dainty garments out for her husband to admire, when he returned from his auction rooms, likewise filled with satisfaction over the day's accomplishments.

Between them, they somehow lost sight of the fact that Telcide was developing a new interest.

Among the suitors whom they had not seriously considered was a young Frenchman of excellent family but slender means, André de Blondville. He had first come to New Orleans because, as an ardent Royalist, he had not been made welcome during the régime of the First Empire. Much of his life had been spent in exile, for, as a small child, he had been smuggled to England, at the time of the French Revolution, in which most of his family had been guillotined. But he had always cheerfully and resourcefully adapted himself to conditions which many persons would have found depressing and discouraging. He had become an accomplished scholar, and he was not above teaching French to the Americans who were invading the city and changing its character beyond Canal Street. He had also become a skilled swordsman, and was not above giving fencing lessons to anyone who would take them, whether American or Creole. Above all, he was essentially a musician, and nothing delighted him so much as an opportunity to play and sing, whether he were paid for doing so or not. When Telcide told her parents that she would like to take lessons from him, they readily gave their consent; it would take her mind off her grievances if she spent more time at her harp and her piano; and, of course, her sister Amélie or one of her aunts would always be present when M. de Blondville was instructing her.

It was unfortunate that Amélie, who was jealous of Telcide and did not like to see her enjoying herself so much, failed to accept this responsibility as seriously as she should have and that an aunt, not otherwise unoccupied, would not always seem to be available. The result was that André and Telcide were frequently quite unsupervised and the inevitable happened; the day came when their fingers strayed from the keyboard and the strings and became interlaced. In another minute, they would have clasped each other in an ardent embrace if fate, in the form of Alonzo, had not opportunely intervened.

Vague rumors had been coming to his ears and, though he was at first not disquieted by them, he eventually decided that, mourning or no mourning, it was time he resumed his courtship on a more personal basis. The Le Carpentiers had concluded the sale of their house on Bourbon Street and were preparing to move out of it; but they still had not done so because, though the new house on Chartres Street was furnished, it was not yet decorated to their entire satisfaction; besides, they had continued to cling to the idea of having a wedding or at least a formal betrothal ceremony for their housewarming. Hence, when Alonzo knocked, it was at a door which led directly into the parlor—an arrangement which, as Don Diego had pointed out, had its disadvantages. Telcide and her teacher let go each other's hands and Telcide sprang forward to open the door, overturning the piano stool and scattering music as she did so. Alonzo had no difficulty in taking in the situation at a glance.

"Good evening, Telcide. Good evening, M. de Blondville," he said coolly. Then he looked at the clock. "Is this not the hour when you generally hold your fencing class, Monsieur?" he continued. "Your other pupils must be waiting for you. I am sure this one would not wish to detain you." And when André had taken his graceful and apparently unhurried leave, Alonzo addressed himself, still coolly, to Telcide. "Since you have so much leisure to devote to music," he said, "I take it that all your preparations for our wedding must be complete. Let me see—this is the thirteenth. Shall I suggest to your father that, if convenient for him and your mother—and, of course, if agreeable to you—we shall meet with our friends and relatives on the twentieth to draw up the marriage contract? In the new house, of course. I believe it has always been understood that the first celebration there should be in some way connected with our union and I can think of no arrangement that would suit me better."

Having made this announcement, standing at a respectful distance, Alonzo crossed the room and put both arms around Telcide, drawing her close to him. He had never done anything of the sort before and he knew, as well as she did, that it was most improper he should, until they were man and wife. But, after all, André de Blondville had been on the point of doing it and that would have been far more improper. So, once he had started, Alonzo did not come to a halt when he put his arms around his fiancée. He kissed her, not gently on her cheek and brow, as he had occasionally done before, but very hard, on her mouth, over and over again. She still had not spoken a word and, if she had been incapable of doing so when he first entered, she was doubly so now, because it was literally impossible to open the lips he had so completely sealed. When at last he released her, he looked down at her and laughed. It was the first time she had heard him laugh since his father died.

"And now," he said, "of course we must be married at once. Any other course would be unthinkable, considering the liberty I have just taken. Besides, you are now twenty-two years old and, presently, people will begin to refer to you as an old maid. Such references would not be agreeable to me in connection with my future wife. I shall request a special dispensation of all the banns but the first, and ask M. l'Abbe Moni if it would be agreeable to him to perform the wedding ceremony on the twenty-first."

MARRIAGE CONTRACT

BETWEEN

A. M. MORPHY AND L. T. F. T. LE CARPENTIER.

Appeared before Joseph Arnaud, Notary Public at New Orleans, in the State of Louisiana, in the presence of witnesses of legal age hereinafter named and whose signatures are affixed:

Mr. Alonzo Michael Morphy, of legal age, living in this city, born at Charleston, legitimate son of the late Mr. Diego Morphy and the late Lady Louise Peire, on the one part.

And the Damsel Louise Thérèse Felicité Thelcide Le Carpentier, of legal age, living in this city, where she was born, legitimate daughter of Mr. Joseph Esaü L. Carpentier and Lady Modeste Blache, on the second part.

The aforesaid Mr. Morphy and Mlle Le Carpentier, accompanied by the father and mother of the bride and their relatives and friends here assembled, have promised and by these presents solemnly sworn to unite themselves in lawful marriage, at the first request of either one, in conformity with the laws of this State and the rites of the Catholic Church, following the religion which they profess; and in view of this marriage have settled and engaged upon the following matrimonial covenants:

There shall be between the future spouses, from the day of the said marriage, partnership in or community of ownership of assets and of profits, compounded, administered and liquidated in conformity with the laws of this State.

The property of the bridegroom consists of the following:

1. A sum of ten thousand piasters, several represented by endorsed notes, and almost all carrying mortgages, which are in the hands of Mr. Louis Pelié in this city, and of which Mr. Le Carpentier, in behalf of his daughter, the bride, has informed himself, as he so declares.   10,000.

2. A plot of land with the framework of a building, in the Faubourg Marigny, facing Crayes Street, measuring forty-six feet in width and one hundred and twenty feet in depth, estimated to be worth two thousand piasters.   2,000.

3. A plot of land in this city, facing St. Peter Street, measuring thirty-five feet in width and ninety feet in depth, between Burgundy Street and the Ramparts, estimated to be worth six hundred piasters.   600.

4. Sundry slaves, to wit:

    Louison, mulatress, a laundress, forty-five years old and
    valued at five hundred piasters.   500.

    Hyacinthe, mulatto, a workman, twenty-four years old,
    eight hundred piasters.   800.

    Honoré, griff, fourteen years old, five hundred piasters. 500.

    Beckey, American Negress, sixteen years old, four hundred
    piasters.   400.

    Jacques, American Negro, nineteen years old, six hundred
    piasters.   600.

    Friday, Negro carter, fifty years old, four hundred
    piasters.   400.   3,200.

Total: Fifteen thousand eight hundred piasters.   15,800.

The property of the bride consists of the sum of four thousand piasters which the bridegroom acknowledges and declares to have received from the aforesaid Mr. Le Carpentier, father of the bride, in the presence of these witnesses, to his satisfaction, from which sum of four thousand piasters thus received as a dowry, the said bridegroom is obligated to make rightful restitution to anyone thereto entitled. Upon dissolution of community property, the bride or her representatives, having cause, shall be entitled to appeal, and in such case to exercise all the rights of recovery provided by law.

Thus it has been agreed in good faith between the two parties.

Said agreement acted upon and entered into at New Orleans at the residence of Mr. Le Carpentier, father of the bride, the twentieth of February, eighteen hundred and twenty-nine, fifty-third year of the independence of the United States of America, in the presence of M. Auguste St. Martin and M. Louis H. Féraud, requisite witnesses domiciled in this city, who have signed with the prospective husband and wife, the father and mother of the bride and their relatives and friends here present, after having read the same.

(*Signed*)	A. Morphy	Thelcide Le Carpentier
	Ernest Morphy	J. Le Carpentier
	Aug. St. Martin	Blache Le Carpentier
		Blache Tournier
	Emma Morphy	Lilia Morphy
	L. H. Féraud	Amélie Le Carpentier
	P. St. Martin	Amenaïde Le Carpentier
		H. D. Peire

Jh. Arnaud, Not. Pub.

(Translation of the original French document on file in the Office of Custodian of Notarial Records, Parish of Orleans, State of Louisiana.)

According to *Le Courrier de la Louisiane*, the *Louisiana Advertiser* and the marriage records of St. Louis Cathedral, the marriage of Alonzo Morphy and Thelcide Le Carpentier took place in the cathedral the following day by special license of the Honorable Justice of the Peace, J. Petot, one bann having been published and the other two dispensed. The marriage ceremony was performed by the Reverend Abbé Moni, Curé of St. Louis Cathedral.

4.

Telcide had been born and reared in the Creole tradition; therefore, she accepted, as a matter of course, that, immediately after the wedding reception, a bride was undressed by her mother, who then clad her in a long-sleeved, high-necked nightgown and saw her safely to bed in the best room of her parents' house; there she was left to await the arrival of her bridegroom, who had meanwhile been told when she would be ready to receive him. Telcide also knew that neither of them was supposed to stir from this room for the next fortnight, that meals would be served to them by an unobtrusive servant, and that they were supposed to spend this time "in getting acquainted," before they emerged to face their relatives and friends, not as separate individuals, but as a united couple. However, her consciousness of all this had been objective; no personal element had invaded it until Alonzo's abrupt declaration that he wanted the marriage to take place immediately had thrown the well-ordered household of the Le Carpentiers into a state of chaos.

Both Joseph and Modeste had protested when Alonzo, leaving Telcide stunned by his violent embrace, had flung himself out on the terrace, where the husband and wife were quietly drinking coffee, and delivered his ultimatum. Joseph had risen in anger, saying that such haste was unseemly, that no *jeune fille bien élevée* was married out of hand like that. Modeste's objection had taken a different form: yes, certainly, the linen was embroidered and initialed; but the wedding dress was not even ordered, or any of the ball dresses, visiting dresses, and *robes d'intérieur* which constituted a suitable outfit. There was not a dressmaker in New Orleans who could prepare them within a week; besides, it had been their intention to order all these creations from Paris, if Alonzo had only given them an inkling that he meant to lay aside his second mourning. Moreover, they were on the very threshold of Lent, which made his attitude all the more incomprehensible. How could they have imagined that he would consider a wedding until after Easter?

"All the more desirable to have it take place before Lent begins; otherwise, there would have to be a delay of five weeks instead of only one."

"But the reception! How can we provide a suitable collation for a large and distinguished company on a few days' notice?"

"You can limit the number of your guests. My mourning will provide a plausible pretext for that. And I am sure Ernest would insist on it in any case."

The mention of Alonzo's brother, who had now Anglicized his name, added fuel to the fire. The Le Carpentiers knew that he did not consider them in his social class, that he would have been pleased to see the match broken off and that, if it must take place, he would be extremely critical of any entertainment connected with it which did not meet his standards. Besides, they had always intended that the wedding feast should be a showy affair. Alonzo interrupted their continued objections.

"Perhaps you would prefer to have M. de Blondville for a son-in-law. Then everything could be done in the French manner, at your convenience."

"That music teacher! That fencing master!" exploded Joseph.

"Telcide is very fond of music. From what I have heard and, indeed, from what I saw, less than an hour ago, she especially enjoys it when she shares it with M. de Blondville. And his skill as a swordsman might be very convenient, in case he were ever called upon to uphold the honor of anyone in the family."

"You are not suggesting—" exclaimed Joseph, still more furiously.

"I am not suggesting anything. However, since you have raised the question, though indirectly, I may state I am surprised that you should have permitted your daughter—and my fiancée—to receive visits from a gentleman—if a music teacher and a fencing master may be so designated—without strict supervision. Certainly you have never done so in my case. But we will let that pass. I have, of course, every confidence in Telcide's complete innocence, or I should ask for permission to withdraw from my engagement to marry her, instead of insisting upon doing so immediately. And I do insist. What I said was not a suggestion; it was a demand."

He bowed and left the terrace, nor did he re-enter the drawing room before taking his departure from the house. Joseph and Modeste Le Carpentier spent the rest of the evening in heaping reproaches upon their daughters. Naturally, Telcide came in for the bitterest of these, but Amélie did not escape. What did the latter mean by leaving her sister alone with that *emigré*, that *parvenu*, that fortune hunter? It was a marvel that all the careful parental projects of years had not come to naught because of their carelessness! As for Telcide, Alonzo was quite right; the sooner she was married, the better. Obviously, that was the only way to keep her out of mischief. But what an inconvenience, what an harassment for her father and mother! To be sure, M. Seignouret had finished the cabinetwork on the *lit à ciel*; but the sunburst of azure satin which gave it its name and lined the canopy was not even begun, much less was the lace chosen for its festoons, or the cherubic figurines which were to secure these in place. And it was all very well to talk about a simple reception! They knew what Alonzo would think—and what Ernest would say—if an unlimited amount of champagne and an enormous supply of *dragées* were not provided, and that was without mentioning innumerable creams, jellies, cakes and pastries. And here they were not even installed as yet in the new house. . . .

"We could have been, at any time for a year now," Telcide retorted. She had emerged from her stunned state and had also recovered her spirits enough to resent the abuse that was being heaped upon her. "After all, it will not take long to put the final touches on the decorations. And certainly there are slaves enough to serve a wedding banquet. As to the *ciel*, what does it matter? That could be added later, if necessary."

"Added later! Just listen to this girl, Joseph! As if the bridal night occurred more than once! You are talking very strangely, Telcide. I hope you have not also been acting strangely?"

"Certainly not. It is Alonzo who is doing that."

They pressed her to tell them what she meant, rightly suspicious that she did not refer only to his precipitate attitude in regard to a wedding. But she lapsed into sullen silence. Nothing would have wrung from her the admission that Alonzo had taken her in his arms and kissed her, as if they had already been married, much less that, though she had been startled, the shock had not been an unpleasant one. Rather, the contrary.

In the hectic week which followed, she began to give more thought to the mysteries that she had never before tried to solve. Of course, she understood that her husband would not enter the room until she was clothed in the fine embroidered nightdress and fully covered with the sheets and quilts of the *lit à ciel* which, despite her mother's anxiety, was now in place, with the pale blue lining of its canopy finished and the lace festoons awaiting only the cherubs to complete the adornment. But what, exactly, happened after that? Surely she was not supposed to remain in bed for a fortnight, still between the same sheets, still clad in the same nightgown! Of course, she would have a deep bath before the ceremony; but she would need to sponge herself off, at least, from time to time after that, and she could not do so fully covered by a nightdress; then there were even more private functions which must, inevitably, be performed. Surely these were not supposed to take place in the presence of a stranger, a man at that! She wondered why she had never thought of all this before and, finally, she summoned courage to ask her mother, blushing as she did so. Mme Le Carpentier answered both practically and soothingly.

"Do not concern yourself, *chère*. As you know, we are giving you and Alonzo the large bedroom nearest the rear, the one connecting with a *cabinet*, which, in turn, leads directly onto the terrace and the patio. For the time being, this will serve as your dressing room. The washstand and Alonzo's shaving stand will be there, and the same slave who serves your meals will empty the basin and other receptacles you have used and bring you fresh supplies of towels and plenty of water. Alonzo has already selected one of his own slaves to perform these duties, Beckey, I believe her name is. He says she is very expert and very tractable. I am sure you will have excellent service."

"But where will Charles and Amenaïde and Amélie sleep if you give up so much space to us?"

"Charles will use the other *cabinet*, at the rear of the banquet hall. To be sure, that will be slightly inconvenient, as we had intended to use that as a pantry, and let him have the one we now propose to give to you. But your needs must come first at such a time. Amélie and Amenaïde, as you know, would both have shared the middle chamber with you, had it not been for this hasty marriage; they will now have it to themselves, and your father and I will occupy the one in front. At least, that will eventually be the arrangement. For the present, I think it is better this plan should be reversed, that Amélie and Amenaïde should not be in the room next to yours."

"Why?"

"Because of what they might overhear. I am sure you and Alonzo will be as discreet as possible, but after all, there is a door between the two rooms and sounds sometimes penetrate, no matter how careful one is. Your father and I have been married a long time, so we will make allowances."

"Allowances for what?"

"Why, for anything that might come to our ears! Newly married couples naturally need to make adjustments, and sometimes such adjustments are not easy, especially for the bride."

"Why especially for the bride?"

"Well, you see the bridegroom is more experienced."

"More experienced? But Alonzo has not been married before!"

Mme Le Carpentier coughed slightly. "No, *chère*, of course not. But men adapt themselves to such relationships more easily than women—or rather than young girls. You are a maiden—a—a virgin. A virgin sometimes finds the transition to wifehood difficult. Only at the beginning, of course. Afterward, she shares her bridegroom's rapture. Do not forget this—if there are difficulties at first."

"What difficulties?"

Mme Le Carpentier became less soothing and more vague, though she remained practical. "You will find out soon enough," she said. "It is not my place to go into too many details. It is the husband's prerogative to initiate his wife into all the mysteries that are sacred to the holy estate of matrimony. Do not forget, either, that whatever he does, he has a right to do. You must not protest or resist. Above all, I hope you will not make yourself ridiculous or bring ridicule on your father and myself by unseemly behavior. There is a story which went all the way up and down the River

Road before it reached New Orleans and then became the jest of the day here. It concerns a bride who rushed into her parents' room in the middle of the night screaming, '*Je ne peux pas me coucher avec ce cochon là, il veut m'enlever la chemise!*' "

In spite of herself, Telcide trembled a little. She had been thinking of that long-sleeved, high-necked nightgown, in which her mother was to clothe her, as a coat of armor. And now, it appeared, her bridegroom could disarm her at will, and she must not run for succor to her parents or she would be the object of ribaldry throughout the city. It was the husband's prerogative to initiate his wife into the mysteries sacred to the holy estate of matrimony, and even the bride's mother must not tell her beforehand what these were. The bridegroom had a right to do whatever he wanted, and there must be no protest and no resistance. What could he want against which she would protest or resist? It had never occurred to her that her wishes and Alonzo's would not be the same. Now it appeared that he might make demands upon her that she would be reluctant to grant, but that, nevertheless, she must do so. She had always thought of love only in terms of ardent but gentle caresses, never in terms of adjustments or difficulties, much less of submission. Sex as a vital and urgent force had never been mentioned in her hearing; she connected it only with charming sentiment and that shyly and hesitantly. She tried to lure her mother into further confidences which would be reassuring. But Mme Le Carpentier protested that she had already said more than was really seemly and, besides, she had a great deal still to do. Not only were the cherubs still unplaced on the lace festoons, but the *accouchement* bed had not yet been brought into the bridal chamber.

The *accouchement* bed, which was placed sideways at the foot of the *lit à ciel*, was another feature of Creole life with which Telcide had always been familiar in an objective way. She knew that when a woman was in the last stages of labor, the midwife, with the help of a slave, lifted the sufferer from her great four-poster to this hard and narrow couch, in order to facilitate the delivery of the baby—not for its mother, but for those who had charge of her. She had never visualized the details of confinement, any more than she had visualized the details of the transformation from virginity to wifehood. But she did know that women not infrequently died in childbirth, because such deaths had occurred among family acquaintances, and that at best it was not a pleasant process. Now it seemed to her not only needlessly premature, but needlessly harrowing that an *accouchement* bed should be brought into her room where she could not avoid seeing it constantly; she knew she would not be able to look at it without a feeling of dread. But her mother watched its installation with supreme satisfaction.

"There!" she said, when it was finally in place. "That was the only thing missing to have everything in readiness. If I am not mistaken, you will be needing it nine months from now or, at least, within a year. Perhaps you will give your father and me a beautiful little grandson for a New Year's present. I am sure that would please Alonzo immensely also, and that it will not be his fault if our hopes are unfulfilled. I hope it will not be your fault, either. What is the matter with you, Telcide? You look as if you were going to faint! Here you have been clamoring for Alonzo, I don't know how many years, and now you act as if you did not welcome the realities of marriage and its natural consequences. Come, help me get these cherubs into place!"

During the week that followed the interrupted music lesson, Telcide made several further attempts to talk confidentially with her mother, all to no avail, and there was no one else whom she could consult; Amélie would be no help, of course. Meanwhile, Alonzo called regularly, but briefly, every day. He did not want to interfere with the preparations for the wedding, he said, and he knew there was no time to spare. He treated all the Le Carpentiers with the greatest respect; but though he kissed Telcide's hand, upon his arrival and departure, he made no attempt to see her alone, much less to take her in his arms again. She wished that he would. Instinctively, she had begun to feel that a less formal and distant courtship would have prepared her more adequately for the mysterious intimacy which was to begin so suddenly. They had never even met without supervision, except on the occasion of that one embrace; and soon she was to be confined in the same room with him for a fortnight! Meanwhile, he did not even bring her flowers, explaining that he was afraid their arrangement would add to the general confusion. But when the day arrived for signing the contract, he brought with him an imposing number of relatives and friends as witnesses, and the terms upon which he and Joseph Le Carpentier had previously agreed were admittedly liberal—the value of the settlement he offered was far in excess of Telcide's dowry; and after the formal ceremony was over, while the witnesses were still foregathered, he presented her with a magnificent diamond bracelet as a betrothal present, thus following the Spanish custom, instead of the French, which would have indicated a ring. The following day, he made a striking appearance as a bridegroom and the carefully selected guests, both at the cathedral and at the reception, remarked to each other that they had never seen a handsomer couple. Contrary to Mme Le Carpentier's fears and prophecies, a dressmaker had been found who could turn out a wedding dress that was not only suitable but elegant and Telcide, though very pale, was looking her loveliest. The collation left nothing to be desired and the assembled company enjoyed it thoroughly. They toasted the newly-wedded pair again and again in the excellent champagne, and lingered as long as was seemly to savor the *dragées*, the creams, the jellies, the pastries and the cakes. But as there was no dancing, out of respect to Alonzo's half-mourning, they could not prolong their stay until the wee small hours, as they otherwise would have done. It was still comparatively early when they took their departure, and Mme Le Carpentier signaled the bride. The moment for the ceremonial disrobing had arrived.

After the removal of the veil and the ornaments which secured it, this was not a lengthy process. Mme Le Carpentier had dismissed the idea of plaiting Telcide's beautiful hair into demure twin braids; it was much more alluring, falling loose in a soft cloud about her shoulders, and Mme Le Carpentier believed in allure, at the right time and in the right place. The fashion of the day was still that of the Empire, between two eras of tight lacing, wasp waists and hoopskirts. There were no rigid corsets to be carefully loosened and unhooked, and only one petticoat, instead of a series of these, over a fine chemise. The low-heeled white slippers dropped almost of themselves from the small cold feet. The silk stockings were peeled easily from the slim white legs. Then the exquisite nightdress was slipped over the girl's head and her mother guided her toward the bed, which had already been invitingly opened, and installed her on one side of it, with a great square pillow behind her head and a soft coverlet drawn over her.

"The logs in the fireplace are still glowing, though they have ceased to blaze. Surely you're not cold, *chèrie?*" Mme Le Carpentier asked with a final show of solicitude.

"No."

"Then why are you shivering?"

"Because I'm frightened."

"Nonsense! There is nothing to be afraid of as long as you behave yourself. Remember what I have told you. Do not protest, do not resist, above all, do not make us ridiculous by screaming. We shall be well aware how you conduct yourself, your father and I. Remember there is only one wall between your room and ours."

"I shall remember."

"Good! I will tell Alonzo that you are ready for him. He is still in the further *cabinet*, which was put at his disposal for the evening."

Mme Le Carpentier went out, closing the door quietly behind her. The dying fire gave a little light and so did the small oil lamp in the *veilleuse* which had been placed on the *vanité*. Otherwise, the room was in darkness. Although Telcide heard Alonzo when he came in, she could not see him clearly until he stood beside her, looking down at her. Then she thought that his expression was one of triumph, rather than of tenderness, and she closed her eyes. They were still closed when he locked her to him in swift and powerful domination.

PART TWO

"The Knight Moves Forward"

1847–1857

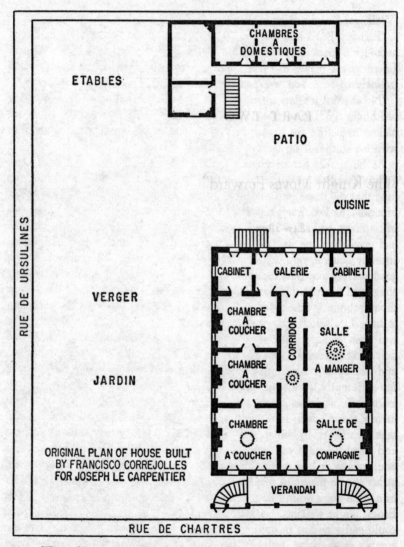

CHAMBRES A DOMESTIQUES

ETABLES

PATIO

CUISINE

RUE DE URSULINES

VERGER

JARDIN

CABINET   GALERIE   CABINET

CHAMBRE A COUCHER   CORRIDOR   SALLE

CHAMBRE A COUCHER   A MANGER

CHAMBRE   SALLE DE

A COUCHER   COMPAGNIE

ORIGINAL PLAN OF HOUSE BUILT
BY FRANCISCO CORREJOLLES
FOR JOSEPH LE CARPENTIER

VERANDAH

RUE DE CHARTRES

This plan is reproduced through the courtesy of the firm of
Richard Koch and Samuel Wilson, Jr., Architects, New Orleans.

5.

"Well, good night, Alonzo. Perhaps you'll have better luck next time."

"Perhaps. But I know as well as you do that chess isn't really a matter of luck—it's a matter of skill. I'm no match for you, Ernest, and I realize it. There isn't a player in New Orleans who is your equal for strength and in analysis. . . . You won't have a glass of wine before you go?"

"No thanks, it's late already. That boy of yours ought to have been in bed hours ago. I'm surprised Telcide lets him sit up this way. Hélène was tucked in before we began our game. You can't expect Paul to do well with his studies if he doesn't get enough sleep."

As he spoke, Ernest glanced at the ten-year-old child who had been quietly standing near the table where the chessboard was set out, all the time that his uncle and his father were playing. The victor did not speak unkindly; it was not his way to be unkind, and, besides, his mood was triumphant and therefore genial. Despite the ungrudging praise Alonzo had given him, he had not won the game easily; his brother, the former attorney general, now a judge on the Supreme Court of Louisiana, was a good player, too. But, though Ernest had never said so, and was slightly chagrined because this was the case, Paul's silent scrutiny irked him. Even though the little boy never spoke out of turn, it was somehow disconcerting to have him watch every move with such a steadfast gaze. If the observer had been someone like their family friend, Eugene Rousseau, who had defeated the great English player, Charles H. Stanley, a year or two earlier, and who often came to play with the Morphy brothers, Ernest would have felt differently. Rousseau was an undisputed master, and much could be learned from him, not only when he was an antagonist, but when he was merely an onlooker; in either case, after a game was over, he would make sage comments, by which one would profit another time. But this intent and watchful child was different; nothing could be gained by his presence and, sooner or later, something would be lost; he could not be expected, at his age, to maintain that attitude of brooding silence indefinitely; it was unnatural for a young boy, and someday nature would assert itself. Then Ernest might well make a rash move, because he was startled and a game could easily be lost through one false play. The possibility of this was becoming an obsession with him, no doubt an unreasonable one; but he could not rid himself of it.

Alonzo put his arm around his son and spoke in his defense. "Hélène is two years younger than Paul," he said. "Telcide still regards her as a baby, and probably will go on doing so, unless, at this late day, we have

another child and I rather hope we won't—four are quite enough to provide for, with the cost of living what it is today. And, as far as Paul's studies
are concerned, you needn't worry about those—he's leading his class and
that's no inconsiderable feat, at Jefferson Academy."

"I suppose not. But the mastery of chess isn't among the required subjects,
is it? If he's going to sit up until all hours, he might concentrate on something that is. Then perhaps he could skip a class and reduce the cost of his
education by finishing school sooner."

"He's skipped two classes already. I don't want him to skip any more and
neither does Edward. It would be embarrassing for Edward to have a
brother, three years younger than he is, in the same class with him."

Ernest shrugged his shoulders slightly. "I didn't mean to precipitate an
argument," he said nonchalantly. "I know Paul's your white-headed boy,
even though we have to use the expression figuratively." His eyes rested
for a moment on Paul's dark, wavy hair; then his gaze shifted to the child's
serious face. Something about its expression made him uncomfortable,
though he could not have told what; it was noncommittal, but it was perfectly pleasant. "Well, as I said before, it's late, even for gentlemen of our
age," he remarked. "Good night, Alonzo. Good night, Paul."

They answered simultaneously and Paul added, "I'll go to the door with
you and put up the bar."

He followed his uncle from the *salle de compagnie* to the wide entrance
hall, opened the paneled door leading to the front gallery and held it ajar
until Ernest had descended the curving staircase. Then he closed the door,
bolted it, and swung the great iron bar, which hung beside it when not in
use, into place across it, fastening it securely. The bar was heavy, but
though Paul was short for his age and rather slightly built, he handled it
without difficulty. When he went back to the parlor, Alonzo had already
set the chairs which had stood on either side of the gaming table back in
their proper places, and had begun to pick up the chessmen, preparatory to
putting the board away for the night.

"You didn't need to lose that game, Father," Paul said without preamble.
Alonzo looked up, a Pawn which he had been on the point of removing
still in his hand. "My dear child," he said, "you don't know what you're
talking about. Edward is fairly good at the game already—that is, for a mere
boy, as my father used to say about me. But though you recognize the different chessmen, you have no idea how to use them, and your uncle Ernest
is generally acknowledged to be the greatest expert in New Orleans. When
he played Queen to her third, everything was all over."

"I know it isn't polite to contradict, Father, but I do have some idea how
to use the chessmen. I've learned from watching you play with Grandfather
and Uncle Ernest and the friends, like Mr. Rousseau, who come here so

often. You play chess with someone at least three or four times a week and you've always let me stay in the room with you. I'm glad you have, because I've loved doing it. *Maman* says you play too often, but I've never thought so. I wouldn't have missed seeing your games for anything. And now I can play with you, too, if you'll let me. I know that when Uncle Ernest played Queen to her third everything was all over. But if you'd played Pawn takes Pawn, instead of Bishop to Queen's Bishop's fifth, the course of the game would have changed."

"I'm afraid you don't know as much about chess as you think you do, son. Had I played Pawn takes Pawn, as you suggest, what would have been my following move?"

"If you let me set up the board again, I think I can show you, Father."

"As you see, I've moved some of the men already, Paul. I don't believe I could put them back exactly as they were. I don't remember all their positions."

"I do. Let me put them back. Please, Father."

The child spoke so beseechingly and earnestly that Alonzo could not help being moved. And it was quite true that Paul had an infallible memory —that was among the reasons why he had progressed so rapidly at school; his reports showed that, once he had learned a lesson, he never forgot the slightest detail of it. Moreover, at home, he frequently recalled to other members of the family incidents, many of them trivial, which they had completely forgotten. He had never made a show of this; it was only when such recollections would in some way be helpful that he supplied the requisite missing link between situations which, otherwise, would have been baffling; but this had happened often enough to impress not only his brother and sisters, but his parents and grandparents. Alonzo, in spite of himself, was impressed now.

"Very well," he said. "Set them up as they were. I couldn't do it myself, but I daresay I'd recognize a mistake in the arrangement, if you made one."

Paul fetched the two chairs which had already been neatly ranged on either side of the double doors leading into the ballroom, and put them facing each other across the table. Next, he took two large volumes from the glass-enclosed bookcase in the corner and placed them on the chair he expected to occupy; he was so undersized that he could not reach the chessmen easily without such an expedient. Then, after waiting for his father to sit down, he seated himself and began to reorganize the disarranged board. His fingers, which were slim and deft, moved quickly. In no time, the pieces were in place and he looked up at his father.

"That was the set-up when you made your first incorrect move," he said.

Alonzo, who had been following his son's swift movements with mingled astonishment and admiration, looked fixedly at the board. "Yes," he said at last. "Yes, I believe you're right. I believe that was the way it was—in fact, I know that is exactly the way it was. From here on, pretend you're playing for me and that I'm playing for your Uncle Ernest. What do you think I should have done next?"

"You should have replied with Queen to her fourth. Then Uncle Ernest would have played Pawn takes Knight. Your next move would have been King's Bishop takes Pawn, Uncle Ernest retaliating with Queen to King's Knight sixth. After that, you could have played King to Queen's second and Uncle Ernest would have castled. Your final blow would have been Queen's Rook to King's Knight square and you would have won."

As he spoke, the child shifted the pieces quickly from place to place. When he moved the Queen's Rook to King's Knight square, he glanced up with a gleam of triumph in his eye. For a moment, his father stared almost unbelievingly at the board and, as if to convince himself that there had been no possible error, he reflectively placed a testing finger on piece after piece. Finally, he met his son's steadfast gaze and held out his hand, laughing.

"You're right," he said. "Right as rain. Rousseau himself couldn't have done better. *Mes compliments, maître d'échecs de l'avenir!* Now, run along to bed. I'm going myself in a few minutes."

Telcide appeared to be dozing when Alonzo entered the familiar room which had been their bridal chamber and which they still occupied together. She often stole little naps, when he and Ernest sat late at chess and, obviously, this was what she was doing now, for she did not instantly sit up in bed, propping her great square pillows high behind her and smile at him in welcome, as would have happened if she had been aware of his presence. He knew he need only speak her name softly, in order to rouse her, to find her alert and eager to meet his mood, whatever this might be. No man could have asked for a more compliant wife. But, at the moment, his mood was reflective, rather than demanding. He seated himself in one of the comfortable armchairs near the fireplace and permitted his thoughts to wander, as his gaze roamed around the room, which the *veilleuse* on the mantel and the coals on the hearth illumined with their soft light. The lace festoons and the cupids had disappeared from the four-poster; but the canopy, lined with fluted silk, which gave it the name of *lit à ciel*, was unchanged, except that the silk had faded and was now silver gray rather than blue. The *accouchement* bed, which had been used four times, was also still in place, though Malvina, the first child born on it, was seventeen years old, and might soon be needing marital equipment herself, judging from the number of suitors who were already clamoring for her attention. Although she was not permitted to go to the semi-public dances at the ballroom adjoining the *Théatre d'Orléans*, she had been to a succession of those *bals de royauté* which had been an institution in Creole families from the earliest Colonial days; and while these were always held in private houses, with carefully selected guest lists, they were so numerous that, in the course of a season, Malvina inevitably met a good many eligible young men, or at least young men who considered themselves eligible, to whose importunities she listened with more attention than her father considered desirable. Of course, she must marry eventually, at some time in the comfortably vague future and, when she did, she would have to be provided with an *accouchement* bed, as well as a *lit à ciel*. But there was no need of worrying about that yet. He had been disturbed, however, because she had come in that evening much later than he approved, from a *soirée* at the St. Martins', who were cousins of his and who had formerly lived next door, but who had now moved to Bourbon Street, which did not permit such close supervision. He had interrupted his chess game to speak to her sharply, and he meant to speak to her still more sharply in the morning, for he could not altogether dismiss her flightiness from his mind, even in his gratification over the surprise Paul had given him. It was a relief to know that she was at last sleeping quietly in the next room, which she shared with little Hélène, and that their slumbers were equally peaceful and unbroken.

He was annoyed with himself, however, because he could not completely dismiss the *accouchement* bed from his mind. His gaze wandered toward Telcide, who was still quietly dozing. Presumably, she would never need it again, as eight years had now passed since the birth of Hélène. Alonzo was rather glad of this, not only because, as he had told his brother, four children were enough to provide for, with the cost of living what it was, but also because he had found Telcide's confinements increasingly harrowing. There was no logical reason for this. It had not occurred to him to dread her first one; indeed, he was slightly annoyed because she did not—as her mother had rightly guessed he hoped—give him an heir for a New Year's present, ten months after they were married; the delay of even two in proving her powers of production had seemed to him unduly long, considering the frequency and intensity of his acts of love, which she had never resisted, much less repelled. Alonzo prided himself that he had been man enough to give her no chance to do the first, and gave her mother credit for counseling her not to do the second. To be sure, it had taken Telcide time to get over her first fright and pain, her first sense of shock and outrage; but that was all to her credit. A passionate bride was an object of suspicion among the Creoles—indeed, one bridegroom of the family's acquaintance had actually asked for a canonical separation from his wife because she responded so easily and ardently to his initial embraces that nothing would convince him she had not been prepared for them by another man; and even a responsive bride was regarded somewhat askance. Alonzo had been greatly gratified by Telcide's abysmal innocence and pleased, rather than concerned, because her acceptance of his advances was based on helplessness and not on free will. But he had not been able to dismiss promptly from his mind the horrors surrounding Malvina's birth, though these had been brought home to him as little as possible. This lack of easy forgetfulness was a source of annoyance, because it had made him temporarily hesitant about resuming the exercise of his marital rights as soon after the birth of the child as he otherwise would have done. But he had had a happy surprise: Telcide—doubtless due, he told himself, to the wise course he had pursued—finally quickened to ardor; he had no reason for remorse for forcing himself upon her when Malvina was still a baby, because, now that a suitable time had elapsed for initiation into the mysteries of matrimony and no reflection could be cast on her maidenly character, Telcide was ready for his embraces; she not only returned them spontaneously, she sometimes even seemed to invite them. He actually dreaded her second confinement more than she did or, at any rate, more than she seemed to. As a matter of fact, there was no reason why she should have dreaded it; she was in labor barely twelve hours when Edward was born, whereas it had taken three days and nights to bring Malvina into the world; with Paul and Hélène, things had been easier still. And yet—illogically, he told himself, since it was only part of an established pattern, Alonzo was glad to think that the *accouchement* bed would probably never be used again, at least by Telcide, and found himself wincing at the thought that Malvina and Hélène would some time need its prototype. Indeed, he shrank from the vision of some unknown young man who might subject either of his daughters to such an ordeal as he had triumphantly imposed upon his own bride, not only during their wedding night, but during the entire period of two weeks when they had never left their nuptial chamber.

Not, he reflected now, by no means for the first time, that he regretted what he had done; everything had turned out admirably. He and Telcide were regarded by their family and friends as an ideal couple, and he knew that she felt, as he did, that their marriage had been a great success. To be sure, he realized that she rather resented his preoccupation with chess, though she never said so; he was almost as tolerant about her preoccupation with the piano and harp, and thoughtfully brought home sheet music whenever he saw anything new displayed in shop windows which he felt might appeal to her. He had prospered in his profession and he was generous with his wife; he provided her with a handsome carriage and permitted her to set a lavish table and buy beautiful clothes without consulting him as to their cost. In addition, he gave her frequent presents of handsome jewelry. She made allowances for certain masculine peccadilloes and did not inquire too closely into what he did with his time when he was not at home. If it ever occurred to her that this was not fully filled with his legal and banking duties and his visits to his brother, she never said so. As far as he was concerned, he was completely confident that she never did anything in his absence that would reflect discredit upon him; he knew she was a loyal wife and a devoted mother, besides being a meticulous housekeeper and an accomplished hostess. Both he and she were satisfied with their *status quo*. But times were changing with the new generation. Perhaps a different approach to matrimony might result in more immediate and more radiant bliss, as far as Malvina and Hélène were concerned. The thought was a recurrent one and forced itself to the forefront of his consciousness even when he should have been otherwise preoccupied. . . .

He was suddenly aware that Telcide had wakened and that he had not even realized when this happened. She was already sitting up in bed, with her pillows piled high behind her, smiling at him. She had a very charming smile. Indeed, the years had dealt kindly with her, despite child-bearing, emotional adjustment and never-ending household responsibilities. She and her elder daughter might easily have passed for sisters. Her color was as fresh, her hair as soft and dark, her form as graceful as ever. Alonzo thought he had never seen her look more desirable than she did now; and though he would expect and receive recognition of his desire later on, he was not yet ready to yield to it and Telcide knew this.

"Did you have a good game?" she asked pleasantly.

"Yes. A surprisingly good one."

"*Surprisingly* good?" she repeated, revealing her own interested astonishment. "I thought all chess games were good, if you won."

"Not if, having lost, you later learn how you might have won and, thereby, learn how to win repeatedly in the future. I am going to explain to you what I mean before we settle down for the night. But, meantime, by way of introduction to my subsequent remarks, I will break the news that we have another chess player in the family."

"Morphy at the age of thirteen played a strong Chess game without sight of the board. Rising step by step to two games, to three, to four and so on, we find him while still in his teens playing twelve games simultaneously blindfolded and against players to whom the champions of the day could not give more than a pawn and move with safety in a set match. More surprising even than the number of games which Morphy could thus play blindfolded at one sitting, was the nature of his play under these seemingly difficult conditions. The brilliancy of the combinations was in most cases matched by their soundness and often by their depth—in the sense of the number of moves over which, with lightning rapidity, he carried his analysis. A veteran player told me of one of these games which he had carefully examined after it was finished because he believed that a certain brilliant stroke could be more successfully met than it had been in actual plays. 'Along every line,' he said, 'but one, I found Morphy's strategy sound, but along that line there seemed to me a safe, though difficult defence, resulting in eventual victory over him. I passed an hour or two every evening for a week, analysing the game along this line, and having satisfied myself it was sound, I mentioned the point to Morphy when next I met him. I was for setting up the board to show him what I meant, but he would not suffer me. "I remember the game perfectly," he said. "Your defence is not sound, though it is the best available; you have overlooked a mate in three, following the sacrifice of my King's Bishop after the fifth move of your defence." ' My veteran friend looked over the position the same evening and found the case was as Morphy had stated.

"Imagine the abnormal brain development in some special though unknown way, which enabled a boy Chess player, ten days after playing a game which was one of the twelve played blindfolded, to correct in an instant and without setting up the position, the result of ten or twelve hours of analysis of the game by a strong and veteran player!"

Richard A. Proctor in the *Louisville Courier Journal*.

6.

The news of Paul's astonishing feat quickly spread beyond the connubial chamber of his parents. Not that he mentioned it himself to Edward; he guessed and rightly, that Edward, who already considered himself quite a chess player, would not be especially pleased at learning he had another rival in the family circle, and that this rival was a brother three years his junior. Paul went quietly to bed, and did not speak of the matter the next day at school, either to Edward or to his only intimate friend, Charles de Maurian. He did not mingle riotously with the other boys, as Edward did; in point of fact, he cared so little for sports or for general companionship, that he usually remained in the classroom during recess, reading or writing alone, though Charles, who was as robust and ruddy as Paul was delicate and pale, continually urged him to join the others. He followed his usual custom the morning after he had so suddenly aroused his father's amazement and admiration.

The rest of the family was more vocal. Before he went to his own office, Alonzo went to Ernest's, explained to the latter what had happened, and urged his brother to come around to the Chartres Street house that evening to see for himself exactly how the game had worked out. Their half-brother, Diego, Jr., had succeeded their father as Spanish Consul, so neither had any responsibilities as far as functions of this office were concerned; but Ernest had become a successful cotton broker and this business, while remunerative, also required intensive attention and long hours of exacting work; however, he listened to Alonzo patiently, if not enthusiastically; he could scarcely be expected to rejoice at finding himself out-maneuvered by a ten-year-old child, especially after having been regarded for some years as the foremost chess player in New Orleans, with the possible exception of his friend and contemporary, Eugene Rousseau. Though his manner toward the judge was marked by a certain coolness, it was courteous; if Alonzo would set up the board again, exactly as he and Paul had left it, Ernest would be glad to see how the results of the match had been altered. There would be no need to set up the board again, Alonzo told him rather smugly; it had been left exactly as it was and Telcide had been warned not to touch it, or to allow her mother, Malvina, Hélène, the two boys or the servants to do so.

In the face of these instructions, it was impossible for Telcide to keep her counsel, even if she had wished to do so. The servants were well trained to unquestioning obedience and the boys were at school most of the day, so they presented no problem. Neither did Mme Le Carpentier, for Telcide was now mistress of her own establishment, to all intents and purposes, instead of a docile member of her mother's. The Le Carpentiers still retained title to the house which Joseph had built with such pride; but after the marriage of Amenaïde to the rising young physician, Edouard Fortin, he and his wife had moved, with Amélie and Charles, to a smaller house in the same block, indicating that, if the Morphys were to remain in the larger one, Alonzo must assume the expense and responsibility of running it. As he had both the means and the desire to do this, and the need of more room for his increasing family, the change caused no regrets, as far as he was concerned, but it had been hard for the older lady to adjust herself to a less ostentatious way of life; she was increasingly prone to sit at home and brood over it. The slave trade was not what it had been, anyway, at her husband's auction rooms; and he had been reckless about purchasing real estate and foolhardy in striving to outdo all his neighbors in the pretentious style of his living. She could not refrain from reproaching Telcide for some of these extravagances, which had been incurred in her behalf; and Telcide was relieved when she did not have to listen to such recriminations, and glad, rather than otherwise, not to see her mother just then, quite aside from the question of the chess table. It happened this was the day, formally set aside, for the reception of guests; her callers would naturally wonder why the *salle de compagnie* was not in its usual state of rigid order; and Telcide was only too delighted at the idea of giving the indicated explanation. On their return to their own homes, the visiting ladies would hardly be able to wait in order to share the tidings of such a phenomenon with their families. Hélène's little playmates were not much interested in what had happened, nor was she able to tell her tale very effectively; the case of Malvina was entirely different: she was attending an afternoon party and found herself the center of a circle so inquisitive that half of the gilded youth there assembled were ready to skip a dance or two in order to listen to her. She was not at all displeased at thus finding herself a center of attraction; the only drawback was that the others did not all want to listen at the same time; they drifted back and forth and kept stopping her when she was about to go on the floor herself. One of her prospective partners, John Sybrandt, who was openly paying court to her, was especially annoyed when this happened.

"I don't see why you have to spoil a dance just to brag about a child's chess playing," he said rather sullenly.

"But John, I haven't spoiled the dance! I've added to the excitement of it! It was threatening to be a dull party when I turned it into a lively one. And I wasn't bragging—that is, not really. I was just saying that Paul, who had been watching Father and Uncle Ernest—"

"Yes, I heard what you said. Do you want to waltz or don't you?"

Malvina did want to waltz; she especially wanted to waltz with John

Sybrandt, whose courtship she was inclined to favor, though she had not yet been able to find out whether her father and mother did so or not. She melted willingly into his arms, her full, frilly skirts billowing out around her, and gazed up at him with rapture. He tightened his hold on her unbelievably small waist and they floated off together. Paul was not mentioned again between them that afternoon.

The case of Edward was quite different. He was much more active, physically, than Paul, but he was also a really good chess player, and was never too tired for a match when he came home from school, if there were nothing else he especially wanted to do. His mother always included some sort of a musical program at her receptions, which caused them to last longer than most of those held in their circle of acquaintances, and her visitors were still in the *salle de compagnie* when he walked through the hall, so he did not intrude. But he overheard scraps of conversation and immediately returned to the rear gallery where Paul, having spent all his recess periods in reading, was now reading again.

"What's the meaning of all this chatter about Father's game with Uncle Ernest last night?" Edward asked abruptly.

Paul partially closed his book, keeping one finger to mark the place where he had left off reading. "I haven't heard the chatter, so I don't know," he said pleasantly but noncommittally.

"Well, you must have some idea. When those visiting ladies aren't singing to their own accompaniment, or playing the harp, or urging Mother to do one or the other, they're all talking their heads off about what a paragon you must be."

"I'm not sure just what you mean by a paragon."

"Oh, a prodigy of some sort! Pity none of us realized it before! I'm afraid we haven't been paying you as much respect as we should."

He spoke scornfully, but there was a note of apprehension in his scorn. Obviously, Paul had done something remarkable, something that he, Edward, had never done. He was almost choked with jealousy.

"Well, it was like this," Paul said with the continued calm that never failed to irritate his brother. "Father and Uncle Ernest played last evening while you were at Grandfather's and I watched them. You know I'd rather watch a chess game than do almost anything else. Father's mind must have been on some decision he's got to make, in the court or at the bank, instead of on the game. So, after Uncle Ernest left, I asked Father if he wouldn't set up the board again and let me show him where I thought he'd made a mistake."

"Damn cheeky of you, I'd call it. He probably didn't remember how the board was set up, as far as that goes."

"He didn't exactly, but I did. And when I put the chessmen back in place, he said, yes, that was the way it was. We played the last part of the game over again. I took Father's men and he took Uncle Ernest's. And I won."

Paul reopened his book and resumed his reading. Edward snatched the book out of his hand.

"A tall tale, if there ever was one! When I see that match played, maybe I'll believe you."

Paul retrieved his book, but before he resumed his reading, he answered in the same quiet way he had spoken before. "When we went to bed last night, Father said he was going to leave the chessboard the way it was, and ask Mother not to let anyone touch it until he and Uncle Ernest could play the last part of the game again. I believe he meant to ask Uncle Ernest to come back tonight. If he did and Uncle Ernest comes, you can watch the game. Then you can decide for yourself about the tall tale. And, as far as that goes, I'll play with Uncle Ernest and you myself, whenever either of you'd like me to. I don't know just why you all thought that all I could do was to tell a King from a Castle. It doesn't take much intelligence to learn more than that, by the time you're my age, if both your grandfathers—"

"One of your grandfathers died before you were born!"

"Yes, I know. But a record's been kept of his major games. And the other grandfather still plays almost every evening—not to mention my father and our uncle Ernest and practically all their friends. I've been watching them for some time."

"Ever since you were a baby in long clothes, I suppose!"

"No, but ever since I could write well enough to keep a record myself—and you know I could write by the time I was six. Well, here are Father and Uncle Ernest now. Why don't you let them tell you—and show you—what happened?"

This time, Paul put his book conclusively aside and ran down the rear steps into the patio. Ernest greeted him affectionately.

"Well, Paul, I hear we have a champion in the family. I'll have to start taking you with me to the Exchange Reading Rooms—there's a special section there reserved for chess players. I'd like to show you off to some of my friends."

"You won't do anything of the sort." Telcide's visitors had at last departed and, unobserved, she had come out on the gallery, where Beckey had already begun laying the table for dinner. "It's one thing to have the child play here, in our own house, but it's quite another to show him off before a group of sports. I've managed to leave the chess table untouched, as you asked me to, Alonzo, so you could repeat last night's game, but first, let's have something to eat. Boys, go and wash your hands and tell your sisters to come out here. We'll have a quiet, unhurried family meal."

The family meal was not as quiet or as unhurried as Telcide might have wished. Hélène, who was a delicate, nervous child, refused to eat; her mother, without success, kept coaxing her to try this morsel or that, and finally decided that she would be better off in bed and that Malvina should sit with her and read aloud to her or sing to her soothingly until she went to sleep. Malvina, who was expecting John Sybrandt to call on her, and later to escort her to a *bal de royauté* was not at all pleased with this arrangement, and her parents were not pleased with those she had made on her own initiative. She had already seen John Sybrandt at a party that afternoon and, in their opinion, he was calling too frequently for anyone who was not officially an accepted suitor; and who, pray, was to chaperone them on their way to and from this dance? Her mother was too tired after her fatiguing reception; her father proposed to play chess. Even after Malvina assured them that a way had been found out of these difficulties, they were not appeased. It seemed she had taken it for granted, considering the circumstances they had just mentioned, that they would not be needing the carriage; and Malvina had approached Mme Le Carpentier, who had willingly agreed to accompany her to the dance, which was again at the St. Martins', who seemed to be entertaining perpetually. It was all too apparent, Alonzo said, that the young people of the present generation had no consideration for their elders and no regard for the proprieties. Mme Le Carpentier was getting on in years; it was too much of an effort for her to stay out until all hours, even if, under pressure, she consented to do so. As for John Sybrandt, the judge proposed to have a serious talk with him at the earliest opportunity. Not tonight, since he would be otherwise occupied, but very soon. Meanwhile, Malvina should discourage his visits and decline his escort.

"As we've told you before, it isn't as if the St. Martins were still living next door," Telcide added reprovingly, "or as if Natalie were at home instead of in Paris. The next thing we know, you'll be asking to go down to Belle Chasse, where that Jewish husband of hers is giving all those ostentatious parties."

"As a matter of fact, that's exactly what I was going to suggest," Malvina retorted, as she scooped up the last of her turtle soup. "Mr. Benjamin likes young people—he always includes some of our crowd in his invitations. He's included John and me in the one for next Sunday."

"Then your father will decline for you in a note personally delivered to Mr. Benjamin's office tomorrow morning," Telcide said, now speaking not only reprovingly but icily. "Of course, what John Sybrandt does is no affair of ours."

"I don't know that I want to go out of my way to offend Judah Benjamin," Alonzo said surprisingly, as he took a second helping of *grillades*. "He's not only one of the best lawyers, but one of the ablest all around men in Louisiana today. Incidentally, he's not a bad chess player. I don't mean that he's in the same class with Ernest and Rousseau, but he's good enough so that they both enjoy having a game with him occasionally. Mark my words, he'll go far in whatever he undertakes; it won't do us any harm to be on good terms with him. Auguste St. Martin always goes to his son-in-law's parties; he thrills the boys and girls with his stories about the bloody slave risings in Santo Domingo when he was a young man; they sit around hanging on his words and shivering with delight. Besides, he dotes on Judah; Auguste doesn't blame him in the least for his separation from Natalie. Of course, she's our cousin and we mustn't criticize our own kin. But, after all, her indiscretions—"

"I wasn't talking about Natalie's indiscretions," Telcide said, in a tone that clearly implied she did not wish Alonzo to do so either, particularly in the presence of their children. "But Malvina's got to have some sort of a chaperone besides Auguste. He's getting to be a garrulous old man, and he probably doesn't notice half of what's going on."

"I understand that Judah's sister, Miss Rebecca Benjamin, is not only a very gracious but a very capable hostess for him," Alonzo said. "To tell you the truth, I'm pleased rather than otherwise that Malvina's been invited to Belle Chasse, though I'd have been better pleased if John Sybrandt had been asked at a different time. She's much too young to be taking any suitor seriously."

"How old was Mother when she began to take you seriously?" Malvina inquired somewhat pertly.

"That has nothing to do with the present question. She was much more mature for her age than you are, and my future was already assured. However, as I said, you may accept the invitation to Belle Chasse, provided it comes in proper form to either your mother or me. Naturally, you will take Tata with you; it is high time that she stopped considering herself a dry nurse and learned to act like a lady's maid. And I will arrange about the carriage. Perhaps we had better consider the advisability of having two and supplementing Friday's services with those of another slave. Friday's getting to be an old man."

"He never was anything better than a carter, anyway," Telcide said testily. "But we don't need another slave. Honoré has not anywhere nearly enough to do—there's no reason why he shouldn't be trained as a coachman. On the other hand, I can't spare Tata. After all, she's always taken full charge of

Hélène, as she did of all the other children from the time of their birth. Hélène's ailing, as you can see for yourself. If she were deprived of her nurse, at a time like this, she might become seriously ill."

"All right, we'll send Beckey and let Jacques do the serving alone for a few days," Alonzo responded. "If Honoré can be trained as a coachman, there's no reason why Jacques shouldn't be trained to be a better butler."

A tempest in a teapot seemed imminent. Ernest had no desire to take sides; indeed, in this instance, he sympathized with both his sister-in-law and his brother. He knew that Telcide had always considered Natalie St. Martin's marriage a mésalliance, not only because Benjamin was a Jew and her Catholic training had been of such a nature that she was bound to misprize him on that account, but because he was a noveau riche. It was easy for her to forget that, until recently, a Le Carpentier had not been considered the social equal of a Morphy and, also, for her to overlook Natalie's "indiscretions," which might have been called by a harsher name. No doubt, Telcide herself would have welcomed an occasional trip to Paris, if not actually a sojourn there, instead of perpetual enclosure in the Vieux Carré; and no doubt she would have enjoyed the society of gentlemen, to a greater degree than her restricted mode of life permitted. It was not only Natalie's exploits which might have made her restless; her lively and scatter-brained sister Amenaïde, who had married young Dr. Fortin, had spent considerable time abroad—in fact, one of her children had been born in Paris and had not been baptized until the *jeune ménage* returned to New Orleans. This delay had scandalized the rest of the family and had given rise to speculations about other possible lapses. Alonzo was still very Spanish in his viewpoint about the degree of seclusion desirable for women, and it seemed likely, judging from Malvina's mutinous attitude, that her father would soon be forced to change this viewpoint, whether he wished to do so or not. Ernest saw no reason why Alonzo should not listen more favorably to John Sybrandt's suit. He was good looking, he had no obvious bad habits, and he was doing well in the Cotton Exchange, as Ernest was in a position to judge. On the other hand, Ernest respected and even shared his brother's opinion that Judah P. Benjamin had a great future before him. He would have enjoyed going to Belle Chasse himself and, unless he were mistaken, Alonzo secretly hoped that the invitation to Malvina might lead to others which would include more of the family. The once unknown Jew had already come a long way: after arriving in New Orleans from Charleston, with hardly a cent to call his own, and a somewhat tarnished reputation regarding his alleged, though unproved indiscretions at Yale, he had won signal recognition in the legal profession, had become a successful sugar planter and a member of the state legislature and had married into one of the first families; there was every prospect that, before long, he would be elected to the United States Senate, and then his position of importance would not be local, but national, and those who had previously been cordial to him might well continue to profit thereby. Moreover, he was affable, hospitable and generous; despite his enormous capacity for work, he never gave the impression of being hard pressed, he found time to entertain delightfully, and his charity to those less fortunate than himself had become a byword. Decidedly, there was much to be said in his favor. But Ernest decided to pursue a safer subject.

"It is good to know that Pierre Beauregard has so completely recovered from the illness to which he succumbed on the very day that our victorious army took possession of Mexico City," he said. "It seemed like the irony of fate that he was obliged to take to his bed with chills and fever after going through the war without any more serious injury than a couple of trifling wounds. However, I gather that everything was made very comfortable and pleasant for him while he had to linger for a few weeks at the Aztec Club, and he certainly had a royal welcome when he reached New Orleans. Now I understand that he and Laure and the children are spending most of their time with the Villerés at Magnolia Plantation and that he is getting a good rest."

"He certainly deserves it!" Alonzo and Telcide spoke simultaneously and, as Ernest had foreseen, the change of subject cleared the atmosphere. "While we are talking about men with a great future," Telcide went on, "we might mention Pierre—a real Louisianian. None of the younger officers in the Engineering Corps has come out of the war with a record comparable to his."

"It is highly creditable," Alonzo admitted ungrudgingly. "But there's also a young engineer from Virginia, named Lee, that I do hear compared to Pierre in prowess. Of course, that may be an exaggeration. Anyway, I met Jules Villeré, Laure's father, on the street just the other day, and he said that whenever I felt like going down to Magnolia—*that's* a place where we know we're always welcome—"

"Oh, Father, couldn't you take me with you?" Edward inquired eagerly. Though Ernest had not failed to observe the slight note of envious sarcasm in his brother's voice, it had escaped the boy entirely. "Then perhaps Major Beauregard would tell us all about the Battle of Chapultepec himself!"

"I'm beginning to think neither of my elder children is satisfied to stay at home," Telcide said rather drily. "If it isn't Belle Chasse, then it's Magnolia. I hope I'm not going to hear next that you want to go visiting somewhere, Paul."

"No, Mother. But I do want Uncle Ernest and Edward to see how Father and I worked out that chess game."

"I think we've all finished dinner now, haven't we? There's no reason why we shouldn't show them right away."

Alonzo rose without waiting for Telcide to give the signal to leave the table, forestalling Edward's request for a second helping of "nectar," as vanilla ice cream, flavored with grenadine and raspberry, blended with *syrop d'orgeat*, was locally known. Hélène was led whimpering off to bed and tucked in with very little formality; then Malvina changed hurriedly into an elaborately flowered evening dress; and, having maneuvered to meet John Sybrandt in the front hall near the entrance door, whispered to him that they would have their tête-à-tête at her grandfather's, as her mother was going to spend the evening with the old gentleman, while her grandmother was at the ball. A tête-à-tête consisted of nothing more than a guarded conversation in one room, with the door open into the next, where the rest of the family sat at attention; but at least it was better than nothing, especially in a case like this, when Telcide was admittedly very tired and might even doze, and Joseph Le Carpentier, less admittedly, was growing quite deaf. The courting couple and the reluctant mother of the self-willed girl were at last on their way down the front steps, and the chess players, sighing inwardly with relief, settled down to their game, with the two boys —Edward fuming, Paul completely composed—seated beside them.

It took only a few minutes to convince Ernest that Paul had correctly sized up the last few plays in the game of the previous evening. He rose from the table, clapped his younger nephew on the back, and said they must have a game together some time the following week; he could not stay any longer just then, as he had already promised to meet his friend James McConnell at the Exchange Reading Rooms—where he proposed to take Paul as soon as Telcide would permit!—and was already late for the appointment. Alonzo, having said good night with equal amiability, was about to put the chessboard away, when Edward sprang forward and put his hand over it.

"You're not going to let Paul get away with it as easy as all that, are you, Father?" he asked angrily. "Let *me* play with him; *I'll* show him!"

Alonzo glanced from one brother to the other, not without anxiety. The air was electric again. But, as in the case of Malvina, it seemed better to temporize.

"Very well," he said. "Your uncle Ernest thinks I permit Paul to sit up too late. But just this once more, I'll make an exception and give him two hours' grace. If you can win or even draw in that length of time, Edward, more power to you! Meanwhile, I'll be the onlooker this time."

The Morphys dined later than most of their friends, especially on the days when Telcide received. The clock was just striking nine as the chessmen were set up a second time. It was chiming the quarter hour before eleven when Edward swept them off the board and gave his brother a furious look.

"I'll never play another game with you as long as I live!" he shouted. "I don't know how you do it, but I do know this: I won't have you bragging all over New Orleans that you can beat your elder brother."

"I wouldn't brag," Paul answered, gathering up the scattered chessmen. "And I'm sorry you don't want to play with me. But, if you won't, I'll see if I can't play with someone else."

Courtyard of the Morphy house on Royal Street,
from a private drawing hitherto unpublished.

7.

Alonzo was too strict a disciplinarian to permit Edward's defiant statement to remain unchallenged. He sternly reminded his elder son that Paul had never been a braggart, and that there was absolutely no reason to suppose he would suddenly turn into one, on the strength of a single feat of skill; it was far more likely that he would minimize this, if he mentioned it at all. However that might be, chess games between the brothers must continue. Nevertheless, as Paul went on, winning game after game, Alonzo relaxed to the point of permitting the periods between Edward's evenings of humiliation to lengthen; and eventually Paul was playing with so many other persons that, without losing face, their father was able to say it was evident there was not enough time left over for the talented boy to waste on matches where the outcome was a foregone conclusion. He had not begun to realize that this would almost always be the case, no matter who Paul's adversary happened to be; but at least it had the merit of freeing Edward from forced participation in a contest which he had ceased to regard as a pastime and now considered an ordeal.

Joseph Le Carpentier, on the contrary, took never-ending pleasure in playing with Paul, much to the chagrin of Charles, whose father had never ceased to regard his son's game with contempt, though it was well above the average. The boy spent evening after evening with the old man, whose activities and interests were becoming more and more restricted. He enjoyed going every morning to the French Market, where he bought the daily supplies for both establishments, since Alonzo, though subscribing, like most Creoles, to the theory that the purchase of food was a masculine prerogative, left all such provisioning to his father-in-law, while he paid ungrudgingly for his share, and never even mentioned the subject of lagniappe, which Le Carpentier appropriated without qualms. Although Joseph was now obliged to lean heavily on a cane, as his weight had become burdensome, he enjoyed the walk down Ursuline to Decatur; neither the intense heat of summer, nor the chill winds of winter, nor the downpour of rain which might come at any season bothered him. As he walked along, he stopped to pass the time of day with various social acquaintances, bent on errands similar to his, and also with several storekeepers, who were apt to be standing at the open doorways of their tiny shops, and with whom he had achieved a cordial relationship, even though it was slightly condescending on his part. When he reached the market, he did not allow either his increasing avoirdupois or his reduced fortunes to deter him from buying large quantities of the best foodstuffs he could find and there were plenty to choose from: glowing fruits, vegetables almost as varied and as multi-colored; great slabs of red meat; small fur-bearing animals such as rabbits and squirrels which had been disemboweled, but not skinned; unplucked poultry and game; huge baskets piled high with crabs and shrimp; iridescent fish hanging from hooks. The vendors were as various as their wares: pure-bred French and Spanish; Isleños from the Deep Delta; Indians and "Red-bones" from Lacombe; stalwart Negroes still as black as the people of the African tribes from which they had been torn; lovely quadroons in whom no outsider would have recognized the touch of the tarbrush, but whom Orleanians were quick to identify by the turbans they were obliged, by law, to wear—all proclaiming their wares in the tongue and the manner most natural to them, from the stolid Indians to the excitable Isleños. The mingled backgrounds of the latter, who had originally all come from the Canaries, but now included Chinese, Malayan, Filipino, Portuguese, Italian, Danish, Swedish, German, Greek and Slav, as well as Creole, had resulted in a dialect peculiar to their region, which was even more baffling, especially when shouted, to those who did not speak it themselves, than the "gumbo French" used by many Negroids. The babel of these voices mingled with the creaking of small carts, the clatter of wagons over the cobblestones and the whistles from the steamboats on the river just beyond the market.

None of this confusion, none of this uproar, disturbed Le Carpentier; he made his way in leisurely fashion from one stall to the next, not for-getting the herbs which formed so essential a part of cuisine—garlic, bay leaves, thyme, basil and the sassafras leaves which would be powdered and used as filé for gumbo—both Modeste and Telcide considered it preferable to okra for this purpose. All these herbs would be gathered together into a "seasoning bunch." Everywhere Joseph selected the best he saw and plenty of it: the mirlitons and cushaws were exceptionally fine and fresh this morn-ing? Very well, he would take two dozen of each. Mallards? Of course; but were there any papabotes to go with them? Indeed, yes, Monsieur; the Indian girl from Lafourche, who is sitting just over there at the right, brought a brace with her. A brace? He would need more than that! Very well, there must be some elsewhere in the market. There, what did I tell you, Monsieur! Busters and frogs' legs, red fish for courtbouillon, pigs' feet and calves' feet for a *daube glacée,* pomegranates and maypops to make sirup for sweet cooling drinks. Yes, and squirrels for the Quarters; he liked those himself, but the other members of the family did not. . . . Perhaps that would be enough for this morning, but he would take one more look around. . . . The hamper of Hyacinthe, the slave who accompanied him, was piled high by the time he halted for a cup of coffee at the Café du Monde before turning toward home; and, although there were plenty of flowers in his own garden, he selected one for his buttonhole and a nosegay for his wife at the Flower Mart before he resumed his pleasant way to Chartres Street, again pausing to chat with congenial spirits.

After this excursion, he rested at home for a while and often took a second rest, at the Cathedral, before going on to his auction rooms. He had never been especially devout, but he found it soothing and pleasant to sit quietly in one of the rear pews, easing his legs and looking at the great fresco behind the altar, which represented St. Louis of France, clad in gorgeous raiment and surrounded by dignitaries of church and state, proclaiming the Seventh Crusade. The picture was no masterpiece. Le Carpentier knew enough about art to realize that. But it was glowing and vital and depicted the sort of triumphant scene he enjoyed, rather than one featuring penances and martyrdoms. That old reprobate, Don Andres Almonester y Roxas, who doubtless needed the Mass which was said for the repose of his soul every Saturday, had, nevertheless, been a constructor and a creator; this cathedral, rebuilt entirely at his expense after a dreadful fire, was a fitting memorial to him; and it looked as if his daughter, Micaela, now the Baroness Pontalba, was a chip off the old block. Her conduct was unconventional, to say the least; but what could you expect? Don Andres had not married her mother until some years after their daughter's birth; the offspring of such parents had a right to be unconventional; and the buildings, with Gallier as their architect, which were to flank either side of the Place d'Armes—no, no, that was called Jackson Square now—for which plans had already been made and which would soon be under construction were the greatest addition to the Vieux Carré which had been made in a long while. Le Carpentier had never had the honor of achieving more than a bowing acquaintance with Don Andres, who, after all, had died when the former was a quite young man; but he had met the Pontalbas through Alonzo, who knew them quite well and would doubtless have seen more of them if they had not spent so much of their time in Paris, not all of this—so it was whispered—together. Moreover, Ferdinand Percy, who had represented the Pontalbas in New Orleans during one of their frequent absences, was an intimate friend of Alonzo, and, through him, other members of the Percy family, which was a very distinguished one, had come within the Le Carpentier-Morphy orbit. Ferdinand's son, Emile, who was Secretary of the Water Works, had a fine house on Esplanade, where the Morphys often went, and he and his wife were frequent guests at the Morphys' great house. Moreover, Ferdinand had an especially fine little granddaughter, Alice, who was just about Paul's age; perhaps, later on, there might be an alliance in that quarter. If so, it would meet with none of the opposition which Malvina was encountering in her desire to marry John Sybrandt; it would be another step upward in the social world.

While he sat thinking of all this in the Cathedral one morning, Joseph also became aware that he had seen there, several times, a girl who made him think of Malvina, though she never sat near him and whose face he could not have seen in any case, since this was always veiled. But something about her carriage and her movements was certainly familiar, and he remembered hearing Telcide say, with gratification, that Malvina was going to Mass very frequently these days. All Masses were over by the time Joseph reached the Cathedral, but this veiled girl stayed on and on, praying very devoutly. Or was she praying? Was she lingering there to meet someone where she could be unobserved? It was not the first time and probably would not be the last that lovers' meetings had taken place in church. Perhaps he had better look into the matter a little more closely. If he left his accustomed pew and deliberately seated himself near this veiled girl, he would soon find out whether or not it were Malvina: if she remained close to him, he would be able to identify her in some way, even though her face were hidden; if she changed her seat or seemed to avoid him otherwise, that in itself would be a betrayal. But he decided against such spying. He shared Ernest's opinion that there was no real reason why Malvina should not be allowed to do what she pleased, as far as John Sybrandt was concerned; if she were thwarted in seeing him at home as often as she wished and forbidden to go to dances with him, she could not be blamed for meeting him in church.

It was often with either the Percys or Malvina in mind, rather than the logical business of the day, that Joseph went on to the auction rooms. They were still profitable, but he had lost his zest for the slave trade, partly because it separated him from the social status to which he had succeeded in raising Telcide, and partly because he had begun to have an uneasy feeling about its ethics. Of course, those Northern abolitionists, whose rantings were sometimes reported in the French daily paper, *l'Abeille*, were just so many fanatics; at the same time, he knew there was a germ of truth in some of their accusations. His domestic servants and those of his family and friends were never mistreated; and, in some cases, like that of Tata, for instance, whom he himself had bought as a nurse for Malvina, had eventually achieved positions of considerable household authority. Moreover, he had never established a charming quadroon on Rampart Street as a recognized mistress, or even had brief carnal relations with any woman of color. In these respects, he could congratulate himself that his conscience was wholly clear. But he knew that some of the plantations—and, as far as that went, some of the town houses—where the chattels from his auction room were sent, had a bad name; he could no longer disassociate his with this. Increasingly, he looked forward to the evenings with his little grandson, when he could forget such disturbing thoughts in his absorption with the chessboard.

But the boy did not come to play every evening, nor could that be expected; and when Paul was not there Le Carpentier found himself more and more the prey of disturbing thoughts, and these did not all center on the slave trade, by any means. Sometime before, he had sold the land on which he had planned his side garden back to his architect, Correjolles. Joseph had at first taken great interest in it; he had ordered quantities of wild iris and lilies, fern and ginger plants brought in from the slave farm in the swamps; and when these began to grow and flourish, after being transplanted, he had been gratified, both because the sight of them gave him personal pleasure and because he received so many compliments on them. This space was unwalled, so everyone passing up and down Chartres Street could look at it freely, and many paused to do so and to admire it; this was a new idea, to have a private garden open like that, instead of having it hedged in by high walls. Besides, iris and ferns and ginger were of themselves novelties in a city where an abundance of camellias and roses were taken for granted. But Alonzo did not share his father-in-law's enthusiasm for wildflowers or relish the idea of having strangers share the pleasures provided by personal property; he clung to the seclusion of the patio and insisted that his wife and children should do the same. Little by little, the side garden was neglected; when Correjolles made a good offer for the land which it covered, Le Carpentier decided to accept this. He would show his fine son-in-law that, if the latter were not pleased with the way he, Le Carpentier, improved his own property, he could and would dispose of it to someone who might build on it, thereby cutting off light and air from one entire side of the great house. Alonzo, needless to say, was furious when the sale, secretly arranged, was consummated; but it was then too late for him to do anything about the matter, unless he himself bought the land back from Correjolles, and that his pride would not allow him to do. Besides, what would be the use of owning a plot, unless he also owned the great house?

This, Le Carpentier had steadfastly refused to sell; now he was beginning to think he might change his mind: a certain John Merle had made him a handsome offer, and Merle's wife, Aloïse, was passionately fond of flowers. The Merles stood ready to buy all the property, both that still belonging to Le Carpentier and that which now belonged to Correjolles; the garden would be restored, not in its original form, but in more approved and conventional style, with a high wall, brick walks and a central fountain. Again Joseph decided to show his fine son-in-law something: namely, that the latter would have to move to a completely new location.

Again, the Justice was enraged, but the auctioneer remained adamant. Alonzo had not been satisfied either with the wild garden or with the division of the property. Very well, now there would be a formal garden in the

French style, and the property, as bought from the Ursulines, would be intact again. It was quite immaterial to Joseph where the Morphys went next. He had changed his original plans for a fine French house in order to suit Don Diego; to all intents and purposes, it had become a Spanish house. Yes, Le Carpentier had yielded, for Telcide's sake; she was in love with Alonzo and, therefore, she did not want any of the Morphys crossed. And now she might as well have been a Spaniard herself; she lived like one, she acted like one. No wonder her two eldest children were mutinous, the girl in her way, the boy in his; Malvina was seeing more and more of her unwelcome suitor; Edward was playing chess more and more infrequently. Hélène was a sickly little thing, doubtless due to the seclusion in which she was kept; she did not have enough spirit to rebel. Only Paul, out of the four, was really a credit to the Le Carpentiers and Joseph did not doubt that Paul would find a way of spending his evenings with his old grandfather, and beating him at chess, when the boy was not elsewhere, beating more prominent men.

It was true that, by now, Paul was playing with a good many adults. Ernest, having had repeated proofs of the boy's prowess, finally persuaded Telcide that she should permit her son to accompany his uncle to the Exchange Reading Rooms, where the boy proceeded to defeat Ernest's best friends and most competent antagonists—Mr. James McConnell, Mr. Eugene Rousseau, Judge Meek, Dr. Ayres, and even the great English master, Charles Stanley. Now a new chess luminary was expected to arrive in New Orleans, a Hungarian by the name of Johann Jacob Löwenthal, and Ernest was sure Paul would put him in his place, too. Of course, there might be some difficulty in persuading such a celebrity to play with a child who was not yet in his teens; but Ernest said he would undertake to bring this about. . . .

Neither Alonzo nor Telcide was particularly interested in the project. Indeed, they both thought Ernest was pushing Paul too far and too fast, and bringing him too much into the company of older men who, though undeniably persons of distinction, were less desirable companions for a little boy than schoolmates of his own age. They had decided to send him the next year to St. Joseph's College at Spring Hill, near Mobile; they were going to send Edward at the same time, confident that, in the company of so many other agreeable youths, Edward would get over his feeling of inferiority and Paul would cease to withdraw so much into himself. Charles de Maurian was going, too; he would help to bring Paul out of his shell, if anyone could, for Paul was really attached to this one friend, and they had been together for several years now at Jefferson Academy. Meanwhile, Telcide was more interested in her new house than she was in chess and she had succeeded in arousing Alonzo's enthusiasm, also. They had found one that exactly suited them, on Royal Street: an immense structure, already old at the turn of the century, where the Banque de la Louisiane had once been quartered in the basement. Later, a Virginian, Martin Gordon, had used all of it as his residence and it was from him the purchase was made at the fantastic price of thirty-five thousand dollars. It had no side garden: Le Carpentier's house was still the only one in the Vieux Carré which could boast that, as well as a patio. But its grilled porte cochere was double the usual width; not only could the largest imaginable coach and four enter it with room to spare; two carriages, going in opposite directions, could pass each other without difficulty in the great paved driveway between the entrance gate and the courtyard. This courtyard and the terraces, galleries, balconies and apartments leading from it were all spacious and beautiful. Outdoors, lattices and pergolas permitted elaborate arrangements of greenery and bloom; indoors, the floors were remarkable for their parquetry, the stairways for their grace. And—as Alonzo and Telcide did not fail to point out to her parents—this magnificent property was to be all their own, to do with whatever they pleased. Family ties were all very well; the Morphys would continue to get together with the Le Carpentiers for Sunday dinners and so on. But they would be independent, and there would be no more talk about who was responsible for building a pretentious house in the first place, or what kind of a garden was suitable to go with it.

In the end, Le Carpentier regretted that he had yielded to spite and felt he had acted rashly; he was afraid he would no longer be encouraged to do the marketing for the two families, and there were more reasons than one why he would miss such an opportunity. He began to look around for a house on Royal Street himself, ostensibly so that he would not be too far away from Paul to make the evening chess games with his grandson feasible and convenient. As a matter of fact, before long, he actually did convince himself that these were more important to him than the marketing. With feelings of desolation, instead of triumph, he watched the Morphys depart and the Merles move into the house of his dreams; and, when the change was complete, he more than once took his stance at the gatehouse of the former Ursuline Convent, which was now the Bishopric and stared across the street with mournful gaze.

"The Merles!" he said to himself, leaning heavily on his cane. "A hundred years from now, how many people are going to remember that John Merle and his wife ever lived there? That house will be known as the one which Joseph Le Carpentier built and in which Paul Morphy was born!"

THE MORALS OF CHESS

Benjamin Franklin

1779

"Playing at Chess is the most ancient and most universal game known among men; for its original is beyond the memory of history, and it has, for numberless ages, been the amusement of all the civilized nations of Asia, the Persians, the Indians, and the Chinese. Europe has had it above a thousand years; the Spaniards have spread it over their part of America, and it begins lately to make its appearance in these states. It is so interesting in itself, as not to need the view of gain to induce engaging in it; and thence it is never played for money. Those, therefore, who have leisure for such diversions, cannot find one that is more innocent . . . but advantageous, to the vanquished as well as the victor.

"The Game of Chess is not merely an idle amusement; several very valuable qualities of the mind, useful in the course of human life, are to be acquired and strengthened by it, so as to become habits ready on all occasions; for life is a kind of Chess, in which we have points to gain, and competitors or adversaries to contend with, and in which there is a vast variety of good and ill events, that are, in some degree, the effect of prudence, or the want of it. By playing at Chess then, we may learn:

"1st, Foresight, which looks a little into futurity and considers the consequences that may attend an action; for it is continually occurring to the player, 'If I move this Piece, what will be the advantage or disadvantage of my new situation? What use can my adversary make of it to annoy me? What other moves can I make to support it, and to defend myself from his attacks?'

"2d, Circumspection, which surveys the whole Chessboard, or scene of action:—the relation of the several Pieces, and their situations; the dangers they are repeatedly exposed to; the several possibilities of their aiding each other; the probabilities that the adversary may make this or that move, and attack this or that Piece; and what different means can be used to avoid his stroke, or turn its consequences against him.

"3rd, Caution, not to make our moves too hastily. This habit is best acquired by observing strictly the laws of the game; such as, if you touch a Piece, you must move it somewhere; if you set it down, you must let it stand."

The Chess Reader, The Royal Game in World Literature,
compiled by Jerome Salzmann. (Greenberg: Publisher, N.Y.)

8.

A group of children were playing blindman's buff in the courtyard at the rear of Judge Alonzo Morphy's house on Royal Street and, for once, his son Paul was romping with the others, instead of sitting in the shade bent over a book.

Charles de Maurian had come back from school with Edward and Paul, which was not unusual; so had their cousin Edgar Hincks and the two Percy boys, Henry Ferdinand and Léonce, who were about the same age; they had brought along their sister Alice, who was slightly younger; that was not unusual, either. But this time they had also brought along a friend of Alice's who, they said, would be a nice playmate for Hélène and liven her up a little. As things had turned out, she had done more than that; she had livened up everyone, including Paul. When he had sat down quietly, in a corner, according to his habit, she had run merrily over to him and, though she did not take his book away from him, or even pretend to do so, she somehow gave him such a strong impression that she thought it was strange for him to be reading, under the circumstances, that, almost without realizing it, he closed it of his own accord.

"You're Edward's brother, aren't you?" she inquired. "I'm not sure I know your name. Mine is Charmian, Charmian Sheppard. Aren't you going to try to catch me?"

He rose slowly and looked at her attentively before answering. She was fully as tall as he, but he realized that she was younger, for she had a certain childish chubbiness, though she was straight and graceful. She was very fair, with sparkling blue eyes, dimpled rosy cheeks and golden curls which framed her pretty face and white neck. Her expression was as arresting as her coloring; her smile seemed to be on the verge of bubbling into laughter. All in all, she did not look in the least like a Creole, even less so than the Percys; she looked like a young fairy princess who had stepped straight out from the pages of a *conte de fées.*

"My name is Paul. I don't usually play any game but chess," the boy answered quietly.

The little girl's smile, which had seemed so close to a laugh, now actually became one. "Chess? But that is a grown-up game! You will have plenty of time for that, and for reading, when you are older. But you won't have time to play then. Come, let me blindfold you!"

She whipped a soft handkerchief from an unseen pocket and, before he could protest any further, bound it around his eyes. Then she took his hand and drew him into the circle which the others were already forming. Her fingers felt very soft and small and yet he could not seem to resist their guidance.

"I persuaded your brother to be the first blindman," she said gaily to Hélène. "Now, Paul, you must turn around three times, and then you must start running and keep on until you catch someone. I don't believe it will take you long. I believe you can run faster than any of the rest of us, if you only try!"

She was right; it did not take him long. But it was Hélène he caught and not Charmian. As the latter took the bandage off his eyes and put it on his sister's, while the others jumped up and down and shouted excitedly, Paul detached himself from the group and started back toward his favorite corner. Charmian tied her knots with extraordinary swiftness and bounded after him.

"Why, we've only just begun!" she exclaimed. "You can't stop *now!* It's only fair to go on playing until someone catches *you!*"

All the others agreed with her, clamorously. Paul might have ignored the implication of being a spoilsport, if the accusation of being unfair had not been coupled with it. And it was true that he could run faster than any of the others; Hélène, after repeated attempts to catch someone—anyone— began to cry and Edgar, who was very tenderhearted, deliberately walked into the reach of her thin, clutching little hands; but, once blindman him- self, he gave no quarter. He seemed to avoid Hélène by instinct, as he rushed madly about in pursuit of the others, and finally succeeded in pinioning Edward who, in turn, caught Alice. Paul began to feel a certain reluctant pride in the fact that his speed in the courtyard was comparable to the speed with which he moved his pieces on the chessboard. However, he wanted to be blindman again, so that he could catch Charmian; she had lured him into this game by asking him if he did not want to catch her, and he found that he did. The only way he could do this was first to be caught himself and he had no intention of pretending that he could not avoid capture.

A sound on the rear gallery diverted him momentarily, and he glanced up to see his uncle Ernest standing there, beside a tall man who wore side- burns and a moustache, but no beard, whom Paul did not recognize, and who was looking down at the courtyard with interest. As a matter of fact, it was not the romping children who had arrested the stranger's attention, but their spacious playground. It was neither overrun with wildflowers, like the side garden Joseph Le Carpentier had originated with such enthusiasm, nor almost bare like the flagstone patio, with a fountain in the center and only enough greenery to keep it from being wholly unadorned, at the rear of the Chartres Street house. It was surrounded by tall magnolia trees, whose huge waxen flowers had burst into fragrant bloom; their scent blended with that of the honeysuckle vines, which were mingled with the ivy as a covering for the walls, and which were just beginning to bud. The peach and fig trees, which were planted in front of the magnolias, around the clear space, would, of course, not bear fruit until later; but the outsider knew enough about horticulture to realize that, before the summer was over, the one would be laden with golden fruit, the other with purple. Next came a border of roses, some already past their prime, some blossoming luxuriantly and some just beginning to bud; it was easy to see that different varieties had been planted with care, so that there should be a supply for every season. Verbena was scattered about and there were separate beds for mint and basil.

"I've been hearing a great deal about basil, of which it seems you have a plentiful supply," the visitor said. "I hear your blacks use it in their voodoo rites; I should like very much to know more about these and, if possible, to see some." He spoke French with complete correctness, but in a guttural voice which betrayed the fact that it was not his native language.

Ernest shrugged slightly. "That can easily be arranged. Such rites take place almost every Sunday in Congo Square; and if you are thinking of remaining in New Orleans, as I hope you are, until St. John's Eve, you can see them in their most extravagant form. That is the date when Marie Laveau, a handsome mulatress, who is sometimes called the Voodoo Queen, holds court in some allegedly bewitched bower, near Bayou St. John. Its location is supposed to be a secret, but it should not be too hard to discover."

"I am not sure that I can remain that long, though I should certainly like to do so," the visitor went on. "Meanwhile, I shall accept your offer to take me to Congo Square some Sunday afternoon. . . . Is the basil planted here for the benefit of your own slaves who believe in voodoo?"

"Partly, I should say. But partly because we use it ourselves for seasoning, and it is not unsightly, growing among the flowers."

"*Unsightly!* I should say not! Permit me to tell you, Monsieur, that this is one of the most beautiful gardens I have ever seen and I have seen many."

Again, Ernest shrugged slightly. "It is even more beautiful when the yellow jasmine comes out a month or so from now or when the violets are in bloom, but those are gone by now; in fact, many of them have been crystallized with sugar, for sweetmeats," he said. "My sister-in-law is very fond of flowers—a taste she inherited from her father, though his ran rather wild." Ernest smiled at his own unremarkable jest, which he made no effort to explain. "And her younger son has inherited it from her," he went on. "Next to a chessboard, he loves a garden, though it is not often he goes tearing around in one, as he is doing today. I cannot imagine what has got into him. But never mind. I have not forgotten why we came out here—it was to discuss neither voodooism nor horticulture." He cupped his hands and called to make himself heard above the hubbub of the children. "Paul! Come up here, please. I want you."

Paul's quick glance in the direction of the gallery had not roused any special interest. Strange guests were no novelty to him; his parents entertained dozens of them and his uncles brought as many as they chose to the house. This might be another allegedly famous musician, discovered by his mother or her bachelor brother Charles, who had now come to live with them and who played the flute incessantly; it might be an eminent lawyer, bringing a letter of introduction from their friend Judge Bermudez; or, for that matter, it might even be a cotton broker, lacking in polish, but tolerated by Ernest because this Midwesterner was shrewd and rich. It did not matter much. Paul was still intent on his game, for he had not yet succeeded in catching Charmian. However, he called back, civilly enough, over his shoulder.

"All right. Just a minute."

The two men left the gallery and disappeared into the house. Paul sidestepped Charles, who was blindman again, and bumped into Charmian, who did not move quickly enough. The next instant Charles had caught her.

So Paul had failed again! He watched Charles bind Charmian's eyes and wavered. Perhaps it was futile to go on playing fair. He had better let her catch him; then he could surely catch her. But he must not pause near her too soon or she and all the others would realize he was doing it on purpose and not because he was out of breath. While he hesitated, the door leading from the house to the gallery swung to with something very like a slam, and Tata advanced toward the railing, the folds of her starched apron crackling, the knotted ends of her *tignon*, which the children called "rabbits' ears," quivering as if she were very impatient or very angry. Neither was unusual.

"Paul, *to jusse gaignin l'air ain bandit jordi*," she grumbled. "*A c't' heure vini cote to'n'onc' et tache pas fai la mine comme ca.*"

"*Mais aussi co faire ous aute embete moin*," he called back. It never occurred to him, or to any of the children, to answer Tata in any other way than in the dialect which they had talked with her ever since they could talk at all, any more than it would have occurred to him to call her by her real name which was Tabitha. She had now told him that he looked and acted like a bandit, that he was to come at once to his uncle Ernest, who was waiting for him. In return, he had asked why she was bent on bothering him. But he decided that he might as well go, first as last; he could not seem to catch Charmian, whatever he did, and if he failed to obey Tata's bidding, his uncle would reappear and reprimand him sternly, before everyone. He reluctantly mounted the gallery steps, glancing backward several times as he did so. Then he suffered Tata to stand over him while he straightened his disordered clothes, washed his face and hands and brushed his hair in the *cabinet*. When he reached the drawing room, he saw that the chessboard was set up, and that his father, his uncle and the strange visitor were all standing near it.

"Paul, this is Herr Löwenthal from Hungary," his uncle said, putting his arm around the boy's shoulders. "He has gone into exile, as a result of the struggle between the Magyars and the Austrians, in which he played a heroic part. We are proud to welcome to him to New Orleans, especially as he is one of the greatest chess players in the world and—"

"And has kindly consented to honor us by playing a game with you," Alonzo said, finishing the sentence for his brother and taking his son's hand.

Paul looked quickly from one man to another. It was easy enough to guess what had happened: his father had said, trying to speak casually, that he would be gratified to have this expert's opinion on the qualifications of his younger son as a chess player; and the great man, since he was a guest in the house, could not very well refuse. He had probably answered, with inward reluctance, but with outward courtesy, that he would be glad to play one game with the little boy, if that was what would be agreeable to his host; but all the time he had doubtless been saying to himself, "This sort of a delusion on the part of a blind relative is really rather annoying." Suddenly, Paul's resentment at having been dragged away from the garden melted into thin air; perhaps he would not have been able to catch Charmian, no matter how hard he tried; but there was no doubt about it, he could beat this man at chess. One simple game! How could that make any trouble for him? He had been playing three simultaneously, blindfolded, for more than a year now. Blindfolded! That did not mean the same thing in chess as in blindman's buff. It only meant you turned your back to the boards, but kept all the different moves in mind. And that was easy enough to do. It was the other that was hard—catching a little girl you could not see. . . .

"Good afternoon, Herr Löwenthal," he said politely, stepping to the further side of the table where the chessboard was set up. "My father is right, this is a great honor. Shall we begin?"

"As soon as you sit down," Löwenthal, who had already seated himself, answered rather curtly.

"If it will not annoy you, I will play standing up. Then we will not have to wait while I bring two heavy volumes from the bookcase and put them in my chair, so that we may face each other levelly."

"But you will get very tired and that will give you a disadvantage."

"It is kind of you to think of that, Monsieur. But I often play standing up."

"Very well then, I will pick up two Pawns, and when I have brought them forward, in my closed hands, you will choose which you would rather have."

"I beg your pardon, Monsieur. Since you are our guest, I would rather the first choice should be yours."

After the opening moves, Löwenthal was convinced he was dealing with no beginner. For the next half hour the game went on with no noticeable advantage to either side. Then Tata came in with refreshments, a cooling beverage among them. She had been taught not to interrupt games, so she set her tray quietly down on a nearby table and as quietly started to leave the room. Paul called after her.

"Pour me a glass of *sirop*, please, Tata, before you go!" he said, almost pleadingly.

He was very thirsty. He had not stopped for a drink when he came into the house, overheated from running about, and now his mouth was so dry that he felt he could not bear it any longer. He seized the glass which Tata handed him and drank avidly, momentarily oblivious of everything except his thirst. His next move was made almost at random, the glass, which he had asked Tata to refill, still in his hand. Then he recognized that his move had been a mistaken one.

"*Que je suis bête!*" he exclaimed angrily. "Here, Tata, take this glass away and, next time, don't interrupt. You've been told often enough not to."

"Tata gave you the drink because you asked for it," his father reminded him rather haughtily. Alonzo was also vexed. Up to that moment, Paul had justified the faith which the judge placed in his son. Now, according to all indications, the boy had lost the game.

"That move ought not to count," Löwenthal said indulgently. "I know you did not intend to make it, Paul. I cannot hold you responsible for such an oversight."

"It doesn't matter whether or not I intended to make it," Paul said stormily. "I did make it. Of course, I cannot win the game as it now stands. But I will not let you win it, either!"

Immediately, Paul gave repeated checks with his Rook and the game was finally declared drawn. Löwenthal glanced at the clock and suggested that perhaps it was not too late to have another. Paul looked toward his father and uncle for directions and they both nodded. He quickly opened with King to King's fourth. Löwenthal retaliated with Pawn to Queen's Bishop's fourth—the so-called "Sicilian Defense." Again, for the next half hour or so of play neither side appeared to have an advantage; then Löwenthal played Queen to Rook's fifth and was not slow to realize that Paul's latest Pawn advance had meant mischief.

"'That move ought not to count,'" Paul said quietly. "'I know you did not intend to make it. I cannot hold you responsible for such an oversight.'"

Löwenthal looked across the board at his antagonist. The little boy's face was masklike; there was not a hint of impudence in it. But, despite this lack of expression, the Hungarian knew that he was being paid back in kind for his condescension and that he deserved the rebuke. He held out his hand. "Touché!" he said. "Now you will beat me fairly and squarely; and you will beat many others who consider themselves masters—in fact, probably all of those with whom you play. Suppose we consider this evening's diversion ended. If you would care to have another game with me, however, on a future occasion, that would be my pleasure. I believe there is to be an Assembly of distinguished chess players at the Exchange Hotel. Would you care to meet me then?"

"Of course, you'll accept Herr Löwenthal's flattering invitation," Alonzo said hastily. He turned from his son to his visitor. "I am sorry that, before we knew of the proposed Assembly, my brother Ernest and I had made another commitment," he said regretfully. "Ordinarily, I would try to cancel any previous engagement. But this happens to be an occasion when I do not feel I can do so. One of our very good friends, Pierre Beauregard, had the great misfortune to lose his beautiful young wife, Laure, a few weeks ago. We attended the touching funeral service and it seemed doubly sad to us because the last time before that, when we visited St. Bernard Parish, it was to go to Kenilworth, the home of the Bienvenus, which is directly opposite the cemetery, for the ceremony attending the presentation to Pierre of a golden dress sword, given him in recognition of his brilliant record in the Mexican campaign. At that time, Laure, a vision of loveliness, stood proudly beside him, with their two little boys, René and Henri, between them. And now the happy memory of this scene is obscured by one of infinite sadness— the sight of her as she looked, still beautiful, lying in her casket before this was closed and consigned to the family tomb, while her bereft husband and young sons remained weeping beside it."

He drew out a handkerchief and wiped his eyes, apparently unable to control his own grief. Herr Löwenthal murmured something appropriately sympathetic and Alonzo went on, "Ah well! I should not burden you with this long and tragic recital were it not for the fact that Ernest and I have not yet paid our *visite de condoléance* on the grief-stricken family, and it so happens that the day of the Assembly is the one that has been fixed for it. Laure's parents, the Villerés of Magnolia Plantation, with whom Pierre and the children are staying at present, have very rigid views on the subject of such visits. I fear they would resent it greatly if ours were postponed. I am sure, Herr Löwenthal, that under all these circumstances, you will understand—"

"Of course, of course. I had already heard both of Major Beauregard's brilliant record and his sad loss. I should not dream of permitting a social gathering to interfere with so solemn an engagement. But perhaps some other member of your family, who is not making this pilgrimage of respect with you, might accompany your son to the Exchange."

"Certainly . . . Paul, I am sure your grandfather would be very pleased to take you."

Paul looked from his father to the visitor. "I appreciate the compliment you have paid me, Monsieur," he said. "I don't much like playing in public. But of course it's for Father to decide. And now, if it's all right, I'll go back to my friends."

When Paul reached the courtyard, it was empty. He went to Edward's room and found his brother there, studying. Yes, the others had gone home, hours ago—did Paul have any idea how long he had been playing that stupid game of chess? No, Edward had not the faintest idea who Charmian was or where she lived. Probably the Percys could give Paul the information. She had come with them and gone with them. No, he had not caught her at blindman's buff. But he had caught Alice twice.

FROM A LETTER TO A YOUNG GENTLEMAN
JUST ENTERED AT OXFORD UNIVERSITY

"Chess, by my advice, you will always continue to practice. If we should meet when you are some years older, I will tell you the various reasons which I have for advising you to play at this game, in preference to any game that depends only on chance. Remember too, that after having been able to learn Chess, you must not complain of an inability to learn anything else."

Anonymous. 1784

FROM THE BOOK NAMED THE
GOVERNOUR

"The chesse, of all games wherein is no bodily exercise, is mooste to be commended; for therein is right subtile engine, wherby the wytte is made more sharpe and remembrance quickened. And it is the more commendable and also more commodiouse if the players haue radde the moralization of the chesse, and whan they playe do thinke upon hit; whiche bokes be in englisshe. But they be very scarse, by cause fewe men do seeke in plaies for vertue or wisedome."

Sir Thomas Elyot. 1531

The Chess Reader, The Royal Game in World Literature,
compiled by Jerome Salzmann. (Greenberg: Publisher, N.Y.)

9.

Joseph Le Carpentier was delighted with the suggestion that he should accompany his grandson to the Exchange Hotel on the occasion of the Assembly. He did not have the slightest doubt that Paul would win another game with Löwenthal; and he welcomed the prospect of seeing the triumph take place in the presence of a distinguished company. The boy felt quite differently about this; it was one thing to play at home or at his grandfather's, or even in the Exchange Reading Rooms, when no one was present there except his relatives and their close friends, whom he had been accustomed to see in the family parlors and at the family tables ever since he could remember. It was quite another to play surrounded by complete strangers, some merely curious, others mildly mocking, still others actually hostile. Paul had always been shy, and this shyness became actually painful when he was in the presence of persons with whom he did not have even a casual acquaintance, especially if large numbers were foregathered. He begged his father to send word to Herr Löwenthal that he was ill and, indeed, this was not a feint; he could not eat, he had a terrific headache, and he began to run a slight fever. His mother tried to come to his defense; the child could not possibly win, she insisted, when he was in such a condition. But her husband laughed at her fears and her father had no idea of foregoing the treat he had been promised, simply because a boy who, by this time, should have outgrown his childish vagaries, might be allowed to have his own stupid silly way. In the end, Paul was almost bodily dragged up Royal Street to the scene of the Assembly.

This was now generally called the St. Louis Hotel, because the despised Americans had built another magnificent hotel on the further side of Canal Street, which they had impudently called The Exchange, although that title was already unofficially pre-empted. To be sure, the full name of the Creole's favorite haunt was *City* Exchange; but their penchant for nicknames also included a taste for abbreviation, and they had long since referred to it merely as The Exchange, and to the apartments where chess was played as the Exchange Reading Rooms. Outsiders were naturally confused by names which, to all intents and purposes, were identical, and often went to keep appointments at one hotel when they should have gone to the other. Among themselves, the Creoles stubbornly clung to the term Exchange and with equal stubbornness refused to preface it by the word City; but, when directing visitors, they had begun to speak of the St. Louis. After all, that was appropriate; their cathedral was named for the holy King of France and so was one of their principal streets. Why not their hotel, also?

Once Paul and his grandfather had crossed the beautiful rotunda and entered the secluded section reserved for private gatherings of a cultural nature, Paul's worst fears were realized. The atmosphere was thick with the fumes of liquor and cigars and the crowded place resounded with the babel of hearty masculine voices. Practically all the men, who were smoking fine Havanas, drinking brandy, and exchanging jokes and stories, were total strangers to the Le Carpentiers and the Morphys. Löwenthal was already on hand, conversing in his careful guttural French with several alien admirers. The circle parted to admit Paul and his grandfather, while the Hungarian and his companions greeted the newcomers cordially, urged them to accept some refreshment, and seemed disposed to continue talking. Paul tugged at his grandfather's sleeve and spoke to him in the patois which he believed none of them would understand.

"Can't we start playing right away and get it over with?" he whispered.

Fortunately, one of the men in the group was as well acquainted with the dialect as Paul. This man turned to the others and spoke to them in a tone that revealed understanding, not only of the boy's words but of their real meaning.

"I think our young fellow Orleanian, Paul Morphy, would like to begin his game with our distinguished visitor, Herr Löwenthal, as soon as it is agreeable to the latter," he said pleasantly. "No doubt, he still has some studying to do today. Shall we clear a place so that the two may be seated? I see that the chessboard is already in position."

Paul looked at his unknown benefactor gratefully. Then, since he could neither ask for big books to bring him up to the level of his opponent nor remain standing, without immediately calling attention to his lack of stature, he sat down opposite Löwenthal, who had acted quickly on the suggestion which had just been made. The chessboard came almost to the boy's shoulders and he had to raise his arms to move his men, which embarrassed him; but at least the disturbing confusion of sounds had ceased. Some of the onlookers were still smoking and drinking, and all of them were crowding as close to the central table as possible; but they were quiet now, watching intently and not even murmuring approbation or disapproval as the game progressed. A long time elapsed before either side gained any material advantage or made an obvious misplay; and still the silence remained unbroken, until Paul suddenly cried out, "*Échec!*"

It was the clear call of a victor, not the bewildered exclamation of a timid child. Löwenthal looked across at him and smiled.

"*Et mat!*" he added amiably.

Pandemonium suddenly broke loose. The spectators, shouting and applauding, crowded closer still to the chess table, wringing the boy's hand and slapping him on the back. He bowed politely to Löwenthal, thanking him for his generosity with his time, which was so much bespoken by those who wished to show him hospitality; then as briefly as he could, without discourtesy, he acknowledged the compliments of the crowd and turned to his beaming grandfather.

"*Allons nous-en, Grand-papa,*" he said.

"But we can't go now. They want you to stay, to congratulate you, to make much of you. They're very proud of you. Of course, they'd be delighted if you'd play another game."

Paul looked up at him miserably. "I don't have to, do I?" he asked, beneath his breath. "I was told I had to play one more game with Herr Löwenthal, but no one said anything to me about playing two. I don't like all this shouting and confusion. Besides, there's something I want very much to ask you. I haven't been able to find out what I want to know from anyone else. I thought I'd go back to your house with you, if you'd let me. Then we could have a game by ourselves, later on."

The old man weakened. He was flattered that Paul should consider him capable of giving information which no one else had been able to supply, and he dearly loved his quiet games alone with his grandson. Without giving any sign of unseemly haste, but still without undue delay, he managed to take his leave of the company and, with the boy beside him, went stumping back to the little house on Royal Street. Once in his own parlor, he settled down in his favorite armchair, with his legs stretched out in front of him and heaved a deep sigh of contentment.

"Your grandmother is taking a nap," he said. "I glanced into our chamber and saw her lying on the bed. She did not answer or even move when I spoke to her and she will doubtless sleep for some time. Your uncle Charles is at Werlein's buying a new flute and your aunt Amélie at church, where she spends most of her time, having nothing better to do. You and I will be quite undisturbed. So tell me, *cher*, what it is you have on your mind."

"I know that you have a great many acquaintances, on both sides of Canal Street, because they come to your auction rooms. I wonder if you have ever heard of a family named Sheppard?"

Le Carpentier drew his brows quickly together. "Albert Sheppard?" he asked in a sharp voice.

"I don't know the man's Christian name. I only know there is a family named Sheppard that lives somewhere in that new American quarter—the Garden District. I thought perhaps they might have bought slaves from you."

"No," Le Carpentier said shortly. "They do not buy slaves from me. They do not keep slaves. It is against their so-called principles."

"You do know about them then?"

"I know something. Probably your father knows as much. Why didn't you ask him?"

"Because I thought I would rather ask you, *Grand-papa.*"

Again, the old man softened. He was more and more gratified that Paul should have come to him for information, but at the same time he wished it had been on some other subject. "They *are* Americans," he said. "So, of course, it is natural that they should live in the Garden District. I understand that they have a very fine house, though I have never seen it. The head of the family is this Albert Sheppard of whom I just spoke. He is quite well-to-do—in fact, I suppose he might be called wealthy. But he is not the sort of person with whom the Morphys would ever associate, even if he were a Creole. He is a shopkeeper."

"What kind of a shopkeeper?"

"Well, I have no doubt he would prefer the term merchant. He owns a large establishment where he sells dry goods of all sorts, especially fine materials for dresses, and the various other articles of apparel that ladies wear—bonnets, gloves, stockings and so on. I do not mean that he sells them himself, over the counter. He has clerks, who are increasing in number all the time, and who attend to such matters as that. And he has delivery wagons, drawn by very handsome horses. I have no doubt your grandmother and mother and sisters have all been supplied by him."

"I've never heard any of them speak of him."

"You wouldn't, of course. Professional men and their families do not mingle socially with shopkeepers." An unwelcome inner voice seemed to be whispering, "Nor willingly with auctioneers, either"; but Le Carpentier succeeded in stilling it. "This Sheppard's store does not carry that name," he went on. "It is called the House of Paris or something ridiculous like that. It is on Canal Street and it has already been enlarged twice, though Albert Sheppard has done business here only a few years. . . . What made you ask?"

"Because Alice Percy, who often comes to our house with her brothers, brought a friend with her the other day—a little girl named Charmian Sheppard. We were all playing blindman's buff together in the courtyard when Uncle Ernest called me into the house to meet Herr Löwenthal. The Percys and Charmian had gone when I went back to the courtyard, and Edward said he did not know anything about her—the strange little girl, I mean—that I had better ask the Percys. But I haven't seen Alice since then and Henry Ferdinand and Léonce say they don't know anything about her, except that she goes to the same school as Alice. So I decided I would ask someone else."

"I see. But why did you care who this American child might be?"

"Because she dared me to catch her. And I never had a chance that day."

"And is that the only reason?"

"Well—" Paul hesitated—"she's very pretty. She has yellow curls and blue eyes and pink cheeks. And a nice laugh. She seems to be very high spirited. I suppose if she'd been plain and sullen or sulky, I wouldn't have cared so much whether or not I could catch her. I don't know."

"I see," Le Carpentier said again. "But you hope you will have a chance some other time?"

"Yes, *Grand-papa*, that's it."

"Well then, we must see if it cannot be arranged. But perhaps this idea of yours had better be a secret between you and me. I don't know that your father and mother will like it very much. They don't always like their children's ideas, you know."

"Yes, I know. For instance, I'm sure Malvina wants to marry John Sybrandt and they don't want to have her."

Le Carpentier stared at his grandson. Despite Paul's prowess at chess, Joseph still thought of him as a child. But of course he was nearly thirteen years old now and he might well be conscious of cross currents in the family.

"Uncle Ernest doesn't feel the same way about it that they do," Paul went on. "He says that John Sybrandt's a very promising young man, that he'd be glad to have him in the brokerage firm later on. Uncle Ernest went on to say that there wasn't any hurry—about the firm or the marriage, either, I mean. He said he thought it might be a good plan if Father and Mother let Malvina go to Europe this summer, with Aunt Amenaïde and Uncle Edouard Fortin. I think they might have let her, too, with the notion that it might take her mind off John Sybrandt, if she hadn't happened to mention Uncle Ernest's idea at the St. Martins'—you know she goes to their house a lot. Then Mme St. Martin or Mr. Benjamin or somebody wrote to Natalie and Natalie answered right away and said she'd love to have Malvina visit her in Paris. And that didn't please Father and Mother at all. They would have been willing to have her go somewhere in Italy or Spain with Aunt Amenaïde, but they didn't want her to visit Natalie St. Martin—of course, she's Natalie Benjamin now—in Paris. They don't approve of her."

Le Carpentier continued to stare at his grandson with increasing surprise. Unwittingly, Paul had presented a number of problems which Joseph realized would be more difficult to solve than those involved in a chess game. He would think over everything Paul had told him about wanting another chance to play blindman's buff with Charmian Sheppard and see if it could not be arranged; as to the possibility of a trip to Europe for Malvina and a visit to Natalie Benjamin, that was something with which he could not attempt to meddle. He told his grandson this and suggested that they might now get out the chessboard.

The evening passed pleasantly enough. Paul won, as usual, but his grandfather enjoyed the game; and when he had seen the boy home and gone to bed himself, he reflected, with satisfaction, on the events of the day. The Morphy family was increasing in prominence all the time. He had taken a hand in allying his own family with it and he was reaping many rich rewards from the connection. For instance, he had been a witness to Paul's public triumph and, moreover, he was the boy's chosen confidant. As for Malvina, that was a situation which was no concern of his, as he had said. . . .

He rose the next morning, refreshed after a good night's sleep, and when he had done the marketing and taken his two brief customary rests, one at home and one at the cathedral, he went on to his auction rooms in better spirits than he usually approached them. He was just entering the door when he came face to face with Mr. Judah P. Benjamin.

"Why, good morning, M. Le Carpentier," Mr. Benjamin said cordially, extending a hand which was firm in its clasp, despite its almost feminine softness. He was noted for the ingratiating smile which was one of his most striking characteristics, and this smile had never been more beguiling than it was at the moment. "I was just coming to call on you," he went on. "That is, if my visit would not be inopportune. There is a little matter I would like to discuss with you. However, if you would prefer to have me return later—"

"I am very much honored by your visit, Mr. Benjamin, as you must know," Le Carpentier replied heartily. "Please come into my private office. Would that chair be comfortable for you? And would you permit me to offer you a cigar, or is it too early in the day for that?"

"It is never too early in the day for a good cigar," Benjamin replied, accepting the Havana graciously. He lighted it and sat puffing away for a few minutes in obvious contentment, speaking inconsequentially of this and that. Le Carpentier had begun to wonder what had occasioned this early call, on a matter which did not seem in the least pressing, when Benjamin laid aside his cigar and reached for the inner pocket of his elegant coat, producing a wallet.

"The enclosed document, which has been in my possession for some time, has just happened to catch my attention again," he said suavely. "I thought it might possibly be of interest to you."

He handed a folded sheet of paper to Le Carpentier and, picking up his cigar once more, leaned back in his chair, the embodiment of leisure and affability. Le Carpentier unfolded the paper and stared at it, unbelievingly. It was more than twenty years since he had given it a thought—not since the death of Don Diego. But here, unquestionably, was the original of the letter addressed to Captain Joseph Clements and signed by Beluche, the copy of which he had so carefully destroyed when he first entered into negotiations with the Ursulines for the property on Chartres Street, the letter which assured the captain that the auctioneer, Le Carpentier, would advance any necessary sums to repair a privateer. . . .

"This must be a farce or a forgery," he said hoarsely, when he managed to speak.

"I assure you it is neither, my dear M. Le Carpentier. I can give you abundant proofs of its authenticity and tell you how it came into my hands, if you wish me to do so. I have all the time in the world. Later, we might destroy it together. But since that would be the culmination of a private and personal agreement, suppose we say that such destruction might properly take place on the day that your charming granddaughter, Malvina, sets sail for Europe to visit my beloved wife, Natalie?"

Vestibule of the Morphy house on Royal Street,
from a private drawing hitherto unpublished.

10.

Paul was glad, rather than otherwise, when the time of departure for Spring Hill finally came. At first, he had felt the natural reluctance of the city born and city bred to spend an indefinite period in the country. Spring Hill was several miles from Mobile, and the number of visits students were permitted to make there was strictly limited to one a month. The description of the college's fine location, so elevated that, even on the hottest days, it was breezy, and of the abundant water supply which, combined with its height, was responsible for its name, left him quite unmoved. The accounts of the magnificent view of the surrounding countryside and the Gulf, like those of the unique opportunities for sports, did not appeal to him, either; there were no finer sights, in his opinion, than those he could see within a stone's throw of the house where he lived, or even by merely looking from a window, whether up and down Royal Street or out onto the courtyard; as for sports, he still disliked and disdained these, and the very idea of swimming in a cold lake made him shiver. Unlike most boys, he did not have to be driven to a tub; indeed, his propensity for bathing was considered excessive and even unwise. But he wanted the water very hot and, when its temperature suited him, he would soak contentedly in it for such long periods that he was frequently hauled out, through main force, either by his father or by Edward. Moreover, the former not infrequently told him that if he persisted in such habits, these would be the death of him. Of course, that was merely a figure of speech, but it had become a tiresome one because it was reiterated so often. Paul assumed, and rightly, that he would hear it less frequently at Spring Hill, without reflecting that hot baths would not be so easily come by at the college, either.

But there were other reasons why he was not averse to getting away from New Orleans. One day, he had taken a long walk beyond Canal Street, which he had seldom crossed before; and, though usually he enjoyed strolling about, as much as his grandfather did, he missed the familiar sights and sounds and smells of the French Quarter, once he had left it. There were no nuns, walking quietly two by two, and no bright-turbaned quadroons or roistering sailors, either; there were no raucous wandering vendors of *calas tout chaud* and *estomac mulâtre*; no booths of *bière douce*, no fruit stalls, no scents of strong coffee and rich food wafted from unseen kitchens and mingling with the fragrance of flowers, both those in half-glimpsed courtyards and those sold in the French Market, in Jackson Square, and up and down the *banquettes*. The gay and vociferous confusion, to which he was accustomed when he went abroad, was lacking in these strange orderly streets which he had now reached, where the colors were subdued, the voices controlled and the pace steadied.

It was a different world which he had entered and he was not sure he liked it, but he had kept on and, finally, he had located the Sheppards' house which, as his grandfather had said, was a very fine one, though totally different from either of those in which he had lived. This one, like those around it, stood in the midst of a great open space, handsomely landscaped. Its portico was also open to the street. What he had heard of Americans must be true: they did not cherish the privacy provided by shuttered windows at the front of their residences and patios at the rear; they wished to make a show of their prosperity with their trim gardens and the great columns which framed their unobscured drawing rooms. To be sure, Paul's grandfather had caused a plot to be planted with wildflowers beside his Chartres Street house; but that was designed to give light and air to his property and to benefit the community as a whole; the Le Carpentier and Morphy families never used it for rest or recreation; and now that the property had been sold to the Merles, and Mrs. Merle had created a garden in the French style, she had discreetly walled it in from prying eyes. But obviously, though no one who could conceivably belong to the Sheppard family was in sight, this great open space at which Paul gazed was their pleasure ground. A man in working clothes, though he was white, was playing the hose, and another was carting away weeds and stray twigs in a wheelbarrow. Paul opened the garden gate, which was on the latch, and approached the hose player. This man gave Paul such a hearty greeting that it was obvious he did not consider the visit an intrusion.

"Howdy," he said, with a broad grin. This disclosed an incomplete set of teeth, and those that remained were discolored by tobacco juice. Nevertheless, the grin was unmistakably cordial, and so was the general expression of the man's unshaven face. "Lookin' for someone, sonny?"

"This is the Sheppards' place, isn't it?" Paul answered, rather formally. His world, hitherto neatly divided between gentlefolk and their slaves, had included no such character as this. He did not wish or intend to be discourteous, but he was at a loss to know how he should speak to a white laborer.

"Sure is," the man replied readily. "But the family's gone for the summer— Mr. Sheppard and Miz Sheppard and the flock."

"The flock?" Paul inquired, not immediately grasping the meaning of the mild jest.

"Yep. Their little white lambs, Charmian and Berenice. They're lucky —ain't got just one ewe lamb, got two. Nary a young ram though. Mr. Sheppard, he takes that hard."

"Do you know how long they'll be gone?"

"Can't say. I judge until about November. Anyways, until I let 'em know this city ain't a fiery furnace no more, and there ain't no yellow fever around. Me and my brother over there, we're their hired men, and we're staying on to look after things. We don't mind getting sweaty and we ain't afraid of no diseases. Besides, we ben with Mr. Sheppard ever since we was young 'uns, and he's always treated us fair and square. 'Twouldn't be the right thing to go back on him now, just because his business brung him to this hellhole out of God's own country."

"What do you call God's own country?" Paul asked coldly.

"I guess most folks figure it's where they was born and raised and their folks before them, don't they? I didn't go for to hurt your feelings, sonny, and I'm sorry if I did. Likely you think *this* is God's own country, cause you don't know different. I spoke too hasty. But for us, God's own country is way up yonder in New England. Ever hear of Boston?"

"Yes."

"Well, that's where Mr. Sheppard lived winters before he come here. But he had a notion to open a new store, anyways; and when the Missus took sick, and Doc Flint said she'd be better off in a warmer climate, Mr. Sheppard made up his mind New Or-leens was the place for that store. Summers, they'll keep right on going to New Hampshire, like they always done. Town by the name of Dublin."

"I thought Dublin was in Ireland. Some of my father's ancestors came from there, a long while ago."

"Well, some of Mr. Sheppard's people come from this Dublin I'm talking about, a different one, a long time ago. So the family's always kept the old place to go to summers. Not that any of the rest of us look down on 'em as summer people. There's been Sheppards in and around Dublin ever since the first settlers come there, and that's quite a while back, I can tell you. My brother Lucas and I was born on Sheppard property, one of the farms; and seeing as how we're a fair-sized family, fifteen in all, Lucas and I figured we wouldn't be missed none, or anyways not too much, if we come along to New Or-leens. I've always liked gardenin' and I'll say this for your city, sonny: all you got to do is to set a plant in the ground and it'll grow, fast as you can watch it. Don't even have to water it much, rainin' like it does a good share of the time. This is the first dry spell I've saw." The gardener picked up his hose, which had lain on the ground in the course of this conversation, while the stream from its nozzle rippled unguided over the well-cut grass; then he bethought him of the basic laws of hospitality, as these were evidenced on his native heath. "Want to have a look round?" he inquired. "No reason why you shouldn't, if you do. Lots of folks is curious about the Sheppards and I'm glad to tell 'em what I know and show 'em what I can. Maybe you'd like a glass of nice cold milk and a sugar cookie? Never saw a youngster yet that couldn't eat a sugar cookie, and it's a hot day, so you need something to wash it down. Nice and cool in the kitchen, too. Wouldn't hurt you to rest a mite."

"It's very kind of you. But I'm not hungry or thirsty, either, and I ought to be getting home."

"Some other day then. Welcome any time. I can cook as good as most womenfolks. Brown's the name—Zeke Brown." He held out a brawny hand.

Paul took it, his initial reluctance to do so overcome by the feeling of friendly firmness which the grasp gave him. Then he said good-bye, speaking less coolly than he had before. Of course, this gardener was an uncouth creature, but he unquestionably meant well. . . . So the Sheppards were Yankees! What a pity! He had really liked that little girl. He had really wanted to see her again. But now that he knew where she came from and how she lived in New Orleans. . . .

He wandered slowly back to the French Quarter from the Garden District, nursing his disappointment and his disillusionment. It was indeed a very hot day; a glass of cold milk and a sugar cookie—whatever that was!—would doubtless have tasted very good. He was already hungry and thirsty, despite his denial, when he had his strange encounter, and he would be much hungrier and thirstier by the time he reached Royal Street. But he looked forward to his return home with no particular pleasure. The place had not seemed the same without Malvina, though, when she was still there, he had thought her both stubborn and silly, and had felt that they could get along very well without her. Her departure had caused him no grief. On the contrary, though, as a rule, he disliked and avoided noise and confusion, he had been so fascinated by the scene at the Hospital Street dock, when he went with the rest of the family to see his sister off, that any pain which the sense of impending separation might have caused him was engulfed in admiration and wonder. Bales of cotton, stacks of lumber, barrels of molasses and countless other varieties of merchandise were piled high along the waterfront; and great drays, driven by shouting Negroes, were constantly thundering up. As these were unloaded they kept adding to the amazing array of goods already there. Strange scents of tar and smoke and sisal mingled with those of coffee and sugar; river packets, as imposing in their way as the ocean-going vessels, were lined up at the landings, and the great stream was crowded with craft of all kinds. From where he stood, Paul could see the full bend of the crescent which gave the city its nickname, and a glorious sweep it made, curving northward toward Jefferson Parish and southward to St. Bernard, with the settlement of Algiers directly across the glittering expanse of water. If there had been no wind, towboats would have been required to get the *Emma Fields* underway. But the weather was favorable for her independent progress and she moved from the dock with her great white sails swelled by the breeze and shining in the sun. It was a splendid sight and Paul watched it entranced, unmindful of the tears his mother was shedding and the set expression on his father's face, as they stood beside him, waving their handkerchiefs to the voyagers until the departing vessel proudly rounded the bend and floated down the Mississippi toward the Gulf.

Afterward, however, there had been an emptiness about the house which only Malvina could have filled. Of course, her bedchamber was vacant, and Paul was conscious of this vacancy every time he went past its closed door; but once, when he had opened the door and looked around him at the beautiful order, which was such a contrast to Malvina's incorrigible untidiness, he felt that she was further away than ever and he did not repeat the experiment. The worst of it was that this new atmosphere of emptiness was not confined to the one bedchamber; it permeated the drawing room, the library, the corridors, the gallery, the courtyard. He found himself listening for the sound of Malvina's laughter and chatter, watching for the sight of her pretty rebellious face and her slim brightly clad figure; even trying to create the illusion that he could still savor the delightful scent which their father had insisted she used too freely, but which to Paul had seemed to typify her gaiety and her independence. . . .

Mr. Benjamin had allowed no grass to grow under his small, shapely and remarkably well-shod feet after his early morning call at Joseph Le Carpentier's private office. The very next day he had reappeared, bringing with him this time no incriminating document, to be sure—that he still had in his possession!—but a neatly folded newspaper which he laid on Joseph's roll-top desk, indicating a marked passage among the other items of shipping news:

"Wednesday, May 1st:—For Liverpool. To sail positively on or before the 15th of May, full or not full—the new and splendid A1 fast sailing American ship *Emma Fields*, Samuel Snow, master, is now loading and has the most of her cargo on board and will positively sail as above. This ship is admirably calculated for passengers, having splendid stateroom accommodations, with other conveniences, and will be a fine opportunity for parties intending to leave about the above time. She can handsomely accommodate 40 cabin passengers and has also superior arrangements for 80 steerage passengers. For terms apply to the Captain on board at Post 28, 2nd Municipality, or to J. P. Whitney & Company."

"It has occurred to me that this splendid vessel would provide ideal accommodations for the members of your family who are about to travel abroad," Mr. Benjamin said suavely. "And, as I happen to have very close and pleasant relations, both with the Whitney Company and the master of the ship, I should be delighted to say a word, which I think might be effective, in behalf of Dr. and Mme Fortin and Mlle Malvina. Of course, if they cared to go to New York, they could take one of the new Cunard steamers—the *Asia*, for instance. But the trip north is so long and tiring, especially for ladies! And they really would not save much time in the end, when you count in that week of overland travel. Besides, I am sure all of you will wish to be on hand to see that they are comfortably disposed in their cabins and to take aboard such little delicacies as may counteract or mitigate possible mal de mer. Of course, there is poultry, confined in coops on the upper deck, for consumption during the voyage, and a ship's cow is quartered in a special deckhouse with padded sides, so the ladies will be well provided with chicken and milk, not to mention fresh vegetables, which are protected from the weather by overturned boats up on the booms. But such foodstuffs are mere staples, to which we must add. Unfortunately, it is too late in the season for oysters, but lemons and other wholesome fruits are abundantly available. Also champagne, the best remedy of all. I had planned to provide a case of that, leaving the other trifles for your personal attention. And, of course, you could not give this nor wish the travelers bon voyage unless they left from New Orleans."

"When you say 'all,' you are no doubt including yourself," Joseph was tempted to say. "You are going to be sure that Malvina is on that ship before you give me the copy of that wretched letter from Beluche." But he was wise enough not to pronounce these words aloud. Instead, he merely remarked, "It is very kind of you, Mr. Benjamin, to take such an interest and show such generosity. But I am sure my son-in-law will wish to provide everything his daughter really needs and he also has excellent connections."

"Of course, of course. No one realizes more keenly than I do the great prestige which Judge Morphy enjoys, and deservedly so. But surely he will allow me to make some slight gift as a mark of good will. And, occasionally, the word of someone outside the immediate family, someone wholly disinterested, like myself, for instance, is helpful to the authorities. By the way, you have, of course, told the judge about our little conference yesterday?"

"Not yet. There was no propitious moment last evening. My daughter was giving a musicale and—"

"Of course, of course," Mr. Benjamin said again. "I have the greatest admiration for her talents and her hospitality. But, after all, time is short, and there is bound to be a great demand for accommodations on the *Emma Fields*. I am sure that when I come to see you tomorrow—"

Benjamin had not said, "*If* I come to see you tomorrow." Le Carpentier knew that he now had no choice. Before they went to bed that night, he would be obliged to disclose to both his daughter and his son-in-law certain disgraceful details of his past, which he had flattered himself would never come to light. All day long, he sat sunk in the deepest dejection, trying—but as he knew only too well, trying in vain—to think of some loophole of escape from confession. He did no work himself and he declined to see his clerks and his lieutenants in trade. Finally he closed and locked his office and went sadly stumping down the street to the Morphys' house.

The ensuing scene was even worse than he expected. He had always dreaded, with reason, Alonzo's cold controlled anger and Telcide's hysterical weeping; he had managed, for years, to avoid more than occasional exhibitions of both. Now he was exposed to their full fury. So the blackmailed couple were to choose between sacrificing their daughter and saving his reputation! Very well, they would make the choice and it would be to let him take the consequences of his misdoings and thereafter cut themselves off from him. . . . And his wife, Telcide's aging mother, Le Carpentier asked. Telcide's sister, Amélie, whose existence was so barren, at best? Her brother, Charles, who was so unfortunate and who had learned to lean so heavily on them? Not to mention incurring the ill feeling of their kinsfolk, the St. Martins, and the St. Martins' all powerful son-in-law, Judah P. Benjamin? If he, Joseph Le Carpentier, were exposed and disgraced, would not this exposure and disgrace spread to the rest of the family and affect Alonzo's important position as a judge? Was it "sacrificing" Malvina to let her take a cultural trip abroad, under the pleasantest possible circumstances, with the experienced Amenaïde and the latter's distinguished husband? After all, the girl would not have to stay long with Natalie St. Martin Benjamin, and Amenaïde would be in Paris at the same time. Surely Malvina's reputation was not so fragile that it would break under such a light test!

In the end, of course, it was Le Carpentier who won; but his was a Pyrrhic victory. He went home exhausted, racked with the realization that no matter how solid a family front was presented to the world, relations would never again be the same between him and his favorite child and with the head of the house to which he had so proudly allied her. Paul, of course, was not told exactly what had happened, nor did his groping conjectures hit anywhere near the truth. But he recognized the strain in the atmosphere, which Malvina's excited preparations for departure did nothing to mitigate; and then she was gone, and though the strain gradually subsided, the vacancy caused by her departure seemed more and more depressing all the time.

It was not only the absence of Malvina which had altered the atmosphere of the household; as Telcide's maternal duties slackened and her smooth-running establishment required less and less guidance and supervision, she gave an increasing amount of time to music, for which she had always had such a decided penchant. The old priest who had taught her

Italian and Latin during her girlhood had frequently exclaimed in despair, *"Fanatica per la musica! Sempre las musica!"* when her impatience to leave her books for her piano became uncontrollable. Nowadays, her husband quoted this, rather wryly, and Paul did not wonder; she spent hours on end studying the science of composition, and tried her hand at writing sonatas, trios and *septuors,* and adapting for orchestration music originally written solely for the piano; now she was actually contemplating the creation of an operatic score. She had succeeded in securing the co-operation of a family friend, M. Placide Canonge, in this enterprise; and she kept rushing back and forth between her piano and her desk, trying out arias, drafting librettos, and consulting her adviser, who was a well-known littérateur, with all the advantages of a Parisian education. Paul knew that by the time he was within half a block of the house, he would begin to hear vague, disconnected sounds, which would become more distinct, but subject to an equal amount of interruption as he drew nearer. Nor was this the worst of it; after dinner there would probably be a concert. It was the rule, rather than the exception, for at least twenty or thirty persons, often more, of different nationalities, all as "fanatic" about music as his mother, to invade the place several times a week. Forty-five music stands were now kept in a closet adjoining the main salon, ready for use, and on the occasion of the more pretentious concerts, these were all grouped around the splendid Erard piano, which had been manufactured especially for Telcide, and transported from Paris to New Orleans with the same care as if it had been a precious jewel—as indeed it was, in its own way. Not that it was as ornate as many similar instruments in the city at that time; its rosewood frame was unadorned; but the harmonies which issued from it were almost overpowering in their volume, especially as the music room was so constructed as to be intensely sonorous, and was outfitted in a way that favored the reverberation of noises, unmuffled by thick carpets, heavy draperies, or furniture of an encumbering nature. Besides the piano, it contained only light chairs; some antique music standards, more valuable than those whose habitat—when not in use—was the closet; a variety of musical instruments, some of them propped up against the walls, some hung upon them in panoplies, and some scattered pell-mell over the chairs; and a vast rosewood bookcase, filled not with literature but with bound volumes of classical music. Several celebrities who had come to New Orleans declared that this bookcase had yielded rare works which they had been unable to obtain elsewhere in the city, and agreed with the heterogeneous performers who frequented the concerts that Mme Morphy was the superior in skill, as well as the guiding spirit of all.

The house was a large one, and if its musical aspects had been consigned to this one salon and its rear gallery, which gave on the garden, these would not have seemed so inescapable. But on the other side was an oval-shaped vestibule, lighted from above by a glass dome, which served to illuminate marble busts of Gluck, Haydn, Mozart, Beethoven, Weber and Mendelssohn —in other words, the divinities of this temple. Here and there the reflection of the dome's golden beams was caught by more music standards, made of copper and shaped in the form of lyres; the same beams fell on ancient brass instruments, installed in the more remote recesses of the vestibule. When the sun shone on all these, the place seemed to glitter; but, at night, when the heavens were overcast, the dome conveyed the sky's quality of darkness to all the objects underneath the transparent vault. On the other hand, when the moon shone on them, these objects assumed the aspect of frightening apparitions. Nothing would induce Hélène to go to the vestibule after nightfall; and, though they would not have confessed this, Edward and Paul entered it with the greatest reluctance and went through it as rapidly as possible, once the sun had set. Only Malvina had frequented it willingly, in John Sybrandt's company; and Paul was old enough to guess that there was an ulterior reason for this: once the guests were assembled in the salon beyond, no one was likely to go through the vestibule until after their departure, for refreshments were served to them through the rear gallery. Moreover, whatever sounds the courting couple made which, after all, were mostly only those of whispers and kisses, these were completely drowned out by the racket around the piano. Yes, it was easy to understand why John and Malvina had found this vestibule so favorable and pleasing a trysting place. . . .

But they were gone across the ocean now, the vestibule was empty, and though preparations for a concert later on were indeed apparent, his mother and M. Canonge were still the only persons in the main salon when Paul entered the house, after his disappointing visit to the Garden District. Edward, he found upon inquiry, had gone to the Percys' and Hélène was in bed with a migraine. The judge was in the library, intent on a book, and looking somewhat tired and strained; Paul realized that the day in court must have been unusually exhausting. Alonzo looked up and nodded; then he resumed his reading; the day was long since past when he was roused to jealousy by the presence of a musician in the parlor with his wife. As quietly as possible, Paul set up the chessboard and was soon bending over it, with his head buried in his hands. After a few minutes, his father looked up and spoke with irritation.

"Good heavens! You look as if you were wrestling with some Archimedean problem! Wake up! Syracuse is about to fall!"

"Wouldn't you like to have a game with me before dinner, Father, and help me solve the problem?"

"No, I would not. I've had enough problems for one day, without inviting any more! Good Lord, is that your uncle Charles playing his flute again?"

"I'm afraid it is. But you know he doesn't have many diversions. I'm sure he tries to be as quiet as possible and, after all, his room's at the other end of the house."

"It isn't so remote that I can't hear his damned flute. If there's one instrument I detest more than any other, that is it, and he hasn't a particle of talent. He ought to realize that by this time. At least, your mother's a fine musician, even if this collection of characters she's attracted is just about driving me crazy. Why don't you ask him to play chess with you?"

"I have, but he's refused. His feelings are hurt because Grandpapa would rather play with me than with him."

"Well, it's no wonder—that your grandfather would rather play with you than with him, I mean. As for Charles, his feelings are always getting hurt. He's such a sensitive plant that there's no easy way to handle him."

Paul tried in vain to think of some adequate reply. He did not enjoy his uncle's flute playing or his mother's "collection of characters" any more than Alonzo did. He had not welcomed the introduction of either into their household. The frequent visits of his father's brother, his uncle Ernest, affected him quite differently; he liked and admired the latter, who was exceedingly successful in his highly competitive business as a cotton broker and who lived an independent life, while still remaining conscious of family ties and appreciative of their importance; he never outstayed his welcome and was always joyfully received as a guest because he was such a good companion, quite aside from his outstanding skill as a chess player. But poor Charles Le Carpentier had none of Ernest's noticeable characteristics; he had not succeeded at anything; even his parents had found his presence so wearisome that they had finally betrayed this and he had asked for hospitality from his sister and brother-in-law, who had grudgingly accorded it. He had then been assigned to the least desirable room in the house and given to understand that the more he remained there, the better the rest of the family would be pleased. In this retreat, he had surprisingly developed a taste for playing the flute—or at least trying to play it. He had even gone so far as to attempt adapting one of Beethoven's symphonies to an arrangement in which this instrument would have a leading part, and had secured Telcide's unwilling permission to have it played at one of her concerts. For a short time, he had been very happy, as he gravely placed on five music stands as many copies of his *chef d'oeuvre,* each bearing the caption, "*Sonate de Beethoven arrangée par Charles Le Carpentier.*" After the disastrous performance was over and the company was recuperating on the gallery, under the benign influence of champagne, some wag had returned to the salon and changed the inscription to read, "*Sonate de Beethoven dérangée par Charles Le Carpentier.*" The wretched man had found the desecrated sheets when the party was over and he had gone to gather up his music; he had never recovered from this blow to his pride and since then he had learned of a crowning insult: the despicable nickname of *Cracheur de Flute.* Nevertheless, he went doggedly on with his practicing. Paul could not help admiring his persistence and feeling sorry for him; but neither this admiration nor this pity could change the fact that Charles Le Carpentier was a bore and a failure and, since the boy realized this all too well himself, he could not very well convince his father to the contrary.

He put away his chessboard as quietly as he had got it out and left the room. The judge had resumed his reading and did not even notice his son's departure. As Paul mounted the stairs, he met Tata coming down and stopped her.

"Fix me a nice hot bath, will you, Tata?" he said coaxingly. And, as she started to remonstrate, he added, "You won't have to do it many more times, you know. Next week, I'll be gone to college. No doubt, you're glad of it."

She burst into vehement denial. Malvina, her first charge, had already deserted her; now the next two—namely Edward and Paul—were also about to go far away; that would leave her only Hélène out of all four nurslings. Why did he speak to her in such a cruel way? Of course, she would prepare the bath. She had only been joking when she pretended that she did not want to do it. And afterward she would bring him a tray. He need not go downstairs to one of those dull dinners, with M. Canonge as the outstanding guest, that would soon begin. . . .

He lay in his tub for a long time, feeling more and more relaxed and content, and by the time he had finished his supper he was already drowsy. He did not hear the commotion caused by his mother's musical enthusiasts, or the pitiable, lonely sound of his uncle's flute. He went to bed and to sleep, at peace with the world. And afterward he dreamed that he was playing blindman's buff again, and that though he had not caught Charmian this time, either, he was so glad to see her, after he thought he had lost her, that he did not care, because she was more beautiful than ever.

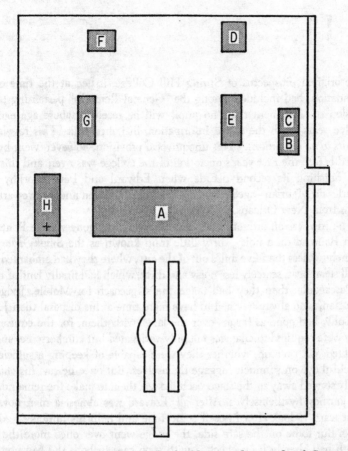

The above plot gives an idea of the buildings and grounds of Spring Hill College as they were in 1839. No radical change took place until 1854 when Father Gautrelet's improvements and enlargements began. Therefore, it is safe to assume that this is the way the buildings and grounds looked when the Morphys and Charles de Maurian entered the college.

A — College Building.
B — Storehouse and kitchen.
C — Stable.
D — Residence of servants.
E — Infirmary.
F — Residence of lay professors.

G — A two-story building, the upper story being used as a storeroom for trunks, the lower story serving as a place for the boys to wash in.
H — Chapel.

The above plan as reproduced through the courtesy of Robert J. Zeitz, Assistant Librarian, Thomas Byrne Memorial Library, Spring Hill College.

11.

The original prospectus of Spring Hill College, issued at the time of its foundation, had included among the "General Remarks" pertaining to admission the statement that "no pupil will be received whose age exceeds twelve years" with the added information, in italics, that *This regulation admits to no exceptions.*" This unequivocal provision, however, went by the board before the first year's operation of the college was over; and this was just finishing its second decade when Edward and Paul Morphy and Charles de Maurian—aged respectively sixteen, thirteen and twelve—arrived there from New Orleans.

The trip was an arduous one. The boys had first gone via the Pontchartrain Railroad on a noisy, dirty little train known as the *Smoky Mary*, to Milneburg, less than five miles out of the city, where they had embarked on a small steamboat, scarcely less noisy and dirty, which had finally landed them at Pascagoula; then they had taken the stagecoach for Mobile. Judge de Maurian, who always seemed to have more time at his disposal than Judge Morphy, had gone as far as "over the lake" with them, for the equipment they were required to take was not only variegated but cumbersome, and he doubted, with reason, whether they were capable of keeping a sufficiently watchful eye on so much luggage themselves. But once he saw his charges safely stowed away in the stagecoach, he left them to make the remainder of the journey by themselves. After all, Edward was almost a man now; he must learn to look after himself some time and help his juniors to do the same. But to be on the safe side, the judge went over once more the lists which had already been checked with such care in both the Morphy and the de Maurian households, in accordance with the requirements which stated: "Every pupil will furnish himself with a bedstead, mattress, and the necessary bedding: (moscheto bars are entirely unnecessary), a pillow, 2 pairs of sheets—also a wash-bowl and a stand, and also 12 shirts, 6 cravats, 6 napkins; 6 towels, 12 pocket handkerchiefs, 3 summer suits and a suit for winter, consisting of a blue cloth dress coat, a surtout and two pairs of pantaloons, also a silver fork and table spoon."

Judge de Maurian folded the slip of paper on which the list was written and handed it to Edward for safekeeping and further checking. "Sure you have everything, boys?"

"Yes, sir."

"Well then, good-bye and good luck to you."

Although none of them would have admitted it, they watched his departure with sinking hearts. None of them had been away from their families before and the last link with these was a wrench. Besides, the trip at best was a hard one, and the day was unusually hot, even for July. Their enrollment had begun with the summer term, for the report that the location of the college made it immune to yellow fever and other epidemics, which decimated the low-lying towns and cities during the torrid months, had spread quickly; and anxious parents—the Morphys and de Maurians like many others—had welcomed the opportunity of safeguarding the health of their sons by permitting them to reverse the usual order of vacations and take these in November and December.

The anxious parents had, to be sure, entertained some misgivings on other grounds: St. Joseph's College at Spring Hill had first opened under auspicious conditions, with the Right Reverend Michael Fortier, Bishop of Mobile, as its founder, ten students from New Orleans, as many from Alabama and Florida, three from as far north as Philadelphia, and one from over the border in Mexico among its pupils. Admission to it was regarded, and rightly, as a great cultural privilege, for at the time there was no other college in Alabama and only two others in the Gulf states—one in Mississippi and one in Louisiana, neither of which offered a full collegiate course. But its prestige decreased as two different religious orders—the Fathers of Mercy from Lyons and the Eudest Fathers from Rennes—successively gave up its direction. Eventually, it had been temporarily closed, and it had only recently been reopened and taken over by the Jesuits, who had their detractors in the American South, as they did elsewhere in the world. Even such a Catholic stronghold as New Orleans had viewed them with misgivings after their expulsion from France, and had continued to do so. But it was impossible to overlook the excellence of their educational system, and they had the support not only of an outstanding cleric, Napoleon Perche, who later became Archbishop of New Orleans, but also of the secular newspaper, *l'Abeille*, the only daily in general circulation among the Creoles. Though only eighteen pupils were enrolled at Spring Hill when Father Francois Gautrelet, delegated by the Provincial of Lyons in the name of the Company of Jesus, took over his responsibilities as Rector and President in 1847, together with a distinguished faculty, there were ninety-three before the end of the next year. These were students from Cuba, Ireland, France, Yucatan, Martinique and even one from Boston, which seemed still more extraordinary to the denizens of the Deep South, though they did not recognize the importance of his name, which was Oliver Shaw. But the names of the Orleanians enrolled were weighted with significance—Beauregard, Bermudez, Ducros, Forestier, Freret, Villeré and many others. A year and a half later, when the Morphy brothers and their friend Charles de Maurian descended from the stagecoach, travel stained and weary, the number of pupils had more than doubled, and attendance at Spring Hill was regarded not only as a spiritual and cultural advantage, but as a distinct social asset.

Scholastically, the newcomers adapted themselves without difficulty to their unaccustomed regime, for they had been well prepared at Jefferson Academy; and though all their lives they had been lapped in luxury, they regarded the primitive condition of their dormitories and washrooms as amusing rather than annoying, and their somewhat fantastically cut blue and white jackets and pantaloons as uniforms of distinction. The requisite that "every able-bodied student, be he son of governor, senator or aristocrat, must work one designated day of every week on the college farm" went somewhat harder; neither Edward nor Charles had ever seen a white man doing hard manual labor, and the only glimpse Paul had had of such activities had been those of Lucas and Zeke Brown at the Sheppards' establishment in the Garden District. However, such work, like the high scholastic standard, was part of the college tradition: at the time of its foundation, Bishop Fortier had not only walked back and forth between Spring Hill and Mobile every day, literally taking the ten miles in his stride; he had helped, between classes, to clear the land, cutting down trees and spading up the ground. The students had naturally fallen to and helped him and, as a reward, the day's strenuous activities had ended with football.

Charles and the Morphys admitted that this had all been very praiseworthy, at the time; but now that the farm was productive, the grounds around the buildings neatly landscaped, and the buildings themselves adequate—though the Rector kept making plans for further improvements and additions—neither they nor any of the other Orleanians could see any reason why this sort of work should be carried on. The days of pioneering were over. The original two-story frame houses, one occupied by the Community and the other by the Seminary, had very soon been converted, the one into an infirmary, the other first into workmen's quarters and later into a storeroom for trunks with washrooms below. A wooden chapel had speedily been added, and the main college building, which would have done credit to any institution, had almost immediately taken form and substance. It was more than a hundred feet long, it was made of brick, it was three storys high not counting the basement, it had long windows and double doors and a colonnaded façade. The faculty officers and students had long since had this building to themselves; the lay professors had a residence of their own; the servants were provided with one almost as commodious; the storehouse, kitchen and stable were all adequate. Regular rows of splendid trees and a large variety of shrubs overshadowed the somewhat haphazard arrangement of all these buildings, and green lawns stretched among them to the edges of the woods where, on Tuesdays and Thursdays—and sometimes on Sundays—the boys walked through the sylvan paths, two by two, in the wake of a prefect, to a "chosen place of recreation." This prim arrangement was somewhat counterbalanced by the fact that they could, if they chose, go swimming every day. This was another precedent Bishop Fortier had established.

Edward and Charles chose to follow this precedent; Paul did nothing of the sort. But he quickly made his mark scholastically. He began by winning First Premiums in Latin, Greek and English, and Second Premiums in Christian Doctrine, French and Arithmetic, and he steadily maintained the excellence of this record. Edward and Charles made equally impressive showings in their respective courses, besides doing well in the limited field of recreation and accepting the weekly exercise of manual labor philosophically. An epidemic of measles, which slowed down some of their competitors, failed to affect them, for they had all passed safely through most of the so-called children's diseases before they left New Orleans. However, Paul found the intermittent but excessive cold hard to endure and took little pleasure in the rare snowfalls which delighted many of his fellow students, Charles among them. When the two simultaneously complained of sore throats, the physician of the college announced, rather acidly, that their ailment was doubtless due to the fact that they had coddled themselves too much; if, instead, they had braved more exposure, they would soon have been able to tolerate inclement weather; as it was, he supposed he would have to send them to the infirmary.

Paul obeyed orders docilely enough, thankful for the comfort of bed and the escape from noisy companionship. Charles tried to protest, with reason, that he had not coddled himself; he had gone swimming practically every day, despite the cold; he had not only built snowmen, but engaged in snow fights. Nevertheless, like Paul, he had a bad headache as well as a sore throat and neither one wanted any supper; it hurt to swallow and, besides, they were not hungry. Before morning, they had begun to vomit at frequent intervals, and though they spoke to each other very little, because talking hurt, too, each noticed that the other kept alternately throwing off and pulling up his blankets. When the physician of the college came in to see them the following morning, he knew, almost at first glance, that he had two seriously sick boys on his hands. He had made a mistake in scoffing at their sore throats; obviously, these were not merely the result of a failure to toughen themselves; something more serious was presaged. Nausea, chills and fever had already set in; he did not like the look of their tongues, which were red and swollen; he must watch for the next symptoms and, meanwhile, he must see that there were no visitors to this part of the infirmary.

He did not have long to wait; when he made his next visit, his patients' faces were not only flushed but blotched. He undid their nightshirts and saw that their chests and stomachs were dotted with red. He fastened the buttons again, told the boys sternly to lie very still until he returned, and went out to inform the Rector that they had two cases of scarlet fever on their hands.

The Rector had no mind to risk an epidemic; measles, the year before, had been bad enough; this could be even worse. Of course, Paul and Charles could not be taken out of bed, in their present condition; it might well cause their death. They would have to be given the best care available and no one must go near them except the infirmarian and the physician of the college. By no one, he meant no one on the faculty. As to the student body, that would be dismissed, until all danger of contagion was past.

The severity of this measure aroused feelings that diverged very markedly; the boys who lived in Alabama, Mississippi and Louisiana were overjoyed at this fortuitous holiday; those who had come from Mexico and the West Indies were presented with something of a problem, those from Europe with a still greater one. Fortunately, the Gulf states lived up to their reputation for hospitality; the stranded strangers were kindly received in the homes of their classmates, and it was Spring Hill, rather than Mobile or Jackson or New Orleans, that became a desolate place. For a week or more, it was also pervaded with grave anxiety. Charles was a vigorous boy, who should be strong enough to throw off almost any ailment; Paul's case was entirely different. He was naturally delicate and he never took enough exercise or spent enough time in the fresh air; when he was struck down by anything serious, such as scarlet fever, it went hard with him. The Rector felt it necessary to advise his parents that his condition was critical, coupling this information with a sharp warning that neither of them must try to see their son. Paul would have the best possible care, but the college was quarantined. . . .

Fortunately, it was not long before he was able to write a more reassuring letter. The worst was over and now that the fever was abating, Paul actually gave the physician less cause for concern than Charles, because he was not so restless. He accepted without complaint the fact that convalescence would be long and tedious, whereas Charles was inclined to kick against the pricks. Eventually, the Rector wrote a third letter, this time to the de Maurians as well as the Morphys. The contents of the two letters were almost identical.

It seemed that a young Mexican by the name of Rafael Carraquesde had brought a chessboard with him when he came to college, and had succeeded in rousing the interest of Louis Landry, a classmate from Louisiana, in the game, which previously had never figured in the activities of Spring Hill. When quarantine was declared, the Louisianian had invited the Mexican to be his house guest, and in the enforced haste of their departure, the chessboard had been left behind. Paul had never shown much interest in their contests, though occasionally he had acted, upon request, as their referee; indeed, he had never even mentioned the subject of chess, as far as anyone on the faculty, with one important exception, could remember, until he began to sit up, for brief periods each day, during his convalescence. Now he asked the infirmarian if, by any chance, Carraquesde's chessboard was still at the college and, when he was told it was, requested that it be brought to him. Charles, instead of being pleased when it arrived, asked an impatient question.

"Will you please tell me how it is possible for two intelligent human beings to sit for an hour or more moving little figures around on a board and actually get some fun out of it?"

"I'm not going to tell you, I'm going to show you, if you'll let me," Paul answered calmly.

Charles would not even look at Paul as the latter set up the chessmen; the younger boy was not amused, he was vexed. But at last, as Paul said nothing more, but simply continued to sit quietly on one side of the chessboard, with no sign of impatience or annoyance, Charles drew up an easy chair to the other side and flung himself into it.

"All right," he said, in a tone of exasperation. "I suppose we've got to do something to kill time, while we're shut up here, as if we were in prison for some crime. You might as well show me the moves. Mind you, I'm not saying I'll play a game through."

Spring Hill was one of the few colleges at the time where the letters the students wrote their parents were not subject to the inspection of the Rector or the faculty; therefore, the one which Charles sent his father, when he was allowed pen and paper, was dispatched to New Orleans as soon as he had sealed it. Judge de Maurian was not without a sense of humor. A few days thereafter, the Rector received a letter from him.

"Reverend Father:

"I thank you for yours of the 12th inst. telling me of my son's satisfactory progress toward recovery and some of the contributing causes for this. I may, in reply, quote a few lines from a letter he has just written me.

" 'You know I never thought I should like to play chess, but for lack of anything else to do, I let Paul teach me the moves. Then we played several games for study, while he explained the reasons for these moves. After these sittings, I changed my mind and my opinion and now I do not see how a man who did not play chess could be happy. As soon as I get out of the infirmary, I am going to get a chessboard of my own and ransack the bookstores in Mobile for chess books. I wish you would have similar stores ransacked for me in New Orleans.'

"I am complying with my son's request in the hope, however, that he will not give more time to the study of chess than he should, especially when one considers how much he has lost from his regular curriculum because of illness.

"With respectful regards, believe me, Reverend Father, to be

> Faithfully yours,
> Charles Amédée de Maurian, Sr."

"I have long loved her, and I protest to you bestowed much on her; followed her with a doting observance; engrossed opportunities to meet her; fee'd every slight occasion that could but niggardly give me sight of her . . . I have pursued her as love hath pursued me; which hath been on the wing of all occasions. But whatsoever I have merited, either in my mind or in my means, meed, I am sure, I have received none; unless experience be a jewel; that I have purchased at an infinite rate; and that hath taught me to say this:

> Love like a shadow flies, when substance love pursues;
> Pursuing that that flies, and flying what pursues."

Merry Wives of Windsor, Act II, Scene ii.

12.

The change of heart which Charles had abruptly undergone proved a boon to both Paul and himself. His enthusiasm not only gave him a new interest, different from any of those he had experienced before, but it strengthened the tie between him and his best friend. As long as his major concern had been with sports, which Paul disliked, though there had been no friction between them, there had sometimes been a lack of mutual understanding; now this lack had been supplied. But possibly, of the two, Paul profited more even than Charles.

Subconsciously, he had resented the intrusion of Löwenthal into the quiet pattern of his life. The Hungarian had begun by breaking up the first outdoor game which Paul had ever really enjoyed and preventing him from bringing it to a happy close. His triumph at chess was only one more after many previous ones; but if he could have caught Charmian, that would have given him a new sense of elation. Then the public exhibition at the Exchange had been an ordeal for him; he had suffered agonies of embarrassment in that great room filled with hard-drinking, heavy-smoking men, watching him like hawks, ready to scoff and mock if he failed and to slap him on the back and guffaw uproariously if he succeeded. It had been torture to serve as the center of attraction for such a group, to be regarded as an oddity—a prodigy, to be sure, but an oddity just the same. He still winced at the recollection of that afternoon; and as if one such match had not been bad enough, a match was next arranged with General Winfield Scott, an accomplished amateur who visited New Orleans and asked to meet "the best there was." The best was Paul and the General did not conceal his feeling that he had been offered an affront when the boy was presented to him. Paul had won and won again and the General's attitude became, if anything, one of still deeper resentment. This was why Paul had never wanted to play chess at school—the wound had been too deep to heal easily. However, the news of his prowess had, of course, penetrated to Spring Hill and, one day as he was leaving the chapel, the priest who had officiated, overtook him and suggested a game. Paul had heard it rumored that there was "a top chess player" on the faculty, but it had not occurred to him that one of the teachers, especially one of the clergy, would approach a student with such a proposal. Though he could not decline it, his surprise, mingled with his displeasure, resulted in an answer which lacked the respect he would normally have shown for the cloth.

"Very well, Father, if you insist. But I'd like to make a condition—and a prediction."

"I'd be interested in hearing both, my son."

"If we play, I'd like you to take half an hour after I've moved before you do so. Every time. That's the condition. The prophecy is that I'll beat you in fourteen moves."

"You're very sure of yourself, my son."

"Yes, Father."

He had hoped, of course, that the priest would withdraw his suggestion; even if the withdrawal had been coupled with a rebuke, he would have preferred this outcome to the other which he foresaw as inevitable. But the priest was equally sure of victory and convinced that, in the case of his pupil, pride would come before a fall and a haughty spirit before destruction. The game began and, after his first move, Paul looked at his watch, rose, bowed and left the room. His antagonist saw him go down the steps of the college building and stroll off among the trees. In exactly half an hour, he was back again. This process was repeated thirteen times, but long before this point was reached, the priest had ceased to feel amusement. He never suggested a second game and, in his subsequent association with Paul, he never referred to this one. If the news of it leaked out, this was promptly suppressed—Paul would have been the first to silence it. As in the case of his victory over Löwenthal and Scott, this one had been a source of chagrin, amounting almost to pain. The very thought of future experiences, similar to these, revolted him. If Edward's attitude had been different, his might have been different, too; but Edward had never once played with him willingly since the first defeat at his younger brother's hands, and Spring Hill had released them both from parental coercion on that score. Now that Charles could and would play chess with him, Paul's whole outlook changed.

Nor was this only in regard to chess. That relaxation having been provided, he could relax in other ways, too; since the last barrier to complete companionship with Charles was removed, he could accept and even invite companionship with others. He had been elected vice president of the Thespian Society during his first year at Spring Hill, and had played the part of the duke's son, Charolois, in *Gregoire* at the commencement exercises; but he had accepted the position and taken the role with hesitation, and had consented to both largely because refusal to do so would have made him more conspicuous than acceptance. However, the following year, though he would certainly have preferred a male role, he made no objections to acting Portia in *The Merchant of Venice* and ended by throwing himself into the part with enthusiasm. Shortly thereafter, he became a member of the Philomathic Society, of which Edward, who had now been graduated, had been successively secretary and vice president. Eventually, he was persuaded, without too much difficulty, to give one of the principal addresses at commencement; and, having taken his Bachelor's Degree, with honors, he decided to stay on at Spring Hill for another year, since Charles was still there, and study for his Master's Degree. Charles had been gradually creeping up on him in the number of premiums secured; but, far from resenting this, Paul rejoiced in Charles' steady advancement.

As the vacation periods took place in November and December, the boys were in New Orleans for Christmas, which was largely given over to religious observances; and for New Year's, which marked the beginning of the social season, though they were absent for Mardi Gras. Edward was, by this time, going to the balls at the Théatre d'Orleans, the theatrical performances at the St. Charles and similar entertainments, besides spending considerable time, like most of his associates, at one or the other of the famous fencing academies on Exchange Alley; he mingled generally with the gilded youth of the city, while maintaining his closest ties with the Percy family. Paul was too young to share in most of their diversions; but he had accepted a challenge from Charles de Maurian to the effect that if he, Charles, could learn to play chess, Paul could learn to fence. Consequently, he began to accompany Edward on the latter's excursions to Exchange Alley, where he watched the sword play with the same attention that he had watched his father and his uncle at chess, before he attempted to play himself. He also went frequently to the theater, less for amusement than for enlightenment; if he were to do credit to his class at Spring Hill, through his acting, it behooved him to see how the leading performers of the day played their roles. His attention was the subject of mild amusement to the other members of his family; however, they had learned that mockery was not only wasted on Paul, but very often proved a boomerang.

As a child, though he had always been grave and studious, he had also given the effect of daydreaming much of the time, for he had a habit of sitting with his head resting on his hands while he gazed off into space. The fact that this dreaminess was deceptive had long since been evident. Now it was no longer a characteristic; he sat up straight and looked the world in the face. His eyes and hair were as dark as Alonzo's and Don Diego's, who greatly resembled each other; but the aquiline severity of their features, so typically Castilian, had been softened in Paul's case. Except for his coloring, he looked more like his mother than his father; and there was something very winning about him that his Spanish forebears had lacked. He had remained short for his age, as well as slim, but his figure had both grace and dignity. Every time his grandfather looked at him, the old man's heart swelled with pride. He had wanted to raise his family to the ranks of the aristocracy and he had done more and better than that; thanks to him, Telcide and Alonzo had bred a boy who, in every sense of the word, was a gentleman.

With his ever-increasing self-confidence, Paul no longer retreated from association with girls and boys his own age and, like Edward, he saw a good deal of the Percys; but he found, to his regret, that Alice had lost sight of Charmian Sheppard; they no longer went to the same school and, though Alice did not say so, Paul gathered that the "Yankee" had failed to make the grade in the more exclusive Creole educational circles, partly because she was a Protestant and partly because her father was a shopkeeper. Indeed, Alice said, with a toss of her head, she was not at all sure Charmian had not been sent north to school. Many "Americans" did that with their children; they maintained that schools in New York and New England had a higher scholastic standard than those in New Orleans, which was, of course, ridiculous. Paul had confirmed the report of Charmian's absence by wandering off to the Garden District again and renewing his acquaintance with Zeke and Lucas Brown, who had not forgotten him and who welcomed him warmly. Yes, the ewe lambs—this time, Paul did not fail to catch the allusion —had been sent off to other pastures. But they would be back, come Christmas.

Paul not only held fast to the hope of seeing Charmian again; he steadfastly sought to do so. Two Christmas seasons came and went without success; but he was patient and persistent, as well as eager, and at last he had his reward.

Like so many sought-for goals, this one was apparently reached by mere chance. He had wanted to see Ben Le Mar as Falstaff, and his grandfather was the only member of the family whom he could persuade to accompany him to the St. Charles Theater. One of Telcide's frequent concerts was taking place that evening at the Morphys' Royal Street house and, as some of the participating musicians were really celebrities in their way and had come from a distance, Alonzo had consented to make the occasion a *soirée de gala* and to receive with his wife. Edward was committed to a supper party given by Pepe Llulla, a native of the Balearic Islands, who was one of the most fashionable *maitre d'armes* and who frequently entertained his more important pupils, after business hours, on a lavish scale. Hélène, as usual, was ailing. Ernest, to his nephew's great regret, was busy with preparations to leave New Orleans for Cincinnati, which he proposed to make his future headquarters. Mme Le Carpentier, though in vigorous health, had become more and more of a recluse. But old Joseph, now so lame that he required the support of two canes instead of one, in order to get about, was still game for an outing and still delighted to be his favorite grandson's chosen companion. He lowered himself into his comfortable seat at the theater, stretched out his aching legs, and prepared to snooze, if the performance should prove to be over his head, as those chosen by Paul very frequently were. His state was one of such ease and contentment that he was almost asleep before the curtain went up at all. Therefore, he failed to notice that his grandson's attention had been diverted by two young girls, seated on either side of a lady, at Paul's left.

Paul glanced at the girl nearest him, at first casually and then incredulously. It did not seem to him possible that in the whole world there could be more than one human being with all the attributes for which he had been watching so long: the cascade of golden curls, the rosy cheeks that curved so delicately toward full red lips, the quick grace of every movement, the soft but insistent voice, the light irrepressible laughter. He looked past her to the lady and the other young girl beyond. The lady was elegantly dressed in violet silk, and her hair, arranged with elaborate artfulness, instead of streaming in shining waves over her shoulders, gave the same effect of spun gold as her daughter's tresses, though it lacked their glow. Her face, too, must once have been very beautiful and still had a faded loveliness, which bespoke delicate health rather than advancing years; she seemed to be a comparatively young woman. The girl on her other side was more sturdy and less striking, and she was whispering excitedly to the fourth member of the party, a thick-set man with a square jaw and strong stubby hands. This must be the father of the family, Paul instantly decided, and the girl who was talking to him resembled him more than she did her mother or sister. But, while she did not have their exceptional charm, she, too, was arresting, in an inescapably vital way; perhaps she would be the type that would be called "very handsome" when she had filled out a little more and acquired more poise; as it was, she could only have been called very vivacious. She seemed to bound on her seat as she settled her cloak behind her and spread out her hoops; in the process, she dropped her program and bent over to retrieve it with an unsmothered exclamation of annoyance.

"I can't get it," she said impatiently, straightening up again. "It's slipped way down underneath the seat in front of me."

"It serves you right, Berenice. You never can hold on to anything," the square-jawed man beside her said rather curtly, without offering to help her recover her program.

Berenice! Then he had not been mistaken! That was the name of the second ewe lamb. Paul seized upon the unseen advantage her loss had given him.

"Won't you take mine?" he asked the girl who was sitting beside him. "I have an extra one and you can pass yours on to your sister."

"Why, that's very kind of you!" she said, accepting the proffered program without hesitation. She acted quickly on his suggestion, but Paul felt sure that however rapid her movements, she did not drop things as she changed her position. She looked back at him and laughed. "I don't see the extra one, though," she said.

"My grandfather's. He won't be needing his. As a matter of fact, I don't need it, either. I've seen this play several times already and I've studied it at college, in our Shakespearian course."

"You *have?* I've studied it, too, at school, but I haven't seen it before. I'm terribly excited about coming here tonight. . . . Do you live in New Orleans? Where do you go to college?"

He answered the last question first. "Spring Hill, near Mobile. But I do live in New Orleans—on Royal Street. As a matter of fact, I think you've been to my house."

She shook her head, laughing again. "I don't believe so. I haven't been invited to any of the houses on Royal Street." She spoke quite without rancor, simply as if stating a fact.

"Didn't you go to one several years ago, with Alice Percy and her brothers? And play blindman's buff?"

She wrinkled her brow a little, as if trying to remember. "Why, yes, perhaps I did," she said after a moment's thought. "Alice Percy . . . well, I haven't seen her or her brothers, either, in a long time. I don't go to school in New Orleans any more—I'm only here for the holidays. But I seem to remember vaguely . . . are you the boy who didn't want to join in the game, who didn't want to play anything but chess, until I said there'd be plenty of time for that later on, and dragged you out to the courtyard?"

"Yes, I'm the same boy—Paul Morphy. You're Charmian Sheppard, aren't you?"

"*Paul Morphy!*" the girl repeated. "Then you did—you do—" It was evident the name meant something to her and she leaned forward and laid her hand on her mother's. "Mama, who do you suppose that is, sitting beside me? It's—"

"Hush, darling. The curtain's going up." In a lower voice, she whispered, though not so softly that Paul failed to hear her, "You mustn't talk to strangers, Charmian."

"But he isn't exactly a stranger! He's—"

"I said hush, dear."

The curtain was indeed rising, but Charmian could whisper, too, and she did so. "It's Paul Morphy. You know, the boy everyone talks about. The chess prodigy who beat that Hungarian—Löwenthal, was that his name? Papa saw him do it. His father's a judge or something. His mother gives musicales all the time. They have a lovely house and they're great friends of the Percys. They're terribly important. Oh, Mama, do speak to him when the curtain goes down! Do ask him to come to our house!"

So that was the way it had come about, apparently by accident, after the long, long search. During the first entr'acte, Mrs. Sheppard spoke to Paul cordially and, before the play was over, he had been introduced to Berenice and Albert Sheppard, too, and asked if he would care to go home with them, for some light after theater refreshments. He hesitated, looking in the direction of the somnolent Le Carpentier.

"I'd like to very much. But you see, I'm with my grandfather—"

"Wouldn't your grandfather come, too? We'd like to have him. Or, if he doesn't want to, would you rather wait and come some other night?"

Paul was torn between loyalty and longing. In the end, loyalty won. But again he had his reward. His grandfather had roused sufficiently to hear the invitation. He might be lame, he might get sleepy when he went to a play like this one; but there was still nothing the matter with his hearing or his understanding. He glanced in the direction of the Sheppards and took in the situation instantly. Then he struggled to his feet and managed to make a very creditable bow.

"I thank you, madame, in my grandson's name and in my own. We shall both be very happy to accept your kind invitation. You have your carriage here, of course? We also have ours. I shall tell our coachman to follow yours."

"I know the way, *Grand-papa*," Paul told him.

"Her [Madame Begue's] second floor establishment, reached by way of a winding stair at 207 Old Levee (now known as Decatur) needed no advertising. The fame of the mouth-watering meals served there so spread from one person to another, that it was necessary for anyone not a regular patron, or one wishing to bring a guest, to make reservations days ahead of time. People were turned away constantly. Yet she refused to modernize or enlarge her set-up, saying it would only spoil the place, and anyway they were not trying to get rich.

"Begue's had no written menus, so it was impossible, even for those who frequented the place regularly, to be sure what would be set before them next. Of one thing all were certain, however: Breakfast, the only meal served at Begue's, would start promptly at 11 a.m.; and long after one thought he could not possibly put away even one more mouthful, another and still another course would be brought on and consumed with great enjoyment.

"There was something about the food prepared by Madame Begue, and washed down by good red wine served in water goblets, that made it delightful to eat, easy to digest, and so broke down one's resistance to 'plenty,' that one would stay on and on, eating away through each tempting course until the sudden realization that three or four hours at the table has passed!"

Sue Baker in *The Times-Picayune New Orleans States Magazine*—February 27, 1949.

13.

If Mr. and Mrs. Albert Sheppard had not been quite adamant in their viewpoint that their daughters would be better educated in New England than in New Orleans, and if they had not been equally determined that Charmian and Berenice should have the best possible cultural advantages, it is quite likely that, even if Charles de Maurian were doing so, Paul might not have remained at Spring Hill an extra year, to take a Master's Degree. However, since his only chance of seeing Charmian was during her Christmas vacation, when he was in New Orleans anyway, it required no great exercise of will power for him to stay at college. In fact, he had grown accustomed to its routine of studies and content in its general atmosphere. He found the subjects which he had always enjoyed—History and the Languages—increasingly absorbing, as he plunged more deeply into them, and he began to take a keener interest in Mathematics and Philosophy. Moreover, he had achieved a more thorough appreciation of the architectural aspects of the college and its natural advantages than he had experienced at first. The enlargements and improvements which Father Gautrelet was making on the buildings were outstanding, and included greater facilities for hot baths, which were not the least of their attractions, as far as Paul was concerned. The landscaping had achieved a pleasing harmony; the woodland avenues and paths were ideally suited to quiet contemplation; and, indifferent as he was to athletic sports, Paul had always loved to wander about and to gather flowers. He had been allowed to bring the chess set of lemonwood and ebony, on which he had first played, and several other personal possessions which were dear to him, from Royal Street to Spring Hill, and had been allotted a nook of his own in which to keep them. All in all, he really preferred Spring Hill to Royal Street, except when the latter was the natural approach to the Garden District.

The social hour at the Sheppards', after Le Mar's performance as Falstaff at the St. Charles Theater, was only the first of many that Paul enjoyed there. He found the whole family congenial and the huge house surprisingly attractive. Albert Sheppard was entirely unlike any man Paul had ever known; the New Englander did not pretend to have polish, but he had unlimited energy, will power and ambition and he was remarkably astute in all practical matters. "There's an old saying up in New Hampshire, where I come from, that if you ain't educated, you got to use your brains," he told Paul, early in their acquaintance. "Well, I'm not educated, I know that and, believe it or not, it's rare in my part of the world. Most of the boys in our neighborhood get to college somehow, Dartmouth mostly, but every now and then to Harvard, even if their folks have to scrimp and save so's they can. My family's about the only one I know well that never had much book learning—land, that's what they liked, and all they wanted, until my father came along and took a notion to set up store, too. That's what gave me the idea—only I wasn't satisfied to set up store in Dublin. I wanted to try my luck in Boston and it's been darn good luck, I'll say that for it—good enough for me to branch out wherever I wanted to. I guess I wouldn't have thought of New Orleans if it hadn't been for the Missus—maybe Zeke told you that. But when we found she just couldn't stand zero weather any more, no matter how many fires we kept going, I said to myself, 'Well, so long as I'm going to start another store somewhere and it better be in some warm place, it might as well be the "City of Sin" as anywhere else.' To tell you the truth, I was kind of curious to see what a city of sin was like. I'd never been in one."

He grinned and chuckled and his manner was so genial that Paul found it impossible to take offense.

"I like it down here, too, first rate," Albert Sheppard went on. "Not that I've done any more sinning than I ever did before. But the House of Paris is coming along fine. I couldn't ask to have it show bigger profits—the fact is, I didn't expect to have it show them anywhere nearly as big as they are, not for a few years yet anyway. But there was a good opening here for a store of just that kind. And the Missus has improved right along—that is, as far as her health is concerned. I think she's kind of lonesome sometimes though."

"I'm sorry to hear that," Paul said quite sincerely.

"Well, the truth is people in New Orleans don't seem to be very neighborly. And having the girls gone so much of the time . . . but then, we want they should have every advantage. And talk about all the boys we know getting to college! Why, the *girls* are starting to do the next thing to it! That seminary of Mary Lyons at Mount Holyoke is about the same as a college already. And that's where Berenice is headed. She's like me—she makes up her mind she wants to do something and she does it, come hell or high water. And what she wants to do is go to Mary Lyons' Seminary, so I guess she will. Maybe it would have been a good thing if I'd felt the same way about Dartmouth, instead of being in such a hurry to branch out and have a store in Boston. My Missus' family are all educated and they're in comfortable circumstances, so it didn't matter whether they used their brains or not; but we Sheppards had got to the point where we were land poor." He chuckled again, and Paul could not refrain from smiling, too; much as he appreciated Mrs. Sheppard's ethereal loveliness, he failed to visualize her as showing any of her husband's initiative, which he was beginning to admire very much. "Just the same, her folks couldn't have given her all the

comforts I have," Mr. Sheppard continued, looking with pardonable satisfaction around the spacious, handsomely furnished room where he and Paul
were sitting. "We've kept the house I bought in Boston—it's on Beacon Hill,
where most of the old families live. Lots of the newcomers have gone to
South Boston, but it was the hill, cobblestones and purple glass and all, that
the Missus wanted, so that's what I got for her, and her sister, who's a fine
woman, stays there and looks after it for her when she's not there—looks
after the girls, too. And of course there's always been the property in Dublin
and always will be, as long as there are any Sheppards. She can take her
pick as to where she lives, if she doesn't get to coughing; and she has all the
help she wants. I don't mean slaves. I mean hired men and hired girls. Well,
you've met the Browns—people of that sort, who think they're just as good
as we are and, by gum! they are."

"I see what you mean," Paul said slowly, though he was not quite sure
that he did.

"The Missus is thinking of taking the girls on the Grand Tour, too,"
Mr. Sheppard went on. Now that he had started, he found it hard to stop.
"I'd miss them, but I wouldn't stand in the way of their going. I'm sorry to
say I couldn't leave my business long enough to go with them."

"Wouldn't the Grand Tour interrupt their school schedule?" Paul inquired hopefully.

"Well, the way we figured, they could go the year before Berenice entered the seminary—she isn't ready yet to leave Miss Hersey's, the day
school where she goes in Boston. And Charmian doesn't hanker to go on
studying Latin and History and such forever, and to be in a place where
there's just girls. Some nice finishing school might be her ticket, maybe one
abroad. That's not decided yet. But like her Ma, she doesn't find New
Orleans over and above neighborly. I think the Grand Tour may be just
the answer for her."

This conversation was disturbing to Paul; as a result of it, he approached
his mother on the subject of the Sheppards. The consequences were not
wholly satisfactory.

"I've met some people I like very much," he said hesitantly, one day when
he believed the occasion was favorable. "Their name is Sheppard and they
live in one of those big new houses in the Garden District. I thought perhaps you might call on Mrs. Sheppard and—well, invite them all here to one
of your concerts."

"Where did you meet them?" Telcide asked suspiciously.

"As a matter of fact, one of the daughters of the family, Charmian, came
here to our house several years ago with the Percys. Perhaps you didn't see
her. She was out in the courtyard with the rest of us when Uncle Ernest
called me in to play chess with Herr Löwenthal and when I went out

again, the Percys and Charmian had left. But I happened to sit next to her at the theater a little while ago and I recognized her. She's—she's very pretty and so is her mother. Anyway, Charmian's sister, Berenice, who's pretty, too, but in a different way, lost her program, so I offered mine and Charmian and I got into conversation. *Grand-papa* was with me that night and the Sheppards asked us to go home with them after the theater for a light supper. We had a very pleasant time. I'm surprised *Grand-papa* hasn't told you about it. I've been to see them several times since."

"No, your grandfather hasn't told me anything about it," Telcide said, speaking rather sharply this time. "Perhaps there was some reason why he didn't. These Sheppards you're talking about—they're not any connection of the man who owns the House of Paris, are they?"

"Yes, that's just who they are."

"But, Paul, you wouldn't expect me to call at their house! You wouldn't want me to invite them to one of my concerts!"

"I don't see why not. They've been very courteous and very hospitable to me."

"Naturally. They'd like nothing better than to be received socially in New Orleans. But they won't be, not if they stay here fifty years."

"I don't see—" Paul began again. But the trouble was, he did see. He knew that the Sheppards were Yankees. He knew they were in trade. The fact that they were kindly, that they were rich, that the girls and their mother were charming and cultured and the father of the family vital and successful would not make any difference. He could not remind his mother that her father had long been connected with enterprises far less creditable than those of Albert Sheppard and that Le Carpentier's education was no better. Her feelings would be hurt and to no avail. She would say it was not the same thing, as indeed it was not, but her meaning would be different from the one Paul had in mind. Joseph Le Carpentier could have kept a quadroon mistress, cozily installed in a neat little house on Rampart Street, without giving rise to criticism; and though, as far as Paul knew, he had never done so, it would have been regarded as quite natural if he had. He could have frequented any of the numerous gambling establishments in the Quarter, and lost every cent of the fortune he had so painstakingly accumulated, and that would have been considered natural, too. He could have killed a man in a duel, and that would have added to his réclame, rather than detracting from it. He actually had been an auctioneer and might even have dealt secretly with privateers; and though these activities were regrettable, they were condoned. He was still a Creole, whose wife had come from a well-established family and he had seen to it that his daughters married into distinguished ones; his grandchildren were aristocrats. There could not now be any connection, however casual, with persons of lesser consequence, as far as Telcide was concerned. Above all, with persons who belonged to a different world. Yankees. Shopkeepers.

Having failed with his mother and recognizing that any attempt to appeal to his father would only meet with a rebuff, Paul next approached his never-failing ally, his grandfather. Joseph Le Carpentier had enjoyed his midnight supper with the Sheppards; the weather had been unusually cool for New Orleans, and he had relished the hot buttered Medford rum and pumpkin pie with which he had been served and had found visiting with the family easier and pleasanter than he would have believed. Of course, their French was negligible, but he had not been named the "Double Tongued" for nothing, though it was a long while since he had taken satisfaction in this title. Not unnaturally, the Sheppards' known attitude toward slavery irritated him; but the subject was avoided and he accepted, without dwelling too much on the matter, the proffered refreshments from a rather grim looking, middle-aged white woman, who wore a large starched apron over her print dress, but no cap on her severely dressed hair, and who was, as Mr. Sheppard put it, the mainstay of their hired help. When it came to a question of returning such hospitality, which he eventually accepted several times without mentioning this to either his wife or daughter, Joseph was at a loss. Mme Le Carpentier received very few visits and went out even less, even among her old friends; that she could be persuaded to enlarge this restricted circle with strangers was almost inconceivable. Joseph hedged and, fortunately, circumstances provided him with a convenient pretext for doing so.

"Your *grand'maman* isn't up to making visits," he told Paul sadly over the chessboard. "Her embonpoint makes it hard for her to get around. Yes, I know, I'm not a featherweight myself; but a man can carry his poundage better than a lady and he isn't so sensitive about leaning on a cane. You know that, except for family dinners on Sundays, your *grand'maman* hardly ever has anyone to a meal any more. Of course, a visitor's offered coffee and cakes—a visitor that's received at all. But half the time, your *grand'maman* sends word by Fifine that she's lying down, that she has a migraine, anything for an excuse. Why, you don't always see her yourself, when you come here evenings! Of course, I could ask Mr. Sheppard to dinner at Antoine's with me any time, and I could probably find a few other men to join us, even if your father wouldn't. Or I might manage a Sunday breakfast at Begue's, though that's getting harder to arrange all the time. Madame wants the reservations made a long way ahead and what's more, she wants to know who's going to be in the company. I don't think she'd turn Sheppard down—he's getting to be quite a figure in his way. But then again she might, and that would be very embarrassing."

"You could talk to her about it first, you could make her feel complimented because you were consulting her."

"Yes, I could. But listen, Paul—you know as well as I do that it isn't dinner at Antoine's or breakfast at Begue's that people like the Sheppards are after. They want to be invited to our houses, the ladies as well as the men—I mean the gentlemen," he added hastily, noticing the hurt expression on his grandson's face. "The girls want to go to the *bals de royauté*. Well, I just don't see how it can be done. I'm sorry, Paul, very sorry. This girl you like so much—"

"Well?"

"Well, she's a beauty if I ever saw one and she has *esprit*, too. It's amusing to talk to her as well as pleasant to look at her. And she's got good manners—good enough to take her almost anywhere. So has her mother, so has her sister. Her father—well, he's not quite in the same class, but after all—" Joseph Le Carpentier hesitated a moment and then came out with a statement he had never made before. "But after all, I wasn't in the same class with your grandmother when I married her. Or even afterward, when I built that house on Chartres Street. I'm not now."

"I think you're the best grandfather a fellow ever had."

"Well, that's as may be. What I started to say was, and I'm just as sorry to say it as you can be to hear it, the Sheppards don't fit into our pattern. I don't believe you can make them, no matter how hard you try. Now let's not talk about them any more. Let's get on with our game. I see my Knight's cornered. What's your next move?"

Paul's next move, apart from those he made at the chess table, was to appeal to his aunt Amenaïde. As the wife of a physician, she was less bound by caste than the wife of a Supreme Court Judge; her long sojourns abroad had served to liberalize her ideas; and, in any case, these had always been less rigid than Telcide's. She liked good food and good company and she welcomed any excuse for dressing in her best and making merry. Yes, she said readily, she would call on Mrs. Sheppard; and if her father really wished to give a breakfast at Begue's, she would act as his hostess. She though she could persuade her old maid sister, Paul's aunt Amélie, who, poor old thing, didn't get much fun out of life, to attend the party, also, and she presumed that Paul would invite Charles. In that way, both the young American girls—Charmian and Berenice, were those their names?—would have a *beau cavalier*. And what about Edward and Alice Percy? No, Paul said regretfully, he had already talked with Edward, who was not interested. Well, never mind, Aunt Amenaïde replied soothingly; she and her husband, her father and her sister, the four Sheppards and the two boys—that would make ten and ten was an ideal number—large enough to make the occasion seem like a party and still small enough for general conversation. She would speak to Mme Begue herself. And about the call—just where was it the Sheppard family lived? Oh yes, on First Street. . . .

The call went off smoothly, the Sheppards accepted the invitation to breakfast with alacrity and the party at Begue's went off smoothly, too. Amenaïde, attired in crimson silk of the latest fashion, was an exuberant hostess. The red wine, the "cap" bread, the "tub" butter, the veal cutlet, the tender liver, the broiled tomatoes—all were served with a flourish and savored with appreciation, to the accompaniment of lively conversation. Mrs. Sheppard returned Mme Fortin's call, and the Fortins, M. Le Carpentier, Amélie, Charles and Paul were duly invited to the Sheppards for dinner, it being politely understood that Mme Le Carpentier's state of health and Mme Morphy's responsibilities in connection with her musicales did not permit them, to their great regret, to accept invitations to such functions. The fare at the Sheppards was as excellent as that at Begue's, though it consisted of entirely unfamiliar dishes as far as their Creole guests were concerned: a hearty fish chowder, hot baking powder biscuit, a huge roast of beef with Yorkshire pudding, roasted "Irish" potatoes, mince pie and three kinds of frosted cake served with floating island. The wine that accompanied this Gargantuan feast was not on a par with the food and the coffee would hardly have passed as such in any Creole household. Lacking the proper amount of stimulus, conversation flagged somewhat and involuntary yawns were stifled by everyone except the four young people, though exemplary politeness continued to prevail. But Paul did not need to be told that now the amenities had been observed, these would not ripen into a continuous round of hospitality; any serious attempt in this direction would be a strain for all concerned.

Fortunately for him, though the Creoles considered their own houses well-barred fortresses against alien intrusion, they were liberal in their outlook as far as their sons' independent diversions were concerned and youths were permitted to pursue these freely even before they had fully emerged from adolescence into manhood. It was tacitly understood that Paul, like Edward, would go to the *salles d'escrime,* the gambling houses and the public balls, if he felt so inclined, and few questions were asked as to how he spent his time after dinner and before he reached home. If his mother guessed—as his grandfather knew—that a good deal of this time was agreeably whiled away at the Sheppards', she did not say so, nor did she discuss the question with her preoccupied husband; and Charles, who was also aware of the situation, forbore to mention the matter to his friend until the latter was spending his last year at Spring Hill. Then it was done as tactfully as possible.

"Now that you'll soon be in New Orleans all the time, I suppose you'll be going out more, won't you?"

"You mean, I'll spend my evenings at other houses besides the Sheppards'?"

"Well—something like that."

"I don't believe so. I think that until Charmian gets back for the Christmas holidays, I'll probably play chess with *Grand-papa* in the evenings that I'm not going to the theater or helping Mother with her musicales or studying. I imagine I'll have to study rather hard."

"Yes, I suppose so. Just the same, I envy you the chance you've got to read law under Christian Rosellus and Randall Hunt. There isn't a better firm in New Orleans than theirs."

"You'll have just as good a chance, with just as good a firm, next year. Look how Edward Bermudez is coming along! He'll be Chief Justice of the state one of these days."

"If you don't beat him to it."

"Nonsense! Father seems to take it for granted that I ought to be a lawyer and I presume I should, especially now that Edward's definitely decided he doesn't want to. He'll probably match Uncle Ernest's success as a cotton broker, but I'll never match Father's on the bench. Anyway, I can't be admitted to the bar until I'm twenty-one. That means I've got three more years to go."

"And, meantime, what are you going to do besides studying and playing chess and helping with your mother's musicales and going to the theater?"

"I just told you. Only now, I'll see Charmian during her Easter holidays, as well as her Christmas holidays. I couldn't up to now, because I've always been at college during the spring. And perhaps some time I could go north during the summer. I've always wanted to play at the New York Chess Club anyhow, and there must be some such club in other cities, too."

"Boston, for instance?"

"Yes, Boston, for instance. In one way, it's been nice having our vacations in midwinter. But in another, it's turned things topsy-turvy with our hardest work all through the hottest months and graduation in October."

Charles started to say, "There are any number of things to do in New Orleans besides those you're planning on. And any number of girls, more available and more suitable than Charmian Sheppard and just as attractive. Why don't you do some of those other things, why don't you see some of those other girls?" But, as he glanced at his friend, he knew it would be worse than useless to say any of this; it would be offensive. Paul's sensitive face betrayed no anger; but there was a fixed look about it that precluded argument. He did not intend to alter, in the slightest degree, the course he had set for himself.

Paul took his Master's Degree, as he had taken his Bachelor's Degree, with highest possible honors. The commencement exercises were held on a perfect autumn day, and the blue sky and warm sunshine seemed to lighten the solemnity of the occasion and mitigate the consciousness of impending separation. Charles delivered an address on "The Pursuit of Wisdom" with appropriate dignity and earnestness, but with no note of mournfulness in his voice. And Paul was very proud of him; for the moment, his regrets at leaving the place where he had stayed so long and so contentedly were submerged in a glow of achievement, his friend's as well as his own, and in the rewarding praise of his teachers. "Of all the youths I have met in my long years at this college," his professor of Philosophy told him, pressing his hand, "I can truthfully say that I have never known anyone who was your peer in strength and capacity of intellect, Paul." The old scholar paused for a moment and then added huskily, "I shall miss you, my dear boy."

"I shall miss you, too, sir," Paul said and his voice had begun to be husky, too. After that, he did not linger over his preparations for departure. The trip to New Orleans was no longer the arduous one that it had been when he first came to Spring Hill; he had to go by stagecoach only as far as Mobile, where he took the steamboat, *James L. Day*, for the so-called inland passage, paying five dollars for his berth. The ship sailed out of the beautiful Bay of Mobile in the evening, with sweeping gulls following after it; the air was warm and hazy and the water was smooth as glass. As darkness fell, the haze cleared and the stars were brilliant. It was very still.

Paul stood on deck for a long time, looking first at the sea and then at the sky and then at the sea again. He was not sorry to be alone for a while, though at first he had been disappointed, because Charles had been delayed by some unforeseen last minute duties and had not been able to make the trip with him. His parents had gone to Spring Hill when he took his Bachelor's Degree, so they had suggested that they should not come there a second time and he had not urged them to do so. His extra year had seemed to have no special connection with them, but now, the next morning at daybreak, he would be entering Lake Pontchartrain by a narrow passage and then, after skirting its southern shore, he would reach Milneburg and disembark there. Afterward, he would board one of the cars of the little railroad, which was built on piles, and pass over the swamps shaded by tall moss-hung cypress trees. In less than an hour, he would be in New Orleans, unless he stopped for breakfast at the Elysian Fields Coffee House. But he hardly thought he would. Now that Spring Hill and everything it had meant to him was behind him, he wanted to get settled in his own room at home as soon as possible, ready to begin work the next day in the office of Rosellus and Hunt. He intended to work very hard, to qualify as soon as possible for his bar examinations, even if he could not practice for another three years. And, after all, he was not thinking three years and a half ahead—only two months. This was the 11th of October. On the 11th of December, Charmian would be coming to New Orleans for her Christmas holidays.

Paul Morphy's bedroom, reproduction of a private
drawing never previously photographed.

14.

Though he had fully expected to do so, Paul did not find the work at the distinguished but rather dingy offices of Rosellus, Hunt, McCabe and Hennen very hard. His infallible memory permitted him to retain, word for word, practically everything he read; it was obvious that he would know the Code Napoleon by heart in record time. But though the labors, which he had been told would be so onerous were, in his opinion, surprisingly light, he found them excessively boring, and it was with difficulty that he refrained from expressing this opinion in his father's presence. Moreover, the theater had lost much of its allure for him, now that he did not have the incentive of watching famous professional players with the ulterior purpose of perfecting his own technique. His mother's musicales had always annoyed him almost as much as they did his father, not because he lacked appreciation of music, for which he had an excellent ear, but because the heterogeneous groups she assembled were uncongenial to him; and none of the usual pleasures pursued by the young men about town whom he knew had the same appeal to him that they did to Edward. More and more frequently, as soon as he had finished his dinner, he walked the short distance from his parents' house to his grandparents' and spent the rest of the evening at the chess table.

With the arrival of Charmian and Berenice, this schedule underwent an abrupt change. Though they had failed to penetrate the fastnesses of the French Quarter, they had now made a good many friends in the Garden District, where Yankees were flocking in larger and larger numbers, and where the House of Paris was not regarded as a social stigma, but as an outward and visible sign of tremendous success. Moreover, the enormous balance which Albert Sheppard kept at both the Louisiana State Bank and the Commerce Bank commanded such respect that a strong movement was already afoot to invite him to become a director in one or the other; he could count not only fellow merchants, but fellow financiers among his acquaintance. These men were not slow to realize that their wives and daughters, no less than their sons, would be well advised to rescue the Sheppards from the comparative isolation in which they had lived at first. A slight change in their status had already taken place when Paul met the family at the theater. When he made his first call of the season, the year that he began the study of law, he found the huge house on First Street already thronged with a gay company. Mrs. Sheppard, whom he had never previously visualized as a musician, was playing a lively tune on the piano; Mr. Sheppard was presiding at a brimming punch bowl; and a dozen laughing couples were alternately waltzing and pausing for welcome refreshment.

Paul was greeted, as usual, with cordiality; but he recognized, almost immediately, that he should have called sooner. The seven day trip from New York to New Orleans, by combination stagecoach and railroad, was considered very fatiguing; and he had taken it for granted that young ladies required a certain amount of time to recuperate from this, especially as there was a good deal of strain connected with the unpacking of Saratoga trunks and the disposition of their contents in armoires; so he had allowed for all that before presenting himself. Apparently, the other boys and young men whom he had never met before and to whom he was now introduced, entertained no such scruples; he gathered that they had arrived at the front door, bearing camellias, bonbons and sheet music, almost as soon as the Sheppards themselves arrived and had gained a firm foothold. Though he succeeded in snatching a waltz with Berenice, he hardly wedged in a word sidewise with Charmian until the dancing was temporarily suspended for musical chairs. Then he was ruled out early in the game and, to his great satisfaction, she was the next to be eliminated by the abrupt cessation of crashing chords. He had been hopefully watching for such a possibility and rushed to her side before anyone else could reach it.

"I've hardly seen you at all," he said, and instantly realized that he had made a mistake by saying this reproachfully rather than regretfully.

"Well, it's your own fault. I've been here three days, plenty of time to have lots of visitors and plan for lots of parties."

"I thought you'd be tired. I thought you'd want to rest after your long journey."

Charmian threw back her head and laughed—the laugh he had always found so entrancing and in which, for the first time, he detected a slight mocking note. "*Tired!*" she echoed. "Why, I'm never tired! I don't see why you should have thought I wanted to rest. I'm not fragile, like Mama. You don't think I look sickly, do you?"

"I think you look perfectly lovely, as you always do."

She tossed back her curls, which she still wore in a shining cascade over her shoulders. "Then you must tell me so, once in a while."

"I'd like nothing better than to tell you so every day. But I can't very well do it when—"

The music had stopped again, with the same suddenness as before, and another youth, to whom Paul took an instantaneous dislike, was charging in their direction. Disregarding Paul completely, the intruder seized Charmian's hand and pulled her in the direction of the rear gallery. "I'm roasting to death, after all that tearing around in a hot room!" he complained. "You must be, too. Come on, let's get a breath of air!"

She glanced archly back at Paul over her shoulder, but she did not resist the arrogant interloper; indeed, she seemed pleased rather than otherwise at his importunities. It would never have occurred to Paul to burst in on a conversation in that way, much less to drag off a girl who was talking to another young man, without so much as a by your leave. He considered it the height of discourtesy, not to say boorishness and, in his resentment, he tried to tell himself that if these were Yankee manners, it was easy enough to understand why gentlefolk did not want to put up with them. But a moment later, when Berenice joined him, his ill feeling melted in the face of her buoyant bloom. She was not beautiful, like Charmian; she still looked more like her father than her mother, but, added to his vitality, she had a charm of her own. She was singularly free from airs and graces, and her candor was entirely untinged with coquetry and was permeated with good will. She instantly recognized that Paul's sensibilities had received a shock and set about to make amends.

"You hadn't met Chester Rollins before, had you?" she said. "Mama thinks he's rather a rough diamond, but Papa likes him—he says diamonds are diamonds whether they're rough or not and that, sooner or later, they get smoothed over. I expect he's right. Just the same, I don't think it would hurt Chester to have someone take him down a peg. If Charmian doesn't do it, maybe I will myself."

"No, I hadn't met him before," Paul said, purposely confining his answer to her question. "Is he a Bostonian, too?"

"Goodness no! I think his family came from somewhere way out West, Ohio, maybe. But they've lived in New Orleans longer than we have and they just bought a house in the next block. Chester's father is in the shipping business. I believe he means to go into that, too. . . . How do you like law?"

"Not much."

"Then why don't you do something else that you do like? I mean, most of the Sheppards were farmers, but one of my uncles used to say my father couldn't tell one end of a cow from the other. Of course, that was just his way of teasing, because Papa would rather have measured yard goods than do the milking, when he was a boy. So that's what he started out by doing. And just look at all he's done since!"

"Yes, I know he's been very successful," Paul said guardedly. "But in my case, I don't know exactly what I would do, if I didn't go on with what I've begun. I don't know of anything I'd like better—that is, if I've got to have a profession, and I suppose I must."

"But, Paul, there are sure to be some things you like to do!"

"Yes, I still like to study, even if I don't have to any more, and I like to read and go on long walks and play chess. And—" he added hastily "—I like to come and see you and Charmian very much. Do you suppose that tomorrow evening—"

"I'm afraid that tomorrow evening we're going to a party at the Emorys'. But what about Sunday dinner?"

"Well, Sundays we always have dinner with my grandparents, or else they come to us. But perhaps for once . . . yes, I will come. Thank you very much."

He did so, but his departure from established custom was viewed with great disfavor, not only by the Morphys, but by the Le Carpentiers. For the first time, even his grandfather failed to find excuses for him. He reflected, bitterly, that he might have committed almost any folly to which the city's gilded youth was addicted without bringing down so much censure on his head as he had done by failing to appear at the family board when he was supposed to be there. But neither the censure nor the bitterness prevented him from taking a much bolder step: he accepted an invitation to spend Christmas Eve with the Sheppards.

In the period that had elapsed between his first disappointing visit and this gala occasion, he had managed to see a good deal of Charmian or, rather, he had managed to be in the same house with her a good deal. As a matter of fact, he had found Berenice more responsive to long friendly talks than her sister. It was from the elder girl he learned that the time for their departure on the Grand Tour had been set for the end of the spring term at school and that they would probably be abroad for a year and a half; their father would join them, briefly, during the next winter and, perhaps, during their second summer in Europe as well. When they returned, Berenice was going to Mary Lyons' Seminary, as she had so long hoped to do. She was not sure how Charmian would spend her time after she got through finishing school—perhaps in New Orleans, if Mama's health did not improve. And Mama had not seemed quite as well as usual, lately. A note of anxiety crept into Berenice's voice, but she suppressed it quickly. Of course, it was just that Mama tired easily, when they had so much company. Berenice didn't mean Paul, he was welcome at any time, and he was always so pleasant and quiet. But some of the others who came there. . . .

"Like Chester Rollins, for instance?" The words were on the tip of his tongue, but he managed to suppress them, just as Berenice had managed to suppress her expressions of anxiety. He could well understand that a fragile lady, like Mrs. Sheppard, might find Chester Rollins exhausting and, as far as that went, he, Paul, found the shipping magnate's son repulsive. But probably both tolerated Chester for the same reason: Charmian found him amusing rather than otherwise and they would not interfere with anything that gave Charmian amusement.

She was now extracting a good deal of it, not only out of Chester Rollins, but out of life as a whole. Paul had never seen her in such high spirits as she had been since she came home this time. In the brief interludes that he had alone with her, that bubbling quality of merriment, which was the first thing he had ever noticed about her, besides her beauty, made itself felt more and more insistently. He could not pin her down to serious conversation, as he could Berenice. But, in the end, it was she who, to his surprise, was the one who suggested that he should spend Christmas Eve with them, and that he should come early, before the other guests, so that he could see the tree in all its glory and the other decorations while they were still fresh: laurel—holly—mistletoe. . . .

"The tree?" he asked, puzzled.

"Yes, of course. You don't mean to tell me, Paul, that you don't decorate a tree at your house and light candles and hang presents on it Christmas Eve?"

"No. You see Christmas Eve's a—a very solemn vigil with us. We fast and then we go to Midnight Mass. We don't give each other presents until New Year's, sometimes not until Three Kings' Day."

"That sounds to me like an awfully dull way of celebrating a holiday. You'd better let me show you how we do it."

"Thank you. I'd be delighted to."

Since Christmas presents were apparently in order, he gave serious thought to the subject. The nature of the gifts considered suitable for a young man to give a girl was extremely limited; and certainly Charmian could not wear any more flowers, or eat any more candy, or use any more sheet music than she was already supplied with. But books; yes, he had heard that books—carefully chosen, of course, so that they would not in any way offend against propriety—were also permissible. He would buy books for both Berenice and Charmian, but the one for Charmian should be just a little more elegantly bound, a little more elaborately illustrated, than the one for Berenice. And Berenice would understand, just as she understood everything and, far from taking offense, she would feel he had done the natural thing. And surely he might offer a lace scarf to Mrs. Sheppard and a box of exceptionally fine cigars to her husband.

He took considerable pleasure in the selection of these gifts and wrapped them with care; then he stacked them neatly on his dresser, in preparation for the great evening. It did not enter his head to hide them, though he had made no mention of his plans. If he had been questioned, he would have answered candidly, sorry that, for the second time, he was to be the cause of hard feeling for failing to remain with his family, but still determined to pursue his own way. Since it did not occur to anyone that this would be a departure from precedent, the subject was not mentioned, and it seemed to him that probably the simplest course would be to drop out at the last moment, when it would be too late for argument. He might have been successful if his mother, who did not often enter his room, of which Tata took entire care, had not come there unexpectedly late on the afternoon of the twenty-fourth. He had been closeted so long that she was afraid he was ill. Instead, when he answered her knock, she found him standing in front of his shaving stand, wearing black dress trousers and a stiffly starched frilled shirt and engaged in carefully arranging his white cravat.

"Why, Paul!" she said in surprise. Her quick glance flashed from his *costume de rigeur* to the wrapped parcels. "Haven't you been preparing your New Year's gifts rather early, *cher?*" she asked. "And surely you didn't intend to go out to some social function, apart from all the rest of us, before we went to Mass?"

He finished the arrangement of his cravat and reached for his dress coat, which was neatly hung over the back of a chair, before he answered her. Then he faced her with that fixed expression which everyone who knew him realized meant unalterable determination.

"Those aren't New Year's presents, they're Christmas presents," he said steadily. "For the Sheppards. I'm having family dinner with them, before a party. In fact, I promised to get there a little early, to see the decorations. It seems they're something very special. Will you excuse me, Mother? I think Honoré has the cabriolet ready for me."

"Paul—you're not serious!"

"I never was more so."

"We deplored your absence from Sunday dinner, but we condoned it. This is something we can't condone. The most solemn fast of the year—the most glorious Mass—and you're going to eat dinner with outsiders and attend a *soirée de gala* at their house!"

"I'm sorry, Mother, that you don't approve. I know Father won't, either. I love you both very much and I mean to be a dutiful son. But, after all, I'm not a child any more. There are some decisions I have to make for myself. This is one of them. There will be so many different dishes, I couldn't possibly do justice to all of them and no one will notice which ones I leave untouched. I'll go to Mass the first thing in the morning. I'm not overlooking my obligations to the Church or to my family. Please believe me and please don't be angry with me."

He leaned toward her, meaning to put his arms around her and kiss her cheek. She pushed him away.

"If you go out of this house tonight—"

"I'm sorry, Mother," he said again. Then he gathered up his little packages and quietly left the room.

When he reached the Garden District, he saw that not only the Sheppards' house but all those around it were aglow with lights. The shutters had not been drawn or the shades pulled down, and he could see great glittering trees, hung with colored balls and silver tinsel and surmounted by shining stars or wax cherubs, rising in the stately drawing rooms beyond the pillars of the porticos. The front doors were decorated with great wreaths, tied with mammoth bows, and laurel was festooned over their lintels. He threw his reins to Zeke, who was standing, grinning, near the front gate, evidently awaiting him; and responded heartily to the hired man's greeting of "Merry Christmas." Then he bounded up the steps, cradling his packages in the crook of his arm. Just before he actually reached the festooned door, it swung open to admit him.

Inside of it stood Charmian, dressed in crimson silk, with a wreath of crimson flowers on her flowing hair. Her neck and arms were bare, except for a garnet necklace and garnet bracelets; and, although her hoops stood out full around her, falling to her feet, her tight-fitting bodice was cut so low that its bertha of fine lace barely veiled the swell of her young breasts. She put a finger warningly to her lips.

"Hush!" she said softly. "I wanted the fun of coming to meet you myself, before any of the others knew you were here. You've brought us some presents, haven't you? I knew you would! But put them down on that table for a minute and—come on—toward me. Then stop when I do."

He looked at her unbelievingly. There was something unreal, something close to magical, about her manner, her voice, her appearance, the subtle fragrance which enveloped her. Almost without conscious action, he placed his gifts on the table, as she had directed, and advanced slowly toward her, while she as slowly retreated. Then she stopped and laughed.

"Look up!" she said. "And see where we are."

Again he followed her directions, but he understood her meaning no more clearly than before. They had come to a halt underneath a huge crystal chandelier, blazing with lights. This was decorated not only with garlands, but with a small cluster of foliage, which was dotted with white berries and which swung tremulously from a ribbon attached to the pendant of the chandelier. As he looked from this to Charmian, she laughed again.

"Don't you see that we're under the mistletoe bough?" she whispered. "Aren't you going to kiss me?"

He put his arms around her and drew her toward him, still unable to believe in the reality of what seemed to be happening. Far from resisting him, she nestled closer to him; she was almost as tall as he, so she did not need to raise her face for him to reach her mouth, but, at first, it did not occur to him that he might venture as far as that. However, when he had kissed her brow and her cheeks, he realized that her lips were waiting for him, too, and he pressed his against them, at first gently, then harder and harder, and still she did not draw away. Almost beside himself with rapture, he tightened his hold on her waist; and having kissed her throat again and again, found that his lips had strayed until his face was buried in the smooth beauty of the cleft whiteness that rose above her bodice. Suddenly aghast at his boldness, he lifted his head to gaze at her and still saw only laughter in her eyes.

"I thought you never, never would!" she whispered. "I've tried every way I could think of—teasing you, taunting you, running away from you. Finally, I saw there was only one thing to do, so I did it. Now please begin all over again and, this time, don't stop so soon."

OBSERVATIONS

Particulièrement
Relative Aux Femmes.

"Une stature généralement moins élevée que celle de l'homme, mais plus de légèreté et d'élégance dans la taille, des formes moins tranchées et plus arrondies, des traits plus délicats, la peau d'un tissu plus fin, plus de souplesse, de lenteur et de grâce dans les mouvements, la douce expression du regard, l'accent enchanteur d'une voix moins grave et plus sonore: dans tout cet ensenble, je ne sais quel irrésistible attrait d'abandon et de faiblesse qui demande un appui: tels sont les caractères auxquels l'homme, des le premier aspect, reconnaît la céleste compagne qui doit partager avec lui les plaisirs et les peines de la vie."

Etudes de l'Homme by J. A. Perreau.

(This particular book was once in the private library of Don Diego Morphy.)

15.

Paul kept his word, both in regard to the letter—if not the spirit—of the Christmas Vigil and early Mass the next morning.

His abstention from most of the delicacies for the Sheppards' holiday feast subjected him to some teasing from his contemporaries and many expressions of genuine concern from his kindly hostess, beside whom he was seated. Didn't he like roast turkey? Could she have something else cooked for him instead? He didn't like mince pie, either? Why, he would go home hungry! Wasn't he feeling well? It did not reassure her when he helped himself liberally to mashed potatoes, squash, onions and cranberry jelly with the main course and, later, to plum pudding, ice cream and layer cake. She belonged to the school of thought that believed in "tempting" her guests' appetites and, as a Unitarian, the rules and regulations of Catholic practice were either unknown to her or distasteful, or both. Paul tried, as tactfully and unobtrusively as he could, to explain the dietary limitations placed on him by observance of the Christmas Vigil; but he could see that Mrs. Sheppard was at first bewildered, then hurt and, finally, a little aggrieved, so he gave up the effort. Ordinarily, he himself would have felt disturbed by her attitude; as it was, he was still so enraptured by the memory of Charmian's kisses and the anticipation of further and still more ardent embraces, that nothing anyone else said or did had much effect upon his sensibilities.

He went straight from the Sheppards' party to the cathedral, reaching there for the five o'clock Mass, and he did his best not to add inattention to his other venial sins of omission and commission. But he was still tingling with amorous excitement, and he rose and knelt and crossed himself mechanically, scarcely aware of what he was doing. He could not communicate in any case, since he had failed to go to Confession within the previous octave. Fleetingly, he realized that this would be regarded by his parents as another serious failing; but he could no more keep his mind on them than on the priest at the altar. All his consciousness was flooded with blissful thoughts of Charmian—Charmian—Charmian. . . .

He suddenly perceived that the five o'clock Mass was over and that preparations were already underway for the next one and, in the same automatic way that he had done everything else, he left the rear pew where he had taken a seat, genuflected, dipped his fingers in Holy Water and went out into the cold darkness of Jackson Square. It took him only a few minutes to reach home and, after letting himself in with his latchkey, he removed his patent leather shoes and tiptoed through the hushed house to his own room. Once there, he stripped off his clothes, permitting them to land haphazardly, instead of arranging them, according to his habit, with meticulous care. Then he flung himself into bed, where his stirred senses were gradually submerged in rosy dreams, almost as vivid as reality.

It was noon before he was roused to unwilling wakefulness by the arrival of Tata, who appeared at his side with coffee and a message from his father: it seemed that the judge had asked for Paul several times already and was becoming impatient; though she did not put it quite this way, it was evident Tata thought Master Paul would be well advised to go, as quickly as possible, to the library.

"An' you ain't got time for no tub," she added warningly.

"If it isn't already prepared for me, I suppose I haven't. But I've got to shave anyway, so I may as well take a sponge bath here, too. I'll feel a lot better when I have," Paul answered, without any signs of haste. "You can bring me hot water, while I'm drinking this coffee. And please pick up all those clothes that are lying around and bring me some clean underwear and everything else that I'll need."

"I done tol' you, the judge—"

"I heard you. I'll go to the library just as soon as I'm properly washed and dressed. It won't make the judge feel any better if I present myself looking like a tramp."

Tata continued to murmur, but she did his bidding and, when Paul went to his father, forty minutes later, he was immaculately turned out. The judge was pacing up and down, his arms folded across his breast. As he turned toward his son, Paul saw that his expression was ominous. His face had become more highly colored as he grew older, and anger reddened it still further; his long straight nose quivered. It actually seemed to Paul that even Alonzo's thick wiry hair, brushed forward over the ears, was bristling with rage. Everything about him was forbidding. Nevertheless, the boy managed to speak as if nothing out of the ordinary had happened or was about to happen.

"Good morning, Father. Tata says you want to see me."

"It's a little late to say good *morning.* I've been waiting for you for some time. I want an explanation of your extraordinary conduct, if you have one to give me."

"I accepted an invitation to spend Christmas Eve with the Sheppards, as I've already told Mother. I didn't realize that such an acceptance required an explanation. You don't ask for one if I go to a *salle d'escrime* or a gambling house. You wouldn't even ask for one if I went to a quadroon ball."

"I advise you not to address me disrespectfully, Paul."

"I don't mean to be disrespectful. I don't wish to be. I do mean and wish to be logical. I thought that was one of a lawyer's first duties."

"You're not a lawyer yet. You're a minor, subject to parental control."

"I don't want to say anything that will hurt your feelings, Father. But may I ask you a question?"

"Yes, if it's a proper one."

"I believe it's a pertinent one. If I'm not mistaken, you and Mother told Malvina that she was a minor, subject to parental control—which, of course, was perfectly true. But she found a way of overcoming the handicap of her youth and she escaped from your supervision. My question is this: do you think any of us are any happier than we would have been if she'd been allowed to receive her suitor here and, in due course, married him from her own home?"

Paul was well aware that the question was a dangerous one, calculated to rouse the judge's wrath to a still higher pitch, but he was also aware that his argument was unanswerable. Malvina had never returned to New Orleans, from the day she set sail on the *Emma Fields* with the Fortins. She had found one pretext after another for prolonging her stay abroad after her visit to Natalie St. Martin Benjamin was over: Aunt Amenaïde had discovered just the right piano teacher for her there in Paris, it would be a shame to abandon the lessons which would help her achieve musical ability comparable to her mother's. Uncle Edouard was going to attend a medical congress in Rome; he proposed to take his family with him, for Aunt Amenaïde made friends so readily, anywhere and everywhere, that he had found her likability a great asset in his work; of course, Malvina was included in the party; she would never again have such a wonderful opportunity to see Italy under the best auspices; they had any number of invitations from delightful Italians and they might even have an audience with the Pope! They were returning to France by way of Switzerland and, as they were all debilitated after the heat and the social activities of the Eternal City, Edouard and another physician with whom he had conferred, both felt they would be well advised to spend several months in the cool bracing air of the Alps. It was in Switzerland that John Sybrandt had joined them and that Malvina had married him under the sponsorship and with the full knowledge and consent of her aunt and uncle. John now had an excellent position as a cotton broker in the great English manufacturing city of Manchester, and Malvina was not only a happy wife, but the proud mother of a baby boy whom she had never brought to visit her parents. There was no assurance when they would see their elder daughter again or make the acquaintance of their first grandchild. The knowledge of this was bitter to them both.

Alonzo did not answer Paul's question angrily; in fact, he did not answer it at all. It was far too evident that, though Paul was not yet a full-fledged lawyer, he could argue a case very well and that, though he might be a minor, subject to parental control, he could not be browbeaten. There was an adamantine element underlying Paul's deceptively tractable disposition and peaceloving character. His sensitive face could become very firm. The judge, irritated by his own inability to dominate his son mentally, when he had so easily and so long dominated his wife physically, unwisely resorted to sarcasm.

"I trust you are not about to tell me that your mother and I are once again to suffer the pangs, sharper than a serpent's tooth, as the Scriptures say, of having a thankless child?"

"I don't believe Malvina is really a thankless child, only a free spirit. I certainly am not thankless. But if you mean are you again faced with the possibility of an engagement in the family, of which you don't approve, I am afraid I shall have to say yes."

"An *engagement!* At your age!"

"Well, an understanding which would lead to an engagement, if you prefer to have it that way. I meant to tell you today, of my own accord, that I'm deeply in love with Charmian Sheppard. I didn't intend to wait until you felt you had to force such an admission from me."

"You don't know what it means to be in love!"

"I think I do. As a matter of fact, I believe I've been in love with Charmian since the first time I ever saw her, when I was thirteen years old."

"You can't expect anyone to believe that a thirteen-year-old boy knows what it means to be in love!"

"I didn't expect you to believe that I could show you how to beat Uncle Ernest at chess when I was ten." He did not add, "And neither of you has ever won a game from me since—nor my grandfather, nor my elder brother, nor any of our friends. And not even the great Löwenthal." Nonetheless, the unspoken words forced their way into Alonzo's angry thoughts. "I managed to convince you of that, so I hope I will convince you of this, too," Paul continued calmly. "You know I've never looked at any other girl. But whether or not I was in love with Charmian when I was thirteen, I'm certainly in love with her now."

"That Yankee! That shopkeeper's daughter!"

"Mr. Slidell was a Yankee and for all we know his people were shopkeepers. He doesn't say much about them. But his career's comparable to yours in importance and he married Mathilde, one of those beautiful Deslonde sisters, with the full approval of her family."

Again, Paul had scored. John Slidell, who had come from New York as a complete stranger, had achieved an almost immediate success in Louisiana, both as a lawyer and as a politician. He had represented the state in Congress for two years and, afterward, had been appointed United States Minister to Mexico. Though that country had declined to accept him, when diplomatic relations were severed before the outbreak of the Mexican War, he had speedily overcome this temporary setback and was now an outstanding member of the Senate. Indeed, he was credited with being influential in advocating the nomination of James Buchanan for the Presidency and, if the latter should be elected, Slidell would be a power in the administration. As to his marriage, there was no question that an alliance with the Deslondes, the hereditary owners of vast sugar plantations in the Parishes of St. James and St. John the Baptist, was quite as much of a social triumph as any he had won in legal and political fields.

"And then of course there's his partner, Mr. Benjamin, who married our cousin, Natalie St. Martin," Paul went on.

"John Slidell isn't a beardless boy," Alonzo interrupted angrily, refusing to embark on the still more unwelcome subject of Judah P. Benjamin's successes. "When you become a senator, you can marry whom you please. I'll be dead by then. I shan't be able to prevent you."

"I know I'll never be a senator and I want to get married while I'm still a young man. You did, didn't you? What's more, you married a French girl, though Spain and France were traditional enemies—the daughter of an auctioneer."

"I forbid you to speak in this way about your mother."

"I haven't said anything against my mother. Nothing would induce me to. I love her dearly. I also love Charmian Sheppard dearly. I hope you won't say anything I can interpret as casting aspersions on her."

"I shan't mention her name at all and I shall insist that you do not, either, in this house. What you do with your own time, out of it, is, as you have reminded me, something I have not hitherto questioned. I shall not question it in the future. But if you continue to go to the Sheppards' house, it must be with the distinct understanding that neither this girl with whom you are infatuated—Charmian, is that her name?—nor any of her family will ever be received here."

"I'm sorry to hear you say that. I'd meant to ask you, as soon as I'd told you I was in love with Charmian, if you and Mother wouldn't call on her parents and tell them you would be glad to welcome her as your daughter, when the proper time came."

"There never will be any such time."

"I'm sorry to hear you say that," Paul repeated. "Because I'm already committed."

"What do you mean, committed?"

"I mean I have spoken to her of love. I have embraced her."

"No doubt she invited you to do both. In that case, you are not committed."

For the first time in the course of the painful interview, Paul recognized that he, and not his father, was at a disadvantage. It was quite true that Charmian had invited his embraces, and that she had done so even before he had openly declared himself. But his astonishment, because of this, had been entirely submerged in his joy, though he knew only too well he could not explain anything of the sort to his father. However, the judge was quick to press the advantage given him by his son's momentary silence.

"It is only what I should expect of a girl with her lack of breeding," the judge said, again speaking sarcastically. "By all means, continue to see her, if you wish to. I know that young men must sow their wild oats."

"I am not sowing wild oats. I am conducting an honorable courtship. And I will not stay here and listen while you talk in such a tone about the girl I want for my wife. There are some things no man has a right to say to another, even if they are father and son. You have just done so. I must ask you to excuse me."

He turned on his heel and left the room. His father made no effort to detain him. Both were equally aware that they had reached an impasse.

Paul knew that Charmian would expect him to return before the day was over, and he hoped that he might have a chance of speaking quietly to Mr. Sheppard sometime during the course of the visit. This hope was defeated. The house was full of company, both young and old, and no one, not even Charmian, was enjoying the atmosphere of gaiety more than the man who was now very generally recognized as a merchant prince. To entertain on this lavish scale, without giving a thought to its cost, suited his temperament perfectly; such hospitality had been an integral part of his goal, no less than the establishment of the House of Paris. His own house must be symbolical of the great emporium's success.

It was not until almost the eve of Charmian's departure for the North that Paul was able to lure Mr. Sheppard into his so-called "den" long enough to have a serious conversation with him. Meanwhile, the boy had been alternately experiencing interludes of gloom and gaiety. His father did not again bring up the subject of Paul's defection on Christmas Eve or his attachment to an unsuitable *partie* and his mother avoided the mention of both; but the atmosphere of the Morphys' house was glacial and Paul spent as little time in it as was humanly possible. Fortunately, Charles de Maurian was home for his vacation from Spring Hill and it was taken for granted that Paul would spend a good deal of time with him. Edward Bermudez, who had been graduated several years earlier, and who was forging ahead rapidly in his legal career, was another college friend who was always glad to see the young law student. The St. Martins and their son-in-law, Judah, continued to keep open house; and now that Pierre Beauregard's long period of mourning was over, he had become an outstanding social figure, whom his juniors followed with admiration and around whom they flocked. It was logical that Paul should be in their company. All this made life easier. Besides, at the Sheppards', he was caught up in the continual round of merriment and when he could get Charmian to himself, she was quite ready to have him make love to her; she even created a few opportunities which he would have considered it presumptuous to seek. Though stolen kisses were sweet, Paul could not suppress the feeling that anything clandestine was unworthy of them both; hole in the corner fondling was not the sort of caress he sought or desired. Moreover, Charmian did not seem to attach the same importance to their relationship that he did. She continued to laugh, to tell him not to be a sobersides, to ask him if they weren't having fun, instead of assuring him that he meant the world and all to her, as she did to him.

Mr. Sheppard, though cordial to the point of joviality, was also obviously disinclined to treat Paul's courtship as a serious matter. When finally cornered, he listened pleasantly to everything the boy had to say, as he sat with his legs stretched out before an open fire, a glass of brandy on the table beside him, and an excellent cigar, from which he took occasional puffs, in his hand. At last, draining his glass and sitting up a bit straighter, he began to talk in his turn.

"Well now, I'm not surprised that you and Charmian have taken a liking to each other," he said genially. "But you're both pretty young. Neither of you has had much time to look about yet. You've hardly been away from New Orleans, except to go to that Catholic college in Alabama, where they kept a checkrein on you. Charmian's been to New York a few times and stagecoaching through the White Mountains and she's spent a season at Saratoga Springs, so she's had more of a chance to mingle with different kinds of folks than you have. But she ought to be given her head a while longer. When she's gone through finishing school and made the Grand Tour—"

"I don't want to interfere with any of that, sir. After all, I haven't passed my bar examinations yet. But I did hope that, before Charmian went back to Boston, we could have some kind of an understanding. Especially, as she won't be back here until April."

"Well now," Mr. Sheppard said again, "the Missus and I have been talking things over and we've about decided not to have the girls come to New Orleans for their spring vacation. By April, it's begun to warm up some in New England, though not much, I'll admit. Land! I've seen good sleighing in Dublin at that time of year! But it's some warmer anyway. And the Missus thought she wouldn't mind the cold too much if she went north then; she figures it will take quite a while to get everything ready for that long trip of theirs. They want to get off just as quick as Berenice graduates from school. That'll be in June. Of course, they're going to take one of the new Cunarders and—"

"But in that case, I won't see Charmian for two years!"

"No, I guess you won't, Paul. So all the more reason why you shouldn't be hasty about anything now. In two years you might see someone you fancied even more than you do Charmian."

"I don't 'fancy' Charmian, sir. I—I love her. I've never loved anyone else. I'm sure I never shall."

"I know that's what you think. But I've never met a boy yet that didn't fancy—and I'm sticking to that word—more than one girl before he settled down for good. I like you, we all do, but I'm not prepared to say you're much different from the average, when it comes to taking fancies. I hear you're quite a prodigy at chess. But Lord! that hasn't anything to do with nature!" He laughed, not unkindly. "Now I think the world of my Missus. But I don't mind telling you, as man to man, that I've had other fancies, both before and after I met her. Fancies—yes, we'll let it go at that. But this time it isn't so easy to stick to the one word. Some would use a different one."

"I told you, sir, that I preferred to use a different one."

Sheppard laughed again. "I know you did. But when you and I said a different one, we weren't thinking of the same word. Well, suppose we talk about something else. What are your prospects? How soon do you suppose you could support a wife? I mean in the right style: plenty of hired help— no slaves, mind you!—half a dozen new dresses whenever she wants them, trinkets and gewgaws galore. And, of course, a nice house of her own."

Momentarily, Paul was nonplussed. He had given absolutely no thought to anything so material as worldly goods; his father was a wealthy man and the Morphy house was enormous. The desirability of an independent income for a young husband, the idea that a bridal couple should have an establishment of their own, had not entered his head. Mr. Sheppard, with habitual shrewdness, was quick to realize this and to press the advantage it gave him.

"Of course, the Missus and I expect to give our girls as fine a trousseau as money can buy," he said. "Clothes, linen, silver, china, jewelry—all that we'd supply as a matter of course. But once they're married, we'll look for their husbands to support them—wouldn't dream of consenting to any other arrangement. Oh, I don't mean that we wouldn't give them an occasional present or a special treat or an extra luxury now and then, of course! But when it came to the grocery bills and the servants' wages or the purchase and upkeep of a house, that wouldn't be any part of our responsibility. And, of course, we wouldn't think for a minute of having them live with us after they were married—we'd miss them like everything, but we'd know they'd be better off by themselves. As for letting them live with their husbands' families—why, that isn't to be thought of, not even if their in-laws doted on the very ground they walked on! And you and I don't need to talk about this—I wouldn't wonder if it isn't sort of a sore subject with you as well as with me. But we both know what your family thinks of us Sheppards."

Again Paul had no adequate reply. It was easier for him to cope with his own father than with Charmian's. He looked at Albert Sheppard with such mute misery that the kindly man was actually sorry for him.

"There, maybe I ought not to have come right out with that, even though it's true enough," he said. "I'll tell you what, Paul, you go ahead with your studies and find yourself some kind of a law practice, even if it's a small one. When we got down to brass tacks, I wouldn't mind helping out some on the grocery bills, in spite of what I just said. I might even give Charmian her house. But I'm not going to promise anything or let her promise anything—and mind you, she hasn't told me she wants to—until she's through school and finished her Grand Tour and you've hung out your shingle. So that's that. Now come on and let's see what the others are doing. From the sounds, I'd say there's lots of fun going on in the parlor. We been cooped up here long enough."

Paul left the Sheppards' house sunk in deep gloom and he saw no prospect that this would lighten before Charmian went back to Boston. But some slight assuagement of his despondency came from two unexpected quarters.

He had not played much chess with his grandfather lately, partly because he had been so intensively occupied elsewhere, and partly because he knew that Joseph, like Alonzo and Telcide, was resentful of his absence from the family circle on the occasions when it was taken for granted he would form a part of it. But when he reached home, after his disheartening talk with Albert Sheppard, Tata, who had waited up for him, handed him a small sheet of paper, folded in the shape of a triangle.

"Mlle Amélie, she give me this," the old slave told him. "She said you was to read it when wasn't no one else looking."

Paul accepted the note and, when he reached his room, read it by the light of the *veilleuse*. It was written with lavender ink in a fine Italian hand and smelled faintly of musk.

"Dear Paul,

I should like very much to have you come to see me tomorrow. The time when *Maman* takes her siesta will be best, as Papa is also at his office then.

Your loving aunt,
Amélie."

He could not imagine why this forlorn old maid should suddenly express a wish to have him visit her secretly. As a matter of fact, he had no inclination to do so. Like all the rest of the family, he considered her a nonentity—though not a nuisance, like poor Charles, because she was so self-effacing that one was hardly aware of her existence. She was a mere wisp of a woman, literally more or less concealed, much of the time, by her corpulent parents. She invariably wore nondescript gray dresses which merged into her background, and her soft, shabby shoes made no sound as she walked. When it came to that, she walked very little; most of the time, she remained secluded in her room, the smallest and least desirable in the Le Carpentiers' house. She went regularly to Mass, at the hours when the cathedral was least frequented, but aside from this, she seldom stirred abroad. Paul could not remember seeing her, except, shrinkingly, at Sunday dinners—no, he was wrong! She had been to that breakfast at Begue's, a long time before, and to the Sheppards' house afterward, when they had all had so much to eat, imperfectly seasoned, and so little to drink, none of it vintage wine. When he remembered this, it crossed his mind that, for some strange reason, Amélie wanted to talk to him about Charmian.

He was right, but he was very far from guessing beforehand the turn the conversation would take. Amélie was watching for him at the window when he reached the Le Carpentiers' house, and let him in herself, enjoining silence, as she did so. His grandmother was asleep and Fifine, Mme Le Carpentier's body servant, was slumbering, too, on the pallet in her mistress' room; the other slaves were all in the quarters. But it was just as well to be careful. Amélie led him into her chamber and closed and locked the door. Then, before seating herself, she walked over to the *coiffeuse* and, opening her modest jewel box, removed from it a small piece of tissue paper, folded as neatly as the note had been and evidently containing some trifling trinket.

"I've been thinking about the Sheppards," she said in her soft quavering voice. "They were very kind to me, you know—inviting me to that fine dinner, at their beautiful house. I wanted very much to see them again, but *Maman* said, after I'd made my *visite de politesse*, that I mustn't go back. So I thought . . . I understand those lovely girls are going away in a day or two and that they're not coming back for a long while. . . . You know your parents and your grandparents talk about them—"

"Yes, I know," Paul said, trying to speak with a degree of resignation which he was far from feeling.

"Well, and I know you go to see them just the same, no matter what Alonzo and Telcide may say. And I thought that, perhaps, as a parting gift from me—of course, it wouldn't be proper if it came from you—you might take them these."

She handed him the scrap of tissue paper and he unfolded it carefully. Inside lay two insignificant ornaments. One was a small brooch made from finely woven hair, stiffened to form semi-spherical globules, encircled and fastened with narrow strips of gold; the other was a heart-shaped locket, with a single turquoise in the center.

"If you gave presents to *both* girls," Amélie went on breathlessly, "and from *me*—why, there couldn't be anything wrong in that, could there? The hair was *Maman's*, when she was a young girl. She gave the brooch made from it to me on my fete day, the year I was sixteen. The little heart was also a present to me about the same time. It was given to me secretly. Of course, I hoped . . . but that was a long time ago. I don't need it to remind me of the past. I don't want to think of the past, any more than I have to. But, perhaps, it would mean something to you in the future—do you sometimes venture to call Charmian *mon coeur*, when you speak to her, or at least think of her that way?"

"Yes, Aunt Amélie, I do."

He was infinitely moved, so touched that he hardly knew how to express his gratitude and his emotion. But she did not seem to expect or even want him to do so. Now that she had made her little offering, she was fearful that his presence would be discovered and questioned.

"I'm sorry I haven't a proper box to put them in. But you can carry them just as they are, can't you?"

"Of course, Aunt Amélie. And please let me say—"

"No, no, don't say it. You must hurry along. Your grandmother or Fifine might wake at any moment."

He kissed her, wondering if the tears on her face were all hers. Then he put the two trinkets in his waistcoat pocket and went straight to the Sheppards' house.

It was still fairly early in the afternoon. Like his grandmother, Mrs. Sheppard lay down after lunch, while Mr. Sheppard spent this period at the House of Paris; and the grim gray-haired woman who opened the door for him said that no other company had as yet arrived and that the two girls were upstairs, packing their Saratoga trunks. She would tell them he was there. The next instant Charmian came bounding down the stairs and flung herself into his arms.

"Oh, what luck!" she said joyfully. "Not a single soul around, for once. Let's go into the den, shall we?"

If he associated this, briefly, with his previous session there, the impression lasted only a minute. The den was not like the drawing rooms, which gave on the street and opened into each other and into the main hall; it was tucked away by itself, under the stairs, and it had only one door, which Charmian not only shut, but locked, just as Aunt Amélie had shut and locked her door an hour earlier. And yet it was not the same, except that both had made sure there would be no intrusion. Poor Amélie had wanted secrecy only in order that she might be undiscovered while she made her pitiful little offering. Charmian wanted secrecy in order that Paul could pay court to her, more boldly than he had ever done before.

She flung herself down on the sofa, making room so that he could sit beside her and, by leaning over, put his arms around and behind her waist and kiss her, from her brow to her breast. Involuntarily, he realized how easy it would be to loosen her bodice or even the fastening of her belt. Then he saw that her fingers were already unknotting the light scarf with which her lownecked dress was finished and, almost abruptly, straightened up.

"*Mon coeur,*" he said gently, "you are so generous—so lovely—so innocent —that you cannot guess how you tempt me. For you do not know, either, how greatly I desire you. Much more than I have a right to. I want you for my very own—for my bride. But we have been told that we must wait to fulfill our love and, therefore, we should not caress each other like this. I—I might forget myself. I might even forget that I must prevent you from responding to me. This"—and he suited his action to his words—"must be our last kiss today. But look, I have brought you a little present!"

He took the small package from his pocket and unfolded the paper. "I have called you *mon coeur*—my heart," he went on. "Perhaps you did not know that, with us, this is the tenderest term which any man can use in speaking to his sweetheart. But it is. And now, thanks to my Aunt Amélie, I have a little golden heart to give you, one that you can wear all the time until we are together again—until we can love each other with no restraint. Will you accept it, darling, with that understanding?"

The two trinkets were still lying side by side in his hand. Charmian sat up, fastening her fichu, straightening her skirt, and swinging herself upright on the sofa. Her hair was tumbled and she reached up to smooth it. Then she touched not the heart, but the little brooch.

"What's that funny thing?" she asked. "Is that for me, too?"

"No, that's for Berenice. You see, Aunt Amélie—"

He told her about the note his aunt had written him and the visit he had made her. The story lost nothing in the telling. But the touching episode did not seem to move Charmian as deeply as it had him.

"Since you've got a present for Berenice, too," she said, rising, "I'd better go and get her, so you can give it to her."

"But, darling—aren't you going to take yours first?"

"Yes," she said, almost carelessly. "I'll take mine first. It hasn't any chain, has it? Well, I'll find one for it. I've got lots of charms and lockets and things like that; there must be an extra chain somewhere among them."

Abruptly, Paul was conscious of the great variety of ornaments he had seen her wearing, and realized that most of them were far more valuable than this simple little gold heart, with a single small turquoise imbedded in it. He could not help wondering if there were a slight sting to her words, if the gift did not mean as much to her as it had to him, if in some way he had disappointed or even failed her. Then he saw that she was slipping the little heart into her bosom and smiling at him, more sweetly than she had ever done before; and his fears vanished into thin air, even before she said, "Couldn't we have just one more kiss—a real one—for good luck before I start upstairs?"

She went out of the room, leaving the door open this time and, a minute later, he heard her laughing. She had met Berenice in the hall, so she had not needed to go to the second story to fetch her sister. She told Berenice that Paul was waiting in the den with a present for her, and then went singing on her way.

Berenice came into the room and stood quietly while Paul told her about his Aunt Amélie and the two presents. When he finished, he saw there were tears in her eyes, just as he feared there had been in his own not long before, and she took the little brooch and fastened it carefully to her lace collar.

"I'll always wear it, I'll always treasure it," she said earnestly. "You won't forget to thank your aunt for it, in my behalf, will you? I don't quite dare write to her, since she wanted to keep this a secret. Someone else might see the note."

"Yes, you're right. And I won't forget to tell her."

The doorbell rang, jangling through the house. Berenice sighed.

"I'm afraid that's callers, beginning to come," she said. "I'll have to go out and meet them—Mama's still lying down. She doesn't seem to be getting any stronger. I hope when Charmian and I have left she'll get a good rest. But, Paul, before I say good-bye, may I tell you how much your friendship has meant to—to all of us? Perhaps Papa—" she hesitated and then went on, speaking with her usual candor. "Perhaps Papa was a little hard on you the other day. He told us, afterward, he was afraid he had been. But it's only because he loves Charmian so much, because he wants to be certain she has happiness and security when she makes a choice. She's so lighthearted herself, she might not be careful enough, if he didn't safeguard her. I know you wouldn't want him to feel any other way."

"No," said Paul, "I wouldn't. Because I feel the same way myself. But

I'm not sure I've made her understand that, though I've tried. Will you help me to do it, Berenice?"

"You know I will. You know you can depend on me to do anything I can for you."

Strangely enough, it was because he felt so sure this was true, even more than because Charmian had put the little gold heart in her bosom, that Paul left the house with hope and happiness permeating his entire being.

To the Honorable P. H. MORGAN,
Judge of the Second District Court of New Orleans.

The petition of Telcide Le Carpentier, widow of the late Alonzo Morphy of this City, respectfully shows:

That on the 22d Instant, the said Alonzo Morphy, your Petitioner's husband, departed this life in the Said City of New Orleans, as will more fully appear from the annexed certificate of his death.

That he died intestate, leaving as his only heirs four children, viz: Malvina Morphy, wife of John D. Sybrandt; Edouard Morphy, Paul Morphy and Helena Morphy; the two latter being minors.

That by law your petitioner is entitled to the tutorship of her said minor children, and that an under tutor must be appointed to them by your honorable Court.

That as Tutrix aforesaid your petitioner is bound to cause a faithful inventory to be taken of the property belonging to the Succession of the deceased.

Wherefore she prays that she may be admitted to take her oath as Natural Tutrix of her said minor children; that an under tutor be appointed to them and sworn as Such; that the Said inventory be taken by Theodore Guyol Esq., notary public in this City in the presence of all the parties interested, and that two appraisers be appointed and sworn to value the property to be inventoried; and as in duty bound, etc.

(*Signed*) Martin Blache,
of counsel.

Order.

Let the Petitioner be confirmed as the natural Tutrix of her minor Children within named and Let Letters of Tutorship be delivered to her on her taking the oath required by law. Let Charles Le Carpentier be appointed & sworn as the under tutor of said minors. Let the Inventory within prayed for be made by Theodore Guyol Esq.; not. pub. in the presence of all parties interested or them duly called and let Louis Marette & Francis Charles be appointed & sworn as appraisers to value the property to be inventoried.

New Orleans 26th Nov. 1856.
(*Signed*) P. H. Morgan
Judge
A true copy. V. Wilz
Cy. Clk.

No. 704
17th & 27th DECEMBER 1856
INVENTORY
OF THE ESTATE OF THE LATE
ALONZO MORPHY

I.

BY VIRTUE of and in obedience to an Order of the Honorable P. H. Morgan Judge of the Second District Court of New Orleans, bearing date the Twenty-sixth day of November Eighteen hundred and fifty-six, and directing an Inventory of the property and effects belonging to the Succession of the late *Alonzo Morphy*, late of this City, deceased, to be taken by the undersigned Notary: which order was rendered on the Petition of *Mistress Thelcide Le Carpentier*, widow of the said deceased: duly certified copies of which said Petition and order of Court are annexed in the margin hereof for reference. . . . .

Be it known that on this Seventeenth day of the month of December in the year of our Lord One Thousand eight hundred and fifty-six, and of the Independence of the United States of America, the Eighty-first. . . . .

I *Theodore Guyol*, a Notary Public duly commissioned and Sworn for the Parish of Orleans State of Louisiana, accompanied by *William G. Sarham* and *Paul Abat*, witnesses of lawful age and domiciliated in the City of New Orleans, proceeded to the late residence of the said deceased, No. 89 Royal Street in this City where I found assembled the following named persons to wit: . . . .

1. The said Mrs. Morphy, acting in her capacities of widow in Community of the said deceased, usufructuary of his Estate, and Natural tutrix of their Minor children, named *Paul Morphy* and *Helena Morphy*—and *Charles Le Carpentier*, their Under Tutor:

2. *Mistress Malvina Morphy*, of lawful age, wife, of *John Darius Sybrandt*, of this City, and herein duly assisted and authorized by her said husband.

3. The said John Darius Sybrandt, acting in his capacity of Administrator of the Estate of the said deceased.

4. *Edouard Morphy*, of this City, of lawful age, son and one of the heirs of the said deceased. . . . .

5. *Louis Marette* and *Francis Charles*, of this City, the experts duly appointed by the said Court and sworn by me, said Notary, to appraise the property of the said Succession to be inventoried. . . . .

In the presence of which said parties and witnesses, I, the said Notary, proceeded to take a true, faithful and correct Inventory of all the property and effects belonging to the Estate of the said late Alonzo Morphy, in this Parish, together with the valuations thereon affixed by the said Experts in manner and form following to wit: ....

HOUSEHOLD FURNITURE

IN THE LIBRARY

[Here follows a detailed description of the entire contents, each item valued separately.]
Total Value $ 364.75

IN THE HALL

[Here follows a detailed description of the entire contents, each item valued separately.]
Total Value 10.00

IN THE PARLOR

[Here follows a detailed description of the entire contents, each item valued separately.]
Total Value 1,129.00

IN THE DINING ROOM

[Here follows a detailed description of the entire contents, each item valued separately.]
Total Value 605.00

SILVER WARE

[Here follows a detailed description, each item valued separately.]
Total Value 216.00

IN THE OTHER DINING ROOM

[Here follows a detailed description of the entire contents, each item valued separately.]
Total Value 67.00

IN THE CABINET

[Here follows a detailed description of the entire contents, each item valued separately.]
Total Value 11.00

IN THE BED ROOM

[Here follows a detailed description of the entire contents, each item valued separately.]
Total Value 778.00

IN ANOTHER BED ROOM

[Here follows a detailed description of the entire contents, each item valued separately.]
Total Value 55.00

Amount Carried forward $ 3,235.75

| | | |
| Amount Brought forward | $ | 3,235.75 |

IN ANOTHER BED ROOM

[Here follows a detailed description of the entire contents, each
item valued separately.]

| | |
| Total Value | 55.00 |

IN THE KITCHEN

[Here follows a description of the contents and their appraised
value.]

| | |
| Total Value | 30.00 |

Amounting in all to the sum of Three Thousand
three hundred and twenty dollars and Seventy-five cents $ 3,320.75

SLAVES

Charlotte, a Negro woman, aged about twenty-three years valued at One Thousand Dollars   1,000.00

Dailey, a Negress, aged about Fourteen years, valued at Seven
hundred Dollars   700.00

Amounting together to the sum of Seventeen hun-
dred Dollars $ 1,700.00

CASH

Amount to the Credit of the said deceased in the Louisiana State
Bank, as per Bank Book, Fifteen Hundred and eighteen Dollars
and fifty-two cents $ 1,518.52

And now, at the hour of Six o'clock P.M. of the day and date aforesaid,
there not being sufficient time to finish this Inventory, I, the said Notary, adjourned the further taking thereof until the Twenty-seventh day of Decem-
ber instant. . . . .

In testimony whereof I have hereunto signed my name, together with the
said parties and witnesses on this Seventeenth day of December Eighteen
hundred and fifty-six.

F. Charles   J. D. Sybrandt
L. Marette   Ch. Le Carpentier
W. Sarham   Edw. Morphy
                  T. Morphy
                  M. Sybrandt
Theo. Guyol

And again, to wit, on this Twenty-seventh day of December, in the year
of our Lord One Thousand eight hundred and fifty-six, I, the said Notary,
pursuant to the adjournment aforesaid, proceeded with the taking of this
Inventory, in the presence of the said parties and witnesses, as follows, to wit:

Stocks

[Here follows a detailed list.]

Total Value $ 44,220.00

Real Estate

[Here follows a detailed list.]

Total Value $ 87,925.00

Bills Receivable

[Here follows a detailed list.]

Total Value $ 7,478.27

On a careful examination of the papers of the said deceased it was found that they consisted principally of old memoranda, notes presented and other documents which were considered to have no value whatever: and all which, together with the aforesaid Bills receivable and the Titles to the Real Estate and Slaves were left in the possession of the said John D. Sybrandt. . . . .

And now, the said parties declaring that they knew of no other property, rights, credits or effects in this Parish, belonging to the Succession of the said deceased, and to be included in this Inventory, I, the said Notary, closed the same with the following Recapitulation.

Recapitulation

Amount of the appraised Value of the Household Furniture, Thirty-three hundred and twenty dollars and seventy-five cents   3,320.75

Amount of the appraised value of the Slaves, Seventeen hundred dollars   1,700.00

Amount of Cash, Fifteen hundred and eighteen dollars and fifty-two cents   1,518.52

Amount of appraised value of the Stocks, Forty-four thousand two hundred & twenty dollars   44,220.00

Amount of the appraised value of the Real Estate, Eighty-seven thousand nine hundred and twenty-five dollars   87,925.00

Amount of Bills Receivable, Seven thousand four hundred & seventy-eight dollars & twenty-seven cents   7,478.27

Making a Total of One hundred & forty-six thousand one hundred and sixty-two dollars and fifty-four cents $146,162.54

In testimony of all which I hereunto subscribe my name with the said parties and witnesses on this Twenty-seventh day of December A. D. 1856.

L. Marette	Ch. Le Carpentier
F. Charles	Edw. Morphy
P. Abat	T. Morphy
W. G. Sarham	M. Sybrandt
J. D. Sybrandt	Theo. Guyol

16.

Paul received his diploma as Bachelor of Law with the same ease that he had earned his previous degree. In fact, he had been with Rosellus, Hunt, McCabe and Hennen less than a year when he knew the Code Napoleon by heart in its entirety; and, rather ruefully, the distinguished gentlemen who headed the firm admitted there was nothing they could teach him that would justify him in remaining with them any longer. Since, because of his youth, two years must still elapse before he could be admitted to practice, he found himself rather at loose ends. Of course, there were all the diversions New Orleans habitually offered and, now that Charles de Maurian was home for good, Paul could be sure of congenial companionship. Moreover, the entente cordiale had been re-established between himself and his grandparents and, though there was still a certain degree of detachment in his relations with his father and mother, the atmosphere of the house had undergone a definite change for the better since Malvina and John Sybrandt had returned for a prolonged visit. It was now understood that they would spend part of each year in Europe and part in the United States; John's increasingly important stature as a cotton broker required close connections on both continents. With the healing of the breach between Malvina and her parents, Paul was also happily conscious of lessened stiffness and strain in the same quarter; and he was greatly distressed, on returning from one of the long rambles about the city which gave him increasing pleasure, to find his mother very badly upset and, apparently, with some cause.

"The house must be kept absolutely quiet," she said warningly. "Your father has met with an accident."

Paul might well have been forgiven for reminding her that it was not he who usually disturbed the quiet of the house, but he was too greatly concerned to do so.

"What kind of an accident?" he asked quickly.

"Why, a group of men were standing on the banquette outside the courthouse when one of them, who was wearing a Panama hat, turned abruptly. The edge of the brim struck your father in the eye. It seemed like a very slight mishap, but he's suffering a good deal of pain, and some inflammation has set in already. Dr. Matas has been here and has told me your father must stay in a dark room, with cool bandages on his head. Either Tata or I will remain with him and change these bandages every hour. She's there now, so that I'd be free to come and meet you and tell you what had happened."

"Do you think he'd like to have me go and speak to him?"

"I believe he's been given something to lessen the pain and that's made him drowsy. Perhaps tomorrow would be better."

Tomorrow, however, did not prove to be any better; indeed, it proved to be definitely worse, for the pain was more severe and the inflammation had become more pronounced. No amount of medication seemed to relieve either one. At the end of a few days, it was evident that Alonzo Morphy was a very sick man and that the cause of this was no longer confined to his eye. Before his startled family had fully grasped this fact, he died from congestion of the brain.

Though Paul was well acquainted with the rigid rules governing the observance of mourning among Creoles, this was the first time they had affected him closely, for his father's parents had died before he was born and his mother's parents were still hale and hearty. He was not only genuinely grieved; he was acutely upset. His mother seemed to change almost overnight from an active, spirited and attractive matron to a drooping figure of crepe-clad woe. None of her children had ever meant as much to her as her husband. Malvina had disappointed and deserted her, and was now preoccupied with her husband and baby, Hélène was a whiner and a weakling, and both the boys lived in worlds of their own. To be sure, these worlds were entirely different. Edward's was that of the cotton brokerage, the subscription balls, the fencing academies, the gaming houses and any and all pastimes in which Alice Percy might be suitably included; Paul's was that of chess, of classic scholarship, of legal lore, of contemplation and of ill-starred romance. Telcide was excluded from both worlds, to practically the same degree. Moreover, Alonzo was the only man she had ever loved, and though marriage had not fulfilled all the rosy dreams of her girlhood, she had cherished these for a long while; she now reverted to them, as if they had never been troubled, much less damaged. Nothing which had happened between herself and her husband had been a departure from the pattern of the time and place in which they lived. How could she ever have resented the unfounded jealousy which had transformed a deliberate and respectful courtship into the imperious demand for an immediate marriage, the ruthlessness with which her innocence had been shattered on her bridal bed, and the passion which, once fully roused, remained insatiable year after year? How could a man, free to follow his impulses without restraint or censure, realize what the initiation into the mysteries of sex meant to a helpless girl or its dominance to a defenseless wife? She told herself that Alonzo would have been lacking in both spirit and virility if the manner of his wooing and wedding had been different; and it would have been a reflection, first on her unsullied virginity and then on her wifely duty, if she had not suffered from his initial vehemence and submitted to his subsequent requirements. She bitterly repented the fact that, when she had been married a little less than a year and had ceased to shrink from subjection, but had become frightened by the presage of the quickening within her womb, she had gone weeping to Father Moni, the priest who had performed her marriage ceremony and who was an old friend of the family, and had bared her heart to him. Instead of answering her with compassion, he had done so with severity: the Church, he reminded her, followed the mandates of Scripture which, from the earliest times, ordained that women should be ruled by their husbands and bring forth their children in sorrow. Then he added, less sternly, that there was another line in the same Biblical passage, wherein the Lord said to Eve, "Thy desire shall be to thy husband."

"In good time, my daughter," Father Moni had told Telcide, "the same shall be true of you. Meanwhile, be patient. Above all, be obedient and of good courage."

She had never been advised, much less enjoined, to study the Bible herself, so she had not read the passage the priest quoted; but she had lived to learn that it was true not only in its harsher parts, but in its happier ones. The day came when she looked forward to the night without dread, and soon thereafter she began to respond to Alonzo's passion—at first hesitantly, then willingly and, at last, ardently, in exactly the sequence and to exactly the degree expected and desired of her by her husband. If he had not actually told her this in so many words, he had nonetheless revealed it by his attitude toward her; and he had been still more gratified because it was she who had indicated—delicately to be sure, but still unmistakably—that there need be no delay in the swift resumption of marital relations after her first dreadful experience with childbirth. How could a man, she asked herself reasonably, to whom procreation meant simply the triumphant pleasure of begetting, visualize the desperate agonies of parturition? She answered this question for herself, just as she had answered the earlier ones, not only to her own satisfaction, but to her husband's relief, for, as a matter of fact, Alonzo had been more conscious of her sufferings than she realized. But the horrors of her first *accouchement* grew dim with time in the minds of both and did not haunt them again for a long while. Mercifully, Telcide did not conceive almost annually, like many of the women she knew, until they were past the age of childbearing or had succumbed to it. There were nearly four years between Malvina and Edward, three between Edward and Paul, two between Paul and Hélène. Telcide was able to tell herself, convincingly, that she did not have to pay too heavily for the joys of union, and to confess that, even if she had been so obliged, they would have been worth the cost. What had been first a shock, then an ordeal, then a duty, had ended by becoming a delight.

Afterward, she had felt secret shame because she craved caresses which became less and less frequent and demanding. Her senses were now fully awakened, while her husband's passion, so long insatiable, was at last beginning to burn itself out. Again, she told herself that this was natural: desire for a woman died a natural death, once it had run its course. And after all, jealousy still survived. Otherwise, why should he insist on the almost Moorish seclusion in which she lived, confined to her house and patio? Surely this was a sign that he still loved and cherished her! She clasped this belief to her breast and music, which she had always loved, now became a channel of emotional release. Though Alonzo did not share her fondness for this, he made no objection when she devoted an ever-increasing amount of time to it. She was proud to be the wife of a man who provided her with every material comfort, who played the host with a prodigality that made him a general favorite, and who achieved widespread recognition as a public figure embodying brilliance, learning, justice and dignity; that he had never talked to her about his work seemed to her no lack of confidence; legal matters were beyond her comprehension and she had not resented or missed the lack of this communion. When he died, there was nothing assumed about her grief; it was genuine and deep.

To a certain degree, Paul recognized his mother's sense of bereavement and shared the respect, accorded by the community at large, to the memory of a striking personality which had abruptly disappeared from its accustomed place, creating a void which could not be filled by others of less distinguished bearing and achievement. But Paul was less understanding than Telcide and less impressed by popular acclaim. He conscientiously sought to think only of the advantages which had been provided by a good home and a good education, to dwell on the love of books and of chess which he had shared with his father; but, try as he might, he could not dismiss from his mind bitter thoughts of Alonzo's attitude toward Charmian. Unlike his mother, he could neither forgive nor forget.

It was almost a year now since he had seen his one and only love. As long as Mr. and Mrs. Sheppard remained in New Orleans, he had continued to call on them occasionally, and they had never failed to receive him courteously and cordially. But they had left together the previous April and only the faithful Browns remained in charge of the otherwise deserted property. Paul went to see them sometimes, too; he no longer felt above accepting a sugar cookie and a glass of milk or, for that matter, any other refreshment they might offer; and, often, they had more news of the family than he did, for Mr. Sheppard sent his hired men businesslike directions every week. Charmian wrote occasionally, and her letters would have made amusing reading for any disinterested person; but they were so filled with references to merrymaking that, to Paul, they seemed to accentuate his

loneliness. Berenice wrote more regularly and more seriously: she was studying hard, she did not go to as many parties as Charmian, she was almost
sorry that the Grand Tour must intervene before she could enter Mary
Lyons' Seminary; but she was sure, once they were on their way, that she
would enjoy every minute. The letters that came after the Sheppards
reached Europe bore out this expectation, but mails from the Continent
were slow and uncertain. This was no surprise to Paul, for Malvina's correspondence had always been intermittent; nevertheless, it was a disappointment. When the news of Alonzo's death reached the travelers, they all sent
suitable expressions of condolence; but Paul thought he could detect in
these the realization that they were writing about a man whose loss propriety obliged them to observe, but who they realized never had been and
never would have been their friend. And after that, the letters became
fewer and farther between.

The great house seemed terribly empty to Paul. Telcide and Alonzo had
continued to occupy the same room as long as the latter lived; now Telcide
insisted she could not endure the loneliness of an unshared bed, again persistently choosing to remember only those intervals which had given her joy
and fulfillment; and believing that such a move might prove some assuagement to her sorrow, she took Hélène in with her. This meant an empty
chamber. The musicales had, of course, come to an immediate end with
Alonzo's death, so the parlors were unused, except when Telcide could be
persuaded to receive a *visite de condoléance*; and the library seemed to
Paul, in some ways, even more deserted, for it was there that the judge had
habitually sat by preference and hence the one which his son associated
most closely with him. The chessboard had already been set up in readiness
for a game the evening that Alonzo met with his accident; and, eventually,
Paul found he could not any longer stand the sight of it where it was, and
removed it to his own chamber. This was a commodious room, with a large
bookcase in one corner and a hooded fireplace in another, and it provided
ample space, despite the size of its canopied bed, for a chess table in the
center. Here, withdrawing more and more into himself, Paul sat alone,
evolving new patterns of play; increasingly, these became his one absorbing
interest.

The prescribed period of mourning was hardly underway when Charles,
the family failure, appeared in the midst of a doleful gathering, looking abnormally cheerful, and announced that he was at last getting married. The
fortunate lady was Mlle Marie Eugénie Alexandrine Lassus—a mere acquaintance of the other members of the family—and the ceremony would
take place as soon as the banns had been duly published—this with a side
glance at Telcide, who had been married by special dispensation. Understandably aggrieved by this reference to her hasty wedding, she was even

more so by the proposed infringement on an inflexible custom: to celebrate a marriage during first mourning was unheard of! Yes, hers had taken place during second mourning, but the circumstances were unusual. So were these, Charles replied triumphantly; he had been an object of charity and derision in his brother-in-law's house; now he would have a home of his own.

Paul had never imagined that he would be sad to see Charles depart and not glad to be relieved of listening to inept flute playing; but now here was another empty room, another source of silence. Malvina, to be sure, was back in hers, but her husband and her baby shared it now; brother and sister did not drift back and forth, companionably, between each other's rooms; as far as Paul was concerned, she might just as well have been still in Europe. He took to watching the mails more closely than ever, hoping against hope that, sooner or later, he would receive a letter from Berenice about something more cheerful than ruins and museums; it was too much to hope that he would receive one from Charmian, telling him about scenery, instead of about this charming marquis and that delightful count whom she had met. At last, when his father had been dead almost a year, and plans had been made to observe *Toussaint* with appropriate ceremony by a visit to the family tomb, Paul received a communication postmarked New York, and tore it open so hurriedly that he did not even stop to look at the letterhead printed in the upper lefthand corner of the envelope. Because this was what he wanted to do, he leaped to the conclusion that Mrs. Sheppard and Berenice and Charmian had come back to the United States sooner than they expected, and that he might soon be in frequent and easy touch with them, even if he could not actually see them. The letter was not the one for which he had hoped and, for a moment, every other sensation was drowned in his disappointment. Then he reread it and experienced, if not a feeling of rapture, at least one of satisfaction.

Frederick Perrin, the secretary of the New York Chess Club, wrote that the first American Chess Congress was to take place there. It would be a source of pride and pleasure to the officers and members of this exclusive society if Mr. Paul Morphy of New Orleans would come to New York as its guest.

PART THREE

"The King of Games"

1857–1859

"What shall I say of the crowning excellence and glory of the Congress—the wonderful playing of our 'young Philidor'? No, I am wrong; for though I believe I was the first to give him that appellation, yet it is a misnomer. Philidor but shadowed forth the mightier chess genius which it reserved for America to produce, in the person of our young friend, Paul Morphy, in whom we all take such national pride. He verifies the truth of the poet's line:

'Westward the star of Empire takes its way.'

"He charms us no less by his quiet, unobtrusive deportment, modest and refined nature, gentlemanly courtesy, elegant manners and genial companionship, than by his wondrous skill at our noble game. Thoroughly conversant with all the openings and endings, he shows that he has laid every writer under contribution to increase his stock of 'book knowledge'; but it is his own matchless genius which embraces and enlarges them all, that wins the victory, and that enables us, *as we intend to do,* to challenge the world to produce his peer. He reminds us of the noble river on whose banks he lives, which, gathering in its course the contributions of various tributary streams, pours at last its own current into the ocean, deep, clear, and irresistible."

Excerpts from the speech made by Mr. W. J. A. Fuller, editor of the Chess Department of Frank Leslie's *Illustrated Newspaper*, at the dinner given at the Hotel St. Denis by the New York Chess Club.

"Mr. President and Gentlemen of the Congress—I sincerely thank you. To one, to all, I tend my expression of my warm and heartfelt acknowledgments. Much, however, as I feel honored, I must be permitted to see in this gathering of chess celebrities something more than a tribute to merit, whether real or supposed. Gentlemen, we have come together for a noble purpose; we meet at this festive board to rejoice at the success of a grand undertaking. Great, truly great, is the occasion. For the first time in the annals of American Chess, a Congress is being held which bids fair to mark an era in the history of our noble game. Chess, hitherto viewed by our countrymen in the light of a mere amusement, assumes at last its appropriate place among the sciences which at once adorn and exalt the intellect. We have met this night to hail the dawn of a true appreciation of its manifold claims to regard. And, gentlemen, may we not cherish the hope that this, the first great national gathering of the votaries of Caissa, may prove but the forerunner of many yet to come? Should time realize this fond anticipation, to you, gentlemen of the New York Club, will belong the praise of having taken the lead in the glorious cause. You have, in political phrase, set the ball in motion. From the New York Club—from the altar where you worship—has gone forth the first note of praise, destined soon to swell into a mighty anthem to the achievements of our kingly pastime."

Excerpt from speech of Paul Morphy, made in response to a toast at the dinner given at the Hotel St. Denis, by the New York Chess Club, October 17, 1857.

The Book of the First American Chess Congress by Daniel Willard Fiske. (Rudd & Carleton, N.Y.)

17.

Creoles were not essentially great travelers; they were so content with their own little world that they had no driving urge to enlarge it. Only Paris seemed superior to New Orleans as far as sights, pastimes, fashions, sophistication and culture were concerned, and these they sought there either directly or indirectly. It was not unusual, in the first half of the nineteenth century, for a wealthy family to charter a ship, proceed en masse to the "City of Light," and return with a full cargo of furniture, carpets, paintings, porcelain and miscellaneous objets d'art, all acquired for personal use. In the course of such leisurely sojourns, ladies naturally replenished and augmented their wardrobes, bridal trousseaux were provided and even layettes were prudently anticipated, while both plantation houses and town houses were being outfitted in their entirety. Husbands and fathers took an active and interested part in all this wholesale shopping; it did not occur to them to be bored or annoyed by it and, indeed, as often as not it was they who made the more important selections. Nor were trips made primarily for purchases of such character by any means the only ones undertaken. Superior educational advantages, rather than luxury items, were often the end in view. French universities, French lycées and French convents, like French furniture and French couture, were considered a cut above those in Louisiana. What was more, all such institutions, but more especially the lycées and the convents, provided convenient sanctuary for the creamy skinned, silky haired children who were the products of those liaisons to which no reference was made in polite society but concerning the existence of which no one was in ignorance. These children were sent quietly, in the competent care of priests and nuns, and frequently never returned—not because harm befell them, but quite the contrary: a happier lot awaited them in France than they ever could have had at home. Their half-brothers and half-sisters, however, came back to add distinction to great family names.

Strangely enough, considering this Creole predilection for Paris, the first Morphys and Le Carpentiers never returned to Europe after coming to Louisiana; and it was not until the exigencies of Edouard Fortin's medical duties took him to the continent that his young wife, nee Amenaïde Le Carpentier, also went there, thus providing an excuse for their niece Malvina Morphy to join them and facilitating her marriage to John Sybrandt. Neither Alonzo nor Telcide had ever crossed the Atlantic or even sought to diversify their mode of existence by holiday trips to seaside or mountain resorts. They were quite satisfied with furniture by Mallard and Seignouret and fashions by Sophie. The opera provided them with all the entertainment they required beyond that provided by their family and friends; and they had not considered a French education desirable, much less necessary, for any of their children. Edward and Paul had done very well in Jefferson Academy and Spring Hill, Malvina and Hélène at Madame Girard's and the Ursuline Convent. When Paul started for New York, to attend the first American Chess Congress, at the age of twenty, he had never been farther from New Orleans than Mobile.

He set out hesitantly both for this reason and for several others. Like all the rest of his family, he felt no urge to travel, to see strange sights and meet strange people. Since his graduation at Spring Hill, he had once returned to Mobile, to engage in a match with Judge Alexander Meek, whose friendship he had achieved while he was still in college and who, through the kindliness and courtesy of his bearing, had done much to help Paul overcome his aversion to playing chess with older men. He had enjoyed this interlude; but a well-ordered life in New Orleans, which he felt sure was without peer among cities, represented his ideal of urban existence and he had never outgrown the shyness of his childhood. He clung to his old friends, but he avoided making new acquaintances. Besides, he was very conscious of his mother's reliance on him. Both Edward and Malvina had a greater number of pursuits than he did; they were not at home so much; and Hélène was a care, not a help. He felt it would be selfish of him to leave, at least before the period of first mourning was over. But shattered as she was by her husband's death, Telcide did not find the atmosphere of the great house as depressing as Paul did; it was her natural haven and, little by little, she began to take interest in it again and to find comfort and cheer in the presence of her first grandchild. When Paul realized this, he reflected that perhaps, after all, a change was what he needed. Moreover, all the men whose opinion he asked—his grandfather, his uncle, Eugene Rousseau, James McConnell—kept urging him to accept Mr. Perrin's flattering invitation. At last, he decided to do so.

It would have been possible, of course, for him to make the trip to New York by rail; for some reason, the Sheppards had always preferred to do so. But this involved many changes, with poor connections, and accommodations which provided only a minimum of comfort were very costly. It was much less expensive and much less trouble to go by ship. Accordingly, Paul took passage on the *Philadelphia*, with Captain S. P. Griffin, Commander, which made Havana a port of call, in preference to selecting a steamer following a coastwise course; and was rewarded by the splendid sight of a magnificent harbor at sunrise, a few days after the equally thrilling experience of leaving the mouth of the Mississippi, where water and land merged so harmoniously together that it was almost impossible to tell where one left

off and the other began, and a full moon was shining directly overhead as
the ship slid into the Gulf.

Unfortunately, he proved to be a very poor sailor and, consequently, most
of the time between these two great spectacles was spent miserably in his
berth. Brief as was his stay in Havana—a scant twenty-four hours—it provided a merciful reprieve from nausea, besides giving him a glimpse of a way
of life which he found fascinating. His paternal grandfather, as Spanish
Consul in New Orleans, had maintained many close Cuban connections
and his uncle Diego, succeeding to the same post, had enlarged on these
through the years. Friendships had continued to flourish, partly through
correspondence and partly through the officers of Spanish vessels and gentlemen who traveled with them, either for business or pleasure. The news of
Paul's invitation to New York and of the route he was taking had quickly
reached Havana, and when the *Philadelphia* entered the harbor, between
the grim batteries of La Punta and El Morro, a welcoming committee was
already waiting to receive him, despite the early hour. In fact, he found himself engulfed with hospitality. The young captain of a battleship, who had
been entertained by the Morphys when his man-of-war was in New Orleans, clamored for the honor of acting as host. Rather grudgingly, this
privilege was accorded him by a prominent banker and a merchant prince
who were also frequent visitors to Louisiana, and by two or three others in
the delegation who were known to Paul as outstanding chess players. But
the captain was not to imagine he could monopolize Señor Morphy all day.
Yes, they would gladly breakfast at the former's house to make plans; afterward, they would see. . . .

It had already begun to be very hot when they drove away from the docks
and Paul found himself envying the others their cool linen suits as their
carriages went clattering through the narrow streets; but when the grilled
gates of the captain's high blank house opened to admit them, he found the
shadowy galleries and luxuriant patio cooler than those of Royal Street in
similar weather. There were luscious fruits, mangoes and pomegranates
among them, as well as small crisp rolls and excellent coffee for breakfast;
and it seemed to Paul that they had hardly finished this when the captain
began to concoct a drink by mixing rum and sugar and lime juice with
water, which he drew from a hanging jar, half concealed among the greenery. As he filled the glasses of his guests, he added more fruit to the mixture
before inviting them to drink.

"And if you don't say that a planter's punch rivals a mint julep in excellence, I shall never invite you to my house again!" he said, holding a
glass to Paul with a flashing smile.

"And that will give the rest of us a better chance to welcome him in
ours!" the banker laughed.

They were still chatting and jesting, drinking planter's punches and smoking strong black cigars when luncheon was announced—a luncheon of omelette with tomatoes and green peppers slipped in between its fluffy folds, pompano fried in olive oil and guanábana sherbet. After they had done this meal full justice, it was, of course, siesta time, and Paul was conducted to a cool bare room, high ceilinged even by New Orleans standards, sparsely furnished in bamboo, and as restful in its shadowy stillness as the gallery had been. He slept a long time and woke to an awareness of great content, so great indeed that he would willingly have lain where he was for another hour or so, drowsily listening to the distant but unceasing tinkle of street players' guitars; but he had promised to be ready at five for a sightseeing tour and, afterward, there was to be a *merienda,* followed by an evening of chess, at the residence of Don Francisco Fesser which, Paul had been given to understand, was not a "simple colonial house" like the captain's, but a *morada,* an establishment of great elegance.

In Paul's estimation, nothing could possibly have been pleasanter than the house he had already visited; but he was duly impressed by the arcades of the *Ayuntamiento,* the sheer walls of La Fuerza, the graceful spire of the cathedral and, indeed, by all the outstanding landmarks of the early colonial era, not only in the Plaza de Armas, but scattered throughout the old section of the city; and, upon arrival at the *morada,* he found the reports of the elegance maintained by Don Francisco were by no means exaggerated. Here the furnishings, instead of being of bamboo, were the heavily carved, richly upholstered Spanish type, the chandeliers dripping with crystal, the *merienda* served on gold and silver; as for the "evening of chess," one game succeeded another, as Paul had rather expected it would, until time for him to rejoin his ship. As he stepped into the waiting carriage, drawn up at the garden gate of the *morada,* the perfume of the night-blooming *damas de noche* was almost overpowering in its fragrance; the mingled scents of tobacco, sugar and coffee, of which he had been so conscious in the daytime, though these still persisted, were submerged by it. The tinkle of guitars continued to follow him as he drove along the narrow streets and, through the open doorways of the cafés, he could see carefree groups still drinking and dancing though, by the time he reached the docks, the lights of the city had begun to pale, while sunrise illumined the sky. The *Philadelphia* was leaving Havana, as she had arrived there, at daybreak and he stood for a long time on deck watching this radiance blaze through the gloom that so briefly preceded the dawn. He was not aware of weariness, only of exhilaration; it was midmorning before he remembered that he had been up all night, that it was high time he thought of sleep again.

Unhappily, the ocean again proved inimicable and, by the time the ship rounded Cape Hatteras, Paul had not only lost all sense of exhilaration, but was miserably convinced that nothing which awaited him at his journey's end could possibly be worth the wretchedness he was enduring. However, he again found unexpected excitement and a sense of reward as the skyline of New York came into view. Here was no overwhelming beauty, such as had transported him at the mouth of the Mississippi and in the harbor of Havana; but the power and promise of the great city seemed to reach out toward him, drawing him to it, capturing him and challenging him with its own vital force. In New Orleans, it had still been summer when he left and in Havana it was apparently never anything else; languor was a normal part of the way of life; but here a brisk breeze was blowing as the *Philadelphia* came into the river, the trees on its banks were already scarlet and golden and the tang of autumn was in the air. As Paul stood on deck, breathing in the stimulating freshness, he was suddenly conscious of new life and energy.

He was stationed near the gangplank, waiting for the crowd to thin a little before attempting to descend, when a determined looking young man, who had made his way quickly through it without apparent effort, cast an enquiring glance about him and then approached Paul without hesitation. "Mr. Morphy?" he said in a pleasant and purposeful voice. "I'm Fred Edge of the *New York Herald* and I'm also acting as one of the secretaries for the Chess Club. Delighted to see you. We've been afraid your ship might be delayed, that you'd miss the first meeting. I've got a hack waiting right along side, we'll go straight to headquarters."

"It's very kind of you," Paul said, somewhat taken aback by such a show of haste. "But I think I ought to go first to the hotel to leave my bags and register and so on. Then afterward—"

"Oh, I'll send your grips along to the St. Denis," Fred Edge assured him, propelling him, willy-nilly, down the gangplank. "And you're registered already—of course, I attended to that. But you'll have to hurry if you're going to take part in the Grand Tournament, and everyone wants to have you. The meeting this afternoon is being held on purpose to make the final arrangements . . . well, here's our hack. Please jump right in, Mr. Morphy. Driver, the Chess Club, 19 East 12th Street, and we've no time to spare. Did you enjoy your stay in Havana, Mr. Morphy? What are your first impressions of New York? Do you find it very different from New Orleans? I'd like very much to get a short piece about you in tomorrow's paper, so I'll just ask you a few questions as we jog along and jot down your answers while they're fresh in my mind."

The hack was rattling over the rough cobblestones at what seemed to Paul breakneck speed, rather than "jogging," and he found it difficult, while lurching about on the seat he was trying hard to keep, to word what he considered satisfactory replies to the questions hurled at him in such swift succession. Mr. Edge, however, did not seem to expect any very deep or prolonged comments. Instead, after scribbling a few notes on a dog-eared pad, he himself began to impart information.

"Judge Meek from Mobile has been here for a month already. Remarkable man, charming, too. I understand he holds very high rank among the proficients of the southern states. You know him, perhaps? Yes, yes, I remember now—you played against him in Mobile last winter and won every game in the match. So you must hold still higher rank. Mr. Kennicott of Chicago and Mr. Allison of Hastings, Minnesota, arrived last Saturday—both leading players in their section of the country, of course. But Mr. Paulsen of Iowa has been stealing the limelight, giving exhibitions of playing without seeing the board. 'Playing blindfold,' it's called, isn't it, though his eyes aren't bound at all? Do you go in for that, too, Mr. Morphy?"

"I've done it experimentally. I haven't done it in public."

"Oh well, you will, I'm sure, while you're here. I'd better say in my piece that you have it in mind. Ah, here we are and everyone's waiting to welcome you and then plunge right in with the business of the day, so that they can get a head start on tomorrow's."

He must be making a very poor showing, Paul told himself, as he went the rounds of the waiting gentlemen, under the aegis of Frederick Perrin. Only Judge Meek, who welcomed him warmly, was not a stranger, and all were considerably older and taller than he, all formally dressed in clothes of different cut and heavier texture than garments to which he was accustomed; moreover, the men who were not clean-shaven trimmed their beards and moustaches differently from his acquaintances in New Orleans. To him they all seemed personages of imposing stature, figuratively as well as literally, and he stood in awe of them. It was unfortunate for his peace of mind that, in his turn, he did not guess they all found his looks attractive, his manners pleasing, and the modesty of his bearing definitely reassuring. Though Judge Meek had already sung his praises, it came as an agreeable surprise to discover that a young man of his much heralded attainments, while composed and courteous, could be so wholly unassuming.

Presentations and greetings over, the group proceeded to organize. Colonel Mead, President of the New York Chess Club, was asked to act as Chairman, and Doctor Fiske, Editor of the *Chess Monthly*, as Secretary. Twelve gentlemen, Paul among them, had already signified their willingness to enter the lists the following day, and four others now agreed to engage in the contest, so that the requisite number of sixteen might be reached. Several methods of play were next discussed. It was remembered that there had been great disappointment, at a tournament held in London, because some of the best players had been drawn against each other in the first round or section; as a result of this, several who would otherwise have

won prizes were eliminated at the beginning. To avoid any such mishap, it
was proposed that the eight winners in the first round should play for first
and second prizes and the eight losers for the third and fourth. But both
this suggestion, made by Mr. Calthop of Bridgeport, and a similar one,
made by Judge Meek of Mobile, were eventually rejected and it was decided to abide by the original plan of pairing the contestants off by lot.

The discussion, though amicable, was protracted and, by the time it was
over, Paul wanted nothing so much as a chance to retire to the privacy of
his own room, sup quietly there and get early to bed. His hospitable and
energetic hosts, however, had not the slightest idea of permitting him to do
anything of the sort; he was to be their guest at dinner; later, they were
depending on some passages at arms between him and the redoubtable
Charles H. Stanley, who, though English born, had long been considered
chess champion of the United States. Indeed, large numbers of persons,
who were counting on such a spectacle, were already beginning to crowd
into the clubroom. Without being downright discourteous, there was no
possible way in which Paul could decline to fall in with these complimen-
tary but exhausting plans. When he finally escaped, and made his way
wearily to the St. Denis Hotel, declining the persistent escort of Mr. Edge,
he was almost frantic with fatigue. It was with relief that he learned he
was not expected to appear at the first formal meeting until eleven o'clock
the following morning.

He had also been advised that this meeting, and others of the Congress,
would not be held at the headquarters of the Metropolitan Club, which
were not spacious enough for such large gatherings as were foreseen, but in
the so-called Descombes Rooms at 764 Broadway, which had been rented
and outfitted especially for the occasion. As he entered these, coming from
his hotel—a walk which he found bewildering, though he had been obliged
to traverse only a few blocks—Paul was again overwhelmed with a sense of
inadequacy. The new quarters were overpowering, just as the men with
whom he was now associated and the noise and bustle in the streets were
deafening. The main hall was at least eighty feet long, and at one end of
it was a raised platform, over which hung the American flag with its thirty-
one stars, draping the bust bearing the name of Franklin—the first known
chess player of the New World. Along each side of the hall were hung
other national banners, inscribed with the names of famous players: Labourdonnais for France, M'Donnell for England, Lopez for Spain, and so on.
At the foot of the hall, French and American colors were entwined with
the great name of Philidor stretched across them; and, above the banners,
on scrolls, the names of living leaders in the chess world were set forth
in letters of silver and gold: Lewis, Staunton, Walker, Von der Lasa, Anderssen, Löwenthal, Harrwitz, Petroff and Jaenisch. Two rows of marble

tables extended the entire length of the hall and, on these, were placed large
inlaid boards and the chessmen classically designed by Staunton, the greatest of English players; while a huge telegraphic chessboard, for repeating
games of more than ordinary interest, hung at the further end of the hall.
Beyond this was a lavish but puzzling arrangement of committee rooms,
lunch and retiring rooms. Paul was thankful when the Congress was called
to order by Colonel Mead, and he could be sure of sitting still for a few
minutes, without the obligation of speaking to anyone.

He felt a thrill of pride for the South when the name of Judge Meek
was put in nomination as President of the first American Chess Congress,
and that of his first-found friend in New York, Fred Edge, for one of the
Assistant Secretaries. All nominees were unanimously elected, and Judge
Meek made an appropriate address in accepting the chair. Several special
committees were appointed, on one of which—that of the chess code—Paul
was surprised to discover his own name; he still found it hard to believe
that he could be considered an authority by men so much more experienced
and important than he was. He had not recovered from his astonishment
when he heard the motion to adjourn, and immediately thereafter the drawing of lots for antagonists began.

Paul's opponent proved to be James Thompson, like Stanley a native of
England, who had now adopted New York as his habitat. Paul had found
him especially congenial when they met the previous evening and was
pleased by the prospect of playing with a man whom he knew to be a general social favorite as well as an outstandingly brilliant player. Thompson's
agreeable personality assured him there would be no unpleasantness about
the game; and if he had met his match, as far as skill at chess was concerned,
it was with a foeman worthy of his steel. Again, weariness seemed the
greatest drawback to his enjoyment; the game went on and on and, with
the approach of evening, the room was crowded with onlookers. Although
these were constrained to observe the rule of silence, imposed on players
and spectators alike, the very presence of so many strangers added to Paul's
feeling of malaise; he was obliged to make a determined effort to maintain
inward, as well as outward, calm. But at midnight, when the rooms closed,
the score stood zero for Thompson and two for Morphy. At the end of the
second day it was the same. At the end of the third, it still stood zero for
Thompson, but three for Morphy and his name was added to the list of
victors.

By this time, the sensations of shyness and strangeness were beginning to
abate. The conditions under which he was obliged to play—the crowds, the
publicity, the tenseness of the atmosphere—were becoming familiar; and he
was less disturbed than he had been at first by the comments he overheard
when the spectators, released from the obligations of silence, voiced their

opinions as they were leaving the hall. Sometimes they paused, clustering together in small groups; at other times, they walked rapidly along, expatiating with vehemence on what they had observed. At times they caught sight of him, showered him with congratulations, wrung his hand and asked him to confirm their conclusions; at others, thanks to his small stature and unobtrusive bearing, he slipped unnoticed among them. "Morphy's fourth move of King's Knight to Bishop's third was better than the usual one of Pawn to Queen's third. I could tell right then he would be the winner." . . . "Nonsense! You couldn't have known that soon. After all, there were twenty-one moves before Thompson resigned, even though they played fast —just an hour, the game lasted!" . . . "Stanley's maneuver didn't help Thompson much, did it? And when he played Queen to Queen's Bishop's second, with the idea of preventing Morphy's move of Pawn to King's Bishop's fourth, he overlooked Morphy's next certain move—Pawn to Queen's fourth."

There was no mistaking the friendliness of such attentive interest or the admiration his associates felt for him, both as a man and a player. They continuously urged him to join them, after the sessions were over, at Taylor's Saloon, which, oddly enough, was a great social mecca, characterized by such splendor of furniture and appointments that a distinguished English visitor remarked these were "suited to a fairy palace rather than a sublunary café and restaurant." Paul had never even tried to drink whiskey before and did not care for wine, but he recognized the true cordiality of the invitations and accepted them gladly. In an atmosphere of geniality and relaxation, the games just finished were reviewed move by move. On the fourth day of the Congress, it was announced that Mr. Paulsen would play four games simultaneously, without seeing the board and men; he immediately requested that Mr. Morphy should be one of the opposing players. No greater compliment could have possibly been paid him. Paul flushed with pride and pleasure as he accepted.

It was arranged that he and Paulsen should sit back to back on the platform at the end of the hall, with the four boards arranged across the room, and Mr. W. A. J. Fuller, Mr. Denis Julian and Mr. C. H. Shultz as the other contestants. Public interest, which had already been very great, now rose to fever pitch. So many persons, unconnected with the Congress, not a few of them outstanding in pulpit and bar, clamored to see the extraordinary exhibition, that the Committee on Management issued tickets of admission at a dollar each. By noon there was hardly standing room in the main hall; and shortly thereafter Mr. Paulsen began the performance of his much heralded blindfold feat.

It more than fulfilled the great expectations of the crowd, for not once did his memory fail him; he retained an unerring knowledge of the pawns and pieces on each board. But just before midnight, at the twenty-eighth move, Paul announced checkmate in five moves. He had won the game.

The meeting was adjourned in an atmosphere of wild excitement. It was unthinkable that the two remaining games should be played then and there, not only because the hour was so late, but because they would have been inevitably anticlimatic in character. Moreover, Mr. Shultz, convinced of his inability to cope with the situation, had resigned from the contest; and it was not until the following Monday that Mr. Paulsen's blindfold match, in which he won a game with Mr. Fuller and drew one with Mr. Julian, came to a conclusion. By that time, however, Mr. Julian had other matters on his mind. He was not only a superb chess player, he was a superb hotelier, and most of the visiting celebrities were quartered at the hostelry which had been placed under the protection of his patron saint and given his Christian name. To him had logically been entrusted the arrangements for the banquet in honor of distinguished guests.

The results more than justified the confidence placed in the host. The menu was headed by the representation of a board and men and featured such dishes as *Filets de boeuf à Meek-Mead, Dindonneaux au Congrès, Bastion de Gibier à la Palamede, Chartreuse de Perdrix à l'Echéquier, Vol-au-Vent de Cervelles à la Paulsen, Pommes de Terre à la M'Connell, Gâteaux à la Julian, Pudding à la Franklin.* The walls of the dining room were adorned with emblems of chess and inscribed with the names of its leading ornaments; but these decorations were insignificant compared with those which ornamented the table. A temple to Caïssa and a monument to Philidor had been created of glittering confectionery. A statuette of Franklin was done in ice, those of Kings, Queens and Knights in jelly, and those of Bishops, Castles and Pawns in cream. The huge cakes were in the shape of chessboards. Fortunately, none of the convivial spirits seemed to be surfeited by food or overpowered by magnificence. Mr. Julian and Judge Meek had both composed songs especially for the occasion, which were sung with great éclat. Mr. Stanley, on rising to lament the absence of Mr. Paulsen, which was deeply regretted, suggested that all the rest of them might take comfort in the thought that, since this gentleman could play chess without seeing the board, he no doubt had the power of eating dinner without seeing the table; probably, at that very moment, he was exercising his peculiar psychological genius in some lonely chamber and enjoying the evening's entertainment with as much zest as any of the confreres present! This and various other jesting remarks were all received with hearty applause and some of the postprandial speakers contrived to be witty as well as felicitous in their remarks, notably Judge Meek, who continued in his role of Presiding Officer.

"It is not often at chess," he said, "that I complain of having the *first move*, but at the present time and under such flattering circumstances I can scarcely deem it an advantage, for it necessarily places me in a *crowded position* and forces me to adopt a *close* rather than a *brilliant style* of play. Still, acknowledging the honor of the great *odds* allowed me, I must say that to me this is an occasion of deep and peculiar interest. What the patron fathers of our fraternity so anxiously desired has to some extent been realized in this country. This convocation of chess magnates from all portions of our union is an evidence of the wide diffusion of our game. They have come, with fraternal impulses, from New England, the middle states, the illimitable West and from my own golden and sunny section. They have met as brothers and friends. Ties of congenial taste and sympathy have been established and must exert no insensible influence in eradicating sectional prejudices and uniting each and every part of the country, like the separate squares of the chessboard, in one harmonious whole. A band of brothers, we now meet in cheerful mood around the altar which our host of the St. Denis—a true Philidorian problem himself—has so tastefully and artistically decorated. Here he has fashioned his most graceful *pâtisseries* into the images and implements of our own craft. To *solve* these felicitous devices is certainly more easy and agreeable than to unravel the *two move* and *three move* enigmas with which he has perplexed our modern searchers into Sphinxean mysteries. But I linger too long. A 'winking spirit' from the glasses before me cries check to *my move* and warns me to beware or I may make a *stale*. I therefore conclude with an expression of my gratification at the auspicious prospect open for chess in the United States by the establishment of our national association."

Murmured expressions of appreciation mingled with applause as Judge Meek took his seat and Colonel Mead rose to respond to the speech. After referring briefly to the moral and intellectual aspects of chess, he dwelt more at length with its social aspects and stated that, "though he had been playing for more than a quarter of a century and come into contact with thousands of chess players, at home and abroad, he could truthfully say that he had never met but one person to whom he could not extend the right hand of fellowship as to a brother." He paused for a moment, as if giving his hearers the opportunity of guessing to whom he referred; then, shaking his head and smiling, he dismissed the subject and, instead of referring to anyone else anonymously, proposed a single toast:

"To the health of Mr. Paul Morphy, the refined gentleman, the accomplished scholar, the master chess player."

When the Congress entered its third week, Paul's star was still in the ascendant. He had already played against Judge Meek in the second section, "a truly imposing specimen of a man. . . ." "As they took their seats opposite each other," the ubiquitous Edge wrote in next day's *Herald*, "one thought of David and Goliath; not that the Judge gasconaded in any wise after the fashion of the tall Philistine, for modesty adorns all his actions; but there was as much difference in cubic contents between the two antagonists, as between the son of Jesse and the bully of Gath, and in both cases the little one came out biggest. Judge Meek sat down with an evident conviction of the result, and although he assured his youthful opponent that, if he continued mating him without ever allowing him the least chance, he would put him in his pocket, he consoled himself with the reflection that Paul Morphy would serve everybody else as he served him."

At the end of the third week, Morphy and Paulsen had won an equal number of games, namely three, and each had drawn one; neither had been defeated. Therefore, in accordance with the terms of the prospectus the time had now come when they should play against each other for first and second prizes. Public interest, which had flagged slightly after the blindfold contest, rose to new heights. The rooms were more crowded than ever and many ladies, including Paulsen's sister, believed to be the strongest amateur of her sex in the country, were now numbered among the onlookers. Several of the male observers were also outstanding: Charles Mackey, the famous British poet; Richard Grant White, the learned Shakespearean scholar; Oliver Byrne, the widely known mathematician; John Van Buren, son of the ex-President. The press, spurred on by the example of Fred Edge, devoted more and more space to the Congress. Public imagination was captured by the spectacle of the two personable young men, so peculiarly gifted, not only in the usual accomplishments of a chess player, but with the art of conducting more than one game at a time without seeing the boards. Both were courteous in their attitude to each other; both had the pleasing attribute of modesty. Either would have been welcomed as a winner. Nevertheless, when the contest between them came to an end, after two full days of play, it was evident that the highest hopes had been placed on Paul. The announcement that he had won five games and had been awarded first prize met with unrestrained enthusiasm.

Sonorously, the President read off his name and those of the others who had won prizes in both the Grand Tournament and the Minor Tournament. The first prize was a service of plate, consisting of a pitcher, four goblets and a salver. The pitcher and the goblets bore the initials P. M. The salver was inscribed:

This Service of Plate
is Presented to
PAUL MORPHY,

The Victor in the Grand Tournament,
At the First Congress
of the
American National Chess Association,
New York, 1857

Above the inscription was a representation, copied from a photograph by Brady, of Morphy and Paulsen playing chess together. On the same table where the silver service was set forth lay a gold medal in the shape of an American shield, having on the obverse a design showing Paulsen playing five simultaneous games without the sight of the boards. The reverse bore the inscription:

Presented

to

LOUIS PAULSEN

by

Members of the National Chess Congress
October, 1857.

At the request of the subscribers, it was Paul who made the speech for the presentation of the medal. He was not at his best. He was essentially too generous to resent sharing his moment of glory, but he lacked the ability to do so vocally, and his thoughts, like his gaze, instinctively turned toward his own trophy. Inevitably, the words he pronounced, sincere as they were, sounded stilted, rather than spontaneous, in the beginning and, as he went on, became extravagant and flowery rather than restrained and dignified. "Mr. Paulsen, in behalf of several members of the First National Chess Congress, I present you with this testimonial," he began. "If measured by the admiration it is meant to convey of our estimation of your wonderful blindfold play, it will not be deemed of little value. Sir, I claim you for the United States. Although not a native of America, you have done more for the honor of American chess than her most gifted sons. Old Europe may boast of her Stauntons and Anderssens, her Harrwitzes and Löwenthals, her Von der Lasas and Petroffs; it is the greater boast of America that the blindfold chess of Paulsen has not yet been equaled. What if Labourdonnais played two, Philidor three, and Kieseritzky four games at one time? We have in our midst one whose amusement it is to play five, and who will soon fulfill his promise of playing seven blindfold games of chess simultaneously."

Suddenly he found himself shouting. His voice, usually so quiet, no longer seemed to be his own. "We fling our proud defiance across the waters. Come one, come all! Let the superhuman feats of our Paulsen be performed with equal success by the much-vaunted European chess knights! Let the much and deservedly extolled Harrwitz enter the lists! We challenge him —we challenge all the magnates of the Old World!"

As he reseated himself, unconsciously reaching for one of his silver goblets and gazing at it exultantly, he was only dimly conscious of Paulsen's heartfelt thanks and of the applause that was ringing around them both. He was already asking himself a burning question: in "throwing down a challenge to Harrwitz and all the magnates of the Old World," who was it that he hoped might enter the lists against them—Paulsen or himself?

There was only one honest answer to this question.

RACE BETWEEN THE *DIANA* AND THE *BALTIC*

Drawn from a lithograph of the original oil, painted by George F. Fuller, Louisville, Kentucky, 1858.

"The *John C. Fremont* operated mostly in the through trade between Pittsburgh and New Orleans. This was a modest-sized sternwheeler owned principally (4/7) by Capt. Jackman Taylor Stockdale, then a young man, who lived at Georgetown, Pa., not far below Sewickley, a town which still exists in pristine isolation without benefit of railroad, bus or waterworks. The *Fremont* was not pretentious; she was a family boat, which is to say that the crew was composed, for the most part, of Georgetown persons, related to the captain.

"A passenger, going on board the *Fremont* at Pittsburgh, might well become dissatisfied and change boats, provided dates could be worked out all right. There would be a wonderful opportunity for him to take, at Louisville, Kentucky, the elegant side-wheeler *Diana*, Capt. Edward T. Sturgeon, which departed on its maiden voyage from Louisville on December 24, 1857, bound for New Orleans.

"The *Diana* became, later, celebrated. In March, 1858, she ran a race all the way from New Orleans to Louisville with another side-wheeler, the *Baltic*, almost an even draw. A painting of this race was lithographed and still is one of the more celebrated representations of the old steamboat days. It was the *Diana* also, which picked up survivors of the *Pennsylvania* explosion at Ship Island, June 13, 1858, a catastrophe which Mark Twain has attended to in some detail inasmuch as his brother was one of the victims. Captain Sturgeon earlier built the *Eclipse* which was the longest side-wheeler ever built for the Mississippi, and perhaps the fastest.

"Both the *John C. Fremont* and the *Diana* were used in Civil War service in the early 60's. The *Fremont* was at the battle of Pittsburgh Landing, Tennessee River. The *Diana* was a troopship."

Extract from a private letter written by Captain Frederick Way, Jr., Editor of *The Inland River Record* and one of the greatest living authorities on inland waters travel. This letter was written in corroboration of previous statements made by Leonard Huber of New Orleans, another great authority on the same subject.

18.

Because he was essentially so sincere, Paul could not avoid giving the honest answer for which the question called; but he did so only in his most secret thoughts. When he heard it asked, in general conversation, as he did several times during the next few weeks, he brushed it smilingly aside, and those who asked it were sufficiently tactful to see very quickly that he had not the slightest intention of saying or doing anything which would detract from the réclame of his most formidable rival. But they found other ways of making him understand that they entertained the same hope he did; and even though they refrained from discussing the matter further with Paul, their feeling about it was soon an open secret, not only in chess circles throughout the United States, but throughout the world. The comments temporarily suppressed in New York found open expression elsewhere. In London, Löwenthal stated that, "The graybeards were fairly pushed off their pedestal. Youth and genius proved more than a match for age and experience. All went down, almost without a struggle before the conqueror from New Orleans. Americans are in ecstasy at the brilliance of the star which has risen in their midst, regard him as invincible, and are ready to defy the world to produce his equal." In Paris, Harrwitz was saying much the same. Echoes of these pronouncements inevitably reached Paul's ears and hard as he tried to dismiss them from his mind, he was only partially successful in doing so. He was finding the fruits of victory unexpectedly sweet; he could not help dwelling in anticipation on those which he had not yet tasted, but which he now knew were his for easy plucking.

It had originally been his intention to leave for home as soon as the Congress was over; this plan, at least, he was easily persuaded to change: so far, he had been nowhere except to the St. Denis Hotel, the Metropolitan Club and the Descombes Rooms; surely he did not intend to come such a distance and then see none of the sights of New York! And surely he intended to give the club members the pleasure of playing a few offhand games with him!

Paul had neither the wish nor the will power to brush aside such attractive suggestions. He lengthened his walks and gradually became familiar with the city's most outstanding landmarks and, in the course of these rambles, he bought presents to take home with him—trinkets from Tiffany, Young and Ellis, silks from Arnold Constable, gifts of all kinds from Evans and Company. He went to the Academy of Music, where the Italian Opera Company of Paris, fresh from its triumphs in Vienna, was performing *La Somnambula* and *Semiramis* to crowded houses, and to Wallach's Theater to see Boucicault's comedy, *London Assurance*. He wrote home that he "found Harlem one of the pleasantest suburbs of the city" and that the Croton Aqueduct and waterworks—completed ten years earlier—were "the principal object of curiosity in or about New York." He took the ferry to Staten Island and the paddle-wheeler *Isaac Newton* up the Hudson to Albany—an excursion made in gorgeous surroundings to the lively accompaniment of popular music from a steam calliope. He played, as requested, a number of offhand games with odds of Knight; then, as the result of these was so much of a foregone conclusion as to rob them of all excitement, he offered odds of Pawn and Move in a match to any of the leading members of the club. According to the terms, the winner of the first seven games was to be declared victor, and the challenge was accepted by Charles Stanley. At the end of the fourth game, marking four successive defeats, he declined to go on and resigned both the match and the hundred dollar stakes.

His resignation struck the first discordant note that Paul had heard since his arrival in New York; it was evident that Stanley was both aggrieved and resentful. He not only withdrew from the match, but, to a large degree, from the club; for several weeks he was almost never seen there. Having been for many years acclaimed the champion of America, he could not accept defeat at the hands of a player years younger than himself and hitherto almost unknown, except locally, with the same smiling philosophy as Paulsen, who, like Morphy, was still a young man, and whose outstanding skill had only recently been given recognition. James Thompson, with whom Paul had secretly hoped the match might be played, proved equally difficult to deal with; unequivocally he declined to accept the odds which Paul had offered and the latter, usually so imperturbable about chess and almost everything else, except when his painful shyness among strangers was involved, unburdened himself in a long indignant letter to Charles de Maurian. "Do not hastily infer that there exists the smallest degree of ill feeling between myself and most of the New York players," he wrote. "But Mr. Thompson seems to think it beneath his dignity to accept odds of a player who has won every game contested with him. The result of his conceit is that we never play together."

Paul had hardly posted this letter when he realized that he, too, was beginning to feel aggrieved and resentful, and that such an attitude was not worthy of the ungrudging admiration he had received from all but two men. Perhaps he had trespassed too long on the hospitality of New York; in any case, it was high time he went home; he had been away much longer than he had intended. Despite everything that had happened in the meanwhile, he had not been able to forget the deathly seasickness which had marred his voyage on the *Philadelphia* and he began to make inquiries about al-

ternate routes. He could, he found, go from New York to Pittsburgh by rail
in the course of a single long day; from there he could proceed the rest of
the way to New Orleans by river packet, either direct, if he were fortunate
enough to make connections with one of the few steamboats which plied
both the Ohio and the Mississippi, or by changing from one packet to another somewhere along the way. If he followed either of these plans, he
would not only avoid the discomforts of ocean travel; he would see a great
deal more of the country. His outlook had undergone a great change since
he left home; he no longer felt that there was probably little worth seeing
or doing outside of New Orleans—Havana and New York had taught him
the fallacy of this. He was now eager for more new sights and new experiences.

He did not disclose his decision to leave until he had completed all his
arrangements; when he did, protests arose on every side. Fred Edge, who
had improved all possibilities of being with Paul, was particularly vehement
in his objections; he was victimized by an especially bad case of hero worship. And James Thompson, secretly ashamed of his poor sportsmanship,
asked for the privilege of presiding at the farewell dinner which was hastily
arranged. Only Stanley remained sulking in his tent and Paul, genuinely
distressed, realized that he would never be able to enjoy the profits of the
stakes he had won in the unfinished match. After giving the matter careful
thought, he decided to have the money sent, as unobtrusively as possible,
to Mrs. Stanley, after his departure from New York. It was his hope and
belief that no one would know of this except Willard Fiske, the editor of
the *Chess Monthly,* with whom he had now agreed to work as co-editor.
But Fred Edge, who was much too alert a reporter to permit anything of the
sort to escape him, got wind of it and, in due time, persuaded Fiske to allow
him to show Paul a copy of a letter Fiske had written to a close friend, which
read: "The score standing Stanley none, Morphy four and one drawn
(drawn through Morphy's carelessness) Stanley resigned the match. Loving
Morphy as I do, it is a pleasant thing for one to tell that, before leaving
New York, he sent the stakes, accompanied by a kind note to Mrs. Stanley,
who, poor lady, sadly needs them. Stanley would have drunk it all up, but
now his wife and children will be benefited by the money. When the world
shall have lost the glorious Paul (which God send, may not happen for
half a century) and someone shall write his biography, I hope this, and
some other incidents I note of, will find a place in the narrative. They will
show that his heart is as great as his intellect is acute. But he will not let me
speak of them now."

Though the existence of this letter was not known to him before he left
New York or, indeed, until long afterward, Paul could not fail to recognize
the general warm-heartedness with which he was sped on his way. The

farewell dinner, less ostentatious than the one that had marked the climax of the Chess Congress, was equally convivial and, despite the ungodly hour at which his train left for Pittsburgh, a large and genial gathering was at the station to see him off in one of the "Silver Palace" cars run by the Central Pennsylvania.

A greater contrast to the clattering *Smoky Mary* of the Pontchartrain Railroad, to which Paul's experience with "taking the cars" had hitherto been confined, could hardly have been imagined. The "Silver Palace" was both clean and quiet, and the stops at Harrisburg for dinner and Altoona for supper gave him a chance to stretch his legs and broke the tedium of the trip. For several hours, the train progressed through level landscape, now shorn of the autumnal foliage which, a few weeks earlier, had given it brilliance and beauty; the scene might have appeared monotonous to Paul, if his mood had not been such that he was prepared to find everything about the journey enjoyable; and though dusk was already descending when they reached the mountains, he made the most of such glimpses as he could get of them, for they, too, like the harbor of Havana and the skyline of New York, represented a strange and wonderful sight. But he had become very tired before the train finally pulled into the Pittsburgh depot, and he was still more weary by the time he had fought his way through the crowds there, in the wake of a runner from the Monongahela House, who steered him into a waiting bus. Then, after a jolting passage through noisy, sooty streets, this functionary led him down a long passageway, flanked on either side with cigar stores and lined with plush-covered sofas, and ushered him triumphantly into the lobby of the hotel.

He had been offered letters of introduction from his new-found friends in New York to acquaintances of theirs in Pittsburgh, but had declined these, as the departure of the *John C. Fremont*, the steamboat he had chosen, was tentatively set for the day after his arrival and his passage was already engaged. He had been warned that there were often unforeseen delays, as the packets on the Ohio followed no regular schedule, but came and went "on the rise," as river conditions permitted. But luck was with him: plentiful rains had kept the water high and mild weather had prevented the formation of the ice that, only the year before, had seriously interfered with winter travel. The downpour which, like the soot, perpetually obscuring the atmosphere, had seemed to him so depressing, was actually a blessing in disguise; it enabled him to start on the next lap of his journey thirty-six hours after his arrival in Pittsburgh; and, as he had found little to do in the meanwhile, besides conscientiously visiting "The Point," Fort Duquesne and Mrs. Morgan's Place, all seen through the gloom which, apparently, never lifted, he was glad to be on his way.

His first impressions of river travel, however, proved no more rosy than those of the prosperous and vital city which he was leaving with so few regrets. The waterfront was even more drab and dirty than the rest of Pittsburgh, the crowds even more clamorous and disreputable than those that had thronged the Union Depot. Paul fairly fought his way to the gangplank and made his way through a press of ill-mannered passengers up the so-called "grand staircase" to the boiler deck. The clerk in the little office beside the uncarpeted entrance tossed him a key with no other greeting than the information that he was to share a cabin with another man; and when he reached this temporary refuge, after a walk down a long dingy saloon, he began to feel more kindly about the *Philadelphia* than he ever had before. His nostalgia increased when he saw that the quarters assigned to him contained nothing but two narrow bunks, a built-in shelf, equipped with a bowl and pitcher, and one three-legged stool. He painfully made his way back to the office, intent on asking to have these accommodations changed; but the indifferent clerk pretended to busy himself with other passengers for so long that Paul was turning around in discouragement, when, to his great surprise, he heard someone addressing him by name.

"Mr. Morphy? I believe you and I are to be cabinmates. But I have found the space allotted to us quite unsuitable and I have already insisted that it must be changed. Shall we step into the bar while a satisfactory adjustment is made? Allow me to introduce myself—Clyde Batchelor of St. Louis."

The speaker, a fresh-faced, handsome man, elegantly if somewhat flamboyantly dressed, smilingly held out his hand as Paul, with the painful flush which always accompanied embarrassment on his part, tried to express his appreciation of such kindness on the part of a stranger. "I'm a stranger to you, of course," Clyde Batchelor went on pleasantly, "but the name of Paul Morphy is known to everyone who so much as glances at a newspaper these days—and though I'm not much of a reader, I'm a little more thorough than that. Besides, though I can't qualify as a serious player, I know enough about chess to recognize the importance of the contribution you've made to it in New York—why, thanks to you, its status in the United States is entirely changed! Captain Stockdale should be greatly complimented that you've chosen his little stern-wheeler for your river trip."

"That wasn't entirely a matter of choice. It seemed to be the only one going direct from Pittsburgh to New Orleans."

"Yes, I can see that that might seem to you a convenience. On the other hand, you may prefer to change into something more luxurious somewhere along the line. No need to decide right away. I am sure there wouldn't be any trouble about making a transfer and, if you did, you'd be better able to choose another time what type of transportation you preferred. Mind you, I've nothing against the *Fremont* and I like young Stockdale who, incidentally, is her principal owner, as well as her master. She's what we

call a family boat; that is to say, her crew's composed for the most part of
Stockdale's relatives from Georgetown, the small place where he lives himself, near Sewickley. But the new side-wheeler, *Diana*, Captain Edward T.
Sturgeon, is leaving Louisville on her maiden voyage Christmas Eve, and
she'll put on a celebration worth your seeing, unless I'm greatly mistaken.
. . . Well, now for another bout with our friend the clerk, and if his attention still strays we'll try someone else. One thing is sure: the world's
champion chess player isn't going to make his first river trip in that cabin
they tried to give us."

"I'm not the world champion, Mr. Batchelor. Only—"

Batchelor laughed. "I realize you don't know it yet, Mr. Morphy, but
you are. Now, if you'll excuse me just a minute—"

It was hardly more than that before he returned with the information that
the so-called "bridal suite" was providentially vacant, and that he had taken
the liberty of ordering Mr. Morphy's baggage, as well as his own, moved
into it. Paul had no inclination to dispute with his benefactor and, as the
voyage continued, he became increasingly grateful. Though the river was
free from ice, there were already patches of snow on its banks and intermittent flurries of this in the air; even when no wind was stirring—and most
of the time it came in chilly gusts from the east—the weather did not lend
itself to pastimes on deck and heat from the pot-bellied stove near the office
did not extend into that part of the saloon where bountiful but unimagina-
tive meals were served. Paul had no desire to linger over these repasts, which
he found tepid and poorly seasoned, especially as he had discovered few
congenial table companions; and, being an extremely moderate drinker, he
had no desire to while away hour after hour in the bar, where the company
was still less to his liking. All in all, the spacious privacy of the bridal suite
was a godsend and Batchelor made an ideal roommate—companionable but
unobtrusive, jovial and considerate. As he had seemed from the beginning
very well informed about the "world's champion chess player," the latter
was not surprised that Batchelor asked very few leading questions; and
though Paul would have liked to know more about his new-found friend,
he hesitated, under the circumstances, to show much curiosity and this remained unsatisfied. Beyond the original information that he came from St.
Louis, Batchelor did not mention this city again; and though his familiarity
with river travel seemed to indicate that he spent a great deal of time in this
way, the reason for it was by no means clear to Paul. He somehow gathered
that Clyde was a cotton broker and, on this assumption, asked if he had
ever met either Ernest or Edward Morphy. No, unfortunately, he had not,
Batchelor answered regretfully; but of course both were well known to him
by reputation, especially Mr. Ernest Morphy, who had proved himself one

of the most substantial citizens of Quincy, Illinois. Batchelor hoped he still might have the pleasure some day. . . .

Young Captain Stockdale seemed duly impressed when he found he had a celebrity aboard his stern-wheeler and went out of his way to be agreeable. But neither he nor any member of the family which comprised his crew could play chess or was able to discuss it intelligently. The same was true of all the passengers whom Paul drew into casual conversation. For once in his life he found that the greatest embarrassment was not on his side, but on the side of those who felt unequal to fraternizing with a famous figure. Much as he enjoyed voluntary seclusion, Paul began to feel oppressed by isolation and finally mentioned this to Batchelor.

"They're not really unfriendly and they don't mean to be boorish, but they're in awe of you," Batchelor said in his pleasant way. "Most of them are rather plain people—well, you must realize that. It isn't just your chess playing that sets you apart from them, though that would be enough to do it. You're an aristocrat, you're a scholar. They're self-conscious when they try to talk to you."

"Yes, I noticed that. But I'm sure I've never been discourteous, that I've never given any of them the idea I felt superior."

"Of course you haven't. Just the same, they know you *are* superior, it's an inescapable fact. You're superior not only to the passengers on this boat; you're superior to most people in every way. It's been a privilege for me to be associated with you, even very briefly."

"You're much too kind. But if you really feel that way, I don't see why the association has to be brief. I'd like very much to have it continue."

The natural rejoinder to this statement, Paul thought, would be one from Batchelor to the effect that he would like this, too. Instead, though he nodded and smiled and said thank you, he changed the subject by asking if Paul had given any further thought to a transfer at Louisville.

"Why yes, I have. I think I'd like very much to make it—at least, if you're making it, too. Otherwise, unless I'm imposing too much on your good nature, I'd rather continue on the *Fremont*."

"No, I decided quite awhile back I wanted to be aboard the *Diana* when she made her maiden voyage. I shan't be able to go all the way to New Orleans, I'm afraid. But I can go as far as Memphis. And soon after that you'll be back in your own climate, among your own people—no more harsh winds, no more snow flurries, no more unseasoned food, no more rude Yankees."

He continued his jesting banter for a few minutes and then left the suite for the bar, as he was apt to do periodically, without asking Paul to accompany him. The procedure in no way suggested lack of congeniality, but rather respect for his companion's probable wish to have their cabin to himself occasionally, so that he might attend to correspondence or work out chess problems undisturbed; and, despite the fact that Batchelor had disclaimed any intentions of being a serious player, he not infrequently made a comment which revealed more than ordinary understanding of the game and, at last, consented to try one at odds of Pawn and Move—the same that Stanley had refused to accept in New York. Paul won, of course, but not so easily that the game was without challenging interest. After that, they played chess together regularly.

It was snowing so hard when they reached Cincinnati that neither went ashore; but the next morning, when they arrived at Louisville, though the air was brisk, the sun was shining brightly and the landing was full of interest to Paul. A dozen or more boats were drawn up at the waterfront and there were as many Irish and Dutch dockhands as Negroes. These workmen moved with extraordinary agility and dispatch among the mule-drawn drays and the great hogsheads of molasses, piles of tobacco and rawhides, and bales and boxes of every description consigned to western steamboats, while every few minutes some new arrival contributed to the cheerful congestion. Eventually, a large wagon, well laden with children and furniture and drawn by two huge horses, came plunging forward, while its driver shouted, above the din, that he was a Kentuckian, moving to Texas with his wife and family and would be obliged to anyone who could tell him when the *Baltimore* would be leaving.

"She's advertised for three o'clock this afternoon," one of the workmen shouted back. "Me, I don't look to see her leave before tomorrow evening."

"Doesn't it add to the confusion if boats don't follow a schedule?" Paul asked Batchelor as they picked their way along. "It isn't like Pittsburgh, where everyone knows they have to wait for the rise."

"No. But misrepresentations like that one are a common practice to get passengers. Often the boat's smoked up, the bell tolled, and other indications of imminent departure staged, while all the time there is no intention of leaving until the freight cargo is filled. Don't worry about those Texas children. They'll be a lot happier tearing around the deck of the *Baltimore*, even if she doesn't move an inch for the next twenty-four hours, than they are cooped up in that wagon. What's more, their parents will be happier, too."

"The *Baltimore* looks rather like a Noah's Ark to me—no, that isn't a correct statement. The animals aren't going in 'two by two.' There must be at least a hundred sheep aboard already, besides all those horses and mules and cows. I don't believe there'll be much room left for passengers."

"You'd be surprised. . . . Well, shall we get along to the Gault House? I think you'll find it very comfortable. And we can check from there on the departure of the *Diana*. It should be tomorrow morning."

"I declined to accept any letters of introduction for Pittsburgh," Paul said hesitantly. "But I think perhaps I ought to take the initiative and visit the Chess Club here. It was founded by a Dr. Raphael, who won the fourth prize in the Grand Tournament at the Congress. I didn't have the pleasure of playing against him myself—his opponents were first Kennicott and then Paulsen; and as he wasn't staying at the St. Denis, I didn't see as much of him as the men who were. But, of course, I saw *something* of him, between matches, and at the big dinner and other celebrations, and he struck me as being a very remarkable man. He's a celebrated doctor, who spent eighteen months in the Paris hospitals and, during the same period, managed to play regularly at the Café de la Régence with Kieseritzky and St. Amant. He moved from Louisville to New York for good last spring, but his leading associate, Mr. Bland Ballard, lives here and it might seem ungracious if I went through without even making my presence known."

"Of course, it would! Just as soon as we've checked in at the Gault and found out exactly when the *Diana* leaves, you should send Mr. Ballard a note announcing your arrival."

"And say I have a friend with me?"

"No, if you'll excuse me, I'd rather you didn't do that."

"But certainly you'd enjoy a game at that club! And certainly any number of its members would enjoy having one with you!"

"I'm doubtful on both scores. I'm not in the same class with you and your friends, Mr. Morphy."

"You're my friend, one I value very highly. These men I'll meet here are all strangers to me. I wouldn't seek them out if I didn't feel such an omission might seem discourteous."

"And it would, as I've already told you. So, though I'm very pleased—I may say very touched—that you've accepted me as a friend, I'm going to speed you on your way to meet Mr. Ballard, while I attend to other pressing matters. We'll play chess again on the *Diana*—at least, if you're not persuaded to spend Christmas in Louisville. That's more than likely to happen, you know."

"You're wrong. I'm looking forward to spending Christmas with you."

It was not for lack of urging that he did not change his mind. If he had been favorably impressed by Dr. Raphael, the latter had been equally impressed by him; his praises had been sung long and loudly at the Louisville Chess Club and, though he secured a room at the Gault House, he was not permitted to occupy it, except for sleeping and dressing, from the time his note to Bland Ballard was delivered. Indeed, so overwhelming was the hospitality shown him, he was glad that he had taken the precaution of asking to have his baggage taken to the *Diana* at the same time as Mr. Batchelor's;

as it was, he barely caught the boat on the morning of the 24th after a festive breakfast. Batchelor was standing on deck, close to the gangplank, watching for him, with an expression of pleasure and amusement on his handsome, ruddy face; and, thrusting out a strong shapely hand in welcome, he linked his arm in Paul's and drew him through the crowd.

"I want you to come down to the main cabin right away," he said. "You can explore the rest of the premises later. But the ritual of setting the tables, on a boat like this, is a sight worth seeing—a very different process, I assure you, from that of preparing the 'foundering' dinner on the *Fremont*, where the only object is to get enough 'shells' on the table to completely cover the cloth. Here, everything is done with military precision, in direct charge of the Second Steward."

They hurried down the stairway, arriving at their destination just in time to see more than a dozen white-coated waiters engaged in setting up as many tables, under the watchful direction of the dignified Second Steward —a fine looking colored man whose elegant black attire might have seemed somber had it not been relieved by the touches of gold supplied by his heavy watch chain and the rims and hooks of his moonlike glasses. Two waiters were assigned to each table and, after bringing out folded tablecloths from the pantry, they stood at attention awaiting the signal to lay the cloths. This came when the steward twice clapped his hands smartly together; then suddenly every table turned white. Still moving with military precision, the waiters paraded back to the pantry, returning with the "silver boxes" holding the cutlery for which each was responsible. Again they lined up in position and, after a repetition of the awaited signal, the silver went down on all the tables in perfect cadence. Preparations for serving a feast were complete. Meanwhile, not a word had been spoken between the steward and his crew.

"Interesting, isn't it?" Batchelor asked, turning to Paul with his ready smile.

"It's more than that, it's amazing! Such perfect coordination! How many of us achieve it in our human relationships?"

"Very few, I'm afraid. . . . Well, now for the rest of the sights. You won't have time to take them all in before the bell rings for dinner. That bell ringing is another rite in itself—not every man can put the necessary gusto into doing it and get the best rhythm. It has to be someone who has a lot of feeling for the act, who can make it seem like an invitation and give it appetite appeal. And the dinner will be a fine one, served with the same ceremony that you saw when the tables were set. But the real feast will be tomorrow, of course."

That afternoon, when Paul left the main cabin in all its magnificence of glittering chandeliers, rich carpets and rosewood furniture, he felt that, for once, Batchelor must be mistaken; it would be impossible to provide a meal more lavish than the one of which they had just partaken. But Batchelor had been right, as usual. They had been invited, because of Paul's prominence, to take seats "back on the plush," though this was the section from which unmarried men were generally excluded, as it was supposedly reserved for families and ladies traveling alone; and, as they sat down on Christmas Day, they were handed fancily printed and ornamented menus, at first glance rather resembling valentines. These were inscribed with no sentimental verses however; instead, a formidable array of dishes was listed, each with its separate heading.

SOUP

Oyster soup a la Plessy, rice a la Florentine, quenelles of fowl a la Marie Louise.

FISH

Baked red snapper a la creme, trout a la Gonthier, broiled sheepshead, oyster sauce, broiled flounder, Dutch sauce.

BOILED

Corned beef, turkey, oyster sauce, leg of mutton a l'Allemande, ham, tongue.

ROAST

Beef, mutton, pork, turkey, veal, pig, saddle of lamb a la Dauphine.

ENTREES

Boned turkey a la Lucullus, sweetbreads a la Parisienne, turban of filets of fowl a la Prince de Galles, timbale of macaroni a la Milanaise, braized ham, sauce champagne, calf's head a la financiere, chicken a la cardinal, oyster pie.

COLD DISHES

Boar's head with apple jelly, aspic of fowl a la Macedon, gelatine pig with aspic jelly, hunter's beef, currant jelly; salmi of ducks with aspic jelly, gelatine poulards with aspic jelly, Yorkshire pig, chicken salad, lobster salad.

GAME

Roast saddle of venison with red currant jelly, wild goose a l'Aberdeen, braized teal ducks with stewed peas, braized snipe a la princess, rabbit pie with fine herbs.

Relishes

Pickles, Worcestershire sauce, French mustard, horse radish, sapsago cheese, John Bull sauce, olives, guava jelly, Soyer's relish.

Vegetables of the Season—Pastry and Dessert.

Puddings

Ice pudding a la Chesterfield, pudding a la Viennoise, English plum pudding.

Pies and Tarts

Mince pie, fanchonetts, apple pie, champagne biscuits, gooseberry pie, peach cobbler, damson pie, strawberry tarts.

Cakes

Pound, jelly, almond drops, Boston cream, fruit, sponge, lady fingers, lady cakes.

Creams and Jellies

Charlotte a la polonaise, Celestine, strawberry cream, Macedoine of fruit, orange flower cream, panachee jelly, variegated jelly a la Victoria, maraschino jelly, champagne sherbet.

Dessert

Pyramid of cream candy with pink web, pyramid of macaroons with silver web, basket of cocoanut drops with French kisses, croquante of English walnuts, croquante of oranges, vase of nougat a la Chantilly, grosse meringue of pistachois, horn of plenty.

Fruit

Apples, pecans, almonds, figs, English walnuts, oranges, prunes, raisins, filberts, bananas.

Coffee, Tea

"It's all I can do to *read* through it," Paul said, laying the fantastic sheets down on the table again. "I don't see how any human being could *eat* through it—and remember, I was brought up on Creole cooking, which no one ever called light! I think I'll just settle for oyster soup, roast turkey and plum pudding—all appropriate for Christmas."

"What, no boar's head with apple jelly, no wild goose a l'Aberdeen, no fanchonetts, no orange flower cream, no macaroons with silver web!"

"I'm afraid not. But I'd be pleased to watch you eat them."

"All right, I'll do my best to oblige."

The meal was a merry one, eaten to the accompaniment of excellent music by a colored orchestra. From the beginning, the passengers had proved more congenial than those on the *Fremont;* in fact, several of them were very distinguished. The children that Paul and Clyde had seen on the wharf at Louisville were among many whom the Head Steward had delighted with a Christmas tree and an impersonation of Santa Claus; the *Baltimore* had been abandoned for the *Diana* when the deception about the former's sailing time had been discovered, and the indignant wagoners had persuaded several persons of their acquaintance, also Texas bound, to make the same change they did. These were pioneering people, hardy and purposeful. For the most part, however, those who had chosen the *Diana* were travelers of considerable wealth and importance, or honeymoon couples for whom this would be the great trip of their lives. The *Diana* was definitely in the luxury category; the average traveler would be content to accept one of the older boats, like the *Susquehanna,* the *Ohio Belle* or the *Fanny Bullit.*

"Perhaps that accounts for the fact that I haven't seen any of the types that traditionally dominate the river boats," Paul said to Clyde, when they had returned to their cosy cabin after their Gargantuan Christmas feast. They had been invited to join some other gentlemen who proposed to spend the afternoon "trying their rifles," by shooting at driftwood and ducks. But they had declined, on the ground that they were not equal to even that mild exertion. As a matter of fact, they had interrupted a game of chess to respond to the dinner bell and they both wanted to go on with it. "Your move, I believe, Mr. Batchelor."

"Yes, I believe it is. . . . Just what do you mean when you speak of 'traditional types'?"

"Why, light ladies, soldiers of fortune, profiteers of all kinds! Now I think of it, they're the sort that are supposed to have the most money though, aren't they? Probably they're just part of a legend—they and the gamblers. I haven't seen a gambler, either."

"Are you sure?" Clyde asked, looking at Paul steadily across the chessboard.

There was a long silence. With devastating suddenness, Paul remembered Clyde's unexplained absences on the *Fremont,* his evasion when a continuance of friendship had been offered him, his refusal to be seen at the Louisville Chess Club. So that was the explanation! This pleasant, helpful man, who had provided for his comfort and cheered him with companionship was actually one of those professional thieves who plied their nefarious trade up and down the inland waters! And he, Paul Morphy, had failed to recognize the miscreant for what he was, because he did not dress, as gamblers were "traditionally" supposed to do, in black broadcloth and fancy linen with diamond studs! Because he was not pallid, slim and raven locked, but ruddy, stalwart and fair haired! No, those were not the reasons, he would not admit for a moment that he had been such a simpleton. He had failed to recognize Batchelor as a miscreant, because Clyde was not one. A gambler—yes perhaps, even a professional gambler, but a thief never. Paul drew a deep breath and returned Clyde's steady gaze.

"Yes," he said, "I am sure. Shall we go on with our game?"

The *Diana* reached Memphis about two in the morning on December 29th and a number of her passengers disembarked there, among them Clyde Batchelor, who slipped out of the cabin so quietly that Paul did not even hear him when he left. The weather was mild now, the sun bright; the region of cotton fields had been reached and, occasionally, planters' spacious houses and clusters of Negro huts could be seen on either side of the river. Presently, trees draped with Spanish moss came into view and the plantations were more numerous and extensive. At midmorning on the 31st, the *Diana* passed Vicksburg and later stopped at a wood yard to take on fuel, which caused a considerable delay. Well, so Paul would not get home to celebrate New Year's Eve, as he had hoped. Doubtless that was why he felt the latter part of his trip was disappointing, despite the fact that he was nearing New Orleans. But again, as when he had made the speech of congratulation to Paulsen, he found he could not avoid giving an honest answer to a question he himself had raised. He knew he had ceased to find happiness in the trip because he, for whom it was so hard to make friends, had parted from Clyde Batchelor and because he realized the parting was final.

"The enthusiasm created in 1858–1859 by the victorious career of *Morphy,* was far reaching. Well do we remember those times when *Morphy* was in Europe on his first venturesome expedition! These were our college days and though we then affected Chess and were accustomed to while away many a leisure hour over our chessboard, playing occasionally with a member of our family, we did not know among the entire circle of our acquaintances a single Chessplayer or of the existence of such a thing as a chess club. Merely the reverberation of the applause *Morphy* received for his contest of *Paulsen* in the tournament of 1857 had reached our ear; and *Morphy* went to Europe. We well remember the moment when it first dawned upon us that it was something to be a chessplayer like him! His name began to appear in red letters in the headlines of the newspapers; every steamer from Europe brought fresh news of greater triumphs, his name could be heard in the omnibuses on Broadway, in the lobbies of the theatres, in hotels and barrooms. As the enthusiasm grew, we began to discover, to our surprise, that nearly every one we knew either were chessplayers or were going to learn to be; it became all at once a 'big thing' to be a player of that game in which our countryman was beating all creation, and he who could best explain the ins and outs of the full reports of *Morphy's* various matches which appeared in the *Herald* and other city papers was the centre of the attraction in every place of public resort. Chess was all at once decidedly the fashion; those who today observed the public interest and enthusiasm excited by the recent triumphs of the American horses on the English and French turf will be surprised to learn that at the time of which we speak the popular interest in the chess events then taking place abroad was much more marked and much more lasting; for, whereas the victories of Iroquois and Foxhall were the occasion of a week's interest, among our general public, the triumphs of *Paul Morphy* extended through months, and the news of each succeeding exploit added to the steadily increasing enthusiasm. At this time when so many were learning the game, when so many who had abandoned the practice of it were renewing their acquaintance with it, there arose, naturally enough, inquiry for proper facilities for play, which soon became a demand, a pressing want. Out of this sprang the conception of the '*Morphy* Chess Rooms' (realised in the spring of 1859), a Chess resort of which every disciple of Caïssa was proud etc."

Brentano's Chess Monthly as quoted in
Paul Morphy: Sein Leben und Schaffen.
Von Dr. Max Lange.
Leipsiz. Verlag von Veit & Comp., 1894.
Leipzig

19.

Hearty as had been his send-off in New York, it paled in comparison with the welcome that awaited Paul in New Orleans. By the time the wharf itself was visible, he was aware of familiar figures standing there, waving and shouting to him: his grandfather, leaning on his cane, but indignantly shaking off tenders of other support; his uncle Charles, alone in the group fluttering a handkerchief instead of choosing a more masculine signal of enthusiasm; his brother Edward, his brother-in-law John Sybrandt, his cousin Edgar Hincks and his friend Charles de Maurian—all these as a matter of course; but less expectedly, such local celebrities as Mr. Rousseau and Mr. McConnell. They could not wait for him to disembark; they came swarming up the gangplank before it was firmly in place, wringing his hand, clapping him on the shoulder, seizing his arm; nor did they have the slightest idea of releasing him to go quietly home. Carriages for all of them were waiting alongside; as many convivial spirits as possible squeezed into the one where he managed to install his grandfather and uncle and seat himself; the others followed close behind, singing rollicking songs as they rode through the streets. When Paul reached home, he found that his mother, far from being disconcerted, had expected this boisterous influx. She had prepared a copious spread, complete with champagne, and Paul saw with pleasure that she had not only lightened the gloom of her mourning attire, but that she was beaming with joy over the return of her son, instead of dwelling with grief over the loss of her husband. The presents bought in New York were distributed amid exclamations of enthusiasm; the new silver service was hastily unpacked and put to immediate use; everyone crowded around to admire it, everyone clamored for the first chance to drink out of the goblets. Telcide and Malvina went to the piano and Hélène to the harp; Charles Le Carpentier produced his flute, everybody sang. It was late at night before the final toasts were drunk and, even then, the music did not cease for the night. Paul had hardly sunk into bed when he heard strains of it again, this time coming from the street below his window; his brother, his brother-in-law, his cousin, his uncle and all his friends were serenading him.

In a day or two the excitement would subside, Paul told himself. He had been pleased and touched by the reception which seemed to crown his triumphs in New York; but now he wanted and intended to settle down seriously to work. In accepting the co-editorship of the *Chess Monthly*, he had not done so lightly, with the mere idea of "lending his name" to a periodical already distinguished; he hoped and believed that his contributions might be valuable enough to give it added prestige. With equally serious purpose, he had accepted the presidency of the New Orleans Chess Club and gave the most careful attention to directing it. Moreover, everything about life in New Orleans seemed perfect and complete to him. Though she would not go to see Edwin Booth in *Richard III* and *Much Ado About Nothing* at the Gaiety or Hackett in *The Merry Wives of Windsor* at the St. Charles, his mother was persuaded to occupy with him a *loge grillée* at the Orleans Theater, where two grand and two comic operas were given each week; indeed, she could not very well decline, for such *loges*, screened as they were from public gaze, were almost universally accepted as suitable for persons of both sexes who were in second mourning, as well as ladies who were *enceinte*. The season was a brilliant one, including such offerings as *William Tell*, *Robert le Diable*, *Il Trovatore* and *Les Huguenots*. It was seldom that Paul, who loved opera, missed a performance. He likewise took up fencing again, practicing regularly at Pepe Llulla's *salle d'escrime* in Exchange Place, where he had taken his first lessons; and he was never missing at the family dinners and the informal soirées given by his friends. All these diversions were a source of genuine pleasure; so were the long rambles which he managed to make part of his daily routine. The sights of the city streets held his rapt attention, their sounds were music to his ears. He seldom passed a flower vendor without buying a nosegay for his mother or a boutonniere for himself and he was almost as likely to accept a small brown paper square containing the typical rice cakes known as *calas tout chaud*. He resisted the siren song of *"Eks! Fresh eks! Tres por oun dima,"* for fresh eggs, like salty oysters would be delivered straight to the door; but sometimes he succumbed to the cry of *"Glace à la vanille!"* and, accepting the peddler's glass, ate the ice cream as soon as it was scooped from the freezer. He also usually paused when he heard the musical note produced by striking a metal triangle with a metal bar, thus announcing the approach of the *marchand de gaufres*—the shaving cake man; and the familiar figures of the chimney sweeps, the scissors grinders, and the palmetto merchants were all a welcome and integral part of his life. He never failed to stop and greet them with a smile and the same courtesy that they accorded him. What did New York have to offer that could compare with this pleasant, easy understanding and comradeship between the privileged and the lowly? Nothing, absolutely nothing! People in New York scurried through the streets as if the loss of a single minute was a disaster; there was no time for fellowship. He had traveled and triumphed and it had been a great experience, it had given him a sense of fulfillment; now he was ready to rest on his laurels in the surroundings which he knew and loved. He was, therefore, disturbed, rather than otherwise, when Charles de Maurian brought him a clipping from the *Illustrated London News*.

"Challenge to European Chess Players." he read. "The American Chess Association, it is reported, are about to challenge any player in Europe to contest a match with the young victor in the late passage of arms, for from 2,000 to 5,000 dollars a side, the place of meeting to be New York. If the battle-ground were to be London or Paris there can be little doubt, we apprehend, that a European champion would be found, but the best players in Europe are not chess professionals, but have other and more serious avocations, the interests of which forbid such an expenditure of time as is required for a voyage to the United States and back again."

"Staunton must have a vivid imagination," Paul said, handing the clipping back to Charles. "Of course, there hasn't been any such challenge." Then, noticing a rather strange expression on his friend's face, he added hastily, "That's right, isn't it?"

"I suppose it is, technically."

"What do you mean, technically?"

"Well, perhaps officially would be the better word. As far as I know, the American Chess Association hasn't officially issued any challenge. But you must realize that you had hardly defeated Paulsen when the idea of one began to take form. Didn't you?"

"No—I—well, after I made the speech of presentation to Paulsen when he won the gold medal, I said that I challenged all the magnates of the Old World to enter the lists against him. Of course, I was just talking. But afterward I realized, when I said that, I was subconsciously wishing I could be the one to pick up the glove. However, I never told anyone I felt that way. I was rather ashamed that I had. And I don't any more."

"There was no reason why you should have been ashamed. As you see, other people have felt the same way."

"Then there *has* been a challenge?"

"I told you, not as far as I know—officially. But I think there will be very soon now."

"What makes you think so?"

"Why—this clipping for one thing. And other things, too."

"What other things?"

"Wait and see," said Charles, pocketing his slip of paper. "Want to have a game, giving me odds of Rook?"

He declined to discuss the matter any further and, indeed, Paul did not press him to do so. The former continued to feel disturbed, rather than exultant, at the possible turn of events and Charles was quick to realize this. Accordingly, it was not until after one of the committees of the Orleans Club, of which he was a member, had actually sent a formal challenge to the great English master, that de Maurian showed Paul a copy of it:

"On behalf of the New Orleans Chess Club, we have the honour to invite you to visit our city, and there meet Mr. Paul Morphy in a Chess match.

"In transmitting this invitation, permit us to observe that we are prompted no less by the desire to become personally acquainted with one whom we have so long admired than by the very natural anxiety to ascertain the strength of our American players by the decisive criterion of actual conflict over the board. . . .

"It must now be a matter of general desire to fix, by actual contest with the best European amateurs, the rank which American players shall hold in the hierarchy of Chess.

"For this purpose it was suggested that Mr. Morphy, the winner at the late Congress and the present American champion, should cross the ocean and boldly encounter the distinguished magnates of the Trans-Atlantic Chess circles; but it unfortunately happens that serious family reasons forbid Mr. Morphy, for the present, to entertain the thought of visiting Europe.

"It therefore becomes necessary to arrange, if possible, a meeting between the latter and the acknowledged European champion and to us it is a subject of congratulation that the sceptre of Trans-Atlantic chess is wielded by one who, with respect to regularity of communications between the two countries, and for other reasons, enjoys facilities for accepting our invitation possessed by no other European player. . . .

"Fully subscribing to the wisdom of the proposal made by you in the introduction to the Book of the Tournament, we beg leave to express our entire willingness to insert a clause providing that 'one half at least of the games shall be open ones. . . .'"

With this letter was enclosed a list of propositions for the conditions of the match, to which Staunton was invited to suggest any alterations he might deem advisable. The proposed stakes were $5,000 a side; and, should the English player lose, the sum of $1,000 (£200) was to be paid to him out of the stakes to meet his expenses in accepting the challenge. The winner of the first eleven games should be declared the victor. The place of the match should be New Orleans, and the date of commencement May 1st, or any other day in 1858 agreeable to Staunton. The time occupied in deliberating on any move should not exceed thirty minutes.

As Paul read all this, a flush, which fast became deeper and deeper, spread over his face. When he had finished, he looked up at his friend with genuine consternation.

"I can't think what made you do it, Charles! That is—I know you meant it kindly, I know you and the others who signed their names to it are fond of me and proud of me. But Staunton isn't going to like this at all. I don't like it at all! It's presumptuous, it's preposterous to suppose for a minute that a man like Staunton would come all the way to New Orleans to play with me! 'Family reasons, indeed.' What do you think he's going to say to such a suggestion as that?"

"I'm eagerly waiting to find out," Charles replied calmly. "There *are* family reasons why it would be hard for you to go to Europe, aren't there?"

"Of course there are! Hard! Reasons that would make it impossible. But Staunton won't feel they justify us in asking him to come to New Orleans!"

"Well, then the next step will have to be taken."

"What step?"

"The step that overcomes all the reasons that prevent you from going to Europe."

"Charles, you're dreaming."

"There's no harm in that, is there? Now let's have a game. The usual odds?"

The Carnival season was now approaching its height and Paul was thankful, rather than otherwise, for the fresh diversion that this offered to those he was already enjoying at the opera, the *salle d'escrime* and the soirées. He did not want to dwell on the scorn and sarcasm which would probably characterize Staunton's reply to the presumptuous challenge—if he sent one. The revival of enthusiasm for Carnival celebrations in the circles where Paul moved offered opportunities for a welcome change of thought. During the Forties, the time-honored festivities had deteriorated to a point where many Creoles took only a half-hearted interest in them and no active part. Indeed, some prominent persons felt actually averse to doing so, after unorganized maskers had engaged in a free-for-all fight, through clouds of flour and dust, with the most ruffianly elements of the city; and the general feeling of distaste had found public expression in *l'Abeille*: "Thousands of persons who yesterday had located themselves in the windows, balconies, and upon the sidewalks of the different streets through which the procession of masquers usually pass, were sadly disappointed in their non-appearance," the paper stated. "This long established custom, which in the palmy days of the *Ancien Regime* was wont to be celebrated with grotesque pageantry . . . has, within the last few years, been gradually falling into disuse, not the less so from the abandonment of the old master spirits who led on the merry crowd, than from the lewd and miserable crew who, of late years, have been permitted to join in the celebration. It is the custom, however, 'more honored in the breach than in the observance' and *we hope it will henceforth be regarded 'with the things that were.'*"

Something of a comeback had been staged soon after the Fifties were ushered in, but this was due largely to the fine display of the volunteer fire companies and to the spectacular performance of Jenny Lind, rather than to any carnival organization. It was not until six years later that a welcome new order of things began with the newly-formed Mystic Krewe of Comus, an offspring of the "Cowbellion de Rakin Society" which had long flourished in Mobile. As 1857 had marked the period of the Morphys' deepest mourning, they had heard little and seen nothing of the Krewe's first triumphs; now they shared the gratification of their friends in the revival of what they regarded the true spirit of Carnival through such an appropriate medium. Even though half-mourning still prevented their attendance at the beautiful ball in the Orleans Theater, they joined the enthusiastic crowds to watch the parade, which had for its design "The Classic Pantheon," and in the general excitement which it aroused. For days its *Tableaux Roulants* were the main topic of conversation: Flora in a car of flowers, drawn by butterflies; Ceres drawn by oxen, Bacchus by leopards and Diana by stags. Juno had her peacocks, Venus her swans, Aurora her winged horse. On and on came the floats, lighted by Negroes who acted as torchbearers, and each tableau, as it came into view, seemed to surpass its predecessor in splendor. Everything had combined to make the celebration a success: the weather had been perfect, there had been no disorders, and out-of-town visitors, including many from Mobile, had helped to swell the crowds to some twenty thousand eager onlookers. By night, "the whole city was in motion and both public and private masquerade balls supplemented the more exclusive private entertainments. Like the tableaux, each sought to surpass the others in magnificence and the fancy dress affairs given by the Young Men's Society, in which the 'Celestial Empire Club' arrayed in scarlet Chinese costumes, went through a series of pantomimes and drills, was very generally accorded the highest claim." The following day the *Crescent* hailed this second festival as "The greatest affair of the kind ever gotten up in this city. In years agone," it continued, "there were many brilliant and novel features in the celebration of Mardi Gras; but, in the memory of our oldest inhabitants, nothing which would begin to compare in taste, brilliancy and beauty with that of the Mystic Krewe last night."

Charles de Maurian knew better than to interpolate a false note in the cheerful chatter which at last prevailed again in the Morphy drawing rooms. Therefore, as weeks went by and still no unwelcome answer came to the challenge, Paul concluded that the question had been dropped. At last, however, Charles sought him out again with another copy of the *Illustrated London News* in his hand and passed it over to him without comment.

"We have been favored with a copy of the *defi* which the friends of Mr. Paul Morphy, the chess champion of the United States, have transmitted to Mr. Staunton," he read. "The terms of this cartel are distinguished by extreme courtesy and, with one notable exception, by extreme liberality also. The exception in question, however, (we refer to the clause which stipulates that the combat shall take place in New Orleans!) appears to us utterly fatal to the match: and we must confess our astonishment that the intelligent gentlemen who drew up the conditions did not themselves discover this. Could it possibly escape their penetration that if Mr. Paul Morphy, a young gentlemen without family ties or professional claims upon his attention, finds it inconvenient to anticipate, by a few months, an intended voyage to Europe, his proposed antagonist who is well known for years to have been compelled, by laborious literary occupation to abandon the practice of Chess beyond the indulgence of an occasional game, must find it not merely inconvenient, but positively impracticable, to cast aside all engagements and undertake a journey of many thousand miles for the sake of a chess-encounter? Surely the idea of such a sacrifice is not admissible for a single moment. If Mr. Morphy—for whose skill we entertain the liveliest admiration—be desirous to win his spurs among the Chess rivalry of Europe, he must take advantage of his purposed visit next year; he will then meet in this country, in France, and Germany, and in Russia, many champions whose names must be as household words to him, ready to test and do honour to his prowess."

"What did I tell you?" Paul said angrily, handing back the paper. " 'Could it possibly escape the penetration of Mr. Morphy's friends that if a young gentleman without family ties or professional claims would find it inconvenient to cross the Atlantic, his proposed antagonist, a gentleman engaged in laborious literary occupations, could hardly undertake a journey of many thousand miles for the sake of a chess-encounter.' I'm not surprised at Staunton's attitude—of course, he wrote that article himself; he has free access to the columns of the *Illustrated News!* But he hasn't had the courtesy to write the Committee a personal letter, has he?"

"No," Charles confessed, "he hasn't. No doubt he thought such an admission would discourage us. But that's where he was wrong."

"If he was discourteous, it was only what you deserved for being presumptuous. Besides, what about this trip to Europe next year? This is the first I've heard of it! You've put me in a very awkward position."

Charles had never seen his friend so excited. "Listen, Paul," he said, speaking very earnestly, "you admitted, when you found out we had sent the challenge, that you knew why we had done it—because we're proud of you. And it isn't just New Orleans that's proud of you any more. It isn't just New Orleans and New York. You don't suppose for a moment, do you, that we acted without authority? Why, six months ago, at the dinner of the Congress, Perrin said, in replying to a toast to the living players of France and England, that he hoped and believed the defeats he himself had undergone in those countries would be fully avenged 'whenever Mr.

Morphy visited the Old World.' You were there when he made that statement. You must have heard him!"

"I suppose I did. Yes, I know I did. But I thought that was just talk, too, like my presentation speech to Paulsen."

"It wasn't anything of the sort. The challenge was sent in our name because that was our privilege—you belonged to us first. But you don't any more—that is, we have to share you—with the world. I believe you when you say you didn't realize, in making that presentation speech to Paulsen, that you were secretly wishing that you could be the one to pick up the glove. I know you thought you were just talking. But don't forget there's many a true word spoken in jest. You were speaking some of them that day."

Paul was sitting with his head bent, his whole attitude one of depression, rather than hope. His face was half hidden, but Charles knew it was suffused with the telltale flush that betrayed feelings which could not be controlled; he suspected that tears were very close to the veiled eyes. He put his arm around his friend's shoulder.

"Listen, Paul," he said again. "Fred Edge has resigned from the *New York Herald*. He's already started for England as a sort of *avant courier* for you. He didn't ask your consent, because he knew you wouldn't give it. But he's acting with authority, too." And, as Paul still did not answer or look up, Charles continued, in a gentler voice, "We're counting on you, *cher*. I've already talked to your mother and she agrees that we're right. She wants you to go as much as we do. I've engaged passage for you on that new Cunarder, the *Arabia*, sailing June 9th from New York. All your friends there are delighted at the prospect of seeing you again. And I understand there is an American family visiting in London just now that you won't be displeased to find in England. I hope I'm not being indiscreet when I mention the name of Sheppard. The ladies are being presented at one of the June Drawing Rooms."

"The world that opened upon Paul Morphy, when he set foot upon the eastern continent, could hardly be called a new one. Familiar with the published games of all the living masters, he had examined their style and measured their strength with an acuteness of Chess judgment which has never been equalled, and with a memory which is rarely treacherous. The men with whom he was about to meet were no strangers to him; he had known from boyhood every peculiarity of their Chess character. The foemen before him could have inspired him with no sentiments of fear; for, aware of the strength of their blows, he felt confident that his own would be stronger. In short, whatever doubts others may have felt, Paul Morphy himself could hardly have anticipated any other result to his European tour than that which actually followed. It was the lord of a broad realm going forth, in the pride of his hereditary right, to take possession of his own, with the modesty of youth and the confidence of strength."

The Book of the First American Chess Congress by Daniel Willard Fiske (Rudd & Carleton, N.Y.)

20.

There was not time to take the inland route back to New York; it would have to be the Gulf of Mexico, the Caribbean and the Atlantic again. But, by a happy chance, the *Philadelphia* was about to sail from New Orleans; at least seasickness would be somewhat assuaged amidst familiar surroundings and familiar faces, at least there would be another enchanting interlude at Havana. The misgivings Paul felt as he started on this second journey were not for the earlier part of it, but for the part that was to come later.

This time, too, the ocean was kinder to him than it had been the previous autumn; instead of spending most of his days huddled miserably in his berth, he stayed on deck a great deal and, to his pleased surprise, he found congenial spirits among his fellow passengers. The acquaintances he had already made in Havana could not do enough to show their satisfaction over his return to them and his prospects abroad had been instrumental in causing both the Captain General and the Bishop to include him in invitations to their respective palaces. At the end of the first lap of his journey, it was reassuring to find the St. Denis Hotel and the Metropolitan Club familiar territory, peopled with familiar friends; and even the hustle and bustle of New York had lost the terrifying quality of their tension. Paul's embarkation on the *Arabia* marked a red letter day in his personal life, as well as in the history of American chess.

It was, perhaps, inevitable that there should have been a reaction to this sunny mood, even if he had not again fallen a victim of seasickness. At best, ocean travel seemed to him a monotonous experience, at worst, an endurance test. The size of the *Arabia*—2,400 tons with accommodations for 180 passengers—had at first reassured him, and her estimated speed of thirteen knots was also in her favor; at that rate, the trans-Atlantic voyage should not last much over ten days and that was rapid traveling—or so it seemed beforehand. By the time the ten days were up, Paul had changed his mind. The *Arabia* pitched and rolled in mid-ocean even worse than the *Philadelphia* when rounding Cape Hatteras; the voyage seemed interminable. When Paul finally arrived at Liverpool in a dismal drizzle on the 21st of June, even the almost indomitable buoyancy of Fred Edge, who was again waiting to meet him, was temporarily blighted by Paul's deep depression.

"I'm sorry you've had such a miserable crossing, but that's behind you now and I'm sure you'll enjoy the trip to London," Edge told him with determined cheerfulness. "Lovely countryside, quite unlike any you've ever seen: thatched cottages, village greens, flourishing hedges, rolling pastures, flocks of sheep, herds of fine cattle." And, as none of this seemed to raise

Paul's spirits in the least, he rattled on, "I've engaged rooms for us at Löwe's Hotel on Surrey Street. The proprietor is a German and a fine chess player, so you'll have much the same setup as you did in New York—I mean, Löwe's more or less the counterpart of Denis Julian, as regards both his business and his avocation. The place looks very comfortable to me. Not that you'll be there much. Most of your time will be spent at the clubs, of course—St. George's, very aristocratic; the London Chess, right in the heart of the city; the Philidorean Rooms, only recently opened. Each has its special background and its individual attractions. For instance—"

"Suppose you wait to tell me about them when we're settled in the train. Do you think I could get some coffee? I believe perhaps if I could have a small black—"

Edge doubted this, regretfully. "We can have tea though," he said, still speaking with great good cheer. "It's almost tea time. And the tea's very good—strong, black, India tea. We English drink it with lots of milk and sugar and—"

"*We* English! I thought you'd become an American!"

"Well, I'm about half and half, I suppose. In New York, I feel like an American and in London, I feel like an Englishman. You know the old adage, 'When in Rome, et cetera.' Well, that's what I try to do. New York's a wonderful city, but so is London."

"Is it always as cold as this, the latter part of June?"

"No, not always. . . . Well, here we are at Customs—a mere formality. In just a few minutes now, we'll be in our comfortable railway carriage, drinking nice hot tea. That'll warm you up."

"I don't feel as if I'm ever going to be warm again. And you keep talking about going to *London*. We can't do that right away. We've got to go first to Birmingham. We've barely time to reach there for the beginning of the tournament."

"No, no! The tournament's been postponed until August."

"You must be mistaken. Why, I had a letter from Mr. Thomas Avery, the President of the Birmingham Chess Club, enclosing this item from the *Illustrated London News.*" He took a clipping from his wallet and read aloud from it: " 'Annual Meeting of the Chess Association.

" 'It was noticed in our columns last week that the Chess-players' Derby day was fixed to commence on the 22nd of June. The arrangements of the local committee are, of course, not yet complete, but it is whispered that they have succeeded in insuring the presence of the American chess phenomenon, Paul Morphy, an attraction, of itself, sufficient to secure the largest attendance which has been known for years.' There you are! Surely someone would have let me know if there had been any change."

Fred shook his head doubtfully. "Yes, I should think someone would have. Still, I'm very sure—"

Paul, however, was not to be dissuaded. Eager as he was to reach London for personal reasons, which he had not confided to Edge and which had no relation to chess, he persisted in taking the train to Birmingham. The drizzle by this time had become a downpour, and the long twilight, so beautiful in fair weather, seemed only to prolong a period of gloom between day and night; the charm of the countryside was effectively dimmed by this semi-obscurity and the "good strong India tea" was not at all to Paul's taste. He sat shivering in the part of the railway carriage farthest from the windows, which two English fellow travelers had flung wide open, his warmest overcoat buttoned tightly around him and supplemented by a knitted muffler. Any further attempts to cheer him, Edge finally realized, were doomed to failure.

Even so, he could hardly have foreseen an unrelieved continuance of untoward circumstances. He had been right about the postponement of the tournament; there were no reservations for them at the Station Hotel, no message for them at the desk and no sign of preparation for such an influx of visitors as a tournament would have indicated. They were rather grudgingly accommodated in a small chilly room and, the kitchen having already closed, went dinnerless to bed.

A note, dispatched early the next morning to Mr. Avery, resulted in an immediate call from that gentleman, whose regret at the inconvenience to which Mr. Morphy had been put was genuinely and most politely expressed; but mingled with his apologies was the inescapable suggestion that postal service in the States must leave much to be desired. He had written to Mr. Morphy, advising him of the change in date as soon as this had been made; he could not understand why his second letter had not been received before their distinguished guest left New Orleans. Of course, he would look forward to seeing Mr. Morphy again in August or, if they could prevail on him to stay on now for a few days, Mr. Avery was sure some offhand games could be arranged and Mr. Morphy would be a most welcome visitor, though no official contest could take place.

Mr. Morphy, however, could not be persuaded. Even Mr. Avery's courtesy and cordiality failed to obliterate Paul's first unfavorable impression of Birmingham which, moreover, his first experience with an English breakfast had intensified rather than improved. "Good strong India tea" had again made its appearance, along with porridge, kippered herring, grilled kidneys and toast on a rack to insure its coolness. A beverage presented as coffee had also been served, but Paul failed to recognize it as such and turned from it with repugnance. At a later hour, the bacon and eggs, undeniably excellent, might have placated him, but he did not consider them suitable for early morning consumption. Rain was still falling steadily and the hotel parlor, where he and Fred received their unhappy visitor, seemed to have absorbed much of the dampness in the outer atmosphere; he was cold, hungry and annoyed. It required all his savoir-faire to reply that he appreciated Mr. Avery's kindness, but that there were urgent reasons why he must reach London as soon as possible. Mr. Avery was not to give the matter of the delayed letter another thought; it was probably quite true that the American mail service could not compare in efficiency with that of the British Isles. They parted with mutual respect, if without mutual heartiness.

Fred Edge was not suffering from either hunger or cold, as he had enjoyed his breakfast and was used to the English climate, but he, too, was annoyed. Why on earth couldn't Paul have taken his word about the postponement of the tournament, instead of making this unnecessary stop? The rooms at Löwe's Hotel had been engaged for the night before and Lord Lyttleton, the President of the British Chess Association, together with several members of the St. George's Club, had been expecting to welcome them there. Now the rooms might well have been let to someone else and the reception committee disbanded; it would be hard to straighten these matters out. And what were the urgent reasons why Paul now wanted to reach London which were unconnected with chess and unaccounted for, as far as he, Fred, was concerned? His orderly mind had no room for vagaries such as those in which Paul seemed to be indulging. This time, it was he who withdrew from companionship in the railway carriage. He was very close to sulking; and it was Paul who broke in on the silence into which Fred had retreated.

"Do you happen to know the dates of the Drawing Rooms?" Paul inquired.

"The *dates* of drawing rooms?" Fred repeated. "What drawing rooms?"

"The ones that are held at Buckingham Palace. When young ladies are presented to the Queen."

"Oh—those! No, I'm sure I don't. As I don't know any young ladies who are likely to be presented to the Queen, there's no reason why I should have been interested."

"Do the newspapers announce the dates and give the names of the young ladies beforehand?"

"I don't know that, either. If they do, I haven't paid any attention to such announcements. Why should I?"

"I don't suppose there's any reason why *you* should. But I do happen to be interested. I have reason to believe that some friends of mine either have recently been presented or are shortly to be. I understand that all nationals have to be recommended by their own Ministers. I suppose I can get the information I need from the American Legation. I'll go there the first thing tomorrow morning."

"My dear fellow, you can't do that! At least until we've found out what plans Lord Lyttleton may have made for you!"

"Couldn't we find that out tonight? I wouldn't like to go to the Legation, to make a first call, after normal visiting hours. But surely it doesn't matter how late we go to the club!"

"Normally, it wouldn't. But you see they were prepared to receive you, formally, last evening. Since we didn't show up or send them any message beforehand, we can't simply break in on them now. As soon as I see you settled at Löwe's, I'll go around and find out the lay of the land. Then I'll let you know about an appointment for tomorrow. But that's got to be your first consideration. Otherwise, you might make an unfavorable impression."

Conversation again languished. But, before they reached London, the rain ceased and Paul admitted to himself, although not to Fred, that the fresh verdure of the countryside, the thatched cottages and fine flocks and herds in the rolling pastures did indeed have a great deal of charm. He was also intrigued with the vehicle which Fred selected from a row of similar ones drawn up outside the railway station: a low-hung, two-wheeled, covered cab, drawn by one horse, with a driver perched on an elevated seat at the rear who permitted his reins to fall loosely over the top of the cab, but who started off at a goodly clip, as soon as he had them comfortably enclosed behind doors which folded over them like an apron. This was called a hansom, Fred informed Paul, after a man by the name of J. A. Hansom, who had patented the style of conveyance some twenty-five years earlier. It had become amazingly popular, almost immediately.

"I'm not surprised. I think it's very chic myself," Paul said enthusiastically, and Fred sighed with relief. He had begun to be afraid that nothing was going right with this enterprise on which he had counted so much, which he had indeed made a considerable personal and professional sacrifice in order to further. But if the mere sight of a hansom cab, let alone the experience of riding in one, could improve Paul's mood, surely the comfortable quarters awaiting him at Löwe's Hotel and the welcome he was sure to receive at St. George's should certainly raise his spirits still further.

Dinner, though it lacked seasoning and sauces, at least provided a great improvement on the fare in Birmingham. The sole, the beef, the cheese and the strawberries were really excellent—but did the English never cook potatoes except by boiling? And, as for the "cold shape" and the sago pudding, Paul really did not know which was worse, as an excuse for a sweet! However, he admitted that he was adequately nourished when he and Edge left the dining room and said he would start unpacking while Fred went on to the club to reconnoitre and find out whether or not it was too late to present himself there that evening.

Edge returned with a favorable reply: Lord Lyttleton had departed for the night, but had left a message saying he hoped Mr. Morphy would lunch with him the next day; it was believed that Herr Löwenthal, who was also visiting London, and who expressed himself as being most eager to seeing Mr. Morphy again, might be among the other guests on this occasion. Meanwhile, Mr. Boden and Mr. Barnes—two of the "Five Great B's" who formed such a strong phalanx among London amateurs—were still on hand and so was a rather eccentric clergyman, whose name was actually Owen, but who insisted on being called only "Alter," both in conversation and in the written references to his game. Despite his peculiarities, he was an excellent player. If this would be agreeable to Paul, "Alter" would engage him that very night. . . .

Paul had not the slightest desire to go out again; he had still not wholly recovered from the effects of his seasickness, and his experience in Birmingham had done nothing to improve his condition. But he realized that he had been ungracious to Edge and was eager to make amends for this; besides, the prospect of another drive in a hansom was really inviting. Instead of cutting Edge off short, as he had before, when the latter tried to describe the characteristics of the various clubs, he listened with unfailing interest, as they went clip-clop along the streets. It was apparently so called, partly because George was the Christian name of its founder and partly because its first meeting had been held at Beattie's Hotel on George Street in the province of St. George. It had begun its existence in a burst of prosperity and popularity and, from the beginning, was famous for its cuisine, its wines, and its large, well-proportioned rooms. But, unfortunately, Mr. Beattie went into bankruptcy and St. George's was turned out of doors. For several weeks, the club was homeless; then it found refuge in the Polytechnic Institution, on Regent Street, where one of the chess addicts was a large stockholder. There again it was soon in flourishing condition; its membership became more and more distinguished; and it was in this locale that Staunton played his first match with St. Amant and lost it.

"But he won the second, as I recall it, in Paris," Paul said.

"Yes, and then declined to play again after stakes had been deposited for a third and final match. He pleaded ill health and went home." Edge hesitated for a moment, before adding with obvious reluctance, "It's unfortunate that he's beginning to acquire a reputation for finding some sort of excuse for not playing if he thinks there's a chance that a game may go against him. He's too outstanding a figure in the chess world to permit any risk of such an accusation. Like Caesar's wife, he should be above suspicion."

"But if he really were ill," Paul said tolerantly. "Well, let's forget about him for a moment—I suppose I'll be meeting him within a day or two and then I can form my own estimate of him. Go on with your history of St. George's. Is it still in the Polytechnic Institution?"

"No, its members weren't able to dine there, so they dwindled away. Then they were offered apartments at the New Palace Club Chambers in King Street, St. James's, which suited them to a T. But here we are, so you'll see for yourself."

Paul was more than ready to agree with Edge on that score; from the moment he entered the club, he found the atmosphere of St. George's agreeable and the companionship of his fellow chess players congenial. The informality of his first visit actually proved an advantage. Presentations were made and speeches exchanged without stiffness or ceremony and conversation turned naturally to a variety of subjects: Mr. Morphy's Louisiana background, which was unfamiliar but fascinating territory to his new acquaintances; his various voyages over waters equally unfamiliar and fascinating; his stopovers in Havana, which none of the others had visited and which seemed to them even more exotic and entrancing than New Orleans and the Mississippi River. His stature as a traveler gave him added prestige as a chess player and, to his great relief, interest centered elsewhere than on his first impressions of England. Seated in easy chairs around a coal fire, with decanters and glasses in easy reach, the members of the club surrounded their guest and made him feel that they were honored to welcome him in their midst. The conviction that no contests should be staged and no challenges issued before the morrow was so unanimous that it did not need to be put into words; and the hour for Lord Lyttleton's luncheon was set so conveniently late that Edge could offer no reasonable objection to a call at the American Legation before it took place.

Again, Paul could not feel otherwise than pleased with his reception. Philip Dallas, the son of the Minister and also First Secretary of Legation, welcomed him warmly. Of course they already had word of his coming, this amiable young man assured him, and were confidently looking to him to "twist the lion's tail." He must dine with them as soon and as frequently as his other commitments would allow—what about that night for a starter? And what would Mr. Morphy especially like to do in London, whom would he especially like to meet? What were his major interests, other than chess? Horse racing? Boating? Dancing? The stage? Sightseeing?

Paul was forced to interrupt the seemingly unending flow of hospitable offers. He deeply appreciated the kindness of Mr. Dallas, but he must of course consult Lord Lyttleton before making any binding engagements. Meantime, he would be greatly obliged if Mr. Dallas would tell him where to get in touch with some friends of his who were, he felt sure, well known at the Legation: Mr. and Mrs. Albert Sheppard and their daughters, Berenice and Charmian.

"Why, of course I can!" Philip Dallas exclaimed without a moment's hesitation. "On the rue des Saints Pères—I'm not sure of the number, but that's not in the least necessary—the Hotel d'Ambres is all you require. Luck was certainly with them, having an establishment like that offered them, right in the heart of the Faubourg St. Germain—the most tightly guarded stronghold of the French aristocracy. Of course, when I refer to the *Hotel* d'Ambres, I'm talking about a *hotel particulier*—a private palace—not a public hostelry, and this is said to be a perfect gem of seventeenth century architecture, with some of the finest *boiseries*, tapestries and Louis XIVth furniture in the Capital. But, after all, Jacques d'Ambres won't be needing it himself as long as he's stationed in London as an attaché of the French Embassy, and it's quite in character for him to make a beau geste, especially where lovely ladies are concerned."

"I'm afraid I'm not following you. Do you mean to tell me the Sheppards are in *Paris?*"

"Why yes, my dear fellow, didn't you know that? They left immediately after the Drawing Room last week. They'd had all of May here, as well as a good share of June; they'd got as much out of a London Season as they could possibly hope for, a lot more than most people would expect. So, of course, it was natural for them to get what they could out of a Paris Season before the 14th of July. And I'll wager they'll get a good deal, with the setting and introductions Jacques has provided for them. By the way, he's a mighty good chap, you'll enjoy meeting him. Just as soon as you let me know when you're free for a meal, I'll get in touch with him, too. Now, before you dash off to that luncheon with Lord Lyttleton, Father wants to meet you. Nonsense, it won't take but a minute; his private office is just down this corridor. I'll go ahead to show you the way."

Edge had agreed to wait for Paul at Löwe's, so that they could go on to St. George's together. He sprang up, eager and smiling, as his protégé entered the room; but, even before the latter spoke, Fred realized that something untoward had already undone the good work of the convivial evening they had spent at the club.

"I'm afraid what I'm going to tell you may disappoint you," Paul said. "It may even be rather upsetting to you. I am sorry if it is, but I can't help it. I agreed to come to London for two reasons: to play chess with Staunton and to meet some friends here. I've just learned that my friends have already left for Paris. Of course, I still want to play with Staunton—that is, if he doesn't stall. From the hint you dropped yesterday and from some stray remarks I heard later at the club, I gather that, occasionally, he does. I'll wait a reasonable length of time, I won't give anyone a chance to say I haven't kept my side of the bargain. But I don't propose to be put off indefinitely to no purpose. I intend, as soon as possible, to present myself at the Hotel d'Ambres, rue des Saints Pères, Paris."

"Cherished chess! The charms of thy chequered chambers chain me changelessly. Chaplains have chanted thy charming choiceness; chieftains have changed the chariot and the chase for the chaster chivalry of the chessboard, and the cheerier charge of chess-knights. Chaste-eyed Caïssa! For thee are the chaplets of chainless charity and the chalice of child-like cheerfullness. No chilling churl, no cheating chaferer, no chattering changeling, no chanting charlatan can be thy champion; the chivalrous, the charitable, and the cheerful are the chosen ones thou cherishest. Chance cannot change thee; from childhood to the charnel-house, from our first childish chirpings to the chills of the churchyard, thou art cheery, changeless chieftainess. Chastener of the churlish, chider of the changeable, cherisher of the chagrined, the chapter of thy chiliad charms should be chanted by cherubic chimes, and chiseled on chalcedon in cherubic chirography."

ANONYMOUS. 1857

The Chess Reader, The Royal Game in World Literature,
compiled by Jerome Salzmann. (Greenberg: Publisher, N.Y.)

21.

30, Vincent Square, Westminster, London, July 24, 1858.

Chas. A. de Maurian, Esq.

Sir, At the request of Mr. Paul Morphy, I undertake the pleasant task of informing you relative to the events which have transpired in relation to him since his arrival in England. Mr. Morphy, as you will easily understand, being so much at the mercy of this or that Knight errant desirous of breaking a lance with him, as to be precluded any chance of corresponding with his friends. And I think, too, that 'the eternal fitness of things' would demand that Achilles should not be his own Homer.

The postponement of the Birmingham meeting from June to August has given your compatriot the advantage of measuring swords with a number of our leading amateurs. On his arrival in London, Morphy immediately sought out the St. George's members showing extreme desire to test his skill. The fatigues of an Atlantic voyage had, however, told somewhat upon him, and although he vanquished every successive opponent, it was not, at first, in that startling proportion which he has since realized. Up to the present moment, he has played nineteen games with Mr. Barnes of which the latter scored six to Morphy's thirteen, but the final eight were gained, one after the other by the last named gentleman, proving conclusively a certain superiority. Mr. Boden who ranks among the ten principal European players, has tested his powers nine times, winning one, drawing three and losing five. The Rev. John Owen, whose *nom de guerre* is 'Alter,' won the first game through Morphy's carelessness, but lost the following four; his opponent assuring me that he could easily give him pawn and move. Other antagonists, of almost equal ability have 'bit the dust,' and I beg to refer you to the Postscriptum for a correct list of the casualties.

Boden enjoyed the reputation of being the leading player at the Grand Chess Divan in the Strand, perhaps the greatest Chess Forum in the world, where still linger the memories of Kieseritzky, Anderssen, Heyderbrandt and others. Boden, then in all the pride of ambition, replied with Mephistophelian sneer that 'Morphy would soon find his match.' The first two games between them came off at the Divan, relinquished afterwards for a private room, the former gentleman not wishing to peril his reputation further, as the result was Morphy 1, drawn 1, Boden 0, and as he expressed himself as highly disgusted at the score becoming public, as he purposely played private to obviate publicity. A prominent member of the St. George's Club stated a few days ago that he could not have believed that any man could beat Boden in such proportion; to which observation he saw that 'the proof of the pudding is in the eating' may very properly be quoted.

Morphy crossed the ocean, and threw down his gauntlet in the very sanctum of his adversary—the den of the dragon—the St. George's Club. No way now for Staunton to refuse. Accept he must, but play, will he? And men are now betting odds of 5 to 4 at the St. George's, the London and the Divan, that Staunton will find some pretext for not playing. He does not like the present appearance of things, for during the past fortnight although Morphy has been playing right and left, with men of all shades of strength, he has not lost a game, more especially in view of the match now progressing between Morphy and Löwenthal. Löwenthal was the proposer of this match, which was offered by him in the most friendly spirit, with an eye, also to wiping out his former defeat by a boy of thirteen years old, which, you of course, remember. The game was well played on both sides. The first game was a draw, and the other two being easily won by Morphy. The fourth was one of our hero's happiest efforts; from the first to last Löwenthal never had a chance, and he resigned after two hours and a quarter play at the thirty-first move. Löwenthal has acted throughout, Morphy states, in the most friendly manner.

Morphy's scores with leading players here, in off hand games, stand as follows: (Staunton will not publish them in the I. L. N. they being too much in Morphy's favour.)

Morphy		13	Barnes		6	Drawn		0
Morphy		5	Boden		1	Drawn		3
Morphy		4	Owen		1	Drawn		0
Morphy		6	Löwenthal		0	Drawn		0
Morphy		2	Hampton		0	Drawn		0

I promise you, Sir, that during Morphy's stay in Europe you shall be kept perfectly *au courant* of his battles, etc.

I beg to remain, Sir,
Yours very respectfully,
Fred B. Edge.

Edge had been so engrossed in the composition of this letter that he had not even heard Paul enter the room. Now, after signing his name with a flourish and reaching for an envelope, he looked up to see that his friend was seated beside him, also holding a letter in his hand.

"Why, hello!" he said. "You're just in time to see what I've written your friend de Maurian. If there's anything you want to add or change, you can write a postscript." He handed the sheets to Paul, who read through the text attentively and then handed them back, shaking his head.

"No," he said. "There's nothing I want to change or add—as far as Charles is concerned. He'll be very pleased with the picture you presented and I don't want to cause him any unnecessary anxiety. But perhaps I'd better show you a letter I've written myself, before I send it."

The missive which Paul in turn handed over for inspection covered only part of a single sheet.

Howard Staunton, Esq. (Edge read.) As we are now approaching the Birmingham meeting, at the termination of which you have fixed our match to commence, I think it would be advisable to settle the preliminaries during this week. Would you be good enough to state some early period when your seconds can meet mine, so that a contest which I have so much at heart, and which from your eminent position excites so much interest in the chess world, may be looked upon as a *fait accompli?*

I am, dear sir,
Yours very respectfully,
Paul Morphy.

Edge was the one who now shook his head. "I'm sorry that you felt you had to write. But I'm not surprised. Whenever you've *spoken* to Staunton—and Lord knows you've had plenty of chances to do that, meeting as often as you have—he's put you off. I don't wonder you felt the only way to pin him down was to get something on paper. And I don't wonder you're hurt, either."

"I'm not hurt, exactly. But I'm puzzled—for all sorts of reasons. At first, Staunton declined to play with me because it wasn't convenient for him to come to New Orleans. Well, that was easy enough to understand—and even if it *had* been convenient, no one should have expected a mature professional man to leave his home and his work and cross the ocean to play with a boy he'd hardly heard of. He never should have been asked to do so—it was a presumptuous proposal, as I haven't hesitated to tell my friends who made it. I'm not surprised he resented it. But I've tried to make an *amende honorable.* I've shown him I realized it was fitting that Mahomet should go to the mountain, not the other way around. I've been courteous. I've been patient. I haven't hurried him or harried him. I've proved through my games with others that I know how to play, that he wouldn't be demeaning himself by taking me for an antagonist."

"I'm afraid that's just the trouble. I'm afraid you've won too many games while you've been waiting around."

"You mean you think he doesn't *dare* play with me? That he won't risk losing his title?"

"Well, it looks rather that way, doesn't it? A champion doesn't need to beg for 'some weeks of preparation' the way Staunton has. He doesn't need to talk about the pressures of professional commitments along other lines. He has too much self-confidence for that. He's eager to prove his prowess, the way you are."

"It's not so much that I'm eager to prove my prowess. It's that I came to England on purpose to play with Staunton, not with all the famous 'B's,' not even with Löwenthal, though nothing could have been more pleasing to me than to meet him again. I don't like to leave anything undone that I've started out to do. However, as I've told you before—"

"Yes, as you've told me before, you had a second purpose in coming to London and you've found that the only way you can fulfill that is to get on to Paris. You *have* been patient, you *have* been courteous. But can't you go on being patient and courteous just a little longer? As an Englishman, I don't want to have you thwarted in both the projects for which you came to London. Let's see what Staunton says in answer to that letter."

All that Staunton said in answer to the letter was a repetition: he would like a few more weeks to prepare. A second communication from Paul, offering to leave the terms of the contest entirely to Staunton, was still unanswered when the tournament at Birmingham began. And Paul's bewilderment was considerably increased when he received a telegram from Mr. Avery asking him to take the first train from London: Mr. Staunton was already there, the Committee was eagerly awaiting the arrival of Mr. Morphy before making the final plans for the contest.

This time, when Paul sought out his friend, he was almost speechless with rage. Staunton had declared, unequivocally beforehand, that he would play nothing but consultation games in Birmingham; now he had announced his intention of competing in the tournament.

"And if he thinks this is the way he can force my hand, he's mistaken!" Paul shouted. Edge had never heard him raise his voice but once before— in his moment of supreme excitement at the New York Chess Congress. "I agreed not to play because that was *his* agreement! I'm not going back on mine!"

"You don't mean you'll refuse to go to Birmingham!"

"No, I won't refuse to go to Birmingham. I've promised to give a blindfold display there on the twenty-seventh and I keep *my* promises! But I shan't be there when the meeting opens on the twenty-fourth. And if the tie in which I'm drawn for the first round goes by default to my opponent, I shan't dispute the verdict!"

It was impossible to calm him and, after a few minutes, Edge gave up trying to do so. He was still in a state of feverish excitement when they took the train and when they parted for the night at the Station Hotel. When they met the next morning for breakfast, they were hardly seated when Paul made an electrifying announcement.

"You've probably heard that there's going to be a public soirée tonight. I'm going to fling a question at Mr. Howard Staunton in a voice loud enough for everyone to hear. Before all present, I'm going to ask him to fix his date or, if he won't, why not."

"Paul, you wouldn't—you couldn't be guilty of such a gaucherie. It would counteract everything you've done so far. Everything that has won you so much admiration and respect!"

"I don't care. I've stood all I can from Staunton. The time comes when you have to speak to men who are beneath your contempt in their own language, if you speak to them at all. That's when you've made the sad discovery that they don't understand anything else."

"Then it's better not to speak to them at all."

"Ordinarily, I'd agree with you. This is an *extraordinary* occasion!"

He pushed away his plate with even more visible distaste than usual for an English breakfast and did not even pretend to drink his "good strong India tea." Edge, in a last desperate effort to calm him, suggested that they should take a quiet stroll through the courtyard of Queen's College.

"Why not? I don't give my exhibition until this afternoon. It might be a good way to pass the time."

Neither had any idea, in accepting it as such and nothing more, that Caïssa, the patron deity of chess, was at last playing into their hands. They had hardly entered the tranquil enclosure when they caught sight of a group advancing from the further end. It was led by Lord Lyttleton and at his side was Mr. Howard Staunton. Mr. Avery followed with several other gentlemen. Paul glanced swiftly in their direction and quickened his pace. Lord Lyttleton, as usual, greeted him with the utmost cordiality; Howard Staunton, unless he literally walked around Morphy, could not avoid meeting him head on. Thus confronted, as Paul afterward said contemptuously, "His gambit was not good."

"I regret that I've not been able to find a favorable occasion to answer your latest letter, Mr. Morphy," he said rather haltingly. "I am sure you must recognize at least some of the reasons for my hesitation to give a definite reply to your request that I would set a definite date for our contest." And, as Paul bowed without replying, and all the others were obviously waiting attentively for Staunton's next words, he went on still more haltingly, "You see, I'm entirely out of play."

"I cannot believe that you are not still the world's champion, however out of play you may be," Paul said icily, bowing again.

"Yes, but I'm engaged in a very important literary work. I am under bond to my publishers, who are pressing me."

"I would not wish to add to that pressure," Paul, who had heard all this many times before, said still more icily. "Perhaps by October you will have been released from some of the strain under which you are now laboring."

"I really cannot say. We are already almost at the end of August and—"

"November then? Or December?"

The surrounding silence had become oppressive; courtesy compelled

Staunton to put an end to it. Besides, he did not like the way Avery was looking at him, still less the way Lyttleton avoided doing so.

"Well, Mr. Morphy," he began and stopped. But there was no help for it now, he would have to go on. "Well, Mr. Morphy," he said a second time, "if you will consent to the postponement, I will play you at the beginning of November."

"Choose your own time, by all means. As I have said, I do not wish to add to your feeling of strain or deny you time for preparation, now you have convinced me you need that. But whatever arrangements you make, please let them be final."

"Yes, of course. I will see my publishers and let you know the exact date within a few days."

Once more Paul bowed. Then he stepped aside, permitting the group he had confronted to advance. He did not move again until they were out of sight and hearing. Afterward, he turned to Edge and laughed.

"This afternoon, I will give my blindfold exhibition," he said. "This evening I will go to the public soirée—not to make a scene, but to receive congratulations. Tomorrow we will return to London and start packing. The next day we will spend making farewell visits to everyone who has been so kind to us. And the day after that we will be on our way to Paris, where we will remain until early November."

The blindfold exhibition was a brilliant performance before a brilliant gathering, the congratulations with which Paul was showered at the soirée sincere and spontaneous. He left for London in high spirits and the news that Löwenthal had defeated Staunton at the tournament, by a score of two to zero, which reached him a few days later, was not calculated to lower these. Edge was afraid that a paragraph, appearing in the form of an answer to an imaginary correspondent, in Staunton's *Illustrated London News*, might have that effect, but judged it wiser to show this to his friend himself, rather than let Paul discover it or hear it from some outside source. Nevertheless, it was with many misgivings that he handed over the paper.

"As you surmise, 'knowing the authority,' the slang of the sporting paper in question regarding the proposed encounter between Mr. Staunton and the young American is 'bunkum.' In matches of importance it is the invariable practice in this country, before anything definite is settled, for each party to be provided with representatives to arrange the terms and money for the stakes. Mr. Morphy has come here unfurnished in both respects; and, although both will no doubt be forthcoming in due time, it is clearly impossible, until they are, that any determinate arrangement can be made. 2. The statement of another contemporary that the reduction in the amount of stakes from £1000 a side to £500 was made at the suggestion of the

English amateur is equally devoid of truth; the proposal to reduce the amount having been made by Mr. Morphy."

"I hope you'll ask for an immediate retraction of those unblushing misstatements," Edge said hotly, as Paul contemptuously tossed the paper aside. "Why, without mentioning Englishmen, of whom there are plenty, I'll take my oath that there are any number of Americans in both London and Paris who would assert you could be backed against Staunton for ten thousand pounds and that the money could be raised within twenty-four hours!"

"I don't doubt that you're right. And since that's so, why do we need to bother with an answer? Besides, when a man resorts to such measures as these, he won't stop until he's committed himself irrevocably. The best thing to do is to let him go on and do it."

It was in this nonchalant mood that Paul continued his packing.

L'HÔTEL MEURICE EN 1855.

"L'Hôtel MEURICE, installé au n° 223 de la rue Saint-Honoré devint, à l'époque de la Restauration le rendez-vous des Anglais, avides de visiter ce Paris où, pendant plus de vingt ans, s'était joué le sort du monde.

"Deux annonces, conservées à l'hôtel, et datant, l'une de 1819, et l'autre de 1827 constituent deux documents curieux sur les formules de publicité d'autrefois et sur la manière dont jadis, on comprenait le confort.

"La première s'énonce ainsi:

" 'MEURICE exprime tous ses remerciements aux Anglais qui l'ont honoré de leur patronage, et s'efforcera de continuer à mériter leur bienveillant appui.

" 'Il vient d'ouvrir quatre nouveaux appartements, en face le Jardin des Tuileries, dans l'un desquels on pourrait, si cela était nécessaire, installer jusqu'à 30 lits; et des appartements plus petits à un seul lit, à 3 francs la nuit. Les prix du service, fixés à l'avance et très modérés, sont indiqués sur des imprimés placés dans chaque chambre. MEURICE se flatte qu'aucun hôtel en Europe n'est mieux réglé, ni mieux organisé pour donner le plus grand confort aux Anglais, dont il a le souci constant de respecter les habitudes et les traditions, et il espère continuer à mériter toujours leur approbation.'

"En 1827, l'annonce s'exprime ainsi:

" 'Pour un voyageur anglais, aucun hôtel de Paris n'offre autant d'avantages que l'Hôtel MEURICE, n° 223, rue Saint-Honoré. Il est situé dans un endroit joli et agréable, près du Palais et du Jardin des Tuileries.

" 'On y peut avoir un appartement à la journée. Les petits déjeuners sont servis dans le café ou dans les chambres, et les voyageurs peuvent prendre leurs repas à table d'hôte ou dans leurs appartements. Un tarif est présenté à chaque étranger, sur lequel sont inscrits tous les frais du service. La note est réglée chaque semaine. Le linge est blanchi à trois milles de Paris, au savon, et, ni battu, ni brossé, comme c'est l'habitude généralement en France. La plus grande régularité est observée pour la relève et la distribution des lettres, et les renseignements de toute nature sont fournis au bureau.

" 'Du 1er Novembre à la fin de Mai, Monsieur MEURICE fait des prix spéciaux pour personne seule ou familles, comme pensionnaires, au jour ou au mois, soit à table d'hôte, soit dans les appartements, vin et tout compris, excepté le bois que les clients ont la liberté d'acheter.

" 'Il accepte aussi de loger sans pension, au jour, à la semaine ou au mois.

" 'Dans cet hôtel il y a aussi un bureau pour les changes, des courriers privés, *des interprètes. On peut y retenir des voitures pour Calais, Boulogne et n'importe quel endroit du continent.'*

"*La rue de Rivoli est, en 1835 achevée jusqu'aux Tuileries. MEURICE s'est installé dans des bâtiments neufs, en façade de la rue.*

"*Pendant la Monarchie de Juillet et le Second Empire, le voisinage des Tuileries et de la Cour attire à l'hôtel une clientèle brillante et choisie qui consacre sa renommée; mais, bien que pendant plus d'un demi-siècle il ait été la maison la mieux fréquentée de Paris, cette renommée est aujourd'hui éclipsée par le succès sans précédent du nouvel Hôtel MEURICE.*"

From pamphlet privately printed by the Maison Devambez for the Hotel Meurice.

22.

Despite his many triumphs and the kindness and courtesy with which he had been treated during his two months' stay in England, Paul was still smarting with resentment against Staunton when he finally set out for France. Nothing about the trip was calculated to raise his spirits. Edge, who by this time had become his alter ego, did not succeed in rousing him until it was too late for them to catch the morning train; hence, since their belongings were already packed, they strolled about aimlessly until early afternoon and finally reached Dover in time to take an evening boat. But when they landed at Calais, they found they could not get to Paris that night. Paul had been dreadfully seasick during the crossing, and his initial experience on French soil was unfortunate: he spoke the language so fluently and with such a complete absence of accent, that the landing officials could not be persuaded he was an American citizen, entitled to the passport which he presented for examination. Not until he had given them a summary of the settlement, manners and customs of Louisiana did they consent, after much shrugging of shoulders, outspreading of hands, and whispered consultation among themselves, to return his *papier reglé* to him. Even so, the price of this release was the confiscation of most of his under-linen, a procedure which the officials assured him "was customary."

Having made their escape from the customs house, the two young men started out to the Hotel Dessin, secured rooms for the night and, after dinner, went for a stroll, which instead of refreshing them, depressed them still further. Cynically, they agreed that Calais might have been a magnificent town "before the discovery of architecture," but if William the Conqueror were to revisit it, he would find it unchanged, except that it was now dirtier than it could have been in his day! Their general malaise at least had the effect of serving as a spur to get them on their way as soon as possible, and they did not miss their morning train a second time. At quarter before eight, they were on one of the dingy cars which, with frequent stops, crawled along for ten hours before it reached Paris. Again, at the Gare du Nord, an inspection of baggage took place; but fortunately, this time, Paul's French aroused no suspicions and his remaining underwear was not claimed as a forfeit. He and Edge were released without argument and were free to take a fiacre to the Meurice.

The very sight of the brilliant streets and the luxurious apartments of the beautiful hotel acted as a stimulant; and after an excellent dinner at the Restaurant des Trois Frères Provenceaux, Paul needed no urging from Edge, who already knew Paris well, to win his consent for another stroll. They ambled down the Palais Royal and past the Théâtre Français and, as they went along, Edge gave no indication that he had any special goal in view; but when they reached the Café de la Régence, he stopped and, without consulting his companion, pushed open the wide door and motioned toward the interior.

This was so dense with tobacco smoke that, at first, it was almost impossible to form a definite idea of its size, style or occupants. But through the haze, they managed to make out the massive figure of the patron, Pierre Morel, who was colloquially and affectionately known as the Rhinoceros. He acknowledged their presence without animosity, but also without either curiosity or enthusiasm. As far as he was concerned, they were just two more customers; Paul had emphatically said that he did not wish to announce his arrival in Paris until the next day, and Edge had respected his wishes to this extent, without being able to resist the temptation of showing him the place which had been designated as the scene for his future triumphs. When their eyes became more accustomed to the clouded atmosphere, they were able to see that they were in a large room filled with tables placed so close together that passage among these was difficult; and that, at each table, games of draughts, cards, dominoes and chess were in full progress. This room led into another which was much more ornate; its massive ceiling was decorated in the cornices with shields, three of them bearing the names of Philidor, Deschappelles and Labourdonnais—the most celebrated frequenters of the café. A fourth shield bore only the foundation date, with space for the name of some future customer, deserving of special tribute. Here the air was not so heavy, for smoking was forbidden; but there was no lessening of noise around the two billiard tables, encircled by additional groups of card and chess players. In both rooms, the hubbub was so great as to make anyone, not an habitué, wonder how the concentration required for a serious match could be possible. The variety of strange tongues—German, Swedish, Italian, Greek, Russian—created a veritable babel; and the classes of society represented were as manifold as the languages. The military ranged in rank from private to colonel; the clerical from shabby curés to stately monsignori; men in working clothes brushed against elegantly clad fops. The Italians gave an effect of quarreling while they talked, the Swedes one of calm detachment; and here and there, among the gamesters, a man sat by himself, with a cup of coffee in front of him, quietly reading from a newspaper printed in some language which bore no resemblance to those in ordinary European use.

Paul, at first slightly displeased at having been ushered, without warning, into the place which he had had no intention of visiting until the next day, found himself drawn, against his will, toward a group clustering around two men whose absorption in their game of chess was so complete that they seemed oblivious of their surroundings. Their skill was of no mean order; fascinated, Paul began to watch them, unconscious of the passage of time, but finding it difficult to maintain complete silence; every now and then a play which was either advantageous or disastrous seemed to him so inevitable that some kind of an admonition was indicated. But, like the other observers, he managed to hold his peace. Edge, meanwhile, strolled over to the cashier, the only woman in the room; could this *dame de comptoir* tell him the names of those two experts, he asked. One of them was a M. Journoud, *"un de nos plus forts,"* she told him; she did not know the other. Many strangers came there. In fact, they were expecting an American, a M. Morphy. Their client, M. Arnous de Rivière, had just received a letter, saying that this celebrity was about to leave London for Paris and Herr Harrwitz, a Prussian, who was presently in Valenciennes, would be returning the latter part of the week in order to meet him. . . .

The game between M. Journoud and the stranger had ended in a draw and the crowd around them was breaking up. Paul looked around for Edge and it was a minute or two before he succeeded in locating his friend. Then he spoke with some impatience.

"You know I didn't intend to come here until tomorrow. I've other plans for the rest of the evening."

"Don't you want to come upstairs and see the private quarters of the *Cercle des Échecs?* That's where you'll be playing, unless you'd rather stay in this mob."

"I don't intend to play anywhere tonight and I've seen as much of this place as I want to, for the moment. Do you mind if I call a fiacre and leave you? I'd like to pay a rather private visit."

"Don't be so bashful about it. That's what every young man wants to do when he first gets to Paris—and as long as he stays here."

"We're not talking about the same thing," Paul said coldly. "If what you have in mind attracts you, please don't let me interfere. I'm going to pay my respects to Mrs. Albert Sheppard and her daughters. Suppose we don't try to make connections again until tomorrow morning."

It was a beautiful balmy night, with bright stars shining and a brilliant moon rolling through fleecy clouds which were scattered lightly over a great expanse of clear sapphire sky. Open air cafés, where rubicund waiters bustled back and forth with their trays, were doing a thriving business; and the streets were still thronged with pedestrians. Paul had been fortunate enough to secure an open victoria, instead of a closed hack, and, consequently, could look about him in every direction and savor all he saw to the full. The vehicle was shabby, the horse which drew it skinny, and the driver, who kept muttering unintelligibly beneath his breath, so seedily clad as to emphasize his obvious lack of prosperity. But if his conveyance had been a golden coach, drawn by superb snow-white steeds, and driven by a functionary in elegant livery, Paul's sense of enchantment could have been no greater.

As the victoria rumbled over the cobblestones on its leisurely progress toward the Faubourg St. Germain, the cafés became less numerous and the crowds began to thin. A quiet, not unlike that of the countryside, pervaded these secluded streets; but light still shone from the windows of many houses, including the one on the rue des Saints Pères at which the driver finally drew up behind an elegant, if somewhat somber, private carriage which was already stationed there. As Paul descended from his creaking old vehicle, telling the *cocher* to wait for him, the outer door, which led to a vast courtyard, was opened by a concierge and a tall, bearded man, wearing the ribbon of the Legion of Honor and carrying one of those black bags which, all over the world, signify that their possessor is a physician, came slowly forward from the direction of the monumental building beyond.

"Good evening, *M. le docteur*," Paul said, stepping inside the court, despite the sputtered protests of the concierge, who tried to block his passage. "I'm an old friend of the Sheppards', Paul Morphy of New Orleans. Is it indiscreet to ask if one of the ladies is ill?"

The doctor set down his bag and extended his hand. "M. Morphy? The great chess player whose impending arrival has caused so much excitement?" And, in an aside to the still protesting concierge, he muttered, "*Taisez vous. Ce monsieur est ami de la maison.*"

"I do play chess. I don't know about the excitement," Paul replied, grateful for the prompt intervention and acceptance. "But won't you please tell me . . . it's rather late to be making a professional call, unless there's an emergency."

"Or a social one, either, isn't it?" the doctor inquired with a smile which did much to relieve Paul's anxiety. "But I can understand your concern. The young ladies, I am glad to say, are in blooming health. But Mme Sheppard grows frailer all the time and she suffers increasingly from attacks of faintness, one of which was the cause of my presence here tonight. It is impossible to tell, until such an attack has passed, whether it was merely the result of undue fatigue, emotional strain or a symptom of serious heart trouble. Happily, I have found no indications pointing to a present cardiac disturbance; but I should not have been able to enjoy untroubled rest later on if I had not come when I was called. Madame's circulation is poor at best; she was chilly, even on such a fine evening as this; but when the really severe weather sets in, her condition is bound to cause me grave concern, unless there is a great improvement, which alas! I cannot foresee. She should arrange to leave Paris and go to the Riviera or else return to your New Orleans which, I understand, has a delightful climate."

"And she doesn't want to?"

The doctor shrugged slightly. "I think it is really a matter of indifference to her. She has developed a certain lassitude, an unwillingness to make decisions, especially if they involve moving about. But she has come to have confidence in my treatment of her and, naturally, I must confine my practice to Paris. Undoubtedly, another factor in the situation is that the family is very pleasantly settled here, as you will see when you go in."

"Then it *is* all right for me to go in?"

"Indeed, yes. I hope you did not take my little jest about a social call too seriously. I have given Mme Sheppard a soothing draught, so perhaps it would be better if you did not disturb her tonight. Her elder daughter, Mlle Berenice, is sitting with her and will continue to do so until she is really asleep. But her husband is in town just now and he and Mlle Charmian are in the salon. I have just left them there. Go in, by all means. I am sure they will be delighted to see you. As I am, to have met you."

With a courtly bow and a second word of admonition to the concierge, the doctor passed through the great outer door. Paul saw him walk toward the waiting carriage before he was swallowed up in the dimness of the street. The concierge closed the door, but, though he continued to shake his head and look at Paul suspiciously, he did not try to stop the visitor's rapid progress across the huge paved court, bare except for the low stone posts, looped together by iron chains, which flanked it on either side. Paul was accustomed to large houses built flush to the street, with a patio in the rear, to which a driveway usually led direct; but he had never previously been to one with such a grim and guarded approach. However, the façade which he now faced, though its dimensions were imposing, was less formidable in character than the courtyard; green shutters brightened its dun-colored walls, twin lanterns shone on either side of the entrance and the demilune, by which this was approached, harmonized with its general pattern. Paul needed no second bidding to run up the steps and ring the bell. There was a slight delay about admitting him and he chafed with impatience. Though he could not see them, because of the drawn curtains, he could hear Charmian and her father talking, and it seemed intolerable that he should be made to wait before he was permitted to join them. When the door was finally opened by a manservant, whose startled manner and rumpled uniform both suggested that he had not expected to be summoned again, once the doctor had left, Paul spoke loudly enough to make certain that he would be overheard.

"I am M. Morphy of New Orleans. *M. le docteur*, whom I met, just as he was leaving, assured me that Mlle Charmian and M. Sheppard would be glad to see me."

The words were not out of his mouth before father and daughter appeared in the wide doorway, leading from the drawing room to the front hall, and brushed aside the hesitant servant. Mr. Sheppard wrung his hand warmly and Charmian, without abashment, threw her arms around his neck.

"Come in, come in! Glad to see you! Of course, we're delighted! But we really didn't expect you until tomorrow."

"I'm not supposed to be here, officially, until then. I'm meeting Harrwitz, for the first time, tomorrow noon. But I purposely came a day early, to have an evening—or at least part of an evening—to myself. As a matter of fact, I'd have been here yesterday if we hadn't missed the morning train from London and been obliged to spend the night in Calais—a dismal place, if I ever saw one! Then Fred Edge, who's still with me, played a trick on me; he suggested an after-dinner stroll and, the next thing I knew, he was pushing me inside the Café de la Régence. But at least he had the decency not to give me away and I escaped without being recognized. So of course I came straight here."

"Of course! Come in and sit down. My Missus is a little under the weather and Berenice is staying with her. But I think Berenice will be down in a few minutes. Meanwhile—" He looked from Paul to Charmian and laughed. "Meanwhile, I guess you two wouldn't mind if I went up and had a look at the Missus myself."

"I'm terribly sorry to hear Mrs. Sheppard isn't well. But if you're sure my visit isn't inopportune—"

"Doesn't look that way to me," Mr. Sheppard said, laughing again. Charmian had now taken Paul's arm and, while her father was talking, made small cooing sounds of pleasure.

"Then I wonder. . . . I kept my cab, a victoria. It's such a lovely night, perhaps you'd let Charmian come for a little ride with me, sir."

"*Let* Charmian! I like that! What do you think he is? A sort of jailer?"

"You see," Mr. Sheppard said genially. It was obvious that he was in a very good mood, much better than Paul would have expected on the part of a man whose wife had been sufficiently ill to indicate that a physician should be summoned late in the evening. "No monkey business, though. Paris isn't Gretna Green. And the parsons—I mean the priests—can be pretty shrewd about spotting runaways and pretty stern in dealing with them."

"I assure you, sir—"

"Oh, Paul, can't you ever take a joke? Come, let's go! I don't even need a hat, do I?"

Paul had really hoped to catch a glimpse of Berenice, whom he liked very much and, since Mr. Sheppard had said she would "be down in a few minutes," it was on the tip of the visitor's tongue to suggest that the excursion be delayed that long, even though he had been the one to propose it. But both Mr. Sheppard's joviality which, Paul suspected, might be partly due to the amount of excellent wine he had consumed with the evening meal, and Charmian's unconcealed eagerness to be off, deterred him from making such a suggestion. He shook hands with Mr. Sheppard again and kept abreast of Charmian as she ran quickly down the steps and across the court. She paused long enough to give a few rapid instructions to the concierge, who now looked more surly than ever. But she had leaped lightly into the victoria before Paul could proffer his help.

"I have to sit on your right," she told him. "Otherwise, everyone who sees us out together will think I'm a naturally naughty girl and that you want to let people know you think so, too. You don't, do you? You don't want other people to think so, either, I'm sure."

"You know I think you're the loveliest, sweetest, purest girl in the whole world! You know I'd kill anyone who had the indecency to so much as hint otherwise."

"What are you talking about? You wouldn't kill a fly!"

"Yes I would if—"

"Well, don't let's talk about killing! Let's tell the *cocher* where to go and then settle back for a nice quiet visit with lots of kisses."

"In an open victoria?"

"Of course. Everyone kisses everyone else in Paris, if they want to, even if it isn't any Gretna Green. . . . Have you been to the Bois de Boulogne yet?"

"I haven't been anywhere except from the Gare du Nord to the Meurice to leave my bags and to the Restaurant des Trois Frères Provenceaux to eat my dinner, and down the street to the Café de la Régence where I found myself, as I told you, before I had any idea that was where we were headed. Then I came straight to see you."

"Which, of course, is what you should have done. Now say, 'Cocher, Bois de Boulogne, et allez doucement.' Then you won't need to speak to him again for hours. And, of course, we can put up the top of the victoria, if you want to. But it's pretty dark in the Bois anyway."

He had been completely unconscious of the flight of time, Paul told himself honestly. He could not believe that his watch was right, as he started to wind it, when he was back in his room at the Meurice and saw that the hands were pointing to four o'clock. It was unforgivable that he should have kept Charmian out so long, especially when her mother was ill, that he should have been so late in taking her home that Berenice had long since gone to bed, that only Mr. Sheppard, who gave every indication of having been napping, between brandies, should have good-naturedly waited up for them and said, with a yawn, "Well, I guess boys will be boys and girls will be girls." It was incomprehensible that Paul should have forgotten the real reason why he had come to Paris—to play chess with a formidable antagonist, whom it would require all his skill to defeat. He should have gone to bed early, he should have had a long night's rest; above all, he should have avoided anything that would be emotionally stirring. And instead, he had spent hours riding about a city which, if not actually sleeping—he doubted if Paris ever really slept!—was certainly somnolent, at least in the parts where he had gone in the shabby victoria, with his arm around Charmian's slim yielding waist, and her shining head on his shoulder, except when she raised her lips to meet his. . . .

He undressed and lay down on his bed. But he was too overwrought for sleep. He told himself he must regain his composure, he must stop thinking about Charmian and yearning for her and remember only his obligations to the sponsors who looked confidently forward to his meeting with Harrwitz. But how could he? How could any man, who had spent hours with his beloved after a long separation from her, think of anyone or anything else?

At noon, as agreed, he met Daniel Harrwitz—a small man with a well-developed head and large piercing black eyes—at the Café de la Régence. For the first time, in his long succession of triumphs, Paul lost the game.

SKETCH OF THE GAME OF CHESS

Bon Senior Abn Yachia
Circa 1100

". . . . We have not yet spoken of the woman. She sitteth at the top of the high places of the city. She is clamorous and wilful in her way. She girdeth her loins with strength. Her feet abide not in her house. She moveth in all directions, and turneth about her. Her evolutions are wonderful, her ardor untiring. How beautiful are her steps across the plain!"

The Chess Reader, The Royal Game in World Literature,
compiled by Jerome Salzmann. (Greenberg: Publisher, N.Y.)

23.

Admittedly, the circumstances under which the game was played were unfavorable to Paul, quite aside from his exhausted condition; but he made no effort to justify his defeat by dwelling on these. "Harrwitz won because he made the best moves," he insisted when Edge began to murmur. *"Tu sais, je ne suis pas homme aux excuses."*

He was fond of describing himself in this way when other chess players pleaded illness, lack of preparation, strange surroundings or the burdens of professional duties as alibis for inferior play; and his recent experience with Staunton had made him doubly averse to changing his own attitude. Besides, next to Staunton, there was no antagonist he was as eager to engage as Harrwitz. This Prussian had literally given himself up, body and soul, to chess. He rose early in the morning, went directly to the Café de la Régence, and remained there, playing steadily—except for the brief intermission when he dined—until late in the evening. He followed this schedule with absorption day after day, whereas all others regarded as past masters of the game had supplementary interests and varied pursuits: St. Amant shone in exclusive social circles; Löwenthal was an editor and an analyst; Anderssen a professor of mathematics; Heyderbrandt a diplomat and Löwe a hotelkeeper. True, Staunton had once been as constant in his attendance at the London Divan as Harrwitz now was at the Café de la Régence and had become so rabid on the subject of chess that he actually caused the bosoms and tails of his shirts to be printed with kings, rooks and pawns; but that was before literary pursuits had begun to divert him. There was no possible chance, as far as Paul could see, that Harrwitz could or would find the same excuses as Staunton or invent others. If he, Paul, could beat Harrwitz, he would, in truth, be the chess champion of the world. When his antagonist, delighted with the results of the first game, shook hands with him as they bade each other good-bye, displaying even more cordiality than when they had greeted each other a few hours earlier, and said they had better settle the preliminaries of the match the next day, Paul readily agreed.

"And, in the meantime," Edge said as he and his protégé walked back to the Meurice, "you'll go to bed at once and get a good long sleep."

"I'm sorry to disappoint you. I have an engagement for this evening."

"This evening! Why man, there's no evening left, even by Continental standards! It's night already."

"Very well, I won't argue about phraseology. The point is I want to change my clothes. They're saturated with the smell of smoke. That's why I'm returning to the Meurice. But I'm going straight out again."

"Paul, if you stay out most of the night a second time, the same thing will happen tomorrow that happened today."

"All right then, it will. I'm sure you find this hard to believe, but there are some things that matter to me more than chess."

Again, as when he had been confronted with the deep depression which had engulfed Paul when the latter arrived in England, Edge found that argument was unavailing; and once more it was four o'clock in the morning before the truant returned to the hotel. However, he was ready and waiting for Harrwitz when the Prussian appeared at the Café de la Régence shortly after noon. This time Harrwitz, though he had insisted on playing in one of the large public rooms the day before, willingly adjourned to a private parlor; but, upon arrival there, he began to impose conditions for the match rather than to discuss these. There must be no seconds, he said, and no umpires. Paul, who had not foreseen such a restriction, had already asked two outstanding players from the enemies' camp, de Rivière and Journoud, to act in the former capacity; he was distressed and embarrassed at the idea of withdrawing his invitation; and, though their courteous and understanding attitude did something to assuage his feelings, he could see that these were shared by a newcomer on the scene: Eugene Lequesne, whose supremacy as a sculptor was rivaled by his standing as a chess player. Harrwitz was not popular at the Régence; in fact, many of its habitués had declined to play with him, because of his offensive manners, and he had more than once been obliged to accept a casual visitor to the café as an opponent, because no one else would put up with his insolence. Now, as he delivered his ultimatum, Lequesne glanced anxiously at the outsider; but Paul, despite his chagrin, managed to answer tranquilly.

"I am sorry I did not realize earlier that Herr Harrwitz objected to seconds. But the mistake is mine. I should have acquainted myself better with his habits of play."

"Very well," the Prussian said harshly, "before you make any more mistakes, let me acquaint you further with my habits of play, as you call them —more accurately, the conditions upon which I am willing to play with you. I shall insist that you accept all bets offered and that the winner of the first seven games shall be esteemed the victor."

"Very well," Paul said, still tranquilly.

"And that we shall play only four out of every seven days every week."

"That will suit me admirably," Paul answered, this time smilingly, as he began to visualize more and more leisure for visits to the Hotel d'Ambres and drives through the Bois de Boulogne.

"And the match shall be played in the public part of the café."

This pronouncement was not so easy to meet with a smile. It had been one thing to play with a crowd of onlookers at the tournament in New

York; they were not allowed to approach the contestants and silence was strictly enforced on both groups. At the Régence, there was constant movement, noise and confusion, as in any café; and, to make matters worse, Harrwitz had displayed a rollicking contempt for his antagonist throughout the first game and, at the end of it, had leaned across the table, seized Paul's hand and, turning to the crowd, announced in a jeering voice, "Astonishing! His pulse beats no faster than if he had won!"

To be sure, the public's response to this sally had been less jovial than he had hoped; again, his bad manners had made him offensive to the habitués of the Régence and not a few thought that Morphy would retaliate by refusing to go on with the match and that they would not blame him if he did. Lequesne now felt the same way; although this was his first meeting with Morphy, he had been quick to admire and recognize the other's sensitivity. He was relieved when he heard Paul say, a second time, "Very well," as quietly as he had the first, and add, "Shall we start right away?"

"Why not, now that everything is amicably settled?" Harrwitz responded.

He led the way back to the large smoke-filled main room, selected a table without consulting Paul's choice in the matter and made his first move belligerently. Paul was by this time so weary and so disgusted that his only conscious desire was for escape. Temporarily, he had forgotten that a victory over Harrwitz represented his supreme ambition. He played not only inattentively but carelessly, while Harrwitz smiled sardonically, rolled about in his seat and addressed bystanders in loud and boastful tones. While he did not actually say, "You see? It takes very little trouble to beat this poor young fellow!" the inference was plain and, unfortunately, it was based on fact. For the second time, he was an easy winner.

"Two down and five to go!" he shouted, rising and pushing back his chair.

"Yes, five to go, Herr Harrwitz," Paul answered, gathering up the chessmen.

He still spoke quietly, but there was a different quality in his voice. It was not dull with fatigue, like the infrequent comments he had made during the last few hours; it was steady and purposeful again. He was aware, despite the restrained courtesy of the crowd in the face of the Prussian's boorishness, that he himself had forfeited much of their faith through his listlessness; but, no longer indifferent, he was determined to regain it. He remained where he was for a few minutes, chatting with Lequesne, de Rivière and Journoud; then he bade them good night, said that this time he would follow his mentor's advice about a long sleep, and linked his arm through Fred's as they went out of the door.

"Those chaps will be surprised, won't they," he said, "when Harrwitz starts to lose—and continues to lose from now on?"

Paul was a good prophet. Harrwitz did not win again. During the third and fourth games, Paul scored beautifully, and without hesitation or excitement. At the end of each, he was showered with congratulations from the same persons who, such a short time before, had looked so woefully crestfallen. When he won the fifth game, Harrwitz, whose conduct had become less belligerent, was plainly uncomfortable. In an aside to an acquaintance, he confessed that Morphy was proving stronger than he expected. The next day, Paul received a letter, asking for an "intermission"; Mr. Harrwitz, it appeared, was in "ill health." Paul laughed as he turned the missive over to Edge.

"What are you going to say in reply?" Fred asked with interest.

"Oh, with many expressions of sympathy for his indisposition, I'll suggest a respite of ten days or so. But I think I'll also suggest that when we start playing again, we do so daily, with the exception of Sunday. Meanwhile, I'm not sorry, you know, to have ten days free."

From the beginning, Paul had made no mystery of his visits to the Hotel d'Ambres and, though Fred had at first protested against these, because he saw in them a menace to Paul's prowess at chess, his disapproval had gradually become less outspoken and, as a matter of fact, less intense. When Paul lost the second game with Harrwitz, Fred had referred so angrily to the subject that they had been very close to quarreling; but when Paul agreed to go to the opera with him that evening, instead of rushing off once again to the rue des Saints Pères, he had been somewhat appeased. Paul had not thought it necessary to inform his friend that this change of program did not indicate a corresponding change of heart. Charmian had a previous engagement which she either could not or would not break and, after two rapturous midnight drives through the Bois and the promise of more, Paul had realized that it would be unwise to say or do anything which might cause her to resent a protest on his part. As a matter of fact, if he were not to be with her in a delicious solitude *a deux,* there was nothing which could possibly have given him more pleasure than attending an operatic performance. He had inherited his mother's love for music and might even have excelled her in ability along those lines if he had put as much time and effort into it as she had. Edge, who had not been previously aware of this, was amazed to find how much musical knowledge Paul had acquired, not only while sitting in a *loge grillée* at the Orleans Theatre, but also during the course of the soirées held in the Morphys' drawing room. He listened with respectful attention while his friend informed him that Madame Morphy was herself composing an opera which she had tentatively entitled *Lorraine,* which was still unfinished, but of which they had great hopes; and then went on to analyze, in critical detail, such great works as *William Tell, Il Trovatore* and *Les Huguenots. La Part du Diable,* the production of the present evening, was, of course, rather trivial by comparison; but it served well enough for a pastime, if nothing better offered. . . .

Nothing better offered, as far as Charmian was concerned, for the following evening, either; and again Edge was delighted with Paul's compliance, when the latter consented to accept an invitation for dinner at the residence of a certain Monsieur Doazun, who was himself a chess expert of no mean standing, and who had enjoyed the friendship of Deschappelles and Labourdonnais. Once more Paul's compliance was based not only on a desire to please and placate his friend, but because he was in a favorable position to do so. True, Charmian had been engaged for dinner and the rest of the evening; but she had been free earlier in the day and had suggested that he might like to have tea with her in the garden—it was really worth seeing.

The bait of a garden was quite unnecessary; tea with Charmian, no matter where it was served, would have represented to Paul an ambrosial feast in Elysian Fields. Nevertheless, once seated at a table on a green lawn, near a fountain with a backdrop of an ivied wall and flanked by noble trees and age-old statues, he did not remain unmoved by his surroundings, much less oblivious of them. The severity of the vast entrance court at the front of the palace had left him totally unprepared for the gracious verdure, trickling waters and warm marbles of the grounds at the rear. Actually, it was incorrect to refer to these merely as "a garden"; they comprised a series of gardens, leading from the terrace on which the doors and windows of the ground floor opened. It would have been impossible to believe, beforehand, that such stately spaciousness, combined with such quietude and such luxuriance, could prevail against the noise and crowding of a great city.

Charmian had been waiting for him when he arrived, and had drawn him from the vestibule, paved in great squares of black and white marble— "It looks just like a giant chessboard, doesn't it?" she had asked him laughingly—into a small drawing room for a swift embrace. The others were waiting for them in the garden, she told him; she hadn't been able to arrange, today, for them to have much time alone; they would have to make the most of what they did have. Lacking leisure for the expression of their feelings, they achieved even greater intensity than before; never had Paul permitted himself to clasp Charmian so closely or to kiss her so passionately; never had her response to him seemed so ardent and eager. Neither heard Berenice when she first called from the further end of the terrace, to tell them Papa and Mama were already waiting for them at the tea table; she was obliged to come nearer. Inevitably, Paul realized with some confusion that she must have seen them locked in each other's arms; but this confusion was so permeated with ecstasy that it did not trouble him, especially as Charmian seemed quite unconcerned at the consciousness that Berenice had been a witness to their rapture. Indeed, he told himself triumphantly, this would indicate, more definitely than anything that had happened previously, that he was an accepted and, therefore, a privileged suitor. Berenice greeted him warmly but calmly, her attitude that of an affectionate sister. Surely, everything was well in the best of all possible worlds.

Nevertheless, despite his conviction of this, he was momentarily shocked by the appearance of Mrs. Sheppard. She looked old enough to be the girls' grandmother, instead of their mother, and a grandmother who was ill as well as old. There was not a ray of color in her face, which had lost most of its former beauty; her soft skin had become a mass of wrinkles, and her once abundant golden hair was scanty and had turned snow white. Her loose dress hung in folds on her emaciated form and her heavy rings slipped about so freely on her thin fingers that Paul kept expecting them to fall off. Only her smile was as sweet as ever and her eyes as kind.

"I am so glad to see you, Paul," she said cordially. "Come and sit beside me and tell me about your triumphs."

"I haven't had any in Paris so far, Mrs. Sheppard," he said, accepting the proffered seat.

"Oh, but you will! I do not go out in society any more, because I do not seem to be very strong, just now, and, besides, it is so pleasant here that I am more than content to remain in this lovely garden and Berenice insists on staying with me, most of the time. But my husband and Charmian assure me that everyone regards you as the coming sensation of the season."

"Indeed they do," Charmian agreed. "The reason I couldn't ask you to dine here last night or the night before, Paul, was because we were going to parties both evenings, one given by the Duchess de Trevisse and the other by the Princess Mathilde. And in both places everyone was talking about you. The Princess wants you to come to her next soirée; she told me to invite you. I thought perhaps we could go together. She has a perfectly wonderful house on the rue de Courcelles and receives every Tuesday. You'd like to go, wouldn't you? You'd see everyone worth knowing in Paris there."

"I see everyone I really want to see here and now," he said, glancing happily around the table, "and I can't imagine a more wonderful place than this."

"That's because you haven't been anywhere else yet, except to that horrible café. But you'll change your mind when you see the Princess and her house. Won't he, Papa?"

"He might. And then again he mightn't. I understand this one has some special attraction for him."

They all laughed, as if Mr. Sheppard had said something extraordinarily witty and original. Berenice had unobtrusively taken over the task of pouring the tea, for her mother's frail fingers were now shaking uncontrollably.

But, as her family seemed to be accepting her condition without anxiety, Paul thought that perhaps it was not as serious as it seemed. She went on talking to him in her kindly way.

"You must feel free to come here whenever you have leisure and inclination, Paul," she said. "If my husband and Charmian are not at home, Berenice and I will always be glad to see you. And you have a friend with you in Paris, haven't you? A Mr. Edge? Next time you come to tea, you must bring him with you."

And that could be a very good idea, for more reasons than one, Paul said to himself as he thanked her. Fred and Berenice might take a liking to each other—why not? Fred was a personable, as well as an agreeable fellow, and Berenice could easily have passed for a beauty had it not been necessary for her to bear comparison with Charmian; and not even Charmian had a more delightful manner or more lively intelligence. He appreciated the devotion of Berenice to her invalid mother, but he hoped this would not deprive her of the normal pleasures to which her youth entitled her—pleasures such as he and Charmian enjoyed. But no, that would be too much to expect, because no one in the whole world had as much to offer a man as Charmian, no other man was as fortunate as he.

He glanced across the table and caught her eye. She looked him full in the face, smiled and bit her lip ever so slightly; he could see two white teeth resting on it for a minute and then the lips parted a little before they came together again. The movement was so quick and so subtle that he was sure no one but himself could have noticed it, but in it he read an invitation. Before he left that afternoon, they must embrace again and when he kissed her, it must be not only passionately, but fiercely and questingly. He had not yet proved his power to wound or even bruise in the name of love and she wanted him to do so; his essential gentleness had prevented him from realizing this. He had not yet discovered all the secret sweetness of that beautiful red mouth; his essential reserve had prevented him from seeking it. . . .

He was not sure whether or not he should give her a signal that he had understood. But the sudden temptation to do so was so strong that he could not resist it. He nodded ever so slightly, before turning away to devote his undivided attention to her mother.

"Who is this Princess that Charmian is talking about?" he asked, not caring at all, but conscious that at least he must pretend interest.

"Why, don't you know?" Charmian exclaimed, setting down her cup. The question had not been addressed to her, but it was obvious she felt her mother unequal to answering it. "She's the Emperor's first cousin and a great favorite of his—in fact, when they were both very young, they were engaged, but the match was broken off for family reasons and she married a horrible Russian prince instead. Now she's legally separated from the brute and lives her own life—a perfectly wonderful life. She's rich, she's beautiful, she's the toast of Paris, she has I don't know how many admirers at her feet. But she doesn't care about any of them, except—"

"That'll do, young lady. No need to try and tell Paul about the Princess all at once. Leave a little for him to find out for himself. . . . How about it, Mother? Finished your tea? Beginning to find it a little chilly?"

Mrs. Sheppard had, it appeared, finished her tea and did not care for any cake. Her appetite, she told Paul apologetically, did not seem to be very hearty. And yes, her husband, who was always so thoughtful, was right; she was beginning to notice a change in the air, now that the sun was setting. Perhaps she had better go into the house. But she hoped Paul would not hurry away on that account. And he was to remember they were expecting him back soon and that he was to bring Mr. Edge when he came the next time.

She rose, gathering a shawl of lacy white wool around her and took her husband's arm. Albert seconded his wife's invitation and they moved slowly away in the direction of the terrace. Paul had rather expected that Berenice would go with them. Instead, she poured herself another cup of tea and helped herself to more cake.

"I don't think any of us have told you the history of this house, Paul," she said, "and it's really very interesting. Wouldn't you like to hear something about it?"

Actually, there was nothing Paul wanted less at that moment. He looked from one sister to the other and saw that Charmian was again biting her lower lip and that the expression of Berenice was inscrutable. He swallowed hard.

"Yes, very much," he said, because it was obvious he could say nothing else.

"It was built by the *grand aumonier* of Louis XIII, but he ruined himself with its costly construction. So he was forced to rent it and Queen Christina of Sweden leased it for her Ambassador, the famous Hugo de Groot. After that, it was bought by the Duchess of Villars, who spent another fortune on it. When she died, she left it to her niece, the Marquise de Tourcelles. Eventually, just before the Revolution, it was occupied by the Marquis de Flammaran."

"You're skipping," Charmian interrupted. "If you're bound to tell history, why not the spicy parts as well as the stupid parts? The poor Marquise de Tourcelles never got much fun out of the place, because her mean old husband clapped her into prison and managed to keep her there. He thought she was too frivolous and flirtatious. Just the same, she loaned it to the Marquis de Cavoye, whom she liked very, very much, just as the Princess

Mathilde likes Monsieur de Nieuwerkerque very, very much, even if Papa did shut me up when I tried to tell you about him. By-and-by, this favorite gentleman of the marquise bought it. Lots of people still call it the Hotel de Cavoye, instead of the Hotel d'Ambres, though it's been in Jacques' family a long time now. By the way, did you meet Jacques while you were in London?"

"No, I'm sorry to say I didn't. Philip Dallas very kindly tried to arrange it, but there never seemed to be a time when we were all free."

"Oh well, you'll see him when you go back. You are going back to London, aren't you?"

"Yes, in November."

There was a short silence. Charmian crumpled the last piece of cake to which she had helped herself and glanced first at Paul and then at Berenice.

"Aren't you going on with your history lesson?" she asked her sister. "You haven't told Paul about the *boiseries* yet—that those in the banqueting hall came from the Hotel de Crillon and those in the main drawing room from the Hotel Saint Senoch. I'm sure all that would be vitally interesting to him. And don't forget the marble mantelpieces, either, or the portrait of Villars by Tournière or any of the rest of it."

It was impossible to escape the note of sarcasm that had crept into her voice. Paul tried to do so and, to his distress, found that he could not. But Berenice, if she were aware of it, seemed undisturbed by it.

"Why don't we show him these treasures, instead of telling him about them?" she asked in her calm way. "I think Papa and Mama are right, it is getting a little cool."

"I'm not in the least cool. I think this is the pleasantest part of day in a garden. Don't you, Paul?"

It was, undeniably, very pleasant. The shadows were beginning to lengthen under the great trees and the birds were beginning their twilight twitter; the musical sound of the fountain's trickling water mingled with their chirping. An early moon, still only a slender crescent, shone in a sky which had changed in color from turquoise to sapphire and its beams silvered the statues. If only he and Charmian could be alone here. . . .

A footman came quickly across the terrace and, approaching the table, began to gather up the tea service. As he did so, he spoke in an aside to Berenice and she rose hesitantly.

"Mama has sent for me," she said. "I'm afraid I must go. Are you sure you won't come, too, Charmian?"

"Of course I'm sure," Charmian said shortly.

"Then we'll see the *boiseries* another time, Paul."

Berenice walked slowly in the direction of the house and twice she stopped, as if still doubtful whether or not to go on. Once she turned around and waved to them. Paul waved in return, but Charmian sat stubbornly still.

"Berenice is spying on us," she said angrily. "She saw us kissing each other, before we came out."

"Yes, I believe she did. Just the same, I don't think she was shocked. She realizes we love each other, that I want nothing in the world so much as to marry you."

"I don't know that she was shocked. She may have been, because she's a terrible prude. But that's not the main reason she doesn't want you to kiss me, that she was determined not to leave us. She's jealous."

"Berenice jealous! You're dreaming!"

"Didn't it ever occur to you that she's in love with you?"

"Of course not! She's fond of me in a sisterly way and I'm very glad she is. I'm fond of her, too, in a brotherly way. But—"

"But you weren't ever tempted to kiss her—in a brotherly way?"

"No, of course not. I've never been tempted to kiss anyone but you."

"Do you expect me to believe that?"

"Yes. In the first place, because it happens to be true. In the second place, because I've told you so and I want to feel that you rely on my word."

"All right, I believe you. And now you must believe me when I tell you something."

"What is it?"

"That you need more practice in kissing."

It was hardly a wonder that, when Paul returned to the Hotel Meurice, Edge could not have asked for a more jocund companion. As they dressed for Mr. Doazun's dinner, Paul described the gardens of the Hotel d'Ambres, repeated, parrot-like, what he had learned of its history, and informed Edge that the latter was included in the next invitation to tea. Fred was understandably pleased and flattered. He was also moved to more curiosity about the owner of the Hotel d'Ambres and the reason for its loan to the Sheppards than he had previously felt.

"You say this hotel, as you call it—I must say I think that's a damn queer way to talk about a palace—belongs to the Marquis d'Ambres and that he's loaned it to the Sheppards. How did he happen to do so?"

"I've told you that, too. He's an attaché of the French Legation in London. He won't be needing it for a long time himself and, according to Phil Dallas, there's nothing he enjoys more than making a beau geste."

"I see . . . how old is this noble marquis?"

"Why—I don't know. I didn't ask."

"Is he married?"

"I didn't ask that, either. What difference does it make?"

"None, I suppose. Except that if he had a wife he might not feel so free to make a beau geste in the direction of a family with two marriageable daughters."

"Nonsense! He made it chiefly on Mrs. Sheppard's account. She's a pitiful invalid. She doesn't go out at all. That beautiful garden is a godsend to her. D'Ambres must have known it would be."

"I see," Fred remarked again. "So you're sure he isn't sweet on either of those charming girls?"

"No, I didn't say that. Of course he may be. I imagine a good many hopeful gentlemen are. But I am sure there wasn't any bargain about this, that he wasn't given any encouragement. Because neither of those charming girls is sweet, as you call it, on him. They both have other interests."

"I see," Fred remarked a third time. And the subject was not mentioned again.

As might have been expected, Mr. Doazun's dinner was a great success.

"The gaps in his match with Harrwitz enabled Morphy to meet the amateurs of Paris, against whom he scored his usual success; and the general treatment accorded to him was some consolation for Harrwitz's bad conduct. A correspondent of the American *Chess Monthly* thus describes the situation: 'Behold our young hero in the Café de la Régence. . . . Crowds flock to see him. "Does anyone believe," exclaims St. Amant, "that it is not the season and that there is nobody in Paris? Let them go to the Café de la Régence and glance at the throng of spectators who look on in admiration while Morphy, the young American, displays his wonderful attainments." . . . Honours are showered upon the head of the eminent champion. Famous sculptors like Lequesne ask him to sit for his bust in marble; he is asked to dine with dukes; audiences notice his visits to the theatre; and poets and men of genius flatter him. And amid all this Gallic pride exults in the fact that he is half a Frenchman.'

"After beating Harrwitz, Morphy announced that he would meet no Paris player at less odds than Pawn and Move, though he did not insist on this with Arnous de Rivière, who had become a personal friend. As Harrwitz was in no mood to admit that he had lost the match just terminated by his resignation, Morphy extended the challenge at Pawn and Move to him also, with no result, as might have been expected. The Paris amateurs who, in casual games, accepted these or higher odds all justified Morphy's estimate of their strength as compared with his own. It is true that he let amiable and titled ladies, who eagerly invited him to their *salons*, win games of him—but these, very rightly, have not been preserved for publication."

Morphy's Games of Chess, Philip W. Sergeant. (Bell & Sons Ltd., London.)

24.

At the end of ten days, Herr Harrwitz declared himself sufficiently well to play again and again was beaten, which left a score of Morphy four, Harrwitz two, drawn none. The Prussian immediately suffered another relapse.

Paul had enjoyed every minute of the interval which had been free from chess and, to a lesser but by no means inconsiderable degree, so had Edge. Both had been frequent visitors at the Hotel d'Ambres and Edge had instantly fulfilled Paul's hopes by losing his heart to Berenice. Though her calm cordiality could not be interpreted as encouragement to his ardor, he admired her all the more because, as he put it, inelegantly but effectively, it was plain to see that she was not one of those girls who would drop into your mouth like a ripe cherry. Her devotion to her mother was another attribute which appealed to him strongly; far from resenting the amount of time she spent with the invalid, he was convinced she would reveal the same amount of unselfishness in all her relationships. He did not complain because she did not have more leisure for visitors and almost none at all for going out; he set this down both to her present credit and as a good omen for the future.

As far as Charmian was concerned, he was quite content to leave his friend a clear field. He acknowledged and praised her beauty, but he was sincere in saying that Berenice was more his type. Paul, though puzzled by such a declaration, was so glad to take it at face value that he did not question it. Nothing, he told himself blissfully, could have been more ideal than his present position in relation to every one of the Sheppards. Berenice continued to treat him like a fondly regarded brother, Mrs. Sheppard like the son whom she had desired in vain, Mr. Sheppard like a prospective son-in-law who was wholly acceptable. To be sure, when Paul again broached the subject of an official betrothal, Mr. Sheppard staved him off, but much less emphatically than he had the first time. Now that Paul had achieved his majority, he would, of course, be justified in feeling that his suit should not be dismissed as a boyish fancy; he was old enough to give serious consideration to matrimony and to have such consideration treated with respect. On the other hand, he had not settled down yet, as far as either locale or profession was concerned; he was traveling from place to place, committed to a series of chess tournaments. Once he was back in New Orleans and had begun the practice of law, they would discuss the subject of a formal engagement again, and Mr. Sheppard had no doubt that they would see eye to eye in the matter. Meanwhile, Charmian was getting a good deal out of her European experience, and her father thought it was better to keep to its present pattern, at least for the time being. Once *she* had settled down, she couldn't expect to have her present opportunities, which were educational, as well as enjoyable. Besides, Charmian was the sort of girl—as Paul probably did not have to be reminded—who would need to have her fling some time and it was much better that she should do so now rather than later. Mr. Sheppard did not see that Paul would gain anything by having the engagement announced; as far as her father could make out, Charmian was giving her suitor as many privileges as any man had a right to expect until he was actually married.

It was because this was indeed the case and Paul in no position to deny it, that he did not press his point any further. Whenever he and Charmian were by themselves, she accepted and returned his embraces without hesitation. As a matter of fact, she often seemed to invite them, as she had that first day in the garden. She showed no embarrassment when they were occasionally surprised in each other's arms, and she not infrequently took his hand in hers or leaned against his shoulder in the presence of her parents and her sister, who all seemed to take such caresses for granted. It was unimaginable to any gently bred Creole that a girl of good breeding and good character would permit, much less encourage, such liberties on the part of a man whom she did not regard as her future husband. Indeed, though the code was now somewhat less rigid than in the days of Alonzo and Telcide, Paul felt sure that his brother Edward had never been as "privileged" as he was himself, during the period of courtship. He might well consider himself fortunate—and he did!—because of such discrepancy in customs as apparently existed between those of New England and those of the Deep South. As long as he and Charmian and all her family knew that she was his prospective bride, and he was allowed to treat her as such, what did it matter whether or not the rest of the world knew of his supreme good fortune?

It was, of course, the intervals when they were by themselves that gave him the most intense happiness. He nearly always found Charmian waiting for him in the small drawing room which led from the vestibule with the "chessboard" pavement, and which seemed to him an ideal mise-en-scène for love making. The *grand salon* beyond, with its white *boiseries*, its immense crystal chandeliers, its endless expanse of polished parquetry and its stiff, scattered Louis XIV furniture, struck him as not only formal but forbidding of both aspect and atmosphere; there was always a certain chilliness about it. But the *petit salon*, with its wall covering of crimson brocade, its incidental panels of green and gold, its jewel-toned Persian rugs, its glowing family portraits and its charming bibelots was warm and friendly and intimate. On cool days—and there were soon an increasing number of these— a fire burned under the marble mantel and, at dusk, candles flickered beneath shades of rose-colored silk. Only the firelight and the candlelight illumined the room; otherwise, it was engulfed with kindly shadows.

Next to the sweet privacy of the *petit salon,* Paul came to value the hours spent in the garden, where the tea table was always laid on sunny days and where the Sheppards sat at leisure with their more familiar friends. Paul and Fred quickly became part of the congenial group and, from this, their circle expanded to embrace the *haut monde* at whose soirées they were also welcome guests. The first invitation from the Princess Mathilde was swiftly followed by a second and a third; but next to the Sheppards, the house that Paul was soon visiting most often was that of the Baronne de la Sange, a beautiful West Indian who insisted she was drawn to him "because he was a lazy Creole like herself." As a matter of fact, she had achieved almost as exalted a status as a hostess as the Princess Mathilde; she was renowned as the patroness of the arts, and the most celebrated sculptors, painters and authors flocked to her salon every week. But there was nothing of the pedant about her; she was witty rather than learned and possessed of such abundant health and spirits that she never showed the slightest sign of strain, fatigue or depression. With Morphy opposite her and St. Amant or Lequesne at her side to stop her when she made a serious mistake, she would play game after game, meanwhile keeping the entire company in a state of merriment by her sallies; and when she found that her fellow Creole was almost as fond of music as he was of chess, she included the principal singers from the opera in her guest list, and even prevailed upon the famous baritone, Graziani, to play against Paul with odds of Queen. Afterward, the great singer referred to the match, in which he eventually played not only one game but three, jestingly and at the same time proudly. "I am accused of not taking my lessons with Préti seriously enough," he said. "Hereafter, when anyone asks me if I understand chess, I shall say, 'Certainly; I sometimes play with Mr. Morphy!'"

Before coming to Paris, Paul had been under the impression that the creation, direction and expansion of soirées was wholly a feminine prerogative. He was permanently disabused of this conviction by Count Casabianca, who was "at home" every Friday evening and who, while providing opportunities for whist, écarté and other card games for his guests, was himself always to be found in a corner with the Duke of Brunswick, Count Isouard, Signor Préti—Graziani's teacher—and other devotees of chess. This was the group which claimed Paul as its own, not only at these Friday receptions, but on every other logical occasion and some which seemed far less logical. The Duke of Brunswick declined to be separated from a chessboard even when he went to the opera; and when Paul and Fred were invited to share his *avant scène loge* at a performance of *Norma,* Paul found he was expected to sit with his back to the stage, playing chess from the beginning to the end of the evening!

It was, perhaps, this experience, more than any one other, that made him feel that he had had enough, at least for the present, of being a social lion or, more exactly, merely a social lion. St. Amant had spoken truly when he said Paul supplied a want which Paris had been feeling for some time—the want of a hero. Lequesne had asked for the honor of making his bust; the press of Paris had begun to print humorous bits about him; he never had a free evening. Paul had been understandably pleased and flattered by these various indications of his growing fame, and he neither sought nor desired to change his mode of life during the first "intermission" for which Harrwitz asked; as he told Edge, he was by no means sorry to have ten days free. But when the Prussian asked for a second respite, Paul announced his intention of playing eight blindfold games, simultaneously, in the public café.

The announcement caused great excitement. The press heralded the news; crowds of strangers came pouring into the Régence, eagerly questioning its habitués, who were, at first, no better informed than outsiders as to the particulars of the approaching performance. When it became known Morphy had insisted that, if he played blindfold at all, the café must be open to anyone who chose to walk in, public enthusiasm became almost unbounded and the proprietor, M. Delaunay, was equally delighted: it was easy enough to see that, under these circumstances, the exhibition would draw immense crowds to his establishment. He began to entertain a very friendly feeling for M. Morphy.

It was next announced that the blindfold struggle would begin at noon and, long before this, the crowd of onlookers had begun to assemble. A space had been roped off for Paul at one end of the main hall, beyond the billiard tables, some of which had been removed to create more room, and a large easy chair had been placed for him in the enclosure thus formed. Edge, who was exceedingly anxious about his protégé, tried to assure as much bodily comfort as possible, for his concern was well grounded. Paul was very far from well. He had never cared much for wine and had insisted, against all advice, on drinking the unfiltered Paris water. The consequences of this had already been intermittently disastrous. Now, on this day of days, he was in considerable bodily pain which he was unable to conceal from his friend. Eventually, he did not even try to do so.

"I don't know how I'm going to get through my work," he said despairingly. "I'm afraid I'll be obliged to keep leaving the room. If I do, some evil-minded persons are going to be sure that I'm examining positions outside." Edge did his best to be reassuring, but he, too, was troubled.

The eight boards for Paul's antagonists, forming a redoubtable phalanx, were separated from him by the billiard tables which still remained in the principal room of the café, and by the immense crowd of onlookers. White-aproned waiters, carrying well-laden trays, wove their way back and forth among elegant silk-hatted, frock-coated gentlemen, who were alert to every move; and the shabbier element among the habitués, usually so much in evidence, though now in the minority, also made its excitement evident. A few insatiable readers spread out their newspapers and smoked their cigars, pretending that the exhibition was of no interest to them; but every now and then they failed to resist the temptation of casting covert glances in the direction of the armchair where Paul sat with his back to the assembly, and straining to hear his pronouncements. De Rivière called the moves for the first four boards, Journoud for the second, and everything was soon progressing swimmingly. Potier, playing at number six, rose from his table to show on another board how Morphy had actually "seen" seven moves in advance. Préti, playing at number seven, became increasingly agitated as Paul put shot after shot into his bull's-eye. Baucher, playing at number one, was the first to give in. Bornemann, at number three, soon followed with Préti, Bierworth at number two with Potier; Guibert at four and Lequesne at five effected drawn battles and Seguin at eight was left alone. Though all the combatants were considered masters of the game, he was admittedly strongest of all. It was not surprising that he was the last to go down to defeat. The surprise—to him and to everyone else—lay in the fact that he was not, after all, unbeatable.

When this was proved, pandemonium broke loose. Contrary to his fearful expectation, Paul had not once been obliged to leave his seat. Now he stepped from the armchair in which he had been immovable for ten consecutive hours, without having tasted a morsel of food or taken a sip of water during the entire period; yet he was apparently as fresh as when he sat down. English and American spectators, of whom many were present, burst into lusty cheers and the French joined them as the whole crowd rushed toward the hero of the day. The waiters of the café had conspired beforehand to carry Paul out in triumph on their shoulders, but they could not get near him and were finally obliged to abandon the effort. Huge bearded men grasped his hands, almost shaking his arms out of their sockets, and nearly an hour passed before the gigantic Pierre Morel, assisted by Mr. Thomas Bryant of New York, succeeded in fighting a passage through the crowd. In the street, the scene was repeated. The multitude was even greater than in the café, the shouting even more deafening. Morphy, Bryant, de Rivière and Edge tried to make for the Palais Royal; but the crowd pursued them and, when they reached the Guard House of the Imperial Guard, sergeants de ville and soldiers came running out to see whether or not a new revolution, like that of 1848, was in progress. Somehow a private upstairs room at the Restaurant Foy was finally reached and, as the good companions did justice to an excellent supper, Paul called off the moves of the day's games.

The following noon, he began his next game with Harrwitz and, at the fifty-ninth move, the Prussian "resigned." This time, the resignation proved final.

The health of Mr. Harrwitz was obviously causing him great concern. Paul, who was now really ill, since he was suffering from the results of a severe chill, as well as digestive troubles, was glad enough to be through with this disagreeable antagonist and hopeful that he need never hear of him again, in connection with his own games. However, an unexpected difficulty arose regarding the stakes. The Prussian had not deigned to consult his backers when he threw in the sponge, or even to tell them that it was his intention to do so; they were furious for, like Paul and Fred, they were convinced that Harrwitz was a *malade imaginaire* or, that if he actually were ill, the indisposition was mental rather than physical. When Lequesne, who had acted as stakeholder, arrived at the hotel to turn over the substantial sum of 290 francs to the winner, he made no attempt to conceal the fact that the debts of honor had been grudgingly paid.

Paul was horrified. It had never been his desire to play for money, under any circumstances, and he had consented to do so, in this instance, simply because of the condition that Harrwitz had imposed at the beginning: that Morphy was to accept, unquestioningly, any bets which were offered during the match. Now, considering the generally strange and unpleasant situation which Harrwitz had himself precipitated, nothing would induce him, Paul, to take a penny.

Lequesne withdrew, with understandable confusion, to return a few days later with a suggestion, which he hoped would be soothing to M. Morphy's injured feelings: the different subscribers to the stakes were desirous that he should receive the sums that he had unquestionably won; however, they also felt that Herr Harrwitz should play out the remainder of the match and, to appease his backers, he would consent to do so.

"But he has resigned the contest!" Paul protested, his growing annoyance tinged with bewilderment. "How is it possible to go on with it when he's already put an end to it?" And, as Lequesne shrugged his shoulders without answering, Paul added, "Of course, we could start another match. I'm willing to do that—immediately."

This, however, was not at all what Harrwitz had in mind; he unhesitatingly declined to consider anything of the sort. Meanwhile, letters were pouring in from all quarters, complaining that bets on the result of the contest were influenced by Morphy's refusal to accept the stakes, and when Lequesne frantically brought the 290 francs to him the second time, he consented to receive them. Nothing, however, could persuade him to keep them; he deposited them with M. Delaunay, the proprietor of the Régence, at the same time making a public announcement: subscribers to any part of the sum in question, who were still dissatisfied with the turn things had taken, were at perfect liberty to withdraw from it the amount to which they felt entitled. If, after this had been done, there were any money left, perhaps it could be used to defray the expense to which Adolph Anderssen would be put if he left his Breslau Gymnasium in order to play with Morphy in Paris.

The suggestion was not made seriously. Nevertheless, to Paul's great satisfaction, this was exactly how the money was ultimately used.

For some time, he had toyed with the idea of visiting the principal chess centers in Germany, thus responding to urgent invitations; but as long as there was still a chance that he might return to England in November, for the match to which Staunton had committed himself in Birmingham, he hesitated to put any additional distance between himself and London, still more to move from place to place in such a way that correspondence might be slow in catching up with him, as had happened before. He was convinced that Staunton would be only too glad to seize on any possible pretext for saying that the responsibility for their failure to meet lay at Paul's door. Early in October, he had written a long letter to the Englishman which revealed that he had been deeply hurt by the latter's public sneers about the lack of seconds and stakes, and recapitulating what had passed between them. Then he had added: "Permit me to repeat what I have invariably declared in every chess community I have had the honor of entering, that I am not a professional player—that I never wished to make any skill I possess the means of pecuniary advancement—and that my earnest desire is never to play for any stake but honor. My friends in New Orleans, however, subscribed a certain sum, without any countenance from me, and that sum has been ready for you a considerable time past. Since my arrival in Paris, I have been assured by numerous gentlemen that the value of those stakes can be immediately increased to any amount; but, for myself personally, reputation is the only incentive I recognize."

He might have added that, besides the "numerous gentlemen" who had offered to increase the stakes to any amount, the Princess Mathilde, addressing Edge in the hearing of all her guests, had exclaimed at one of her soirées, "Please tell M. Morphy from me that for ten thousand pounds against Mr. Staunton or any other player in Europe, he must go no further than this house!" Indeed, the temptation to do this had been very strong, for no sponsor in Europe enjoyed more prestige than the Princess. But his adherence to the Creole code of silence, where any gentlewoman was involved, prevented him from making such a proud boast. He contented himself, as far as seconds were concerned, by saying he was sure these could be found at St. George's, and again requested Staunton to fix a date for their match, since "early November" had obviously proved inconvenient. He did not refrain from adding that he was sending copies of his letter to the *Illustrated London News, Bell's Life, Era, Field* and *The Sunday Times*; he was all too sure, by now, that Staunton's sense of propriety would not compel him, on his own initiative, to make the letter public.

Staunton's answer had been prompt, but it had been crushing: he definitely withdrew from any promise he might have made to play a match; his work prevented him from getting adequate practice; perhaps if Morphy visited England again they might play a few games *sans façon*.

That was all.

As a result of this correspondence, an acrimonious wrangle began in the chess columns of English periodicals and, though the great majority of contributors to these were on Morphy's side, his injured feelings and hurt pride, far from being assuaged, were lacerated over and over again as the undignified dispute went on. To be sure, his conscience was clear and it seemed to him that this was also true of his case. He had come to Europe above all to play Staunton, whom he complimented by regarding as the leading master in Europe. Perhaps erroneously, but at least in good faith, he had taken Staunton's statement of April 3rd to mean that the champion was ready to play him in London; and, if he had been mistaken, Staunton could have easily corrected his wrong impression as soon as they met at the St. George's. Far from doing this, he had let Morphy continue to think that a match would be played sometime in 1858 if the young American would wait until Staunton could find a convenient date. And finally, he had ridiculed his opponent as an adventurer without backing and furtively hinted that he was a professional.

If the contest with Harrwitz had ended more happily, Paul could, perhaps, have dismissed easily from his mind his grievance against Staunton. However, though he had not only played with the Prussian, but defeated him, the conditions under which the match had taken place and the hard feeling at the end, about stakes, had depressed him deeply. Now, just as he had hoped that a victory over Harrwitz, who had beaten Staunton, might be a compensation for the contest that had never taken place in England, so he felt that a victory over Anderssen who was, by all accounts, both a gentleman and a scholar, and who had won the International Tournament of 1851, would more than compensate for all previous unpleasant experiences at the chess table. What was more, such a victory would prove, beyond any shadow of a doubt, that he, Paul Morphy, was the Chess Champion of the world.

Under all these circumstances, his tentative plan of a trip to Germany was entirely logical. On the other hand, even after there was no further danger of missing connections with Staunton if he undertook it, there were various reasons why he was loath to leave Paris. One of these was the state of his health. Though he had always declined to use this as an excuse for not fulfilling his engagements and looked with contempt on those who did, he was beginning to suffer the consequences of his refusal to do so. He and Fred had now moved from the elegant Meurice to the less pretentious Hotel de Breteuil, which was also pleasantly located on the rue de Rivoli; and their apartment, facing the Tuileries Gardens, was sunny and spacious. Paul could be kept very comfortable there; and the physician, who was now attending him and who had finally succeeded in persuading him to stay abed, was horrified at the mere suggestion that he might go to Breslau or Berlin, or both. If his patient had not been able to endure the rigors of the Parisian climate, so much more severe than those to which he was accustomed, how could he possibly expect to thrive in cities still further north? The contention was probably more effective because Paul had been leeched and was too weak for much argument. He watched the doctor depart without attempting any, then turned to Edge and asked him, with a wan smile, to hazard a guess as to how much blood had been lost.

"Oh, three or four pints, I should guess," Edge answered cheerfully. "I don't believe there's another drop in my body."

Paul closed his eyes and lay quite still, trying to determine for himself his best course of action. It was true that he felt too ill to undertake a long journey, even though this could be made by train and therefore would probably be less disastrous in its consequences than another sea voyage, and that in winter. But there was another reason why he did not want to leave Paris: a trip to Germany would mean separation from Charmian, whom he now saw daily except when he was actually confined to his bed. Was even a victory over Anderssen worth such a separation? For a chess player, yes, of course. For a lover, no, of course not. Which was he, primarily?

His good sense should have told him. As a chess player, only Anderssen was left to challenge his supremacy and a match between them would quickly settle that question, with the odds in his favor. As a lover, he was still far from his desired goal. True, it had never occurred to him to make Charmian his mistress—marriage, not a liaison, was his aim; and, though he had been tempted, over and over again, to claim her completely, he had so far always succeeded in resisting. It was no thanks to her that this was so; if he had taken her, he could not possibly have reproached himself for seduction; though she had never said this, in so many words, he knew that she was not only conscious of his temptation, but ready and willing to have him yield to it. It was he, not she, who had kept her chastity inviolate. But he told himself that it was her very innocence which was responsible for her attitude. She knew, as well as he did, that many, perhaps most, of the great ladies in the world where she now moved so easily and gracefully had lovers, and she saw no reason why she should not do the same. He found himself unable to explain to her. He could not say that these were matrons, whereas she was a virgin; that would seem to infer that the marriage vow was not one which need be taken seriously, and this was the last thing he wanted to do. When she became his wife, he would expect her to take it seriously, indeed he would feel dishonored if she did not. He often felt that, in all fairness, he should go again to her father and plead for the formal betrothal which would lead, without delay, to the altar. But he had done this twice already and twice had been rebuffed. Albert Sheppard was a man who did not brook interference with his decisions and he had decided that the time was not yet ripe for matrimony; if Paul were too insistent, he might well find himself deprived of his present "privileges" and that would be heartbreaking—for himself and, he fondly believed, for Charmian, also. It was much better to drift along as they were. Mrs. Sheppard, he felt sure, had no idea that such drifting was dangerous for her daughter; possibly Berenice was wiser, but no small part of her wisdom was revealed through her silence.

Edge made no attempt to break in on his friend's reveries. But the day after the leeching, he came into Paul's room and sat down on the bed, obviously the bearer of important tidings.

"You can forget about going to Germany," he said in a triumphant tone.

"What are you talking about? I can't forget it. That's just the trouble."

"It shouldn't be any trouble at all. Anderssen is coming here to play with you."

"Fred, I don't think much of your joke."

"It isn't a joke. Your friends at the Régence have acted on your suggestion that the money from those damned stakes might be used to pay Anderssen's expenses to Paris."

"But I didn't make that suggestion seriously. I knew he couldn't leave his classes."

"Not during term time. There's nothing to prevent his having a vacation when his pupils do, at Christmastime. Or so he says. In fact, he's already accepted the invitation."

"But I can't wait for him that long! I'm supposed to go home for Christmas."

"You're not supposed to do anything of the sort. In the first place, your doctor won't hear of it. If he advised you against a train trip to Berlin, how do you suppose he feels about a trans-Atlantic crossing in December? Well, I'll tell you: he feels it would be suicidal. I've already written your mother to that effect. You ought to be getting a letter from her any day now, saying that she understands perfectly, that she'd be much easier to have you stay where you are. There are plenty of Christmases ahead that you can spend in New Orleans . . . what's more," Fred went on, lighting a cigar, "I've just had an interesting talk with the Sheppards about a Christmas celebration. When I saw you were settling down to take a nap, I decided it would be a good chance for me to pay a little visit at the rue des Saints Pères. And Charmian told me to ask if you remembered a Christmas party at their house in New Orleans that you went to years ago?"

"Yes," said Paul shortly. "I remember it. What else did she say?"

"Only that mistletoe grows in France, too."

ADOLF ANDERSSEN

"Chess supremacy passed into English hands when, in 1843, a twenty-one-game match between Pierre de Saint-Amant and Howard Staunton, the acknowledged successors of De Labourdonnais and MacDonnell, was won by the English master, with a score of 11 wins, 6 losses, and 4 draws. Saint-Amant had won a previous match, and after losing six games of the second match in short order, he had come back so strongly that a third contest was proposed by his backers. Staunton found an excuse not to play, and the French never really conceded his superiority.

"Meanwhile, the standard of chess had risen to a high level in all countries, and it was recognized that only a tournament in which the leading players of the different nations competed could decide where the chess crown belonged. The Great Exhibition of London in 1851 offered an opportunity of organizing such an international contest. It was won by the German Adolf Anderssen, a teacher of mathematics at a high school in Breslau. His play had extraordinary depth and brilliancy, and he was conceded, by all other participants except Staunton, to be Europe's leading master. The latter took his defeat most ungracefully. In the official account of the tournament, which he edited, he tried to depreciate Anderssen's victory and thereby only lessened his own prestige.

"The German master proved his stature in many tournaments which followed, and some of the combinations he made still rank among the finest on record. His accomplishments and his fame were eclipsed only by the spectacular career of a young American by the name of Paul Morphy, a native of New Orleans, who crossed the Atlantic in 1857 and defeated him decisively."

The Adventure of Chess by Edward Lasker.
(Doubleday & Company, Inc., Garden City, N.Y.)

25.

The doctor's verdict against travel, whether by land or by sea, was, as it proved, quite superfluous; his patient had become so weakened that, though he made repeated efforts to rise it was only to find, over and over again, he could not stand on his feet. Part of his debility was unquestionably due to the attack of influenza which he had persistently refused to recognize as a serious illness as long as he considered himself bound to play with Harrwitz. When he finally took to his bed, his fever had already been high for several days, his cough racking and persistent; that he had escaped pneumonia was in itself a minor miracle. But his recovery might have been much more rapid, if he had consented to rest and medication at the beginning of his indisposition, instead of postponing these until his condition was actually alarming. Now, as one dreary December day succeeded another, and his strength still failed to return, it looked more and more doubtful if he could be up and about before Christmas.

Edge, who had watched over him with affectionate anxiety, found some consolation in the fact that Paul, whose moods of depression were so often a handicap both to himself and those who were attached to him, remained relatively undiscouraged throughout this trying period. Day after day, as Fred helped him back to bed when he had been sitting only a short time in an armchair by the window which "gave" so pleasantly on the Tuileries Gardens, he said cheerfully that, after all, he was quite comfortable as long as he stayed between the sheets, propped up with pillows; he was not feverish any more, he was coughing less and less and he was quite free from pain; since there had been this much of an improvement, surely it was reasonable to expect that there would soon be more. Edge had hesitated to let him know when Anderssen actually left Breslau, fearing that Paul would begin to fret over the fact that he was in no condition to meet this adversary; but deciding that the news was bound to reach the invalid sooner or later, and that it was better this should be broken gently, he finally overcame his scruples. Instead of showing the least concern, Paul plumped up his pillows and called for a chessboard.

"I feel a fever coming on," he said gaily.

"What, again?"

"Oh, not the kind of fever you're thinking of—it's time to forget all about that. This is a *chess* fever! Go ahead, be a good fellow. Give me a board and pieces. I'll show you some of Anderssen's games."

The next few hours were spent in re-creating battles, all with different adversaries and with numerous variations. Finally, he dilated at length about a certain game in which, though under the mate, Anderssen sacrificed his Queen and, after several moves, forced his opponent to resign.

"There!" Paul exclaimed, leaning contentedly back among his pillows. "If that doesn't show the master, I don't know what would. You may take away the board now if you want to, Fred. And what about some supper? I believe I'll try to get up for it. I'm getting terribly tired of trays. Our *garçon* could bring in a little table and I could sit in my armchair with you opposite me. You might even persuade me to have a glass of wine, if you tried hard enough!"

Their evening was the pleasantest they had passed in a long while. When Fred bade his friend good night, it was with the happy conclusion that Paul was really on the mend at last; and the next morning, when he entered the sick room at ten o'clock, he found that Anderssen had already arrived to pay his respects and that he had promptly been invited to share Paul's *café au lait*.

He had, he explained, reached Paris the previous evening and had hastened to call at what seemed to be the earliest suitable moment; no one had informed him that M. Morphy was ill. He had apologized for the intrusion, but M. Morphy, as M. Edge could see, had been most cordial and insisted that they must breakfast together; of course, he would leave immediately thereafter, so that there might be no danger of tiring the invalid. He would not think of talking over arrangements for commencing a match until M. Morphy was in a state to undergo the fatigue of one. No, no, Paul protested, polishing off his last *croissant;* of course they must talk over arrangements; he was sure he would be well enough to play any day now—well, almost any day. Herr Anderssen became convinced it would do the invalid no harm for him to prolong his present visit and perhaps they might agree—tentatively, of course—on a date to begin playing. This was the 14th. Well, what about the 20th? He would suggest a later day, but unfortunately his holiday lasted only a fortnight. However, perhaps they might play in this pleasant apartment instead of at the Régence; that, at least, would spare M. Morphy a very considerable effort.

The 20th would suit Paul perfectly—why, given a week, he would feel as strong as a lion! And yes, he was sure there would be less opposition from his physician if they played at the Breteuil, where there would be room for only a few specially invited spectators; after all, the moves could be forwarded every half hour to the Régence. Should they decide now on the number of games in the match? A possible thirteen? That is, the one who first scored seven should be declared the victor? Good! What about stakes? Herr Anderssen desired none but honor? Better and better! That was exactly the way Paul felt about the matter himself! Well, since everything was now amicably settled, as far as chess was concerned, what about a little sightseeing? Paul and Fred understood that this was the first visit Herr Anderssen had made to Paris. Fred would be delighted to take him to the Louvre and anywhere else he would like to go.

The sightseeing, Fred reported to Paul some hours later, had been a great success except for the fact that the Place de Carrousel had been very muddy after the heavy rain of the previous evening, and Herr Anderssen had been much concerned because he could not keep his boots clean while crossing it! They laughed together over the preoccupation with neatness which had prevented the visitor from enjoying, to the full, the treasures of art and architecture so lavishly spread out before him; but there was no division of opinion between them regarding the likeability of this massive, middle-aged German, whose consideration and courtesy formed such a welcome contrast to the boorishness of Harrwitz.

"Did you notice his smile? There's something actually sweet about it, though that seems a strange thing to say in describing a man of his years and experience."

"Of course I noticed it. And I don't think it's strange at all to speak of it in that way. I thought it was in character with the rest of his personality, including his voice. That was sweet, too, like honey."

"Well, there's no doubt that his face is as pleasant as it is expressive and he seems extraordinarily placid. Just the same, I've heard that, as a player, he's very excitable."

"Excitable, perhaps, but reasonable. I don't dread the match with him at all. In fact, I'm looking forward to it very much. I've hesitated to tell you, *cher*, but since all the trouble with Staunton and Harrwitz, I've had moments of feeling I never wanted to play chess again. It was probably just because I was so ill. Anyway, I feel very differently now—physically and mentally both. I'm sure I'll be able to sit up longer today without suddenly starting to pitch over."

His optimism proved well founded. He neither "pitched over" nor grew dizzy in trying to get from the bed to the armchair and he remained at the window for nearly two hours before he confessed to fatigue. The next day, he sat up both morning and evening, received several visitors and called again for his chessboard. At noon on the 20th, fully dressed for the first time, he went with Edge into the small salon where the match was to be played. Anderssen was already there and, far from showing any signs of impatience, asked solicitously for Paul's health before consenting to play, and charged him not to hesitate about calling off the game if, at any moment, he did not feel equal to continuing it.

Within five minutes as many moves had been made; but Edge could not help noticing that Paul had already begun to be restless, instead of playing, as usual, with his eyes fixed steadfastly on the board, his expression impas-

sive and his body immobile. He did not, however, avail himself of Anderssen's courteous suggestion that he might stop at any moment. The game
continued for more than seven hours without interruption. Then, after sev-
enty moves, Paul, who had opened with the Evans gambit, lost it.

He did not seem unduly fatigued by the effort he had made to sit up
so long, or much depressed by his failure to win. Instead, as Edge helped
him back to bed, he chatted about Anderssen's defense, with which he
declared himself charmed. The next day, though his pallor and restlessness
persisted, his spirits were amazingly good and remained so even when the
game was drawn. On the morning of the third day, he walked into the
salon unassisted, his face fresh, his eyes sparkling. He would like to have a
turn at the Ruy Lopez, he said, since Anderssen had found that so favorable
to success. They had been playing only an hour, when Anderssen laughingly resigned, with the suggestion that, since they had spent so little time
at the board, M. Morphy would perhaps give him another chance that
same day.

"Of course. Maybe the next game won't take long, either."

"I'm sure it won't, if you dash along at the same furious rate, M. Morphy."

The "furious rate" was not prompted only by a desire to score brilliantly;
Paul had set his heart on doing some Christmas shopping. He had prudently neglected to mention this beforehand to Edge, who, he was sure,
would raise all manner of objections; in the presence of a comparative
stranger, he would be more inhibited. As Anderssen rose from the table,
confessing a second defeat and saying he must be on his way to the Régence
to expedite reports to his friends in Leipzig and Berlin, as he did every day,
Paul also rose with alacrity and said they might take a fiacre together; he
was going in the same direction as Anderssen, but continuing a little
further.

"Paul, you must be crazy!" Edge exclaimed, leaping up and trying to bar
the door.

"Nonsense! It's a beautiful day for a change and I haven't had a breath
of fresh air for weeks. I'll feel a lot better when I have."

"Is that all you're going out for—a breath of fresh air?"

"Yes, practically. I thought I might do one errand—at Cartier's."

Again Edge realized that this was another of those occasions when argument with Paul was futile. He might be back in bed the next day, but
meanwhile he intended to buy Charmian a present; and if he found something that pleased her, and she made it evident that he had, on Christmas
Eve, he would not care whether or not his shopping expedition eventually
spelled pneumonia.

As a matter of fact, it seemed to do him no harm. He continued to improve in health and spirits day by day and he won the fifth and sixth games in the contest without more apparent effort than he had won the third and fourth. Anderssen had plans of his own for Christmas Eve, which he had been invited to spend with German friends living in Paris. He took a genial leave of Paul and Fred and, having sped him on his way, they set out gaily for the rue des Saints Pères. As their fiacre drew up at the great outer gate, which had gradually come to seem less formidable to them, they were disturbed to see the neat carriage of the eminent physician who attended Mrs. Sheppard drawn up at the curb.

"Is Madame ill, really ill?" Paul inquired anxiously of the concierge, with whom he was now on the friendliest terms.

"Not only really ill, but very ill," the man replied sadly, shaking his head. "*Monsieur le médecin* told her yesterday that she should give up all idea of the party tonight, but she refused. She was sure she would be better. She has much merit, that woman! And now alas! she is worse. There will be no fete tonight. However, the young ladies are expecting the young North American gentlemen. My instructions are that they are to go in."

Considerably sobered, Paul and Fred walked across the vast paved court. Charmian was not watching from the window of the *petit salon* and no fire was lighted there; it was obvious that they were not expected to linger. They sat for a few minutes in chilly silence and then a nun, wearing the habit of a nursing order, came into the room on noiseless footsteps. The clicking of the long wooden rosary which she wore at her side made the only sound.

"I am sorry to tell you," she said in a soft, grave voice, "that it will be quite impossible for any member of the family to see you tonight. *Monsieur le docteur* and another Sister are with Madame Sheppard and her husband and daughters are remaining on call in an adjacent boudoir. They may be summoned at any moment to bid her a last sad farewell. She was advised, long ago, that she should go south, that she should not risk the possible consequences of exposure to cold weather. We can only pray that it may now not be too late for her to heed this advice." The nun paused for a moment and then continued in a different tone, though still speaking very gravely, "Mademoiselle Charmian thought it possible that you gentlemen might be bringing some little gifts to herself and her sister. If she is right and you would care to entrust them to me, I shall be glad to see they are delivered— at a moment more propitious than this one. I shall also be glad to accept any little donation you may care to make for the orphans in our Home. It would make Reverend Mother very happy."

Christmas was a dismal day, but at least it was not shadowed by actual tragedy; to everyone's surprise, Madame was holding her own, the concierge announced, when Paul and Fred went to inquire for her in the morning. Paul sat down for the seventh and eighth games in the contest with more heart for them than he would have believed possible twelve hours earlier and won the first, though the second was a draw. On the 26th, the report from the sick room was the same and Paul was sorry that Anderssen again had plans for celebrations with compatriots. On the following day, although the news was not so good, he managed to win the ninth game. The tenth, which was played the same day, Anderssen carried off in seventy-seven moves. If he were dependent on Mrs. Sheppard's progress to win the match, Paul reflected, he might easily lose it; but that had now become a minor consideration. All that mattered was that this lovely, gentle lady, who had shown him so much kindness, should not be a victim of the dread pneumonia which he himself had so fortunately escaped.

Happily, the bulletins continued to be reassuring and the games went on in orderly fashion, though Anderssen, again proving himself understanding and sympathetic, said he had learned this was a period of great anxiety to his antagonist and if it seemed wiser to discontinue the match. . . . No, Paul assured him, he was better off at the chess table than he would be alone in his room, brooding; he could not possibly put his mind on anything else, and though he went twice a day to the rue des Saints Pères, he could linger at the Hotel d'Ambres only long enough to make inquiries; all the rest of his waking hours were empty except for those he spent with Herr Anderssen; they were, consequently, a godsend. The eleventh game Paul won in seventeen moves and, picking up the pieces, Anderssen laughed in his pleasant quiet way.

"M. Morphy wins in seventeen moves," he said, "I in seventy-odd. That is natural. The surprising thing is that I win at all. They are saying at the Régence that I am not playing as well as I did against Dufresne and I am obliged to reply, 'No, M. Morphy won't let me!' "

Anderssen left for Breslau the same afternoon, with many expressions of heartfelt good will on both sides; and when Paul went to make inquiries at the Hotel d'Ambres that evening, the concierge told him that Madame had passed the crisis and that Mademoiselle Charmian would be glad to see him if he would care to remain.

He crossed the courtyard in a series of bounds, and it was only a matter of minutes before his sweetheart was at last in his arms again. This time he held her tenderly, keeping his passion in check, and murmuring words of comfort and encouragement, rather than of ardor. He saw, with delight, that she was wearing the heart-shaped diamond locket he had bought for her and listened, with rapture, to her words of thanks for such a lovely present.

"It's beautiful, Paul, it really is," she told him. "I'd be proud to wear it any place. I didn't feel quite that way about the little turquoise pendant you gave me so many years ago. Not that I don't treasure it. I keep it safely locked in my jewel box and every now and then I take it out and look at it. But you know how it is in Paris—women wear such magnificent bracelets, earrings and necklaces, and even tiaras, just as we'd wear a string of beads. I'd be a little self-conscious."

"Of course, darling, I understand perfectly. I only wish I could buy you necklaces and bracelets and earrings. Perhaps I can someday."

"Why, Paul, you didn't think I was hinting, did you? This diamond locket is *adorable*, and there's a place in it for a picture, isn't there? Have you had one taken on purpose for me?"

"No, I haven't had a chance, because I have been ill, too, you know. Not seriously ill, like your poor mother, but ill enough so that an old dragon of a doctor, who kept bleeding me, and Fred, who can be a good deal of a fussbudget, managed to keep me in bed for three weeks. That's why you didn't see me for such a long time. But I wrote you nearly every day and Fred brought the notes when he came to see Berenice. Don't tell me you didn't get them."

"Poor Fred! He's wasting his time as far as Berenice is concerned, but I'm glad he brought me the notes. Of course, I got them and they were sweet! I kept meaning to answer, but somehow I never got around to. December was so frightfully gay."

"Yes, I understand about that, too. I'll have a picture taken for the locket directly after the New Year."

"Oh, please do! You've had one taken with Anderssen already, haven't you? I heard you had."

"Yes, I have, but just yesterday and at his request."

"Was it part of his request that it should be taken at the house of the Baronne de la Sange?"

"Yes, by the time it reached me. I think she may have suggested it in the beginning."

"Will she show in the picture? She and all her old statues and things?"

"I don't know. Perhaps. But what difference could that possibly make, darling?"

"Oh, none, I suppose! But I get awfully tired of her silly talk about fellow Creoles. I'm glad there's going to be a picture on purpose for me to put in the locket. I'll have it to remember you by."

"*Remember me by!* Do you imagine I'll give you a chance to forget me?"

"Not really, of course. But *our* dragon of a doctor says we must go south the minute Mama's able to travel, and he thinks that should be in just a few weeks, now that this 'crisis' he's continually talking about is over. It seems that, when you have pneumonia, you keep going downhill for five days and then you either die or start getting better. Well, Mama's getting better, there's no doubt about that, even if the dragon-like doctor and those two dreary grasping nuns do keep on talking and acting as if there still wouldn't be any hope for her unless we did exactly what they said."

"But naturally, you will."

"Yes, naturally. As a matter of fact, I'm not at all sorry that I'm going to have a chance to see Nice. Everyone seems to have a very good time there, everyone in good health of course, I mean. But Mama ought to get some pleasure out of it, too. Papa's engaged a whole floor in the best hotel on the Boulevard des Anglais, and—"

"You won't be away from Paris long though, will you?"

"I don't know just how long. Mama will have to stay south until it gets warm, of course, and Berenice will stay with her. Perhaps Papa and I will come back without them. It all depends."

"On what?"

"Oh, several things. But you won't miss me, will you—I mean too much?"

"I'm not sure just what you mean by too much. I'll miss you terribly, I know that and so do you."

"Well, you should make an effort to see more of other people. That pretty cousin of yours, Natalie Benjamin, keeps complaining that you never come to her house. She *is* your cousin, isn't she?"

"Yes, she was a St. Martin. The St. Martins and the Le Carpentiers are very closely related, but—"

He stopped, embarrassed. He did not like to say that Natalie's reputation for levity was such that he had decided the less he was seen in her company the better. Even by the most liberal Parisian standards, she was extremely indiscreet. Fortunately, Charmian neither noticed his hesitation nor guessed the reason for it.

"Well, now is your time to placate her. And I understand the American Minister, Mr. Mason, is really quite annoyed because you haven't dined with him but once. It seems he's asked you several more times and you've always said you were engaged."

"So I am, darling. I'm engaged to you."

"Oh, that's not what I mean at all and you know it! I mean you always say you're dining somewhere else. Now you won't be dining here at all for a while and that'll give you more free evenings, though I do know you have lots of other invitations. By the way, the Princess Mathilde says the Emperor has expressed a wish to meet you and, of course, once it would have been the easiest thing in the world for her to arrange, as she's his best beloved cousin. But since he married a Spaniard, he's very keen on protocol and says the audience must be arranged through the American Minister, so if you want to meet the Emperor, you'd better improve your standing with Mason."

"I don't know that I especially want to meet the Emperor. But if you think it's an opportunity I shouldn't miss—"

"Oh, I do! And now that you're through with Anderssen—you are through with Anderssen, aren't you?"

"Yes, just. To my regret. He's a wonderful person—the most splendid and chivalrous player I ever encountered. I was sorry to see him leave."

"Then you're champion of the world now?"

"Yes, I suppose so."

"And you won't need to play chess any more?"

"I don't need to, but of course I want to. I'm hoping to play with Mongredien, the President of the London Chess Club, next. He's offered to come to Paris on purpose to play with me, just as Anderssen did, instead of insisting that I should go to London. I didn't want to do that. I didn't want to be parted from you. And now you're going yourself."

"But, Paul, I'm not leaving for Nice right away! Perhaps not for several weeks yet. And I'm coming back just as soon as I can. It wouldn't seem natural if I didn't find you here. You will wait for me, won't you?"

After their first embrace, they had been sitting quietly side by side, in front of the pleasant fire, while they talked together. Now she threw herself into his arms again. When, at last, he released her, he knew what his answer must be.

"Of social engagements, Morphy could have had as much as he liked, for he was still the lion of Paris; but again his bodily condition was against over-exertion.

"His family had obviously grown anxious about his prolonged stay in Europe, and perhaps about news which reached them of his ill-health; for soon after his brother-in-law Sybrandt's arrival in Paris we find Morphy starting on his journey home. On April 4th there was a grand farewell banquet to him, organised by his admirers at the Régence, at which eulogies were heaped upon him and bust, for which he had sat to the well known sculptor, Eugene Lequesne (one of his opponents in the blindfold exhibition in September, 1858) was unveiled. This was crowned with a laurel wreath by Saint-Amant, in his earlier days considered the best player in the world.

"Morphy made but a short second stay in London, putting up at the British Hotel in Cockspur Street. He arrived on April 10th, and left again at the end of the month. As in Paris, social invitations were many; but he had broken his journey in London mainly to meet Löwenthal again and help in the preparation of a collection of his games; though he declares in his introduction to this volume that 'the copious notes are mainly due to Löwenthal's well-earned reputation and assiduity as an analyst.'

"He found time to give two blindfold exhibitions—at the London Chess Club on April 13th, when he was 'off colour' and only finished two games out of eight, wining both, while the rest were agreed as drawn; and at St. George's Club on April 20th, when he did much better, winning five and drawing three of eight games. Also, at the St. James's Club on April 26th he gave a simultaneous exhibition, not blindfolded, against five picked opponents. . . .

"On April 30th Morphy sailed from Liverpool, and on May 11th he reached New York, being escorted off the ship by Fiske and Lichtenhein, who came aboard to welcome him and to invite him to a banquet the same night at the Metropolitan Hotel. The honoured guest was not too tired after the banquet to go to the New York Chess Club and play four games with Frederick Perrin, the secretary, to whom he conceded the odds of Knight, less than which it was his declared intention never to give to an American player. . . .

"On May 25th, there was a great gathering in the chapel of the University, where Morphy was asked to accept a magnificent chessboard and men, and a gold watch.

"The board, which had mother-of-pearl and ebony squares, was of rosewood inlaid with silver, and at each corner were the letters P.M. in a wreath of gold. On a silver plate on one border was the inscription: 'To Paul Morphy, a recognition of his genius and a testimony of regard from his friends and admirers in

New York and Brooklyn, 1859.' On the opposite border was another silver plate, bearing the names of fourteen players with claims to the chess championship of the world.

"The men were of solid gold, representing Romans, and silver, representing Barbarians, and they were mounted on bases of cornelian.

"The watch had a stem surmounted by a coronet, studded with diamonds, and the places of the numerals were taken by representations of chess pieces in red and black. On the case were the initials P.M., the arms of the United States, and the inscription: 'To Paul Morphy from the Testimonial Committee of the New York Chess Club as their tribute to his genius and worth. New York, May 1859.' . . .

"When the presentation had been made, with many flattering words, Morphy expressed his thanks in a speech of which one passage may be quoted:

"'A word now on the game itself. Chess never has been and never can be aught but a recreation. It should not be indulged in to the detriment of other and more serious avocations—should not absorb or engross the thoughts of those who worship at its shrine, but should be kept in the background, and restrained within its proper province. As a mere game, a relaxation from the severe pursuits of life, it is deserving of high commendation.'"

Morphy Gleanings by Philip W. Sergeant.
(David McKay Company, Inc., Philadelphia.)

26.

It was neither surprising nor disturbing to Paul that, during the next few weeks, he saw very little of Charmian. It was natural that the Hotel d'Ambres should be kept as quiet as possible for, even though the invalid remained secluded, the consciousness of much coming and going in the house might excite her and it was essential that all risk of this should be avoided. The stir of preparation for departure was in itself a menace to the complete stillness which the doctor would have liked to impose on the household; and of course it was unthinkable that Charmian should dash from one party to another under the present conditions. For some reason she seemed to have taken a dislike to the Baronne de la Sange or she and Paul might easily have met at her hospitable house on the days she was not officially at home and was receiving only a few friends for lunch or dinner. It was too cold for drives in the Bois and it was not customary for girls of good family to go to restaurants. Besides, Charmian told Paul, at one of their infrequent meetings, she had to spend most of her time, when she could leave the house, with dressmakers; nothing that she or Berenice or their mother had was suitable for wear in the South. She was responsible for three new outfits, since her mother could not and Berenice would not go out to get them. As she and Berenice were about the same size, she tried on dresses for both and minor alterations were made on her sister's clothes afterward. Of course, her mother needed nothing except negligees for the time being, but mercy! that dragon of a doctor—Paul had certainly described him exactly—objected to the presence of a seamstress in the house or even brief visits from a *vendeuse* or a fitter. She, Charmian, really had an undertaking on her hands to see that they all had what they needed when so many obstacles were put in her way. . . .

"Aren't there any dressmakers in Nice?" Paul asked innocently. "I mean, couldn't you get what you need right away and then add to your wardrobes after you reach the South?"

"You talk just like a man! Papa asked that same question. I suppose there are dressmakers in Nice, but we don't know yet who the best ones are and things like that take time to find out. Besides, once we get there, I want to be free to enjoy myself. I might just as well spend my time at the dressmaker's as anywhere else while the weather is so awful and while everyone thinks it would be heartless if I had any fun. Not that I can see why. It was different those five days when Mama's life was actually in danger. She's convalescent now."

Paul started to say that if Charmian did not spend so much time at the dressmaker's she might have more to spend with him, but thought better of it. For a different reason, he refrained from saying he understood that pneumonia often left a patient's heart in a rather tricky condition and that, even though a convalescent's condition seemed to be good, watchfulness was almost as essential as quiet. He did not want to alarm her for nothing. . . .

Several times when he entered one of the drawing rooms which, in accordance with Charmian's expressed wishes, he continued to frequent even though she could not go with him, he was under the impression that the conversation was abruptly terminated or that its subject was swiftly changed at his approach. Once he was very sure that unfriendly remarks were being made about someone he knew and tried to identify the victim. As he thought the matter over, he decided that the talk had centered on Natalie Benjamin and, since everyone knew he and she were cousins, it was natural that this should have been hurriedly stilled. It was unfortunate that her conduct should have become a matter of such general scandal, but, after all, that did not touch him personally. She was older than he, they had never been closely associated. Every family had its black sheep. There was no reason why he should be greatly concerned.

It was finally decided that Charmian, her father and one of the nursing sisters should go before the others to Nice, to make sure everything was in readiness for the convalescent when she arrived; and that Mrs. Sheppard herself should be accompanied by Berenice, the second sister and the doctor. Paul was obliged to acknowledge that this was a logical arrangement and was annoyed with himself because he wished the plan had been made in reverse; if it had, then the necessity for quiet in the house would have been obviated; he and Charmian even might have had a cosy little dinner with her father the night before their departure, relieved to know that the period of preparation was over, Mrs. Sheppard safely on her way in good hands. As it was, of course nothing of the sort was possible. The final visit that he had with her in the *petit salon* was punctuated with tiresome interruptions about shawl straps, tea baskets, chamois-covered traveling cushions and undelivered bonnets. At the station, a dozen acquaintances came to speed father and daughter on their journey; and these well-wishers were not only vociferous in their expression of regret at the Sheppards' departure; they were the bearers of immense stiff bouquets, huge boxes of bonbons and sheafs of reading material. The train was already pulling out of the station before everyone had been properly thanked. Paul did not even have a chance to kiss Charmian good-bye. The depression which he had so far managed to keep in check suddenly engulfed him. He had no idea when he would see her again and he knew, from past experience, that she did not shine as a correspondent. His sense of separation from her was overpowering.

Under these conditions, the arrival in Paris of Mr. Mongredien, the genial President of the London Chess Club, was a godsend. Since the match with Anderssen, Paul had played very little—indeed, there had been a recurrence of the distaste for chess which he had admitted during his illness, and a few offhand games with St. Amant, who had now become one of his most valued personal friends, constituted his only activities in that direction. But the arrival of Mongredien, and the knowledge of the effort this distinguished gentleman had made in order to play against him, had a salutary effect on Paul. He was not insensible to the compliment Mongredien had paid him and which had been duly reported, that while the mature Englishman knew he could not beat the young American he was "unwilling to forego the pleasure of a tilt with him."

As Paul entered the Hotel de Louvre, where Mongredien was staying, he could feel the "chess fever," as he had called it, rising in him again; and he was delighted when he found that, besides Edge, St. Amant and de Rivière were to be the only spectators to the contest. The first game, admirably played by Mongredien, who continued his self-depreciation, resulted in a draw; in the second, Paul scored seven *parties* one after the other; and the third slipped from his opponent's grasp after a ten hour struggle. Mongredien made none of the standard excuses of Staunton and Harrwitz as long as the contest lasted, but, once it was over, he confessed himself exhausted. How Mr. Morphy could still seem not only alert but fresh was beyond his comprehension.

"Why sir, you should have seen him in New York!" Edge exclaimed. "During the Congress, I saw him sit down, day after day, at nine in the morning and play continuously until after midnight, winning over one antagonist after another! And none of this seemed to weaken him in the least."

"Yet I understand that recently he's been seriously ill. Youth is a strong ally and energy and persistence are wonderful qualities in chess or in anything else. But it is an error to mistake them for strength. . . . Forgive me if what I have just said sounds like an impertinence," he added kindly, putting his hand on Paul's shoulder. "It wasn't meant that way, I assure you. It was prompted by concern and, if you will permit me to say so, affection. You've made a good many friends since you came abroad, Mr. Morphy. It is natural that we should be concerned lest you might overdo. Have I told you Herr Löwenthal sends you his best regards? You know, he is one of your staunchest admirers! And he is very hopeful that you can come back to London this spring, to help him with some book he's working on."

"I didn't misunderstand what you said to me, sir. I appreciate your friendship, and Fred shouldn't tell tales out of school like that. Don't put too much stock in them anyway—he always exaggerates." Paul cast a withering glance in the direction of his friend and went on, "I really don't know what to say about London. I'm not sure I should try to return there. Of course, I'm complimented at Herr Löwenthal's suggestion that I might be helpful to him, but I've hesitated to accept his invitation."

"On account of Staunton? My dear fellow, that's absurd! You'll find a royal welcome waiting for you, with that erstwhile champion still sulking in his tent, sore because he isn't included in the festivities and isn't entitled to be."

Paul hesitated, but it did not seem quite fair to let Mr. Mongredien leave with the impression that distaste for even the most casual encounter with Staunton was the only reason for indecision about returning to London. "My family is beginning to feel I've been away long enough," he said. "They understood when my physician told me I shouldn't attempt a trans-Atlantic crossing in midwinter, but the weather will soon be more favorable. And I've rather cogent reasons why I feel I ought to get started with law, now that I'm legally of an age to practice. On the other hand, I've promised to stay in Paris until a—a friend of mine, who had to leave here because of illness in the family, comes back. I'm afraid that when I've kept that promise, I ought to take the first ship home."

"Well, of course you must keep your promise. And I quite understand your family's wish to have you return and your eagerness to get started in your profession. But I'm still not going to give up hope of seeing you in London again this spring. Are you willing I should tell Löwenthal you are giving serious thought to his suggestion?"

"Yes, of course. I'm willing you should do that."

St. Amant suggested that they might all go on to the Régence and, though de Rivière and Edge accepted the invitation with pleasure, Mongredien pleaded the necessity of packing and Paul said that he hoped, under those circumstances, that the others would excuse him, too. He walked slowly back to the Breteuil, so deep in thought that he was hardly conscious of the route he was taking, though this led him through one of his favorite parts of Paris—along the rue de Rivoli and past the Louvre, the Place Napoleon and the Place du Carrousel, where Anderssen had muddied his shoes; he did not realize he had gone by the Palais des Tuileries until he became aware of the Gardens beyond it. Ever since Mr. Sheppard had spoken to him seriously about settling down, as a necessary prelude to matrimony, he had been giving more and more sober thought to it. But as long as he was committed to a series of contests, he could not disappoint his backers, and his ambition to prove himself, indubitably, chess champion of the world, when he was so close to realizing this desire, had not unnaturally been even stronger than the urge toward law. Besides, as long as Charmian was in Paris and he could continue to see her almost daily, under advantageous conditions, he had not felt the postponement of their marriage too hard to accept, especially as he recognized that his prospective father-in-law was right in saying that Charmian would need to have her fling sometime and that it was better she should have it before marriage than after. But now the contests were over, he had no more commitments, he *was* champion of the world and he was not seeing Charmian almost every day—in fact, he was not seeing her at all. It was only his promise to await her return that was keeping him abroad.

His fears that he might not hear from her frequently or satisfactorily had been more than justified. She wrote him hurried little notes, ending with a row of X's for kisses, but giving him very little news. Gradually, he gathered that the hotel of their choice had proven luxurious, elegant and ideally located, but that the wardrobe she had taken such pains to select had not been adequate after all and that she was obliged to spend a great deal of time in supplementing it. The sunshine was splendid, but the days were short and, after the sun went down, Nice was not much warmer than Paris, nor was it nearly as gay as she had expected. There were an appalling number of invalids in evidence, some of them much sicker than her mother, many of them being wheeled about in bath chairs by attendants, which, of course, did not enliven the scene very much. Naturally, they did not know many people in Nice and lots of Americans seemed to feel that the best way of getting acquainted was through sharing in the church activities, which were terribly dull, and taking tea with the Consul's wife, who was an old frump. She really did not know how she would have passed the time, if Jacques d'Ambres, the friend who had loaned them the house in Paris, and who was a perfect dear, had not managed to wangle a holiday just then. Of course, he was an older man and devoted himself mainly to Mama; still he was someone to talk to and ride with once in a while and he could be quite good fun.

Jacques d'Ambres had not been mentioned between Paul and Fred since their first conversation on that subject, and Paul was gratified to find the guesses he had made on that occasion about the Sheppards' benefactor had obviously been correct; the marquis was an older man, devoted to the invalid, and it had been indeed fortunate that he had been able to go to Nice at that time to relieve the tedium of the stay there. What troubled Paul was not Jacques d'Ambres' presence on the Riviera; it was Charmian's indefinite absence from Paris. None of the hurried notes made any reference to her return with her father, in accordance with the tentative plan which had been discussed before their departure. In his own letters, Paul had referred to this several times, but his questions had remained unanswered. He was sorely tempted to break away and start for Nice himself, instead of prolonging his anxious wait. However, it had not been suggested that he should go there and the hesitant hint that perhaps he might do so had resulted in a letter from Mr. Sheppard which, far from encouraging him, quickly disabused his mind that it might be a good idea. If Paul came to Nice, Mrs. Sheppard would insist on seeing him, as he was one of her favorites; and her physician had strictly forbidden visitors; besides, it was probably a very good thing that he and Charmian should be separated for a time; it would give them a chance to be surer of their feelings. . . .

The tone of the letter came very close to being curt and Paul felt that this was unwarranted. Evidently the Marquis d'Ambres was permitted to see Mrs. Sheppard—or was he revealing his "devotion" only at a distance? And Mr. Sheppard knew that no one could be surer of his feelings than Paul; was Charmian's father intimating that she did not even yet know her own mind? Considering her attitude toward her suitor in the last few months, such an intimation was an insult to her. . . .

He was still so deep in these unhappy thoughts that he actually passed the Breteuil without realizing he had already reached his destination. He turned, annoyed with himself at such a careless preoccupation. As he went through the lobby, he was told that he had a visitor and, as the gentleman had said he was Mr. Morphy's brother-in-law, he had been permitted to mount to the apartment. The concierge hoped no indiscretion had been committed. . . .

Paul had always liked John Sybrandt and, on general principles, would not have been surprised to see him at any time in Paris, where he now had such important business connections. However, as months had gone by and there had been no intimation that such a visit was imminent, he had dismissed the possibility of it from his mind. Besides, at the moment, he did not feel equal to entertaining a guest; whatever Fred might think or say, Paul did not leave a chess table, after a ten hour struggle, "as fresh as when he sat down to it." He did his best to make his greeting sound hearty, ordered a good supper sent up and asked for news of home. Everything was about as usual, John assured him, doing full justice to the excellent meal which was promptly set before him. But Paul was very much missed, especially by his mother. Had he set a definite date for going home?

"Did you come all the way to Paris just to tell me that and ask me that?"

"No, of course not. I came to see about getting an apartment which Malvina and I can use as a permanent pied-à-terre abroad. We've had only temporary ones before. But it's evident that I need to be here, more and more, just as it is that New Orleans and not Paris is the place for you."

"I hope you found something satisfactory?" Paul inquired, trying to keep the growing irritation out of his voice.

"Yes, quite so. A rez-de-chaussée, on the rue du Cirque, between the

Faubourg St. Honoré and the Champs Elysées. I'd have preferred something on the first floor, but there's a prospect that there may be a vacancy before long and, if there is, I'm to have the first chance at it. However, as I was saying—"

"Look here, John," Paul interrupted, "I know Mother wants to see me and, as far as that goes, I want to see her. But I have a special reason for staying in Paris right now."

"Really! Would it be indiscreet to ask what the reason is?"

"Not only indiscreet, but impertinent. However, since I know you won't leave me in peace until I tell you, I will. As a matter of fact, I'll be guilty of a breach of confidence in doing so. But—"

"Good grief, Paul, don't get so hot under the collar! This is February. You've been abroad since June, living entirely on family funds, which aren't as plentiful as they once were. Of course, it's very high-minded of you, insisting that you won't play chess professionally; but if you're not careful, you'll exhaust your patrimony faster than you expect."

"I'm proposing to start earning my own living very soon now. I've a special incentive for doing so. I'm not supposed to mention this, because there's been no official betrothal yet. But I'm engaged to be married."

"The hell you are! Is the lucky young lady's name a secret, too?"

"Yes, for the time being. She's been obliged to leave Paris temporarily, because of her mother's serious illness. I promised to wait until she comes back, so that we could make definite plans for our marriage then."

"Well, congratulations! I'm glad to know you've come to your senses. The last I heard from you on the subject was several years ago, when both your mother and father were up in arms because you swore you would never marry anyone but that Yankee shopkeeper's daughter! A blonde bitch if I ever saw one! Talk about our dear cousin Natalie Benjamin—why, Charmian Sheppard could give her cards and spades!"

Paul sprang from the table, trembling with rage. "Get out of here before I throw you out!" he shouted. "And don't come back, to tell me what I ought to do and how much I ought to spend and then go on to insult my fiancée and her family. Maybe you've forgotten, but I haven't, that my father and mother did everything they could to prevent my sister Malvina from marrying you! You never could have done it, either, if Benjamin hadn't pulled off a fine piece of blackmail on Grandfather. And whatever you choose to say about Natalie, it was she who invited Malvina to stay with her in Paris when she first came here and made it possible for you to be with her. But I've never lowered myself by calling you a son of a bitch on that account, never until today! And let me tell you, you miserable bastard, that Albert Sheppard's a merchant prince, just as the Medicis were merchant princes, and that he's welcome in noble houses in Paris, where you've never got your foot inside the door and never will. His wife's a saint on earth if there ever was one, and I only hope she isn't headed for heaven before her time! As for their daughters, they're both pure and beautiful as angels and if you ever say anything to the contrary again, I'll kill you, do you hear? I might even do it now, if you don't get out quickly."

The aftermath of this regrettable scene was understandably one of considerable strain. Sybrandt wrote a long apologetic letter to Paul, saying that, of course, he never dreamed, when he spoke of the Sheppards as he did, that Charmian was Paul's fiancée, or indeed that the old friendship had been renewed. Of course, the stories he had heard must all have been inspired by jealousy, because Albert Sheppard was so immensely rich and Charmian so beautiful, and because of their entrée into an exclusive society which outsiders almost never penetrated. He understood Paul's resentment of malicious gossip and could not begin to say how sorry he was he had listened to it, much less repeated it. Of course, it was true that he had not been considered good enough for Malvina and no wonder; it would have been hard enough to find any man good enough for her. But Paul was a different sort, he was worthy of anyone, even of an angel, and John was sure that Paul had been right to describe Charmian in that way.

The letter was torn into bits and thrown unread into the scrap basket. Three others in succession followed the same fate. Finally, John succeeded in waylaying Paul in the lobby, where the outraged suitor could not make a scene, and following him upstairs, meantime vehemently apologizing and explaining. It was while he was thus pleading his cause that the concierge rapped loudly and handed Paul a letter of quite different character: postmarked Nice, marked *urgente* and heavily bordered in black.

He knew before he opened it what was in it and he felt sure the sad news would be broken to him by Berenice. Charmian, poor stricken child, would not be calm enough to write; her weeping would be uncontrollable. And Albert Sheppard would be too unbelieving, too stunned, too broken; this was the sort of thing that happened to other people—wives of paupers and weaklings, not the wives of rich powerful men who lapped them in luxury and wrapped them in cotton wool. But Berenice would remain calm and competent; the only tears she would shed would be in secret and her hand would remain steady at the helm in any shipwreck.

"Dear Paul" (she wrote in a firm clear hand) "I am writing to tell you that Mama died early this morning. The end came very quickly and painlessly. Her tired heart just stopped beating.

"I think she expected this because, though she had never talked much about death, she told Papa a week or so ago that she wanted to be buried in Boston and, of course, we all want to follow her wishes. We are very fortunate in having Jacques d'Ambres with us at this time, because he is in a position to cut through a good deal of red tape, which sometimes makes it difficult to take an American home for burial. Final arrangements have not yet been made, but we shall go by the quickest possible route to the nearest port where we can get trans-Atlantic passage.

"I know you will want to be with us in our bereavement, but I must ask you to believe that it would be better if you did not try to do so. You might arrive to find we had just left here and there is bound to be a certain amount of confusion, no matter how well everything is handled. The presence of an extra person—even a close friend we value as much as we do you—would inevitably add to this. I hope you will not take amiss what I am saying. It is not meant to be unkind.

"When we get back to Boston, we shall go to our old house on Beacon Hill and stay there for the present. If anything brings you north, after you return to the United States, please let us know. When we are over the first shock of our grief and have resumed an ordered way of living, you will be welcome in our home, as you always have been.

"Charmian sends you her love. She says she is sure you will understand why she is not writing herself. And I am sure Fred will understand why I do not write a separate letter to him.

"Faithfully and affectionately yours,

"Berenice Sheppard."

Paul wiped his eyes, cleared his throat and handed the letter to John. "I'm ready to start back to New Orleans whenever you like," he said quietly.

Afterward, he found that he thought of that spring largely in terms of banquets for which he had no heart, tributes to which he found it difficult to respond and gifts which he had no inclination to use.

Of course, there were intervals between these. There were the weeks of congenial work in London with Löwenthal, though these were darkened because this period also marked the time of his parting with Edge, who was remaining in England, at least for the time being. There was the crossing—as usual, a nightmare and doubly so because of his longing for his friend—on the *Persia* from Liverpool to New York; there was the renewal of good companionship when he reached his own shores, none of which compensated for the loss of the one that meant most to him. But the impressions these experiences made on him were less lasting than the seemingly endless dinners, the still more endless addresses, and the trophies which weighed him down.

First came the banquet at the Régence. He learned, just in time to avert this, of a plan for a monster tournament of a hundred players, divided into five classes, from which the five winners would meet him in a final pool, all receiving odds from him. As originally scheduled, the farewell dinner was to follow this tournament, but the project was so far modified as to permit one without the other. However, before the evening was over, the bust by Lequesne was unveiled and crowned with laurel by St. Amant. Then bust and crown were presented to him with due ceremony.

In London, there was not an isolated banquet, but a series of ovations, in which chess became a mere accessory to personal compliments. He dined at the London Chess Club with a special group, at the St. George's with Lord Cremorne in the chair, at the new St. James's, of which his friend Löwenthal was secretary. He gave another blindfold performance, at which he did not shine, and still another exhibition, at which he was not blind-folded, but played five games simultaneously and scored a brilliant success. And finally, declining dozens of invitations to similar functions, he escaped, actually glad for once that he was going to sea.

He had hardly stepped off the ship in New York when the banquets began again. There was one in his honor that same night at the Metro-politan Hotel; the Union Club bestowed a silver wreath upon him; and then there was a great assembly in the chapel of the University and he was presented with a chess set, whose squares were ebony and mother-of-pearl and whose men were gold and silver. On the same occasion he was given a gold watch, in which jeweled chess pieces took the place of numerals and his initials were picked out on the back in gems, while the stem was surmounted by a coronet studded with diamonds.

At last these ceremonials were over and no more wreaths, no more costly gifts were forthcoming in New York. To be sure, there was still another banquet before him. But to this he looked forward without dread. For it was to be in Boston and in Boston, banquet or no banquet, he would be reunited with Charmian.

"We have met, gentlemen, some of us as members of the local association, some of us as its invited guests, but all of us as if by a spontaneous, unsolicited impulse, to do honor to our young friend, who has honored us and all who glory in the name of America, as the hero of a long series of bloodless battles, won for our common country. His career is known to you all. There are many corners of our land which the truly royal game of kings and conquerors has not yet reached, where, if an hour is given to pastime it is only in an honest match of chequers, played with red and white kernels of corn—probably enough upon the top of the housewife's bellows. But there is no gap in the forest, there is no fresh trodden waste in the prairie which has not heard the name of the New Orleans boy, who left the nursery of his youth, like one of those fabulous heroes of whom our childhood loved to read, and came back, bearing with him the spoils of giants whom he had slain, after overthrowing their castles and appropriating the allegiance of their queens. . . .

"I propose the health of Paul Morphy, the world's chess champion. His peaceful battles have helped to achieve a new revolution; his youthful triumphs have added a new clause to the declaration of American Independence."

Excerpt from the speech made by Oliver Wendell Holmes at the dinner given in Paul Morphy's honor at the Revere House, Boston, May 31, 1859.

27.

The day was warm for a New England May, and many of the passengers in the steam cars had insisted upon opening the windows, thereby letting in not only a breeze, but smoke and cinders. Normally, the trip from New York to Boston took only about nine hours; but a hotbox had caused a long delay, and it was very late at night when the train finally pulled in at the Boston and Albany Depot. Paul was not only thoroughly exhausted, he was thoroughly out of sorts. He had been futilely trying, for hours, to flick ashes from the clothes which had been immaculate when he left New York and, intermittently, mopping his moist face with his fine linen handkerchief; this was now black and so were his hands. The bags, containing his trophies as well as his clothes, were so heavy that he could hardly lift them down from the rack above him, much less carry them with any degree of ease the length of the aisle and down the steps to the station platform. But just as he reached this, laboriously, a watchful figure detached itself from the waiting crowd and hastened forward to meet him.

"Paul! I'd have known you anywhere! Don't you remember me? I'm Oliver Shaw and this is Stephen."

Edward's classmate from Boston, who had been graduated with him, and Oliver's younger brother, who had remained at Spring Hill only one year! The New Englanders who had seemed so alien to the southern atmosphere of the college! Paul had not seen them or heard from them in years and had never expected to do so again. Yet here they were, a welcoming committee of two, on a dimly lit wooden platform in the dead of night.

"Of course, I remember you," Paul said truthfully and thankfully, as he shook hands. He never forgot a face any more than he forgot a fact; but, in the surrounding obscurity, he would have found it hard to recognize his most intimate friend; and, besides, he had been taken entirely by surprise. It had never occurred to him that an old college mate would be on hand to welcome him at such an unseasonable hour. There had been no mention of Oliver or Stephen in any of the communications urging him to visit Boston; of that he felt quite sure; and his long-lost acquaintances did not instantly clarify matters, though their cordiality was unquestionable.

"Here, let me help you with those grips," Oliver was saying. "Father promised our coachman the evening off, to go to a family wedding, before we knew you were coming. But I've got a hack waiting outside. We'll have you home in no time."

"I believe I'm to go to the Revere House."

"Nonsense! You're to do nothing of the kind. The minute we heard you were coming, I told Cousin Lemuel—"

"Cousin Lemuel?"

"Yes, my cousin Lemuel Shaw—he's the Chief Justice of Massachusetts," Oliver said casually. "One of the bigwigs who's arranging the dinner for you tomorrow night. Oh, they'll all be there—politicians, professors, poets, what have you! But, meanwhile, we're going to see that you have a good drink and a good sleep tonight and we'll stand over you like dragons tomorrow morning. Otherwise, your admirers will be pounding on your door at six A.M. and sticking to you like leeches."

Paul was too tired and too grateful for anything except silent assent to the suggestions made by the brothers. He walked wearily along beside his rescuers, down the platform and through the dingy station and sank into the waiting hack with undisguised relief. As they rattled along over the pavements, Oliver gave a glowing account, frequently interrupted by Stephen, of the profound impression made in Boston by the news of Paul's reception in Europe and New York, while the latter answered only in polite monosyllables. But as they left level ground and began the steep ascent which he realized, from what he had previously learned of the city, must be Beacon Hill, he roused himself sufficiently to ask a question.

"Do you happen to know a family named Sheppard?"

"Several of them. Which one do you mean?"

"The father of the family is a Mr. Albert Sheppard. He has two daughters —Berenice and Charmian."

"Oh!" Oliver glanced at Stephen and something in his tone struck Paul as slightly unnatural, though he could not have told just what it was. "I don't know them personally, but of course I know who they are. As a matter of fact, they live not very far from us, when they're home, which isn't often. I believe they're in Boston now though."

"Yes, I'm quite sure they are. Mrs. Sheppard died in southern France, late in the winter, and Mr. Sheppard brought her—her body home for burial at Mount Auburn Cemetery. Of course, his daughters came with him. I'd like very much to call on him and the girls as soon as I can."

"Then write a note the minute you're thoroughly awake in the morning and I'll send it around. Of course, everyone wants to entertain you. You'd better get in your call before you're swamped."

"Yes, I mean to. In fact, I don't intend to be 'swamped' to such a degree that I can't call often on the Sheppards."

"Of course, you must do just as you please." Again, Oliver's voice did not sound quite natural. "Well, here we are. I'm afraid everyone else in the family has gone to bed, and I told Saunders, our butler, not to wait up, either. I was sure Stephen and I could manage to make you comfortable."

He dismissed the hack, picked up the heavy bags again and, taking out a latchkey, opened the door flanked by fluted white columns. Paul had not been prepared for so elegant and spacious a house. A graceful staircase curved upward from the center of an immense square hall, whose walls were covered with the handsomest landscape paper he had ever seen; and the incidental furniture, mirrors and paintings with which this foyer was adorned were equally imposing. The lights were turned low in the rooms on either side, but he could catch glimpses of rich rugs and upholstery, more mirrors, more paintings and quantities of books. Oliver, noticing his surprised and admiring glances, shook his head.

"You'll have plenty of time to see the family treasures tomorrow," he said. "I know you're dead on your feet. Come on up to bed. You've got two flights to go, I'm sorry to say."

The room into which Paul was finally ushered dwarfed all the chambers in the Morphys' Royal Street house, his own included, and he had always thought those commodious in the extreme. It was permeated with a sweet smell, not the heady perfume of jasmine and gardenias and orange blossoms, such as rose from his courtyard at home, but the fresh delicate fragrance of lilacs and the spicy odor of clove pinks, which stood here and there in clear glass vases. Warm as the day had been, the night was cool, and a coal fire in an open hearth shed a welcome warmth and radiance on its surroundings. Drawn close to it was a chintz-covered wing chair, facing a table on which two decanters, one of white wine and one of red, were set out, together with a pitcher of milk, bread and butter, cheese, fruit and a large frosted cake. Beyond, a well-appointed desk stood open and between the windows was a bookcase bulging with volumes bound in half calf. The bed, hung with chintz which matched the covering on the chair and the window curtains, was invitingly turned down. Everything bespoke comfort and friendliness.

"Our room is just across the hall, so if you want anything, don't hesitate to call us," Oliver said cheerily, as he set down the bags. "Otherwise, we won't disturb you until we hear from you. Then we'll get your note out as soon as it's written. We eat big breakfasts in this part of the world, but I know you like a light one and you can have it any time you choose. Good night and good luck!"

Paul awoke to the soothing sound of gentle rain and, glancing at his magnificent new watch, saw with horror that it was nearly one o'clock. He sprang up, snatched the dressing gown he had not bothered to unpack the night before and put it on, then went straight to the desk, where he dashed off a note to Charmian, asking if he might come and see her that afternoon. Not until he had signed and sealed it did he open the door. The one to the room opposite was also open, and Oliver was sitting near it, a newspaper in his hand, but his attitude one of watchful attention.

"Well, hello!" he said cordially. "Mother was beginning to be afraid you'd died in your sleep, so about an hour ago I peeked in on you, very cautiously, and you were slumbering like a baby. So I told her not to worry, you'd probably wake up in time for lunch. Is that the note you want sent out? Give it to me, I'll see that it goes right away. And you'd like some coffee, wouldn't you, while you're dressing? Saunders will bring it to you and fix the fire. You'll need hot water, too, of course. And you might like to have a look at last night's *Transcript*. There's a screed saying what a great man you are and an advance notice about the dinner. I hope you like poetry. Mr. Longfellow and Mr. Lowell have both written some on purpose for the occasion—Mr. Longfellow's is likely to be a little on the sentimental side. But Dr. Holmes is going to be the toastmaster and he's really very witty."

Paul accepted the newspaper and glanced through it, with pardonable satisfaction, as he waited for the promised coffee. It was not as good as he would have had at home, but it was better than any he had found in England or France, the cream that came with it was so thick that he could hardly pour it, and the muffins, butter and marmalade that supplemented it were all so delicious that he consumed everything in sight, disregarding the fact that he would soon be expected to eat a hearty meal with the assembled Shaw family. There was a foot tub beside a washstand, both of which had been hidden by an Oriental screen that was now drawn aside, and a plentiful supply of hot water was unobtrusively brought in while he was devouring his breakfast. When he looked around, he saw that the coal fire was burning brightly again and that a manservant was picking up the clothes which he had dropped haphazardly the night before and carefully unpacking those which were still in the bags.

"Will that be all for the moment, sir?" the man asked as he approached Paul and took the tray.

"Yes, thank you very much."

The man bowed, deferentially. "Mrs. Shaw asked me to tell you that when you were ready, she would like very much to welcome you, sir. She's waiting in the library to receive you. Unfortunately, Mr. Shaw was obliged to remain at his office, but Mr. Oliver and Mr. Stephen have been excused from there for the day, in order to be at your disposal. And, of course, you have only to ring if you should require further services from me, sir."

Decidedly, this was rather like being back in London even to the rain, except that here his hosts created a warmer atmosphere of friendliness than any of the persons Paul had visited in England. He bathed and dressed without the feeling that he would be made uncomfortable because he had upset the regular routine of the household and, when he opened his door a second time, found that Stephen was waiting for him "to make sure he did not lose his way when he went to the library." It was perhaps just as well for, unguided, he would have gone straight on to the ground floor; brief as his glimpse of the rooms on either side of the entrance hall had been, he had certainly seen books there. But these, apparently, were considered quite incidental. The library was on the second floor, stretching across the entire width of the great house and, except for the wainscoted space over the mantel, where a fine portrait hung, it was completely booklined. Paul had never seen so many in any private house before, and was faintly surprised that they did not seem more overpowering. But again the cordiality of the atmosphere, the rich coloring of draperies and upholstery, and the prevalence of fresh flowers relieved any impression of the ponderous. A handsome elderly gentleman advanced with an outstretched hand, and a middle-aged lady, with a pleasant intelligent face, looked up from her needlework with a bright smile.

"Welcome to Boston, Mr. Morphy!" they said almost simultaneously; and the elderly gentleman added quickly, "I'm Lemuel Shaw, and this is my cousin Anna, the mother of your former college mates and, incidentally, of four other sons whom you'll meet later—two are at the Boston Latin School and two are at Harvard." Paul, realizing for the first time that he had kept not only the immediate family, but the Chief Justice of the state waiting while he dallied, flushed with embarrassment; but no one else seemed to feel any, and the Justice continued amiably, "Their father is very sorry that he was detained at the office, but he'll be seeing you tonight —as I shall. Unfortunately, though I could slip away from court for a few minutes, I can't stay for luncheon with you. However, Anna is going to give us all some sherry now. Meanwhile, perhaps you would let me have the pleasure of talking with you in French, since I do not have many opportunities to converse in that beautiful language, though I read it constantly. If I am not mistaken, it really seems more like a native tongue to you than English which, nevertheless, you speak perfectly."

"You're not mistaken, sir—that is, I'm afraid I don't speak perfect English, but it is true that most Creoles still prefer to speak French among themselves, or sometimes Spanish. At our house, it was about half and half, until my father died, because he preferred Spanish. Now it's French, my grandparents' and my mother's language."

"Ah! Then you have had the great advantage of growing up trilingual. I envy you. I was fortunate enough to learn French from a distinguished refugee, Antoine Jay, who, after his return to his native country, founded the *Constitutional*. Since then, I have done a good deal of translation for local papers—a pleasant avocation."

"Lemuel, why do you say you do not have any opportunities to speak French? You know you can do it in this house and in many others, as often as you like!"

"Yes, of course—and be understood and answered intelligently. Still, Anna, you will admit it does not come as naturally to us as to our gifted guest."

Oliver, who had been standing by one of the long windows, came forward while his uncle was speaking and took Paul's arm as the latter, no longer suffering from chagrin, responded to the Chief Justice's friendly overtures and Mrs. Shaw's smiling seconds to these. She now poured sherry into small glasses from a decanter even more elegant than those which had been placed in Paul's room, meanwhile talking easily in very creditable French of inconsequential things until Saunders appeared in the doorway to announce luncheon. Then she rose and, bidding her cousin good-bye, took Paul's arm.

"We thought, since you are going to such a large dinner tonight, that you would rather have a quiet luncheon," she said, reverting to English. "And a simple one, because I am sure the chefs at the Revere House are preparing a really formidable banquet. We want you to enjoy every minute of your stay in Boston, and I'm afraid you would not do so, if we surfeited you with food the first day! But perhaps you would like to take a walk this afternoon, to see something of the Hill and the Common at least. Then we can plan more extensively for tomorrow."

"It's very kind of you. But if I may, I'd like to wait until I get an answer to a note I sent this morning to some old friends, before I go out at all, or make any definite engagements."

"Why, of course! The boys didn't say you had other friends here. They're probably friends of ours, too. If I'd known, I would have invited them to tea. Why didn't you tell me, Oliver?"

"I didn't think. I should have, of course, because they've spent a good deal of time in New Orleans. Mrs. Sheppard did anyway, and I know the girls went there for their vacations sometimes. And then they've been abroad a good deal. You must have seen them in London and Paris, too, didn't you, Paul?"

"I just missed them in London. But I did see them in Paris, before they went to the Riviera for Mrs. Sheppard's health. It's very sad that they didn't go sooner; if they had, she might have recovered."

"These are the *Albert* Sheppards to whom you are referring?"

"Yes—you don't know them?"

"Not personally. But, as Oliver says, they've been away from Boston a great deal. And now, of course, the girls and their father are in mourning. I'm afraid they're not going out, socially, at all, or receiving strangers. But naturally that wouldn't prevent you, as an old friend, from calling. It would only be a proper courtesy on your part."

Again, as when Oliver was speaking the night before, Paul thought he detected a difference in tone when there was a reference to the Sheppards. But though it puzzled him a little, it did not depress him. He and his hosts had now reached the dining room, which was furnished in massive mahogany. Brightly polished silver shone on the huge sideboard and the capacious table; the china was blue Cantonware, the glass Waterford, the linen heavily monogrammed and, again, there were fragrant flowers in evidence, this time tastefully arranged in a low central bowl. Paul was increasingly impressed by Mrs. Shaw; she was very simply dressed, in a dark silk dress with no ornaments of any kind, but it did not seem to require these; and the plain way in which her abundant hair was braided around her head gave the effect of a coronet. The "simple" lunch was very substantial: a fish with which Paul was not familiar, and which was identified to him as scrod, or young cod, delicately broiled and buttered, was served with a species of cabbage salad which they called coleslaw; next came lamb chops, fresh green asparagus on toast, baked potatoes and light homemade rolls; and a rich pudding, to which the Shaws referred as Brown Betty, whose toothsome ingredients no one seemed to feel it necessary to enumerate, brought the meal to an end. Despite the lavish table set by the Sheppards in New Orleans, Paul had somehow gathered that Bostonians' everyday meals, when they were at home, consisted of "boiled dinners" or baked beans and brown bread, the very sounds of which were unappetizing; the delicious fare set before him was as much of a surprise as the impeccable service and the luxurious surroundings. The conversation revealed a courteous and genuine, but incurious, interest regarding his experiences in London, Paris and New York. For the rest, it centered chiefly on music, in which it appeared Oliver was deeply interested, and, more briefly, on books, the China trade and national affairs, with such tactful avoidance of the slavery issue that Paul did not guess how burning a subject it was with them. The Chief Justice had refused, a few years earlier, to release Sims, a famous fugitive, on *habeas corpus*, because he felt bound by the Constitution and the law; though, considering his personal views, his stand had required great integrity and courage in the face of widespread denunciations among his friends and alarming expressions of mob violence. His feelings had never changed and his decision had caused him lasting grief. In other company, he might have made some references to the case; but Anna Shaw knew she could trust him to be silent. However, she had refrained from inviting another young relative, Robert Gould Shaw, to meet him, because she knew Bob could not be kept off the subject. But they did mention the Honorable John Slidell, with generous recognition of his talents and of the tremendous influence he exerted in the Senate, now that he had succeeded in his adroit and outspoken campaign for Buchanan.

"You know him, I am sure," Mrs. Shaw remarked, in her pleasant, cultured voice, as she carefully measured tea leaves from a silver caddy to a heated pot, which she filled from a silver kettle boiling over a small flaming wick. "Indeed, I believe he married a Louisianian, didn't he?"

"Yes, we know him—my father and he were good friends. And yes, he did marry a Louisianian, Mathilde Deslonde, one of four beautiful sisters." Paul thought, with poignancy, of his conversation with Judge Morphy on this subject and tried to dismiss it from his mind by speaking of something pleasanter. "According to my mother's letters, another friend of ours, Pierre Beauregard, is courting Caroline, one of Mathilde's younger sisters. Everyone wishes him luck. His first wife died soon after he returned from the Mexican War, and it's taken him a long while to recover from her loss. He's a wonderful person and deserves all the happiness he can get."

"He'd acquire a very powerful brother-in-law in the Senator if his suit were successful," Mrs. Shaw said thoughtfully. She had begun to pour amber-colored tea into unbelievably delicate cups, doing so with the almost reverent care she would have given a solemn rite.

"Yes. But Pierre doesn't need John Slidell to make him important to us. He's our greatest hero, both as a man and a soldier. He has and is everything we admire most."

Paul launched into the extravagant praise that Pierre Beauregard's name nearly always evoked among his fellow Creoles and the Shaws listened with polite interest. The Sheppards were not mentioned again. But as Mrs. Shaw gave the signal to leave the table, Oliver told Paul that Morton, the coachman, had been instructed to wait for an answer to his note and bring this back with him; however, none had arrived when they returned to the library and, finally, Saunders appeared to say that Morton had returned empty handed. The young ladies and their father were out, the Sheppards' cook had told him; she would see that Miss Charmian got the note as soon as they came in and would be glad to bring the answer herself; after all, Saunders said with a touch of condescension, the cook was a good-natured Irishwoman and it was just a step between the two houses. As a matter of fact, it was a couple of blocks; however, the distance could be covered in a very short time, and Paul declined to go out, even for the constitutional which the Shaws seemed to regard as an essential part of their day's program. He was confident that, at any minute, the hoped-for summons would arrive; but the time came when he could no longer delay his preparations for the dinner at the Revere House, and he was almost frantic with impatience. At last, when he had practically decided to go unannounced and ring the Sheppards' doorbell himself, Saunders knocked at his door and held out a silver salver, on which reposed a small black-edged envelope. Paul seized this and tore it open eagerly.

"Dear Paul," he read and instantly, before even looking at the signature, realized that it was Berenice and not Charmian who had written. His disappointment was like a sharp thrust through his heart, but he tried to ignore this as he read on.

"I am sorry that we were not in when your note came and that we were so late getting home that Charmian had to hurry to dress for another engagement, so she did not have time to answer you herself. But she has asked me to tell you that she will be glad to see you tomorrow afternoon about four. I don't need to add that I shall be delighted, too.

"We congratulate you on all the new honors that you are getting and want to hear more about them. Of course, we shall be especially interested in a firsthand account of the banquet tonight, but we hope you will also bring some of the many trophies you have won and show them to us when you come to see us.

"Papa joins me in kindest regards and I know Charmian would want me to add hers, though, as I said, she went out in great haste and could only leave a short message.

Faithfully yours,
Berenice Sheppard."

Well, he tried to say to himself, it would be less than twenty-four hours before he would see Charmian now and, considering how long it seemed since they had been together in Paris, it should not be hard for him to exercise patience. But he could not entirely rid himself of the pain which had followed that first swift stab of disappointment. He was still suffering from it when he left for the Revere House.

Briefly, as he entered the large private dining room where his hosts and admirers were gathered, one hundred thirty strong, he managed to forget it. Surely this company, which was not seated until nearly nine o'clock, was as distinguished a one as had ever been assembled in compliment to a young man with only a single claim to distinction, and this unrepresented by any of these scholars and statesmen! Scanning the titles and names listed opposite the menu on the satin folder placed at his seat, he read with an increasing sense of awe: the Chief Justice of the Massachusetts Supreme Court, the President of Harvard University, His Honor, the Mayor of Boston, Louis Agassiz, Josiah Quincy, Oliver Wendell Holmes, James Russell Lowell, Henry Wadsworth Longfellow. . . .

Paul's hand trembled with excitement as he laid the folder down again. He managed to respond adequately to the hearty greetings of these important men, all of them much older than himself, nearly all of them bearded and thickset. They were somehow forbidding, not because they lacked friendliness, but because their learning and their fame made them seem overpowering. To be sure, Paul had moved in select social circles all his life—in New Orleans, in New York, in London and in Paris. But these distinguished men were not figures whose standing was dependent on affability or sophistication or birth, much less wealth, or whose legal or political attainments had made them conspicuous, like his father and John Slidell. They were gentlemen of great achievement, not in one isolated field, but in several simultaneously and were widely recognized for this. Poetry by Longfellow was read all over the English-speaking world, he was a famous linguist, and as much at home in Rome and as prominent a figure there as in Boston; Oliver Wendell Holmes, though a leading physician, found time, despite his enormous practice, to write novels and essays. Agassiz, a Swiss by birth, and now a professor at Harvard, stood pre-eminent as a naturalist. Quincy had made his mark in politics, both local and national, and was only one of the many statesmen his family had given to the country. The longer he considered the roster, the more conscious Paul became of superior forces.

Holmes was proposing a toast, a witty one, as Oliver had predicted; but Quincy struck a note of superior originality in referring to Morphy as greater than Caesar because "he came and, without seeing, conquered"—a delicate allusion to Paul's success at playing chess blindfolded. Longfellow was obliged to leave early, without reading his poem; but before doing so, he had invited Paul to visit him at Craigie House. ("If agreeable to you, come in the later afternoon," he said. "I call that the Children's Hour, but I make time then for guests, too, and they generally enjoy meeting my little daughters as well as my wife." Dr. Holmes voiced his approval of this arrangement: "Exactly what I should have suggested, Henry. That will leave Mr. Morphy free to have breakfast with me and find out that I'm not *too* much of an autocrat!") Lowell read his poem most effectively and was enthusiastically applauded. The Chief Justice was cheered when he rose, when he sat down after his speech was over, and at regular intervals during the course of it. As the moment approached when Paul would be obliged to respond to all these tributes, though he also had been cheered again and again, as one laudatory speech followed another, he found himself becoming increasingly nervous. His hands were trembling again when he himself rose; but the impression he made was most favorable. He spoke modestly and briefly, along the same lines that he had in New York, with only a passing reference to chess and with a closing salute "to the literary and scientific men of whom Boston is so justly proud, the stars of the first magnitude that adorn the intellectual firmament of the country."

It was over at last. He could go back to that stately, quiet house on Beacon Hill, where he had been made to feel almost like a member of the family, through the kindness of two former college mates with whom he had never even troubled to keep in touch. And tomorrow—why, it was today, for the feasting and speechmaking had gone on far into the night!—he would see his only love again and, this time, she would become his promised bride as well. His latest letter from his mother had told him not only about Pierre Beauregard's courtship of Caroline Deslonde; she had also told him that Edward Morphy's happy betrothal to Alice Percy would soon be officially announced, and that she hoped Paul would not fail to come home in time for the celebrations that were planned. Oh, he would get there, of course, hard as it would be to tear himself away from Boston! And after Edward and Alice had been duly toasted, he would propose a toast to his own fiancée.

He traversed the short distance between the Shaws' house and the Sheppards' as if he were walking on air and not on uneven bricks. The same grim woman who had been "the mainstay of the household staff" in New Orleans admitted him with no more signs of pleasure than she had ever shown, but this did not surprise him; he was used to her sour looks. The parlor into which she ushered him was handsomely furnished, but it lacked some quality, which Paul could not identify, that every room at the Shaws' possessed in such abundant measure. Perhaps, he told himself, it was only that there were not so many books around, looking as if they had always belonged there, or so many fresh flowers, which also seemed an integral part of the other setting; or perhaps it was the lack of an immediate sense of welcome. To be sure, the note from Berenice had said "about four" and he had arrived just as the tall clock on the stairway was striking; possibly he should not have been quite so prompt. . . .

At last, he heard soft, quick footsteps approaching and rose quickly, with a fast beating heart. But when the long velvet portieres parted, it was Berenice and not Charmian who was disclosed.

"I can't tell you how glad I am to see you, Paul," she said earnestly, advancing to take his hand. "And don't worry—Charmian will be here in just a minute, I'm sure. She's been delayed again somehow." Berenice sat down and motioned to a seat beside her. Despite his first touch of disappointment, Paul realized that he was glad to see her, that her simplicity and forthrightness were as appealing as ever, and he thought, with a pang of sympathy for his friend, how sad it was that Fred had never succeeded in touching her heart. She had on a plain black dress, with white collar and cuffs, not the deep mourning which she would have worn in New Orleans, but nevertheless suitable for her bereavement; and Paul noticed with pleasure that the little hair brooch secured the fastening of the lace at her throat, as it had done every time he had seen her during the interval since he had given it to her. "I hear the banquet last night was a great success," she went on. "Papa rather hoped he would be invited, but of course it wasn't possible to include half the men who would have liked to be there and he realized that. Besides, so soon after Mama's death. . . . While we're waiting for Charmian, won't you show me some of the beautiful things that have been given you? You didn't forget to bring them, did you?"

"No, I didn't forget. Of course, I wear the watch all the time. And I put two of the chessmen—one gold and one silver—in my pocket. I couldn't very well bring the board or the wreath."

He detached the diamond-studded watch from its chain and handed it to her, together with the chessmen. Berenice fingered them with tender care. Then, still holding them, she spoke of her pride in his achievements, her belief that he would go on to greater and greater things. When he questioned her, she said she had no special plans of her own. She doubted if it would be possible for her to go to Mary Lyons' Seminary after all. She thought she ought to stay with her father.

"My aunt, who was here so many years, looking after us while we were in school and Mama was in New Orleans, wanted to go back to Dublin. You couldn't blame her. She was born and brought up there and all her best friends lived in that locality; she only came here to help out. Of course, she stayed until—until we were all settled again."

"You must have had a very sad homecoming," Paul said. His sympathy was genuine and he knew he should have made some such remark before, but his mind had been so full of Charmian. . . .

"Yes, it was sad. But I'm thankful Mama didn't have to suffer any more. I'm afraid she had, more than we realized. But she was very brave."

"You're brave, too, Berenice. And I'm sure Charmian is."

"Yes, she's been wonderful. If it hadn't been for her superb spirit, I'd have given way sometimes."

"You never would have done that! And besides, you had your father!"

"Yes, I had Papa. I hope I'll always have him. Anyway, he'll always have me."

She put it that way because she knows Charmian is going to be married right away and she can't leave her father alone, Paul said to himself triumphantly. He tried to feel sorry for Berenice; he knew for how long she had set her heart on continuing her education. But somehow his sympathy was swallowed in the belief that he knew the reason for her renunciation. He had waited a long time, too. . . .

Again there was a light step in the hall and, this time, it was accompanied by a rustle of silk. Unquestionably, it must be Charmian now. The portieres parted again and she stood before him, smiling. She, too, was dressed in black, but somehow it did not have the appearance of mourning; rather, it gave the effect of emphasizing the blonde beauty of her golden hair and dazzling complexion. Her lustrous skirts billowed about her and, as always, the span of her waist seemed the smaller because her hoops were so large and the swell of her bosom so clearly defined. A lace shawl was draped lightly over her shoulders, but, except for this, they were bare, and the whiteness of her skin was accentuated by the delicate tracery. She was not wearing the heart-shaped diamond locket Paul had given her in Paris, to replace the first poor little pendant with the turquoise in the center; instead beautifully matched pearls encircled her graceful throat and gleamed as they fell in a cascade from the rosy lobes of her ears. Well, he told himself quickly, pearls were more appropriate than diamonds just now. And, after all, it did not matter what Charmian wore. She was *there!* It was unbelievable, but he had only to stretch out his hand to touch her. And she was more radiant, more desirable than ever!

"Charmian!" he cried gladly. "Charmian!"

"Yes, Paul," she said. Her voice was clear and happy, but she did not, as he had anticipated, hold out her arms to receive him. Could it be on account of Berenice? After all, now that he and Charmian were about to be married, surely they could embrace after their long separation in the former's presence. She would be his sister as well as Charmian's! He went quickly forward with his arms outstretched and did not even see that Berenice was quietly leaving by a side door.

"Mon coeur!" he said. "My darling—at last!"

Charmian did not actually draw away from him, but always before she had met him halfway—more than halfway; now she was standing motionless. She was still smiling and there was still that radiance about her, but there was something else that mystified him.

"Don't you want me to kiss you?" he asked in bewilderment.

"Yes, if you want to. But please don't misunderstand."

"Misunderstand?"

"Yes. Listen, Paul—I want to say something before you kiss me—before I kiss you. We've had lots of fun together. I like you very much. I've—I've enjoyed our lovemaking. You can make love very nicely, though sometimes you seem a little backward. But you're so terribly serious about it all!"

"Serious about it all! But marriage *is* serious, darling!"

"I know. That's why I never promised to marry you."

"You never promised—" he began. A terrible fear was mounting in him, a fear unlike any he had ever felt before. And then he saw that the smile on Charmian's face was not loving, but mocking, as he had sometimes fancied, while never allowing himself to believe, before.

"I'm a Yankee," she said, "a storekeeper's daughter. Don't you suppose I know that's what your people have been calling me all these years? They think I'm not good enough for you. Well, it's the other way around. You're not good enough for me. What have you ever done but play chess?

Have you ever earned a cent yourself? Do you ever expect to? I want a man who amounts to something, a man who's a success, like my father. Oh, I know you've won prizes, that stuffy, snobbish people, like the ones you're staying with and who gave you that dinner last night, fawn over you and flatter you; but when you come right down to it, what does that amount to? Nothing, absolutely nothing!"

"Charmian, you can't mean what you're saying! I realize I'm not worthy of you, no man is, but I'll try to be! And you have accepted me as—as a sweetheart for years! You have given me to understand—"

"I've just said, I *like* you as a sweetheart! You can kiss me if you want to and I'll kiss back, but I never meant you to understand that kissing and—and things like that necessarily meant marriage. Perhaps, you *could* have married me, if you'd really tried, if you'd 'forgotten yourself,' as you said once long ago you were afraid you might, and swept me off my feet. But you didn't—either then or later. You went on playing chess. Afraid! You needn't have been afraid! All you had to do in Paris was to go a little further—so far I couldn't have stopped you if I'd tried and I wouldn't have tried very hard. You might have known that. If no one found out, what difference would it have made? And if anybody had found out, my father would have been the very first to say there'd have to be a wedding right away. He'd have stood by me, he'd have given us all the money we needed, so that we could be comfortable and independent of your family. But it would have taken something like that to make him. And nothing like that has happened. I know now that nothing will. If I had a French marquis for a husband—and I haven't decided yet whether I want one or not—I might take you for a lover. It could easily be arranged abroad. But I couldn't have a lover without too much trouble in Boston or even in New Orleans. And I may as well tell you, now as any other time, that I'll never marry a mere chess player!"

PART FOUR

"The Gambit is not Good"

1861–1862

THE QUEENE

The Queene is quaint, and quicke Conceit,
Which makes hir walke which way she list,
And rootes them up, that lie in wait
To worke hir treason, ere she wist:
Hir force is such, against hir foes,
That whom she meetes, she ouerthrowes.

From *The Chesse Play*. By Nicholas Breton, 1593.

The Chess Reader, The Royal Game in World Literature,
compiled by Jerome Salzmann. (Greenberg: Publisher, N.Y.)

28.

"Any more stops before Richmond, Conductor?"

"No sir. Seein' we're so late, we're goin' straight through, leastwise if we ain't flagged."

"Then let's hope everyone's out of flags."

"Could be. On the railroad, that is. Army's got plenty. The ladies are mighty busy makin' 'em for the troops. Cuttin' up their silk dresses and all."

"Yes, I know."

The oil lamp which hung from the dingy ceiling, midway down the dirty aisle, gave only a feeble light. Nevertheless, the conductor could see that the young man who had asked the question, and who now edged slightly toward the window, closing his eyes as he did so, looked weary to the point of exhaustion. His face was white and drawn, even the lips almost colorless, the features pinched; could have been right well favored though, the conductor reflected, if he hadn't appeared to be so puny. His clothes were elegant, too—wasn't often you saw such smooth broadcloth, such fine linen. As far as that went, you didn't see much broadcloth or linen of any kind these days on the Richmond and Petersburg Railroad. Butternut jackets and homespun grays, bearskin shirts and fringed leggings—these were the familiar sights; there were plenty in the car right now. And usually the wearers of such incongruous garments were a noisy lot, their loud laughter, coarse oaths and ribald ditties ringing out above the clatter of the train, the jingle of their spurs, the clanking of their swords and the occasional crash of their bottles. Tonight they were quieter than usual; in one corner a card game was still going on, in another a heated argument over the fitness of Jefferson Davis for the Presidency; and now and then a group, which had been caroling *Lorena*, roused itself and again burst into snatches of song. But for the most part, only snoring broke the silence. Not one of the strange volunteers, however, as far as the conductor could observe, was spent to the same degree as was this one young elegant. The others were all healthily or drunkenly somnolent, that was all.

His curiosity, as well as his interest aroused, the conductor continued to gaze at his peculiar passenger, the only one in the car who had a grimy plush seat to himself. Something about him had discouraged the easy camaraderie of wartime, had made the rough and ready mountaineers avoid him, even if that meant closer quarters elsewhere. Yes, he was a dandy all right, and it was understandable that these sturdy rustics should instinctively shun him and even despise him. But he was not only good looking; there was something actually appealing about his face; perhaps he would have

liked to be friends with the others, if he had known how, or if they had been
willing to let him. He might well be closing his eyes, not only because he
was tired, but because, having failed to find companionship, he was trying
to pretend he did not want it. And either he had seen better days, or he had
been traveling a great distance; his dove-colored coat was rumpled, his frilled
shirt had lost its freshness; they must have been worn, without change, for
some time. Moreover, their style, as well as their condition, suggested that
they were not local products. Although it was obvious that their wearer was
disinclined for further conversation, the conductor's curiosity finally overcame his consideration for the traveler's fatigue.

"Come a far piece, haven't you?" he inquired.

The young man half opened his eyes.

"Yes," he said and closed them again.

"Memphis, maybe?" hazarded the conductor.

The eyes re-opened, wider this time. They were heavily fringed, very large
and very clear; something about them gave the conductor a great shock.
He had expected they would be dull from sleeplessness; instead, their clarity
was disconcerting. He had thought the traveler's skin looked gray; now that
he saw these eyes, he changed his mind. It was the eyes that were gray;
the skin simply blended with them.

"Yes," the young man was repeating. "Yes, I've come from Memphis—
somewhere along the line. Or rather, from Grand Junction, just east of
there." He spoke courteously, but rather coolly. "I've also come from Jackson, from Chattanooga and from Lynchburg, to mention just a few of the
places where I've changed trains since I left home. I believe there have
been ten. However, I didn't start from any of them. I'm not sure I understand why it should interest you so much to know, but since it seems to,
I don't mind telling you that I started from New Orleans."

"New Orleans? New Orleans, Louisiana? Why, that's where old Bory's
from!"

"Old Bory? You mean General Beauregard?"

"Don't I just! That's what we all call him in Virginia!"

One of the men in a nearby seat, who had been dozing on the shoulder
of the man next to him, also half-asleep, suddenly sat up. "Virginia, eh?"
he inquired belligerently. "You all think that's the only state there is, don't
you? Well, let me tell you something: we call him that in Georgia, too, and
down Florida way, where my friend here comes from, they call him the
same. Virginia ain't got no patent on nicknames, not as I've heard." He
rose unsteadily, as if to challenge any such claim, then sank drunkenly back
in his place. Derisively, several others gave voice to similar sentiments, and
two slender young officers, whose smartly tailored uniforms made them conspicuous among their fellow travelers, chanted solemnly:

> "Flashing, flashing, along the wires
> The glorious news each heart inspires.
> The war in Charleston was begun,
> Its smoke obscured the morning sun,
> As with cannon, mortar and petard
> We saluted the North with our Beauregard."

They repeated the last two lines with increasing vehemence; then they, too, lapsed into silence and the conductor spoke even more excitedly than before. "I shook hands with him myself!" he told his unwilling listener. "I had him right here in this very car, from Petersburg north, when he come to Richmond from Charleston."

"Mon pauvre Pierre, comme je te plaigns!" the traveler said under his breath. It would not have mattered if he had spoken aloud and in English; the conductor was now so intent on talking himself that he was not listening.

"I tell you, there's a hero if there ever was one!" he exclaimed. "Not just the hero of Fort Sumter, either—a hero any place you've a mind to put him. You heard what that Georgian said about him and his Florida friend. This war'll be over by autumn, if old Bory's given command like he ought to be and will be, when the President sees the light. He's a military man himself, so I reckon it won't be long now. And what I like best about old Bory is that none of this has gone to his head—I mean ladies pelting him with flowers and bands playing and crowds shouting for speeches every time the train pulls into a depot! He just bows and smiles and then draws back and gets one of his friends to speak for him."

"Perhaps he isn't very good at making speeches."

"Don't you believe it! Why that man would be good at anything! But when he got to Richmond, and found a delegation—all big shots themselves, you understand—on hand to welcome him, and a coach and four drawn up outside, waiting to take him to the Spotswood, what does he do? He thanks everybody and then says, sort of shy like, that of course all this is a great honor, but it's completely unexpected and if it's all the same to these distinguished gentlemen, he'd rather just take a hack and go to simpler quarters, where he can have privacy. Privacy! There's modesty for you . . . say, Mister, ain't you even listenin' to what I'm tellin' you?"

"Yes, I'm listening. If I weren't so tired, I'd be very much interested. But I'm not surprised. I always thought Pierre Beauregard had a keen sense of the dramatic."

"You always thought—you mean to say you know him?"

"I've been a neighbor of his all my life. I'm on my way to see him now."

"You've been a neighbor of his! Well, I declare. What's your name, if it's all right to ask?"

"Quite all right, but I'm afraid it won't mean anything to you: Paul Morphy."

The conductor shook his head. "No, it don't mean a thing," he confessed. "No reason why it should, is there? Just the same, I'm proud to meet you. Anyone that's a friend of old Bory's . . . when you see him, tell him what I've told you—that we all know he can have the Yanks on the run in a couple of months and that we're countin' on him to do it."

"All right, I'll tell him."

"What's more—but there, I know you're tired. Maybe you could snatch a nap before we get to Richmond, like the rest of 'em, if I give you a chance."

He laughed good-naturedly and walked on down the aisle. After having come so close to fame, in the person of old Bory's friend, he had no desire to risk an anticlimax by chatting with others, even if he had noticed anyone sufficiently wide-awake for coherent conversation. But, as he strolled away, he glanced back over his shoulder, and saw that Paul Morphy had moved still closer to the window, and that he was gazing out into the darkness, his elbow on the sill, his chin resting in his hand.

He was absorbed in thought. Perhaps this hideous trip, which had been undertaken on impulse and was at last drawing toward its end, was just another mistake. But that hardly seemed likely. One man could not possibly make so many.

The first, and almost fatal one of course, had been based on the assumption that Charmian was as much in love with him as he was with her. He had not doubted, for one single instant, that this was the case, throughout those blissful weeks in Paris. Now that he looked back on them, he could see that he had been living in a fool's paradise all that time, that she had never told him she returned his devotion, that she had never promised anything; it was not her fault, but his, that he had taken so much for granted. And when he had gone to her in Boston, it was natural that she should have regarded his self-confidence as presumption. What was more, it was natural that she would not feel his prowess as a chess player represented distinction in a profession, and it was right and proper that she should expect and demand this in her husband. Very well, he would show her that he could achieve it, along lines that she would recognize as valid. After all, he had received his diploma as Bachelor of Law with the same ease that he had earned his previous degree; he had known the Code Napoleon by heart when he was only nineteen. This, as he now realized, had been a disadvantage; he could not practice until he was legally of age and in the two years before he reached his majority, he had been rather at loose ends. If he could have gone straight to work, he could have proven the ability which the excellent firm with which he had studied was the first to recognize and applaud. Under the circumstances, however, he had no choice but to drift, at least temporarily. After that, his father's sudden death had left him one of the heirs to a substantial fortune and with the feeling of increased family responsibilities; both had been about equally disastrous as far as his legal career was concerned; he did not need to work and he was needed at home. Then those glittering opportunities for travel and triumph had come to him unsought; was he to blame because he had taken advantage of them?

Certainly, it had not seemed so at the time; now he thought he knew his second mistake lay in his failure to begin the practice of law on his twenty-first birthday. He had gone to New Orleans from Boston by the quickest possible route and the very day after his arrival had presented himself at the office of Messrs. Rosellus, Hunt, McCabe and Hennen. The senior partner had received him warmly; but the warmth had cooled as soon as Paul had made his position clear.

"My dear boy, you should have come to me more than a year ago. At that time, we had an opening for a junior in the firm. Now the place has been filled."

"You might possibly have another, mightn't you?"

"Yes, eventually. But I understood you to say you wanted to start right away."

"I do. It's very urgent that I should. Don't you know of any other firm that might have an opening?"

"I can't think of one offhand. Of course, I'll ask my partners. I'll also make general inquiries in my circle of acquaintances. But at the moment, I don't see how I can give you any definite encouragement."

"Then would you advise me to open an office of my own?"

"Of course, there's no reason why you shouldn't. You've every qualification. Except—"

"Except what, sir?"

"Except that I'm afraid you wouldn't have many clients. You see, most people don't think of you as a lawyer. They think of you—"

"Yes, I know. As a chess player. But they shouldn't any more. I *have* been a chess player. But I don't intend to play another game of chess as long as I live."

He spoke with such vehemence that the older man was startled and tried to answer soothingly.

"Paul, don't say that. You come from a family of chess players—both your grandfathers, your father, your uncle Ernest, your brother Edward. Thanks to them and to you, your friend Charles de Maurian is a good player, too. You are a *great* chess player—a world champion. Chess is an ancient and honorable game. You couldn't have a better means of diversion and you need diversion—everyone does. But you yourself have been quoted, I believe accurately, as saying that chess never has been and never could be anything but a diversion. You've allowed it to divert you too long and to the exclusion of other interests."

"That's why I don't intend to run the risk of doing so ever again."

"But why should there be any risk? You can devote normal working hours to your profession and then, in the evenings—"

"You've just reminded me, sir, that I'm likely to have trouble in building up a practice. I mean to devote my entire time to it—not just 'normal working hours,' but evenings as well."

" 'All work and no play,' you know, Paul."

"All right. Then I'll play occasionally. But not chess."

He had not depended solely on the good offices of Rosellus, Hunt, McCabe and Hennen. He had personally visited every reputable law firm in New Orleans and all those of any distinction in other parts of the state. Everywhere the answer had been the same: there was no opening just then.

He searched for quarters that would not be too costly and when he found some that he thought would serve his purpose, he had cards engraved:

PAUL MORPHY
ATTORNEY-AT-LAW,
12, Exchange Place, Up Stairs
New Orleans

He hung out his shingle and doggedly, day after day, kept long working hours and patiently waited for clients. None came.

Once and only once had he broken his self-made rule not to play chess. His grandfather had begged him repeatedly to drop by of an evening, as he had so long been in the habit of doing, and while away the hours between dinnertime and bedtime with a game. Just as repeatedly, Paul had declined to do so. But, eventually, the old man's hurt bewilderment at his refusal was too much for him. He went straight from his office to Le Carpentier's house, delighted the old couple and their forlorn spinster of a daughter with his gay talk of Paris and London as they dined; and then, as if it were still quite the usual thing for him to do, got out the old chessboard.

Le Carpentier opened and chose to move Pawn to Queen's fourth; Paul replied by making the corresponding move. Le Carpentier's second move was Queen's Bishop's Pawn up one square. Paul reciprocated by advancing his Queen's Knight's Pawn up two squares. Le Carpentier, after careful deliberation, chose his third move to be King's Pawn to King's third square, and Paul quickly moved his Queen's Bishop to Queen two. Le Carpentier retaliated with his King's Bishop to his King's second square and Paul quickly moved Queen's Knight to Queen's Rook's third square.

His grandfather looked at him across the table, amazement in the old eyes that were still shrewd and keen under their beetle brows. Nevertheless, he refrained from speaking, and chose to move on the diagonal his King's Bishop, letting the piece rest at King's Castle's fifth square. Paul's next was Pawn to Queen's Knight five and Le Carpentier strengthened his Bishop's position by then placing his Queen on King's Bishop's three, sensing all the while that, with two ensuing and consecutive King's Knight's movements he would be truly on the offensive. Thereupon Paul threw caution to the wind and played Queen to Bishop's square.

"What's the matter with you, Paul?" his grandfather asked roughly. "If I didn't know better, I'd think you were trying to lose."

"You don't really mean that, do you?" Paul inquired tranquilly.

Without answering, Le Carpentier quickly canceled out Morphy's King's Bishop's Pawn with a maximum vertical sweep of his Queen. Morphy captured Le Carpentier's Queen and, in the same move, toppled his King over in defeat with his index finger. Both players realized that Paul's alternate move of King to Queen square would have been only a short-lived retreat, as Le Carpentier's next thrust would certainly revolve around his Queen's capture of Morphy's Bishop, next effecting a Queen Bishop checkmate after Paul's only remaining move of his Bishop to King's square. Le Carpentier's open Bishop now sufficed and what should have been a royal battle had developed into a pathetic farce. He pushed back his chair, upsetting the chessmen as he did so.

"I'm not in my dotage yet, even if you think I am," he said angrily. "I can tell, as well as the next man, when a game's being given away. I'm not an object of pity, either. To you or anyone else. You needn't come here again. Hereafter, I'll play with Charles."

Well, that was months ago and he had not gone again. Le Carpentier was too proud to ask him, once the harsh verdict had been handed down that his favorite grandson was no longer welcome at his house; and Paul was equally proud; he would not ask for reinstatement in his grandfather's good graces.

Temperamentally, he was not ill-fitted to live a life of seclusion; but the role of recluse, as he had always visualized it, was one devoted to the uninterrupted pleasures of the garden and the library and not to unremitting labor. Nevertheless, he toiled, to no avail, in his second story office, evening after evening, all through the hot summer months. Autumn brought some slight cessation of his voluntary imprisonment, for his brother Edward's long courtship of Alice Percy culminated in a November wedding, and Paul could not decline to attend the correlative festivities. But the happy pair had no sooner departed on their honeymoon than he was working more intensively than ever—indeed, so intensively that he was at first hardly aware of Secession's rising tide. The withdrawal of South Carolina from the Union came as no surprise, nor did it immediately spell war in Creole circles. Some New Orleanians celebrated it noisily, some welcomed it as timely, some deplored it as premature, some underestimated its significance. But, coming as it did, at the height of the Christmas season, the more light-hearted continued their celebrations, either feeling or pretending to feel that it did not and could not affect them too closely and too personally. When Mississippi seceded on January 9th, sentiment was very different; ties between that state and Louisiana were much closer than between South Carolina and Louisiana and these were not based on propinquity alone; culturally and economically the two had much in common. By the time Florida, Alabama and Georgia had taken action, in swift succession, everyone knew that Louisiana would be next.

The news that the State Convention in Baton Rouge had passed the Secession Ordinance reached New Orleans on a fine Saturday afternoon and pandemonium immediately broke loose. The Washington Artillery fired a salute of one hundred guns on the levee and, simultaneously, bells from every church and firehouse began to peal, and the whistles from every steamboat in the harbor began to blow. Even before the first tumult had subsided, Pelican flags were proudly flung out into the breeze from hotels, theaters and other public buildings, and from many private houses as well; and, with nightfall, brilliant illuminations began. The streets were crowded with people, singing the catchy new song called *Dixie*, and the shouts, "Hurrah for Independent Louisiana!" were heard on every side—for, though it had joined other southern states in leaving the Union, it did not immediately enter the new Confederacy, but elected to become an independent republic, functioning under its own flag. Six weeks later it took the almost inevitable step toward affiliation; but, meanwhile, a second great popular demonstration had taken place, with special emphasis on illuminations. At the Louisiana Club a huge single star, richly colored, was surrounded by innumerable brilliant lamps, and the Pelican Club was similarly lighted. The Pickwick Club, on the other hand, was resplendent with a movable transparency in which the Louisiana coat of arms was displayed in different shades of red; and, beneath this, in illuminated colors, was blazoned the motto, "Union, Confidence and Justice." Hotels and commercial establishments vied with private clubs in their elaborate displays, and the Orleans Cadets and the Louisiana Guards were all out on parade. Mardi Gras was even gayer—in fact, gayer than it had ever been. Only the day before, the state had adopted "The Flag of Independent Louisiana" and on the morning of Fat Tuesday, it was unfurled at City Hall before a cheering multitude. A day of wild rejoicing followed and, at night, there was a ball in every available hall, while the streets were crowded with hundreds of merry-makers, awaiting the parade of the Mystic Krewe. As this advanced, the excitement and enthusiasm of the crowd knew no bounds. A great arch, hung with lanterns and bearing the Krewe's name, preceded a transparency captioned *The Four Ages of Life*. The maskers marched in a column of six groups, flanked by Negroes, carrying a chain of platforms, brilliantly lighted with torches. *Childhood, Boyhood, Manhood, Youth* and *Death* were in turn represented with appropriate symbols; and the Comus Ball which followed the parade was even more glamorous than in preceding years.

Without being labeled as a complete spoilsport, Paul had not been able to withdraw completely from the circle of his family and friends during this period. Courteously, if reluctantly, he had joined Alice and Edward, his sister Hélène and his friend Charles de Maurian in the festivities which were so integral a part of Creole life; if only Charmian had been there, he thought, if only he could have seen her delight in such spectacles, he could have shared it! He had never taken any member of his family into his confidence regarding his association with her in Paris or the cruel blow she had dealt him in Boston. Now, for some reason he would have found difficult to explain, he mentioned her to his new sister-in-law as casually as he could when he pronounced her name.

"I don't see what I add to our group. Now, if there were only another girl—"

"Why, Paul, there are plenty of other girls! All you've got to do is to ask one! I know a dozen who'd be overjoyed if you only would. The trouble with you is—"

"I didn't mean just any girl. I meant Charmian Sheppard. She has so much joie de vivre that it's impossible to be dull in her company."

He was immediately conscious of that coolness in the air which seemed to chill it whenever Charmian's name was mentioned.

"Are you talking about that Yankee shopkeeper's daughter who used to come here and try to force her way into society?"

Paul could freeze, too, on occasion. He did so now. "I mean Charmian Sheppard, as I just said. Perhaps you've forgotten that you and she were good friends once. You brought her to our house the first time she came here. She didn't force her way in."

"Well, of course children will play with anyone, unless their parents watch out. Mine did watch out. The friendship, as you call it, didn't last long. Charmian just happened to be in my class at school and that didn't last long, either! Madame Girard found a way of making it clear that her unwelcome pupil would be better off learning her lessons elsewhere! When it comes to livening things up, you know as well as I do that Charmian would never have been invited to one of our parties, Carnival parties least of all, even before this year. And now! Have you forgotten that, besides being commercial and cheap and coarse, Yankees are our *enemies?*"

For a moment he stared at her blankly. Actually, he had forgotten that Charmian must now be classified as his enemy. Up to that time, he had gone on thinking of her only as his lost love, whom he would—whom he must—reclaim. But how was he to reclaim her under existing circumstances? What Alice said was too true—Charmian was a Yankee; she was his enemy; if she had been unwelcome in New Orleans before, her very name was anathema now.

She had never written him since that disastrous meeting in Boston; but from time to time Berenice sent him a chatty little letter and, strangely enough, one arrived to lighten the gloom of Ash Wednesday. She naturally felt very sad, she told Paul, to realize that North and South now seemed to be so irrevocably divided; but she hoped and believed that, even though their two sections of the country were separated, this would make no difference in such old established friendships as theirs. Her father had decided that, until the "politicians and hotheads" had come to their senses, it would be pleasanter to live abroad, so they were going back to Paris. She was not sure they could have the same beautiful house they had occupied before, but when they were settled she would let him know. Until he heard from her again, perhaps it would be better if he addressed her in care of the American Legation, with which they would always be in touch.

"I'm sure there is a great deal to be said on the side of the South," she added in a postscript. "Charmian and I would be glad of any news you feel like sending us. If you see Major Beauregard, please give him our regards. You know how much we have always admired him."

It was, Paul reflected, as he read and reread these last sentences, actually quite a while since he had seen Pierre, at least long enough to have any sort of a talk with him. Of course, they had met at parties, and he personally had not failed to remark the change in the erstwhile brooding widower, which was a matter of such general comment, since the latter had become a Major in the Corps of Engineers and was happily married to Caroline Deslonde. They were living in the house on Chartres Street which had been built by Paul's grandfather and with which his own childhood was so closely associated; it had been loaned them for their honeymoon and then, as the owner wished to spend some months in travel, she had asked them to stay on and they had been glad to do so. Paul had failed to take advantage of several cordial invitations to visit them; now he decided it might not be a bad idea to sound Pierre out on the question of enlistment, which Paul was turning over in his mind. Numa Augustin, a lifelong friend of the Morphy family, who was by temperament a fire-eater, had promptly formed a battalion known as the Orleans Guards; nearly all the gilded youth of the city had rushed to join it, and Edward Morphy and Charles de Maurian had been no exception to this rule; they had been ordered into the service of the State of Louisiana even before this joined the Confederacy. But Telcide had cried out in alarm when Paul suggested following their example: with his delicate constitution, he must be mad to think of such a thing! A little later, when Paul's cousin, Diego, joined the Confederate Guards Regiment and became a sergeant in the Louisiana Militia, Paul broached the subject again and Telcide's protests grew more and more vehement; she was so close to hysteria that he did not dare oppose her openly. But he could not bring himself to believe that there was not some branch in the service in which he could be useful. It was all too plain by now that he would never be a lawyer; very well, he would be a soldier! A dashing officer might very well have more appeal to Charmian than a dull attorney, even if she did not approve his cause. Pierre could tell him how such a miracle could be brought about. With this in mind, he set out for the house on Chartres Street which he still thought of as his grandfather's, though it had now changed hands several times since Le Carpentier had sold it to John and Aloïse Merle.

He lingered for a few minutes in front of the garden on the corner of Chartres and Ursuline Streets, which an open gate permitted him to view unimpeded, despite the high brick wall which now enclosed it. He had loved the wild iris and lilies, the ferns and ginger plants which his grandfather had brought in from the slave farm in the swamps and which, far from drooping and dying as a result of the transfer, had grown and flourished after transplanting, until they eventually achieved something almost jungle-like in their luxuriance. Moreover, he had shared his grandfather's conviction that this small tangled park should be left unhedged, so that it might be enjoyed by the entire neighborhood; and, when the place was sold, he had grieved, not only because it would cease to be a source of family pride and pleasure, but because it would no longer be a source of neighborhood pride and pleasure as well. For a great while, his sensitivity on the subject had caused him to avoid the neighborhood; now, regarding it after time had healed his sorrow at separation from it, he was bound to admit that Aloïse Merle had also brought beauty to it—not, to be sure, that untrammeled sylvan beauty with which Le Carpentier had managed to transfigure a city lot; but a controlled and ordered beauty which harmonized with its urban setting. A fountain, surmounted by a cherub astride a dolphin, stood in the center and the water flowing from the dolphin's mouth fell with a soft musical sound into the circular pool at its base. Neat brick walks radiated from this fountain, encircled the four D-shaped flower beds which made part of a formal pattern and followed the brick wall on all four sides of its interior. A magnolia tree rose above each of the four D-shaped flower beds, and a three foot space between the walks and the wall permitted the thriving growth of more flowers, in abundant variety. With the coming of spring, the camellias had lost their last perfect petals; but some of the roses were already at the height of their glory and the air was heavy with their scent and that of the adjacent tea olive shrubs. Beds of the various herbs, indispensable to Creole cuisine, supplemented the flower beds and fruit trees were espaliered on the walls behind the flowers; lattices and arbors, overhung with wisteria, brought the garden into logical relation with the orchard beyond it and completed the pleasing design. On this balmy day, when the harmonious whole was bathed in beneficent sunshine, Paul felt his heart go out in sympathy to Aloïse; she, too, must have suffered when bereaved of this place. At the same time, his last nostalgic longing for the miniature jungle was submerged in unreluctant admiration for the charm of her creation, embodied in such florescence and fructification.

Realizing at last that, if he continued to linger by the open gate, the acceptable time for calling would be past, he turned away and went up the graceful curved staircase leading to the front door. This was opened by a manservant whose erect bearing and general spruceness suggested training by a military master, who ushered Paul into the *salle de compagnie,* where he had played so many games of chess with his father, his uncle Ernest and his brother Edward. Again, waves of the nostalgia, which, only a few minutes before, he had believed entirely subdued, threatened to overwhelm him; the room, though elegantly furnished, lacked both the allure with which his mother managed to imbue all her surroundings and the atmosphere of culture which his father had been equally gifted in imparting. He was glad when he heard light footsteps approaching and realized that his hostess was not going to keep him waiting and that he would lack time to brood over unwelcome changes.

He had always liked Caroline, as he had liked every one of the charming Deslonde sisters who, like the famous de la Rondes, were not infrequently called the Muses, though, as a matter of fact, while Captain and Madame Deslonde also had nine children, five of them were sons! Paul had been too young to attend the famous fancy dress ball at the Mint, given to introduce Rose and Josephine Kennedy; but he well remembered the sensation Mathilde Deslonde had created when she appeared at this in the elaborate costume of a French marquise and the success, almost as great, which her three sisters had scored in French peasant dress. All this had been the talk of the town. While Caroline was generally considered less fascinating than Mathilde, who had captivated official Washington when she went there as the wife of John Slidell, then Senator from Louisiana, Caroline, too, was a gracious and accomplished hostess; and her reception of Paul was now as courteous and as cordial as he had hoped it might be. But she could not conceal her surprise when he asked to see her husband. Surely he must have heard that, after the abrupt termination of his post as Commandant of West Point and his resignation from the Federal Army, Pierre had gone straight to Montgomery, the newly formed capital of the Confederacy, where he had joined President Davis and where he was now awaiting a new commission! Mr. Slidell and others had recommended him for a Brigadier in the Confederate Army. But whether or not the recommendation bore fruit, he was merely marking time until he received assignment for active duty. He did not expect to return to New Orleans meanwhile; and if he found his absence were to be prolonged, Caroline would not stay on here without him. She did not wish to trespass too long on the kindness of Madame Andry, the hospitable owner of the house, and Caroline's brother-in-law, John Slidell, had very kindly suggested that she and her mother should use his house, on the Esplanade, when it was more convenient for them to be in town than at the Deslonde plantation near Edgard. He and Mathilde were hardly there any more and besides, even when they were, there was plenty of room for all of them. Caroline thought the suggestion represented a generous gesture and the proposed arrangement a logical one. Didn't Paul agree with her? And wouldn't he stay for a glass of wine or a cup of coffee on the new gallery? She did not believe he had been to the house since the original one had been converted to a dining room, thus giving the house a great deal of welcome extra space; he might be interested in seeing the improvements.

"When Pierre gets home," Caroline told him, "we are going to give a big party. We have it all planned. Our guests will enter through the *salle de compagnie* and Pierre and I will stand to welcome them between the columns which divide this from the ballroom. That, of course, is where they will dance. The orchestra will be in the *cabinet* at the rear. If it is a pleasant night, which naturally is what we are hoping for, we will also place an orchestra on the gallery of the slave quarters, and there can be dancing in the patio, too. Those who do not wish to dance, or who want a change from dancing, can stroll in the side garden. We will serve lots of champagne and all the usual *bonnes bouches: petits pâtés aux huîtres, dragées, massepain, langues de chat*, fruit cakes, great platters of salad and ice cream, molds of creams and jellies." She paused for a moment, as if in anticipated appreciation of such a feast. "Of course, Pierre will wear his full dress uniform—his new *Confederate* uniform," she went on, "and I shall wear my wedding dress, changed just a little—for instance, I will have the lace flounces caught up with pink roses instead of white ones. But there, I know you're not interested in details like that! It will be very gala though, don't you think so? We shall count on you to come early and stay late."

He did agree that Mr. Slidell's suggestion was both generous and logical and that the proposed party should, indeed, be a gala occasion. He then thanked her for asking him to remain for coffee, but begged to be excused on the ground that his mother was counting on having him with her at this hour. The plea was a genuine one. Now that Edward had a house of his own, Telcide was increasingly dependent on Paul. But, as a matter of fact, if he had had no valid reason for departure, he would have been tempted to invent one. He did not want to see any more of the house, which he continued to find full of disturbing memories. It had been bad enough to see the altered *salle de compagnie,* even without looking past the Corinthian columns which framed it in the rear and alone separated it from the enormous apartment beyond, which had formerly been the banqueting hall on grand occasions and was now obviously only a ballroom. It would be worse still to see this new gallery supplanting the one where the Le Carpentiers and the Morphys had always taken their pleasant family meals, in fine weather. He knew that any further changes would be unwelcome to him personally, no matter how much they might seem to improve the property. Besides, he felt guiltily conscious, for the first time, that, in his passion for legal achievement, he had lost touch with history in the making, and deeply chagrined because he had not taken pains to be better informed before presenting himself to Caroline. He decided to pursue Pierre to Montgomery, as soon as the pitiful little law office could be closed and other personal matters put in order, and acted as swiftly as possible to do this.

While he was still occupied with the final details, the glad news came through: Pierre was the proud possessor of the coveted promotion and had been sent to Charleston. After that, one event came crowding closely upon another: he became the hero of Fort Sumter; he was making a triumphal progress to Richmond; he was about to receive command of the Army of Northern Virginia. . . .

It was in Richmond that Paul hoped, at last, to make connections with the first hero of the war. He would, he must. And coupled with this was a hope still more daring: since Pierre had become a Brigadier-General, he certainly would require an aide-de-camp. What could be more natural than that he should be glad to grant the request of an old friend who craved the honor of serving him in such a way? Nothing, of course!

It was with this conviction that Paul had started on his journey.

He straightened up in his seat, pulled his coat into place and looked at his watch. The conductor, repeating his ramble down the aisle, stopped again, goggle-eyed.

"That's a might handsome timepiece you've got there," he said admiringly. "Don't know's I ever saw one like it."

Paul detached it from its chain and handed it to him. The conductor's gaze wandered from the diamond-studded stem, surmounted by a coronet, and the initials traced in diamonds on the back, to the simulated chess pieces in red and black which took the place of numerals. He handed the watch back reluctantly.

"Ain't many got anything like that," he said, shaking his head. "Presentation piece, I reckon?"

"Yes. But it has no magic properties for shortening time on journeys. I wish it did."

"Well, cheer up. It won't be more than five minutes now before we're in."

He continued down the aisle, shaking the somnolent passengers into wakefulness. With varying degrees of reluctance or alacrity, they responded to his summons, reaching for their hats, gathering up their bundles and their firearms; then they strolled or slouched along toward the door, yawning and exchanging inconsequential remarks. Paul waited for them all to pass him before he took his own hat from the rack, groped under the seat for his neat bag and drew on his gloves. When he finally reached the station platform, there was not a vehicle in sight.

"Aren't there any hacks or buses at this depot?" he asked a shabby man who stood lounging against a post near the curb, apparently with no fixed purpose of going anywhere.

"Last one left about two minutes ago. Got snatched up quick when the train come in. It's always late, but tonight it's later than common. Everyone was in a hurry to be off."

"Evidently. Is it far to the Spotswood Hotel?"

"Just a few blocks, but it's uphill all the way. Mean to say you've got a room at the Spotswood?"

"Yes, I wrote for one."

The shabby man laughed, not very mirthfully. "Well, you might get space on a billiard table, if half a dozen ain't ahead of you there," he said. "Anyway, I wish you luck. Turn to your left and keep going up Main Street to 8th. This is 14th."

Paul picked up his bag, which had seemed light when he left home, but which had apparently become heavier every time he changed trains than it was the previous time and which was now a dead weight. Before he arrived at the top of the steep cobblestoned hill, he had been obliged to stop frequently to rest and the jostling crowd made the sidewalk almost impassable.

In the lobby of the hotel, conditions were even worse. Large numbers of men, some in uniform, but many in frock coats, were standing in tight little clusters talking so vehemently they did not even notice that someone was trying to pass them, and it was almost impossible to do so. Paul's face was streaming when at last he reached the desk, where a much harassed clerk was telling one applicant for reservations after another that there was no space in the hotel. Finally, he turned toward Paul.

"You heard what I said to all those others," he remarked wearily. "I couldn't get one more man, woman or child into this hotel with a shoehorn. Not even a baby."

"I think you must have a room reserved for me. Paul Morphy of New Orleans. I wrote ahead."

The clerk laughed, as mirthlessly as the lounger at the station. "Mails don't come through very regularly these days, as I should think you'd know," he said. "Even if they did, that wouldn't have made any difference. The hotel's been booked solid for weeks and weeks. . . . I'm sorry," he added more kindly, recognizing weariness even greater than his own in the slender hesitant man who stood before him.

"Could you suggest any other hotel that I might try? It's important I should find a place to stay. I've come to see General Beauregard. He's expecting me."

The clerk glanced toward the clock. "Not at this hour, surely?" he said with a touch of irony. "Listen, of course, I'd be glad to do what I could for you, but I told you the truth; there isn't an inch of space at this hotel or at the Ballard, either. Lots of private houses are taking in people though, and in the morning—I mean later in the morning—I'm sure you could get a room, even if you weren't a friend of the General's. Everyone's doing their best to take care of strangers. Why don't you just leave your bag here in the office and find yourself a chair, if you can, in the parlor? Maybe you could snatch some sleep that way."

While he was talking, a plump, swarthy man, in handsome civilian dress, who was standing near by in one of the tight little groups, turned slightly, looked hard at Paul for a moment and then detached himself from his companions and came forward, his hand outstretched. His beaming face showed no sign of fatigue or uneasiness and he walked with a springing step; indeed, he appeared to be the personification of prosperity and good cheer.

"My dear Paul," he said in French, "why on earth didn't you write to me instead of to Pierre? Everything would have been so much simpler then. I always keep a guest room at the disposal of my friends. Surely, you knew that you could count on Cousin Judah!"

NOTES ON THE SURRENDER OF FORT SUMTER

"Very soon after Major Robert Anderson moved with his command into Fort Sumter from Fort Moultrie, Governor Francis W. Pickens sent James Fraser, of the Charleston Light Dragoons, to me at my plantation fifty miles south of Charleston, with the request that I would assist with my negroes in constructing batteries on Morris Island. Taking my own negro men and others from the plantation of my uncle, Robert Chisolm, and that of Nathaniel Heyward, I was engaged in this work when General Beauregard arrived to take command. I then informed the Governor that it would be necessary for General Beauregard to have an aide-de-camp who was familiar with the harbor and with boating; that I was the owner of a large six-oared boat and six superior oarsmen, that were at his service free of cost. I was thereupon commissioned lieutenant-colonel and ordered to report to General Beauregard.

"Having visited Fort Sumter five times under a flag of truce, and once after the surrender, I became well acquainted with most of its officers. During a visit in company with Captain Samuel W. Ferguson, the officers jokingly complained of being short of cigars and like luxuries. With General Beauregard's approval, the next time duty called us to the fort we presented them with several cases of claret and boxes of cigars.

"April 12th, 1861, I visited the fort in company with James Chestnut, Jr. and Captain Stephen D. Lee, with the demand of its surrender, and heard Major Anderson say in conversation with us, "I shall await the first shot, and if you do not batter us to pieces we shall be starved out in a few days." These words being communicated to General Beauregard, we were again sent to the fort, arriving there about 1:30 A.M., April 12th. After waiting nearly two hours for a reply, we sent word to Major Anderson that our orders did not admit of our waiting longer. He came to where we were waiting in the guard-room, and informed us 'that we had twice fired on his flag, and that if we did so again he would open fire on our batteries.' Under our instructions this reply admitted of no other answer than the one dated April 12th, 1861, 3:20 A.M., which was dictated by Chestnut, written by Lee, and copied by me. Roger A. Pryor was with us on the second visit, but did not enter the Fort, giving me as a reason that his State, Virginia, had not yet seceded. For the same reason he declined to fire the signal shot. Moreover, I believe he was then a member of Congress, and may have been unwilling to compromise himself.

"The facts of the surrender of Fort Sumter to ex-Senator Wigfall are these: General Beauregard, seeing the fort on fire, sent me with a note to General James Simons, commanding on Morris Island, in which I directed him, if he could do so without risk to his command, to offer assistance in extinguishing the fire. I passed down between Fort Sumter and our batteries; delivering my dispatches, I volunteered to go to Fort Sumter, which offer was accepted.

"Colonel Wigfall, of Texas, volunteered to accompany me. While bringing my boat from its moorings in a creek, Wigfall, who was very much excited, jumped into a small skiff. The flag of the fort, which had been shot away, reappeared, and Wigfall was ordered to return, but he was out of hearing. I was ordered to return, and obeyed. Colonel Wigfall climbed through an embrasure, and, assuming authority from General Beauregard, called upon Major Anderson to surrender. Major Anderson did not realize the unauthorized nature of Wigfall's mission until the arrival of Captain Stephen D. Lee, William Porcher Miles and Roger A. Pryor with an offer direct from General Beauregard, similar to the one General Simons was authorized to make. Major Anderson was about to renew the action, when Major David R. Jones arrived with the offer of terms for the surrender of the fort, which were virtually almost anything that Anderson might ask, in order that we might get possession before the fleet could reinforce and provision the garrison.

"I have always been of the opinion that Major Anderson should not have surrendered when he did. The fire only consumed the officers' and men's quarters; the two magazines were uninjured, only one man had been wounded, the walls were secure, and he still had provisions which would have sustained his small command until the fleet could both have provisioned and reinforced him. I was present with Captain Hartstene during the evacuation, and was astonished to see barrels of pork* being rolled out and shipped on board the ISABEL, the steamer furnished by General Beauregard to transport Anderson's men to the fleet. My duty often required that I should pass Fort Sumter and our guardboats at night to visit Hartstene, who commanded the poor boats we used. I was rarely seen and had such a contempt for our guards that on one occasion, having a strong tide in my favor, we did not halt when shots were fired at us. In fact, we were seldom seen until close to the guards of the boat we sought. Captain Hartstene was well aware how easy it was to pass to Fort Sumter and expressed to me his uneasiness on this point; in fact, one bold officer could have easily cleared the way for a hundred barges with men and supplies to pass to the fort. The night but one previous to the surrender was very

---

* Captain J. G. Foster in his report says that the supply of bread in Sumter failed April 10th and the rest of the damaged rice was served at breakfast on the 13th. "The want of provisions," he adds, "would soon have caused the surrender of the fort, but with plenty of cartridges (referring to the lack of material for cartridge-bags) the men would have cheerfully fought five or six days, and, if necessary, much longer, on pork alone, of which we had a sufficient supply."—Editors.

dark. I was ordered to Hartstene between the fort and the fleet in the main ship channel, and my boat touched his guards before it was seen. Later in the war, when Beauregard defended the fort, one of the bravest officers in his command pronounced the work untenable. Beauregard then informed me that if necessary he would go there and hold the fort with his staff; that on no condition would he consent to give it up to General Gillmore. It was after this that General (then Major) Stephen Elliott made his gallant defense of the ruins; when, with the exception of some guns buried under the ruins of the casemate facing Fort Moultrie, but one small gun remained mounted, and that was pointed toward the city, being used merely to fire salutes."

A. R. Chisolm, Colonel, C.S.A.
Battles and Leaders of the Civil War,
edited by Roy F. Nichols (4 vols.), 1957.
(Thomas Yoseloff, Inc., N.Y.)

29.

Hardly waiting for Paul to stammer out his surprise and gratitude, Judah Benjamin propelled him, with seemingly effortless speed, through the crowded lobby and entrance; he smiled and spoke a brief word of greeting here and there as he went along, but he did not pause until he had crossed the sidewalk. Then he indicated a waiting carriage and motioned Paul to enter it, as a smartly uniformed coachman, alert despite the ungodly hour, sprang from his box and opened the door.

"Don't try to talk," Benjamin said pleasantly, slipping his arm around Paul's shoulder. "There isn't time anyway. We'll be at my house in a matter of minutes and you'll be abed in as many more. I'll send a hot toddy and a chicken sandwich up to you. Then sleep as late as you like in the morning. There'll be time enough to discuss your plans when you're rested and fed. And, of course, you'll want a bath prepared—I seem to remember you're a great one for baths. But that had better wait until morning, too—or rather, until later in the morning!"

It was indeed scarcely more than a "matter of minutes" when the carriage stopped before a large house, hospitably lighted. The curtains of the drawing room had not been closed and through the open windows could be seen a card table, with tall well-filled glasses standing among its pile of chips. One of the half-dozen young men who were here companionably foregathered instantly rose and was already at the door when Benjamin and Paul went up the steps.

"Well, Jules!" Benjamin said genially. "You'll be glad your game kept you up so late when you see whom I brought home with me! Our cousin, Paul Morphy! Imagine not letting us know he was coming to Richmond!"

"Outrageous!" Jules St. Martin exclaimed, seizing Paul's bag. "I hope you haven't forgotten your relatives, Paul, now that you're such a celebrity! Oh! of course, Natalie wrote us all about your triumphs in Paris, and you may be sure the story lost nothing in the telling—thanks to Judah's coaching during their courtship, she's a wonderful raconteuse! But come on, it's bed for you right away, isn't it? The garden guest room, I suppose, Judah?"

Paul followed Jules upstairs, his head swimming now with bewilderment as well as faintness. Yes, of course he knew that his cousin Natalie was Benjamin's wife, and that despite her husband's deep devotion to her, she preferred to live chiefly in Paris—in fact, Paul had seen her frequently there. He also knew that Benjamin had accepted this separation not only without acrimony, but with philosophy and that his relations with all the St. Martins had remained extremely cordial. But he had not heard that Benjamin's young brother-in-law Jules was actually a member of the former's household now, or indeed that he had already achieved an ordered and elegant form of living in Richmond. In any case, it would not have occurred to Paul to take the new Attorney General's hospitality for granted on the basis of relationship. . . .

"There you are!" Jules said, setting down the bag on a small mahogany stand. "I'll see that you have something to eat and drink by the time you can get undressed. And by the way, just drop your clothes on the floor as you take them off. That way, they'll be laundered and pressed by the time you want to put them on again."

The spring sunshine was pouring into the room when Paul stirred in his comfortable bed and his first real consciousness was of a clock, striking softly and musically. Half-consciously, he began to count the strokes. Twelve? Impossible! He must have made a mistake! But, as he sat up in bed, rubbing the sleep from his eyes, and looked at the mantelpiece, he saw that he had not. The hands of the delicate little French clock which formed part of the *garniture de cheminée* were indeed pointing to noon and a glance at the "presentation piece" confirmed his fear that it was telling the right time. Before he could rouse himself enough to rise, the door opened softly, and a manservant entered with noiseless footsteps and approached him deferentially.

"Ben watchin' for you to wake this las' hour, sir," he said in a pleasant, husky voice. "But Mr. Benjamin, he say mos' particular to tell you, take you' time. He an' Mr. Jules has gone to they offices, but they be back to dinner, five o'clock. You' clothes is all ready for you, those you lef' on the floor, an' I'll unpack you' bag an' put you' other things to rights soon's I've brought you' breakfast. Does you want that firs' or you' bath?"

This was the same perfection of service in the same type of luxurious surroundings that had so impressed Paul at the Shaw house in Boston; but this time it had the added warmth and grace peculiar to the South. It was doubly welcome on that account and also because Paul stood even more in need of friendly solicitude than he had before. True, he had been travel worn and weary when he reached Boston; but then he had been at the very zenith of his career as a chess player, hailed as a champion by the social and literary leaders of the world, and he had also been a suitor for the hand of his chosen ladylove. Moreover, his hosts had been his former schoolmates, who might reasonably take pride in having the lion of the day as their guest and it was not unnatural that their family should share this pride. Now he was an unsuccessful lawyer, a rejected lover, an idler when he should have been a soldier; he was a failure in every sense of the word; and his rescuer had been a man of renown, much older than himself, and weighted down with the responsibilities of high office in the Confederacy. The favor itself was far greater; the gratitude it inspired correspondingly deeper.

Paul breakfasted and bathed at leisure and, clad in raiment once more immaculate, was about to descend and explore the pleasant garden he could see from his window, when the ubiquitous servant, whose name had been disclosed as Rufus, reappeared and handed him a visiting card on a silver salver. Paul glanced at the engraving uncomprehendingly.

"Colonel A. R. Chisolm," he read slowly and, glancing up, added, "Tell him I'll be down immediately."

"Yes, sir. He did say like he hoped you would be. Seems he in a powerful hurry."

Paul hesitated. Of course, it was not customary to question servants. Yet, this time, he felt justified in making an exception to such a rigid rule of etiquette.

"You didn't happen to gather what he wanted to see me about, in such a powerful hurry?"

"No, sir. Seems like everyone's in a hurry these days, 'ceptin' Mr. Benjamin. He always takes his time, praise the Lord!"

Paul responded to the man's smile with an answering one and with the agreeable sensation that feverish haste was not necessarily an indication of industry or ability. Indeed, he descended the stairs in a more leisurely manner than he had originally intended. The slim, elegant officer who was pacing up and down the drawing room with obvious impatience came quickly forward.

"Mr. Morphy? You have my card, but perhaps my name means nothing to you, as I am not a Louisianian, but a South Carolinian. Permit me to identify myself as General Beauregard's aide-de-camp."

Pierre's aide-de-camp! The post on which Paul himself had set his heart! So he *had* made still another mistake! But with the swift stab of disappointment came the wholesome awareness that his hope had not necessarily been ill-founded. While sound sense should have told him that Pierre would have needed an aide-de-camp long before this, there was, after all, no reason to take it for granted that he would not eventually need more than one, or that the present incumbent could continue indefinitely to give satisfaction. Paul was not favorably impressed with his visitor and hoped that jealousy alone was not responsible for the fact that he found the Colonel's manner lacking in graciousness.

"I fear I owe you an apology. Your letter to the General was overlooked," Chisolm continued, in a tone that did not convey as much regret as Paul would have felt under the same circumstances. "Of course, it is necessary for me to screen his correspondence, which, as you can appreciate, is enormous. And, as you will remember, you wrote in French, which does not happen to be one of the languages I read with the greatest ease." The inference that there were many others which he did read with ease was not lost on Paul, who could not suppress a doubt as to whether or not this were really so; wisely, he did suppress the impulse to say he was sorry he had not written in Spanish, Latin or Greek, which he might well have done. "I therefore put your communication aside," the Colonel went on glibly, "until I could show it to the General at his convenience, and several days passed in which I had no opportunity to talk with him about anything but military matters. Meanwhile, you arrived in Richmond."

Again, the inference was plain: Paul's unexpected arrival in Richmond had been inopportune.

"This morning, the Attorney General called on General Beauregard and asked if the latter had not heard from you," Colonel Chisolm was now saying. "I explained that your letter had been duly received, but that, like dozens of others, it was still awaiting attention. The Attorney General displayed astonishment that there should be such a delay with correspondence —an astonishment which, I confess, I find it hard to understand, though probably he can command more clerical help than General Beauregard; he seems to be very adroit about getting whatever he wants." This time, there was a definite sneer in the voice, which Paul found it hard to disregard; but again he recognized the wisdom of silence and the Colonel hurried on. "To make a long story short, General Beauregard has now read your letter and would be glad to see you at once, if you would care to accompany me to his office. Of course, it is to be hoped that you can make your call very brief, considering the many demands upon his time."

"Did Pierre say that?" Paul asked quietly.

"That he hoped you would make your call brief? Why no, not in so many words. But I thought it best to caution you. I'm sure no stranger to the Richmond scene can possibly realize—"

"Thank you. I felt I must ask, because, if you had been quoting Pierre correctly, I should have felt I must decline to accompany you. I would have preferred not to take advantage of his friendship. As it is, I shall be glad to accept his invitation."

On the brief ride between the Attorney General's house and the hotel, Paul was the more at ease of the two; he commented casually on the beauty of the city, which he was seeing for the first time, and on its apparent suitability for the Capital of the new Confederacy. Colonel Chisolm responded, for the most part, briefly and coolly. However, by the time they had reached the Spotswood, forging their way through crowds which were

even denser than those Paul had battled upon his arrival, the aide-de-camp
had recovered his aplomb.

"We take this corridor to the General's suite," he announced as at last
they emerged from the lobby. "I shall have to ask you to wait for a few
minutes in the outer office—he said he would try to remain disengaged
until you reached here, but of course an unwelcome visitor may have in-
truded while I was not here to guard him. Ah! here we are. Now if you
will just be seated for a minute, Mr. Murphy—I beg pardon, Mr. Morphy
—I will let the General know you are here."

The suggestion of a seat was wholly rhetorical, since there was not a
vacant one in the outer office. Like every other place Paul had seen in
Richmond, except Benjamin's house, it was filled with a motley crowd of
soldiers and civilians. He thought he recognized among them some of the
men he had seen on the train the night before, but he could not be sure
and none of them seemed to identify him as a fellow traveler. In fact, after
glancing in his direction, they continued their conversations without interruption or sat staring aimlessly into space, and he was relieved, rather than
otherwise, not to find himself the object of scrutiny. Besides the uncouth
men in butternut jackets and bearskin shirts, at whose background he could
only guess, were now assembled others whom he had not seen in the latter
part of his journey, but whose uniform was already a familiar sight in the
streets of New Orleans: these were the Zouaves, clad in low cut blue shirts,
scarlet trousers and white gaiters, and whose short bright coats, slung over
their shoulders, added to their air of nonchalant gaiety. They were, for the
most part, guttersnipes of the slums; but—as might have been expected—
they had already proved themselves resourceful, tough and resilient, and
they had made a fine showing when they rallied, six hundred strong, at the
revue held at Pensacola some weeks earlier. Paul, who was now conscientiously following the march of current events in the press, remembered that
President Davis had congratulated General Bragg on the "perfect state of
the Zouaves' drill and efficiency"—a perfection due to the policy of their
immediate officers, a cut above them in the social scale, who gave orders in
a brand of French the privates could understand, and whose rough, often
brutal methods of enforcing discipline were also understood—and respected.
Paul had a casual acquaintance with some of these young officers, though
none of his close friends was among them; and, as he stood looking at the
Zouaves, clustered companionably in the outer office, he wondered why this
was so and felt vaguely sorry that it was. A wave of the nostalgia, to which
he was so subject, swept through him at the sound of the familiar patois
in which the men were chattering and exchanging observations, more or
less ribald, and he was on the point of approaching them and speaking to
them in their own vernacular, when the door to the inner office opened.

"The General will see you now, Mr. Morphy."

As Paul entered the room, Beauregard was affixing his signature to a document which lay before him, atop a pile of similar papers on a laden and rather untidy desk. He rose instantly and held out a welcoming hand.

"*Comment ca va, cher?*" he said cordially. "*Soie le bienvenu!*" Then, as he so often did, he switched from French to English without being conscious of the change. "I am sorry about your letter. But once you're outside of Louisiana, you don't find many persons, even those allegedly well educated, who are bilingual. Better write in English next time and mark your communication 'Personal and Urgent.' Not that I'll guarantee results even then. I don't seem to have the talent for getting good service that Benjamin has." He smiled, good-naturedly; there was none of the sarcasm here that there had been in Chisolm's speech. "Caroline wrote me you'd been to see her," he went on. "I'm very glad. How did she seem to you? I've heard from others that she hasn't been well, though she's never said so herself. I can't help worrying a little."

"She was charming, as always. A little pale perhaps, and thinner than the last time I saw her. But that's not unbecoming or unnatural. And she seemed to be very happily making plans for a party to celebrate your return. But, of course, she's worrying, too."

"Yes, of course. That house your grandfather built is ideal for entertaining, but I don't know that she should be encouraged to keep on planning for a party. I hoped, when I left home, that I'd be gone only a few weeks. Now I'm afraid it may be months, at least, and no one can tell what will happen in the meantime. My luck at Fort Sumter can't hold. Think of it! Not a man lost!"

"The whole South's thinking of it, and talking of it and bragging about it. You'll go down in history as a great popular hero, Pierre! You should have heard my fellow passengers on the train last night, cheering and singing at the mere mention of your name. As to the conductor, he's convinced that you're some sort of a demigod. He charged me not to fail to give you his regards. Of course, you wouldn't know which conductor it was; you've traveled with dozens of them now and no doubt they all feel the same way about you. But it was really quite touching."

"Yes—well—thank you for telling me." Beauregard glanced down at the papers in front of him, frowned slightly and looked up again. "Would you excuse me if I signed a few more of these? They're orders I ought to get out before night if possible. When I've finished, perhaps we could have more of a talk."

"Of course. Or I can come back."

"No, no, stay where you are. I won't be a minute."

He bent over the desk and, as he wrote, Paul observed him, more ap-

praisingly than ever before. So far, he had never given Pierre's looks or
manner much thought; he was a family friend, nothing else mattered greatly.
Now Paul saw a man definitely Latin in type, not very tall, but so strongly
built that, though slender, no one would have described him as dapper. He
had high cheekbones, a straight nose, a strong chin and full lips. His hair,
which curled back above his small ears, though it was otherwise close cut,
and his small moustache were coal black. His swarthy skin was untinged
with the ruddy color which, Paul now remembered, had formerly glowed in
his cheeks, brightening their tan; instead, it had the sallow look peculiar to
such complexions when insufficiently exposed to fresh air, or when the men
distinguished by them lacked regular sleep, exercise and nourishment. His
eyes, too, had changed, Paul realized. They were large and dark and had
once been his handsomest feature—keen, brilliant, merry. Now the lids
drooped over them, as if in weariness, and when these were raised from
time to time, the eyes themselves looked bloodshot and melancholy. Only
transiently was the old sparkle, the old bravura visible. But he still emanated boundless energy, he still personified pride of race, he was still the
supreme militarist. . . .

The door opened and Colonel Chisolm walked in and came over to the
desk without looking at Paul. "The President would like to see you at six,
sir," he said. "And perhaps I should remind you that you have an appointment before that with the Secretary of War. Shall I send word to Mr.
Walker that you've been unavoidably detained?"

"No, no, of course not. It won't take my friend Mr. Morphy long to tell
me what I can do for him. . . . There! That's the last of those signatures
you said you needed, Colonel." And, as the door closed again behind Chisolm's retreating figure, Beauregard said pleasantly, "I was right, wasn't
I, Paul? I'm charmed to see you, of course. But I never seem to get a minute
to myself any more. I wish I did. I suppose it's the price I have to pay for
attracting public attention by what happened in Charleston."

"Of course it is. I realize how important you've become, Pierre, and how
busy you are. I just wanted to say—to ask—"

"Yes, *cher*, go on, what is it?"

"I hoped I might do something to be of service to you."

"What sort of service?"

"I'm afraid I was dreaming, but—"

"But tell me your dream, by all means. Dreams can be important."

"I'm afraid this one wasn't. I'm afraid I've been very stupid. I should have
realized you'd have one already. But I thought if I could be your aide-de-
camp—"

The difficult words were out and he managed not to hesitate or stammer
as he said them. But it required an effort to meet the gaze of the man he

was facing, and he realized he dreaded not only the answer he was awaiting, but the way the words would be spoken. If Pierre mocked him or
chided him—and he realized that either was quite possible—he might not
be able to control himself, he might show his chagrin. Then something that
he had not expected happened; the expression that he saw in the splendid
eyes, now fully opened, was not one of derision or impatience, but of pity;
the answer was so gentle that it might have been given a hurt child with
the hope of soothing him; and the pity and the gentleness wounded him
more than any anger could have done, because if Pierre had been talking
as one strong man to another, he would not have looked that way and
spoken that way.

"My dear Paul, I am so sorry."

"There is nothing to be sorry about. I told you it was just a dream."

"Quand même . . . listen, Paul, you mustn't think I'm not fond of you,
that I don't appreciate all your qualities—"

"But you couldn't make a soldier out of a chess player! That's what you
mean, isn't it?"

"No, it isn't in the least what I mean. What's come over you that you
speak like that about being a chess player? You're a great chess player, the
greatest in the world. It's an achievement. You've got a fine mind, you've
shown yourself to be an outstanding classical scholar. You've got a noble
character. You'd rather cut off your right hand than do anything mean or
shabby. In all those respects, I couldn't ask for anything better in an aide-
de-camp. I'd be proud to have you associated with me. And I could always
use an extra one."

"Then I don't understand. . . ."

Beauregard drew in his breath. "An aide-de-camp's job looks pretty good
here in Richmond, doesn't it, Paul?" he said. "As far as that goes, it didn't
look too bad in Charleston. If it were just a question of accompanying me
to parties, in full dress uniform, or arranging appointments, of guarding the
inner office, of receiving and carrying messages, even of sorting mail—" For
a moment, he smiled and the old gleam came into his eyes; then almost
instantly, he was grave again. "All that, of course, you could do as well
as Chisolm—perhaps better; though it's only fair to say he was aide to
Governor Pickens of South Carolina before he came to me and that he was
highly recommended for social graces. But where I'm going next—" He
picked up a map of Northern Virginia which had been lying in the litter
of papers on his desk and studied it intently, if briefly. Then he tossed it
back among the documents and went on, "The trouble is, you haven't got
the daring or the stamina or the ruthlessness to match your mind and your
spirit, and Chisolm's got those, as well as the other qualifications. My aide
will be needing all of them a week or so from now."

"Couldn't you give me a trial and see if perhaps—"

Beauregard shook his head. "Why, Paul, you've had your chance! You could have enlisted in the Orleans Guard and you didn't. You could have gone to Pensacola with those Zouaves from our slums and you didn't. You could have been one of their volunteer officers, hitting a man over the head with the butt of your revolver if he didn't jump to an order and putting a bullet straight through him without wasting a minute if he were really insubordinate. And Bragg would have backed you up to the limit. *I'd* back you up if you started dealing that way with the hordes of them that are in Richmond right now. I'd put you in charge of a battalion if I had to organize one overnight, provided I thought you could handle it. But I know you couldn't. You know it, too, Paul. That's what I'm sorry about. That's why I had to say so."

"Then there isn't anything more to say, is there?"

"No, Paul, I'm afraid there isn't."

The door opened again and Chisolm came forward, more importantly than ever this time.

"Sir, the Secretary of War," he announced, saluting.

Beauregard held out his hand to Paul. "*Adieu et bonne chance, cher,*" he said, still speaking very gently. "Please go to see Caroline again some time and let me know how you find her. As I told you, I'm very worried about her."

"Benjamin, who was well to do, always managed to live in certain style, surrounded by creature comforts. In Richmond, he had rented a gentleman's three-story residence at Nine West Main Street. Here he maintained bachelor quarters with his brother-in-law, Jules St. Martin, Congressman Duncan Kenner from Louisiana, and two other friends. (His frivolous wife, whom he adored, had resided in Paris for many years.) The house was about a mile from the Executive Offices, and the portly Benjamin enjoyed the clarifying exercise of walking to work. He entertained well, and he kept a guest room for visiting friends, among whom was Colonel Richard Taylor, son of Zachary, who had a plantation in Louisiana. The President found it relaxing and stimulating to dine occasionally at Judah Benjamin's, where the atmosphere was cheerful and the cigars and wines of prime quality.

"As soon as the new Secretary took up his duties, the War Department was invigorated. Davis found that Benjamin could dispatch more business in an hour than many men could accomplish in a day. And he liked his charming manners, his methodical habits, his attention to his duties. For the public morale, Benjamin beamed with confidence, though when he took office the needed supplies for war had been depleted and the expected arms from abroad had not arrived."

Jefferson Davis: Confederate President by Hudson Strode.
(Harcourt Brace & Co., N.Y.)

30.

Paul walked slowly back to Benjamin's house, so sunk in misery that he was hardly aware of what he was doing or where he was going; as a matter of fact, more than once he made an unnecessary turn. Several times, persons in the hurrying crowd that surged to and fro, after he had bumped into them, turned to stare at him and then rushed on again, without waiting to hear his confused but courteous words: "I'm very sorry! So clumsy of me!" But when he stepped off the sidewalk, straight into the path of a great clattering dray, the driver swore furiously as he reined in his huge gray horses, and the shabby passer-by who dragged Paul back to safety was scarcely less vehement in his language.

"Which are you, doped or drunk?" he asked angrily at the end of his profane tirade.

"No—no. Just dazed. Please excuse me."

"*Excuse you!* Maybe I ought to report you. Next thing in your daze, as you call it, you'll be shoving someone else off the sidewalk, instead of stepping off yourself."

"No—no," Paul repeated. "I'll be very careful. I've only a little further to go—I think."

"*You think!* Where are you going anyway?"

"To Nine West Main Street."

The stranger guffawed. "The Attorney General's house? A likely story!"

"I assure you it's true. If you don't believe me, come there with me and see if I don't get in."

Moved more by curiosity than concern, Paul's rescuer acted on the suggestion. As they moved along he was disappointed, rather than otherwise, to see that his charge became gradually less stupefied and went up the steps of Mr. Benjamin's house with something very like self-assurance. The door was instantly opened by Rufus, whose broad beam of welcome dispelled the stranger's last doubts.

"You jus' in time for a nice big julep in the garden befo' dinner, Mr. Morphy. This gen'leman comin' with you?"

Before Paul could answer or thank him for his company, the "gentleman," a rather rough looking character, had beat a hasty retreat. Paul smiled slightly as he watched the disappearing figure out of sight. Then he shook his head.

"I think I'll go to my room, Rufus. I seem to have a slight headache. I really don't care for a julep. And if Mr. Benjamin will excuse me, I won't come down to dinner, either."

"Mr. Benjamin goin' to be powerful disappointed, Mr. Jules, too. They countin' on you, an' it's a fine terrapin stew fo' the firs' course."

"I'm sure Mr. Benjamin will understand if you tell him I'm not feeling well. And I'm afraid I couldn't do justice to the terrapin stew."

He went slowly up the stairs. The garden room was, if possible, even pleasanter in the soft afternoon light than it had been in the brilliant morning sunshine and Paul was grateful for its quietude. A large easy chair was placed close to the open window that "gave" on the garden and he sank wearily down in it. A congenial group of julep drinkers had already foregathered, and the sound of their talk, intermingled with occasional laughter, drifted up to him, along with the singing of birds and the scent of roses. But he was hardly aware of anything except extreme fatigue, the abject exhaustion which is allied with an overpowering sense of futility.

It was Benjamin who aroused him. Paul had been sitting in a characteristic attitude, his head bent, his chin sunk in his hands, when he was startled by feeling a touch on his shoulder and looked up quickly to see his host bending over him.

"No, don't rise," Benjamin said, forestalling Paul's instinctive movement. "I am sorry if I seemed to steal up on you—obviously, you didn't hear me knock. You were deep in thought. However, now that I'm here, if I'm not actually unwelcome, I'll draw up a chair and sit beside you for a few minutes. As you see, I brought my julep with me." He lifted the frosted silver goblet so that it would catch the light and gazed at it admiringly for a moment. Then he set it down on a small nearby table, drew that, as well as a chair, closer to the window, seated himself comfortably and took a satisfying sip.

"Nothing like a julep for refreshment after a hard day's work," he said. "Rufus reports that you aren't feeling well and that you don't want one. But I believe a good drink like this would be just the thing to set you up. In fact, I took the liberty of ordering one for you, in spite of what you said. Surely, you wouldn't condemn me to drinking alone! And I'd like to have a little chat with you. I take it your talk with Pierre wasn't wholly satisfactory?"

Paul laughed bitterly. "He was very kind. He bade me welcome on my arrival and wished me the best of luck when I left. He said he was glad I'd been to see his wife and hoped I'd go again."

"Yes? All that sounds extremely pleasant. What did he say that was disappointing?"

"He told me all the reasons why I couldn't qualify as his aide-de-camp. And they were valid."

"Of course they were. I could have told you the same if you had consulted me instead of Pierre. But that's no reason why you should be so sunk in gloom that you think you can't even drink a julep. Ah! Here is Rufus with yours now."

"Wouldn't you be sunk in gloom if you were convinced you were a complete failure, instead of being a tremendous success, as you are?"

"Probably. But you see, nothing and no one could convince me that I was a complete failure. Many efforts have been made in that direction. They have failed, not I."

Benjamin took another pull at his julep, a longer one this time and, impelled by something in his expression, Paul picked up the second goblet, which Rufus had placed carefully on the table, sniffed the sprig of mint with which the drink was surmounted and, finding the aroma unexpectedly refreshing, began to sip in his turn.

"Pierre is a pleasant fellow," Benjamin went on, "but he looks at everything from the military viewpoint, which is natural enough in his case. Undoubtedly, he left you with the impression that if you had not already joined the army in some capacity, and if you were unsuited, for one reason or another, to be his aide-de-camp and share his triumphs, which may or may not be as great as he now visualizes them, you could not be useful to the Confederacy. In my opinion, nothing could be further from the truth."

"Do you really mean that?"

"My dear Paul, I always say what I mean. My enemies, of whom, I assure you, I have many, do not believe that, because I always try to tell the truth pleasantly, whereas brusquer men seem to feel it is not effective unless it is disagreeable. . . . Did you enjoy yourself during your stay in Paris?"

"Did I *enjoy* myself?"

"Yes, yes. Did you find the setting and the society agreeable, the available accommodations comfortable, the climate reasonably pleasant and so on?"

Again Paul laughed, less bitterly than he had before. "Anyone who did not answer yes to all those questions would certainly be difficult to please."

"Then you would have no objections to returning there?"

"No *objections!*"

"I am very glad to hear you repeat my words so emphatically. Because, as I look ahead, I believe that is the place where you might be of the greatest service to the Confederacy."

This time, Paul could only look at his host speechlessly.

"I think you have already discovered," Benjamin continued smoothly, "that a command of French is not quite as general as it might be, once you are out of Louisiana." A slight twinkle came into his wise and kindly eyes, as he peered at Paul over the top of his goblet. How he could so quickly have become informed concerning Chisolm's alibi was a mystery; yet, from his expression and his tone, Paul could not doubt that it was to this he was referring. "Now I do not need to be told that you are bilingual, my dear Paul. I doubt that anyone else needs such telling, either. But if any doubts should arise on this score, I can quickly set them at rest. Indeed, if I am not mistaken, you are trilingual. Am I mistaken?"

"No, Mr. Benjamin."

"Cousin Judah, if you please. The Spanish is probably less important to the services I have in mind; however, one can never tell. It might be useful, too. The Empress is a Spaniard by birth."

"The Empress?"

"Yes, yes. The Empress Eugénie. The Consort of Napoleon III. The Countess de Montijo de Guzmán. Surrounded as she is by hostile French spies, it surely would be a welcome change for her to converse occasionally in her native tongue with a disinterested friend."

"I was in a daze when I left Pierre's office this afternoon, Cousin Judah, but I thought my mind had become quite lucid again. Now I'm not so sure."

"There is nothing the matter with your mind. You may not be aware of the fact, but I'm a chess player of sorts myself. I admire the type of mentality which alone produces a superlatively good one and I regret that you underestimate your own abilities and decline to make full use of them. You are a very brilliant young man, but you allow yourself to become depressed. If you will excuse me for saying so, that is a bad habit and one which you should try to overcome. But perhaps, because of my enthusiasm for your services to the Confederacy, as I foresee these, I have gone ahead too fast for clarity. I will proceed more slowly. . . . Of course, you know our enemies north of the Potomac are already referring to the present unfortunate conflict as the Civil War?"

"Yes, isn't it—a war between different parts of the same country?"

"My dear boy, that is the last way in which you should think of it—or speak of it. It is a war between the United States of America and the Confederate States of America; two completely separate and different countries."

Paul pondered this statement in silence for a few minutes. "I think I see what you mean," he said eventually. "But is that generally understood and accepted—outside of the Confederacy?"

"No, not yet. But we have every hope that it may be. In fact, that is one of our main objectives. If England and France could be persuaded to recognize the Confederacy for what it is—an independent nation—our cause would be immeasurably strengthened."

Again Paul pondered. Then, instead of answering aloud, he merely nodded, looking Benjamin full in the face and waiting intently for his host to go on.

"It is with that end in view," Benjamin said slowly, "that we have already sent three 'commissioners' abroad—Mr. Dudley Mann, Mr. Pierre Rost and

Mr. William Yancey. I confess I am surprised you were not aware of this and that you had not already grasped the significance of the undertaking. But I know that New Orleans is apt to be somewhat local in its viewpoint and outlook. This is something else you must strive to correct." He smiled so kindly that the words seemed encouraging, rather than critical. "Unfortunately, these gentlemen have not been as successful in their mission as we might have hoped," he went on. "There is no doubt that, in Charles Francis Adams, they have had a powerful antagonist. As long as he remains United States Minister to England—and, unhappily, I see no prospect of his dislodgment—we have very little chance of success there. He enjoys great prestige with both Court and Cabinet, and no wonder—he is extremely able and, despite his misguided views, extremely cultured and high principled. But, in France, we do not have so powerful an antagonist at the head of the Legation in Mr. Dayton and we might do better if we had the right person to oppose him. Mr. Yancey is in poor health and he has allowed himself to become discouraged which, as I reminded you a few minutes ago, is always regrettable. If he should resign, the Commission as a whole might be disbanded and the President might choose new representatives for our cause who could conceivably become more successful, particularly in France."

"You speak as confidently as if the whole matter were already settled."

"I believe it may be, as far as a new Commissioner for France is concerned. There are to be only two the next time, one there and one in England. And I will tell you, of course in the greatest confidence and speaking quite unofficially, as one trustworthy relative to another, who will, I think, be sent to France." He paused impressively and then, without waiting for an answer, spoke the next words softly and slowly. "My former partner—Pierre's brother-in-law—the very good friend of us all—John Slidell."

Paul sprang up, his own goblet still in his hand, but his movement was so sudden that only a swifter one on Benjamin's part prevented the small table on which the latter's drink rested from overturning. Apparently unconscious of the havoc he had so nearly wrought, he stared at his host.

"John Slidell is going to France as our Commissioner!" he said, hardly above a whisper. "And you think—you believe—that I might be of service to him in his mission!"

Benjamin rose in his turn and again laid his hand on the shoulder of his agitated guest.

"We must not leap to conclusions," he said. "Yancey has not resigned as yet, though he has said he wished to do so. Of course, the President cannot appoint anyone else until the expected resignation is a *fait accompli* and there is always one chance in a hundred that, if and when he does, he might not appoint Slidell, even on Pierre's recommendation and mine. There is also the other hundredth chance that John might decline to accept the appointment if it were offered him. I should not have spoken of all this quite so soon, had I not seen how desperately in need you were of encouragement. As it is, I have not been speaking of certainties, only of probabilities, or perhaps I should say of possibilities. But yes—confidentially I do think John will be offered the appointment and that he will accept it. I also think, if he is and if he does, you could be extremely useful to him; not perhaps in any way that would bring you public recognition, but this, I take it, would not matter."

"I'd infinitely rather there were no public recognition!"

"As I thought. Very well then. Do not mention this conversation to anyone. Do not alter your manner of life in any way. Stay on here for a week or more as my guest if you would enjoy doing this, for I would enjoy having you. Meanwhile, I should like to present you to the President and I think there would be no difficulty in bringing about such a meeting. By the way, you will like his secretary, Burton Harrison, a very pleasant fellow, just about your age—perhaps a little older. After you have established a few agreeable and possibly profitable connections here, I suggest you return to New Orleans. I will keep in touch with you there—or elsewhere if you decide to go elsewhere. But if you do, I should like to know how to reach you at any time. Possibly, you would enjoy a short sojourn in Spain. Well, well, we shall see." He picked up his goblet and drained its contents, already greatly depleted. "Shall we go down now and join the others?" he said genially. "I take it your headache is better. Our Congressman, Duncan Kenner, who shares this house with me, had gone to bed when you and I came in last night, or rather this morning, but he is in the garden now and is looking forward to seeing you. Another very pleasant fellow! . . . Did Rufus tell you about the terrapin? I don't know of anything tastier, unless it's canvasbacks, and we're having those, too."

PROVOST MARSHAL'S OFFICE.

New-Orleans, _Oct 1st_ 1862.

This Certifies, That _Mrs Polyxen Reyna_ has rendered a Statement of _her_ Property in accordance with General Orders No. 76. and claims to be an ENEMY of the United States

C W Killorn
Dep. Provost Marshal.

After the capture of the city in April, 1862 any resident of New Orleans who refused to sign the oath of allegiance to the United States was required to render a statement of his possessions and was then certified as "an enemy of the United States."

Original certificate in the collection of Leonard Huber of New Orleans, reproduction courtesy of owner.

31.

"You are quite sure, Mr. Morphy, that you are unwilling to take this oath?"

"Quite sure, sir."

General Bowen shrugged slightly. "You understand, of course, that it is forced on no one. It is far too sacred for profanation by unwilling lip service, for it gives the recipient the unestimable privilege of saying, 'I am an American citizen.' He can claim, like St. Paul, that he was 'born free.'"

"I can claim that, too, sir. In fact, I cannot only claim it, I can prove it."

"Oh, if you want to quibble! Of course, I didn't suppose that you were born in the sort of bondage that you impose on those miserable fellow creatures whom you hold as slaves! And I have neither time nor inclination to enter into an argument with you. For the last time, do you refuse to take this simple oath? After all, you understand you need only to say, 'I do solemnly swear that I will bear true faith and allegiance to the United States of America and will support the Constitution thereof.'"

"Yes sir, I understand. And for the last time I must regretfully refuse to say those words."

Paul stood still for a moment, awaiting a definite signal of dismissal before starting toward the nearest door of the spacious apartment in City Hall which had been converted into an office for the Provost Marshal and the Provost Marshal General. Several large tables were placed at right angles to each other on the handsomely carpeted floor, in such a way as to provide the most abundant light, both from the long windows and from the crystal chandeliers. General Bowen, the Provost Marshal General for the Parish of New Orleans, was ensconced behind one of these tables, with Captain Killborn, the Provost Marshal of the city beside him. Their assistants were busy at other tables. Well-dressed men and women were scattered about the room, some grouped together and chatting in hushed voices, others standing at attention before the various tables; among the latter, a few were signing the papers which had been thrust in front of them and others were discussing these with the confronting officials, as Paul had done. There was no sign of disorder, much less of rebellion; nevertheless, the warm still air was charged with animosity.

Several of Paul's friends were included in the scattered groups and he had paused to join one of these, when he was aware that his name was being called in an unnecessarily loud voice. He turned to see Captain Killborn beckoning to him.

"Mr. Morphy! The General would like to speak with you again!"

Paul excused himself from the friends he had just greeted and returned to the head table. The General now had several documents before him, all of which he seemed to be regarding with interest.

"Have you a brother by the name of Diego Eugene Morphy?" he asked bluntly.

"No, sir, a cousin."

"And your cousin was a sergeant in the Confederate Guards' Regiment of the Louisiana Militia?"

"Yes, sir."

"And was later transferred, by order of Governor Moore, to a regiment commanded by Major General Lovell of the Confederate Army?"

"Yes, sir."

"And served in this regiment when it failed to defend New Orleans before the advance of Commodore Farragut's fleet last spring?"

Paul flushed angrily and bit his lip to keep back an equally angry retort. He knew that General Lovell, bowed down by the sad realization that he could not protect the city with his available military equipment against bombardment from Farragut's warships, had withdrawn in the hope that wholesale demolishment, not to say slaughter, might be averted. This hope had been realized when General Butler was thus enabled to bring his troops into New Orleans unopposed. The captured city was oppressed, but it was not sacrificed. Lovell's strategy had been widely condemned as cowardice by his friends, as well as his enemies; but Paul had been among those who had realized that his action had required a very remarkable brand of courage: he might have been hailed as a hero, if he had been indifferent to widespread destruction of property and widespread loss of life; instead, because of his compassion, he had been branded as a renegade and had accepted his disgrace with dignity. It was hard for Paul to refrain from voicing his sympathetic understanding of Lovell's unfortunate position; but after he had actually opened his lips several times, only to close them again without speaking, he ended by merely saying, "Yes, sir," again.

The General had not failed to observe this struggle. "Do you know what has become of your brave cousin now?" he inquired sarcastically.

"No, sir."

"I am right in believing, am I not, that Diego Morphy is not the only relative you have in the armed forces of the Confederacy?"

"I have a brother, Edward, who joined the Orleans Guards before Louisiana entered the Confederacy."

"You are begging the question. I have told you already that I am not in the mood for quibbling. Where is your brother now?"

"I don't know, sir."

"And these are the only members of your family who are serving or who have served in the armed forces of the Confederacy?"

"No, sir, my uncle, Charles Le Carpentier, my mother's brother, is a Captain in Company E, 4th Regiment, 2nd Brigade, First Division."

"Quite a record of mistaken patriotism, isn't it, for one family?"

The question was sneeringly asked, but, though Paul flushed again, it was courteously answered.

"Of course, you wouldn't expect me to put it that way, sir. May I say it is quite a record of loyalty to tradition and ideals?"

For the second time, the General shrugged his shoulders. "I would now like to ask you a few more questions," he said. "Who are the other members of your immediate family?"

"My mother and two sisters, one married and one unmarried."

"And I believe they are not in New Orleans?"

"No, sir, they are in Paris."

"Just when did they leave for Paris?"

"Last spring."

"Before or after the occupation began?"

Paul hesitated for a moment. "It was shortly after the beginning of the occupation, sir. But the trip had been planned for some time before that. My brother-in-law, John Sybrandt, is a cotton broker—as no doubt you know. His business requires him to divide his time between Europe and the United States. He and my sister and their little son had been in New Orleans for quite a while, and the time had come for them to return to the Continent. They persuaded my mother and younger sister, who are both very far from well, to go with them for a visit."

"Then you are living alone at—" the General consulted one of his papers "—89 Royal Street?"

"Yes, sir."

"A very handsome house, judging from the outside. As you know, I've never had the pleasure of being entertained there. But I understand it is quite elegantly furnished and that the patio contains many rare plants."

Paul bowed without answering.

"Since you would not take the Oath of Allegiance, you will of course be obliged to render a statement of your possessions."

The General pushed one of the papers that lay in front of him toward Paul. "On a form like this—the certificate of a 'Registered Enemy'—which, as you can see, has just been signed."

Paul picked up the form and studied it with apparent attention, then laid it quietly back on the table. "It will take me a little time to prepare such a statement," he said. "My father died intestate. According to Louisiana law, my mother automatically inherited half of his property. The rest, also automatically, has been divided among my sisters, my brother and myself. But the estate has never yet been fully settled, owing to fluctuating values of real estate and stock and bonds. Ours has been a very harmonious family and we have not felt disturbed because our finances were still in a rather fluid condition."

"Especially as the estate was large enough to permit each of you considerable latitude as to expenditures?"

"You might put it that way, sir."

"I do put it that way. You must be aware, Mr. Morphy, that most of the questions I have asked you have been merely a matter of form. I knew the answers already."

"I was aware of that, sir."

The General leaned forward and spoke with increasing emphasis. "You must have also been aware that it has been General Butler's policy, from the beginning, to show all possible leniency. His first proclamation assured former adherents and servants of the Confederacy that those who would sever relations with it and go quietly about their work would not be disturbed in person or property, except as the exigencies of the public service might require. Within a few weeks, however, it was all too obvious that those who were well disposed toward the United States should be distinguished from those who clung to the Confederacy. It was a natural result of this situation that the order went forth requiring that all public officials were to swear allegiance to the United States within five days, and informing all other citizens who 'wished any favor, protection, privilege, passport, et cetera' that they must take the same oath. You did know this, did you not, Mr. Morphy?"

"Yes, sir. Also that the et cetera meant the payment of money, the safeguarding of property and any other benefit that the United States might extend to them, except protection from personal violence."

"Very well. This order was issued early in June. Today is the first of October. Yet, you have not previously been to this office, nor would you have come today had it not been strongly represented to you that you would be well advised to do so."

"That is correct, sir. Since I did not intend to take the Oath of Allegiance, I saw no reason for trespassing on your valuable time."

General Bowen leaned back in his chair, intimating that the conversation had now reached a point where he was prepared to take it in his stride.

"You and more than a hundred thousand others," he said sarcastically. "The outside estimate of those who have taken the oath is twelve thousand and that is somewhat higher than official figures. The 'social influence' of the city has been against it in the circles to which you belong. I understand that certain so-called ladies—the same breed that is responsible for General Order Number 28, which you Orleanians so greatly resent—have refused to receive at their soirées high-minded gentlemen who have taken the oath and that these same ladies have even kept lists, for future reference, of all those whom they suspect of being 'disloyal.' The powerful United States government cannot allow itself to be swayed by petty spiteful little groups with what they imagine to be social influence. That is why the Congressional Confiscation Act was passed in July, ordering the *immediate* confiscation of property belonging to civil and military officials of the Confederacy. All others were given sixty days of grace. Those sixty days, Mr. Morphy, have now passed."

Again, Paul bowed without answering.

"As I have said before, Mr. Morphy, we have endeavored to err on the side of leniency in every case. In some instances, I will admit, this endeavor has been greater than in others. Take Madame Beauregard, for instance, the wife of that notorious rebel General. She and her mother, Madame Deslonde, are living quite unmolested in the handsome residence of that other notorious rebel, John Slidell. Even though Slidell's other property has been confiscated, General Butler, with characteristic clemency, permitted them to remain there when he learned that Mrs. Slidell and Madame Beauregard are sisters and that Madame Beauregard is in poor health."

"All their friends have remarked on this significant gesture, sir."

"Gesture? You call it a *gesture?*"

"What would you like to have me call it, sir? An act of charity toward an elderly lady and her invalid daughter? I assure you that the Deslondes and the Beauregards are not accustomed to thinking of themselves as objects of charity! But they and their friends are not so slow witted that they cannot interpret the true meaning of the word gesture, designed to call attention to an act of so-called generosity which is really a well-directed play to the gallery."

"I advise you to be careful of your language, Mr. Morphy."

"I am trying to be. I realize that we should not discuss debatable subjects. Perhaps you will allow me to leave before I err again."

"Just a minute, Mr. Morphy. You and your family have also benefited by being placed among those who have enjoyed exceptional privileges, despite the fact that you have, or have had, a brother, an uncle and a cousin in the service of the Confederacy. Your father was a judge of great distinction; his brother Ernest is now a highly respected United States citizen, living in Quincy, Illinois; his widow—your mother—is greatly esteemed as a talented and beautiful lady of exemplary character. In short, there has been so much to predispose us in favor of your connections that you personally have been left unmolested for some time. And, I may add, you yourself are not unknown to us by excellent reputation. We have not forgotten that, only a few years ago, your name was in the headlines all over the world, and that no less a celebrity than the great Oliver Wendell Holmes, whose son is now serving gallantly in the Union Army, described you as a friend who 'honored all those who glory in the name of America as the hero of a long series of bloodless battles.'" The General paused impressively before continuing, "I am calling on you, Mr. Morphy, to act the part of a hero again. You are now fighting a bloodless battle—with yourself. And it is a losing one. However, you can win it—simply by raising your right hand and repeating a few simple words after me."

"I know, General Bowen, that some of my fellow citizens do not regard such an oath as binding, when it is given merely in order to protect their property. I don't presume to judge them, if they honestly feel that way. But I don't. Perjury doesn't seem to me like a question of reciting a few simple words. It still seems to me like a major crime."

"Well, I've given you every chance. I've wasted a great deal of time on you and I must say you seem to me most ungrateful. Good afternoon, Mr. Morphy. I'll expect to see you again tomorrow, or the next day at the latest, with that statement regarding your personal property."

This time, Paul did not stop to speak with any of his acquaintances in the groups scattered around the room, and none of them tried to detain him as he smiled and nodded and went on. He was conscious that his long session with General Bowen had, inevitably, aroused curiosity, indeed, that at least snatches of it must have been overheard; this consciousness stimulated the feeling of shyness from which he was seldom wholly free and he wanted to escape the further embarrassment which friendly overtures would certainly cause. He went quickly out of the City Hall and then, more slowly, made his way downtown.

Though the streets were by no means deserted, they seemed to Paul preternaturally quiet. A certain number of Union officers and soldiers were in evidence, some walking briskly, as if bent on errands of great import, at least to themselves, others loitering as if their stroll were simply a means of killing time. Male Orleanians were few and far between and ladies were actually conspicuous by their absence. The gaiety, the insouciance, the friendly warmth of the city were all gone; even its charm was chilled. The houses had a blank secretive look; the doorways of the shops no longer stood wide open to welcome the casual customer; the patios, which had once represented only seclusion, now represented secrecy; they were completely hidden. It was hard for Paul to realize, as he went sorrowfully on his way, that this was the city in which he had been born and bred and of which he would have said the very paving stones were his friends. He felt indeed "amid the alien corn."

The Yankees were not wholly to blame for this, he knew; there had, undoubtedly, been provocations which, being human, they could not help resenting, insults which they could not help avenging; Orleanians would have done the same had the positions of the two groups been reversed. A woman, beside herself with hysteria, had laughed when the funeral procession of a foe passed beneath her gallery; another, still more obnoxiously uncontrolled, had spat in the direction of a Union soldier who annoyed her on the street, perhaps unintentionally. And then, the infamous "Woman Order" had been issued, stating that "Hereafter when any female shall by word, gesture or movement, insult or show contempt for any officer or soldier of the United States, she shall be regarded and held liable to be treated as a woman of the town plying her avocation." It never would have been given, even by as arrogant and ruthless a commander as Butler, if there had been only such slights and discourtesies as those which had occurred when ladies stepped into the street to avoid walking on the same sidewalk as the Yankees and faced indoors when they sat on their balconies. But now the damage was done and what had been honest hatred before had turned to leprous loathing on both sides.

Paul tried to think the situation over logically, as he would have done a chess problem. He was too heavy hearted to do so. His gentle mother, his fragile sister, his brilliant and beautiful sister-in-law, did they deserve the designation of "she-adder," now indiscriminately applied in the northern press to the "fair flower of New Orleans"? Never, never, never!

It was a long time since he had been to see his grandparents, but now, on a sudden impulse, instead of going straight to his own empty house, he walked on until he came to the Le Carpentiers'. The faithful Fifine opened the door for him and, after giving free rein to her delight at seeing him again, imparted the same information that she had done on many previous occasions: Madame was lying down; Mademoiselle was at church; Monsieur would be overjoyed to see the visitor.

"You'd better ask him, Fifine, before I go into the parlor. It's a long while since I've been here, you know. And the last time I came, M. Le Carpentier and I didn't part the best of friends."

She nodded understandingly and left him. As he stood in the entrance hall, he could hear her shouting at his grandfather, in an effort to surmount the old man's increasing deafness, and then his gruff rejoinders. But at last she opened the parlor door triumphantly.

"As I told you, M. Paul. He is overjoyed."

She might well have been right, Paul thought, but his grandfather would have been too proud to admit this, and his continued gruffness could have been a cloak to his real feelings. He was slouched in a deep chair near the fireplace, with a cane conveniently at hand, and he was quite unoccupied. He made no pretense of closing a book or laying down a pack of cards and, though the chess table was still in sight, it stood on the opposite side of the room from him. His clothes were no longer elegant or even neat. He wore no cravat and his collar was soiled, his waistcoat minus a button and his coat spotted. All his garments hung loosely on his frame, for he had become less corpulent in his old age than when he was in the prime of life, and his color had lost much of its ruddiness. But his eyes retained their clarity and shrewdness. The glance he gave Paul was as keen as ever.

"Well," he said grumpily, "so you've come back at last."

"Yes, Grandfather. I'm sorry it's been so long. May I sit down and talk with you a little while?"

"If you've nothing better to do. . . . Something on your mind, I take it?"

"Rather. I'm thinking I might go away. And I didn't want to, without making sure you were all right, or without saying good-bye."

Le Carpentier eyed his grandson still more attentively. "Yes, I'm all right. I suppose you mean have those Yankee bastards bothered me about their damned oath? Well, they've tried to, but they didn't get very far. I was born in France, thank God! I've never been naturalized. They can't make me into an American citizen overnight, no matter how hard they try!"

He grinned broadly, then chuckled and finally broke into a hearty laugh, which Paul found infectious. It had not occurred to him, when he decided to make this call, that it might prove actually cheering. His grandfather had given him a happy surprise.

"I wouldn't wonder," Le Carpentier went on, "if they didn't run up against something of the same sort with John Sybrandt, if he were ever fool enough to come back here while the Yankees are 'occupying' us, as they call it. Not that I think he will, unless it's absolutely necessary on account of his business. Sybrandt's smart. That's why I think he'll say, if he needs to say anything, that he's a Swede. He can even claim that *he* owns the Royal Street house and that, this being the case, it isn't liable to confiscation. I'm sure he can find someone in Paris who'd fix the necessary papers. And the Swedish Consul will back him up, no matter what the truth is, just as Count Méjan is backing me up, though what I'm saying does happen to be true. I *was* born in Paris all right, whether or not Sybrandt was born in Stockholm, like he'll claim. All the consuls are backing up their nationals. Perhaps you know that some of them have gone so far as to set up their own little military establishments. I tell you, they're giving Butler plenty to think about. The fact is, I believe they're interfering with his rest at night. More power to them!"

Again he laughed, and again Paul laughed with him.

"So you don't need to hesitate on my account, if you want to get out of this morgue Butler has made of our fair city," he went on. "And you needn't worry about your grandmother or your aunt, either. Of course, the Yankees have tried to take it out on us because of Charles. But Lord! Even they must know Charles could never be much of a menace to them in the army, any more than he was to you as a chess player. The last we heard from him he was still playing the flute, around the camp fires, and though, as you're well aware, he never was much of a musician, I'll take my oath he was even less as a marksman. Anyway, Méjan will look after us, he's one of the best. And your mother and sisters are abroad already—most natural thing in the world that you should join them. Any trouble about a passport?"

"I've got one, you know. That is, it may be outdated, but that ought to be possible to fix up."

"Yes, I should think so. Sybrandt isn't the only smart one."

"Or I might be able to leave without one."

"You've got some plan?"

"Not really. I didn't want to make one before I talked with you. But the *Vasco de Gama* is in port now."

"You're right, it is. A Spanish man-o'-war. Outward bound for—?"

"Havana. At dawn tomorrow. The Captain came to see me last evening. Just a social call, you understand. After all, I don't need to remind you that my other grandfather was Spanish Consul here and that my uncle Diego succeeded him in that post. So the family has always kept pleasantly in touch with the officers of incoming and outgoing vessels, merchant marine and warships both. I think you know that I've been royally entertained in Havana, both times I stopped off there, on my way to New York. It is fitting I should return such courtesies. So I invited the Captain to have supper with me tonight—it's lonely in that big house, without any company at all. I believe Tata's preparing quite a feast. And it occurred to me that, if the Captain were a little unsteady on his feet afterward—"

"As his host, you couldn't do less than accompany him when he went back to his ship? Well, as I just said, John Sybrandt isn't the only smart fellow around here."

The old man reached for his cane and tottered to his feet. Then he hobbled over to Paul, who had also risen, and put his hand on his grandson's shoulder. "I'll miss you, Paul," he said, "that is, I haven't seen much of you, since that cursed night when you let me beat you at chess. But it's meant something to me just to know that you were in the same city with me—I'm—I'm very fond of you." He felt in his pocket, drew out an enormous and rather soiled handkerchief and blew his nose loudly. "I'm coming down with a cold," he announced belligerently. "I catch them one after another these days. Look, I'd ask you to stay and have a game of chess with me and beat you fair and square, but you mustn't hang around here any longer. So, instead, we'll have our game when you get back. Is that a bargain?"

"It's a bargain. But don't you think perhaps I ought to stay at least long enough to say good-bye to *Grand'mère?*"

"No, it would just upset her to be roused from a sound sleep with news she's bound to take as bad, until she understands. I'll explain to her when she wakes up and say you didn't want to disturb her, but that you left all sorts of loving messages for her. I'll explain to Amélie, too. Of course, you can't wait for her to get back from church. No telling when that would be. You go home and get ready for your dinner guest. You'll be needing a little extra money for your trip—no, don't say anything, I've got some put away I've been wondering what to do with. You won't be able to take many clothes with you, just going to see the Captain off the way you'll be doing. But no one's going to pick your pockets—that is, as far as I know, the Yankees haven't begun to do that yet, though I understand you have to watch the spoons when Butler comes to dinner. I'll send Fifine up to your house with some good wine in a basket, to help the Captain get unsteady on his feet, and you might just look under the napkins carefully as you unwrap the bottles. Might be some gold pieces underneath. Come to think of it, Fifine ought to be able to go to the ship with a second basket; after she's taken the wine to your house. Vegetables and fruit for the voyage! That's the idea, borrowed from Molly Creagh, your other grandfather's first wife! She got herself and her baby both out of Santo Domingo by carrying a basket of produce aboard a warship, didn't she? That's one time they *didn't* find the baby in the cabbages! Why, if you can't get practically everything you need out of the house, I'll say the senior branch of the Morphy family could give the junior branch 'odds of Knight.'"

Le Carpentier blew his nose again, still more loudly this time. "Have a good time in Havana, Paul," he said. "I've always heard it was a very fine city. Good-bye, good-bye. And—God bless you, my boy."

Paul did not have much time to spare. He would have liked to stow away the silver and some ornaments of value himself, in a safe hiding place, before he left the house; but the dining room and the drawing room must be looking their best for the reception of the Captain, so he would have to leave that task to Tata and he knew she would perform it faithfully and as intelligently as her mentality would permit. Personally, he could take care only of the most necessary documents, pertaining to property, and his gold and silver chess set. He did not dare leave these in the gaily painted iron safe which stood in the locked library closet; on the contrary, he drew from it the small supply of negotiable cash which he had in the house, his outdated passport and a few other papers which he thought might be useful to him abroad; then, lighting a hurricane lamp and putting his chess set and the rest of his valuable documents in a small waterproof bag, he descended to the portion of the basement which had been occupied by the Banque de la Louisiane in the early part of the century, but which had remained unoccupied after the building came into the possession of Martin Gordon and later of the Morphy family.

It was years since he had been there though, in his childhood and early youth, he and his companions had sometimes played hide-and-seek and blindman's buff in this part of the premises, which the children had nicknamed Hades, when the weather would not permit them to use the patio; and, as he recalled the floor plan, there was a small room, leading out of the larger one adjoining his father's wine cellar, which was virtually a safe in itself. It had no opening, except into the larger room; and this one opening was concealed by a sliding panel, so skillfully fitted into the rest of the woodwork as to be undistinguishable; in fact, anyone who lacked familiarity with the basement would have taken it for granted that there was nothing behind the paneling but solid wall, that no interior room existed. But it was there, and after a struggle with the sliding panel, which was stuck fast by dampness and disuse, Paul found what he was looking for: a metal door, opening inward to a cubicle with walls of masonry so sturdily built that even the all-pervading dampness of the city had affected them surprisingly little. Imbedded in one of its massive blocks, scarcely discernible, both because of its color and its shape, amidst the darkened flagstones which surrounded it, was a small rectangular safe.

With a deep sigh of relief, Paul unfastened it, thrust the waterproof bag inside and carefully closed the safe again. Then he went out of the cubicle, locking the metal door, pushing the panel back into place, and proceeding through the outer room of the bank to the wine cellar, now sadly depleted of the contents in which Alonzo Morphy had taken such pride, for his widow and his sons possessed neither his interest in fine vintages nor his knowledge of them. Paul was on familiar territory again now; he could grope his way along without the help of the hurricane lamp, so he blew it out. There was very little danger that its feeble gleam could penetrate the batten shutters; but he was taking no unnecessary chances. However, he was wise enough not to set it down until he could put it back on the pantry shelf where he had found it; if anyone else should reach the regions where he had been, its presence there would certainly arouse suspicions and lead to search.

A glance at his watch told him that he might now expect the Captain at almost any time. Fifine had arrived with the basket of wine and, acting on Le Carpentier's instructions, had waited to give it to Paul personally, instead of entrusting it to Tata, as she normally would have done. He removed the bottles, gave careful instructions for serving the wine at the proper temperature, and told Fifine to wait while he repacked the basket to take to the *Vasco de Gama*. When he shook out the napkins, after reaching his own room, he found that his grandfather had more than made good his promise: there were enough gold pieces to keep Paul in funds for a long time.

He repacked the basket with shirts, socks and a change of body linen, covered these articles with handkerchiefs and returned with it to the kitchen, where he watched the two faithful servants pile it high with vegetables, meanwhile giving Fifine rapid instructions. "You understand, don't you? You're to go down to the big Spanish ship—the one with the red and yellow flag—and say you've been told to deliver these vegetables to the Commissary, that they're already paid for. Then you're to come back and get another basket. I'll pack it while you're gone. When I get through with it, there'll be handkerchiefs on top, just as this one has. You and Tata will cover them with fruit instead of vegetables. I probably shan't be able to show you how this time, but you can do it without me, now that you've watched once. Then you'll return to the ship and say the same thing you did before. When you come back here and tell me that both baskets are safely aboard and that no one has stopped you or asked you any questions, I'll give you and Tata each a gold piece."

Fifine grinned, nodded and scurried off. Paul packed the second basket, this time adding a suit and a pair of shoes to another change of linen. The night was cool; he would be able to wear an overcoat without being conspicuous and, thanks to the funds now at his disposal, he could buy whatever additional he needed for a suitable wardrobe in Havana. He stripped, sponged himself off, shaved and put on clean underclothes and a clean shirt. Next he fastened most of the gold, his passport and other papers inside his waistcoat and placed his razor and military brushes in the pockets of his handsomest coat and trousers. Then, fully dressed, he sat down at his desk, drew a single sheet of paper from a drawer and wrote hurriedly:

Dear Cousin Judah:

You asked me to let you know if I should leave New Orleans and to tell you where I should be headed.

If all goes well, I shall sail tomorrow morning at daybreak on the *Vasco de Gama* for Havana. Several eminent Spaniards, who are also devotees of chess, have long been urging me to revisit this city, where I have been warmly welcomed before. A propitious moment for doing so seems to have arrived.

I am sure I shall be welcome to remain in Havana for several weeks, and I shall await word from you there, as I should appreciate advice regarding further travels. Communications may be sent to me in care of the Captain General.

I am putting this letter into trustworthy and capable hands, and have every hope and expectation that it will get safely through the blockade. However, lest it does not, I shall write you again as soon as I reach Havana.

Please give my best regards to Mr. Kenner and Jules and believe me,

Affectionately and respectfully yours,
Paul Morphy.

PART FIVE

Dedication Problem: Set "Strive for Honor!"

1862–1865

"The titular chief of the Northern camp in Paris was the Federal Minister William L. Dayton, who had arrived the previous May in succession to the Southerner Faulkner. Dayton was a New Jersey lawyer, formerly Republican candidate for the Vice-Presidency. Although a man of character and ability, he was prosaic, timid and lacking in magnetism. . . .

"Socially, it was soon apparent enough that the United States Legation was at a disadvantage as compared with the Confederate mission in the Avenue d'Antin, and Parisian society quickly recognised that fact. Slidell's presence, bearing and speech gave him an advantage over his official adversary, and in George Eustis and subsequently Henri Vignaud, he had attractive and competent lieutenants. But his chief asset was his wife, the former Mademoiselle Mathilde Deslonde, and their two pretty daughters Matilda and Rosina. There was also a son, Alfred, still a schoolboy and afterwards a cadet at St. Cyr.

"Mrs. Slidell, intelligent, sympathetic, with charming manners and a gift for music and water-colour painting, made friends easily. According to her daughter she was 'profoundly religious, austere towards herself, indulgent to others.' She had been highly esteemed as a hostess in Washington and she soon occupied her due place in Paris. The girls were fond of music, the opera and dancing, as was the secretary Eustis's young and charming wife, the rich banker's daughter."

John Slidell and the Confederates in Paris (1862–65)
by Beckles Willson, copyright 1932 by B. Willson.
Used by permission of the publishers, G. P. Putnam's Sons, N.Y.

32.

Mr. and Mrs. John Slidell were giving a gala dinner.

Their standards of entertaining were high and, in every way, they were admirably equipped to meet these. Their Paris apartment, on the Avenue d'Antin, was spacious, and elegant not only as to *boiseries* and furnishings, but also as to paintings, statuary and miscellaneous objets d'art. Their drawing rooms and their dining room were characterized both by impeccable taste and lavish expenditure. They had a superlative chef, an accomplished maître d'hôtel and a notable wine cellar, and both husband and wife knew how to make the best use of these. Mrs. Slidell's imaginative and delectable menus, Mr. Slidell's familiarity with the best vintages and prodigality with these, were topics of general and laudatory comment. From the moment of their arrival, the couple had been welcomed in the most delightful and exclusive social circles and, as their acquaintance widened, they were in a position to choose not only among their most distinguished compatriots residing in Paris, but among the members of the French aristocracy in making up their guest lists; their invitations were eagerly sought and invariably accepted. Mrs. Slidell had established a salon which bore favorable comparison with those of the most celebrated Parisian hostesses; in addition, both she and Mr. Slidell made their fellow Americans feel welcome to drop in any day for lunch, without ceremony, and at least once a week they gave a formal dinner. If there were some celebrity whom they especially wished to honor or some event that seemed especially worthy to note, they did not fail to take advantage of such an opportunity; if no such celebrity or no such event were forthcoming, they managed to create the illusion of one or the other, just the same.

This time, there was not the slightest necessity for creating an illusion. Slidell had been patiently engaged for months negotiating in behalf of the Cotton Loan, so-called because the commodity from which it took its name should be used as security; largely due to the good offices of the Count de Persigny, Minister of the Interior, and Emil Erlanger, head of the great banking firm which bore his name, the deal had at last been consummated. Almost simultaneously the engagement of Slidell's beautiful daughter Mathilde to Emil's artistic son Frederick—who had been as patient a suitor as Slidell had been a manipulator—had been announced. The gala dinner was planned in honor of both events.

The Minister of the Interior, Count de Persigny, was gracing the occasion by his presence with his wife, nee Princess Moskova, granddaughter of the great Marshal Ney; so were the Minister of Marine, the Marquis de

Chasseloup-Laubat, and his American-born wife, nee Louise Pilíe of New Orleans, who claimed kinship with General Beauregard. The Erlanger family and southern aristocracy were both fully represented, Napoleonic nobility by the Duke and Duchess de Trevisse. Mathilde and her fiancé, both radiant with happiness, stood side by side, receiving the embraces and the congratulations with which they were being almost overwhelmed. The Slidells' younger daughter, Rosina, and their son, Alfred, kept close by, to direct the flow of conversation, when the time seemed ripe to do so, into other channels; they were already quite at ease at their parents' parties and, like their elders, were fast becoming general favorites. The subject of the Cotton Loan, which, next to the engagement, was naturally that of the greatest current interest, might very well have taxed their powers of comprehension; but no one would have guessed it from their alert expressions and eager answers. Besides, they were ably assisted by Slidell's secretary, George Eustis, and his charming young wife, who both shared in the family's general popularity.

Mrs. Slidell, strikingly handsome in the black velvet dress, gorgeously trimmed with scarlet marabou, in which her portrait had been recently painted, moved graciously among her guests, greeting each with appropriate cordiality. Ropes of pearls were twined among the braids that crowned her head, and festooned the short puffed sleeves, then disappeared in masses of marabou. Twin sprays of multicolored jewels outlined the curve of her corsage at the breast and came together to form a single band extending, in the center, from the top of the bodice to the hips, which were also outlined in marabou. She acknowledged, with exactly the right amount of self-disparagement, the compliments showered upon her. "You are too kind—yes, I am pleased with the model, but of course we must thank Mr. Worth for that." . . . "The pearls were my grandmother's. I shared her jewelry with my three sisters and I was so delighted that these were my portion; but I never thought of wearing pearls this way until recently. In fact, I didn't think of it—it was my husband's suggestion. And then he found the spray in Cartier's window and decided it would put just the finishing touch on this costume. He has such good taste and he is so generous!"

Without abruptness, she detached herself from her outspoken admirers and paused long enough to whisper an aside to her husband behind her painted fan. "Everyone is here now except the de Lixins and Paul. Of course, the de Lixins are always late, but do you suppose Paul could have made a mistake in the address? Or that something unexpected has detained him?"

"No, my dear. Paul wouldn't have made a careless mistake like that. As a chess player, he's far too accustomed to paying meticulous attention to detail. And, if he'd been detained, he'd have managed to let us know—he's the soul of courtesy. After all, it's only just past the hour. Ah! here he is now!"

Before the liveried footman at the door of the drawing room could finish his brief announcement of the latest guest, Slidell advanced to meet the newcomer, wringing his hand and voicing a hearty welcome. "Well, my boy, we were just talking about you! You remember Mrs. Slidell, of course? And Mathilde, who's standing over there with her fiancé? You must join the others who are expressing their good wishes on this happy occasion. Rosina, my dear, will you recall Mr. Morphy to your sister and present him to Frederick? Then see that he meets our other guests. Paul, I'm turning you over to Rosina. You'll be in good hands."

"Oh, Paul, I'm so glad to see you!" Rosina exclaimed, dimpling with pleasure. It would have been difficult to imagine a more charming picture than she made. Her magnificent black hair was arranged in ringlets, some of which were allowed to stray over her white shoulders. A frill of narrow lace, placed above a succession of small crisp satin bows, outlined the bodice of her turquoise colored dress and lay soft and filmy against her still softer skin. The absence of jewels enhanced the general effect of girlish simplicity. Paul, in responding to her enthusiastic greeting, did so with expressions of genuine pleasure and appreciation which he would have prolonged, if Rosina had not interrupted to ask when he had arrived and what he had been doing to prevent him from coming to see her sooner.

"I got here only last night. And I confess I've slept most of today. I found the trip from Madrid rather exhausting."

"Yes, I've heard the trains are terrible. But that's all behind you now. Except for the trains, did you like Spain?"

"Very much."

"I'm sure you'll like Paris still better though. It's the most wonderful place! But you knew that, didn't you? You've been here before."

"Yes, I've been here before and it *is* the most wonderful place. I couldn't be happier than I am about getting back here and finding so many friends from home."

"And not only from home, M. Morphy. You haven't forgotten your French friends, I hope? We certainly haven't forgotten *you!*"

The Duchess de Trevisse had turned from Mrs. Calhoun, with whom she had been chatting and, smiling pleasantly, gave him a gloved hand to kiss. "I shall be receiving tomorrow evening," she told him as he murmured something appropriate. "The same time, the same place as when you were here before. You haven't forgotten, have you?"

"How could I? Ten o'clock? Rue de Grenelle?"

"And you'll come again?"

"How could I stay away?"

She laughed lightly and, as Mrs. Calhoun had now claimed his attention, moved toward another group. His fellow Southerner asked solicitously for his mother. "I'm so sorry she doesn't feel more equal to going out socially. But she's very faithful in her attendance at the Confederate Women's Aid Society. We collect clothing and drugs and little luxuries to send to hospitals and Southern prisoners."

"Yes, my mother told me. She has preferred to live very quietly since my father died and now she's very much occupied with my younger sister, who isn't well, and my elder sister's children, on whom she naturally dotes. But I'm glad she's been helpful. I'll tell her you said so."

"Please do. And please ask her if I can't come to see her, provided she doesn't feel she can come to see me. . . . Ah, Natalie! You know Mr. Morphy, don't you?"

"Do I know him! Why, he's my long lost relative! Paul, how marvelous to see you!"

She threw her arms around him and embraced him with an enthusiasm which indicated that, in her opinion at least, their relationship was such as to place them in the category of kissing cousins. For the next few minutes, the talk was all of the St. Martins, the Le Carpentiers and Natalie's husband, Judah P. Benjamin, about whom she always spoke with effusive affection and whom she welcomed warmly whenever he came to visit her in Paris, though she refused to share his life in America. It was only when Paul managed at last to call her attention to an important looking gentleman, hovering near by, that she finally interrupted herself.

"Oh, I'm so sorry! Good evening, M. le Ministre. Paul, have you been presented to the Count de Persigny? Please permit me!"

As Natalie Benjamin in her turn drifted away, the Minister of the Interior, a swarthy, ruddy-cheeked man with sparkling black eyes and an animated manner, acknowledged the introduction pleasantly and began to exchange agreeable banalities with the newcomer. "I understand you've just arrived from Spain, M. Morphy. What cities did you visit?"

"I landed in Cadiz after a pleasant stay in Cuba and went from there to Seville and Granada, and then to Madrid and, of course, nearby points of interest—Toledo, the Escorial, Segovia, Avila."

"I hope you were cordially received? Spaniards sometimes seem rather aloof to visitors, even the most distinguished."

"I did not find them so. All those I met were extremely cordial to me."

"Did you see the Queen?"

"Yes, several times. She was kind enough to invite me to the Escorial and she's not at all a bad chess player."

"She is rather a debatable figure. I should welcome an account of your impressions."

"She was most amiable and approachable. She gave me the feeling that I was very welcome at the Palace."

"No doubt, no doubt. If you will permit me to say so, M. Morphy, you are a very personable young man and Queen Isabella II has something of a penchant for personable young men, if all we hear is true. I would like to talk with you further about your experiences in Spain. We must arrange a rendezvous. I am afraid we have not time for such a discussion now—at all events, we should not have."

The Minister took out his watch and frowned as he looked at it. "Such tardiness is inexcusable," he said, with no attempt to disguise his annoyance. "If it were some official, detained by affairs of state, who was keeping us waiting for dinner like this, we could make allowances. But de Lixin has nothing in the world to do but make love to his wife. Certain persons are fond of saying much the same thing about me, but though I will confess to deserving the charge that I enjoy it, I do other important things, too, and de Lixin does not. Therefore he could postpone his uxorious pursuits to a later hour. I am sure you are starving to death, M. Morphy, as I am!"

"Fortunately, my mother gave me a good lunch. But you are right, Mr. Minister, it is rather past the hour for which we were invited. May I ask for some information about this gentleman of leisure who is delaying dinner and whose only occupation is so enviable?"

"Gilbert de Lixin—a favorite of Chasseloup-Laubat's—otherwise, I doubt that he'd be invited here." And, as something in Paul's expression betrayed his astonishment at such a comment from a stranger, de Persigny went on, "I can see that you are surprised at my remark, Monsieur. Perhaps I should warn you, at the very outset of our acquaintance, that I'm an incorrigible gossip and am not in the least ashamed of this, even though one of my colleagues has gone so far as to say that, because of this malicious proclivity, I bear as much resemblance to a gentleman as chicory does to coffee. Ah well! it may save you future embarrassment to know that Mrs. Slidell and the Princess de Lixin are not kindred spirits, so to speak. But, as I've just said, de Lixin and Chasseloup-Laubat—"

"Forgive me for interrupting, M. le Ministre. But I do so want to meet M. Morphy. He and my uncle Pierre are old friends. I am hoping he can give me some welcome news from home."

The Count de Persigny had wheeled about abruptly, and Paul realized that, if the effort to save another embarrassment had been wholly sincere, the man who had expressed the hope of doing so had not escaped it himself. The lady who was now speaking to them had come up so quietly behind them, whether by accident or design, that neither had been aware of her approach until she was actually close to them.

"My dear Marquise!" exclaimed the Count. "How delightful to see you!

M. Morphy, the Marquise de Chasseloup-Laubat, one of the most charming of the many charming Americans whom we are privileged to have with us in Paris."

"You are too kind, M. le Ministre. M. Morphy, I am looking forward to a long talk with you after dinner—that is, if we are actually to have any dinner, which I am beginning to doubt! And I hope you will give us the pleasure of spending the weekend with us in the country, some time very soon. Meanwhile, may I repeat my question?"

"About your illustrious uncle? I am sorry to say, Madame la Marquise, it was almost two years ago that I last saw Pierre. Since then, of course, he has become the hero of Manassas, as well as Fort Sumter. And—" Paul hesitated for a moment, but loyalty prevailed over accuracy. "And, naturally, at Shiloh. I saw Madame Beauregard occasionally before I left New Orleans last October. I am very fond of her. She and her mother are living in the Slidells' house, as perhaps you know. I am sorry to say she is very far from well."

"And I am sorry to hear it. May I ask—"

The Marquise did not finish her question, so Paul never found out what she wanted to ask. At that moment, the liveried footman stationed by the door announced the arrival of the Prince and Princess de Lixin and, as if instinctively, nearly everyone in the company turned in their direction, while Mr. and Mrs. Slidell went forward to meet them. The Count de Persigny took out his watch again, and several other gentlemen, glancing expressively toward each other, did the same. There was a subdued murmur among the ladies and Paul caught stray comments, which did not seem to him wholly friendly. "*Mon Dieu,* how did she ever get through the door? Her hoops expand by the metre!" . . . "In the same proportion that her bodices get lower, wouldn't you say?" . . . "To think a little parvenue like that should have achieved one of the proudest titles in France!" . . . "Not to mention one of the greatest fortunes!" . . . "Well, we all know that there are ways and means." . . . "Yes, and the airs she gives herself now! You would think she was born to the purple." . . . "Her supremacy may not last long. Gilbert is susceptible, but no one has ever yet accused him of fidelity."

Paul, looking fixedly toward the door as he tried to close his ears to such lamentable malice, saw coming toward him a tall slender man with sleek black hair, unremarkable features, a pale skin and an expression at one and the same time supercilious and languid. His evening clothes, which he seemed to wear disdainfully, were the last word in cut and elegance. Beside him was a beautiful blonde woman, in a dress of dazzling white, whose golden hair was surmounted with a diamond tiara and whose throat and wrists were also encircled with diamonds. Everything about her seemed to sparkle and, as she came gracefully forward, acknowledging the greetings of her fellow guests, it was clear that this impression of brilliance was not due only to jewels. She emanated it in her own person.

There was only one woman in Paul's known world who could look like that, who could give that impression. The one woman was Charmian.

"*Bien qu'elle [Princess Mathilde] se vît obligée à recevoir souvent Persigny, elle en limita les occasions. Elle avait pris en aversion ce petit homme noiraud et coloré, bavard avec indécence, suprêmement content de lui. Le charme de ses yeux noirs, brillants et animés, son originalité fougueuse n'excusèrent plus son indulgence et elle adopta la formule de Viel-Castel: 'Persigny ressemble à un homme de bonne compagnie comme la chicorée ressemble au café.'*"

"*Elle apprit ainsi que Persigny était fort amoureux de la princesse de la Moskowa qu'il venait d'épouser, que cette dernière se conduisait ridiculement, soit qu'elle sanglotât dans les bras de son époux pendant l'hallali, soit qu'elle restât enfermée avec lui au lieu de descendre à table.*"

"*Quand Mathilde repart, enchantée de sa journée, elle a promis au critique de recommencer pareille fête et lui a même proposé d'assister en personne aux déjeuners qu'il préside chaque semaine au restaurant Magny, rue de La Contrescarpe, et qui réunissent des écrivains d'avant-garde. Une question de dignité se pose cependant. Ne va-t-elle pas se faire confondre avec une duchesse de Persigny, allant au bal Mabille avec Gramont-Caderoussel Son entourage lui déconseille une telle audace. Sainte-Beuve qui tient, malgré tout, à sauvegarder la liberté de ces déjeuners de garçon où chacun se comporte à sa guise, le lui fait sentir: 'J'ai repensé a l'idée du Magny, elle est charmante, et pourtant . . .' Pour dédommager la princesse il lui promet de lui amener, rue de Courcelles, les plus marquants des convives du Magny, des littérateurs comme Flaubert, les Goncourt, Taine, Renan, Gautier, Saint-Victor; des artistes comme Gavarni.*"

Extracts from *La Princesse Mathilde* by Marguerite Castillon Du Perron
(Amiot-Dumont, Paris)

33.

He felt a swift stab of pain, as if his heart had been pierced by a delicate, deadly dagger; then the sharp pointed weapon seemed to plunge deeper and deeper into all his vitals, piercing these again and again. I'm going to disgrace myself by fainting, he thought, the fear flashing through his brain with the same speed that the knife penetrated into his body; I can't continue to stand here, smiling and bowing, while I'm in such agony from these attacks; the strain will cause me to lose consciousness and, shameful as such a betrayal of weakness will be, I'll at least be delivered from my anguish. But though his head was swimming and he swayed a little, the swoon did not come; and presently the pain began to pass, to be succeeded by merciful numbness. By the time Charmian and her husband had reached the place where he was stationed among the waiting guests, instead of feeling too much, he was feeling too little; indeed, he was so deprived of all sensation he was not sure that he had really inclined his head and bent his back and lifted her hand to kiss.

"*Tiens, le petit* Paul!" she said, laughing lightly, as the Duchess de Trevisse had done. In fact, there was so much superficial resemblance between the two laughs, that Paul, had his condition enabled him to be analytical, might easily have guessed that the one was a deliberate attempt to copy the other. But if it were there, the attempt had failed; the Duchess' was the gay, carefree laugh of an experienced and sophisticated woman, so sure of herself and her station that she could afford to be, at one and the same time, casual and cordial; Charmian's still had the mocking quality which had marred it when she was younger; and though Paul had deliberately closed his consciousness to it then, he found he could not do so now. Surprisingly, he was able to retort in kind to the condescending greeting.

"*Tiens*, Charmian, *la grande dame!*"

She laughed again and, this time, there was no mockery in the sound, but imperfectly suppressed resentment. Then she gave her husband an arch glance and spoke in honeyed tones.

"You remember, Gilbert, that I mentioned M. Morphy to you? We sometimes played together as children, when I used to go to New Orleans. That was long, long ago, wasn't it, Paul? And now, of course, you've become very famous . . . you know all about Paul's triumphs, don't you, my love?"

The indifference of the Prince's response suggested that, if he had actually heard any reference to these, he had dismissed it from his mind as being of no importance in his scheme of living. Again, to his great surprise, Paul found himself ready with a quick retort.

"Even if you have told the Prince only that we played together as children, he has the advantage. You have told me nothing about your association with him."

A brief spark of surprise, mingled with curiosity, flickered across the Prince's face. Who, he seemed momentarily to be asking himself, is this insignificant outsider who has the presumption to imagine that he should have been given information by my wife? Then, as if even this much mental effort were too much of a nuisance, his expression again became one of languid indifference; and, as Charmian, flushing slightly, opened her lips to reply for him, Rosina joined them, addressing herself first to Paul.

"You're to take me in to dinner! I'm so pleased! . . . M. le Prince, I think the Countess de Persigny is awaiting your escort . . . Ah! *tant mieux*, M. le Marquis! I was sure you would not delay another instant before claiming the fairy princess."

Guests were already beginning to file into the dining room and find their places at the great oval table covered with a *point de Venise* cloth. Epergnes of silver gilt, alternately filled with fruit and flowers, rose between the tall candelabra on either side of a centerpiece which took the form of a miniature fountain. The place plates and cutlery, like the epergne, were of silver gilt, the delicate crystal goblets edged with gold; the soup plates, which the liveried servants now began to set down, were of finest Sevres porcelain. As Paul picked up his spoon for a first taste of a delectable *potage à la reine*, the goblet nearest the edge of the table was unobtrusively filled with pale wine, its bouquet as fragrant as the aroma of the soup.

He hoped that Rosina was really as pleased at having him as a dinner partner as he was with this arrangement. The more he saw of her, the more delightful he found her; and, as he looked across the wide table at her sister, he thought Mathilde equally charming. Her dress was a duplicate of Rosina's as to cut and trimming, but was made of stiff garnet-colored grosgrain, instead of soft turquoise silk. The difference seemed suitably to accentuate the slight disparity in their ages and Mathilde's emergence from the juvenile status of *jeune fille de la maison* to the more advanced position of promised bride. Moreover, unlike Rosina, Mathilde was wearing jewelry —a locket, earrings and bracelets of turquoises and pearls and a magnificent diamond ring, surely the gift of her fortunate fiancé. But both girls wore their hair in the same becoming way, with a few glossy ringlets straying over their white shoulders; both had the same dimpling smiles, both the same unaffectedness of manner and spontaneous cordiality of speech. Inevitably, it would not be long, Paul told himself, before Rosina was also claimed in marriage; indeed, he thought he had detected ardor, as well as admiration, in the glances the young Count de St. Roman kept casting in her direction, and would not have been surprised to learn that this gentleman was only waiting for a favorable opportunity to advance his suit. Meanwhile, Paul congratulated himself that she was free to receive general attention. He would not fall in love with her, because he was unfortunately so constituted that he could do so only once and that for all time; but he realized that St. Roman or any other man to whom she gave her heart and hand would be greatly blessed.

She chatted on, relieving him of any conversational effort. "You don't mind sitting way 'below the salt' like this, do you? There's so much rank here tonight!"

"I couldn't have asked for another place that would please me as much as this one." He lowered his voice slightly. "But I'm afraid I haven't been presented to the young lady on my other side. Won't you make the necessary introductions?"

"Why, you don't really need any! We often follow the English custom of assuming that fellow guests of the same host, if they don't already know each other, are entitled to do so. But I'll tell you, it's Rachel Erlanger, one of Mathilde's future sisters-in-law. She's a dear, you'll like her."

Paul found that he did, very much. Rachel, too, was extremely pretty, besides being affable and approachable; she, too, chatted so easily and pleasantly that conversation with her presented no strain; he allowed himself to be carried along smoothly with it. The first pain he suffered at the sight of Charmian was assuaged to a degree that he would have believed impossible; the numbness had passed completely. He was relishing his food, savoring his wine, appreciating the magnificence of the table appointments, enjoying the engaging companionship of both Rosina and Rachel and the radiant vision of Mathilde. He had actually ceased to feel that, until the riddle of Charmian's present position had been solved for him, he would be unable to think of anything else, when, gratuitously, the answer was given him.

"You knew Charmian de Lixin before, didn't you? I overheard what she said about playing with you when you were both children, but you'd seen her since then, too, hadn't you?"

"Yes, in New Orleans, when we were in our teens and then later on, both here in Paris and in Boston."

"Then isn't it strange that she should have spoken about your friendship in such a remote offhand way? That is, it would seem strange in anyone except Charmian—she's a rule unto herself, and no one can understand why she makes such *unusual* rules. Oh! I'm sorry! I didn't mean to hurt your feelings! I just forgot for a moment that you and she were such old friends."

"You didn't hurt my feelings, Rosina. I don't believe you ever hurt anyone's feelings, do you?"

"I don't mean to. Well, of course, I wasn't in Paris when she was here
the first time, before her mother died. But Rachel was." She leaned across
him, and he was agreeably aware of the perfume she was using and the
curve of her young breasts under their soft frill of lace and sequence of
satin bows. "Rachel, when Charmian de Lixin was here in the late fifties,
didn't everyone think she was going to marry the Marquis d'Ambres?"

Rachel smiled. "I don't know that everyone did. But I'm almost sure he
did. Otherwise, why should he have loaned her family that wonderful house
of his on the rue des Saints Pères? The poor man was terribly criticized for
doing it, but he must have thought she would be its next chatelaine."

"Oh then, you believed that was his expectation?" Paul asked, bitterly
recalling both his conversations with Edge on the subject and the letter
Charmian herself had written him. "I had understood that he was an older
man, that he was especially devoted to Mrs. Sheppard."

Rachel smiled again. "I don't know just what you mean by 'an older man.'
Jacques must be about thirty. His devotion to Mrs. Sheppard was probably
sincere enough, as far as it went. Maybe he stressed it a little, because, as
I've just said, the loan of the house was rather *mal vu*. Of course, the Sheppards were very nice, Berenice especially, but I don't need to tell you that
locality is the stronghold of the old aristocracy and it seems Mr. Sheppard
was in trade."

The old accusation, Paul told himself. But there was no sting in the way
Rachel spoke, as there had been when his mother and Alice Percy had done
so on the same subject. Indeed, it was hardly possible that there could
have been. Rachel herself did not belong to the old aristocracy and, on her
father's side, neither did Rosina; one was the daughter of a shrewd and successful banker, the other the daughter of a shrewd and successful politician.
But Paul had a feeling that, whatever their background, they would not
have spoken spitefully.

"I always liked Jacques d'Ambres," Rachel went on. "And I know he was
quite inconsolable when Charmian left Paris—that first time, I mean. But
of course he realized that on account of her mother's death . . . anyway, I
understand that when she returned to Boston, she corresponded with him.
She gave him reason to hope that when her period of mourning was
over . . . in fact, he told me so himself. And he was quite beside himself
with joy at her return. And then, almost immediately after that, she met
Gilbert de Lixin. He had been in the Orient when she was here before;
his father was Minister to China then. And, of course, Gilbert is ever so
much richer than Jacques and his rank is much more exalted."

Paul now asked a question. "And that was what counted for her in marriage?"

"Why, yes, I think so! Don't you, Rosina?" Rachel was tossing the conversational ball back to Rosina, who picked it up with characteristic ease. "I think the title especially," she said. "Of course, the Sheppards are tremendously rich anyway; Charmian didn't need money. But I suppose it's always possible to use a little more—Papa says that seems to be the way his wife and daughters feel." The dimpled smile came into play again. "Not that we ever need to tease him. He's so kind and generous that all we have to do is to express the slightest wish."

"I'm sure it's his pleasure to grant it. But to go back to Charmian—"

"Oh yes, to go back to Charmian! Well, as I said, I think it was the title she really wanted. It was as if—well, as I said before, I don't want to hurt your feelings. She's an old friend of yours."

"And as I said before, I don't think you could possibly hurt my feelings or anyone else's."

"It's as if she wanted to make up for not feeling secure—socially secure, I mean; as if she's been slighted because she wasn't. She seemed to be grasping at that—social security, social supremacy; and as if she wanted to snub other people because she's been snubbed herself—not necessarily by them, but by someone. Why, she even sounded that way when she spoke to you, Paul! That's why I said she was strange! Because of course everyone's so proud to claim your friendship, everyone's so pleased that you've come back to Paris!"

A salad was being served, a salad which was a work of art, accompanied by great slices of pâté de foie gras. The fish course, the entrée and the roast had all been passed while the triangular conversation progressed. Mathilde leaned forward from her place across the wide table and, even though he was not as close to her as to Rosina, Paul was again pleasantly conscious of delightful perfume.

"You three have been whispering like conspirators," she said. "I'm sure the girls have been indulging in naughty gossip, Paul. You mustn't let them lead you astray."

"They haven't led me astray. They very kindly set me straight about several matters. But there are others concerning which I am still in the dark. Will it be very *mal vu* if I ask some more questions?"

"Not after the girls each talk for a little while to the neglected man on the other side. You're much too charming, Paul! And, of course, the lion of the hour! I'm really rather jealous of you. I thought this was to be *my* great night—mine and Frederick's, of course!"

She looked fondly toward her fiancé and he returned her glance; Paul had the impression that they had managed to clasp and press each other's hands under the table. That marriage certainly isn't founded on ambition and revenge, he thought with relief. Rachel and Rosina had taken Mathilde's hint and each was devoting herself to the "neglected man" on her other side, though as one was George Eustis and the other Alfred Slidell, both girls claimed they really didn't need to bother, since everything was all in the family anyway. Nevertheless, Paul had an interval for uninterrupted reflection. Yes, he had learned a great deal, but there was still much that he did not know and that he wanted to know. Charmian had met Gilbert de Lixin "immediately" after her return to Paris, that was to say, two years earlier. Yet from the stray remark he had heard before dinner, he gathered that she had not long been married. What had caused the delay? She could, as he well knew, be almost irresistible. Was this languid prince she had finally ensnared so lacking in virility that he had been a slow, even a reluctant suitor? No, that could not be the answer, either, for de Persigny had said of de Lixin that he had nothing to do but make love to his wife. The inference was certainly that he enjoyed doing so and, in Paul's opinion, no normal man could very well help it, if he were married to Charmian.

Another mystery was troubling him. No mention had been made of the other Sheppards, except for the passing remark that Berenice had been especially well liked. He had written her several times in the past few years and he had heard from her once or twice after her return to Paris. Then her letters had ceased; of course, mail to New Orleans had often been lost or intercepted since the Federal Occupation, but that had not quieted his anxiety. He had been sincerely attached to Berenice and had looked forward to seeing her again in Paris, for she had still been there when she had written the latest letter he had received. Now she and her father had completely disappeared from the scene. He must find out why and when. . . .

Mrs. Slidell was giving the signal to leave the table before Paul was able to recapture the attention of either Rosina or Rachel long enough to satisfy himself on any of these baffling points. An interval followed when the ladies were left by themselves in the parlors and the gentlemen withdrew to the library for port, cigars and masculine conversation. Most of them were personages of considerable importance, a good deal older than Paul; the exceptions were Alfred Slidell, Frederick Erlanger, George Eustis and St. Roman; they formed a group on which he would not have hesitated to intrude if they had not been joined, just as he was hoping to do so, by de Lixin. He was beginning to tell himself that his other questions would have to go unanswered, at least that evening, when the Count de Persigny approached him and invited him to continue their interrupted discussion about the Queen of Spain. After Paul had succeeded in satisfying the Minister's curiosity and there was a slight pause, he ventured to change the subject.

"Before dinner, M. le Ministre, you made one or two remarks that led me to believe you knew the Princess de Lixin fairly well. Do you, by any chance, know her family, too? Her father and elder sister are both old friends of mine and no one has mentioned them to me since my arrival."

"I do not know them personally, but I know that they have left Paris. I believe they have gone back to New England. That is where they came from, isn't it?"

"Yes . . . and was this some time ago?"

"No, it was not until after the younger sister's marriage."

"And that was—"

"Just before the New Year."

And this is only May, Paul said to himself! So there *was* a delay! And it was caused by—?

"As I told you in the course of our previous conversation," de Persigny was saying, "I am an incorrigible gossip. Nevertheless I might not have spoken to you so candidly about your beautiful compatriot if I had not known you were a great friend of the Slidell family. But I could see you were very much interested in my reference and, if I am not mistaken, you and the two fascinating young ladies between whom you were seated at dinner were further discussing the same subject. What is there that they did not tell you that you would like to have me tell you now?"

Paul saw no reason for circumlocution. "They told me that Charmian Sheppard met Gilbert de Lixin 'immediately' after her return to Paris two years ago and that, to speak plainly, she dismissed another suitor in his favor. I can't help wondering why her marriage to de Lixin was so long delayed."

"I will inform you at once: he was encumbered with an invalid wife. She died only last autumn. Meanwhile, your beautiful compatriot played her cards extremely well. She could not afford to be as careless as your other friend, the Queen of Spain. And she knew it."

The Minister smiled, nodded and moved away. He could have hardly been expected to say any more, if as much, and indeed Paul had no trouble in putting together the final pieces of the puzzle. Charmian had made up her mind "immediately" after meeting Gilbert de Lixin that she would be a princess and took the first cautious steps to satisfy that ambition; she gave her victim ample opportunity and ample provocation to fall in love with her. Perhaps she had not actually used the same words that were widely attributed to Eugénie when the Emperor laid siege to her: "Sire, the only door into my bedroom leads through the church." But she might well have done so and whatever words she did use had conveyed the same meaning. She had no mind to risk the coveted title and she had managed to keep the prince dangling for almost two years. Now they both had what they wanted. His air of languid indifference could easily be a cloak to passion which, once roused, might be almost uncontrollable; and such passion could take many forms besides that of desiring a woman for herself. Among these could be the form of desiring to dominate her completely, not only physically, but mentally and spiritually. Paul would not have been the child of Alonzo Morphy and Telcide Le Carpentier if he had not known this; he would not even have been a typical Creole. His mother had deeply loved his father and yet her life with him had been far from easy. Charmian, who did not love Gilbert de Lixin, might sooner or later find hers very hard, especially as it was not only possible, but likely that her husband was abnormally jealous as well as abnormally sensual, and that once his jealousy was roused, his passion would be for revenge as well as for dominion. Paul was ashamed to find himself hoping that this might be so; but his shame did not still his hopes. . . .

John Slidell was asking his male guests if they would not like to rejoin the ladies. The gentlemen put down their glasses, extinguished their cigars and made their leisurely way back to the drawing room. As they entered it, the Marquise de Chasseloup-Laubat claimed de Lixin's attention; he could not refuse to give it to her, but his glance strayed toward his wife. Paul had been right: the man was still in the grip of unsatiated passion, that would never be satiated as long as his passion for her lasted, and this might be for years—or it might be for only months or weeks. However, if Charmian were aware of the glance she was undisturbed by it. She waited until her husband was on the other side of the room. Then, without haste, but with unmistakable purpose, she strolled in the direction of Paul.

"Have you noticed that cabinet in the front drawing room?" she asked, indicating a handsome piece of marquetry that stood in a far corner. "It contains quite an interesting collection of miniatures. Rosina has suggested that you might like me to show them to you. I am supposed to have become quite an authority on miniatures, in a small way of course. Shall we go and look at them? I will try to answer any questions you may care to ask about them." Then, as he acquiesced, endeavoring to conceal his astonishment, she said casually, "You see I decided against marrying a marquis after all. You may remember that, the last time I saw you, I told you I was not sure whether I would or not."

"Yes, I do see. And I do remember."

"Do you remember anything else I said?"

"I certainly do. You told me you wouldn't consider marrying a mere chess player."

"I didn't mean that silly speech. You're not holding it against me, are you, after all these years? Please don't—please forgive me. Of course, I shouldn't have said that. I'm sorry. But I was in a very nervous state. My mother had just died. I wasn't happy in Boston. You know how fond I've always been of you, Paul."

They had been talking in low tones as they walked forward, but even so, Paul was conscious of a new quality in her voice. It was no longer mocking; there was a gentleness, almost a sweetness in it and, as he looked at her, he saw a corresponding gentleness and sweetness in her face. He could not bring himself to say that he had not forgiven any more than he had forgotten; he murmured something unintelligible.

"Shall I tell you what I did mean when I asked you if you remembered what else I said?"

He should have been forewarned, he knew that she should not say anything more, that he should not listen if she did and that, in any case, he could give no credence to a word she uttered. For some reason of her own, as yet unexplained, she had singled him out; it must be a selfish reason, it boded him no good; she was false through and through. But the old magic was already at work; he was completely under its spell. Evil this might be, but it was nonetheless irresistible. Again he murmured something, but though the words were indistinct, they were not unintelligible. He was signifying that he was ready to listen.

They had reached the cabinet which contained the miniatures and Charmian had opened the glass doors, thus shielding them from close view and muting the sound of their voices. She selected one of the tiny ivories, framed in brilliants, and held it up for his inspection. To anyone who happened to look toward them at the moment, as Gilbert de Lixin was doing, she would have appeared intent on showing him one of Mrs. Slidell's choicest treasures and identifying it as a certain likeness.

"I said that if I married a marquis, I might consider taking you for a lover," she said in a voice that was now only a vibrant whisper. "Of course, the same is true now that I have married a prince instead."

"The years which Slidell passed as Confederate commissioner at the court of Napoleon III were more conducive to fame than to contentment. Talents of a high order were requisite for success, and these Slidell possessed and exerted. But success in negotiation was predetermined by success on the battlefield. It was impossible that the diplomat succeed where his country failed. As in Mexico, where Slidell had won his spurs in diplomacy, the difficulties were insurmountable. If greatness depended wholly upon good fortune, Slidell's claim to recognition would be limited to his various achievements in moulding Louisiana to his will, and in nominating his friend Buchanan to the Presidency. But greatness is also measured by the amount and intelligence of effort put forth, as well as by results achieved, and by such a test the vexations of an impossible mission reveal the incumbent at his best. Certainly Slidell recognized at Paris the opportunity of a life time to serve the South, his country, and to win laurels for himself."

"The only avenue for really constructive developments lay in semi-official and private negotiations with ship contractors. And 1863, in France as in England, was a year of activity in this direction. The cotton loan made shipbuilding possible, and Slidell soon turned his attention to this auxiliary development of his mission."

John Slidell by Louis Martin Sears (Duke University Press)

34.

"Don't hurry away, my boy. I've been looking forward to a chat with you after the other guests have gone. We'll have a nightcap in the library. Why don't you make your official farewells and then slip away and wait for me?"

Paul nodded, understandingly. He knew that John Slidell wanted to have a confidential talk with him as soon as it was conveniently possible after his arrival in Paris, but he had not expected that it would take place that night at the apartment; he had thought he would be summoned the next morning to the office located around the corner. Better, much better, that it should be now; he could not have slept in any case. He only hoped that he would be able to concentrate on whatever the Commissioner said to him, that Charmian's inviting eyes and vibrant words and the visions that all these implied would not keep darting and flashing across his consciousness.

The quiet in the library was welcome after the hubbub of the drawing rooms and Paul sank gratefully into a comfortable chair drawn close to the hearth, where a cheerful fire was burning. A decanter and glasses stood on a table beside the chair, as if inviting him to take a drink. He poured one of more generous proportions than he generally allowed himself and sat sipping it slowly, as he watched the flames and tried to steady his thoughts and subdue his emotions.

He still had no idea what form the mission for which he had been called to Paris might take, but he did know his work would require a deep sense of responsibility, even of dedication, and that he would not be able to justify the confidence Benjamin had in him unless his mind were alert and his feelings under control. Yet, how could any normal man fail to be the prey of overwhelming agitation after the scene which had just occurred? To be sure, Charmian had made no promises and he already knew, to his cost, that she was adroit at extricating herself from a situation where circumstances pointed to the existence of pledges, even if these had not been voiced. On the other hand, her extraordinary suggestion had not been made as the result of anything that he had said to her, indeed of anything he had so much as imagined; in his wildest visions he would not have dreamed that he could intimately re-enter her life, even if she had not already been married; his failure to succeed in the law and on the battlefield had stifled that hope forever. Now, on her own initiative, she had revived it. For she had not spoken mockingly or even lightly; there had been an earnestness, almost an urgency in her manner and her voice that had never been there before. She, who had not once previously admitted regret or repentance for anything she had said or done, had actually begged his forgiveness for wounding him. She had moved him to pity by reminding him of her mother's death, of her loneliness in an alien and unfriendly city. Never had she seemed so appealing. Never had she been more desirable. . . .

Paul's code of honor was rigid. Even if his lasting love for his childhood sweetheart had not prevailed against carnal indulgence, it would have been against his principles to make love to another man's wife—to a shutter girl, yes, perhaps, except for that deep early attachment; he thought nonetheless of his companions who took their pleasure in that way, or who established their exquisite quadroon mistresses in neat little houses on Rampart Street. Very few, if any, of the young men about town that he knew lived continently or thought of doing so; it was a fastidious disinclination rather than a moral standard that had kept him free from the entanglements they welcomed. But a married woman was something else again; she was sacrosanct among respectable Creoles. He had never heard a breath of scandal against any of his acquaintance. And not only were their persons inviolate; gentlemen rarely mentioned them by name and then only with the greatest respect; duels had been fought, men had been killed, for no greater reason than some slight infringement of this rule. Paul had been as uncomfortable as he was astonished, early in the evening, at hearing Charmian so freely discussed; yet later he had encouraged such discussion, he had even joined in it, with no feeling of personal guilt or of resentment toward the men who spoke of her slightingly. How could this have happened? There was only one explanation: her critics did not regard her as belonging in that sacrosanct category and, though he had not realized this before, it must be that he did not, either. He had permitted her name to be bandied about in his hearing and now he had gone a step further; he was permitting himself to think of being her lover. . . .

Even now, the idea that this was blameworthy, as far as her husband was concerned, did not cross his mind. He felt nothing but contempt, suspicion and revulsion toward Gilbert de Lixin. It was not the fault of the Prince that there had been no illicit love affair with Charmian; it was only her caution that had kept him from faithlessness to his invalid wife, as far as Charmian herself was concerned; doubtless he had been faithless enough with others; he had all the marks of a voluptuary. And what was there about that weak and dissolute face which somehow suggested the saddist as well? Paul did not know, but involuntarily he found himself shuddering. Were there elements in his prospects that were gruesome as well as tantalizing? And was he not mad, even to think of becoming implicated in such a sordid situation, when he was about to embark upon the greatest adventure of his life—one in which not only his own fate, but that of his nation was involved?

The door of the library opened and Slidell came toward him, treading softly across the thick carpet of the booklined room. "No, no," he said, as

Paul sprang up, "sit still, right where you are. I'll have a drink, too, before we start our talk. I'm glad to see you had the sense to pour one for yourself. It's good to get away from all that clackety-clack, isn't it? I enjoy having company as much as the next man and of course, as you know, we had two special reasons for a big celebration tonight. Just the same, I'm glad it's over and that you and I can get quietly down to business."

He settled back into a chair even deeper and more heavily upholstered than the one Paul had chosen and poured himself a drink twice the size of his guest's. He did not seem inclined to enter into immediate conversation and Paul waited, without impatience, for him to begin. Besides being glad of further respite to regain his self-control, Paul welcomed the opportunity of studying his host more carefully than he had hitherto had a chance of doing. The Morphy and Slidell families had been on friendly terms for years; but he himself had seen the Commissioner only as a young and in-experienced man sees one much older and more important—that is, at a respectful distance. Now it was essential that they should come closer together.

Despite the complete lack of tenseness in his manner, Slidell gave the effect of great physical and mental power. He wore his hair, which was already white, rather long, and the scant silky locks tended to produce a benevolent aspect, which, without these, he might have lacked, for his lips were firm and thin, his eyes piercing under heavy black brows and all his features clear cut. His skin was noticeably ruddy, but it suggested robust health and an equable disposition rather than an over-indulgence in food and wine. He was a heavy man, but he carried his weight well; he might have been described as portly, but never as obese. In like measure, though as a senator he had not been renowned for his eloquence or the profundity of his classical learning, he had proved himself a statesman of superior education and intellect. Paul knew that in Buchanan's administration, he had often been called the power behind the throne. Now he was coming more openly into his own. Many of his admirers liked to compare him with Franklin, in looks as well as in capability and in the character of his mission; undoubtedly, such resemblance existed. But Paul did not feel that Slidell needed to borrow distinction from any source, even one as renowned as Franklin's; he had enough and to spare of his own.

"Before we begin to discuss the situation here," he finally remarked, "I should like to hear something about your experiences in Havana. You could not possibly have begun your wanderings in a place about which I am more eager to have a first-hand report. Did you play a good deal of chess there?"

"Yes, the same devotees of the game, who were so cordial to me on the occasion of my two previous visits, were equally hospitable to me this time— Medina, Fesser, Sicre, Dubouchet, Toscano—and, of course, there was a great deal more opportunity for hospitality in two weeks than two days! Don Francisco Fesser again entertained me delightfully at his *morada*—a charming house set in a wonderful garden. I can still taste the flavor of his guanábana sherbet and smell the fragrance of the *damas de noche*. I played against Sicre first—and won after thirty-four moves—I've kept a record of the game, in case you'd like to see it. It was the most interesting one I had in Havana, though I enjoyed playing with Medina and Toscano, too. Fesser contented himself with acting as host. Besides the pleasant *meriendas* for which he was responsible, there was an elaborate banquet at the Hotel Hermitage for which he was largely responsible, too, though not entirely. I gathered that all the leading chess players and some of the dignitaries of the city had a hand in it and, when I embarked for Cadiz on the mail packet, *Cuidad Condal*, they all gave me a wonderful *despedida*."

"By dignitaries, you mean—"

"Well, the Captain General, of course, and the Bishop—personages like that. I'd met them before, too."

"Did you, by any chance, happen to meet a Marylander by the name of John Benjamin Belt?"

"Tutor to the Captain General's children? I did, indeed. He seems to be a very general favorite. He was among the guests at the Hermitage banquet."

"Did you gather whether or not he was confining his activities entirely to teaching the children of the gubernatorial family and shining in society?"

"Yes, sir, I did. It is an open secret that he was charged by Jefferson Davis to swing the sympathies of Cuban officials to the Confederate cause, if he could, and that he's been very successful at it. Southern ships don't seem to be having any trouble at all about finding space in Havana Harbor for refueling or making repairs. And the Captain General is getting medical supplies, which are very badly needed, through to our army."

"Ah! That's the good news I was waiting for. I've had reports before, of course, but they haven't been confirmed by a reliable witness who saw what was actually happening. Your chess connections in Havana have been extremely helpful to us, Paul."

"I'm very glad, sir."

There was a short silence, during the course of which Slidell sat with his head bent and appeared to be reflecting, with satisfaction, on what he had just heard. Then he looked up and spoke emphatically.

"Now that my mind is at rest, at least about the way things are going in Havana," he said, "I want to talk to you about the Cotton Loan that has just been consummated here. That is, I do not propose to go into a long exposition of how it was arranged, who opposed it and who favored it, why the rate of interest was so high, and so on and so on. All these facts and figures are available at the office and you can go there and pore over them with

Eustis. You should, of course, have them at your finger tips in case you are not already familiar with them and someone begins to ask you detailed questions about them. But first of all, I should tell you how I want to use the money available through the loan and why. The greatest need of the Confederacy at the moment is for ships. I propose to see that it gets them."

He paused impressively, but as he did not seem to expect an answer, Paul did not attempt to reply. He merely nodded, leaning forward attentively.

"There will be obstacles in the way of carrying out such a project," he said. "Napoleon's Proclamation of Neutrality, which followed closely that of Her Britannic Majesty's two years ago, set forth, in five clauses, the precise and specific acts that were forbidden French subjects. It is the third clause which is important to us. In case you are not familiar with it—and there is no reason why you should be as yet—I have had it copied for you."

He drew a small sheet of neatly folded paper from his pocket and handed it to Paul. The text was brief and to the point: *"Il est interdit à tout Français de prendre commission de l'une des deux parties pour armer des vaisseaux en guerre, ou d'accepter des lettres de marque pour faire la course maritime, ou de concourir d'une manière quelconque à l'equipement ou l'armanent d'un navire de guerre ou corsaire de l'une des deux parties."*

"Admittedly, that is quite explicit," Slidell said, as Paul looked up after reading the paper. "Happily, it is not as final as it seems. France is governed by an Autocracy, and no matter what enactments are made or policy proclaimed, these can be modified, or even disregarded in practice, without causing any public excitement or legal protest. It did not take me long to grasp this fact." As he glanced toward Paul, his guest was aware of something very like a twinkle in the shrewd old eyes. However, Slidell's voice was grave as he continued.

"I therefore wrote to Captain Bulloch, our Naval Agent in England, telling him that, in my opinion, there would be little official interference if vessels for our purpose were built in France, and no interference at all if, once built, they attempted to leave on some plausible pretext. Are you following me without difficulty so far?"

"Yes, sir. And needless to say, I am deeply interested."

"Unfortunately, Bulloch was not. He was already committed to some English shipbuilders for the construction of four so-called 'Rams' which the Federal authorities were watching with eagle eyes; he thought he had enough problems on his hands without inviting more. But as the prospects for the Cotton Loan were already bright, I took matters into my own hands and approached a member of the Legislative Council, on friendly terms with the Emperor, who is also a naval architect. His name is Arman and his sympathies are with the Confederacy; but his shipyards are in Bordeaux." Again the little twinkle came into Slidell's eyes. "He suggested that the services of a fellow Deputy, a certain Voruz, who lives in Nantes, might be useful, since the latter is not only a political power, but an iron founder, and Voruz was accordingly admitted to our conferences. It was soon decided among us that only one formality was now necessary to assure the success of our venture: a positive declaration from the Minister of Marine that, when the ships were built, they should be permitted to arm and go to sea."

"And the Minister of Marine is the Marquis de Chasseloup-Laubat, whom I met here tonight, isn't he? The husband of General Beauregard's relative?"

"Exactly. You see how neatly the pieces of the pattern begin to fall into place. Arman felt very hopeful that the necessary assurance from Chasseloup-Laubat would be forthcoming—in fact, he was prepared to guarantee that it would be. But still I could not convince Bulloch that it would be better to try the French shipyards than to depend on the 'wavering policy of the British Ministry and the probable delay, expense and publicity of a lawsuit.' I used those exact words in my official communication. But Bulloch still wanted me to wait until 'the state of our finances would admit of fresh operations.' Well, the loan has now been floated. Bulloch cannot possibly stall any longer. He will certainly arrive here within the next few days— perhaps tomorrow. He will give the necessary orders for the construction of such vessels as he sees fit. Among them will certainly be two ironclad ships suitable to enter the Mississippi. The Confederate Congress, anticipating the Cotton Loan, has already appropriated two thousand pounds for such a purpose. I have seen to that—along with further details for which Bulloch will no doubt get the credit, now that I have done the work. Not that it matters."

This time, the Commissioner did not limit himself to a twinkle. He laughed and Paul found it easy to laugh, too.

"Of course, this does not mean that nothing but smooth sailing—and I say that literally as well as figuratively—lies ahead of our ships. The time when we could have been sure of smooth sailing is, unfortunately, past. Our government neglected to establish mercantile relations with Europe at the very outset of hostilities. If it had then seized our own ships and offered inducements to foreign shippers to transport cotton abroad, we would have been provided with ready money to equip the Confederate armies. Cotton worth millions of dollars was still on our wharfs. The ports were still open. Only foresight was lacking—during the five months after the secession of South Carolina and the fall of Fort Sumter, little or nothing was done. It is this lack of logical action at the crucial moment which forces us to more stringent measures now. I have reason to hope, however, that they need not be desperate measures—that is, unless our government goes on making mistakes."

He shook his head and, in the soft candlelight and firelight, his silvery locks took on a new luster. The resemblance to Franklin seemed more marked.

"There are sure to be complications, however. In fact, there has already been a misunderstanding on the part of Congress. It labored under the delusion that ironclad vessels could be purchased ready-made from the French navy. I have been obliged to write quite emphatically that I did 'not see how the negotiation could be opened in such a way as to get the proposition before the Emperor unless it should appear that he had determined to recognize the Confederate Government independently of England,' that there was 'no evidence he intended to take such a decisive step alone,' and that, under the circumstances, therefore, Bulloch would have to be 'content with the covert intimation that no shipbuilder we might employ would be prevented from despatching the vessels to sea when they were completed.'"

He paused to give his next words emphasis, but he pronounced them with cheerful conviction. "I assure you Bulloch *will* be content, quite content. He will order not only the two ironclads, but several corvettes as well. In order to expedite matters, construction work will be divided between Bordeaux and Nantes, though the greater part of it will probably be done in Bordeaux. He will write Mallory, our Secretary of the Navy, that negotiations will have to be carried on through 'intermediaries' and Mallory will accept the statement at its face value. Then Bulloch will proceed to act through the intermediaries. In this undertaking, a great deal of caution will be required and a great deal of help will be needed."

There was another pregnant pause and Paul thought that Slidell was about to disclose something definite, as far as his visitor was personally concerned. Instead, with characteristic thoroughness, the Commissioner proceeded to present further aspects of the general situation in Paris.

"I consider myself rather favorably situated," he said. "I was warmly welcomed when I came here by nearly all the people and by the great majority of the press. A delegation made up of both American and French sympathizers, led by M. de la Garonnière, a member of the Senate, was at the station to meet me and a number of students had also foregathered, intent on giving me a hearty reception. They had even composed a song, which began,

> *'Bienvenu, notr' grand Slidell*
> *Au coeur loyale et l'ame fidèle!'*

That was only the beginning. Before I was really settled at the Hotel du Rhin—long before I was installed in a suitable apartment—callers of all sorts and conditions began to stream in. There is a large American colony here and, for the most part, its sympathies are with the South. Moreover, there is, of course, a natural affinity between Creoles and Frenchmen; they call us *Nos frères de la Louisiane*. Furthermore, such prominent personages as de Persigny, whom you met here tonight, and Drouyn de Lhuys, the new Foreign Minister, doubt, like Thournaval, his predecessor in office, the power of the North to restore the Union. So does the Duc de Morny, the Emperor's 'intimate,' as he is sometimes discreetly called. But why should we not speak plainly? He is Napoleon's half-brother, the son of Hortense de Beauharnais and Flahaut de la Billarderie. The sound sense of all these gentlemen naturally influences their sympathies. As to the Emperor himself, he will not make any definite move toward recognition of the Confederacy, I am afraid, until he is assured that England will do the same. He is obliged to proceed with caution—just as we are. But, meanwhile, he has shown himself not only unprejudiced and well-informed, but friendly. You have heard, I suppose, that he has already received me twice very cordially, the first time at Vichy and the second at Saint Cloud?"

"Yes, sir. And, of course, the whole South has swelled with pride at your reception, not only by the Emperor and the outstanding members of his family and his cabinet, but by the French people. The warm feelings of your fellow Americans could have been taken for granted."

"All the same, I should be surprised if you had heard about my first meeting with Napoleon. It is not the sort of encounter that is usually featured in official communications, or permitted to leak into the press. But I believe it might interest you and also be important for you to know. . . . Did you ever hear of a fellow Orleanian of yours by the name of Sophie Bricard?"

"I think so, sir. She's a singer, isn't she?"

"Soubrette would be the more accurate term perhaps. But she does have a voice of sorts besides—ah—other attractions—a voluptuous form and melting eyes, for instance. She scored quite a success here early in the war, singing such songs as *La Bannière Bleue, Salut O mon pays, Aide-Nous, O France aimée,* at musicales and bazaars. Then she secured an engagement at the *Bouffes Parisien.*"

"Offenbach's little theater?"

"Exactly. I was asked to be one of the patrons there for her debut in *Florian* and, under all the circumstances—her background, her zeal for the Cause, and so on—I felt I couldn't very well refuse. So I took a box for the première. Then, the day before this was to take place, I was advised that the Emperor was to attend, and that the only other *avant scène loge* was permanently reserved for the Duc de Morny, who is Offenbach's most prominent patron. The Duc would have been perfectly willing to yield his box to Mrs. Slidell and her party, but that lazy ignoramous of a United States Minister, William Dayton, sent a message that he wanted a box for himself and Mrs. Dayton. Of course, there was nothing to do but give it to them, since he is the official representative of the Federal Government and the Confederate States have not yet been formally recognized. However, Eustis and I took seats in the stalls and I received quite an ovation when I entered the theater. I was obliged to rise and bow twice before the curtain went up, acknowledging salutations. When Dayton entered his borrowed box, he was hissed. Then, of course, a counter-demonstration had to be staged. If there had been any actual disorder, after the Emperor's arrival, he would naturally have been obliged to leave immediately. Fortunately, though he was expected every minute, he was not there yet and the *gendarmerie* saw to it that the few sympathizers began to applaud, so that the United States Minister would not be entirely eclipsed by the Confederate Commissioner. Mr. Dayton bowed from his *loge—my loge—*and order was restored. But the situation was still ticklish. Dayton is completely without savoir-faire. His predecessor, Faulkner, was a Virginian and, of course, a gentleman, and I am bound to say that Bigelow, the present Consul General, is a very able man—a good linguist, which Dayton is not, a good mixer, which Dayton is not, and a clever propagandist for the United States. That is one reason why we need equally good ones for the Confederacy."

Again Paul hoped that Slidell might begin to give him some definite instructions. Then he realized that everything so far said about the contretemps at the *Bouffes Parisien* was merely introductory.

"From the viewpoint of the applause, which was led by the Emperor, the opening scenes of *Florian* were quite a success, though Eustis and I both thought it was rather blatant. As I said before, Sophie does not really have much of a voice—her attractions are of a different order. However, when we were invited backstage at the end of the second act to congratulate our 'fair compatriot,' we could not very well refuse; and when we reached the Green Room, whom should we see but Napoleon himself, at that very moment smilingly taking Sophie's hand! At the same moment she caught sight of me and, withdrawing her hand, struck a dramatic attitude and exclaimed, 'Voilà, Sire, *voilà le représentant de mon pays souffrant!* The South is fighting for freedom. On my knees, I supplicate Your Majesty. Give us the friendship of France!'"

"And then?" Paul asked, seeing that this time Slidell expected such a question.

"Then naturally the Emperor frowned and stepped back. He did not speak again to her or to anyone else in the company—about a dozen persons were present. But, before he left, he turned to me and shook hands, calmly and politely, as if we were already on terms of the cordial and pleasant acquaintance, which, as you know, we achieved shortly thereafter. I really think this very unconventional meeting helped to break the ice and pave the way for the present unstrained relationship between us."

"Then it was really a good thing in the end?"

"Certainly not a bad one for me. But, of course, Offenbach was furious over the episode, especially when it was remarked, at the close of the third act, that the Emperor was no longer in his box. Then the rumor that there had been a scene in the Green Room began to spread like wildfire, with the addition of all sorts of extravagant fables: *la petite* Bricard had brought the Emperor and the Commissioner together; thanks to her, an entente cordiale was now established between their countries—indeed, Napoleon had promised Sophie, as she knelt before him, that France would espouse the cause of the South! Needless to say, nothing like that had happened and her dramatics did Mademoiselle Bricard no good. Dayton complained to the Foreign Minister, he in turn complained to the Prefect of Police, and she was told to curtail her provocative actions—she was even forbidden to wear a Confederate flag in her bosom! As a matter of fact, her professional career —that is her *stage* career—came to an end very shortly thereafter. *Florian* had a short run and, at its close, she disappeared from Paris for a time. When she returned, it was not as Sophie Bricard, but as Mrs. Eccles. There is no Mr. Eccles in evidence; he is supposed to have gone to Richmond to offer his services to Lee, but that is all rather vague. Anyway, he seems to have left the lady well provided for; she has a handsome suite at the Hotel du Louvre and, as she entertains extensively, she does not appear to be leading a lonely life. Dayton's secretary, Pennington, is one of her more frequent visitors. It is quite possible that, thanks to association with him, she may be losing her enthusiasm for the Confederacy and thinking better of the Union cause. I am glad to say that Eustis is more discreet in the company he keeps. I couldn't ask for a better secretary."

"I'm sure you couldn't, sir. I took an instant liking to him this evening."

Slidell nodded, drained his glass and reached for the decanter on a nearby table. "I'm going to have one more drink," he said, "better let me fill your glass, too. Yes, Eustis is a fine young man and his wife, whom you met, too, a lovely girl, and a great asset to him in every way, just as my wife and daughters are to me. She was a Miss Corcoran, as perhaps you know, a daughter of the Washington banker by that name. Well, as I said, I couldn't ask for a better secretary and he has a good staff working with him. Besides Eustis and the others in the office, I have various official associates and several quite eminent colleagues. Among these are Mr. Dudley Mann, one of the original Commissioners, who has remained in England in a semi-official position; and Commander Matthew Fontaine Maury, the great hydrographer, who could have been our Ambassador to Russia—after looking over the foreign field, he decided he could be more useful by remaining here instead. Captain Bulloch and Major Caleb Huse, his army counterpart, are both doing good jobs, too—that is, Huse would do a good job if there were anything down his alley at present and Bulloch needs all the help he can get to do a job which is too big for him, or for any one man, however competent. That is where I hope you will be able to fit into the picture. You have been very attentive and very patient while you have been listening to me. If you can be equally attentive and patient about everything you hear in the next few months, the services you may render the Confederacy could be almost inestimable."

"I don't need to tell you, sir, that I'd give my right hand to be of the least service. But I still don't see what I can do."

"That is what I am now going to tell you. I had to give you the background first. The persons to whom I have just referred are all well known in their connection with the Confederacy. You, too, are well known, but not in that connection. It is important that you should not be and I do not think this will be too hard. Your health is not robust; the state of it prevented you from becoming a military man. You have abandoned the law, which you did not find a congenial occupation. You have never held a public office, and you are no better fitted to do so than to be Pierre Beauregard's aide-de-camp or a member of the firm of Rosellus, Hunt, McCabe and Hennen. But you are a great chess player. Paris was the scene of some of your most conspicuous triumphs, a few years ago. What could be more natural than that you should seek to repeat these, in the same agreeable setting, now that you are rather at loose ends? Especially as your mother, your two sisters and your brother-in-law are living in Paris and such a program would give you a chance to visit them? Oh, yes, I know, you have said you would never play chess again! But you broke that self-made rule, in the interests of expediency, when you were in Havana, and factors much more vital than expediency are now involved. You have also said you would give your right hand to serve the Confederacy. This is the time to tell me which you really mean."

The impact of this ultimatum was far more forceful than Slidell, for all his shrewdness, could have guessed. There was a long silence, while Paul endeavored, first to recover and then, to think the situation through, not only rationally, but sacrificially. It was true that, in Havana, his resumption of chess playing had been prompted by expediency; but it had also represented his resumption of a major role, in a royal game, among worthy antagonists who were his social equals. He had been hospitably received as an honored guest, not despite his avocation, but because of it. Every courtesy shown him—his invitations to the great plantations and town houses, the *meriendas* at the mansion of Don Francisco Fesser, the magnificent banquet given in his honor at the Hotel Hermitage, the *despedida* when he left for Spain on the *Cuidad Condal*, with Cadiz as his next port of call—all these

were a tribute to his supremacy in an art in which such great Spaniards as
Sicre, Medina and Toscano also excelled. But, in Paris, there would be no
question of meeting again the great masters like Anderssen and Harrwitz;
the Café de la Régence, not the drawing rooms of duchesses, was their
natural habitat; true, St. Amant and Isouard were welcome in the most
exclusive society, were indeed themselves to the manner born; and the Duke
of Brunswick, whose soirées were the epitome of excellence, was positively
fanatical in his devotion to chess, as Paul had discovered at the performance
of *Norma*. But, in the drawing rooms of most ladies of quality, including
that of the lovely lazy Creole, Baronne de la Sange, chess was simply another
amusing parlor trick, like the ability to write witty little impromptu verses
and perform legerdemain. The charming ladies, the elegant gentlemen for
whom he would be called upon to perform sought only the most frivolous
types of amusement; and they would never have welcomed him warmly as a
chess player had he not been, as the Count de Persigny put it, a very personable young man, well born, well bred, good looking, agreeable and un-
attached. Worse, far worse than this: the liege lady of his steadfast devotion
would not tolerate him as a chess player, even with all these other acceptable
attributes; it was his skill, his absorption in the game that had cost him her
love. What wonder that it had become anathema to him? How could he,
in the very moment that she had at last shown herself kind, risk losing her
favor again? And yet, what else could he honorably do? He was, indeed,
involved in something more vital than expediency. He faced the Commissioner squarely and, though he spoke in a low, hoarse voice, he did not
falter as he answered.

"I mean, of course, that I want to help the Confederacy."

"Very well. I believe you had several attractive invitations this evening, to
salons, soirées, country estates and so on. I hope you will accept them all.
You will be asked to play chess wherever you go, or at least in most places
where you go; I hope you will never decline. You are admittedly out of
practice, you can lose a game now and then without raising doubts as to
whether or not you are doing this on purpose; you will probably be well
advised to do so, if you are to remain socially acceptable. But you will not be
spending all your time at the chess table. In the course of your visits you
will hear a great many conversations, you will learn a good deal about French
feeling, and I hope at least a little about French policies. These feelings and
policies you will report."

"To you, sir?"

"For the present. You have the fortunate position of being a friend of
the family—fortunate for you, but fortunate for me, too. It is natural that
you should wish to come often to see Rosina and Alfred, that you should
take an interest in Mathilde's wedding. Eustis and you are about the same

age; it will also be natural for you to see a good deal of him. Another man of whom it would be natural for you to see a good deal, since he is also about your age—a few years older, but not enough to matter—and an Orleanian to boot, is Henri Vignaud. He would have been among our guests tonight had he not been dining with Princess Mathilde. Perhaps you know him already?"

"Not personally. Isn't his father a dealer in clocks and watches, some of which he repairs and some of which he makes himself? I believe my mother's one of his regular customers." Paul hesitated, fearful lest the statement, as he had made it, sounded as if he could not have been expected to know Henri Vignaud personally, since they would not have moved in the same social circles. But he saw no way to remedy this possible impression and went on, rather hastily, "And didn't the son create rather a stir when he insisted on changing his unwieldy baptismal name—Jean Heliodore or something like that—to Henri? I think he taught in New Orleans for a while, meantime writing incidental articles for the newspapers before going to Thibodeaux to edit *L'Union de Lafourche*."

"That's the man. Are you familiar with the rest of his dossier?"

Paul considered for a minute, then smiled and nodded. "Yes, afterward he edited *La Renaissance Louisianaise* and tried his hand at drama. He actually had two plays produced—*Jane Grey* and *Veillesse de Mousquetaires*. Neither made much of a stir, but I saw them and enjoyed them. Later, if I'm not mistaken, he was commissioned a captain in the Sixth Louisiana Regiment and was captured after the fall of New Orleans. I've never heard what happened to him after that. I supposed he was dead."

"He escaped," Slidell said rather drily. "He found out that he was destined for a military prison where most of the inmates did die—of starvation. Somehow he succeeded in persuading a Yankee officer to give him a *laissez passer* through the lines. 'Give' isn't quite the word—it cost him two hundred and fifty dollars, which was practically all the money he had in the world. But somehow, he reached Richmond and Benjamin sent him on to me, just as he sent you. That is, Vignaud didn't make the trip quite as comfortably as you did, under friendly Spanish auspices, with an agreeable interlude at Havana. He managed to get on one of the ships that ran the blockade and took sixty-three days for the crossing—seasick all the time. However, he finally arrived and I immediately put him on my staff, chiefly in a journalistic capacity, though he has—ah!—other duties also. He writes for the *Index*, our Confederate organ published in London, and for the *Memorial Diplomatique*, a Paris weekly. He acts as musical and dramatic critic for that."

"I see."

"No doubt you will enjoy attending concerts and plays with him," Slidell remarked. Again, the twinkle came into his eyes. "Apparently, besides having a good ear for music, he's quite observant. At all events, he has already won the praise of Mr. Henry Hotze, who is in charge of Confederate propaganda. Perhaps you can profit by Vignaud's observations. I hope so."

"I'll do my best, sir."

"I'm sure you will. Now, I have not yet spoken to Bulloch about you, because I wanted to wait until you had actually arrived, until I had talked with you, before doing so. But, as I told you, I am expecting him to reach Paris within the next few days. I will see that you and he meet each other promptly. I will also see that you meet Arman and Voruz. It might be well for you to go to Nantes and Bordeaux; you could include those cities in a pleasure trip which would take in other points of interest and therefore rouse no suspicions. The project of shipbuilding is one of paramount importance to us at present. It must take precedence over everything else and everything that bears on it, directly or indirectly, will be of interest to me. Do you understand?"

"I think so, sir. Do you mean that even in cafés and hotels, in railway carriages, at theaters and so on, I might overhear snatches of conversation which would provide valuable clues?"

"Exactly. None of these possibilities must be overlooked. But your greatest opportunities will be through your contacts and your chess playing will be your most dependable open sesame."

Again he drained his glass and this time he did not refill it. Instead, he took another small piece of paper from his pocket.

"My former partner, Mr. Benjamin, has a very high regard for you," he said. "I believe he is a relative of yours by marriage, isn't he? At all events, as you know, it was he who recommended you to me. In this connection, I think it may be of interest to you to read this letter which I recently received from him."

He handed over the paper and Paul read: "I have arrived at the conclusion that a sufficient sum of secret service money has not hitherto been placed at the disposal of our diplomatic agents abroad. With enemies so active, so unscrupulous; and with a system of deception so thoroughly organized as that now established by them abroad, it becomes absolutely essential that no means be spared for dissemination of truth, and for a fair exposition of our condition and policy before foreign nations. It is not wise to neglect public opinion, nor prudent to leave to the voluntary interposition of friends, often indiscreet, the duty of vindicating our country and its cause before the tribunal of civilized man. The President, sharing these views, has authorized me to place at your disposal twenty-five thousand dollars which you will find to your credit with Messrs. Fraser, Trenholm & Co. of Liverpool, and which you will use for the service of your country in such way as you may deem most judicious."

"In time, I hope to have a Secret Service staff of at least a hundred persons. Paris is much the best place from which to disseminate propaganda," Slidell said, as Paul returned the letter to him without comment or question. "At the moment, however, there are only a few persons so employed and I do not feel it necessary that they should be made known to each other; therefore I shall not tell you who your co-workers are, except for Henri Vignaud, whom we have already discussed. I do not think your duties and those of the others will overlap, but if they should no great harm will be done. I do think it important for you to know, however, that you will not be hampered for lack of funds. I realize that the Federal occupation of New Orleans may have caused you some financial embarrassment. You may draw on me for three thousand dollars immediately and when that sum is exhausted—or rather, when it shows signs of becoming exhausted—you should apply to me for more. It will be forthcoming. I know you are welcome to remain with your sister and brother-in-law, as their guest, as long as you like, but it occurs to me that it might be more practical for you to have a small apartment of your own, a bachelor establishment. Eustis will be glad to help you find one."

He rose, walked over to one of the long windows and, drawing back the heavy draperies, threw it open. The air which streamed in had the freshness which comes with dawn and the first faint rosiness of this tinted the sky. Slidell stood for a moment, breathing deeply and looking out over the house-tops of Paris. Then he came back and put his hand on Paul's shoulder.

"We have talked all night," he said. "I should feel guilty over keeping you up like this, if I did not know something of the hours you have kept in the past, as a chess player. Now you are going to keep them again, and you will be playing, not only with gold and silver chessmen, like those in the set given you by the famous New York club, but with human beings as Kings and Queens, Bishops and Knights—all Pawns. The castles where you stay will be real ones. One last word before you go: if I am not mistaken, you and the Princess de Lixin are old friends?"

"Yes," Paul said, his throat suddenly dry.

"I think I overheard de Persigny telling you that her husband is a great favorite of Chasseloup-Laubat, the Minister of Marine. I cannot imagine why. I see no reason why Gilbert de Lixin should be a great favorite of any-one. But that is the way the land lies. Chasseloup-Laubat's co-operation is what we need more than anything else in this chess game we are playing. Doubtless you will be asked to his house, too. Your lifelong friendship with his wife's relative, General Beauregard, would indicate some courtesies in that quarter. But with their many official obligations, the Chasseloup-Laubats will be less free to entertain you than the de Lixins, nor would they naturally be as inclined to do so as a lady with whom you played as a child. You have already seen enough of Parisian society to know that married

women of unassailable standing are permitted much more latitude in regard
to male guests than is customary among Creole ladies. It is taken for granted
that any accomplished hostess receives guests of both sexes and, indeed, her
husband would feel she *lacked* accomplishment if she were not at ease in
the presence of gentlemen. You should encounter no difficulties as far as
de Lixin is concerned and through him you should be able to see more of
Chasseloup-Laubat than would otherwise be likely. I take it for granted that
you would find the entrée at the Prince's château very pleasant. It could
be very profitable for all of us."

Petites Boutiques des Boulevards. The illustration was taken
from *En Remontant Les Grands Boulevards* by Jacques Castelnau,
published by Le Livre Contemporain, Paris.

"*Les bois de Boulogne, sous Louis-Phillippe, était si maussade que les Parisiens
n'osaient se risquer dans cet 'impitoyable desert.' Dès le début du second Empire, Napoléon III, qui se souvenait de Hyde Park, fit tracer des routes sinueuses,
planter des arbres, creuser des lacs et une rivière serpentine, construire des restaurants, kiosques et chalets. Bientôt, nous dit la comtesse d'Agoult, 'dans les
allées élargies, bien sablées, bien arrosées, se croisaient, aux heures de la fashion,
quatre ou cinq rangs d'équipages, phaétons, victorias, calèches, paniers et huit-
ressorts . . .' Désormais, ce fut par le nouveau bois que les invités de Napoléon
III et d'Eugénie se rendirent au château de Saint-Cloud.*"

Le Grand Siècle de Paris by André Castelot (Amiot-Dumont)

35.

No fiacre was in sight when Paul went out into the street, but he would have waved it aside, even if some *cocher,* less somnolent than most of his kind, had signaled. Paul wanted to walk, to walk rapidly; he had the strong sensation that his footsteps should outpace his thoughts and these were racing. The street lights now shone dimly in the reluctant crepuscle of pre-dawn and the few prowlers and revelers still abroad were blurred figures almost lost in the semi-obscurity; he was not even conscious of them as he rushed past them. But more than one, alerted by the strange hurrying apparition, were roused from the stupor of drunkenness or driven to precautionary furtiveness when he swept past them.

He had, as he told Rosina, slept most of the previous day after his exhausting train trip from Madrid; but this period of rest could not, in itself, account for the fact that he had no sensation of weariness, much less of drowsiness as he sped along. Ordinarily, it would have taken him several days to recover from the fatigue of a long journey, for he had never succeeded in building up reserves of bodily vigor. Moreover, the dinner party, with its renewal of old friendships and its introduction to portentous personages, its medley of chatter and rich food in exotic surroundings, would have constituted a strain on his nervous system, even without the experience, for which he was wholly unprepared, of coming suddenly face to face with Charmian. Her astounding suggestion and the realization, becoming clearer and clearer as Slidell talked to him, that opportunities, rather than obstacles, lay ahead of him if he tried to take advantage of it, might also have precipitated an emotional crisis. He had never been so conscious of such quickening of physical and mental strength as he was now; it seemed to be coursing through his body and illumining his mind; and never but once—on the day of his great victory in New York—had he been so convinced of his ability to triumph. He was no longer a weakling, a nonentity, a failure, except when he faced an antagonist across a chessboard. The very fact that he was unfitted for the battlefield, instead of being a disgrace, was an asset; he had been selected for a special type of signal service to his country, an honor to which only a man of exceptional gifts and complete integrity could aspire. Great patriots like Judah P. Benjamin and John Slidell trusted and respected him; they were confident that he could cope successfully with a delicate and difficult mission. He might, after all, emerge as one of the heroes of the victorious South. . . .

It was already daylight when he reached the Sybrandts' pied-à-terre on the rue du Cirque and let himself in, as quietly as possible, with the latchkey

John had loaned him. Despite his every precaution, however, his mother heard him when he tiptoed down the hall and opened the door of his room. Instantly, the door of hers, which was next to it, opened also, and she stood on the threshold, robed in a dressing gown of soft lavender wool, her hair, still beautiful and abundant, hanging in long braids over her shoulders, an expression of deep solicitude on her faded, gentle face.

"Paul, I've been so worried about you! Where *have* you been all night? The dinner party can't have lasted until morning. I was sure there must have been an accident or a robbery—I made up my mind, if I heard the clock strike again, I'd ask John to call the police."

Paul managed to check the expression of annoyance that was already on his lips and spoke to her soothingly, advancing to put his arm around her shoulders and kiss her cheek. "No, the dinner party didn't last until morning," he said. "But it did go on and on—I'll tell you about it tomorrow or, rather, later today. It was very festive. I'm sure you'll enjoy hearing about it. Any number of celebrities were there, and a very pleasant lady, a Mrs. Calhoun, spoke to me highly about you and said she wished you'd go out more in society. I think she expects me to see that you do and I've promised to try. . . . Well, anyway, after the other guests left, Mr. Slidell asked me to join him in the library and we got to talking about this and that without realizing the passage of time. However, when I finally left his apartment, I came straight home and nobody tried to rob me or even speak to me along the way. Why should you have been so worried? It never troubled you to have Father or Edward or me out late in New Orleans."

"Yes, it did. I tried not to let it show, but it did. And I'm not as good at concealing my worries as when I was younger. Besides, none of you has ever been out *this* late and Paris is different. . . . Wouldn't you like me to make you a nice hot drink, *cher?* Cocoa, perhaps? The cocoa here is so delicious! And there's a chill in the air at this hour."

"Thank you, Mother, but I don't want a thing, except to get some sleep and to have you get some. Good night and sweet dreams."

Decidedly, he thought, as he flung off his clothes, John Slidell is right: I must see about getting a bachelor apartment and I'd better do it at once; I can't have Mother sitting up all night worrying, and I can't have her asking me a lot of awkward questions. His conviction of the need for greater independence increased with the events of the day; not unnaturally, he slept late, and as soon as he had dressed and breakfasted, he went straight to the Commissioner's office on the rue Marignan, where Eustis and Vignaud were both awaiting his arrival, if not exactly with visible impatience, at least with the air that it was high time they got down to cases together. It was quite out of the question for him to interrupt the ensuing conference by going back to the Sybrandts' to lunch, and he knew that his mother would be anxiously waiting for the promised account of the dinner party, which he had excused himself from giving her early that morning. He felt guilty at disappointing her; but he knew he would feel still more guilty if he did not begin his search for an apartment that same afternoon. Then, that evening, he must go to the soirée of the Duchess de Trevisse; she would think he did not appreciate her invitation if he did not appear there; and, meanwhile, he must make his *visite de politesse* to Mrs. Slidell. Moreover, he certainly did not intend to let the day go by without leaving cards on the Princess Mathilde and the Marquis and Marquise de Chasseloup-Laubat—not to mention the Prince and Princess de Lixin. It was going to be a full day; he should never have made such a promise to his mother.

His conviction of this became still stronger when he rushed into the Sybrandts' apartment, late in the afternoon, intent only on changing his clothes and rushing out again. Telcide was in the drawing room, obviously waiting for him; and though she said very little when he told her he was sorry, that he could not stop to chat with her just then, it was evident that his failure to keep his word was a real blow to her. Fortunately, he had a free hour between family dinner and his departure for the Duchess' soirée; and though he realized an account of his activities would mean less to his mother, given in the presence of his sisters and his brother-in-law, than if he could have talked with her cosily and privately, he decided that, in the end, it would be kindest to let her know without further delay that his time would not be his own from then on.

The experiment was not altogether happy. He began with what he hoped would be a glowing account of the dinner, only to find himself cut short when he spoke of the Marquise de Chasseloup-Laubat as General Beauregard's niece.

"She isn't anything of the sort," Malvina said acidly. "I know whom every one of Pierre's brothers and sisters married. This new-found friend of yours has only been a marquise for two years, and her husband's old enough to be her father—in fact, almost old enough to be her grandfather! You can't tell me she was anyone important before her marriage, that all she wanted wasn't just to get a title. She was nee Marie Louise Pilíe. Did you ever hear of any Pilíes in New Orleans?"

"No, but that's no sign she didn't come from there or that she may not be related to the Villerés or the Deslondes. If she were Laure's niece or Caroline's, she'd have a right to say she was Pierre's niece, too—she couldn't be expected to keep saying 'my uncle by marriage.' Anyhow, she is now married to the Minister of Marine, one of the most powerful men in France, and she's very witty and charming."

"That's what you say about every woman you've met here."

"Well, they are very witty and very charming. And some of them are very beautiful. But you'd never guess who was the *most* beautiful woman at that dinner."

"Well, who?" Hélène inquired.

"The Princess de Lixin."

"I never heard of her."

"Yes, you have. Only the last time you did so her name was Charmian Sheppard. And don't answer me by exclaiming, 'That Yankee shopkeeper's daughter!' Or say that, anyway, you're thankful that *I* didn't marry her! You may not have thought she was good enough for the Le Carpentiers and the Morphys; but she's now the member of one of the proudest families in France, she's received everywhere from the Tuileries to the great provincial estates, she's one of the reigning belles of the Empire!"

The atmosphere of the Sybrandts' drawing room was becoming increasingly tense. Paul decided that, instead of continuing his description of the dinner party, he might better break the rest of his news.

"I'm sorry you don't seem to approve of the Slidells' guests. Personally, I felt very much complimented to be included among them last evening and it looks as if I might be thrown with some of them a good deal during the next few months. I told you last night, Mother, that the reason I didn't get home earlier was because the Commissioner asked me to stay on, after the others left, for a talk with him. Well, I went to his office this morning, to go over some of the ground we discussed and it's settled that I'm to take advantage of my stay in Paris by doing some incidental work for him."

"Work! What kind of work are you fitted for?" John Sybrandt asked sarcastically.

"Apparently, Mr. Slidell suggested to Eustis and Vignaud that I could be helpful along the lines of historical research. The Commissioner's trying to assemble notes for a book and his secretaries both have their hands full already."

"But you haven't had any experience at all along those lines!"

"He knows that, of course. But he also knows—"

"That you're the world's greatest chess player!"

"Probably. Yes, of course, he must. After all, that's quite generally known. But what Vignaud and Eustis said was the Commissioner had reminded them that I was graduated with honors from Spring Hill, both as a Bachelor of Arts and as a Master of Arts; that I knew the Code Napoleon by heart and that I'd passed my bar examinations in the State of Louisiana; that I'd been an associate editor of a periodical with international circulation and that I'd helped a very distinguished author edit a book. Also, that I'm trilingual. Benjamin told me he thought I might be helpful because of that, when I saw him in Richmond almost two years ago, and now Slidell seems to feel the same way. Eustis is a capital fellow, but his French is still rather

the homemade brand and neither he nor Vignaud speaks any Spanish. I
am starting work with them tomorrow."

"In the Commissioner's office?"

"No, that's overcrowded already and I need quiet for my type of work.
I'll have an office of my own."

"*An office of your own!* Where? There's hardly room for one here, I'm
afraid!"

"Of course there isn't. In any case, I wouldn't dream of imposing on you.
My office will be in my apartment on the rue de Rivoli. I've been fortunate
in finding exactly what's needed with no delay at all. I'm moving in there
tomorrow."

The break with his family was even harder than Paul expected. His
mother and Hélène both wept uncontrollably. Malvina made invidious remarks to the effect that, now he was the intimate of duchesses and cabinet
officers, it was natural he would think that persons without rank or official
position were not in his social class, even if they were his blood relations; she
supposed he would soon be satisfied with nothing less than an entrée at the
Tuileries Palace. John, who could see that Paul's new connections might
be of benefit to himself as a cotton broker, urged his brother-in-law to re-
consider the decision to move; after all, with a little rearrangement of quarters, it would be perfectly possible to make room for a *bureau* where they
were; if he could watch Paul's comings and goings and those of his associates, he, John Sybrandt, might well make influential acquaintances. Paul
was genuinely sorry to have distressed his mother and his younger sister.
He tried to console them by telling them he would of course drop in frequently to see them, and that he would also arrange for them to have some
little outings with him, to pleasant places where none of them had been;
it might even be possible for them to arrange an extended trip to the South
of France. As far as Malvina and John were concerned, he had no regrets;
he was convinced that the less he saw of them, the better, not only for his
own peace of mind, but as far as the character of his work was concerned.

Once settled in his small furnished apartment, he rejoiced in his independence to a degree which he admitted to himself was selfish, but which
was hardly clouded at all on that account. The apartment in itself was unremarkable, its furnishings tasteful but rather shabby, its plumbing negligible, its artificial lighting inadequate; but it "gave" on the Tuileries Gardens, the outlook which he had learned to love while at the Meurice and the
Breteuil, and the resourceful Vignaud had found him a manservant of
multiple talents and unbounded good will. Early every morning Louis did
the marketing, returning, before Paul was awake, with all necessary supplies, which he had secured at surprisingly small cost; his ability to make

the best possible use of these was almost unbelievable. Paul's rooms and clothes were alike kept in perfect order. Best of all, his bath was always prepared for him without reference to the effort involved in securing hot water or in carrying heavy cans and pails immense distances. Paul had no worries and no disturbances as far as his modest ménage was concerned; it was in a carefree, as well as in an exultant, mood that he prepared for the revelation of Paris in the springtime.

He had not previously seen it in this guise. True, when he had been there before, September nights had still sometimes been mild enough for long drives through the Bois in an open victoria, September afternoons sometimes sunny enough for outdoor teas. But the presage of autumn was already in the air, and soon thereafter dry dusty leaves had begun to fall, long driving rains had set in, the days had grown shorter and shorter, gloomier and gloomier. Now all the trees were misty with fresh green and many of them were in blossom; there were flowers everywhere—not merely in the great gardens, but on the window sills, in the stalls around the Madeleine, in the pushcarts of the humble vendors who hawked their wares up and down the streets. Balloon men were doing a thriving business, too; the multicolored balls, floating in bunches above the vendors' heads before they were distributed among young eager customers, seemed to typify the buoyancy and brightness of the general atmosphere. Punch and Judy shows were playing in the open air to throngs of excited children in charge of uniformed nurses. Other children were flying kites or sailing little boats in the lakes of the Luxembourg or the Bois. There were rowboats on the lakes in the Bois, too, lovers as well as children were reveling in the water and the woods, family groups were seeking out the best places for picnics in the pleasant groves and settling down for leisurely lunches or *gouters*. The crowded boulevards were lined with booths where everything from shoes to sausages could be bought for a song. The sidewalk cafés were crowded, and white-coated waiters were hurrying to and fro with *sirops*, with coffee, with absinthe; they served patrons who sat endlessly over a single order, reading the newspapers or gazing at the passing scene, with the same attention that they gave to grave groups of intellectuals or pretty chattering *grisettes*.

This was a Paris new to Paul, and not only because of its general animation and its loveliness. Hitherto, he had been absorbed at the Régence, except when he was confined to his room by illness, attending the opera or visiting great houses; he had seen little or nothing of life as the average Parisian, whether young or old, spent it publicly, in simple pleasures. Now it was an essential part of his work to learn what people were talking about, not only at soirées, but in the parks and cafés and the boutiques along the boulevards. Some evenings he was able to report definite expressions of opinion about national and international affairs: the struggle between State

and Church in Italy was as frequent a topic of conversation as the War Between the States; so was the puppet Empire in Mexico and the government
in France itself, which some felt hardly more secure. Slidell commented on
Paul's observations as clear and comprehensive. But when he said, regretfully, that he had heard nothing worth repeating, that people seemed to be
talking only about the weather, the races, the latest scandals and the most
recent openings at the theater, Slidell told him not to worry. No one could
hit the bull's-eye every time, especially if there were no bull's-eye there to
hit! And there was no telling when it would be staring one in the face
again.

The fascination which the passing scene had for him did not prevent
him from renewing the associations he already enjoyed with Napoleonic
nobility and benefiting by the acquaintances he had made at the Slidells'
to expand these. One of the cards he had left the first day after the dinner
resulted in immediate response: the Princess Mathilde was delighted to
hear of his return; she did not want to wait until the following Tuesday—
still her official day at home—to see him. She now supplemented her soirées
with informal dinners twice a week. Would he not come to her *en toute
intimité* on Friday?

Paul was always mildly amused by the term *en toute intimité* as Princess
Mathilde and other members of her family used it; anything less "intimate"
than her manner of living in the magnificent house, which had once been
the residence of Queen Christina, could hardly be imagined. Like most
visitors, he was deeply impressed by the monumental staircase which led
to an entrance hall where a white marble bust of Napoleon gleamed against
a background of purple silk. This, in turn, led to a vast succession of reception rooms, their windows, doors and mantels draped with green velvet,
their walls hung with red damask, their jewel-toned furnishings richly upholstered. With all this splendor for a setting, the Princess herself achieved
a dramatic contrast, by wearing white dresses of delusive simplicity but
supreme elegance, designed for her either by Beaudrand or Worth, and confining her jewels to pearls. In the background hovered her ladies-in-waiting,
appropriately gowned in rich but subdued raiment. In the case of Madame
Espinasse, this secondary effulgence was not hard to impose; her husband,
a general of great valor, had been killed at Magenta and she was draped
in the deepest mourning. Madame de Serlay, a daughter of the Duke of
Rovigo, was more difficult to eclipse; she was a blooming blonde, as justly
admired for her beauty as for her affability. Even when she confined herself
to pale blue or Nile green, both were so vastly becoming to her that she did
not need more striking colors to set off her charms; and her jewels, carefully
blended with her dresses, were notable.

None of this familiar staging had been materially changed since his last stay in Paris, Paul discovered, when presenting himself at Mathilde's *hotel particulier* on the rue de Courcelles the Friday after his arrival in Paris; and he found his fellow guests chosen for their distinction along the same lines that had always characterized their selection. Besides the inevitable Count Emilien Nieuwerkerque—now Director of National Museums and quite logically an honored guest in this capacity, besides that of a privileged personal favorite—there were among them, on this occasion, Senator Le Brun, representing politics; Silvestre de Sacy, editor of *Debats*, representing journalism; and the Dumas, both father and son, representing literature. The atmosphere was genial, the conversation brilliant; though Paul learned nothing specific that could be of value to report, both Le Brun and Sacy gave him the general impression of being favorable to the Confederate cause; and their expressed desire to see more of M. Morphy led him to believe that, on some future occasion, he might hear definite references to the stand they might be expected to take publicly; concerning the amount of influence they might wield, if so disposed, to sway French opinion, there could be no possible doubt. This might also well be true as far as the Dumas, both *père* and *fils*, were concerned. True, they had no voice in the Senate Chamber, no periodical of wide circulation in their control; they were without official or journalistic position, they wrote only popular fiction, which would, most probably, be without enduring vogue. Moreover, they were both vain and self-centered and the elder was vulgar in both manner and speech and repulsive in appearance. But they went everywhere, they knew everyone; their value in sounding out opinions might be incalculable. Having now heard so many favorable to the South, Paul began to give thought to the desirability of discovering who felt otherwise and why. This could be all too easily overlooked, since it was human nature to listen most attentively to that which one preferred to hear. He must steel himself against this inclination. . . .

"You are not listening to me, my dear M. Morphy." He was suddenly aware of the Princess, breaking in on his unwelcome and inopportune revery about Yankee sympathizers. "I am inviting you to St. Gratien."

"Excuse me, Highness. St. Gratien?"

"Yes, my rural retreat. It was built under the first Empire, for the Marquis de Custine—just a simple little country place, but quite pleasantly located on the Lake of Enghien, near the famous Baths. It's only about twenty kilometres from Paris on the route to Pontoise. I spend the greater part of the spring and summer there nowadays—in fact, I shall be going there next week for over Sunday. It would give the Count and myself great pleasure if you would join us there. I can promise you good company and quiet diversions."

"I cannot think of anything that could possibly be more delightful. Everything *en toute intimité*, I presume."

"How naughty of you to laugh at me! Yes, I assure you, that is how it will be. I understand that your two compatriots, the Princess de Lixin and the Marquise de Chasseloup-Laubat, intend to lure you away to their rural retreats. I do not propose to let them get ahead of me."

"Of course, they could not do that, Highness, no matter how hard they tried and no matter in what direction."

"Oh, still the great flatterer! I must not neglect my other guests by listening any further to you now. But I shall look forward to hearing a great many sweet nothings a week from Sunday."

Paul was undeceived by the reference to "a simple little country place." He was not surprised when the Château of St. Gratien proved to be a large square house, whose two main drawing rooms, hung with flowered chintz, were separated from the library and the billiard room by an antechamber of Empire design; the many bedrooms, elegantly furnished in carved and inlaid mahogany, were brightened by cretonne draperies; the gardens stretched out interminably toward the lake in one direction and the woods in another. The inside of the house revealed the tastes and talents of the Princess as an interior decorator; the grounds, Nieuwerkerque's tastes and talents as a landscape architect. He had planted flower beds, laid out garden walks and built a boathouse; now he was discussing with the Princess the best color and form for additional walls and she, in turn, was consulting him about the color and form of the frescoes with which Giraud was adorning the walls around the main staircase. They seemed a thoroughly congenial couple, their relationship so regularized as to suggest absolutely nothing illicit, much less furtive. Enviously, Paul watched them together and allowed himself to daydream: if Mathilde could be granted a canonical separation from a brutal Russian Prince, surely it should be possible for Charmian to secure one from a degenerate French nobleman! His former scruples about the inviolability of the marriage vow, as far as a woman was concerned, had undergone a change, since he had seen more of the interpretation put on it by certain great ladies of France, among whom Charmian must now be numbered. Naturally, such a step as he was confident she could take could not be in the immediate future; but what did a little more delay matter, when he had waited for her so many years already? He visualized himself living with her, not, of course, in a château like St. Gratien, surrounded by celebrities, but in a secluded manor house where their idyll, though duly sanctioned, would be free from intrusion. He imagined Charmian delighting in the management of their home while he occupied himself with the improvement of the grounds, like his present hosts. He reveled at the prospect of long hours devoted to music and reading with a tender companion at his side. Most rapturously of all, he thought of long silent nights, moonbeams streaming in through a great window, an alcove dominated by a wide soft bed, Charmian relaxed and responsive in his arms. He had been reading Keats:

> ". . . still stedfast, still unchangeable,
> Pillow'd upon my fair love's ripening breast,
> To feel for ever its soft fall and swell,
> Awake for ever in a sweet unrest. . . ."

The weekend passed, given over to those quiet diversions which the Princess had promised. On Sunday morning, everybody, or nearly everybody, went to Mass in one of the two nearby villages, Deuil and Epinay. After lunch and a siesta, the guests read or conversed while the Princess spent a couple of hours in her studio, painting under the direction of Giraud, whom she had commissioned to build an annex to the ground floor, where great palm trees should be sketched against garnet-colored walls and inlaid cabinets would eventually add to the generally exotic note. Her paint boxes and paint brushes were scattered about in what her teacher called "amiable disorder," and the basket in which her two pet dogs, Tine and Tom, were ensconced, stood on the floor between her easels. At five, she left the studio and, with the little dogs yapping at her heels, led her guests in a procession toward the lake, where a small flotilla of boats and barges awaited their pleasure. Some of the company took advantage of such craft; others preferred to continue their walk, wandering through the shady avenues in the woods, either by themselves or in small groups. There was no regular reunion until dinner time and, even then, little formality about the meeting. In one respect at least, Mathilde had given a correct impression, in speaking of St. Gratien: here her guests could be natural and she herself was without restriction; all were delivered from the ceremony imposed on them by the imperial pomp of the rue de Courcelles.

Nevertheless, it was at St. Gratien that Paul heard the first definite and disturbing expression of personal opinion against the South.

He knew, of course, that part of the press was inimicable, that no less a person than Mathilde's brother, generally known by the silly nickname of Plon-Plon, who controlled *Le Siècle* and *La Presse,* made no secret of his disagreement with his imperial cousin and with the powerful de Persigny, who owned *Le Constitutionale,* and used it freely for the expression of his views regarding recognition of the Confederacy. But Paul had not allowed himself to be distressed by this. After all, Plon-Plon was out of favor and de Persigny stood, literally and figuratively, at the right hand of the throne.

Paul gauged the influence of other papers, pro and con, as corresponding to the comparative power of these. The conversation which he now overheard, while enjoying a solitary ramble through the woods, was much more upsetting to him, even though he could not guess the identity of the fellow guests who were concealed from him by the luxuriant foliage.

"The Emperor will never move first; he will wait until he is sure what England is going to do."

"Granted. Everyone knows that. Why should you speak as if you'd discovered some important secret? But all recent speakers in Parliament have followed Gladstone's lead and you know what he said: 'We may have our opinions about slavery; we may be for or against the South; but there is no doubt that Jefferson Davis and other leaders of the South have made an army; they are making, it appears, a navy; and they have made what is more than either, they have made a nation!' "

"Yes, but that speech was delivered eight months ago. Granted that the Confederates have an army; it has had some very great reverses since then. Chancellorsville was nominally a victory for them, but Jackson died of wounds received in it and Lee has not been able to replace him with anyone equally competent. Besides, that new Federal general—Grant, is that his name?—seems to have been winning in Mississippi." The speaker stumbled over the name before continuing, "And where is the navy that 'appears' to be in the making? We have seen nothing of it so far. And that statement about slavery is a key sentence. The Emperor has his opinion about it, too. And nothing is going to change that opinion, whatever England does."

"Perhaps. Meanwhile, suppose we change our topic of conversation. To be sure, even if we were overheard, which is unlikely, we have said nothing incriminating or even indiscreet. The Emperor's views on slavery are well known, so we are not divulging any secrets. But there is a lack of *delicatesse* in speaking of them here, since Mathilde, out of consideration for her southern friends, pretends she doesn't know these opinions."

"But are you certain that Mathilde agrees with the persons for whom she shows consideration and not with her cousin, the Emperor, or even with her brother, the Prince?"

"No, of course I am not certain. There are very few certainties in this unstable world. But you must admit that she actually goes out of her way to show her sympathetic preference for southerners. Otherwise, would we find *ce petit* Morphy among those invited to St. Gratien? Most assuredly not. But, as I suggested before, let us change the subject."

That was all. Paul tried, when the company reassembled for dinner, to identify the voices of the two men who had spoken, not only with such conviction, but with such authority. He found himself unable to do so. His efforts, later on in the drawing room, were equally unsuccessful. He told himself it was probably just as well. If he had known who the disputants were, he would have been sorely tempted to ask why they were so sure there was no navy in the making, and that, of course, was the very last thing he should say. He returned to Paris with a sense of defeat, the first he had suffered. At his apartment, he found awaiting him a letter from Charmian that rapidly changed his train of thought.

She had, as usual, been dashing from one party to another; she was sorry she had not been able to get in touch with him sooner. (The words had a reminiscent ring, but he closed his ears to it.) Now she and the Prince were preparing to leave for the country, so it was not the best time for visits; nevertheless, she would be glad to see Paul, briefly, if he cared to come in for tea the following day. Of course, it was not really *à la Parisienne* to serve tea, but she seemed to remember that Paul enjoyed it. There would be one or two other guests. . . .

His first impression, after arriving at the Hotel de Lixin, was that he would never reach the scene of the tea party. If he had thought the courtyard of the Hotel d'Ambres forbidding, this one was actually menacing in its size and severity. Once inside the house, a succession of liveried lackeys waved him impersonally forward. Again he thought of the Hotel d'Ambres; how could he have felt that its *grand salon* was colorless and chilly? Every one of the rooms in this endless succession was more enormous, more sparsely and stiffly furnished, more dominated by white marble than that had been. Mathilde at least mitigated her "Napoleonic pomp" with richly colored rugs and draperies, glowing canvases and jeweled bibelots, and all these were impregnated with her vivid personality. These rooms made Paul think of the apartments in some palace long disused and perhaps because of a tragic reason; it was hard to believe that anyone actually lived in them or wanted to live in them. Then he remembered, unwillingly, that the Prince de Lixin's first wife had been an invalid and that it was probably all too true the state apartments had been closed for some time before her death and that, until now, Charmian had lacked the time and the strength to animate them. Perhaps her husband preferred to keep them unchanged; Paul would not have put it past him to forbid Charmian to exercise her own fancy. . . .

At last he reached a room where a small tea table, which looked more or less lost in its vast setting, was placed in front of a stiff sofa, on which Charmian was sitting, with Madame de Chasseloup-Laubat in the seat of honor at her side, and a strikingly handsome man in uniform, whom Paul had not met before, installed in one of the equally stiff armchairs drawn up beside the sofa. Charmian was again in white, as she had been at the Slidells' dinner; and Paul could not help wondering if she were effecting this because it was undeniably so becoming; or whether she was consciously or unconsciously taking her cue from Mathilde, just as he had previously felt she was imitating, either consciously or unconsciously, the mannerisms of the Duchess de Trevisse. At all events, she had achieved a contrast in costume worthy of Mathilde's most successful efforts, for Madame de Chasseloup-Laubat was in magenta, the purplish red which owed both its designation and its vogue to the bloody French victory in the Italian town of that name. In Paul's opinion it was a macabre fashion, and he could not control an inward quiver of revulsion whenever he saw it so displayed. But its present wearer had the complexion and the figure to carry off the trying color, inevitably so unbecoming to most women, and she, like Charmian, greeted him with a cordial smile.

"I am delighted to see you again. I have been hoping to get in touch with you myself, since receiving your card, but my poor husband is overwhelmed with work these days and, as perhaps you know, I have a small baby, who naturally demands a great deal of my attention. However, if you are free for luncheon next Sunday? Yes? How fortunate! . . . Charmian, have M. Morphy and Jacques met before? I am under the impression that presentations are in order! . . ."

"They are indeed! How inexcusable of me! Especially as I am so happy in bringing together two great friends of mine who are still strangers to each other, but who, I am sure, will themselves become great friends. M. Morphy, the Marquis d'Ambres—dear Paul, I am honored to present you to dear Jacques!"

This time, the inward quiver, suppressed without too much difficulty as far as the magenta dress was concerned, proved harder to quell. Despite Rosina Slidell's statement that Jacques d'Ambres was about thirty years of age and that, in loaning the Hotel d'Ambres to the Sheppards, he had done so under the impression that Charmian would be its next chatelaine, Paul had continued to cherish a slight hope that she might be mistaken, that the Marquis really was an older man, that he had visualized himself as a *cavaliere servente* for the mother, rather than as the suitor for one of her daughters. A single glance at the dashing officer before him put an end to any such fragile dream: Jacques d'Ambres was the embodiment of every normal woman's beau ideal of a supremely eligible man. And a new mystery instantly came crowding to the forefront of Paul's consciousness: why, when Charmian might have married d'Ambres, had she chosen de Lixin instead? Was the title of Princess so infinitely important to her that, as Rosina and Rachel had intimated, everything else was subservient to it?

With charming courtesy, the Marquis expressed himself as delighted at making M. Morphy's acquaintance at last; Charmian had long been loud in her praises of her compatriot. He, Jacques, was on leave from his London post for a few weeks. He hoped very much that M. Morphy was not so bespoken that they could not arrange for a little dinner at the Hotel d'Ambres; at all events, they would be seeing each other again at the Chasseloup-Laubats' on Sunday and could discuss it further then, if M. Morphy did not have his engagement book with him. M. Morphy pleaded this omission, but he appreciated the invitation and would give a definite answer on Sunday, if that much of a delay would cause no inconvenience. He was making tentative plans for a short trip and he was not yet sure when he would be leaving Paris. He had never seen anything of the provincial cities or the charming French countryside. The beautiful weather they were now having seemed ideally suited for such an expedition, especially as he was hoping that his mother and his young unmarried sister would accompany him. The territory would all be new to them, too, so they were sharing his pleasure in the prospect; but as neither was in robust health, he had to consult their convenience as well as his own. He hoped the Marquis would understand.

Of course, of course, Jacques hastened to assure him. Two or three other guests came in and conversation became general; also unprovocative and unenlightening. The Prince de Lixin did not put in an appearance and no excuses or explanations were offered for his absence. The tea had become rather tepid and the cake dish was depleted, but nothing was said about replenishment. Madame de Chasseloup-Laubat rose, in a rustle of magenta taffeta flounces and said she must go home to her baby; she would be pleased to have M. Morphy escort her, if he had no other immediate plans. It was inconceivable that he should decline. He accompanied her through the long succession of uninhabited-looking apartments by which he had approached the tea table. He had the feeling that, within a few minutes, the additional nondescript guests, who had contributed so little to the occasion, would also excuse themselves and that the Marquis d'Ambres and Charmian would be left to enjoy a solitude *à deux*.

For the second time since his arrival in Paris, he went to bed a victim of depression and defeat and passed a sleepless night.

"It has always appeared to me a serious omission on the part of historians of the American Confederacy to have left untouched, or touched upon so slightly, the ceaseless activities of the able agents, emissaries and champions, paid and unpaid, of the Lost Cause in Europe. . . . I have presented the salient facts of these activities in so far as they concern Slidell and France as I have gleaned them from every source made available to me. . . .

"Amongst my authorities, Professor Sear's excellent monograph on Slidell, although instructive about his subject's character and political career in America, contains only a few pages about the Paris Commissionership. It is unfortunate that the mass of official correspondence which accumulated at the Confederate office in the rue Marignan, was destroyed by Slidell himself about the year 1866, for fear of compromising the authors; but there still exists in Washington the Slidell-Benjamin correspondence, the Slidell-Mason correspondence, and other valuable letters and papers. I have also made use of various letters and memoranda belonging to the Eustis family, as well as other material compiled by the late Henri Vignaud. I have availed myself freely of the Memoirs of Captain J. D. Bulloch and other naval officers and, most of all, of Consul-General (afterwards Minister) John Bigelow's three portly volumes dealing with his Paris consular and diplomatic experiences. I have also consulted the newspapers and pamphlets of the period. On the whole, then, I feel that my pages convey a fair idea of the protracted arguments, efforts and intrigues, directed by a man of ability and experience, to obtain official recognition for his country from the Emperor, Napoleon III, as well as to promote the naval and other interests of the Confederacy in France."

Excerpt from the Foreword of
John Slidell and the Confederates in Paris (1862–65)
by Beckles Willson, copyright 1932 by B. Willson.
Used by permission of the publishers, G. P. Putnam's Sons, N.Y.

36.

Sunday luncheon with the Chasseloup-Laubats followed the standardized pattern with which Paul was becoming so familiar that it was no longer intriguing to him: as always the setting was elegant, the guests distinguished, the conversation brilliant, the cuisine superlative. He was mildly surprised, however, to find none of the Slidells in the company and managed to say as much in an aside to Charmian. She opened her beautiful blue eyes very wide, as if to indicate much greater astonishment than he felt.

"Why, they couldn't be, of course, since this party is really for Jacques!"

"You mean because they outrank him?"

"Of course not, stupid! Because he doesn't recognize the Commissioner as *having* any rank! As far as he's concerned, that dull, middle-class Mr. Dayton and that nosey Mr. Bigelow are the only American representatives in Paris. Jacques' chief, the French Ambassador in London, and the American Minister, Charles Francis Adams, are thick as thieves. It's natural he should be what you call 'a Northern sympathizer.'"

"I see," Paul said thoughtfully, though he was not quite sure that he did. Then, still more thoughtfully, he added, "I can see how you might have been though. I wonder I didn't think of it before."

"You're not so silly as to imagine that Jacques would influence my views!"

"No, of course not. But, after all, you are a Northerner by birth and so are all your people. Your father and your sister live in Boston, when they're not in New Hampshire."

"Yes, but I married a Frenchman. I'm a Frenchwoman by adoption, I live in Paris when I'm not in the country."

"You've just pointed out that the Marquis d'Ambres, who's a Frenchman, a very distinguished one, and who'd live in Paris if he weren't on post in England, is a Northern sympathizer."

"Paul, you're getting tiresome. Jacques is the *only* one in our circle who feels that way, and he wouldn't if he were here among his own kind of people, instead of being in England. Really, you're hurting my feelings, intimating that I wouldn't sympathize with the South, especially when the South to me means *you*."

The big blue eyes were now brimming with tears. And, at this point, de Lixin, who, on this occasion, had accompanied his wife, joined them, looking more bored than ever, and the conversation shifted to other channels. Charmian, for once, was not in white, but wearing a dress of soft blush rose muslin and a wide malines hat wreathed in roses which matched her dress. Everything about her suggested a delicate perfection of such gossamer-like quality that this might evaporate if a mere man touched her sleeve or brushed against her skirts; Paul, deeply disturbed by his conversation with her, made no attempt to do either.

Jacques d'Ambres was by far the most arresting man at the party; as if his exceptional good looks were not enough in his favor, he was animated, witty and obviously well informed. Paul tactfully tried to draw him out on political sentiment in England and Jacques as tactfully side-stepped the questions. He renewed his invitation to dinner and Paul declined it, with many expressions of regret, because he would be leaving Paris before the suggested date.

In his final conference with Slidell before his departure, he referred, somewhat reluctantly, to his conversation with Charmian on the subject of the views held by d'Ambres. He still retained his inbred conviction that a lady's name should not be brought into conversation between gentlemen, and this feeling was, of course, all the stronger when a personal element was involved. However, he found Slidell quite willing to discuss the matter with him and inclined to do so dispassionately and, on the whole, optimistically.

"Jacques d'Ambres is a good fellow," the Commissioner said ungrudgingly. "And I think Charmian is right in saying that, if he were in Paris instead of London, his views might be different. However, I am not greatly disturbed by them, because I am sure they are in the minority, and I believe you will be, too, when you have acquainted yourself more thoroughly with French views generally, which you will have an excellent chance to do in the course of your forthcoming trip. Industrial France is dependent upon cotton from the South and its seizure by Federal blockaders is throwing thousands of French operatives out of work. It is also dependent on southern tobacco and both these commodities were used in exchange for French silks. Quite aside from these considerations is a widespread belief that the success of the Confederacy would redound to the political prestige of France. As to all this, I do not think there can be much argument. As to the minor point— Charmian's own personal views—I'm inclined to take what she said with a grain of salt—in fact, 'methinks the lady doth protest too much.' It seems to me possible that her opinion might be affected by d'Ambres. As you probably know, he wanted very much to marry her and, though she turned him down in favor of de Lixin, a woman often has a soft place in her heart for a discarded suitor—that is something else I should not need to tell you. But her views would not carry much weight, even if they veered in the direction that I suspect they may, because her husband's are quite different from her—ah—admirer's and, in this case, it is the husband's that count. To tell the truth, I should not be surprised if Charmian were a little afraid of de Lixin."

"Afraid! Why should she be afraid?"

"Oh, probably afraid is not the word I should have used! I mean, I think she would hestitate to differ with him publicly, like any discreet wife." Slidell seemed to be choosing his words with care and, as he did so, Paul's anxiety increased. "She is not a favorite with the ladies in my family—someone has probably told you that already, too. I am inclined to judge her more leniently—the masculine viewpoint, you know, toward any outstandingly beautiful woman. And I do not think, as I have said, that her private opinions on international questions are important. In the first place, I do not think she is mentally qualified to form them with intelligence and, in the second place, even if she were, I think she would be wise enough to see that it is to her advantage to keep them to herself. I credit her with at least enough sense to do that. Perhaps I made a mistake in suggesting that you should go as frequently as you could to the de Lixins'. I confess I believed your early friendship with Charmian might be an asset to us, but I was thinking of it as a logical means of entrée to a great house and not because of Charmian's views. It is de Lixin's which are of moment to us, because he is so close to Chasseloup-Laubat."

"Yes sir, I understood that. But even if you did make a mistake, it wouldn't particularly signify, because that small tea, which I've already reported, has represented the de Lixins' only gesture of hospitality to me so far."

"Really! I was in hopes there might have been some you had not reported." And, as the Commissioner noticed a slight stiffening in Paul's expression, he added hastily, "I mean, of course, not *yet*."

"I try to make all my reports promptly, sir."

"I know you do, I know you do. And I'm sure the one you're going to make on your travels will be very valuable to me."

Paul left the Commissioner's office with a troubled mind. In making his report on the tepid tea, he had not failed to mention the chilling effect that the vast gloomy series of salons had made upon him, and Slidell had admitted that Paul's guess had been correct: the character of these apartments had not been modified since the death of de Lixin's first wife and they had been used very little during the long period of her invalidism. As a matter of fact, they were used very little now; Slidell was slightly surprised that Paul had been invited to the semi-deserted *hotel particulier* on the rue de Varenne, instead of to the charming place near Auteuil; that was where the de Lixins spent most of their time and, for Slidell's money, it was much more attractive than Princess Mathilde's "rural retreat" at St. Gratien. To be sure, it had no lake; on the other hand, in addition to the château itself, there was, among the *dépendances*, an exquisite pavilion which Charmian had been allowed to redecorate completely.

"*Allowed?*"

"Well, de Lixin seems to have a rather marked dislike for changes in his property, especially changes which he does not instigate himself—witness that morgue on the rue de Varenne, which Charmian has never succeeded in brightening up. But she did persuade him that this particular pavilion I mentioned was ideally suited for a 'love nest'—I believe she actually used that ridiculous expression—and that everything about it must reflect an amorous mood. He had been trying to get her for a long time, there is no doubt of that, and when she made him see it as a setting for her capitulation, he capitulated in his turn—about the décor, I mean—and let her have her own way. Also, about settling the servants in a separate *dépendance,* a chalet type, and having them come to the 'love nest' only at the periods when they are actually needed. I believe she thinks she is taking her cue partly from Madame de Pompadour and partly from Marie Antoinette, and she is not really qualified to play either role successfully. She does not have the savoir-faire to match her looks. In a word, she lacks class. And I think she may have got more than she bargained for in the way of lovemaking. I believe that de Lixin might be almost insatiable when it came to demands upon his wife, until something happened to turn his thoughts in another direction—and that hasn't occurred yet."

Paul remembered, with aversion, the statement of de Persigny on the occasion of the Slidell's dinner: "De Lixin has nothing to do but make love to his wife." He visualized, all too vividly, Charmian as the recipient of a sensualist's "insatiable" desire. To his distress, he was unable to dismiss the thought that she might have almost deliberately invited such unbridled passion, first by arousing it and then by denying it satisfaction until it was safeguarded, as far as she was concerned, by a marriage ceremony, and that afterward she might herself be enough of a voluptuary to enjoy it. Bittersweet memories of hours that he had spent with her gave credence to both possibilities without alleviating his present pain, and with the pain came puzzlement: if he were right, and the long hours she was spending in the pavilion with her husband brought her the same satisfaction that they brought to him, why had she made that daring and provocative suggestion the first time he, Paul, had seen her after their long separation? And why had she made it so conveniently logical for d'Ambres to linger when other guests were departing and Paul himself had not exchanged a single word in private with her?

All these questions were still unresolved and still disturbing when he started on his trip, though he did so without reluctance, as far as Charmian was concerned, for there was obviously no further chance of seeing her in the immediate future. She had told him, as they were saying good-bye at the Chasseloup-Laubats' luncheon, that she was going to the country very soon thereafter and had expressed only a vague hope of seeing him once she was really settled; and, as far as his travels were concerned, he suffered no disappointments. Acting on Slidell's advice, he avoided giving any impression that Nantes and Bordeaux were his objectives; and as neither Telcide nor Hélène was physically strong enough to travel rapidly, he had every excuse for proceeding in leisurely fashion. They went from Paris to Chartres and thence by easy stages to Tours and Saumur, stopping to visit not only the most noteworthy cathedrals, but several of the most outstanding châteaux and the famous cavalry school, where laudatory letters of introduction resulted in numerous pleasant invitations. Between Saumur and Nantes they found less to delay them, historically and architecturally speaking; but the courteous hospitality continued and the Loire Valley was in itself a spectacle of such surpassing loveliness that they learned to watch for the sunsets, spreading over the quiet waters and the green fields beyond, with the realization that these were sights, the memory of which they would always cherish. From Nantes, Paul went, very naturally, to see the shipyards at St. Nazaire, an excursion on which M. Voruz, to whom Chasseloup-Laubat had given him a letter of introduction, very kindly accompanied him; he was thus able to improve the opportunity of inspecting the two corvettes which were building there; but he also improved the opportunity of learning more about Anne of Bretagne, on her home territory, than he had ever known before, and of planning short excursions here and there in Brittany, on which Mr. Slidell desired copious notes for his historical brochure. After leaving Nantes, the Morphys permitted themselves a real holiday on the beach of Sable d'Olonne and a detour to see the Cognac country; it would have been impossible to say which they enjoyed more.

They had agreed beforehand that it would be ridiculous not to proceed as far south as Biarritz, which the Empress Eugénie was now making so fashionable as a summer resort. However, the day after their arrival in Bordeaux, Paul told his mother that he had been noticing signs of fatigue, both on her part and on Hélène's; would it perhaps be better to stay there a little longer than they had originally planned and then return to Paris by still easier stages than they had come south? Telcide agreed that, after all, this might be a better plan. She *was* a little tired. The trains were dirty, the stagecoaches jolting, and the connections between the two often left much to be desired. The constant process of packing and unpacking was wearisome; and though she supposed the provincial inns where they stopped were as comfortable as could be expected, even those in the larger towns could not bear comparison with really first-class metropolitan hotels. What route did he have in mind for their return? Angoulême, Poitiers, Tours again, Blois and Orléans? Well, no doubt, they would all be very interesting, but she had never even heard of those places, except, of course, Orléans. She thought Paris would look very good to them. And she had hesitated to say so before, but she had missed her grandchildren lately. Had Paul enjoyed the second shipyard he had been to see and did he think it compared favorably with the one he had seen near Nantes?

As far as he could tell, it compared very favorably, he said casually. Of course, he did not know much about shipyards, so he could hardly judge their relative merits. As in the case of the other, he had only gone to visit this one because the owner was a friend of Mr. Slidell, whose acquaintance the Commissioner thought he might enjoy making; and, indeed, he had found M. Arman, like M. Voruz, a most agreeable man. M. and Mme Arman would be very pleased to receive all three Morphys the next day at their private residence and Paul thought his mother and sister would enjoy going there. As a matter of fact, he would enjoy it himself.

The visit took place to the satisfaction of all concerned. The occasion was wholly social. No reference was made to a letter which M. Arman had dispatched that very day and of which he had thoughtfully given Paul a copy. The letter was addressed to the Minister of Marine and read as follows:

"Bordeaux, June 1, 1863

"Mr. Minister:

"I request of your Excellency authority to equip with an armament of from twelve to fourteen thirty-pounders four steamships, now constructing of wood and iron.

"These ships are destined by a foreign shipper to ply the Chinese and Pacific seas, between China, Japan and San Francisco.

"Their specific armament contemplates their eventual sale to the governments of China and Japan.

"The construction of these ships has been in progress since the 15th of April last. I beg your Excellency will be good enough to accord to M. Voruz, as early as possible, the authorization which I ask, as prescribed by the Royal ordinance of July 12, 1847.

"Arman."

Paul read the letter through twice with careful attention before making any comment. Then he had ventured a question. "This says that the ships are destined for a foreign shipper to 'ply the Chinese and Pacific seas, between China, Japan and San Francisco' and that 'their specific armament contemplates their eventual sale to the governments of China and Japan?' "

"*Eh bien?*"

"Excuse me, Monsieur, but is that statement strictly in accordance with the facts?"

"My dear M. Morphy, what would you expect me to say? That these ships are to ply the Atlantic coastline and the Mississippi River?"

"No, I suppose you couldn't say that exactly," Paul replied slowly. "But couldn't the sentence just read, 'These ships are destined for a foreign shipper' and stop there?"

"Certainly not. Very awkward questions would ensue because I had not been more specific. Believe me, Monsieur, the letter must go as it is to get any results. After all, you do not know that the Confederacy may not *eventually* use the ships as I have specified, do you?"

"No. But—"

"Then pray do not concern yourself further. Remember that you are inexperienced in your present métier. Also, that all is fair in love and war."

Paul had tried to accept this assurance at face value and was annoyed with himself because he was not altogether successful. He was worried on two scores: first, because the still small voice of conscience declined to be quieted; and second, because he was completely in the dark as to the form the answer made by the Minister of Marine would take. Although he had promised that the return trip to Paris should be made by easier stages than the journey south, Paul found himself unable to keep his word. He was in a fever of impatience and anxiety and he knew this would not abate until he could see the answer to Arman's letter. At last, he made an aching tooth a plausible reason for leaving Telcide and Hélène in Orléans, where they had been fortunate enough to find exceptionally fine quarters and to make the acquaintance of friends of friends; it would do them good, he said, to prolong their holiday. Meanwhile, he would rush on to Paris, but he would return in a week or so, or at least as soon as that good Dr. Evans had dealt successfully with his aching tooth. Then he would see them safely back to the rue du Cirque.

This was by no means the first time that a visit to Dr. Evans had been used as an alibi and Paul knew this; but fortunately his mother did not. He hastened, not to the dentist's office, but to the Commissioner's, and there, to his great relief, found the hoped for copy of the Minister's letter to Voruz.

> "Ministry of Marine
> Paris, June 6, 1863

"Sir:

"I hasten to advise you in reply to your letter of the 1st instant that I willingly authorize you to equip with an armament of twelve thirty-pound guns the four steamships now constructing of wood and iron at Bordeaux and Nantes. I will thank you to inform me in time when the ships will be ready for sea, that I may give the necessary instructions to the heads of the departments in these two ports.

> "Chasseloup-Laubat."

The Commissioner invited Paul to join Eustis and Henri Vignaud in toasting the success of the great venture on which they were now embarked. The celebration lasted far into the night. Since all the others were obviously more than satisfied with the two letters, Paul felt he could not be such a spoilsport as to raise questions regarding the accuracy of Arman's statement about the purpose and destination of the four ships building at Bordeaux and the total omission of any correspondence from Voruz concerning those building in Nantes. The celebration was also unmarred by the knowledge that an obscure Alsatian named Petermann, whose very existence was unknown to them, but who acted as confidential clerk to Voruz, was, on that same night, acting to betray both his employer and the Confederacy.

"The slightest acquaintance with chess shows one that it is a play-substitute for the art of war, and indeed it has been a favourite recreation of some of the greatest military leaders, from William the Conqueror to Napoleon. In the contest between the opposing armies the same principles of both strategy and tactics are displayed as in actual war, the same foresight and powers of calculation are necessary, the same capacity for divining the plans of the opponent, and the rigour with which decisions are followed by their consequences is, if anything even more ruthless."

Extract from *Essays in Applied Psychoanalysis*
by Ernest Jones, M.D., F.R.C.P.
(The Hogarth Press Ltd., London)

37.

The Honorable William L. Dayton, Minister of the United States of America to France, whom Charmian had not hesitated to characterize as dull and middle class and who, unfortunately, deserved both designations, was also a disappointed and discontented man.

His depression was partly due to the fact—and he was not so dull that he didn't recognize this as a fact—that the Confederate Commissioner, John Slidell, was infinitely more popular and more influential than he was, both with the *haut monde* and with the hoi polloi. All his efforts to undermine this popularity and this influence had miscarried—even the request, which he had thought so adroit, for the only available *avant scène loge* at the *Bouffes Parisien* had proved a boomerang: Slidell had received an ovation when he had appeared in the stalls and had ended up in the Green Room, where he had been unceremoniously and advantageously presented to the Emperor! The memory of this lamentable episode was among the many that rankled in the Minister's breast.

A still greater grievance lay in the fact that he could not bear comparison with the American Minister in London, Charles Francis Adams, who enjoyed the same prestige with the Crown and with Parliament that Slidell enjoyed with the Emperor and his Cabinet. What was possibly even worse, Dayton could not bear comparison with his own Consul General, whom Charmian had designated as nosey, and who was a thorn in the Minister's flesh—and a thorn, he reflected bitterly, for which he himself was largely responsible. He was hardly installed in his Legation on the rue Circulaire, at the Étoile, when he wrote a letter to Secretary Seward, complaining that, during the administration of President Buchanan, American Legations and Consulates had been filled "largely, if not exclusively, with men of doubtful loyalty," and that "London and Paris were swarming with Confederate emissaries." This, of course, was true and he had only done his duty in reporting it; but coupled with the report had been the request that a competent person should be sent to Paris to counterbalance the propaganda of such emissaries. This, too, had been eminently proper; but he had not realized that, in responding to his request, Seward, the Secretary of State, would provide him with a Consul General so competent as to completely overshadow the Minister himself and, indeed, to make him a mere figurehead. The new appointee, John Bigelow, had long been associated with William Cullen Bryant on the New York *Evening Post* and in the process had become not only experienced, but wealthy. He had spent considerable time in Paris as a journalist before he was sent there officially; he had a wide and distinguished acquaintance there and spoke French fluently; moreover, he was on terms of close friendship with both Seward and that almost equally powerful figure, Senator Sumner. Dayton, though he had once been a Vice Presidential candidate, had no talent for languages, no social graces, and no outstandingly influential connections, either at home or abroad.

Even his secretariat would not bear comparison with Slidell's. In this connection, the Commissioner had certainly been lucky past any man's deserts: first with Eustis, who was an aristocrat to his finger tips and whose young and charming wife had an immense fortune at her command; next with Vignaud, who knew the journalistic world inside out and could smell a secret halfway across a continent; and now with this new fellow, Morphy, whom Dayton had tried to dismiss from his mind as a fanatical chess player and who had been engaged merely as a historical researcher, but who apparently had half a dozen languages at his command and connections in Paris even more extensive and important than those of Slidell himself! And all the while he, Dayton, had no one but that fellow, Pennington, of whom Bigelow had not hesitated to write, not very confidentially, to the Secretary of State, "His ignorance is profound; he has neither the desire nor the capacity to learn anything; his habits are not so very good; he is careless and untidy in his person and boorish in his manners; he writes an illegible hand and is incapable of inditing the simplest sort of note in a satisfactory way."

This wholesale condemnation was, perhaps, a little too severe; still the situation was serious enough to require improvement. But Pennington was neither replaced nor reinforced and Dayton labored, conscientiously but inadequately, to make up for his secretary's deficiencies. This labor constituted another grievance; in accepting the Paris post he had imagined it would be more or less of a sinecure and, with advancing age and corresponding portliness, both mental and physical effort were alien to him. He had no intention of changing the leisurely way of life to which he had become accustomed and resented the alertness of Bigelow, while longing for an opportunity to "put him in his proper place." Unfortunately for the Minister, when the opportunity arose, he failed to recognize it as such.

He was sitting in his office, brooding on the slights which had been shown him, when Pennington ambled into the room and casually announced a visitor. Hoping that someone of importance had at last sought him out, Dayton asked for the caller's card.

"He didn't bring one. From his looks I doubt that he ever owned one."

"What do you mean by saying that he doesn't look as if he ever owned one?" Dayton asked irritably, wishing he knew of some way to force Pennington to address him as sir.

"Why—I can't explain exactly. It's just an impression. The man's what we sometimes call shabby genteel. Middle-aged. Timid. Almost apologetic. He says his name's Petermann and that he's come all the way from Nantes on purpose to see you about a matter of great importance."

"I haven't a single acquaintance in Nantes, and I never heard of anyone named Petermann. Probably some crank. You'd better get rid of him."

"Just as you say."

Pennington withdrew to return a second time. "The man says he has in his possession information which would be very important to the United States government," he announced, speaking a little less casually than he had before.

"You mean he's trying to sell us something?"

"Why yes, I suppose that is what he wants to do. He also said he had close connections with some very important persons."

"I still think he's a crank. But if he's telling the truth, that's the sort of business the Consulate deals with, not the Legation. Send him to Bigelow."

"Very well, sir."

Dayton was so pleased that Pennington had at last addressed him as sir that he dismissed the rest of the conversation from his mind.

Mr. Bigelow was not brooding over slights when Mr. Petermann of Nantes was announced. In the first place, he was too busy to waste time in brooding; in the second, he was not aware of any slights. The Consul General received his visitor briskly and promptly.

"I'm very much interested in what my secretary tells me about your mission, Monsieur. Won't you be seated?"

"The matter's quite confidential in character," the visitor said, almost in a whisper, glancing at the waiting secretary and the open door. He was, as Pennington had tried to tell Dayton, a rather mousy looking little man, and his manner, as well as his words, betrayed his nervousness. He waited until the secretary had been dismissed and the door closed before accepting the proffered seat and propping up a small attaché case beside it. Then, still speaking under his breath, he said, "I've a nephew in the shipping business who's been to America. A Marine he met there told him that if the South had only two or three warships it could blow Boston and New York and Philadelphia to bits. It was all so frightening that I haven't been able to dismiss what he told me from my mind."

"It is rather a frightening thought," Bigelow agreed soothingly, without permitting anything in his manner to suggest that, since he had never heard of even Mr. Petermann before, he could hardly be expected to feel much concern over the views of such a remote figure as the stranger's nephew. "Or rather, it would be," Bigelow continued, "if we didn't know the South doesn't have any warships and can't get any. England and France have both forbidden such construction. England attempted it and was foiled. Fortunately, France hasn't even attempted it."

"But it has. That's just what I've come to tell you," Petermann whispered, clutching the arms of his chair.

"Well, I must say that's very kind of you! Would it be indiscreet of me to ask where you got your information?"

Petermann swallowed hard, but finally managed to find his voice. "I'm the confidential clerk of M. Voruz, the iron founder," he murmured.

"Ah yes, I recognize the name. He is also a Deputy, I believe?"

"Yes, Monsieur. And the correspondence which I am handling daily, between my employer and the Confederate agents here in Paris, proves that certain vessels now building in both Nantes and Bordeaux are destined for the Confederate government."

"Very interesting! Can you tell me what type of vessels?"

"Some are armor plated. Four are equipped with twelve thirty pound guns each."

"But no such vessel could be built in France without official authorization from the Ministry of Marine!"

"True, Monsieur. And there was such authorization. But it was obtained through false pretenses and therefore could be revoked."

Bigelow appeared to ponder. "What you say might be of some importance to my government, if it can be substantiated," he said after due reflection. "But it would have none at all without proofs which are irrefutable. Can you give me such proofs?"

"Assuredly, Monsieur. In the form of both certified copies and original documents. I am prepared to leave some of these with you now, so that you can examine them at your leisure. Others, I can bring with me in a few days. But at the same time—"

"At the same time, you'd feel information of such importance has a certain monetary value?"

"It would be a *manque de tacte* to press that point, Monsieur. Nevertheless—"

"Perhaps you have in mind a sum you think would be suitable under the circumstances?"

The mousy little man was growing bolder. This time, he did not hesitate as he answered.

"I had thought of twenty thousand francs, Monsieur."

Again Mr. Bigelow appeared to ponder and, in the absence of an immediate reply, Petermann guessed, and rightly, that no such sum would be forthcoming unless he could not only convince the Consul General that the documents in his possession were indeed very valuable to the United

States, but also that he did not propose to part with them unless this was made very much worth his while.

"The acquisition of certain papers now in my possession represents considerable risk," he said with increasing boldness. "Even the copying of others has represented a great deal of time and trouble. I have had to leave the office of M. Voruz in order to come to Paris, which involves an absence of several days. I have no guarantee that I shall be paid my usual small salary during that time, even though I pleaded illness and said I needed to consult a specialist. M. Voruz is very averse to granting absences to members of his staff, especially those who are in key positions like mine."

"You're quite sure you didn't say you needed to consult a dentist? Dr. Evans?"

"Oh yes, Monsieur! I mean, oh no, Monsieur! We have very good dentists in Nantes."

"I am sure of it. I was merely permitting myself a little jest. It has become greatly the vogue to consult Dr. Evans in moments of political perplexity and he has quite often been able to suggest a happy solution. But perhaps you did not know that."

"No, Monsieur, I did not. I had in mind a very serious pulmonary complaint." Petermann paused and managed to cough quite effectively. "And then, of course, the expense of the trip, the fare on the railroad, even third class, the cost of a respectable *pension*."

"Yes, I can see that would run into money. Hardly to twenty thousand francs, however."

"Ah, but there is then the chance that I might lose my position because of my disclosures, if the source of these became known."

"I admit that possibility. But since, of course, your gesture is prompted by patriotism—"

Petermann blinked without giving an immediate answer and coughed again, still more effectively this time. "There is something else I might mention," he said at last. "I have referred to my nephew. He is much more fortunately placed in the world than I am and is received in houses where I could not possibly venture to go. Even in places where he is not on visiting terms, he is cordially regarded as a neighbor. He has a small property near Auteuil which adjoins one of the great estates and, when he and any of the princely family meet, coming out of church, for example, or at some civic celebration, or in the course of a horseback ride along rural roads, they always stop and pass the time of day with each other. When I told him how greatly upset I had been by the information he had given me and said that I, in turn, had information at my disposal, he offered to relay this, by word of mouth, the next time such an accidental meeting took place, while out riding, to a certain lady." He paused, coughed and went on. "She is an

American by birth, what I believe is called a Yankee, but she is married to a French nobleman—the one whose property adjoins my brother's. He did as he had suggested, and this lady said, without hesitation, that he should advise me to come to you."

"This is all becoming somewhat vague and involved, Monsieur Petermann. You have not even told me your nephew's name."

"You may assume that it is the same as mine, since he is the son of my brother."

"Very well. I will so assume. But you have not mentioned the lady's name, either, and that I must *assume* you are not at liberty to do."

"On the contrary. Provided, of course, I have your word of honor that it will not be disclosed in the course of our transactions."

"We have not yet reached the point of 'transactions.' But you have my word of honor."

M. Petermann leaned forward and whispered. Bigelow burst out laughing.

"I am afraid you have lost your chance of convincing me that you have something valuable to offer me, Monsieur. The husband of that lady is hand in glove with the Minister of Marine. If Chasseloup-Laubat has ordered the construction of armored vessels, whether or not the authorization was obtained under false pretenses, she would never advise giving away such a secret."

"Excuse me, Monsieur. I see that you are not fully informed. The husband of this lady is, indeed, hand in glove with the Minister of Marine. But the person whose opinion she values most is her *bel ami* and he is not. That is to say, he and Chasseloup-Laubat are old friends and see each other socially on the rare occasions when this gentleman comes to Paris; but they have long since agreed to disagree politically. And there is nothing on earth that would make this gentleman happier than to know you are in possession of the papers I am offering you and his happiness would be shared by the lady in question."

There was a short silence. Then the Consul General permitted himself a question.

"You are very sure of your facts? I mean both in regard to the lady's possession of a *bel ami* and to his identity and his political views?"

"Completely sure, Monsieur. The lady's name I have already told you in confidence. It will not be necessary for me to mention that of the gentleman when I tell you that he is the Naval Attaché of the French Embassy in London."

This time, it required all of Bigelow's sang-froid to answer casually. However, he succeeded in doing so.

"You are aware, of course, that your premise—I can still regard it only as a premise—is extremely damaging to the lady's reputation, from many points of view? That charges, such as you have made, might lead to serious consequences?"

"I am aware of all that, Monsieur. But in this case also, I am in possession of proofs."

"And in this case, I would suggest you would be wiser to forget them—or destroy them."

"I will be guided by you in that respect if you will take these papers which I am offering you."

Petermann reached for the small attaché case which he had put down beside his chair when he seated himself and held it out toward the Consul General. There was another silence, much longer this time. Then Bigelow stretched out his hand for the case.

"Very well," he said, "I will take them and look them over, as you suggested. You may return in two days, with the others you are prepared to submit to me. I still think twenty thousand francs an exorbitant price for whatever you are putting at my disposal, but if I find it convincing, I will pay you fifteen thousand. It goes without saying that whatever else is made public, a certain part of our conversation is to be kept profoundly secret."

"Tis all a Chequer-board of Nights and Days
Where Destiny with Men for Pieces Plays:
Hither and thither moves and mates and plays,
And one by one back in the Closet lays."

The Rubáiyát by Omar Khayyám,
translated by Edward FitzGerald.

38.

"Pardon, Monsieur. A messenger has just arrived from Monsieur Vignaud who says this *petit mot* must be given you *en toute vitesse*, even if I have to rouse you to do so."

Paul sat up in bed, blinking and rubbing the sleep from his eyes with one hand, as he stretched out the other for the note Louis was extending toward him. There must be some real emergency, he instantly realized; he had not been asked to change the habits of late rising, natural to a chess player who was apt to sit up most if not all of the night, when he undertook "research" for Slidell. It was understood that he might suit his pleasure and convenience as to working hours, as long as the task was done.

It took him hardly more than a second to read the note. It was not only written on a single sheet, it comprised a single line.

"Dear Paul: Hell has broken loose. Hurry out here. Henri."

He tore the note into small pieces as he swung out of bed. "Please call a fiacre, Louis," he said. "I'll be dressed by the time it gets here—or if I'm not tell the *cocher* to wait. Monsieur Vignaud requires my immediate presence."

"M. Paul will go without his coffee? Without his bath?"

"Without his bath, assuredly. If the coffee is already made, I'll gulp down a little as I dress. But get hold of that fiacre before you bring it to me."

Ten minutes later he was advancing along the Champs Elysées at a smart clip. Within a quarter of an hour he entered Slidell's office, where Bulloch, Eustis and Vignaud were already assembled. The Commissioner, almost purple in the face, was standing in front of his desk, on which he was pounding with both fists as he shouted at his associates.

"Benjamin keeps telling me I should be prepared for anything!" he bellowed. "He reminds me that I am so far removed from the scene of the outrages perpetrated by the North that I do not realize their crimes are a disgrace to civilization! Therefore, I suppose he would take it for granted that the Federal emissaries here in Paris would suborn perjury, commit theft and forge documents! I confess that I did not. The error is mine. I shall never again make the mistake of believing in the elementary decency of most human beings—even Yankees!"

Paul had not before seen the Commissioner when the latter lacked complete self-control; this display of unbridled rage appalled him as much as it bewildered him. The mystery, however, was soon clarified; Slidell, who had apparently taken no notice of Paul's quiet entrance, now turned in his direction and, without seating himself or lowering his voice, continued his tirade.

"You are no doubt wondering what all this is about, Paul, since you have only just arrived. You may well wonder. That unprincipled super-spy, John Bigelow, has taken a whole sheaf of stolen documents to that stupid bungler, William Dayton, and he has fallen for them, hook, line and sinker and, in turn, has submitted them to Drouyn de Lhuys. The Foreign Minister has expressed himself as 'surprised and vexed' at their contents—as well he may be. To say that *I* am surprised and vexed is putting the matter more mildly than I am capable of doing. If Dayton had gone to de Lhuys with a complaint and with duplicates of certain letters, supposed to justify it, the damn Frenchman might have said, 'These are alleged copies of the private correspondence of two highly respected French citizens. They could have come into your possession only through treachery or bribery. I cannot therefore accept them as evidence, unless and until you produce the originals and tell me how you got them.' That I could have understood, that I could have regarded with tolerance as far as de Lhuys is concerned. Of course, it is inconceivable that I should regard with tolerance anything done by Dayton. But what happens? De Lhuys does accept these documents as evidence. And now he tells Dayton that he is 'surprised and vexed.' "

Slidell paused, literally out of breath. Vignaud now turned to Paul and spoke quietly.

"Perhaps all this is still not clear to you, *cher*. It seems we are in trouble about those ships which have been under construction at Nantes and Bordeaux. There has been a leak about them some place. There, I did not mean to make a bad pun! But—"

"I should hope not," Slidell interrupted. "This is no time for jesting, Vignaud, and you know it. Besides, what you have said to Paul cannot possibly clarify the situation for him. He may as well get the straight of what has happened first as last. Dayton and his spies have corrupted a clerk in the office of Voruz and have rewarded this miserable worm for his stolen documents with enormous sums of money."

"Excuse me, sir." It was Captain Bulloch, the Confederate Naval Agent, hastily summoned from England, who was speaking now. "Perhaps I do not fully understand the situation, but according to the report of it which has reached me, Petermann, the clerk from the office at Nantes, acted completely on his own initiative. He was not 'corrupted' by anyone—in fact, this was unnecessary, since he was corrupt already. And when he went to see Dayton, the American Minister refused to receive him. He never got past Pennington. It was Bigelow's secretary who let him in and Bigelow who bought the incriminating papers."

"Very well, have it your own way. It all adds up to the same thing in the end, since it is Dayton, acting ostentatiously in his official capacity, who has shown the correspondence to de Lhuys and demanded an inquiry. And de Lhuys is 'surprised and vexed!'"

"Excuse me, sir," Bulloch said again, "but isn't that just a figure of speech? After all, the government authorized the building of those ships."

"No, no! That's where you're mistaken. Chasseloup-Laubat authorized it."

"But he is the Minister of Marine!"

"Yes, and that's *all* he is! He doesn't represent the whole Cabinet, much less the whole government."

"However, Voruz and Arman are both Deputies, aren't they?"

"Yes, yes, of course they are Deputies. Are you bent on arguing with me, Bulloch? And, of course, Chasseloup-Laubat knew he had them with him. Shipbuilding's their bread and butter, isn't it? No man gets rich in the Chamber of Deputies, if he's honest, any more than he does in our Congress, and I haven't had any specific reason to doubt their legislative honesty so far. But two voices don't go very far in that Assembly—again, any more than they would in our Congress; and if we suddenly had the whole pack from the Quai d'Orsay unloosed on us, we'd be in a bad way."

"The Minister of Marine must have acted with the Emperor's tacit approval, or even at his direct request, don't you think so, sir? I doubt that Chasseloup-Laubat would have dared to do what he did without this."

"You're right. But the Emperor could easily deny it, wash his hands of the whole matter and throw us to the wolves, and he wouldn't hesitate to do this if he thought it was the best policy. Then de Lhuys would disavow the whole transaction. Napoleon's told the Minister of Marine to send for poor Arman and God only knows what will come of that interview. If it's as unfavorable to us as I fear, Chasseloup-Laubat will also wash his hands of the whole affair."

"How can he? His letter of authorization was specific enough. . . . What is it, Mr. Morphy?"

Paul had been listening to the heated discussion with distress, which only increased as the sad situation became clearer to him. The last thing he wished to do was to add further fuel to the fire of the Commissioner's rage, which Bulloch's arguments, respectfully though these were voiced, had only served to inflame.

"Nothing, sir. That is, nothing that I ought to say, probably. It's just that Chasseloup-Laubat's letter seems to authorize the building of four ships at Bordeaux. I was wondering if there was any sanction for the two building at Nantes. As you know, I saw a copy of Arman's letter. I was in Bordeaux when he wrote it. I mean the one he sent to Chasseloup-Laubat. I ventured to tell Arman—"

"For God's sake, Paul, speak up!" shouted the Commissioner, breaking in again. "This is no time for shilly-shallying, no matter what you wondered! What did you tell Arman?"

"I wondered if it were wise to say the ships were destined to ply the seas between China, Japan and San Francisco and that their specific armament contemplates their eventual sale to the governments of China and Japan. I told Arman I couldn't help doubting the wisdom of such a statement."

"And what did he say in reply?"

"He asked me if I expected him to write the Minister of Marine that they were intended to ply the Atlantic coastline and the Mississippi River. And when I said of course not, and asked if it couldn't have said that the vessels were merely destined for a foreign shipper and ended his statement there, he said no, very emphatically, that wasn't definite enough, it would only have resulted in a lot of awkward questions; and he asked if I knew the Confederacy might not eventually dispose of these vessels as he'd indicated."

"Naturally, you didn't know anything of the sort. He was right and you were wrong about the wording. You realized that afterward, of course?"

"I realized, even without his reminder, that I was new at this métier. Just the same, I couldn't help feeling—"

"Feeling what?"

"That Arman's letter was—misleading."

"Well, damn it all, what else did you expect it to be?"

Paul, who had turned very pale, did not answer. The silence in the room suddenly became even more electric than the previous turmoil. At last the Commissioner spoke, no longer heatedly, but coldly and cuttingly.

"In chess, don't you use every known device to win?"

"No, sir. You use strategy. But it's honest strategy. There's no deliberate intention to deceive. There couldn't be. The chessmen are all kept in plain sight. That's the kind of a game it is."

"Well, I see I was wrong in saying you'd be playing the same kind of a game here in Paris that you'd played before. I'm afraid you're not as well fitted for the task with which you've been entrusted as I thought you were."

Paul rose and bowed. He was trembling and his pallor had now become so marked that Vignaud, who had been sitting beside him, was afraid he was going to faint. But his voice was quite steady as he answered.

"I'm sorry that I've disappointed you, sir. If you feel I can't be of any further service to you, perhaps you'll pardon me if I leave."

"Oh, for God's sake!" Slidell said again. "Sit down and stop acting and talking like a child! As Arman says, you're new at this métier, but you haven't done badly at all so far, not badly at all, and I've no doubt that in time you'll learn to do better. You're observant, you're welcome everywhere, you write very clear reports of what you see and do, and you see and do a good deal. All you need is to become a little more realistic."

"You're in charge here, Mr. Commissioner, and we all respect your authority." Bulloch was speaking again, somewhat more emphatically than before. "But I'm not new at this métier and, if you'll permit me to say so, I think Mr. Morphy has a point. In fact, two points. In the first place, of course we should have official authorization for all six ships, irrespective of where they are built. In the second place, if Arman's letter had stopped as short as Mr. Morphy felt it well might, it could have been pronounced too indefinite and there might have been more correspondence on the subject. That wouldn't necessarily have been a disadvantage. I know the time element is important, but occasionally it's better to make haste slowly. If the Minister of Marine had insisted that we enlarge on our original statement then something else could have been added."

"What, for instance?"

" 'Coast defense on the South Atlantic,'—which could mean anything from Virginia to the Straits of Magellan. 'Protection of inland waterways threatened by enemy invasion'—which could be the Amazon as well as the Mississippi. I may be wrong, but I don't think the Foreign Minister would have objected to a little ambiguity—in fact, I think he might have welcomed it as a loophole. I believe he would really be glad to help us. But when we began to talk about the China Seas, that was putting it on a little too thick."

"We didn't talk about the China Seas. That was Arman's phraseology."

"We encouraged Arman to go ahead in any way he thought best. Now we're using him as our whipping boy."

The Commissioner drummed on the table with his fingers and glared at Bulloch, but he knew he could not ride roughshod in that quarter as he could, if it suited him, in some others. Bulloch had told the truth when he said he was not new at this métier. He was an ex-Naval Officer, who, at the outbreak of the War, had been in command of a mail steamer plying between New York and New Orleans. He had returned the steamer to its owners, presented himself to Mallory, Secretary of the Navy for the Confederacy, and forthwith volunteered for service. Upon being told he was needed in Europe and asked how soon he could leave for a foreign post, his answer had been, "Immediately." Though his cautious attitude in regard to rash measures often irritated Slidell, he was a favorite of the Administration generally and no useful purpose would be served by antagonizing him at this moment.

"Well," the Commissioner said at last, "perhaps you have a point."

"It was Mr. Morphy's point that I was trying to stress, sir."

"All right, all right. Now let's stop crying over spilled milk and decide what to do next."

Since it was the Commissioner who, so far, had done the loudest crying and Bulloch's respectful objections to his more heated statements had been angrily brushed aside, no one else in the room was inclined to offer suggestions. In fact, Paul, who had reseated himself after a grateful glance at the Naval Agent, but who was still pale and trembling, was quite incapable of doing so. Bulloch decided to make a further attempt at pacification and reassurance.

"Wouldn't it be wisest, sir, just to sit tight and await developments? Neither Arman nor Voruz has had an interview with Chasseloup-Laubat yet and it's still not hard to believe that they will be allowed to proceed unobtrusively with their building program, once this current excitement about it has died down. If they can do that, we can meet the next hurdle—how to insure the actual departure of the ships—when we get to it. They would not be ready to sail for several months, in any case. If by then our cause is on the ascendant—"

"On the ascendant!" exclaimed Slidell, his voice rising again. "After the Battle of Gettysburg! After the Fall of Vicksburg! What are you talking about, Bulloch?"

"About the future, as you advised, sir. I don't underestimate the South's losses and failures. But neither do I feel they're going to continue indefinitely. The North is having its troubles, too. Remember those draft riots in New York! And reports are just coming through that there's been an unsuccessful naval assault on Fort Sumter. If that's true—"

"Yes, if that's true, and I believe it is, we can afford to be more optimistic." The Commissioner appeared to consider and, when he next spoke, it was less vehemently. "As you say, perhaps we'd better just mark time for the present. Yes, certainly, that's the wisest course. I'm sorry I blew up. But Dayton always did get under my skin, damn him! As for Chasseloup-Laubat, well, I won't go into that again. The meeting is dismissed, gentlemen. You may proceed with the routine duties of the day. If, later on, I feel it necessary or even advisable, I will call you back. And I will remain where I can be instantly reached in case any further disquieting bulletins come in from our Federal friends. Of course, this means I shall have to revise my social program somewhat. Let me see. Mrs. Slidell and I are giving a dinner tonight in honor of the Danish Minister and his wife. Well, there's no reason why we should cancel that; it might give us a valuable opportunity to find out the general reaction to this treachery. Of course, the news of it will be all over Paris before night. But I am afraid I cannot leave the office long enough to go to that Benefit Concert at the Salle Dourlans under the auspices of the Societies of the Sons of the South and the Daughters of the South. Paul, will you represent me?"

He held out his hand, smiling. It was obvious that his rage had cooled as rapidly as it had risen, that he was completely himself again—benign, competent, collected. His glance, normally so keen, had failed, a few minutes earlier, to note Paul's agitation, which had been all too obvious to the others. Now that he observed it, he realized that the sensitivity of his latest disciple had received a shock, perhaps an actual wound. He was honestly eager to make amends for his harshness.

"Certainly, sir, if that's where you feel I can really be of use," Paul answered.

His manner was completely respectful, his voice still quiet and steady. But, apparently, he failed to notice the Commissioner's outstretched hand.

The concert to which Paul had been assigned was similar to several previous benefits, given under different patriotic Southern auspices, which he had already attended, not heretofore because Slidell had asked him to do so officially, but because it was one of the few types of entertainment which his mother still enjoyed, and he had been glad to take her; in fact, they had attended together a similar concert, given in the same place and under the same auspices, to celebrate the birthday of Jefferson Davis, the previous June. He would have asked her to come with him today, except for his conviction that he would not be able to conceal from her his state of tremulous excitement and decided it would be better to go alone. He was doubly glad he had done so when, greatly to his surprise, he saw that Charmian was in the rather sparse audience.

As usual, she was dressed in the height of fashion, this time in crimson satin and cream grosgrain; a small hat of crimson feathers, with its stiff wings pointing backward, set cockily on her golden hair, gave her the effect of being poised for flight. He did not trust himself to go to her at once, but took a seat diagonally behind her, where he could feast his eyes on her without apparently making any effort to do so. Beside her was an elderly woman in puce color, whom he recognized as one of his nondescript fellow guests at the tepid tea party and who, he believed, was a distant relative of de Lixin's. As the places on either side of them were vacant, it seemed probable that they had come together, and this impression was confirmed as they chatted occasionally with each other between the musical numbers. If this had been Madrid, instead of Paris, Paul would have quickly set down the older woman as a *dueña* and, despite the fact that, here, the idea of such supervision seemed fantastic, it persisted.

The program was unstimulating and Paul was not surprised to see Charmian yawning from time to time behind her fan; indeed, he would have welcomed such a shield himself. However, the very mediocrity of the performance was soothing to his jangled nerves. When, at last, it was over, and the polite but unenthusiastic applause had died down, he stepped forward to greet Charmian and her companion.

"Why, Paul!" Charmian said cordially, "what a pleasant surprise! I didn't see you come in. Have you been here all the afternoon?"

"Most of it. I was a trifle late, so I took a seat in the rear. It never occurred to me that you'd be here, or of course I'd have planned to join you, if you'd been kind enough to give me permission. I didn't think you cared much for entertainment of this sort."

"I don't. But Gilbert thought I should come as a mark of interest in the Confederate cause. He couldn't come himself, because of some tiresome meeting called by the Minister of Marine, but his kind aunt was good enough to accompany me. You remember the Countess of Bonamour, don't you?"

"Of course and, needless to say, I'm delighted to see her again."

He smiled, in his most winning way. The visage of the Countess became, momentarily, less dour, but it could hardly be said that she smiled in return and, when she spoke, her voice was severe.

"My dear Charmian, if M. Morphy will excuse us, I think we should be on our way. Have you forgotten that we must do an errand on the rue de Grenelle before we return to Auteuil?"

"No, I hadn't forgotten. But perhaps M. Morphy would be kind enough to come with us. I do not think the refreshments here are going to be very sustaining or the company very exhilarating and, after all, we have done our duty to the Confederacy by putting in an appearance. Why not see what the Hotel de Lixin could provide in the way of a *gouter?*"

"My dear Charmian," the Countess said again, "the staff is not expecting you for *gouter*. There will be no proper preparations. You are only supposed to give instructions about the tapestries."

"Yes, yes, I know. But it would be interesting to see what the staff can do on the spur of the moment, without any time for preparations. After all, with twenty servants on duty, you would think they might do something. Don't *you* think so, Paul?"

It was obvious that she expected him to agree with her and he did so. It was also obvious that the elderly Countess was not as pleased as she might have been with the turn things were taking, for she was still making objections to the *gouter* when they reached the magnificent carriage, emblazoned with a coat-of-arms, which was waiting for them. With less sympathy than he knew he should have felt for her disability, Paul now saw that she was very lame, that she was obliged to lean heavily on the parasol which matched her dress; he had thought at first it was an accessory to this, but now found that it was, in reality, a sturdy cane, disguised by an encircling framework covered with fluttering flounces. He tried, as gallantly as possible, to give her additional support, which she accepted with no show of gratitude, much as she needed it for getting into the carriage; indeed, she made it plain that she actually preferred the help of the footman who sprang from his place beside the coachman on the box. She took no part in the conversation as they went on their way and, as they approached the Hotel de Lixin, she renewed her warning that they must not linger there, that they would be late in reaching Auteuil.

"If you feel that way, Aunt Stephanie, why not go straight on? It is so hard for you to get in and out of the carriage. And I can take the smaller one and follow you as soon as I see the *gouvernante* about those old draperies which she says are being devoured by moths. Really, she should be able to deal with details like that alone! What is the use of a housekeeper if she has to keep sending for the chatelaine all the time? I shall give her a piece of my mind. And I must have something to eat and drink, I am dying of hunger and thirst. Since you are not, of course it is much better that you should be on your way. Poor Gilbert will probably be detained for hours yet at that tiresome meeting, but if he arrives before I do, assure him I shall be home as soon as I have dealt with the tapestries, in accordance with his wishes."

Too late, the Countess realized her mistake in objecting to the *gouter*. Charmian had leaped lightly from the carriage before the footman, alert as he was, could spring to help her, and was giving rapid directions, both to him and the coachman. In a trice, the superb black horses were in motion and the carriage was underway again, with both men on the box and the old Countess still helplessly ensconced on the rear seat inside. She leaned forward, voicing her angry protests through the open window. Charmian waved to her smilingly, as if the arrangement were one that had been made to their mutual satisfaction. Then, as the carriage swung out of sight, she took Paul's arm and laughed.

"We will now have the tête-à-tête that is already several months overdue," she said gaily.

". . . en privé, [il] la battra et, en public, lui donnera des gifles. . . .

"Rien de plus vil et de plus bas ne peut être imaginé! . . . Faux, lâche, enfin tous les vices, sans une seule qualité!"

Viel-Castel, as quoted in
Le Grand Siècle de Paris by André Castelot (Amiot-Dumont)

39.

The fact that he had not yet recovered from the scene in the Commissioner's office must be responsible, Paul told himself, for the fact that he felt no exultation as he crossed the courtyard by Charmian's side. They were, as she had said, alone at last, and she had maneuvered to bring this about in a way that was actually daring if, as he suspected more and more strongly, the Countess was supposed to act as her *dueña*. She would not have done this without an impelling reason and unless she were willing to take the chance of displeasing her husband by dismissing her guardian. Displeasure! Anger would probably be a better word, and he shrank from the thought of any further show of this, especially from the thought of being its cause.

If Charmian felt any latent uneasiness, however, she gave no sign of it; and that her errand was a genuine one had become obvious, not only because the Countess was the first to mention it, but because a liveried manservant was standing at the entrance to admit her, and immediately informed her that the *gouvernante* was already waiting for her in the suite where the draperies were giving such cause for concern. She turned to Paul and spoke rapidly in English.

"Won't you come with me? I hate to go to that part of the house alone."

"Why yes, of course, if you need me. But why—"

"I'll tell you why later."

The next minute he was sorry he had consented. She was informing the servant that M. Morphy was a great authority on Arras, that she had asked him to give an expert opinion. Paul tried to expostulate with her as they went up the grand staircase, but she shook her head, reiterating that she would explain later, that as soon as this awful tour of inspection was over, they would have a happy visit together. It was futile, indeed it was practically impossible to argue with her. The mere effort of keeping pace with her left him breathless.

The doors leading from the upper hall into the suites of bedrooms, with their correlative anterooms, dressing rooms and sitting rooms, were all open, and Charmian rushed quickly through several of these before coming to a stop in the one where the *gouvernante* was waiting for her. This woman, dressed in the conventional neat black of her calling, was no less severe of aspect than the Countess de Bonamour; and her expression did not soften as Charmian explained again that M. Morphy, an old family friend, was also a great authority on tapestries and that, having had the good fortune to meet him that afternoon at the Benefit Concert, she had prevailed upon him to accompany her to the Hotel de Lixin and give his opinion on the damaged hangings.

"*Madame la Princesse* will pardon me. I do not need another expert opinion. May I remind her that we have had several of these already? All authorities say the same. These rooms need to be aired more frequently and the draperies need to be taken down, at regular intervals, for careful cleaning. The airing is very seldom done. The cleaning has not been done since the death of the *Duquesa*. I have tried several times to remind the Prince of this and he has declined to discuss the subject."

"You cannot blame him for finding it painful. He still declines to discuss it. That is why I am here today. But it is painful to me, also."

"As I can well understand, *Madame la Princesse*. But as I have never been given authority—"

"Very well, I will give it to you now—on the condition that you will never trouble me with the matter again."

"Some of the hangings will have to be destroyed to safeguard the others which, so far, have not been attacked by moths. Do I understand that I have the permission of *Madame la Princesse* to use my judgment about the amount of destruction that is necessary?"

"By all means. In fact, it would not disturb me if you destroyed them all."

"But they are priceless heirlooms!"

"I know, I know. But they are also moth-eaten and in my opinion they are hideous anyway. If they were destroyed it would be good riddance of bad rubbish."

The *gouvernante* flushed painfully and pressed her lips together. Then she spoke in a tone which, though subdued, was still harsh.

"I shall give the matter immediate attention, *Madame la Princesse*. And I take it that henceforth I am to have these apartments and the others in my charge aired as often as I consider this advisable."

"Certainly."

"Then I do not need to detain *Madame la Princesse* any longer. . . . But I should like to express my gratitude to her friend who has been so kind as to favor us with his expert advice," the *gouvernante* added, as Paul and Charmian started to leave the room.

Charmian turned quickly, but something in the *gouvernante's* face deterred her from voicing the sharp reprimand which rose to her lips, and she stalked out of the room without another word. However, once she thought they could not be overheard, she fairly spat out her resentment.

"That woman should be whipped for her insolence until she cries for mercy. I'll see that she is yet."

"Charmian, how can you say such a dreadful thing, even in jest?"

"I'm not jesting. Don't try to tell me you've never heard of a woman being whipped!"

"I've never heard of it without horror—and never in connection with a white woman. Only in connection with maltreated slaves. And that sort of abuse is one of the disgraces of our so-called civilization, one of the main reasons why France won't recognize the Confederacy!"

He was trembling again, no less violently than he had that morning, and his voice was shaking, as well as his shoulders. For all her haste, Charmian could not fail to notice his agitation.

"Let's get out of this dreadful house," she said impulsively. "I never come here if I can help it, and never stay any longer than I have to when I do come. I didn't mean to give that stupid tea here. I'll explain how I happened to. There are lots of things I want to explain. Couldn't we go to your apartment?"

The suggestion startled him. Such an idea had never entered his head, nor would he have dreamed that it would ever enter hers. He stammered out an answer.

"Why yes, I suppose so, if that's what you really want to do. But are you sure?"

"Does your servant speak English or understand it?"

"No, not a word."

"Then I can't think of a better place. I'll order the carriage at once and say I'm going to the rue de Rivoli to do an errand on my way out to Auteuil. That's true enough anyway, and I won't have to account for the time I take to do an errand. On the other hand, I might be asked how I happened to stay here so long, now that the question of those horrible tapestries is settled."

Again, she gave necessary directions quickly and again her orders were carried out with dispatch. Paul, fighting for self-control, found himself seated beside her in a closed carriage almost before he could have believed such an arrangement possible. He was struggling to suppress the utterance of confused and distressed questions, hoping against hope that the answers to these might calm his troubled spirit; yet he was all too conscious that he should let Charmian take the initiative in explaining a situation that was as complex as it was appalling. He felt rewarded for his restraint when, of her own accord, she began to enlighten him, as the carriage rolled along in the direction of the Pont Neuf.

"You must be consumed with curiosity. I'll try to put an end to it. You don't even know who the *Duquesa* was, do you?"

"No."

"She was Gilbert's first wife—a Spaniard by birth. Of course, she was addressed socially as the Princess de Lixin, but in her personal household, she always insisted on being called by her own title. She considered it much more important than her husband's. Naturally, that irritated him. I imagine a good many things about her irritated him."

"Why should you imagine that?"

"Oh, she was a mournful sort of person! Even her name—Dolores—was mournful. But it suited her. And then she was sick so long. Gilbert might just as well have been a widower for years before he actually became one, with a wife like that on his hands. No wonder he had a succession of mistresses."

"I should think he would have been very, very sorry for her."

Charmian shot him a questioning glance. "Hasn't anyone ever talked to you about her—about him—I mean about that marriage?"

"Only to say what you've just told me: that she was ill a very long time—not even the nature of the illness."

"I think it must have been partly mental. I don't mean she was insane, but as I've said, she was a mournful sort of person and she brooded over her wrongs."

"Which wrongs? The succession of mistresses?"

"Oh, I think she took those for granted! I really don't know what else. Probably many of her troubles were imaginary. But I guess it wasn't a very successful marriage from the beginning and that she blamed Gilbert for everything that kept it from being one, instead of taking part of the blame herself. And then she developed some sort of a heart condition."

"So she died of a heart attack?"

"I suppose so. Yes, of course she did."

"Suddenly?"

"No-o. That is, the end came suddenly. But not until she had dragged on and on. Are you sure no one spoke to you about that?"

With startling clarity, the comments made at the Slidells' dinner came crowding back into his confused thoughts. "Why, now that you remind me," he said hesitantly, "I do remember hearing that the Prince de Lixin was—very much attracted by you and that the situation was a sad one because—"

"Because he was already saddled with a wife and I declined to accommodate him by joining the succession of mistresses?"

"Charmian, of course it wasn't put to me that way."

"You mean you chose not to interpret it that way. But I don't imagine for a minute that the tale was glossed over in the telling. Besides, that *is* the way it was."

"I'm very sorry," Paul said slowly. He knew all too well that the answer was inadequate, but he could think of nothing else to say and he felt Charmian would interpret silence as condemnation.

"So now you know why I hate that house," Charmian went on. "It was *her* house—that is, of course, it is de Lixin property, but it is where she lived, all through that long drawn-out married life, and the place grew stiffer and stiffer and gloomier and gloomier because she did. People can do that to a house, don't you think so? That is, if they're pleasant, attractive people, they make the places where they live pleasant and attractive, too, and if they're the opposite, their houses take on those personalities. Especially, in the case of women. Gilbert hates the place on the rue de Varenne as much as I do, but he won't change it himself—he almost never goes there —and he won't let anyone else change it or even supervise it, unless he gives directions. That's how those horrible tapestries got all moth-eaten. He wouldn't go into the *Duquesa's* rooms himself to tell the *gouvernante* what to do with them and it wasn't until today that he made me go and tell her instead."

"He *made* you go?"

"Well, he told me to, and when Gilbert tells anyone to do something, it's much better to do it right away. Otherwise, he's apt to be pretty disagreeable."

This time, Paul could not find an answer, though he tried hard to do so. But it did not matter, because this time Charmian did not really want one.

"I know you think I ought not to talk that way about my husband," she said hurriedly. "But I've got to talk to someone. I'm desperately in need of a friend. You are my friend, aren't you, Paul?"

"You know I am."

"Then you'll let me talk to you freely and not misunderstand anything I say?"

"Naturally, you may say whatever you think best. I can't promise to understand everything."

"Oh, please try! First, about that wretched tea party: I want to get the explanation for that out of the way and then go on to more important matters. Gilbert thought it was going to be at Auteuil—that's why he wasn't present. There was some confusion about the arrangements. You see, I found it would be much more convenient for Jacques, who was in Paris just a short time and of course dashing madly from one place to another, to come to the rue de Varenne. We were rushing around so fast, too—I mean, Gilbert and I—that I must have forgotten to tell him that the plans had been changed. Anyway, he sat waiting for the guests to arrive at the pavilion and all the time they were at the hotel. He was simply furious when he learned about the confusion."

Again, Paul found a ready answer impossible. It was inconceivable to him that Charmian had really forgotten to tell her husband about such a change of plan, or that she would have made it simply for the convenience of a guest who would have been more than glad to conform his social schedule to hers; and, hating the hotel as she did, she must have had some very strong reason, so far unconfessed, for giving her tea party there. But, of course, he did not really need an explanation; it was all too plain that she had schemed to see d'Ambres alone and that she had been able to contrive only one way of doing so. And something else was also distressingly plain: she was not free to entertain when, where and whom she chose. That was why Paul himself had never been invited to the pavilion, why de Lixin had consented to d'Ambres' invitation only because of his inclusion in a group, and then under false pretenses.

"And in the end all my careful planning came to nothing," Charmian went on. Apparently she had forgotten that only a few minutes before she had been talking about "confusion"; now it was "careful planning." . . . "The Countess de Bonamour stayed on and on—Paul, did you ever hear of such an inappropriate name? Can you imagine anyone less fitted for 'good love' than Gilbert's Aunt Stephanie?"

"No," said Paul. "I can't. But that isn't what you started to say, is it?"

"I started to say that, finally, Jacques had to leave, because he was dining at the British Embassy. So I never saw him alone after all, which was the whole idea of the tea. And, afterward, the old cat went around gossiping, because she had caught on to that, and now Gilbert insists on sending her with me wherever I go, so that she can spy on me. But I got rid of her today all right, didn't I?"

"Are you sure it was wise? If you're as restricted in your actions as I gather, wasn't it very imprudent?"

"It may have been, a little, but I tell you I was desperate. And besides, those tapestries! I did go to see them. I did tell the *gouvernante* what to do about them. I am going to stop for an errand on the rue de Rivoli. And there's nothing so terribly improbable in presenting you as an expert."

"There may be nothing improbable about it, but it's completely untrue and you know it."

"Oh, Paul, don't take that tone!"

Her eyes were brimming again and, this time, large tears were beginning to roll down her cheeks.

"Charmian, you know I want to help you if I can. I'm sorry you're so terribly unhappy, but I hate lying, I always have, and there seem to be so many lies involved—in all this." He had almost said, "in everything I'm connected with," but had succeeded in biting back the words. "Isn't there some way of playing fair, even if that is hard to do?" he ended slowly.

"No, there isn't. That is, I don't know of any. Perhaps you can think of one."

"I'll do my best. . . . Will you signal your coachman to stop? My apartment is in the middle of this block."

She picked up a tiny tube at her side and spoke through it. The carriage came to an easy halt and the footman sprang down and opened the door, saluting smartly as he did so. There had again been two men on the box, a coat-of-arms on the lacquered door, a pair of handsome black horses. The carriage was slightly smaller than the one in which the Countess de Bonamour had taken her unwilling departure, but it was no less elegant. And Charmian had spoken of twenty house servants. De Lixin must indeed be an enormously rich man. . . .

"I'm afraid you'll find it quite a climb to my apartment. It's on the fourth floor. Do you mind?"

"No, why should I? Don't you know I'm very good at climbing?"

Her tears were dried and she smiled at her own jest as she took Paul's arm, though he found that he could not. As they went up the long flights of stairs, he was all too conscious of her nearness. She had said several times, with great apparent feeling, that she needed a friend; there had been nothing to indicate that this visit was to assume a clandestine character and he was torn between relief and frustration because this was so. Long as he had dreamed of consummated love, the vision had been untinged by any element of shabbiness and furtiveness; he could not bear to have it so tarnished now. At the same time, there had been that daring spontaneous promise, already long unfulfilled, and there was the abiding fear that another man might have been more privileged than he ever had been or ever would be. Her recent talk had been of friendship, only of friendship, and her need of that—nothing else. On the other hand, she had been the one to suggest that she should come to his apartment and she could not be blind to the implications of such a suggestion. If he did not take advantage of them now, the opportunity might be gone forever. . . .

The faithful Louis was already at the door, before Paul had time to turn his key in the latch. If the servant was surprised at seeing a lady with his master, there was nothing in his respectful manner to indicate this; Paul guessed—and rightly—that such surprise as Louis felt was based on the fact that no ladies had previously been visitors at the apartment, rather than on the fact that one was there now. He lingered briefly, awaiting orders, and when none came, took the initiative in hinting at hospitality. Paul looked inquiringly at Charmian.

"I don't know about tea. Louis has never made it for me. But he does make very good coffee. Wouldn't you like some? Or a glass of wine with some ladyfingers? I know we have some of those on hand. You spoke of *gouter* and that was more than an hour ago. I'm afraid that you're going to be very late for dinner, that you'll be very hungry."

"When I spoke of *gouter*, it was just a pretext. I thought you realized that. I shan't be hungry. I'm never hungry any more."

She had spoken in English. Paul turned to the servant.

"Thank you, Louis, but Madame says she does not care for any refreshment."

"Then if Monsieur does not require anything at present, it would perhaps be a good time to do the errands?"

Of course he thinks this is an assignation, Paul said to himself wearily, as Louis withdrew with a broad smile and a deep bow. Charmian had gone to the window and had stood looking down at the pleasant gardens of the Tuileries, where frolicsome children were taking brief rides on the small patient donkey available for hire, and flying the multicolored balloons that their nurses bought for them from a ragged vendor. Then she had turned and her glance had taken in the details of the well-worn, but well-ordered furnishings of the little salon: the fragile furniture which needed repainting, but which had graceful lines; the upholstery which was frayed, but which had soft colors; the porcelain figurines of amorous shepherds and coy shepherdesses, charming in spite of the incongruity of their fanciful costumes; the prints of Versailles and Fontainebleau hanging in faded splendor against the delicate, though peeling, wallpaper. She sighed.

"You're happy here, aren't you, Paul?"

"I have been."

"But you're not any more?"

He could all too truthfully have said, "It's been a very upsetting day from the beginning"—truthfully, but as he realized, unwisely, for that would have invited questions which he could not answer. It was still truthful to say, "How can I be, when you're in such distress?"

"Well, I know—you're too kind hearted for that. . . . My head aches, do you mind if I take my hat off?"

"Of course not."

"May I put it on your bed, or are you superstitious, like most Creoles? Do you think it brings bad luck to put a hat on a bed?"

"Don't we all have some superstitions, whether or not we're Creoles and even if we pretend we haven't? Not always the same ones, but some?"

"What are yours?"

"Telling a bad dream before breakfast. Bragging that I've had exceptionally good luck—sitting thirteen at table."

"But not putting a hat on a bed?"

"No."

"Then I'm going to put mine there."

The door leading into the bedroom was already ajar. She pushed it open and went in, tossed the crimson-winged hat on the bed, which was covered with toile de Jouý, and walked over to the dressing table, which was draped to match. She sat down in front of this and, after fluffing out her hair and approving the results of this by looking in the mirror, she fingered the military brushes that lay in neat sequence on the glass covered surface of the table, and rearranged them slightly, as if with housewifely care. Then she came back into the salon and looked at him appealingly.

"We could have been happy *together* in a place like this, couldn't we, Paul?"

"I could have been happy with you anywhere, Charmian. You know that. It was you—"

"Yes, yes. It's all my fault. I know that now."

She sat down and buried her face in her heavily ringed hands. He could hear her sobbing again. Resisting the impulse to cross over to her and put his arm around her, he spoke to her very gently.

"You said you wanted to talk to me, Charmian. We can't talk if you keep crying."

"Yes, yes," she said again. "If I can only confide in someone, I'll feel better—at least I hope I will. And I'll try to stop crying. But I can't talk with you if you sit on the other side of the room. Come here beside me, won't you?"

She made a place for him on the loveseat and took his hand. Then she began to speak, in a strangled voice.

"I want to go back to the very beginning, Paul."

"Is that necessary? Won't it be painful—for both of us?"

"I'm afraid so. But I still think it's necessary."

"Very well then."

"You remember—in New Orleans? Your family didn't think I was good enough for you?"

"It wasn't that exactly. It's just that Creoles are very conservative, that they haven't got used to Americans, even yet."

"But *they're* Americans now."

"Yes, I know. Just the same—"

"Well, let's not labor that point. You know and so do I that it wasn't just Creole conservatism that kept us apart. Your family looked down on my father because he was in trade. And they looked down on me because they thought I was fast."

"Please, Charmian—"

"No, I've got to say it. He was in trade, and I would have been fast, as they called it, if I hadn't been so well protected. Not just by Berenice, either, though she always knew I'd bear watching. By you."

"But Charmian, I respected your innocence."

"You mean my virginity. I wasn't really innocent. That is, I was free from a certain kind of sin, because I'd been so well protected. But I wasn't free from the knowledge of what it was or the desire for it."

"I wish you didn't feel it necessary to talk this way. I loved you very much. I'm a normal man, of course I desired you. But even if I'd realized you shared my desire, which I didn't, I wouldn't have taken advantage of it. I didn't want to seduce you. I wanted to marry you. I've tried to explain all this to you before."

"And, like most men, you wanted your wife to be a virgin."

"Yes, that's natural, too."

"Natural! It's an obsession!"

"I'm afraid I don't know what you mean."

"I'm trying to tell you. Well, you wouldn't seduce me and your family wouldn't accept my family and, eventually, we left New Orleans. I made up my mind then I'd get even with you."

"How could you do such a thing, if you loved me?"

"I didn't love you enough to forgive all the slights we'd suffered. I don't mean that you personally had slighted us. Of course, you never did. But you were one of—of a tribe. And you let me go when you could have had me. I didn't understand then, as well as I do now, this male obsession I've spoken of. So, when I had the chance, I struck back."

"It was a very cruel thing to do."

"I am cruel. Haven't you found that out yet? Of course you have. You've known it for a long while and you've been reminded of it once already this very afternoon—when I spoke about having the *gouvernante* whipped until she cried for mercy."

"Don't speak of it again. And I don't see that any of this is doing either of us any good, Charmian."

He tried, quietly, to free his hand from hers. Immediately, her grasp tightened.

"It's doing *me* good, not to have all this bottled up inside of me any longer and, besides, I'm getting now to something else. You see, when we came abroad everything was different. We had good introductions, we were received in the best society. It wasn't just in New Orleans that we hadn't been, before, it was in Boston, too, for very much the same reasons. But once we got to Europe, no one bothered about Papa's shopkeeping any more. No one realized I was fast. New Orleans and Boston are a long way from London and Paris anyhow, and, in addition, Papa's personal connection with his big stores had been a thing of the past for years. He is a very agreeable man and an enormously rich one. He entertained magnificently and gave lavishly to charity. He had a lovely, refined wife, who was all the more appealing because she was so fragile, and two pretty daughters of marriageable age who'd be very, very well dowered. Dallas, the American Minister in London, didn't hesitate a moment about sponsoring us. And almost right away, Jacques d'Ambres fell in love with me."

"And almost right away, you realized you cared more for him than you did for me. Or was it that he was a marquis and I was a chess player?"

She did not appear to resent the bitterness in his voice and, for once, he could not doubt the sincerity of her answer. "That was partly it. I've told you about the old grudge. And then, he is very attractive—you've seen that for yourself. I did think I might like to marry him. I let him think so. That's how he happened to say, when he found we were looking for a house in Paris, that we could have his. You've been told that, I know. And I enjoyed living in it, I enjoyed doing all the things and meeting all the people his beau geste had made possible. It was fun—playing the role of his fiancée."

"And simultaneously playing the same role as far as I was concerned. Letting me have the impression that d'Ambres was an 'older man.' That the beau geste, as you call it, and as I've heard others call it, was made largely for the benefit of your mother."

"Yes, I did all that. I've admitted I'm a climber. I've admitted I'm vengeful. I've admitted I'm cruel. You don't need to have me admit I'm sensual. You know it. I reveled in every minute of the interlude with you. I wanted you to make violent love to me."

"But if you were engaged, or practically engaged, to Jacques d'Ambres—"

"Jacques treated me with even greater respect than you did. He didn't make violent love to me. It never occurred to him that he might easily seduce me. Even if it had, he wouldn't have done it. He wanted an unviolated bride, too."

"Charmian, you say dreadful things."

"I'm talking about a dreadful situation. While you and Jacques and one or two others who don't count were all being so noble, I met Gilbert de Lixin. And he hadn't the least idea of being noble. He tried, the very first time we were alone together, to take me by force. He didn't succeed because of an inopportune interruption to our solitude *a deux*—inopportune for him, I mean. Of course, he was furious because he'd been thwarted and he made up his mind he was going to have me. But I'd learned my lesson from you and Jacques—about virginity, I mean. I knew that if he succeeded then he'd never marry me. And neither would anyone else I'd want for a husband."

"Charmian, I simply can't listen to any more. It's too awful, the things you're talking about, the way you're talking about them. And the last thing you've said isn't true. If you'd been the victim of some degenerate creature, you know I'd have felt nothing but the deepest sympathy for you, that it wouldn't have affected my love for you in the least."

"But would you have believed I'd been victimized? Wouldn't you, after your own experience with me, have believed I'd invited what had happened?" And, seeing the signs of deep depression on his face as he tried to protest, she went on hurriedly, "Of course you would have, and I wouldn't have blamed you. And besides—besides, I was fascinated by Gilbert. He cast a sort of spell over me that no one ever had before. I recognized that, in lots of ways, we were alike. I kept him at arm's length because I had enough sense to realize that I'd lose everything I'd gained by my climbing and my vengefulness and my cruelty if I didn't. But it was almost as hard for me to wait as it was for him. If his wife hadn't died when she did, I don't see how I could have."

"And yet, just a few months after your marriage, when you met me at the Slidells', you told me—"

"Oh, don't you understand? Haven't you realized by now that living with Gilbert de Lixin is like living in hell? Can you blame me if I was snatching at the first chance I saw for tenderness and devotion after submitting day after day and night after night to a sadist?"

She was weeping uncontrollably now, and these were not the pretty tears, shed for effect, which he had seen brimming from her eyes and falling gently over her soft cheeks. They were tears which disfigured her lovely face and shook her beautiful body by their violence. Paul could do no less now than put his arm around her, murmuring such words of love and comfort as his trembling lips would permit him to form. Everything he had suspected, everything he had feared, about de Lixin, was true. Only it was worse, much worse than he had guessed. And now that he knew the whole truth, what could he do? How could he rescue Charmian from this habitation of evil in which she was imprisoned? Her helplessness seemed comparable only to his helplessness.

Little by little, the storm of weeping subsided. The sobs came further apart, they shook her less forcibly. At last she looked up, wiping her eyes and pressing her cheek against his.

"I'm sorry," she whispered. "I didn't mean to give way completely like that. But I told you—it's been bottled up inside me so long I couldn't stand it any longer. And I couldn't have talked this way to anyone but you."

He hoped with all his heart that it was humility and not jealousy which prompted the next question. But whatever the undetermined motive, he had to ask it.

"Not to Jacques d'Ambres?"

"Oh no! I think the world of Jacques, he's a wonderful friend, too. But I couldn't have talked to him like this for all sorts of reasons."

"For instance . . . ?" Paul was ashamed of his insistence. But again he felt he had to know and somehow he believed that this time Charmian would tell him the truth.

"Well, in the first place, he wouldn't have understood—all that about Boston and New Orleans and their prejudices, I mean. In the second, I couldn't have said those things about myself to him; I'd have been ashamed to admit I was a climber, that I was cruel and vindictive. You see, he's idealized me, rather, and I'd like him to keep his illusions, while you know how bad I am and love me just the same. In the third place, I couldn't have said what I did about Gilbert—not just because I shouldn't anyway, but because if I did, Jacques would certainly kill him and he wouldn't be careful about it—"

"Careful!"

"Yes, plenty of people get away with murder, and I mean that literally, but Jacques wouldn't be one of them, so then he'd be tried and executed. I know you don't think I stop at much of anything, and when it's just a matter of right and wrong, it's true, I don't. But I couldn't face such a horror as that. I've faced too many already."

"But you meant to talk privately to d'Ambres about something. You schemed to do it the day there was that 'confusion' about the tea party. Or was there some other reason why you were determined to see him alone?"

Paul knew that he should not have asked her that, either; this time, humility had nothing to do with the question; it was prompted only by jealousy. Her manner of answering was unexpectedly disarming. A strange expression, one that he had never seen before on her face, made a curious change in it and she shook her head slowly before answering.

"I suppose you mean that if I didn't want to talk with him confidentially, then I must have been trying to give him the chance to make love to me. I know you'll be surprised at what I'm going to tell you, perhaps you won't even believe me, but it happens to be true; Jacques has never tried to make love to me since my marriage and I've never tried to give him an opening to. I know most people think I would have him for a lover if I weren't afraid Gilbert would find out and kill us both. I know some people think I've taken the risk, that he is my lover. Of course, I know he still cares for me deeply, but when I told you he'd always been very respectful, I wasn't talking just about his courtship; I meant what I said: *'always.'* So now perhaps I've told you one thing that could make you happy."

"You don't know how happy."

"Then I'm sorry to destroy that happiness, but I'm afraid I'll have to. No, I don't mean that I was lying to you: I've never been Jacques' mistress, I never shall be. But I did want to talk to him privately, about something I'm sure you wouldn't approve."

"Do you really need to? The minute I met Jacques d'Ambres, I knew he was the man you ought to have married. He's high principled, he's distinguished, he's charming, he's—"

"I know. He has all the qualifications for both a lover or a husband and it's my loss that I've never had him for either. However, general opinion to the contrary, there are some Frenchmen with very rigid standards when it comes to love affairs. We don't need to talk about that any more. But yes—I do think I need to tell you why I wanted to see him privately. I'm sorry, because you've understood everything so far and you may not understand this."

"I think I shall."

"And it may hurt your feelings."

"You couldn't hurt my feelings after what you've just told me about Jacques."

"I'm not so sure."

For a few moments she was silent, as if carefully choosing her words. Then she began to speak very slowly.

"Do you remember what I said at the Chasseloup-Laubats'? That you couldn't be so silly as to imagine Jacques could influence my views?"

"Yes, very well."

"That was true enough in a way, because he hasn't influenced them. They were the views I held anyhow. But what *you* said was really true— not just true in a way, but wholly true. I'm a Northerner and so are all my people. My father and sister live in New England."

"Yes, but—"

"Oh, I know what else I said! That I was married now to a Frenchman, that I was French myself by adoption, that I lived in France and that Jacques was the only one in my circle who wasn't a Southern sympathizer. And that was also true. The place where I began to lie was when I said that the South to me meant *you*. It doesn't. It doesn't mean anything personal to me at all, except an old grudge. If it had, I wouldn't have done what I did."

Fear suddenly quivered through Paul's body and, with shame, he realized that he was beginning to tremble again. The fear was baseless, it was actually fantastic. Moreover, any betrayal of it might be disastrous. At all costs, he must prevent Charmian from seeing how greatly she had disturbed him, he must speak and act with complete detachment, complete self-control. Somehow, he managed to answer her quietly.

"What did you do, Charmian?"

"It didn't seem like anything very important in the beginning. In fact, it's only begun to seem important today, now that all Paris is talking about a *Nantais* named Petermann who sold some stolen papers to the American Minister. That's why Gilbert's been called into consultation by the Minister of Marine."

So the fear had not been baseless, it had not been fantastic; and it was not a quiver any longer, it was a fiery dart. The next words came haltingly, because the effort to pronounce them was so permeated with pain.

"This time, I'll be the one to say you'd better begin at the beginning. Otherwise, I'm afraid I *won't* understand."

"All right. It began this way: there's a funny little man who lives near our place at Auteuil—a *petit bourgeois*, who's prospered a lot, so that he could afford to travel and who's now settled down to indulge himself by pretending he belongs to the landed gentry. Of course, we know him by sight, since he's a neighbor, and we always stop and pass the time of day with him for a few minutes when we meet him. It would be very much resented, not only by him, but by everyone in the locality, if we didn't. Until recently, we've never spoken about anything but the crops and how things were going in the outlying villages—things like that. But a few weeks ago, when I was horseback riding—"

"Alone?"

"Yes, Aunt Stephanie wasn't in the picture then. I told you it was the tea party that roused Gilbert's suspicions and this was before that. The meeting on the country road led up to my maneuvers to talk with Jacques alone."

"I see. Go on."

"Well, I met this funny little man and after we'd reined in our horses and chatted about the usual things, he said if he might detain me for a minute, he'd like to tell me something that might be of importance to the Marquis d'Ambres who, he knew, was a friend of mine. There was nothing offensive in the way he said it. He isn't an offensive man, just rather ordinary."

"Yes?"

"So I thanked him, and asked him what it was. Please remember he hadn't said this piece of news, whatever it might be, could be of interest to anyone but Jacques. I thought it must be something about property. Jacques has a place not far from ours, too, and he's been hoping to get some additional arpents to enlarge it. I've wanted and wanted to do something for Jacques, to make up, in a small way, for cheating him. Because I did cheat him, just as I cheated you. Do you see how I feel about that?"

"I think so."

"If I'd supposed what he had to tell me had anything to do with Dayton and Bigelow, I wouldn't have listened to this neighbor of mine. You know what I think of them, even if I am what you call a Northern sympathizer."

"Please go on, Charmian."

"You see? You didn't think I needed to tell you this and now you're really interested. My neighbor went on to say he had an uncle who's a confidential clerk in the office of a shipbuilder at Nantes, and that when he, the nephew, I mean, told his uncle about some of the conclusions he'd reached regarding the comparative strength between the North and the South, as a result of a trip he'd made to the United States—what's the matter, Paul? Aren't you feeling well?"

"Yes, but this is quite an exciting story of yours, isn't it? Don't keep me in suspense about what happened next."

"Why, *nothing* happened exactly, then. He said his uncle began to brood over what he'd been told and decided he ought to reveal the contents of some correspondence that was passing through his hands. I thought he meant, reveal it to *Jacques*, so I figured it might be a fine idea. Here was my chance, at last, for that good turn! Then I found out that, in order to get to Jacques, this correspondence should pass through diplomatic channels. And diplomatic channels, in this case, meant Dayton, whom I despise as much as you do."

Paul tried to turn his head away from her and failed, because her cheek was still pressed to his. He also failed to prevent her from realizing that he was trembling.

"Paul, don't take this so hard!" she cried out. "I said I knew you wouldn't approve of what I did, I warned you I might hurt your feelings, and still you insisted you wanted to know why I felt I had to see Jacques privately. And I decided that, in a way, it might be a relief to you if you knew it had nothing to do with lovemaking. And I swear it didn't. All I wanted was to tell him about this roadside meeting, to prepare him for hearing something in the way of a naval secret that might be helpful to him. My plans went awry the day of the tea party because of Aunt Stephanie, as you know; but I managed to get in a few words alone with Jacques the day of the Chasseloup-Laubat luncheon—enough to give him a hint of what was in the wind. Paul, you said I made you happier than you'd been in weeks by telling you that Jacques had never been my lover, that he never would be. Can't you say now you're a little glad that the meeting I tried to arrange was just something about ships?"

He never knew how he managed to answer her, what words he used, what conviction they could have carried, no matter how he chose them. Actually, he was beyond choosing, beyond all coherent thought. Charmian, the one love of his life, was a traitor to his country; if she were capable of one treacherous act, she might well be capable of others. He had sworn he would give his right hand to help the Confederacy. It was his duty to denounce her, to let Slidell, who, through his own assertion, regarded her opinions on international questions as valueless, know the damage she had already done, the further damage she was capable of doing. And he knew he never would. To that extent, from henceforth, he would be a traitor, too. Moreover, he, who had boasted that he could not endure deception, who had sat in judgment on the prevarication of others, would be living a lie for the rest of his life. Yet, despite his confusion, despite his misery, he did not hesitate in making his decision.

Through the mist of his wretchedness, he realized that Charmian was speaking to him again. He still was not sure what he had said to her, but she must have found it not only reassuring, but consoling.

"I'll never forget your loving-kindness to me, Paul, never as long as I live," she was saying. "I must go now. I'll be in trouble if I don't—I mean deeper trouble than I was already. Don't worry, nothing that's happened today will add to it. I'm sure I can explain my delay in getting home very satisfactorily this time. And perhaps you won't blame me quite so harshly any more, if you find I haven't been altogether truthful."

"Darling, you know there's no blame for you in my heart. Only infinite compassion, infinite love."

"Yes, I know that. If I didn't, I couldn't face the future."

"We'll find some way to change the future. I'll keep trying until I do. And, just as soon as I've succeeded, I'll get in touch with you somehow."

"That ought not to be too hard. If nothing were any harder—"

She turned her head and kissed him, lightly, on the cheek against which hers had rested. Then she half freed her hand, pressed his again, freed it altogether. "I'll go back in your room and get my hat," she whispered. "Perhaps I'd better wash my face, too, so that no one can see I've been crying. I'd love to see your *cabinet de toilette*. It makes me feel more as if we lived together. Afterward, I'll be on my way. Please don't come downstairs with me. Remember, I've been in a shop all this time, selecting draperies."

"The time has now arrived when it is comparatively of very little importance what Queen or Emperor may say or think about us. A plague I say on both your houses. I have an autograph letter of the Emperor to a friend, saying that he *had* given an *order* to let the *Rappahannock* go to sea. The letter is dated 7 inst. and yet the permission is still withheld by the Minister of Foreign Affairs."

Extract from a letter written to Mason by Slidell as quoted in *John Slidell* by Louis Martin Sears. (Duke University Press)

40.

Paul could have sworn that, during the next few months, he did not once fall into a deep dreamless sleep. There were nights which he seemed to pass in a sort of stupor, half-waking and half-sleeping, but which were shot through every now and then, with strange fears, the more frightening because they lacked form and substance. There were other nights when one horrible dream succeeded another and he was awakened by his own cries; and there were also occasional periods when he caught himself nodding at his desk, from sheer exhaustion, and called to Louis for coffee, so that he could try to shake off his drowsiness. But neither the stupor nor the dozing really refreshed him and the memory of the nightmares haunted him so vividly that he was not always sure where actuality ended and fantasy began; and with mounting uncertainty came mounting tension. He was no longer surprised to find his hands and his voice trembling; increasingly, it became an effort to prevent them from doing so.

His mother, inevitably, noticed these evidences of mental distress and physical weakness, as he had feared she would, even when they first manifested themselves, the fateful day that he learned of Petermann's treachery —and Charmian's. Telcide was sure he was working too hard or going to more late parties than were good for him, or both. Anxiously, she told him that he should get away from Paris again, this time not to travel rapidly from city to city, but to rest at some quiet place, preferably in the South, where the climate was comparable to Louisiana's. If he liked, she would be glad to go with him; she had heard Pau highly spoken of for such a respite as she was suggesting. He tried to reassure her: his work was not hard at all; it must be the late hours which made him look a little tired. But he enjoyed them, they made a pleasant change from research; he would, however, cut down on them somewhat. As he had no real intention of doing this, his only alternative was to avoid the Sybrandts' house; his absence from it only added to his mother's concern—and to his. He loved her, he would not willingly have made her rather meaningless life more empty than it was already. But he seemed to have no choice.

It was Charmian, of course, who dominated his anguished mind; and it added to his shame that he thought of her first, not as the traitress to the cause of which he should have been the blameless champion, but as the prisoner of a pervert from whom he was powerless to rescue her. True, nothing occurred which might lead him to believe that the conditions under which she lived had changed for the worse; indeed, soon after the scene in his apartment, he was invited to Auteuil for the first time and was able to see for himself the almost unbelievable luxury in which she was enwrapped. The occasion was a great reception and, as the weather was abnormally mild for September, the grounds, as well as the château and its *dépendances*, were utilized for a fairylike fete. The setting, the illuminations, the music, the banquet were all permeated with enchantment; if evil were mingled with the magic, the merging was so skillful that it baffled detection even by one who was watching for it.

Inevitably, considering all he had heard of it and all he had divined without being told, it was the classic pavilion which had the greatest fascination for Paul. It was, unquestionably, the most striking ornament, architecturally speaking, to the property, and its décor was in harmony with its general design. But, for his taste, there were almost too many crystal chandeliers, too many sweeping pastel colored draperies with matching upholstery, all softly padded, too many delicate porcelain figurines, too many genre pictures by Boucher and his disciples. Practically the entire house had been thrown open to the guests, so he did not think he could have missed finding a library, if there had been one, or a billiard room, either; the accent was not on culture or on skill; it was on the pleasures of the senses. It came as no surprise to him that of the several bedrooms available for inspection, each in turn seemed more ornate and more alluring than its predecessor. He assumed that Charmian's chamber was not among those shown; but, after seeing the others, he could visualize it with such clarity that he felt if he were to open a closed door, he would instantly know whether or not he had entered, unbidden, her most private realm.

None of his wandering had been done in solitude. Throughout the evening he had been a member of a group, not always the same as to identity, but much alike as to sophistication and surface gaiety; and, except for failing to respond to some of the broader jests, during the tour of the second story, he had kept up his end of the conversation everywhere and had seemingly entered into the mood of his companions. Since Charmian received her guests and took leave of them while standing at her husband's side, he had no chance to speak with her alone through the greater part of the reception. However, there was a brief interval when they moved separately through the company and, during this time, Paul managed to get in a few words with her surreptitiously.

"Have your father and sister been to visit you in this beautiful place? No? I should think they'd enjoy seeing it and that you'd enjoy having them. I know your father likes Paris."

"He used to, but he tired of it. When he left the last time, he said he didn't ever want to come back and I can't induce him to change his mind. Of course, it didn't seem the same to him after Mama's long hard illness. . . . Oh, Rosina, don't run away like that! I've hardly had a word with you all evening! Is it true that Mathilde is *enceinte?* How thrilling! Is she hoping for a boy or a girl?"

So that was that; Charmian had already appealed, directly or indirectly, to her father and he had refused to come to her. Probably he had favored d'Ambres as a suitor and had disapproved of her marriage to de Lixin, without realizing how grave were the grounds for his disapproval. He might well have told her that she had made her bed and she must lie in it, failing to know the bitter truth of those terrible words. As for Berenice, in this instance, she would have agreed with her father, also because she had no idea why she should disagree. Paul might take a desperate risk and write to her himself. But the mails were not safe any more. If such a letter as he had in mind were intercepted and its contents made known, the consequences might be extremely grave; it would not be safe for him to interfere in that way and he could think of no other. The Shaws were the only people he knew in Boston and he remembered that their attitude toward the Sheppards had been one of marked coolness when he so much as mentioned the name. Charmian was right; she and her family were no more highly regarded in Boston than in New Orleans. And, in New Orleans, there was certainly no one to whom he could appeal.

The conviction of this made it harder and harder for him to enter into the spirit of the fete as this became increasingly gay. But he was growing more skillful in dissembling his true feelings, except during those attacks of uncontrollable trembling and, fortunately, he was spared that tonight. As he was saying farewell, de Lixin detained him for a moment.

"I am glad you have found your way to Auteuil at last, M. Morphy. You are always so bespoken that it is hard to discover a time when you are free. We must really try to get you some evening when we could have a talk about tapestries. I understand you are an authority on them."

"I felt very much complimented to be called into consultation as an expert, but I really can't claim to be one. However, as you know, I am doing research for the Commissioner and he's especially interested in the relative merits of the products of Beauvais and Arras. He asked me to make a careful study of those."

"Ah! Most interesting! We'll plan a small select dinner, not a mob scene like this, and have you for our guest of honor."

"Thank you. Of course, anyone would welcome an opportunity to dine in this beautiful place. But I hadn't felt it was a mob scene tonight. It's been a fete in fairyland."

There was no time for de Lixin to say anything further or for Charmian to say more than, "Good night. Yes, do come to dinner soon." It was already almost morning and other guests were crowding forward, suddenly impatient to be gone after having stayed far past the point of exhilaration and having reached the point of acute fatigue. Quite aside from his keen regret at having been forced into still another falsehood, Paul was disturbed. The reference to the tapestries troubled him deeply. Had the *gouvernante*, who, he felt sure, was inimicable to Charmian, reported his visit in an unfavorable light? Or had Charmian herself gone too far in her reference to an expert and an errand on the rue de Rivoli? The reason he had not been to Auteuil before was because this was the first time he had been invited and, of course, de Lixin knew that as well as he did. Why this sudden show of hospitality? Was there something sinister about that, too?

As so often happened, he did not get to bed until dawn was breaking and never had his nightmares been so terrible. He dreamed that he saw Charmian chained to what he first thought was a bed and then discovered was a rack. Her cries were bloodcurdling and, when he tried to rescue her, the masked torturer who stood close by tightened the screws and laughed. This went on and on. When he finally waked, screaming himself, as he had so often done before, he could not stop this time, even after he was fully awake. He was still screaming when Louis came to make his coffee. It was a long while before the terrified servant succeeded in calming him.

Although the de Lixins' fete was the most splendid to which Paul went that autumn, there were many others, almost as elaborate; and after *Toussaint*, when the season officially opened again, they increased in number and brilliance. All through the winter, he dragged himself to them, both because attendance at such functions was one of the ways in which he was supposed to make himself useful, and because it was only in general society that he could hope to have a glimpse of Charmian. The invitation to dinner at the pavilion never came and he decided with increasing anxiety that de Lixin, having shot his first bolt about the tapestries, intended to leave his prospective guest on tenterhooks as long as possible. Every now and then, however, Paul was able to snatch a few words with Charmian at a party elsewhere and once when this happened, she whispered something that gave him a ray of encouragement.

"I'm afraid from what I said to you once that you think I'm being physically mistreated. I'm not."

Paul was so startled with the abrupt statement that he answered with equal abruptness.

"How did you guess about my dream?"

"I didn't guess anything about a dream. What dream?"

"I dreamed you were being abused—tortured. It was horrible."

"Well, haven't you ever heard that dreams go by opposites? Forget it. You worry too much, Paul. Gilbert thinks I'm beautiful and he enjoys my beauty. He wouldn't do anything that might lessen it."

"Of course, you're beautiful—the most beautiful woman in the world. Do you mean to tell me that the only reason he doesn't abuse you is because, if you were disfigured, it would interfere in his pleasure with you?"

"I don't know. Yes, I suppose so. But things aren't getting any worse. Hush, we mustn't talk any more!"

She was becoming more beautiful all the time, there was no doubt of it and Paul tried to convince himself that, since this was so, her life could not be too hard after all. He never saw her twice in the same dress and each new creation seemed more splendid than the last. As cold weather came on, she went about wrapped in fabulous furs, sable and chinchilla and ermine. She had more and more jewels, too; with these she outshone even the Empress. He was not so dull witted as to be unaware that such extravagances as these could do much to assuage a woman's hurts, even deep ones; he also knew that they sometimes represented a gesture to compensate for such hurts. From the first premise, he could draw some consolation; from the second, he could find only cause for further anxiety.

It was, however, not only his solicitude for Charmian that made any show of gaiety distasteful to him; he could no longer reconcile the light-hearted pursuit of pleasure on the part of Parisians, and Americans living in Paris, with what was happening at home. News from the battle front was growing worse and worse: General Thomas, "the Rock of Chickamauga," in command of the Left Wing, had managed to hold; but the army had finally retreated to Chattanooga, and near there, at Lookout Mountain and Missionary Ridge, the Confederates had been driven from their besieging position.

There had been only one minor Confederate victory, at Olustee, Florida, to counterbalance these reverses; and where there was not actually death and destruction, there was the lack, either voluntary or imposed, of normal comforts and even simple necessities. During the current session of the Confederate Congress, the importation of luxuries and the private exportation of the South's main products had been officially forbidden. In some instances, such orders were no doubt necessary, but Paul believed that, in the great majority, they were not. Throughout the South women of all ages and men who were either too young or too old to fight—and that meant under seventeen or over fifty, except in cases of physical or mental disability —were, of their own free will, denying themselves all but the barest essentials of decent living, and sometimes even those, in order that the army could be fed and clothed. Taxes on property and profits had been increased and a partial repudiation of paper money, with an issue of new notes, had made this type of currency practically worthless, though the costs of all commodities were soaring. Families which had never known hunger before were half starved now. Moreover, almost every house throughout the South was one of mourning for a father or a husband or a son who had been killed. Paul asked himself how it was possible, under these circumstances, for a genuine patriot to eat and drink and be merry in Paris with a clear conscience. Was his failure to denounce Charmian any more damaging to the cause than the failure of many others to make any material sacrifice?

He knew that the Commissioner would have disagreed with him on this score as on several others; but there had been no open friction between them since the scene about the ships and he was still made welcome as a guest by all the Slidells, who continued to entertain on their usual lavish scale. Indeed, he was actually dressing for a dinner of theirs when Louis brought him one of those little notes marked urgent, the sight of which he had come to dread, because he was convinced that, sooner or later, one would bring him bad news from Charmian. This one, however, was from Rosina, and he read it through, not with relief because it had failed to tell him what he had feared, but with a sense of mounting tragedy.

"Dear Paul: Our dinner tonight is canceled for a very sad reason and I know that, loving Pierre as you do, you will share our sorrow.

"We have just learned that dear Aunt Caroline died more than three weeks ago. You know how slowly news comes through nowadays. She has been taken to Edgard for burial. The last wish she expressed was that her tombstone should be marked with the words, 'The country comes before me.' That was the way she felt. That was the way she had always encouraged Pierre to feel. She never allowed her invalidism to serve as an excuse for keeping him at home.

"Of course, Mama will now be in deep mourning all the rest of the spring and there will be no more formal entertaining. But we will hope to see you very soon in a quiet way. I will write you again when it seems possible to suggest a time. Affectionately yours, Rosina Slidell."

Paul folded the note slowly and laid it down on the table beside him. Then he sat for a long while, in the gathering dusk, thinking of the last visit he had paid Caroline Beauregard. How cordial she had been to him personally, how cheerful about the war! He remembered her plans for a party to celebrate Pierre's triumphant return. And now it was she who had died! Of course she had been delicate for a long time, but her condition had not seemed to be serious; and even "Beast" Butler and his lieutenants had left her unmolested through respect; her home had actually been spared confiscation! If any woman in the South had been safe, Paul would have supposed it was Caroline. And Pierre, who had been exposed to constant danger in battle after battle had, so far, come through unscathed. *So far!* What assurance of safety was there in those words?

That night, Paul dreamed that the party was really taking place at the Beauregards' house, that Pierre and Caroline were standing, as she had planned, between the beautiful columns that divided the *salle de compagnie* from the ballroom and welcoming their guests to the strains of dance music. The men were all in full dress uniform, the women in pastel colored dresses with flowers in their hair. On the gallery, champagne and *bonnes bouches* were being served, happy couples were strolling through the patio and the garden was sweet with the scent of roses. . . .

This time, Paul did not wake screaming; instead, his first semi-consciousness was hazy with happiness. Then he had a dreadful thought: in this dream the host and hostess and their happy guests were not living creatures, they were ghosts, all ghosts. The next letter would bring word that Pierre, as well as Caroline, was dead. . . .

However, the next letter brought no sad tidings and neither did any of those that followed soon thereafter. Instead, there was an innocuous succession of information and instructions about routine work, invitations, and appeals for charity. When bad news finally came, it was brought in person by Vignaud, who burst in unceremoniously upon his colleague and collapsed in the nearest chair.

"You were correct and I was wrong," he said. "The game is up. We've lost the ships."

Bulloch had been right in his surmise that if there were no further excitement, after the first frantic flurry of this, the building program would be allowed to proceed without interference, provided the work were done unobtrusively. Rumors regarding it were rife in both London and Paris; but these were neither confirmed nor denied officially and no pressure was brought to bear on the Commissioner to make any positive statement to the French government. For six months, the situation remained unchanged, and hope persisted that when the ships were finished they would be allowed to leave France unimpeded, their destination and purpose unquestioned. With the New Year, this hope had become stronger. Then, early in February, the long-dreaded but long-averted blow fell like a bolt from the blue: Arman and Voruz were formally notified that the ironclads would not be permitted to sail at all, and that though the corvettes could be sold, it must be as unarmed vessels, destined to be used for ordinary trading purposes.

Paul had not been summoned to the conference which Slidell called at this juncture and concluded, not without reason, that the Commissioner did not want to risk a further expression of such views as had caused disharmony at the September meeting. But Paul learned from Vignaud, with whom he was always in close touch, that Arman had proposed a nominal sale of the corvettes to a Danish banker, with provision for redelivery to a Confederate agent at some foreign port. This suggestion had been rejected by Slidell. Since a similar strategy had been attempted in the case of some English-

built ships and had failed, there seemed no sound reason for believing that
a Danish man of straw might be the answer to the problem. The question
was how to find an alternate answer.

Eventually, Slidell had consented, with reluctance, to the sale of the ironclads, and the Confederate naval authorities whom he consulted advised
him to sell the corvettes also. They pointed out that the original intention
had been to use these in conjunction with the ironclads for the purpose of
raising the Southern blockades; since this was no longer practicable, their
potential usefulness was greatly impaired, if not entirely lost. But he remained unconvinced and, at last, a compromise had been reached: the disposal of the ironclads was to be through genuine sale, but that of the corvettes was to be entirely fictitious. Again, matters drifted for several months
without official action of any sort; then Arman had come to Bulloch and
laid a wholly new proposal before him.

This was based on a contract to sell one of the ironclads to Denmark and
a tentative agreement from the Danish government to buy the other. Since
Denmark was at war, however, the Swedish government had agreed to take
over the rams in behalf of its neighbor and Arman, in turn, had agreed to
deliver the vessels at Gothenburg. Such an arrangement would permit him
to send the ships to sea under the French flag and in charge of his own
crew.

"It sounds more and more complicated to me all the time," Paul had
said, shaking his head when Vignaud brought him the report of the conference at which this proposal had been accepted. "Also more and more
hopeless."

"It may be more complicated, *cher,* but I don't think it's necessarily more
hopeless. Arman insists that if we consent to the bona fide delivery of the
first ram, the second can be saved for us."

"How?"

"Well, when the first is ready to sail, the American Minister will probably
ask the Swedish Minister if the vessel belongs to his government and the
answer will be yes. Then she will depart unmolested and arrive at her destination according to contract. This will avert all suspicion from the second
ram and, when she sails under similar circumstances, Arman's crew will take
her to any rendezvous on which we have all previously agreed."

"Do you know what this sounds like to me?"

"No. What?"

"One of those imaginary conversations in foreign language textbooks
which are supposed to help you get all the correct answers to any questions
you may choose to ask, and in which the questions and answers never really
fit. For instance, your question is, 'Where can I find an experienced *accoucheur* for my wife, who is about to be confined?' The answer in the

book would be, 'Monsieur, Doctor X has no peer as an *accoucheur*. He resides at number ten rue de Ste. Marthe and his regular hours for consultation at his office are between ten and one every day, except when he is actually out on a confinement case. In this event, his very able assistant will give him a message and he will come to see your wife as soon as he has delivered the infant which he is now bringing into the world, and assured himself that its mother is doing as well as can be expected. You may have entire confidence in him.' But, instead of being like this, the answer should read, 'Monsieur, there is no experienced *accoucheur* in this miserable village. Your poor wife will have to depend on an ignorant *sage-femme*.'"

In spite of himself, Henri laughed. "I know the kind of book you mean. You and I can be thankful we never had to try learning French that way. Also, I admit I can see the point you are making; but perhaps, in this case, the questions and answers really do fit. Let us hope so. Anyhow, Slidell and Bulloch have both agreed to the scheme with a warning to Arman that they must be assured the government will permit the vessels to leave when they are ready to move, and Arman says there isn't a doubt of it. He's scheduled to have an interview with the Emperor within a fortnight and we are hopeful that will allay all fears."

"There's an awfully wide gap between hope and assurance."

"Yes, but Bulloch has now called in a new-found friend, a certain Emile Tessier, in whom he has a great deal of confidence. By the way, do you know him? It seems he came from New Orleans originally."

"The number of Orleanians who have found their way to Paris is certainly surprising; and it's evidently on the increase all the time. No, I don't know Tessier. Do you?"

"I didn't, until I met him with Bulloch. But that isn't so odd—you and I didn't know each other in New Orleans, either. The Justice's son and the clockmaker's son, you know."

"I wish you wouldn't drag that in."

"Sorry. Anyway, I gather there are various reasons, unrelated to what his father did for a living, that might have prevented us from knowing Tessier. He hasn't been in New Orleans for a long while. At one time, he commanded a Mississippi steamboat and, since then, he's seen much and varied service in all parts of the world. Now he's turned up in Paris and Bulloch's entrusted him with the final details of carrying out this new deal. Tessier feels quite sure he can handle them."

"Do you?"

"Well, I'm not quite such a pessimist as you are, though I confess I'll feel a little easier when those ships are actually out at sea. But I still believe they'll weather the storm."

Vignaud's ability to look on the bright, rather than the dark, side was a great asset and one that Paul envied him. Nevertheless, the latter could not avoid the conviction that the ship situation was too involved to be promising; and though there was again an interval of respite, he did not expect it to last long. However, he was still unprepared for the suddenness and violence of its end, the evening Vignaud burst in upon him with the news that the ships were lost.

It appeared that he had just come from Arman's apartment at the Grand Hotel, whither he had been hastily summoned and where he had found the shipbuilder in a state bordering on frenzy. Captain Tessier, who had been passing a convivial evening with some seafaring friends, had also been located and dragged away from his genial companions. Bulloch, under the impression that everything was under control, had gone back to England. Slidell, apparently under the same impression, was nowhere to be found. He and his family had taken advantage of the lull to have a little holiday. Even Eustis did not know where they could be reached. How any man, let alone a man in a position of such responsibility could go off like that at a time of crisis. . . .

"Here, have some brandy," Paul said, fetching a decanter and glasses from the sideboard. "Then tell me what has actually happened. I suppose they thought there wasn't any crisis—that's what you've been saying to me: Arman had assured Slidell and Bulloch everything was under control, Tessier was competent to handle the details, in short—"

"Oh, for God's sake, don't rub it in!" Vignaud exploded, gulping down the brandy. "Arman finally saw the Emperor and was lucky to escape with his life. Well, it wasn't quite that bad, but he was threatened with imprisonment if he didn't act immediately. The ships are going to be sold tomorrow—tomorrow, do you hear?"

"Yes, I hear. Sold by whom to whom?"

"The government has offered one of the rams and two of the corvettes to Prussia, the second ram to Denmark and the two Nantes corvettes to Peru. All these offers have been accepted. Arman is receiving his official orders from the Minister of Marine. The Confederacy is completely out of the picture."

"Even when a direct hit was scored by the *Alabama* upon her adversary the damage was comparatively slight. Once a seven-inch shell lodged in the stern-post of the *Kearsarge*—the most vital point of the vessel. If it had exploded it would have shattered the wood-ends which form the counter of the hull and the ship would probably have floundered. But it did not explode. Twenty-eight times did such shells strike the enemy, but the *Alabama*'s powder had deteriorated through being kept too long in a bad climate and also in the wrong place on board.

"Captain Semmes wrote afterward: 'Perceiving that our shells, though apparently exploding against the enemy's sides, were doing him but little damage, I returned to solid shot firing; and several naval experts who witnessed the engagement from the hills near Cherbourg have told me that they were struck with a difference in the appearance of the flame and the smoke produced by the explosions of the shells from the two ships. Those from the *Kearsarge* emitted a quick bright flash, and the smoke went quickly away in a fine blue vapor, while those from the *Alabama* exhaled a dull flame and a mass of sluggish gray smoke.' "

" 'The loss of the *Alabama*,' wrote Secretary Mallory to Bulloch when the news reached Richmond (July 8th), 'was announced in the Federal papers with all the manifestations of joy which usually usher the news of great national victories, showing that the calculating enemy fully understood and appreciated the importance of her destruction. You must supply her place if possible, a measure which, important in itself, the information conveyed by your letter renders of paramount importance.' "

"It is pleasant to be able to add that several of the French mariners who went to the rescue of the *Alabama*'s drowning crew, one pilot named Mauger having saved twelve men, were granted gold and silver medals by the Emperor and cited in the *Moniteur*. For saving others of the crew, including the captain and several officers, the English yachtsman, Lancaster, was held up to opprobrium by some of the Federal newspapers, and the pleasant dictum of Secretary Seward, 'It was the *right* of the *Kearsarge* that the pirates should drown,' was widely approved in the North."

John Slidell and the Confederates in Paris (1862–65)
by Beckles Willson, copyright 1932 by B. Willson.
Used by permission of the publishers, G. P. Putnam's Sons, N.Y.

41.

"Our military position is promising in the extreme, and I do not think I go too far in saying that the Federal campaign of 1864 is already a failure. We may have met with reverses, but nothing at present indicates any danger comparable with the menacing effect of affairs prior to the success of our noble army in repulsing the repeated and desperate assaults of the Federal Army with a slaughter perfectly appalling."

Slidell read the letter, just received from Benjamin, through a second time and turned to Vignaud. "You had better take a careful look at this, too," he said. "Then perhaps you will stop singing that mournful dirge of yours to the effect that the Confederacy is as good as finished, just because we have been double-crossed by a soi-disant diplomat who is actually only one cut above a charlatan, and an opera bouffe imperial actor."

Vignaud accepted the letter in silence, read it and returned it to Slidell without comment. He had been back only a few days from Cherbourg, where he and Eustis had both been sent by the Commissioner when a battle seemed imminent and inescapable between the *Alabama,* which had taken refuge in the harbor, and the *Kearsarge,* which was lurking at the breakwater to attack her. The *Alabama* had been at sea for two years, always on the alert, with no rest for her boilers and little or no chance to supply deficiencies or repair injuries, capturing an occasional prize, but finding fewer and fewer all the time, as shipping became an increasingly hazardous venture. Finally, as her Commander, Captain Semmes, put it, she had "come limping in after a long chase, like a weary foxhound," hoping the French authorities would allow him time to refit her. The news of her arrival was immediately wired to Paris by the American Consul at Cherbourg; and Dayton, with equal promptness, ordered Captain Winslow, the Commander of the *Kearsarge,* which lay fully armed and equipped at Flushing, to start at once for Cherbourg. Upon reaching there, he did not even anchor; before him, at last, was his eagerly awaited chance to grapple with the enemy.

He did not have to wait long. Captain Semmes had been tempted to try stealing out, under cover of darkness, as he had often successfully done from other ports, and had decided against it, as a covert action unworthy of him in this instance. With a gesture characteristic of Confederate bravado, whether in the cavalry or the navy, he had notified Winslow, through the American Consul, that he would come forth and fight as soon as he had finished coaling. Early in the morning of June 19th, the *Alabama* steamed out of Cherbourg harbor. Only a few hours later, Eustis and

Vignaud, who, like hundreds of others, had watched the battle from the hills above Cherbourg with field glasses and telescopes, saw the *Alabama* slowly sink into the Channel, while the *Kearsarge,* her crew almost unscathed, steamed away with flying colors.

It had soon been apparent that gunnery was to be a decisive factor and Semmes, who had been troubled because his crew lacked target practice, had recognized his inferiority in this respect and had tried to maneuver closer to his enemy. But the *Alabama* had received terrific punishment almost from the first. At least twenty eleven inch shells crashed into her sides and through her decks, while the amount of damage she was able to do in return was comparatively slight. The *Kearsage* was protected amidships by cables of steel chain, which were stowed outside and which hung vertically over the engine space, forming a cover for it. All too quickly, it was evident what the outcome of the battle must be; the hull of the *Alabama* was riddled, and the sea was pouring into her through huge holes near her water line. Nine men had already been killed and twenty-one wounded. Captain Semmes made a last desperate attempt to save his ship by eking out her dying engines with sails; but it was already too late when a last searching broadside raked through her. She filled so rapidly that the fires were extinguished in the furnaces and Semmes, hoping to prevent further loss of life, hauled down his colors and dispatched a boat to inform the enemy of his condition. The tragic wreck of the *Alabama* was now only about four hundred yards from the proud *Kearsarge,* but five more shots were fired after the colors had been struck. The waist boats were already torn to pieces, but the quarter boats still held out; and into these the wounded were lowered by men unable to swim, who remained with them. The rest of the crew, in obedience to a previous order, jumped overboard at a given signal. No help came to them from the enemy; the boats of the *Kearsarge* had apparently suffered more damage than was supposed. At all events, ten members of the *Alabama's* crew had already drowned before any of these boats were afloat and even then only two came to the rescue. It was due entirely to the prompt action of a private English yacht and some small French fishing craft, which happened to be in the harbor, that Captain Semmes and some of his officers and men reached shore alive.

After watching the battle from the hills, Vignaud, still stunned by the roar of the guns and appalled by the slaughter he had seen, had gone down to the quay to join the crowd which was waiting to help the survivors ashore and receive the corpses of those who had drowned, to prepare them for burial. It was not made up of mere onlookers any longer. These Frenchmen had brought food and wine and clothing with them, they rushed forward cheering and shouting to clap the haggard and water-soaked on the back and to embrace the wounded. The American Minister's son, who had been sent to support the Consul, promptly reported this as an "indecent spectacle on the part of the Cherbourg population toward pirates and rebels." It had seemed to Vignaud, on the contrary, a very touching one, on the part of an essentially warm-hearted people toward the victims of a major disaster. He had been tremendously moved by it; and, when Slidell handed him Benjamin's cheery letter, he had not even recovered from the effects of this scene, the terrific impact of the battle itself and the sight of the drowning, unrescued seamen struggling through the waves which finally engulfed them. . . .

He was suddenly aware that the Commissioner was speaking to him, speaking rather irritably. "What's the matter, Henri?" Slidell asked. "Haven't you any comment to make on such an important communication?"

"Yes," Vignaud said slowly. "Of course, when Benjamin wrote that letter, he hadn't heard about the battle at Cherbourg. If he had, he wouldn't have said philosophically, 'We may have had some reverses,' as if these didn't amount to much. He'd have said mournfully, 'We've had very serious reverses.' After the news does get to Richmond, I think he'll admit it or that Mallory will do it for him. I think one of them will say we've got to try to make up for the loss of the *Alabama* somehow if we're to carry on with any hope of success."

"We could have made up for it with those ships at Nantes and Bordeaux, if it hadn't been for a kind of crooked diplomacy that should have died out with the last century."

Vignaud refrained from a direct reply. He thought no useful purpose would be served by reminding the Commissioner that the "crooked diplomacy" had not been entirely one-sided. True, it had been hard to reconcile the virtuous indignation and vast astonishment, recently expressed by the Minister of Marine regarding the character of the ships under construction, with the formal authorization, given a year earlier, to arm four of these very ships with an armament of twelve thirty pounders each. That he should now write as if he had made a startling discovery would have actually had a comic side, if the general situation had not been so serious that it was hard to find anything amusing about it. As Bulloch had pointed out, the Commissioner and his associates had encouraged Arman to go ahead in any way he thought best; and, as Morphy had pointed out, it was a way of deception. The Commissioner's heated refusal to see matters in their true light did not alter the facts of the case.

"I doubt that the ironclads and the corvettes would have compensated for the loss of the *Alabama* in any event," Vignaud said at last, still speaking very slowly. "Materially, perhaps. Spiritually, no. They're foreign ships and our people would always have thought of them that way. The *Alabama* was almost bone of our bone and flesh of our flesh, if you know what I mean. When the Paris press came out with the headline, *LA MORT de l'ALABAMA*, I wished I had thought of writing about it that way myself, instead of just an insignificant piece based on a chat I had with one of the survivors, who'd been two years afloat and who was now left stranded in a strange land, without a *sou* to send to his wife and children in Mobile. Of course, I could help him out, as far as that was concerned, and I did; but what the hell? His ship is dead, even if he isn't and she's his beloved dead —*our* beloved dead, too. It's as hard to bear as if she'd been a human being. Everyone in the South is going to feel that way about the *Alabama;* but no one would feel that way about those ships at Nantes and Bordeaux if they went down the way she did."

"They'd have kept a lot of other human beings from meeting their death."

"Granted. So does a levee. But you don't think of it as having or giving life."

"Henri, you're beginning to talk like Paul. I had a whole week of him in this office while you and George were away. I'd have sent him to Cherbourg, instead of you, but I knew he'd collapse completely if he actually saw the carnage of a battle or even listened to the roar of one. He's on the verge of a nervous breakdown anyway, just from hearing about those on the other side of the Atlantic. Oh, he was all right as a pinch hitter! He did a good enough job. He's no shirker when it comes to hard work, even if he has allowed himself to get into this morbid state. And he's reasonably intelligent—no, hang it all, he's very intelligent. But I'm fed up with high ideals and dramatic figures of speech. No matter how silent Paul is, you know the high ideals are there, and when he does start talking, in come the dramatic figures of speech. I've been glad to feel the office was getting back to normal again. Don't disappoint me."

"I'll try not to. But I'm afraid you're right about Paul. He doesn't seem well. And he's a congenital worrier."

"Well, show him this letter from Benjamin."

"I'm also afraid it wouldn't be any more encouraging to him than it was to me. Whatever Benjamin says, the generals leading our noble army haven't repulsed quite as many Federal forces as they should have, in order to give us a certainty of sustained success."

"Good God, what about Lee at Spotsylvania Court House? What about Beauregard at Drury's Bluff and Petersburg? Incidentally, when you take that tone about our generals, you might remember that Lee is one of the Lord's Anointed, if any man ever was, and that Beauregard is my brother-in-law."

"I do remember it, sir. But you said you wanted me to be realistic. What about Butler's advance toward Richmond from Fortress Monroe? What about Sherman's advance toward Atlanta from Chattanooga? What about Grant's steady march south?"

"Well, what about them? Advances aren't battles. I'm sorry I even bothered to show you Benjamin's letter. You don't recognize good news when you hear it any more."

Slidell picked up the letter again, as if to feast his eyes on it and Vignaud took this as a signal that he might return to his own desk. He was worried himself, not only about Paul, who was unquestionably very far from well, but about the Commissioner. Ever since the first defection of the Minister of Marine, which had occurred ten months previously, the fate of the ships had preyed on Slidell's mind and, with each successive crisis in regard to them, his attitude had been more resentful, until now his natural geniality seemed to be more or less permanently embittered. And his mental mood had also been affected by a hostile demonstration directed against him personally, the first to indicate that his great personal popularity might have been impaired.

Near the close of the previous year, he had received a communication signed only, "Your sincere well-wisher, L. D., a student at the Lycée," which read:

"I write this letter to put you on your guard against a plot on the part of a number of American students (Yankees) at the Lycée Conderset, to make a personal demonstration against you on New Year's Day. Knowing that you habitually leave your residence in the Avenue d'Antin every afternoon for the purpose of visiting your office, they propose waylaying you and subjecting you to indignity. They intend carrying a banner (which I myself have seen) inscribed, 'Down with Slidell the Slave Driver,' with an insulting caricature of yourself dragging a slave in chains. They have also composed a song of most vituperative character which they intend to sing. I do not think they intend any personal assault (they are too cowardly for that), but it is well that you should not be taken by surprise."

Upon receipt of this missive, Eustis advised the Commissioner to inform the police, but he laughed at the idea, saying he did not object to letting these young firebrands have their prank and that anyway, it might be only a *canard*. On New Year's Day, after Eustis and Vignaud had left the office to pay the customary calls, he set out, as usual, for his stroll and noticed a group of about twenty at the corner of the Champs Elysées. They were carrying a banner which answered the description in the letter and they immediately began catcalling and singing insulting songs. Some of them were armed with peashooters, but only one or two of these missiles actually found their mark. However, a few of the youngsters grew bolder and aimed wads of paper straight in Slidell's face. This was too much for the Commissioner; he turned quickly, caught one boy by the collar and cuffed him soundly. As the youngster wriggled to get away, he lost his coat, which remained in Slidell's clutches; and when the Commissioner reached home, he showed it to his family with the humorous comment that it was a trophy representing a brush with the enemy! The coat had the name of its owner on the lining, and the next day was returned to the Lycée with Mr. Slidell's compliments.

Although, at the time, he had treated the episode as a joke, there was no question that it had added to his bitterness. His office force and, indeed, all his associates were conscious of this change in him; but Paul, who was more sensitive than any of the others, and who had offended the Commissioner by his stand on the ships, suffered most by the loss of that fatherly friendliness which, at first, had been shown him in such abundant measure. Slidell did not mean to be unkind, but his shortness of temper revealed itself in a dozen ways, some of them more deeply wounding than he realized. Among these was a question about the de Lixins.

"How much have you seen of Charmian and Gilbert lately?" he inquired one day as Paul was leaving the office.

"Almost nothing. Does it matter?"

"Only in one respect. As you know, my main reason for interest in de Lixin, whom I despise, lay in his closeness to Chasseloup-Laubat. Now that the Minister of Marine has gone back on us, I should like to know whether or not de Lixin has followed him into the Yankee camp. I think it's quite possible. After all, Charmian is a Yankee."

Paul's heart missed a beat. "Yes, that's true," he said. "But if I understood you correctly, you thought her views weren't important anyway."

"I believe I did say something of the sort, when I was sure her husband was with us. But if she found he had changed his policy, that might make a difference; while she was silent on the subject before, she might now begin to talk about it. I can see that she could do some damage after all. If you have a chance, or could make one, I'd like you to sound her out. Yes, you'd better make one."

"I think the de Lixins are in England right now, sir."

"That's so, they are. You do keep informed, don't you? Do you happen to know whether or not they are to be gone any length of time?"

"No, sir. I'll try to find out."

"I think you'd better. Especially as their views, if these are given expression there, might do us even more harm in England than in France. What we need now are French advocates for the Confederacy, not enemies of it, with the English."

Paul did not dare make direct inquiries, either at the Hotel de Lixin on the rue de Varenne or at the pavilion in Auteuil. At the former place, he would certainly be recognized; his call would be reported and very possibly given more significance than he would wish. And he rightly guessed that uninvited guests at the pavilion were always discouraged and often suspected. He decided that Madame Chasseloup-Laubat would probably provide his best source of information, that she would attach no undue importance to a polite but casual call, and that whatever her husband had done, as a matter of expediency, her Southern birth and her relationship with Beauregard would still have weight with her. He was fortunate in finding her at home, playing in the garden with her baby and without other visitors. She welcomed him warmly and soon gave him to understand that he had been right in his surmise. In fact, she even went so far as to say she was sorry there had been trouble about the ships and that she still hoped and believed some way might be found of giving official support to the Confederacy. Eventually, it was she who brought the name of the de Lixins into the conversation before Paul had been obliged to ask any questions.

"Apparently, they're having a very gay time in London; of course, this is still the height of the season. . . . Aren't they funny, French and English both, with their insistence on spending the most beautiful time of the year in town, instead of enjoying it in the country? Can you imagine staying in New Orleans all summer if you had a plantation on the River Road?"

"No, I can't. . . . And I'm interested to hear you speak of the French and the English as if you still considered yourself an American."

"Well, I do. Doesn't Charmian?"

"I don't know. Does she?"

"Oh, I'm sure she does! Of course, she's tactful and I try to be, too. She wouldn't dream of expressing any views that might embarrass her husband. I mean, publicly. She might if she were talking to you confidentially, the way I did just now when I told you how I felt about the ships."

"I'm very much honored by your confidence. I'm not sure, however, that Charmian would speak to me so candidly."

There he was, trapped into another lie. Charmian had bared her heart and soul to him and had thus given him a memory which he would keep to the day of his death. Madame de Chasseloup-Laubat answered guilelessly and unsuspiciously.

"Why, I think she would, if you asked her a candid question! She knows as well as I do that you're completely trustworthy."

"I hope and believe she does. But somehow I've got the impression—perhaps mistakenly—that she isn't encouraged to have private talks with her old friends."

Madame de Chasseloup-Laubat smiled. "I'm afraid you're right about that, if the old friends are delightful bachelors. Gilbert's almost insanely jealous. Now if it were my husband, who's more than thirty years older than I am, it would be more understandable—I mean, more forgivable—

wouldn't it? But I'm thankful to say there's nothing of the green-eyed monster about him."

"Which is greatly to his credit."

"And a little to my credit too, isn't it? I've never given him the slightest cause for anxiety and never shall. Whereas Charmian—well, I'm devoted to her and I know you are—but we both know she's something of a flirt, don't we? And Gilbert had to wait for her so long that now he's got her he wants to keep her very much to himself. My husband and I are hoping that after a year or two he'll be more reasonable. But that won't do you any good as far as finding out her present views is concerned, will it? That's what you really want to know, isn't it? Or rather, whether or not she'd be willing to express them if they're different from Gilbert's and, incidentally, what his are now?"

"Since we're speaking frankly and trusting each other, I may as well tell you that's exactly what I want to know."

"Then if you like I'll be glad to ask her myself, as soon as she gets back from England, and pass on the information to you the next time you come to see me after that. I hope I won't have to wait too long for your next visit. We Orleanians must stand together, mustn't we? I mean the Slidells, Natalie Benjamin, Henri Vignaud and you and I."

"Do you include Tessier in this tight little group?"

She laughed. "Now that might be expecting too much of me! No, don't look so upset! After all, I hardly know the Captain. The rest of us are old friends."

Paul was afraid the Commissioner might think he had been indiscreet by talking so freely with the wife of the Minister of Marine. On the contrary, Slidell praised him for handling so skillfully the thorny question of the de Lixins' views. A week later, when they returned from England he was able to report, thanks to Madame de Chasseloup-Laubat, that the Prince was maintaining a rather indifferent attitude in regard to the ships, while still inclined to favor the cause of the Confederacy in his usual tepid way; and that, as far as was known, Charmian shared her husband's views and certainly had not expressed herself publicly to the contrary.

"Good!" the Commissioner said heartily. "I'm more relieved than you'd guess to know all that. De Lixin may seem indifferent and tepid and so on and so on, but he's fantastically rich, and the day might come when he could be persuaded to part with some of his wealth in a good cause, if he could see an advantage for himself in it—not a financial advantage, he doesn't need that, but something else. And, quite aside from what you found out concerning the de Lixins, you've done me a very real service by getting me that statement about Orleanians standing together from Marie Louise. She does have influence with her husband. He not only adores her; he respects her. What's more, she's given him an heir. If anyone can swing him back into our camp again, I believe it would be his wife."

Slidell was definitely pleased with Paul's report, and his entire staff benefited by his change of mood. Moreover, when he sat down to compose his next letter to Benjamin, written after an amicable encounter with Napoleon at the races in the Bois de Boulogne, he was able to express himself in a more happy vein than would have been possible a short time earlier:

"The Emperor, after making enquiries about my family, asked me what I thought of our military position, especially in Georgia, and of the effect of the fall of Atlanta. I said I was happy to assure him that the abandonment of Atlanta was a much less serious matter than was generally supposed in Europe, as we had removed all the valuable machinery and material weeks before Sherman took possession; that the only effect of Sherman's advance was to increase the distance from his base of supplies and make his communications more liable to interruption; that I did not think it at all improbable that we should soon hear of his falling back upon Chattanooga. He asked if the report of the surrender of Mobile was true. I said that I was confident not only that the report was premature, but that we should be able to hold Mobile as we had Charleston."

Admittedly, this opinion was given tongue in cheek. Nevertheless, the Commissioner found himself able to continue in much the same vein.

"I went on to say that we might soon expect stirring news from the armies near Petersburg, and I doubted not that Lee would give a good account of Grant. He expressed his admiration and astonishment at what he had achieved against such enormous odds, and his confidence in our ability to maintain ourselves; he spoke of the impossibility of occupying a territory like ours, and his regrets that our many victories had not been followed by more decisive results. I answered that this was susceptible of easy explanation; that we were always fighting against superior numbers and had no strong reserves to follow up our successes; that the troops that had been engaged were generally exhausted by fatigue; that our great battles had usually been a series of desperate fighting for several days, and while we had inflicted much heavier losses on the enemy, we had necessarily been much crippled ourselves. Besides, our cavalry, from the difficulty of renewing our stock of horses, was much less numerous and efficient than it had been, and we were unable to pursue and harass a beaten and retreating enemy with such effect as would be expected in Europe under similar circumstances."

He read the letter through with satisfaction, signed it, sealed it, and handed it to Eustis for dispatch, just as his secretary approached his desk to announce a visitor.

"Captain Bulloch is calling, sir. He's had a new idea about the French ships. He thinks possibly something may be retrieved from the wreckage after all."

"Well, haven't I kept trying to tell all you crepehangers that things were bound to take a turn for the better, sooner or later? Send him in, send him in!"

As usual, Bulloch was cautious in his comments, but it was evident that his views were illumined by a feeble ray of hope. The sale of the ships had gone through without a hitch, Voruz and Arman had been liberally paid, and for some days Prussian and Danish naval officers had been engaged in walking about the decks of their newly acquired property, supervising the finishing touches on it, and seemingly feeling no personal animosity toward each other, even though their respective countries were enemies. Hardly had two of the corvettes and one of the rams been hurried off to Prussia, however, when an armistice was declared; there was now every prospect that the war might come to a sudden end. The remaining ram had not been delivered to Denmark and Bulloch thought that the Danish government might consider making a deal for her, since her immediate usefulness to it had passed. To be sure, she might have been equipped in a way that would not suit the service of the Confederacy and the equipment could have progressed so far that it would be impractical to change it. But if this could be ascertained. . . .

"You mean you'd like to go to Bordeaux and find out for yourself whether or not we could use her?" Slidell inquired with eager interest.

"No, I don't think that would be wise. I'm afraid my presence might arouse an instant suspicion. What about sending Mr. Morphy again?"

"Heaven forbid! Have you forgotten what happened the last time we did that?"

Eustis tried vainly to signal Slidell. In his usual unobtrusive way, Paul had just entered the office and was standing in the doorway, a sheaf of papers in his hand. The Commissioner was far too excited by what Bulloch had just told him to notice the new arrival.

"I thought you might say that," Bulloch, who had not noticed him, either, went on practically. "My sober second thought was that we might send Captain Tessier. Arman knows him already, so he'll be given every facility for finding out—well, whatever there is to find out. I think Arman would really welcome the chance, because he was mortified over the last debacle. Another advantage is that almost nobody else knows that Tessier was connected with that."

"I believe you've got a very sound idea. Start Tessier on his way to Bordeaux as soon as you can. . . . Why, hello, Paul! When did you get here?"

"Just this minute," he said, coming forward with his sheaf of papers.

A lavender lie such as that did not matter very much, in comparison with the web of dark falsehood in which he was inextricably caught. In fact, nothing seemed to matter very much, not even the fact that he was no longer considered capable of undertaking a delicate mission, because he had told the truth about the first one with which he had been entrusted. He was sorry to see this one confided to such a soldier of fortune as Tessier. The Confederacy deserved better than that of its representatives. Aside from this, he had no feeling about the matter.

His headache was worse than usual today, his trembling more uncontrollable. He did not ask to go home before his usual time, but finally the Commissioner suggested it. Slidell did this kindly, but the very kindness would have added to Paul's sense of humiliation, if he had been capable of any such feeling at this point. As it was, he merely thanked the Commissioner without any secret feeling of resentment and left the office.

He was too tired for the walk which he normally enjoyed, so he hailed the first passing fiacre and sat slumped on his seat until he reached his destination. He mounted the stairs slowly, stopping to rest at the end of each flight. As he did so, he thought with nostalgia of the evening when he and Charmian had gone up these same stairs together, while she jested about being a good climber, all the time holding fast to his arm, so that he could feel her pressing against him. How long it was since he had seen her, how ardently he wished that they might be together now, that in the glory of her presence he might forget his inadequacy, his loneliness and his despair!

He unlatched the door and saw her sitting in the salon waiting for him.

I TELL MY HEART

I tell my heart (and yours)
That love, like truth, endures:
Thorn-crowned and scourged, can bend its back and bear
Its cross to each new station of despair.

I tell my heart love's beauty can outlast
Nailed hands and feet,
And when the passion of the grief is past,
All that was sweet
Shall have its resurrection
In termless Easters of our recollection.

But oh, I am afraid
That love so crucified must surely die,
And of the beauty nothing will remain.
And only the black remembrance of this pain
Shall stand, a cross against a crimson sky.

Georgie Starbuck Galbraith
(The New York *Times*)
March 26, 1958

42.

Instinctively as she rose to greet him, he rushed forward and took her in his arms, holding her close and covering her face with kisses, before he even began to murmur words of love or to voice his joy in her presence. "It's almost as though you knew how much I was longing for you, darling," he said at last. "While I was climbing those endless stairs, I kept thinking. . . ." He broke off, his heart clutched by fear. "You shouldn't be here!" he cried. "You know that as well as I do. Suppose one of your acquaintances saw you come in and told your husband? For that matter, your own coachman might do so."

"My own coachman didn't bring me. I came in a fiacre. Yes, I know it's imprudent, but it isn't actually dangerous, not this time, Paul. Gilbert's gone back to England, or rather to Scotland, after grouse. He's never gone anywhere without me before, but this shoot was to be all men and none of the others were taking their wives, so he couldn't very well insist on taking his. And it's just the kind of sport he dotes on. He left me in charge of Aunt Stephanie and thank God she takes long naps."

"But someone must have seen you leave the grounds!"

"Yes, on horseback. For a quiet ride over country roads. That hasn't been actually forbidden yet, though a groom usually goes with me. As a matter of fact, he did this time. But after we'd gone just a kilometre or so, I told him to take my mount back to the stable, that I felt more like a walk today than a ride after all. I saw him out of sight before I went on to the *Place* and got a cab."

"It still sounds dangerous to me. The groom would know you couldn't walk for hours; when you didn't come back, he'd start a search for you. And you're a very familiar figure in Auteuil and you'd be doubly conspicuous in riding clothes."

"Paul, I know all that, but I *had* to come. I'm frightened. I needed to talk to someone and you're the only person I can trust. I've told you that before. Your nice servant let me in without any question at all and now he's gone to do errands. He tactfully told me he expected to be gone for hours. Won't you invite me to sit down again and let me tell you what the matter is?"

"Oh, darling, I'm sorry! But I was so overjoyed—and then so startled—that I forgot—"

"Never mind, let's sit side by side on the sofa as we did before, shall we? With my hand in yours." And, when they were seated, she added in a whisper, "Do you remember the *gouvernante*—that awful woman we saw when we went to the *Duquesa's* rooms?"

"Yes, of course. I also remember that when I was telling you good-bye, the night of your fete, the Prince said I must come to dinner some night soon so we could talk about tapestries. I've worried about that ever since, thinking there must be something sinister connected with it, wishing I knew what it was, yet dreading to find out."

"I know. A mystery seems more and more like a threat the longer it's drawn out, doesn't it? Well, this is a threat."

"Of what, Charmian? You said you were going to explain."

"I am, but it's all so involved, so hideous."

He saw that, for the moment, it was actually impossible for her to go on and did not attempt to hurry her. "I asked Gilbert to discharge that woman—for insolence," she said at last. "He controls everything about household arrangements, but usually, if I mention some minor preference, he humors me in it. Actually, he indulges me in a good many small ways. When he asked me what she'd been insolent about, I said the care of the *Duquesa's* rooms. I didn't think he'd ask any further questions, because he's always avoided discussing anything about the *Duquesa*, and I didn't think he'd refuse to do what I'd requested, because it's the kind of small favor he's always been willing to grant before. Well, he didn't ask any questions. After all, he didn't need to, since Aunt Stephanie had already told him that you'd gone to the Hotel de Lixin with us, and the maître d'hôtel had innocently revealed that, after she'd left, you'd gone upstairs with me to give an expert opinion on the tapestries. Gilbert was annoyed at that and sarcastic about it, but he wasn't actually angry—it was obvious we hadn't been alone a single minute. But he refused to discharge the *gouvernante*. I couldn't imagine why, but I didn't press the matter. I didn't think I'd have to see her again very soon, and I didn't worry about your visit to the Hotel de Lixin, even when Gilbert spoke the way he did about the small dinner. I felt sure that, if you didn't know anything about tapestries before that, you'd start learning immediately and be prepared for a conversation on the subject."

"You were right about that, of course."

"Then, just this morning, the *gouvernante* came to see me. It seems she asked the coachman where he took me when you and I left the Hotel de Lixin, and he said to a shop on the rue de Rivoli where tapestries are repaired and sold. I don't think for a minute he was trying to betray me; I think he believed what I told him, that I was going shopping, and saw no reason why he shouldn't make exactly the answer he did. Next she asked him which block he took me to and he told her that, too. Then she made careful inquiries and found there isn't any tapestry shop in this block. And finally she found out this is where *you* live."

"I see," Paul said, fearing more and more that he did.

"Now she's threatened to tell Gilbert, as soon as he gets back, that I came to see you. He was angry because you'd gone to the *Duquesa's* rooms, not so much because you'd gone with me, under all the circumstances, but because he doesn't want anyone to go there. However, he didn't actually make me suffer on account of that, except by keeping me in suspense as to exactly what he was going to do when he invited you to dinner. But if he finds out I came here, he'll take it for granted that you're my lover. Nothing could persuade him you're not, and it wouldn't be strange, either, considering the sort of life he's led himself. And if he believed that—"

She broke off, but Paul did not need to have her finish the sentence. He knew that if de Lixin believed that, he might commit almost any outrage. Charmian was not weeping now, as she had been when she came to him before, but she was rigid with terror. The very fact that she had not yet lost her self-control was in itself alarming, because he feared that when she did lose it, after so much repression, her state would be hysterical and there would be no telling what she might say or do. It required a tremendous effort for him to remain calm himself, to question her collectedly, so that he might understand the whole dreadful situation better and, therefore, be able to advise and, if possible, act more intelligently and effectively.

"There are still one or two things that aren't entirely clear to me, darling. I suppose the *gouvernante* is trying to blackmail you?"

"Yes. She claims she isn't paid enough. She's asked Gilbert for a raise in salary and he's refused to give her another."

"Another?"

"Yes, he's kept raising it, steadily, ever since we were married. I know that, not through him, but through servants who've kept coming to me, claiming that they were entitled to higher wages, on the ground that if the *gouvernante* gets more and more, there's no reason why they shouldn't, too. And, on the whole, he's been very liberal, I'm bound to admit that. Stinginess isn't one of his faults. But the *gouvernante's* demands are something astronomical and he's finally refused to go any higher. She insists that I must make him. And of course, if I try to, he'll ask how it happens I'm pleading her cause, when just a little while ago, I wanted him to discharge her. I won't be able to give a very satisfactory answer to that and then he'll go to work to find out why. He'll succeed, too. Don't ask me how. But he will. He'll find out that she's been to me and that she's threatened me and what about."

Charmian was becoming more and more rigid, her voice more and more unnatural. Paul found himself fighting for sustained rationality.

"I still don't understand completely, darling. Why should the *gouvernante* hate you so, why should she want to harm you? You've never actually abused her, have you? You know you said you'd like to, in a horrible way, that day as we were leaving the *Duquesa's* rooms. But she couldn't have overheard, that is, I don't see how she could have, and if you've never—"

"No, she didn't overhear, and I've never actually abused her, though I meant what I said. I'd like to see her whipped, whipped until—"

"Don't say it again, Charmian. Just tell me why she does hate you."

"Because I married Gilbert. Because I supplanted the *Duquesa*, whom she adored."

"But the *Duquesa* was dead!"

"Yes, the *Duquesa* was dead. But that only made matters worse."

"You mean that if you'd consented to be de Lixin's mistress, instead of becoming his wife. . . ."

"No, not exactly. . . . Yes, of course that's what I mean."

"Please, Charmian, don't begin to be evasive! I haven't understood fully so far, but that's not your fault. You've tried to make everything clear to me. Now, when you say first one thing and then another—"

"I told you before that the *Duquesa* died very suddenly. And you know that Gilbert and I were married very soon after."

"I can understand that the *gouvernante* might have thought such a prompt marriage was disrespectful to the *Duquesa's* memory, that it might be resented. But that wouldn't make it reasonable for her to hate you and hound you. You weren't responsible for the *Duquesa's* sudden death!"

"No, but I believe—I'm afraid she thinks I was."

"Charmian, what are you trying to tell me?"

The hysteria which he had been dreading suddenly overcame her completely and, with it, his own attempt at self-control was destroyed. They could only cling to each other while she wept with utter abandonment and he sat trembling from head to foot. How long this nightmarish interval lasted, Paul never knew; but to his shame, Charmian was the first to recover and speak coherently again.

"Of course, I don't mean she actually thought I killed the *Duquesa*. How could I? She never saw anyone except her priest, her doctor, her nurses and her husband. But after dragging on forever, her illness came to a very sudden end. You've been told that, over and over. Can't you see that if I wouldn't become Gilbert's mistress, and the only way he could get me was to marry me, and he saw no prospect of freedom, that he might be tempted—"

"But you'd never have married a murderer!"

"No, I'm thankful you realize that. At least, I wouldn't have married a man I suspected might be one. I swear that such a suspicion never entered my head. But since I've been married—since I've realized all the atrocities of which Gilbert is capable, I've wondered . . . I haven't been able to help it. And when he refused to dismiss the *gouvernante*, I wondered more than ever. That was when I began to think, not only that he might have had—

some hand in the *Duquesa's* death, but that he knew the *gouvernante* suspected this and that he was actually afraid of her—afraid of what she might say to the doctor or even to the police. That would explain why he kept giving her more and more money, until she became so grasping and belligerent that one day he lost his temper and refused. Don't you think that's possible?"

"Yes," Paul said, swallowing hard.

"And don't you think it's possible she might believe that I was as guilty as he was, if a murder had been committed, because I'd been indirectly responsible for it?"

"Yes, I can see that, too."

"Then you must understand why she hates me and hounds me. But she hasn't anything to prove against me, as far as murder is concerned. On the other hand, she does know that I've been here to see you and that I've stayed several hours. That's why she's planning to attack me through you."

Her voice was weary now, weary with the exhaustion that goes with devastating fear. Paul tried to think of something he could say that would restore and reassure her. Before he succeeded in doing so, Charmian went on speaking with increasing evidences of exhaustion.

"I told you that Gilbert is capable of extreme cruelty. Anyone who's capable of that is capable of murder, too. I don't think for one moment that he would hesitate to kill the *gouvernante,* so that she wouldn't be a threat to his peace of mind any longer, if he could think of a way to do it without being found out. He hasn't yet. That isn't saying he won't."

"But if you're afraid he murdered his wife, he must then have thought of a way that would be hard for anyone to find out."

"Oh, that would have been simple! He knows all about poisons, just as he knows all about torture. The *Duquesa* was taking drugs to relieve her pain; the doctor was ordering them, the nurses were administering them. And the nurses weren't suspicious of Gilbert—he seemed to them like a very devoted husband, hardly leaving his wife's side. Nothing could have been easier for him than to slip a little extra laudanum into her sleeping draft, or something like that, when they were out of the room for a minute. Even if there'd been an autopsy, foul play probably wouldn't have been discovered, since the *Duquesa* was being so heavily drugged anyway. And, of course, there wasn't any autopsy."

"But you think the *gouvernante* may know something—or suspect something."

"Yes, though I've no idea what. Any more than I know how Gilbert will find out my reason for wanting her salary raised, after I wanted her discharged."

"That isn't so hard to guess. When you've made your request, he'll send for her and say he's surprised and displeased she went to his wife, after he'd refused her the increase. And then she'll say, with apparent reluctance, that she needed extra money for a special purpose and that she had reason to believe the Princess might be willing to help her, when the Prince wouldn't, because it was the sort of thing that women understand better than men. And then, still with becoming hesitation, she'd tell him what the reason was. In the end, while talking to him instead of you, she might change her tactics completely, soft-pedaling the blackmail very effectively, and laying her disclosures all to the fact that he ought to know his wife was deceiving him and should be so grateful for the information that there'd probably be a suitable reward."

"Yes, yes. I can see how it might be that way in the end. What am I to do, Paul?"

"God knows. I wish I did."

There was silence for a few minutes, while he sat miserably turning over various schemes in his mind and as miserably dismissing each one as impractical, if not wholly fantastic.

"We'll have to think of some way for you to explain your presence in this part of the rue de Rivoli," he said at last. "There must be someone in this block whom you might have gone to see besides myself, someone with whom you're acquainted, however slightly, or who could be—persuaded—to pretend knowing you."

The dark web of falsehood was closing more tightly around him all the time, but this did not cause him pain now, since in it might be the means of saving Charmian. "I'll see what I can do, and I'm convinced you ought to confide in another friend who might be more resourceful and more powerful. Perhaps Jacques d'Ambres after all—I think you're mistaken about him, I think he might understand. Possibly, Marie Louise de Chasseloup-Laubat. I'm almost sure she would. Think it over and I will, too. And there must be some way in which you and I can get in touch with each other—some way you could send for me if you're suffering more than you can bear, or if actual danger becomes imminent."

"Yes, of course there must be. I'll let you know. And I'll think over what you've said about Jacques and Marie Louise. You may be right."

She freed her hand and rose slowly. This time, she did not kiss his cheek, as she had before. But as he rose, too, and held out his arms to enfold her, she went quickly into them and remained for a long time, quiescent in his embrace. He remembered what she had said before about seeking refuge and finding sanctuary with him. The only ray of comfort which penetrated his grief and his horror and his fear was the realization that, somehow, he had given this to her.

"My action in the matter offended Bulloch intensely. We had been warm friends. I saw him but once or twice afterwards, on one of which occasions he simply—and very rightly—said, 'Well, you might have had confidence enough in me to have told me what you intended doing. Your success would have been my disgrace. I deserved better treatment at your hands.' All of which was true and he was justly offended.

"But what was to be done must be done quickly, and I had been my own master so completely for the whole war and had succeeded so completely in everything I had undertaken, that I came insensibly to run everything by my own will, taking counsel of nobody."

"My plan was simply to sail the ship to Charleston or Wilmington and I have no doubt one of two things would have happened, either we should have gone to the bottom or got there. . . . I must have arrived, if at all, in time for at least the *time* of the ending of the war to be delayed and possibly the final result would have been different. There is no denying that the *Stonewall* was a very formidable ship, and it is safe to say that her arrival in a Confederate States port would have given new life to the South and it is hardly too much to believe that under a skilful commander she would have opened the principal ports at once and even had things her own way in offensive operations.

"Had the *Stonewall* arrived at all under my command she would have been on the coast *at least* two months before she did arrive at Havana; indeed I believe she would have appeared on the coast by the middle of February."

Extracts from a letter written by Major Huse,
printed in full in Bigelow's *Retrospections of a Long Life*.

43.

The first reports of Tessier's visit to Bordeaux proved disappointing. Although the war between Prussia and Denmark was over before the one remaining ram could be launched, the Danish Minister of Marine showed no disposition to get rid of her and she was started on her way. Bulloch very logically decided that this was the end of the matter. A few weeks later, however, a caller was announced who introduced himself as Baron de Rivière and said he had the honor to inform the naval agent she was now at the disposition of the Confederacy.

The tale he had to tell was a tall one and Bulloch listened to it with more than his customary caution, for his visitor did not inspire him with confidence, even before the latter had begun to explain his extraordinary statement. According to his own flamboyantly disclosed dossier, de Rivière, a former captain in the Engineering Corps of the French Army, had lived in India, China, Mexico and Peru, not to mention Bolivia, where he owned a tin mine, and Chile, where he had been an officer in the army. Despite these many wanderings and occupations, he had kept in touch with Arman, a lifelong friend; and, chancing to be in Bordeaux shortly after the departure of the ram, he had expressed his sympathy with the Confederate Cause and offered to accompany the shipbuilder to Copenhagen for the delivery of the vessel; perhaps, between them, they could devise a scheme for getting her away from the Danes.

"I have just returned from this trip," he informed Bulloch with a flourish, "and I repeat that the ram is now at the disposal of the Confederacy."

"Then something must be the matter with her. What is it?"

De Rivière coughed and then proceeded to explain. En route to Copenhagen, the *Stoerkodder*, as she was now called, had been given a trial run, and Arman and de Rivière, acting as hosts, had invited a group of Danes to luncheon; then, while drinks were circulating, de Rivière had slipped below and opened a bilge cock, thus filling one of the compartments and greatly reducing the speed and smoothness of the vessel. Inevitably, the Danish engineers aboard soon complained that she was running badly and that it was clear she did not come up to specifications. The bargain was repudiated, the *Stoerkodder* condemned. She was now anchored at Copenhagen. There was nothing on earth to prevent the Confederate agent from authorizing her purchase and starting her on her way again under a different flag.

"Nothing except my unequivocal refusal to have anything to do with such lawless proceedings," Bulloch retorted angrily.

"You mean to say you won't do it?"

"I certainly won't. And that is my last word on the subject."

"Then let me remind you that there are others who will not hesitate to take advantage of this glorious opportunity to serve the Cause."

Having failed with the Navy, to his great and indignant surprise, de Rivière decided to try the Army, and fortuitously ran into Major Huse, the military agent, almost immediately. Huse was not inclined to dismiss the scheme quite so abruptly as Bulloch had done; after a long period of inactivity, he was chafing at the delay in proving his patriotism. Although he conscientiously objected that he had no right to embark on the "glorious adventure," that his colleague was the man to whom it should be entrusted, his scruples were quickly overcome when he learned that Bulloch categorically refused to have anything to do with it, and he hurried off to consult Slidell.

The Commissioner was finding it increasingly hard to pretend he believed the Federal campaign of 1864 had been a failure. The battle of Cedar Creek had ended in a Union victory, though at first a surprise attack by Early had seemed to promise this to the Confederates. Sheridan was devastating the Shenandoah Valley. Rumors were circulating that Sherman was preparing to leave Atlanta for a march to the sea and that he would be virtually unhindered because there was no one left to oppose him. If there had ever been a time for snatching at straws, this was one.

"I've already had a letter from Bulloch about this new scheme," Slidell said, turning to the pile of correspondence that lay on his desk and lifting a sheet from the top. "Just this morning in fact, so I haven't had time to give the matter much thought. But I take it Bulloch turned the offer down because this man de Rivière didn't inspire him with much confidence."

"I'm afraid you're putting it rather mildly, sir. I gather he hates to deal with such an unmitigated scoundrel as he believes de Rivière to be."

"And is that your opinion of him, too?"

"Well, I wouldn't put it quite that strongly. I think he's unscrupulous, but I also think he's accomplished. If he hadn't been, he never could have pulled off such a coup."

"So you might be willing to go to Copenhagen?"

"Well, of course I'm no sailor. My wife makes fun of me because I'm nearly always seasick. But I haven't had a chance to do a damn thing in this war and here it's been going on for three and a half years while I've been comfortably cooling my heels in Paris and London. If Pierson were only here to go with me—"

"Oh yes, Major John Pierson. He's a great friend of yours, isn't he?"

"Not only that, sir—he *is* a sailor. One of the best. And what he's accomplished in the way of shipping arms from Europe to the Confederacy is something phenomenal, as I don't need to tell you. If he'd take on this new job with me, I'd be almost willing to guarantee that, between us, we could make a go of it."

"But you've no idea where he is now?"

"No, sir, it's weeks since I've heard from him."

Slidell reflected for a few minutes. "Well, suppose you think the matter over for twenty-four hours. No doubt you'd also like to consult your wife. I'll think it over, too. Come back tomorrow morning and we'll compare decisions. If they're the same, as I rather think they will be, you may start for Denmark as soon as you can get ready."

"Very well, sir."

He turned from Slidell's desk and, on his way out of the office, stopped to chat briefly with each of the young men who were working at the others. The desk nearest the door was kept available for Paul, who used it only intermittently; but this morning he had come in with a special report and when Huse approached him, he was already standing.

"I couldn't help overhearing what you said, sir," he stammered. "And I feel just the same way—that I've been comfortably cooling my heels while others have been dying for our cause. I envy you the chance you've got now."

"You're sure? I thought you were the young man who felt we didn't play fair about the French ships. Or have I confused you with someone else?"

Silence had fallen on the office, as it so often seemed to do when a hum of activity could have saved Paul acute embarrassment. All the unwelcome signs of this—the flushed face, the trembling hands, the hesitant speech—were betraying his distress now. But he persevered in his answer.

"No, sir, you haven't confused me with anyone else. I still think we didn't play fair."

"Well, this latest trick is a lot dirtier than any that was played in the beginning. Or didn't you gather that much from what you overheard?"

"Yes, I did. But I'm starting to realize that Mr. Slidell was right when he said you couldn't win a war the way you win a game of chess—with all the moves aboveboard in every sense of the word."

"The realization has come a little tardily, I'd say."

"Yes, sir. I know that, too. But please let me repeat that I envy you your chance to save this last ship for the Confederacy and I'll pray your mission may be crowned with complete success."

"If I do go, you wouldn't care to come with me, would you? I could use an extra helper."

The silence had become more profound. Paul knew that if his answer were no, all his protestations of wanting to be of service would ring false, that the condescension with which the Commissioner now regarded him would lose the element of tolerance, which, so far, had saved it from becoming contempt. But if his answer were yes, the summons from Charmian, revealing her desperate need of him, might come while he was out of reach. He had not heard from her in several weeks, but the last time he had seen her, she had managed to tell him that her decision had been against taking anyone else into her confidence; therefore, he was her only hope in case of emergency. She had also told him that although the *gouvernante* had not yet carried out her threat of telling de Lixin about her visit to Paul, the evil woman had hinted that this was because, when she did talk to the Prince, it would be on more than one scandalous subject and that she was gathering evidence in regard to the second. Charmian could only conclude that her indiscretion, as far as Paul was concerned, might now be tied with much darker deeds. At this, his anxiety had mounted to such fever pitch, that he had at last persuaded her to let him send a letter to Berenice, or rather a line. He would say only, "You are greatly needed in Paris. Please come if you possibly can." And, since this message would be signed with his name, there would be nothing to connect it with Charmian if it were intercepted. The note had gone, but as yet there had been no answer to it. Until he knew that the Sheppards were in Paris, and fully informed as to the danger Charmian was facing, he would not dare to leave. . . .

He was aware of Huse still standing beside the desk, waiting for an answer. The expression on the military agent's face was faintly mocking.

"I'm sorry, sir, but I've personal responsibilities here in Paris right now," he said quietly. "My mother isn't well and she's very dependent on me."

Huse gave a short laugh and, with his hand already on the doorknob, glanced across the room at Slidell, who shrugged his shoulders. No one in the room spoke. Huse had hardly closed the door after him when Paul opened it again and went out, still surrounded by complete silence.

He was thankful for the conviction that nothing in the office required his presence there the next day and that actually nothing urgently required it elsewhere. He sat huddled before the cheerful fire in his salon, refusing the food and drink with which Louis periodically tried to tempt him, a prey to gloomy and desperate thoughts. When the early dusk of November set in, he told the servant not to turn on the gas, that he preferred to sit in the dark; and when Henri Vignaud, who was genuinely fond of him and genuinely worried about him, dropped in, it was to find that the dying coals were giving the only light in the room.

"What the devil. . . ." Vignaud exclaimed, striking a match. "Look here, Paul, don't give me another turn like that! My nerves won't stand it. When I first saw you sitting there. . . . What about dinner? Let's go to the Restaurant Foy and have a good hearty meal. I'm at loose ends this evening. I've been counting all day on a good visit with you."

"I'm sorry, I'm not in the mood for going out."

"All right then, won't you invite me to have dinner here with you? I'm practically starved, I haven't eaten a mouthful since five o'clock."

"I'm afraid I haven't much to offer you. Louis must have left and—"

"But no, Monsieur, nothing of the sort," announced Louis, suddenly appearing in the doorway. "In one small minute, I can have a meal ready for the two gentlemen—not a feast, that is well understood, but a double consommé, an omelette, steak with *frites*, a salad, Pont l'Eveque—"

"There, there! Before we know it, you'll have us gorged like Strasbourg geese, destined to become paté de foie gras. Now just build up the fire for us, like a good fellow, and bring us something in the way of an apéritif that we can be drinking while you are assembling this modest meal of yours. You don't mind me giving Louis the orders, do you, Paul? You yourself seem rather lacking in initiative and, as I've said once already, I'm starved."

"Has Huse gone to Copenhagen?" Paul asked suddenly, without even answering Vignaud's question or taking any notice of Louis' activities.

"He is going tomorrow. A most remarkable thing happened. You know he said at the office yesterday that he wouldn't hesitate to undertake the mission if only he could have Pierson with him. Well, this morning, when Huse came downstairs, there was Pierson, waiting to have breakfast with him. Just in from Texas, via Havana, with no idea that Huse had any special or immediate need of him. Merely making a social visit. So now everything's arranged and they'll be off in a cloud of dust."

"And I suppose everyone at the office is saying that, when I had a chance to prove I was something besides a chess player, I had to hide behind a woman's skirts."

"No, Paul, they're not saying anything of the kind. But they are saying—and so they should—that you aren't well, that you ought to see a doctor."

"There's nothing a doctor could do for me. I'm not sick, I'm just discouraged and depressed. If something would happen that would give me good cheer again, I'd be all right."

Vignaud refrained from saying that the trip to Copenhagen might have done exactly this, but that Paul had failed to improve the opportunity. Instead, he urged his friend to take it easy for a few days, promising to visit him frequently, so that he might be kept abreast of the news from Copenhagen and advised if there were anything that required his presence in the office or the field. He was as good as his word, and when he next made a report, he did it with a grin.

"Who do you suppose the first person was that Huse and Pierson saw when they got to Copenhagen?"

"I can't imagine. Who?"

"Bulloch. He changed his mind and decided he couldn't keep out of the game after all. Of course, he says that, on sober second thought, he realized the *Stoerkodder*, which I understand is to be rechristened the *Stonewall*, is now clear of French interference and that Danish purchasers are anxious to annul their bargain. As a matter of sober fact, I don't think he wanted the Army to get credit for something the Navy could have pulled off and didn't. You know how much jealousy there always is between the two branches of the service. I can't believe it was a matter of *personal* jealousy —Bulloch and Huse have always been good friends. But Huse and Pierson, greatly disappointed and chagrined, are back in Paris, so you wouldn't have been able to share in the great adventure, even if you had gone with them. Bulloch's taken over completely."

"At least, I might have shown my willingness to serve. . . . Who's Bulloch putting in charge?"

"Well, de Rivière's still on the scene, and our fine friend Tessier has reappeared. Then there's a newcomer, a certain Captain Thomas F. Page."

"I never heard of him."

"It seems he's kept pretty much out of sight since he's been in Europe and that he's considered especially well suited for secret service because he has that particular faculty. Also, he's one of those strong silent men—he hardly opens his mouth even when he is seen. What his other qualifications are for the job I wouldn't know. When I find out, I'll tell you. But I'm having hard work to keep up with this merry-go-round. Bulloch in and out, Huse and Pierson out almost as soon as they're in, Bulloch back again with Tessier in tow, Page rushing to join them. Do you remember telling me once that the situation then reminded you of the questions and answers, in a textbook, which didn't fit? Well, the situation now reminds me of amateur theatricals—the kind where the actors keep bumping into each other, coming and going through the exits and entrances, and still go on pretending that these encounters never took place and, also, still go on expecting the audience to do the same."

Vignaud hoped the comparison, which he felt rather apt, might bring an answering smile from Paul, but he was disappointed. Nothing seemed to cheer Paul these days and, anyway, the next report was not about progress, but about a series of complications. The Ile d'Houat, opposite Quiberon Bay, had been secretly selected as the place of rendezvous between the Danish crew, with which the *Stoerkodder* was to leave Copenhagen, and the Confederate complement for which this would be exchanged. The transfer was an exceedingly delicate proceeding, which involved the acquisition,

by Bulloch, of a steam tender to carry the ordnance and the new crew
alongside the *Stoerkodder;* and the Confederate exchequer was so low that
he was at his wit's end how to find the wherewithal to do this, until an old
blockade runner put his vessel at the agent's service. Bulloch was able to
select officers and a crew without too much difficulty, as Paris was full of
seamen who had been discharged from other Confederate ships, but getting
them out of the country was something else again, as every port was riddled
with spies; and, meanwhile, de Rivière was having considerable trouble in
his attempts to assemble a Danish crew. Some of the men he approached
had got wind of a plot and flatly refused to serve; others had to be bullied or
bribed. When—or if—the *Stoerkodder* would get out of Copenhagen was
becoming a moot question.

Before it could be answered, all Paris was talking about something entirely different, and the southern contingent, troubled as it was about the
War, had been temporarily diverted from its worries by gossip and conjec-
ture. When Vignaud appeared much earlier in the day than usual, and
asked Paul if he would like to hear a tale that had just broken, about
scandal and sudden death in high circles, he leaped to the conclusion that
the *gouvernante* had already gone with the story of her suspicions to the
police and that startling disclosures and overwhelming tragedy might be expected at any moment. He had hard work to conceal his relief when he
learned that the sudden death had been that of the American Minister who,
according to rumor, had not breathed his last at the Legation, as officially
reported, but in the apartment of the notorious Mrs. Eccles who, as the
chanteuse Sophie Bricard, had been responsible for the first informal meeting between Slidell and the Emperor. Since then, she had not only ceased
to be a singer and become a pampered lady of leisure; she had changed her
colors, allegedly because her services to the Confederacy had not been appreciated. It was true that the more conservative members of the Southern
colony had cold-shouldered her, and it was believed that their attitude had
been influenced by a warning from Benjamin to Slidell, which suggested
that they would do well to "wash their hands of her," because she was a
"young woman of dubious morals whose championship would compromise
the Cause." Her indignation at this slanderous accusation was such that
she promptly shifted her allegiance to the Federals, who did not fail to
make use of her talents for secret service, which were not as questionable
as her chastity; and among those who were admittedly much in her company was Dayton's secretary, Pennington. He had always resented the fact
that his own role as a zealous intermediary had been by-passed because
Dayton had refused to see Petermann and Bigelow had captured all the
credit for the disclosures about the ships at Nantes and Bordeaux. Now he
saw a golden opportunity to make up for this loss of face, and had been

happily improving it when a letter was brought to his Chief one evening early in December while the Daytons were at dinner. The Minister opened it and read:

"Sir:

"This is to inform you that your Secretary of Legation, Mr. Pennington, is jeopardizing your prestige and the honor of the United States by his scandalous liaison with the former Sophie Bricard, now known as Mrs. Eccles and a rebel spy. The writer knows for a fact that Pennington will be spending the evening alone with this *lady* at her apartment at the Louvre Hotel. This ought to be stopped. It is your duty, sir, to stop it.

"An outraged American."

That Mrs. Eccles had lost favor with self-respecting Southerners and the reasons for this had not failed to reach the American Minister's ears; and though rumors that his own secretary was seeing a good deal of her had also come to him, he had tried, with ostrich-like blindness, to convince himself that these visits were untinged by any special personal attraction, but were made wholly in the interests of obtaining information serviceable to the United States. Now, in a burst of righteous indignation, he decided to see for himself whether or not the charges against Pennington had any foundation in fact and, if they did, to demand that the disgraceful liaison should come to an end.

Much of the story which was running through Paris like wildfire was reasonably well authenticated. Mrs. Dayton, beside herself with shock and grief, had freely admitted the receipt of the anonymous letter; in fact, she said the Minister had passed it over to her after reading it and she had agreed with him that he must go to the Louvre Hotel at once. She saw no reason for denying any of this or for withholding general knowledge of the letter's contents. Her greatest concern was that Pennington, whom she hated, should be blamed for her husband's death, since he was indirectly responsible for it, and the letter would prove that Dayton had not gone to the Louvre Hotel because of any desire to see an infamous woman, but to rescue his secretary from one. Dayton had been seen entering the lobby by a number of persons, including a responsible concierge, who had directed him to Mrs. Eccles' apartment. An equally large number of persons had seen him leave, but there the mystery began: he was certainly unconscious when he did so and both the doctor, who had been hastily summoned, and the manager of the hotel, insisted that, though he had had some kind of a violent seizure, he was, of course, still living. They could be counted on to stick to their story, since the removal of a dead body from a hotel, without notifying the police, was a criminal offense; and their deception, if it were a deception, was certainly excusable: the scandal that would result from proof that the American Minister had died in the rooms of an adventuress would shake diplomatic circles throughout the world. The police had apparently taken this into careful consideration, for no attempt was made to contradict the official announcement that the Minister had died at his home of an apoplectic stroke. But hardly anyone believed this, partly for the reason that hardly anyone wanted to believe it. At the most aristocratic soirées, as well as in the most plebeian cafés, the main topic of conversation during the Christmas holidays was the strange case of the American Minister.

"I should never have expected scandal in that quarter," Slidell announced to his secretarial staff, whom he had invited to gather in his library for some hot buttered rum before joining a larger group assembled around the Christmas tree. "Whatever else may be said about Dayton, he seemed the soul of respectability. However, there are others whom I never would have suspected, either, and nevertheless vague rumors about clandestine visits in which *they* are involved are beginning to circulate." Paul thought the Commissioner's glance fell on him for a moment and his heart stood still. But Slidell continued without a pause and Paul decided that he had imagined the glance. "Personally, I am very sorry Dayton is dead, however and wherever he died." And, as murmurs of surprise followed this statement, Slidell went on to explain. "Dayton's removal and Pennington's disgrace will almost certainly mean that Bigelow will be made American Chargé d'Affaires. And there is nothing ingenuous or easygoing about him. It wasn't too hard keeping our movements secret from Dayton—remember he didn't even have the wit to receive Petermann. But the story's going to be a different one from now on, I can tell you. We'll be lucky if Page gets away from Copenhagen without being stopped."

To that extent the Confederacy was undoubtedly lucky and, surprisingly enough, the luck seemed to hold. The *Stoerkodder*, as she was still called, made her getaway from Copenhagen on January 6th and managed to give the slip to the *Niagara*, though this was on watch at Dover; stopped to coal at Niewe Diep and reached Quiberon Bay on the 24th of January. The English tender had already been waiting four days at the Ile d'Houat, despite delays caused by a terrific storm which had obliged her to take perilous refuge at the Cherbourg breakwater; and the transfer of crews was safely made. With a hundred and twenty-five Southern sailors aboard, the *Stoerkodder*, now rechristened the *Stonewall*, set out on her voyage of expected triumph and destruction.

The news of her escape reached Bigelow, who, as Slidell had predicted, was now the American Chargé d'Affaires, just two days later, and his protest to the French government was prompt and vehement. It appeared, however, that there was no way of giving him practical satisfaction. Bigelow pointed out that the transfer had occurred in French waters, that the *Stonewall* had been secretly coaled from a French steamer, and that intelligence of these facts had reached him indirectly through a French government official. The Minister of Marine replied that the waters in which the vessel was lying were not under government surveillance, and nothing that Bigelow could say changed his attitude or spurred him to action. Meanwhile, Slidell was receiving congratulations from many of his French friends, including more than one member of the government, upon the successful escape of the *Stonewall*, and hopes were expressed that she would arrive safely in American waters. Moreover, these expressions were actually supplemented by a letter from Chasseloup-Laubat, informing Slidell of all Bigelow's indignant representations, outlining the manner in which he proposed to deal with that functionary and revealing considerable private satisfaction over the clever getaway!

By this time, the Confederacy was admittedly in sad straits and its last hopes were centered in that one ironclad hull and its eager crew. The *Stonewall's* voyage was almost the sole topic of conversation in the Commissioner's office and, when it was learned that she had sprung a leak and had been obliged to put into Ferrol, near Coruña, anxiety about her fate was widespread and unrepressed, especially after it was learned that the *Niagara* and the *Sacramento* had also steamed into the harbor. But again the *Stonewall's* luck held. She evaded them both and slipped out into open ocean.

Paul entered wholeheartedly into the rejoicing over this. He had finally received a letter from Berenice, saying that she and her father were taking the next ship out of New York and, with this assurance and the expectation of their early arrival, his spirits rose immeasurably. They had never been higher than when the long-awaited note from Charmian finally was delivered.

"Dear Paul:

"I want very much to see you. Can you come to me this evening around ten? No one will try to stop you when you enter the pavilion, for, as you know, the servants sleep in a separate building. I shall be alone and eagerly waiting for you.

"Love, Charmian."

It was nearly nine when the note reached him, but he was fortunate in securing a fiacre immediately and this he dismissed at the great outer gate of the property. Then he walked rapidly through the silent grounds. The front and rear entrances of the château itself were lighted on the outside, but otherwise it was in darkness. This did not surprise him since he knew it was very little used for residential purposes. The lights at the doorways were obviously designed to give such illumination as was needed for easily reaching the pavilion. One or two of the dependencies also showed lights; some of these were in the upper stories, suggesting that a few of the servants had taken advantage of a night when there was no entertaining to get early to bed; others were in what he judged to be kitchens and commons. The pavilion itself was brilliantly illuminated.

At the entrance gates, the silence had seemed to him uncanny, but as he neared the dependencies, he heard voices in the servants' quarters and ceased to feel that there was anything strange. Now the stillness seemed eerie again. The sound of his footfalls as he mounted the stone steps was the only one he could hear. Involuntarily, he slackened his speed to listen for something that would change this noiselessness and make it seem more normal—the splash of a fountain, the barking of a dog, the rustle of shrubbery stirred by the breeze. But there was nothing. Only stillness which seemed to deepen minute by minute.

The door of the pavilion opened easily at his touch and, though he thought he closed it quickly behind him, a sudden gust of cold air chilled him before he could get it tightly shut. He had not realized that there was any wind—indeed, he thought the complete absence of it must account, in part, for that curious disturbing stillness. He could not explain to himself why the draft should have seemed so strong.

He called Charmian's name, at first softly, because by now he had begun to feel that any noise was out of place in these surroundings; then he spoke more forcefully and insistently. He had expected that she would come forward to meet him as soon as he entered and, when she did not, he decided that she had not heard either his arrival or his call and that he must go in search of her. The reception hall was very large, but it was sparsely furnished; he could not possibly have missed seeing her, if she had been there, nor did he see how she could have missed hearing him if she had been near by; he must search the salons. He went from one to another, still calling as he went. Everywhere was the same emptiness, the same stillness.

It had never before occurred to him that she would await his coming in her bedroom, but now it dawned on him that this was what she must be doing. The nameless fear that had been growing more and more intense as he went from one brilliantly lighted room to the next was engulfed in a sudden quickening of the senses. Of course! "I shall be alone, eagerly waiting for you." Not in a formal drawing room, where there could be no real feeling of privacy, even though no one else were present. But in a place where seclusion had its prerogatives.

He had now made a complete circuit of the salons and was back in the hall. Without hesitation, he started up the stairs. He was no longer searching, glancing this way or that for something which might have escaped him and that would give him a clue as to Charmian's whereabouts, even though she herself were not visible. He knew now that he would see her, in all her beauty, the beauty he had known and loved so long, the beauty that was still unrevealed, but upon which he was at last to gaze. He walked rapidly, his step firm, his head held high. Then, just as he reached the top of the stairs, he stumbled.

A careless servant must have left a heavy rug there, rolled in readiness to move from one apartment to another. That anything so cumbersome should block his triumphant progress would have been ridiculous if it had not been so annoying. This unwieldy bulk was out of place in a realm of romance. He tried to kick it away and found it was so heavy he could not do so. He would have to bend over and lift it to remove it. As he bent, he saw it was not a rolled rug, but a man. Then he realized that the man was Gilbert de Lixin and that he was dead.

The evil face had become no less depraved in death. The parted lips still seemed to sneer, the dull eyes to gloat with malicious pleasure; the pallid skin was scarcely more ashen than it had long looked. There was no blood on the immaculate evening clothes, no sign of struggle in the posture. The dead man lay on his back, his arms at his side, his feet encased in patent leather pumps, neatly crossed. Whatever had caused his death, it had come quickly, almost painlessly and it had not been accidental. It had been carefully planned.

Paul straightened up, the stupefaction of his first horrified recoil riddled by a dozen conflicting questions, all clamoring for an immediate answer. Who could have killed Gilbert de Lixin and by what means that would have left so little mark? Having been killed, why had the man been left, fully exposed, in a place where he would inevitably soon be found, instead of being dragged to some secret spot where the crime could be concealed? Was it Paul's duty to notify the police at once, so that a search for the criminal could begin without the delay which might very well mean failure to find him? And then, with what seemed like lightning clarity, he thought he knew the answer to all these questions. Charmian had killed her husband, because she could not endure the torment of life with him any longer and saw no other way of escape. She had found one of the poisons with which he would not have hesitated to destroy some victim of his own and had learned how to use it. She had left the body where it was so that Paul, whom she was awaiting, would see it when he came to her and would know, without asking, what had happened. And he would not notify the police, because he and she would hide the body together and it would never be found. He would now hasten to her, he would tell her he understood, that there was nothing more to fear, nothing to forgive.

He rushed through the beautiful bedrooms that he had visited on the night of the fete, knowing that this time there would not be even one closed door, that these would all be open to expedite his coming. He had been sure, before, that when he came to Charmian's he would recognize it; and, as soon as he reached one he had not seen previously, he knew that his conviction had not been without foundation, that this was her secret realm of love. The ceiling was adorned with painted cupids and in a lighted niche gleamed a marble statuette of Venus. The rug was patterned with garlands of flowers and the draperies over the windows were of rose-colored brocade. The great golden bed stood on a raised dais, like the beds of royalty, its rose-colored curtains closed. Just before he parted them, he called her name softly again. Then he saw her.

She was lying naked on bloodstained sheets, her knees drawn up convulsively, her arms pressed against her bosom, as if in a last desperate attempt at self-defense. Nothing remained of her beautiful face but a pulpy mass of battered flesh. She had been beaten to death.

A. Medina.   Mr. Paul Morphy.   F. Fésszer. F. Sicre. B. Dubouchet. G. Toscano.

DIARIO DE LA MARINA
19 Oct. 1862

A las siete en punte comenzó la primera partida, llevando
Mr. Morphy las negras y el Sr. D. Félix Sicre las blancas.
He aquí como se verificó

	Blancas Sr. D. Félix Sicre				Negras Sr. D. Pablo Morphy	
1	PK4	19	KtKKt sq	1	PK4	19	QKKt4
2	KtB3	20	QRQsq(1)	2	KtQB3	20	QKtQ2(2)
3	BQKt5	21	Q her 2	3	QRP3	21	QR her Q sq
4	BR4	22	QP4	4	KtB3	22	QBP4
5	QP3	23	KP4(3)	5	QBB4	23	QxQ(4)
6	Castle	24	RxQ	6	QKtP4	24	QBPxP
7	QBKt3	25	KRQ sq	7	QP3	25	KBPxP
8	QBP3	26	KtxKBP	8	KRP3	26	BQ4
9	QBKt3	27	QBPxP(5)	9	BxB	27	BxKt
10	PxB	28	PxP	10	Castle	28	RxR
11	QKt her Q2	29	RxR	11	QP4	29	KRB8
12	PxP	30	PK6	12	KKtxP	30	KKt 2
13	QR2	31	RQ4	13	QBK3	31	PK8
14	BxKt	32	RQ2	14	QxB	32	KtQ4
15	QKtK4	33	PK7	15	KBP4	33	KB2
16	QKtKB2	34	KRB2	16	Q her sq	34	KxP
17	QKtP3	35	se rinden	17	KKtP4		
18	KRsq			18	KKtP5		

Terminada esta partida se sirvieron helados á los consurrentes, que fueron
objeto, de las mayores atenciones por parte de los Sres. de Fésser y se
comenzó otra entre el mismo Sr. Morphy y el Sr. Toscano dando el
primero un caballo al segundo. El resultado es fácil de adivinar.

Envoi

El resultado es fácil de adivinar

May, 1865

"You are sure, Don Francisco, that sixteen thousand dollars is the outside price that the Cuban government can pay for the poor *Stonewall?*"

"I regret, Señor Belt, but I am sure. My bank has tried to make the most advantageous terms for the loan. But what can we do? The Cuban government is not too sound; we must safeguard our private clients."

Belt sighed. "That sum will hardly suffice to pay off the members of the crew. It will leave the rest of us nothing."

"Again I regret, Señor Belt. Of course, if a loan to you personally would help, you know you only have to call on me. But how can my bank make a loan to the Confederacy when that has ceased to exist as a government?"

"It can't, I realize that. And many thanks for your offer to me personally. But I can manage. I'm remaining in Cuba, in a new capacity."

"As all Cubans are happy to know."

Belt thanked him again and rose to leave. Fesser held out a detaining hand.

"Pray be seated, *amigo mio.* I hoped you would regard this visit in the light of a friendly call, as well as a business conference. That is why I asked you to come to my home instead of to my office. We will be having refreshments in a minute and there are several matters I would like to talk over with you. Perhaps I can do something for those unfortunate sailors, not as a banker, but as a humanitarian. I will try. But I confess I am puzzled about the *Stonewall.* Unless I am misinformed, she left Copenhagen the 6th of January. She successfully evaded the *Niagara* at Dover. She steamed away from the Ile d'Houat, without impediment, around the 25th of January, and finally she got past both the *Niagara* and the *Sacramento* at Coruña, where she had been delayed for some weeks because she had sprung a leak. After that, she was headed for the open seas. Why should it have taken her months to cross the Atlantic?"

"It shouldn't have. I am just as much in the dark as you are about that, Don Francisco. Why should it have been necessary for her to take on coal at ports as near together as Lisbon and Teneriffe? Why should she have stopped at the Bahamas before coming here? She could not have reached Port Royal in time to save the Confederacy; but she could have at least assuaged the agony of its death struggle by her presence."

"I do not mean to be critical . . . but surely her captain?"

Belt shook his head sadly. "That is part of the mystery. He was most skillful, as you have pointed out, at evading capture. But he never seems to have taken advantage of his good fortune, he appears to have had no sense of urgency, or even of responsibility, for reaching his destination as soon as possible. I cannot explain it, because I cannot understand it."

A white-clad servant came into the parlor with tall glasses of planter's punch and little cakes, put them down on the marble-top table at which the two men were sitting and quietly withdrew. Fesser picked up a glass and raised it as if for a toast, motioning that Belt should do the same.

"To the Lost Cause!" he said gravely. "Perhaps, as time goes on, we shall find it was not entirely lost after all. History has a way of repeating itself, and that has happened before. But now, let us speak of other things. I should like to ask you a question. As you know, we have several times been privileged to receive as our guest in Havana a very delightful and remarkable young man by the name of Paul Morphy. In fact, the last time he was here, you were one of his hosts. He was then on his way to Paris and, as far as I know, he is still there, for I assume that if he did return to the States, it would be via this route. He wrote me several interesting letters from Spain, telling me of his cordial reception there by Queen Isabella and other important personages. I also heard from him once or twice after his arrival in Paris, where he seemed very pleasantly located, though it was not quite clear to me what he was doing. Then the letters ceased. I liked him so much that I've regretted losing touch with him. So I have been hoping that you could give me news of him."

Belt set down his glass, its contents still almost untasted. "Yes," he said, "I can, but it is sad news."

"I am very sorry to hear that. Would you rather not talk about it?"

"No, I realize that you were his friend, that you and others in Havana showed him many kindnesses. It is fitting that you should know about his present condition, so that you may be prepared for it. He has not yet returned to the States, but the latest letters from Paris lead me to believe that he will soon be doing so. With his mother. It is also possible that he may be accompanied by some old friends, a Mr. Sheppard of Boston, and his daughter, Berenice, who have been of great comfort and support to him in Paris. And, as you say, his route will take him through Havana."

"You speak of his 'condition.' Do you mean that he is ill?"

"He has had a very severe nervous breakdown. So far, he shows no signs of recovery from it."

"When you say a nervous breakdown, are you trying to tell me, euphonically, that he is mentally affected?"

"I am afraid so. Not that he has become violent. If anything, he is more gentle and kindly than ever. But he has dreams and delusions. He is suspicious. He imagines that he has enemies, that attempts are being made to poison him. In fact, he dwells a great deal on poison, which perhaps is not altogether strange under the circumstances."

Belt paused for a moment. Fesser made a gesture of sympathy, but did not attempt to interrupt or hasten the narrative.

"It was a bitter disappointment to Paul that he could not take an active part in the war," Belt went on. "He was turned down for military service because of delicate health. He had hoped to become aide-de-camp to Pierre Beauregard, an old friend, but that hope was defeated. However, Benjamin thought he might be useful to us in Paris in—ah—something the same way I've served the Confederacy here. At first, it seemed as if he could. But he found it hard to reconcile his conscience with his duties. This preyed upon his mind."

"I can understand that it might cause him distress. But not to such an extent that it would affect his superb mentality. Remember that I have been a witness of this."

"Yes, I know. Perhaps, in itself, it might not have, though his incessant brooding was certainly doing him no good. But, aside from his disappointment and chagrin in connection with the war, he had personal worries. These also preyed upon his mind. Then he received a great shock, so horrible that it might unbalance any man, at least temporarily, even a man far less sensitive and high-strung than Paul Morphy."

"And the nature of this shock was—?"

"I do not know the whole story; I have only been able to piece together parts of it, bit by bit, from what I have heard through Slidell and others. But it seems that ever since he was a boy, Paul has been deeply attached to a certain young lady. She refused to marry him, on the ground that she could not accept a mere chess player for a husband."

"A *mere* chess player! The greatest in the world! A man who had been hailed as a champion on two continents!"

"I know, but she did not see it that way. Apparently, she was very ambitious, in a worldly sense. At all events, when Paul returned to Paris in sixty-three, he found her married to a nobleman of tremendous wealth, but great depravity. This man's first wife had died under suspicious circumstances. Eventually, a dissatisfied employee threatened to go to the police with evidence that he had been responsible for her death. To avoid discovery and disgrace, he poisoned himself. But not until he had killed his second wife, through jealousy, in a horrible way. Paul had received a letter, begging him to come to her rescue. Evidently, he had been expecting such a summons for a long time. It did not occur to him that the note was a forgery. As I told you, I still do not know the whole story. But when he went to the pavilion where they lived, he stumbled over the corpse of the husband on the stairs and found the mutilated body of the beloved woman in her bed."

Belt bent his head, unable to continue or to look his hearer any longer in the face. Don Francisco reached across the table and took the hand of his friend in a firm grasp. For a few minutes, neither attempted to say a word. Then the Cuban spoke, his voice charged with emotion.

"How incredibly ghastly! Yes, *amigo mio,* as you say, such an experience might well unbalance the most steady mind, the least sensitive human being. And that poor boy—the peerless champion, the incarnation of honor!"

Again there was a protracted silence, and again it was Don Francisco who spoke first. "In case I should not hear of it myself, Señor Belt, you must not fail to let me know when Paul comes through Havana with his mother. I will do everything I can to ensure their comfort while they are here. Of course this also applies to his friends, the Sheppards, if they are here. Perhaps it would be a good idea for them to stay at my house. If so, they would be more than welcome. Alas! there would be no gathering of congenial spirits as there was before. Those other great masters, Medina, Sicre, Dubouchet, Toscano, will not be with us this time. But I hope you will permit me to tell them what has happened. They, too, will wish to pay some tribute to the man whom they recognized as *their* master. I am sure they have all treasured souvenirs of him, as I have. Look, I will show you something!"

He rose, and walking over to a *bargueño* on the opposite side of the room, opened it and took from it a folder of embossed leather. Then he returned to the table and spread out its contents: a single sheet of paper bearing two neat rows of capital letters and figures.

"That is the record of the last game Morphy played in this room," he said almost reverently. "I have kept it all this time and, every now and then, I take it out and look at it and ask myself what I have done to deserve the honor of having Morphy for my guest, of seeing him achieve one of his signal triumphs in my house. I will not give you this slip of paper, Señor Belt. But I will have the record copied for you, so that you may keep it among your treasures, too."

He closed the folder and restored it to the *bargueño* with a gesture as reverent as his words had been. Then, coming back to the table, he looked down on the glasses, still almost untouched.

"We will drink together another time, *amigo mio,*" he said. "I know today, after telling me what you have, there is nothing I could offer you that would not choke you as you tried to swallow it. But there will be days to come when time, the great healer, will have done its work. Meanwhile, I will see what I can do for those poor sailors of the *Stonewall*—in tribute to Paul Morphy. I promise you that I shall not forget. Go with God."

Belt left the house and walked slowly through the garden. The perfume of the *damas de noche* followed him as he went out into the street.

"Chess is thousands of years old—among those to whom its invention has been ascribed are the Greek philosopher Aristotle, the Persian astronomer Shatrensaz, the Chinese Mandarin Han Sing, and the chaste, prudent, just, liberal and learned Zenobia. The Golden Age of the royal game began with Philidor, the French musical composer, who died in 1795, and ended with Anderssen and Morphy. Anderssen, like Morphy, was noted for beauty of combination; he was beaten in his prime by Morphy, who never did but scratch the surface of his marvelous ability. Beyond a doubt, Morphy was the most extraordinary player who ever lived; his brilliancy exhibited was unequalled. Nor can we guess what either he or Philidor might have accomplished by turning these remarkable faculties to useful pursuits. The many sidedness of genius is too well known to permit the assumption that Morphy, whose legal education was superior, could not have distinguished himself at the bar had he so willed. But it is the misfortune of genius almost always to lack perseverance."

The Daily Picayune. Friday morning, July 11th, 1884.

EPILOGUE

Shāh-Māt

July 10, 1884

It was early, so early that the light which filtered in through the closed shutters still had the softness of dawn and not the hard brilliance that would come when the sun climbed high. Nevertheless, it was already very hot, even for July. Paul threw back the linen sheet which he had pulled up to cover him when Tata brought in his coffee, though he had slept—fitfully, as usual—with nothing over him. Then he drew aside the mosquito bar and stepped out of bed.

With deliberation, rather than purposeless dallying, he went through the orderly process of shaving, bathing and dressing. His fresh linen was laid out for him, the studs already in his frilled shirt; his well-brushed coat and well-pressed trousers hung over the back of a chair; his fine cambric handkerchief and pearl-colored gloves lay side by side on his dresser. Tata was a very old woman now, just how old no one knew; she had been a child when she was bought with her mother by Le Carpentier, and no one bothered, in those days, to determine the exact age of small slaves. For that matter, not many persons bothered, even in these days, to determine the exact age of old servants. Her face had a withered look and the crisp strands of hair which escaped from under her neat tignon were as white as her apron; her body, always slight, was now skinny; but she was still strong and wiry and she still did a surprising amount of work. No upstart of a valet could have possibly ministered to Paul's tastes and needs with the foresight which she did, even if such a man had possessed the will, no less than the ability to do so; and Tata knew only too well that such will would be lacking in any newcomer to the household, which was no longer a rich one. Tata did not understand what had become of all the wealth which had once made life so easy and pleasant in the big house and which had apparently melted away into thin air. She did not try to. She only understood that she must stand by, that Miss Telcide and Miss Hélène and, above all, Mr. Paul must have the same kind of service she had always given them and which she would continue to give them, unquestioningly, as long as she lived.

Paul adjusted his monocle, picked up his gloves and his walking stick and, in the same measured, unhurried way in which he had dressed, went out of his room, down the stairs and through the hall. His mother and sister did not rise as early as he did, but he made no special effort not to disturb them; this was unnecessary, for his movements were naturally quiet. He unbolted the front door, opened it wide and stood for a moment looking about him with calm appreciation. Then he closed the door carefully behind him and stepped out into the street.

It was still relatively empty, but his favorite news vendor was already stationed at the corner of St. Louis and Royal Streets; and Paul stopped as usual, not only to buy a paper, but to pass the time of day with the man who sold it, a genial and courteous creature. The weather and other items on the front page furnished them with ample topics of conversation.

" 'The indications today for the West Gulf States are: Fair weather, variable winds, generally from the south in the southern portion; stationary temperature except in the extreme eastern portion; lower temperature.' I'd say it wasn't any lower here yet!"

"And I'd say the same, sir."

"I see there's a change of bill at the West End opera and for the better, according to the *Picayune*. *Madame Anget's Daughter* opens tonight. *Patience* continues its run at the Spanish Fort opera. I must plan to go to both."

"I hope you'll enjoy them, sir. I can't say opera's much in my line."

"Here's some alarming news—cholera has broken out in France again!"

"Yes sir, so it seems."

"The Board of Health is wise in deciding to quarantine all vessels coming from Toulon and Marseilles. As the *Picayune* says, too much care is impossible."

"I daresay it's right, sir."

"A dispatch from Chicago says the indications are that Cleveland is going to get the nomination for the Presidency. There's a lack of cohesion in the opposition."

"Well as to that, of course I wouldn't know, sir."

Paul refolded the paper which he had opened in order to scan these items and tucked it under his arm. Then he bowed ceremoniously to the news vendor, who nodded cheerfully in response, but shook his head thoughtfully, his smile fading, as he gazed after the retreating figure.

"Too bad," he muttered. "Too bad. If he wasn't so pleasant, maybe you wouldn't feel so sorry for him. But it's such a waste, a fine gentleman like that."

Paul's leisurely progress next brought him to the St. Louis Hotel. He entered it by the narrow corridor running between two shops on the Royal Street side, paused for a moment in the courtyard beyond, skirted the bar-room and vestibule on his right and paused again in the rotunda on his left, as he had done hundreds of times before, to admire the famous ceiling decorations by Canova. Then he settled down with his newspaper in the reading room, which was sparsely occupied by a few other early risers, also absorbed in the morning news. One of these glanced up from his paper, looked at Paul fixedly but surreptitiously for a moment, and shook his head in much the same sad way as the news vendor, before he resumed his reading. Two others, who were seated near each other, at some distance from the place chosen by Paul, spoke together in hushed tones.

"Do you know who that man is that just came in?"

"The dandy with the monocle and the walking stick? No, who?"

"Paul Morphy."

"You don't mean the one who used to be the world's greatest chess player?"

"The same."

"But didn't I hear that he'd had some kind of a terrible shock, that his mind was affected?"

"He did have a bad breakdown; perhaps it was caused by shock. I don't know. Whatever it was, it happened abroad. Some say he was violent for a while, that his family thought they'd have to lock him up; others say that he just had queer fancies; thought his brother-in-law was stealing from him; then that someone else was trying to poison him. Wouldn't eat anything except what his own nurse cooked for him. But that's all past and done with now. He wouldn't hurt a fly and he's got over his suspicions. He's shy, always was—and doesn't like to meet strangers. Just the same, he's always polite. And he's kindly. People like him. But they're sorry for him."

"I should think they might be. What does he do with himself?"

"Nothing much. Likes music and flowers. Goes to the opera when it's here. Visits from *loge* to *loge* during the entr'acte, sometimes invites the ladies he's known for a long time to walk with him in the foyer and have light refreshments. Takes a walk every day and stops to buy from his favorite vendors—always ones who are familiar to him; as I said, he doesn't like strangers. Comes here every day to read his paper."

"Pretty aimless, eh?"

"I'll say it is. See here, he can't possibly hear us, but I think he's guessed we're talking about him. He keeps looking at us over his paper. Maybe we'd better stop."

It was true that, as the hushed conversation continued, Paul glanced in the direction of the whisperers from time to time. It did not occur to him, at first, that they were talking about him; he only felt that they were disturbing the quiet of the reading room, where silence should have prevailed; then he decided that he was the subject of their conversation. He was tempted to show his displeasure by rising and intimating to them, in some way, that their behavior was inconsiderate. But, upon reflection, he decided he could not convey this impression without actually speaking to them; besides, he had not finished reading his paper and it was not yet time for Mass. It would disrupt his schedule if he left now.

The two men who had incurred his displeasure themselves rose, and Paul thought he heard them murmuring something about the bar, though it was surely too early in the day for that. However, they were gone; this was all that really mattered. He continued his leisurely reading undisturbed. He had just finished reading his paper when the bells of the cathedral began to ring. This was as it should be, everything in orderly sequence. Again he refolded the paper, but, this time, instead of tucking it under his arm, he tucked it in the corner of his chair, between the cushions of the upholstery. Then he left the reading room, bowing to the scattered occupants as he passed them, with the same meticulous courtesy that he had bowed to the news vendor on the corner of Royal and St. Louis Streets.

He had his favorite seat in the cathedral, and seldom failed to find it vacant; he felt almost as if it were awaiting him, on the righthand side of the center aisle, near the pulpit; from this vantage point he could not only hear the announcements without effort and sermons which he liked to follow attentively; he could also plainly see the painting above the altar, which represented St. Louis of France proclaiming the Seventh Crusade and which Paul Morphy, like his grandfather, greatly admired—perhaps because it was Joseph Le Carpentier who had first called his attention to it, when he was brought to the cathedral as a small child. As he gazed at the picture now, his grandfather, who had been dead so many years, still seemed very close to him.

He knelt and rose and crossed himself at all the proper times, and neither his attention to the sermon nor his interest in the painting prevented him from having a coin ready to drop in the long-handled pouch when the *Suisse* came by for the collection after the Credo. The *Suisse*, a glorified verger, dressed in a gay red uniform trimmed with gold braid, rather like that of a military man, had also been familiar to him ever since his childhood; at least, the present one might not be the same as the one with whom Paul had first made acquaintance forty years earlier, but he seemed the same: a gorgeous and authoritative and, at the same time, a benign figure. Mass would not have been complete if the *Suisse* had not been there to show Paul to the seat that he regarded as his anyway, and to collect the coin that he carefully extracted from his *portemonnaie* as soon as the Credo began. He did not miss his grandfather any more, because of the strong impression that the old man knelt and rose and sat beside him; but he would have missed the *Suisse* if that resplendent figure had not been visible.

The sun was blinding in its brightness when Paul went out into Jackson Square after Mass. Several persons whom he knew were standing near the doorway. They greeted him cordially, but they did not urge him to linger with them, chatting, or to go home with them for an absinthe frappé before a family dinner. He was not unconscious of a certain murmuring as he left them and turned down Chartres Street, but it did not annoy him like the whispering in the reading room; it was natural that friends and neighbors should cluster around the doorway of the cathedral for a little visit after Mass; but he had no desire to join in their chitchat any longer than courtesy required, and he felt no curiosity as to what they were saying after he left them.

It was far too hot now to sit for a time in Jackson Square, as he liked to do in more temperate weather; and he skirted the lower Pontalba building, where the protruding balconies provided some shade, while making his way toward the French Market. As he approached this, an attractive young flower girl hailed him by name and ran forward to meet him.

"*Tiens! ma gentille petite bouquetière!*" he exclaimed cordially. "*Tout va bien,* Rose?"

"*Tout va bien,*" she answered gaily, taking a flower from her basket and pinning it in the lapel of his coat. It was one of her prettiest, fresh and fragrant, but she shook her head and began to protest vehemently when he reached for his *portemonnaie.*

"We are friends," she said in rebuke.

"Yes, of course. But it should be the other way around: I should be giving you flowers."

"Not when I have them and you do not."

"Well, as you like. Will you come with me as I make purchases from those who are not as prodigal of their wares as you are?"

He offered her his arm and she accepted it. One or two passers-by who were strangers to the Market turned to stare at them, but to its habitués the sight was not only familiar but natural. Rose stayed with Paul only until he stopped for the second time, before two vendors of yard eggs and dairy products. They were a mother and son, not long since come from Gascony, and the boy, Pierre, had an understanding with Rose that, as soon as Mr. Morphy began to make his selections and chat with the old peasant woman, the young girl would slip away, unobtrusively. Paul did not notice when she left them and did not ask for her after she had gone. He was now engrossed with *fromages à la creme.*

He stopped again before the Indian squaws who sold herbs which Tata found invaluable for seasoning and lingered to address baby talk to the tawny-skinned, black-haired papooses, strapped on the backs of their mothers. Sometimes he chucked these beguiling babies under the chin and waited for an answering smile, such as he had learned to watch for in his little nephews and nieces; but the papooses stared back at him, unblinkingly and without merriment, and it was now nearly noon, zero hour for buying and selling. He would go to Tante Zizine for a cup of *café au lait* and then he would stop at Himbert's *charcuterie*, to buy a bagful of little cakes, which Edward's children expected him to bring with him when he came to dinner.

These family dinners were a source of great pleasure to him. How foolish he and Edward had both been, he reflected as he strolled along, to let the trivial question of superiority at chess cause friction between them when they were boys! How thankful he was that this question had long since been dismissed! It was years now since they had even mentioned chess, though once a week, at the very least, he dined with Edward and Alice and their children. Children! They were not children any more. The son, named for his father, was himself engaged to be married to that charming girl, Emma Merlin; the daughter, Regina, was receiving marked attentions from a young man by the name of George Voitier. But he still thought of them as children. He continued to carry the little paper bag, filled with buttery cakes—carefully to avoid soiling his gray kid gloves—from Himbert's whenever he went to dine at Edward's on Rampart Street.

He turned from Decatur Street into Barracks and passed the cross sections at Chartres, Royal, Bourbon, Dauphine and Burgundy, keeping as much as possible under the shade of the balconies all along the way. It was, undoubtedly, a very hot day. But it would be cool in the grape arbor back of Edward's house; he would sit there and rest, in his favorite rocking chair, enjoying the shade and the flowers. One by one, the others would join him there: Edward, so purposeful and genial, such a successful man, such an exemplary citizen; Alice, still as pretty, in Paul's eyes, as when she had come to play, during her childhood, in that other garden, the one back of the Royal Street house where Paul and Hélène still lived with their mother. At one time Alice and he had had differences, too; but he could not even remember now what these were about, so they could not have been very important, after all, any more than the differences about chess with Edward had been important. George and Regina, Edward Junior and Emma, all so touchingly in love, would be coming, too, and he would be glad to see them. But he hoped there would be no one else. The family circle was so harmonious, so complete, that it had no need of outsiders to complement it.

In fact, he could not help feeling that the presence of outsiders was an intrusion, and when there were guests who were strangers to him, he would find a pretext for excusing himself and go home, even though that would mean missing the excellent dinner for which Alice would have provided beforehand and the music she would provide afterward when they had left the dining room and gone into the drawing room. Alice knew all his favorite songs and sang them delightfully to her own accompaniment on the piano. But they always sounded sweeter when there were no distractions, such as were inevitably caused by strangers on the scene. Of course, his feeling about this did not apply to Charles de Maurian and Edgar Hincks. Dear Charles! There had never been a break in his friendship with Paul for more than thirty years now, never a misunderstanding, never a strain. He seemed like one of the family. As for Edgar, of course he was one of the family: the son of Aunt Emma Morphy who had married David Hincks and, therefore, Paul's own cousin. Like his father who, before the war, had been Collector of the Port of New Orleans, Edgar had held a number of important civic positions, which he filled not only competently but buoyantly. He was ruddy and robust, with a heavy black moustache, a charming smile and courtly manners. Paul appreciated his social graces; but it was Edgar's tremendous vitality, his inexhaustible heartiness, that roused the deepest admiration, because he knew those were qualities he lacked. But he was not envious. Edgar was his favorite cousin. . . .

Today, happily, no strangers were present when Paul arrived and none came later. He was especially glad because his walk had tired him, for some reason, more than usual. Merely the heat, of course, he told Alice, as he handed her the bag of little cakes and told her he thought the children would enjoy them after dinner. Of course they would, she answered pleasantly. The children had not come in yet and neither had Charles and George; but they would all be there soon. Meanwhile, Paul's chair was waiting for him. . . .

He must have dozed a little, after he was seated in the arbor, for eventually he was aware that Charles and Edgar were both there, too, and he had not heard them come in. He was conscious of hushed voices before he was conscious of any actual presence, and he opened his eyes quickly, because he did not want to be guilty of eavesdropping, however involuntary, especially as he had a feeling that his lifelong friend and his favorite cousin were discussing him, though why he should have thought so, he could not have told. He had experienced the same feeling that morning in the reading room of the St. Louis Hotel, when a man whom he vaguely recognized as someone he had known a long time before, but whose name he could not recall, and another man, who was certainly a stranger, had talked in similarly hushed voices. Now he hastened to greet the newcomers, and they responded heartily to his greeting; then they drew up chairs and seated themselves beside him. The three remained in the pleasant arbor talking of the heat and other inconsequential things until the butler came to announce dinner and they all went together into the dining room, where Edward and Alice, George and Regina, Edward Junior and Emma were awaiting them.

The dinner was bountiful and delicious and Paul, like all the others, did full justice to it, with leisurely enjoyment. Afterward, when coffee had been served in the drawing room, Alice went to the piano and began to sing the songs Paul liked best, as he had hoped she would do, and Edgar, who had a good voice, joined in some of them. When the singing was over, Regina went to the piano and played the *Paul Morphy Waltz,* which she had composed herself. She has inherited my mother's talent, Paul told himself, recalling, with nostalgia, the composition of *Lorraine;* that had been too ambitious, as well as too sentimental, and had never reached the operatic stage, as Telcide had so fondly hoped it would. Regina's gift was surer, as well as more spritely, it would not overreach itself. This waltz was already a popular success. And what a compliment Regina had paid him in naming it for him! He was really very much moved. As he sat listening to her music —his music, in a way, since it was dedicated to him!—he regarded her with great tenderness. She was not only talented, she was lovely. With her exquisite coloring, her large dark eyes, her graceful figure, she seemed the embodiment of everything that represented true Creole aristocracy at its best. He felt that he would be contented to gaze at her indefinitely. But he must have been more tired than he realized, for presently he dozed again and, when he woke, it was with the feeling that, delightful as were his present surroundings, he would like to go home and spend the rest of the day in the privacy of his own room.

"It's the heat," he said, excusing himself to Alice. "Perhaps I walked farther than usual this morning, without realizing it, though I thought I was following my regular route. Or perhaps the temperature really is higher. I'll have a nice refreshing bath, and then—"

"You'll rest first? You won't take a bath as soon as you get home, when you're overheated? Certainly not a cold bath?"

"Why no, I suppose not. Not immediately. You're right, I should rest a little first."

Charles stepped forward. "I'll walk along with you, Paul, if Alice will excuse me. I meant to ask her if she would, even before you suggested leaving. I have some unfinished work at home that needs to be done before night."

"Well, Charles, if you really meant to go anyway. You know I'm always glad of your company."

They made their adieus together and, arm in arm, as they had done so often when they were schoolboys, traversed the familiar streets. When they reached the corner of Barracks and Royal, Paul paused for a moment.

"Would you mind going one block further and walking up Chartres? I haven't been past our old home in a long while. I've a fancy I'd like to have a look at it."

"I'm afraid the look won't give you much pleasure. The place isn't what it used to be, you know. But of course, if that's what you'd enjoy doing—"

"I would, rather. I haven't been there since Pierre lived there, as a lodger, for two years after the war. I went to see him then and he looked unbelievably old and forlorn. It was very sad. He'd been so happy there with Caroline, just after they were married. They'd planned a very gala party. Of course, they never had it. And then he was so alone, after she died. If the woman you love dies, there isn't much left to live for, is there?"

"There are always memories."

A look of pain appeared on Paul's tranquil face and he shook his head. "Sometimes those are corroded," he said sorrowfully. Then almost instantly, he brightened. "But Pierre still had one more day of glory, when he reviewed the remnants of the Louisiana troops from the front gallery. I'm glad I saw that. It was a glorious sight. And, of course, since then, he's retrieved his fortunes, too."

"And lost his good name!"

"Oh no, Charles, don't say that! You can't lose a name like Beauregard just through association with a lottery. And he was desperately poor when Howard approached him. You know that."

"I know you would have starved to death before you'd have stooped to anything dishonorable."

"But it wasn't dishonorable. Only—only—" He groped for the right word and failed to find it. "And you don't know everything I've done, Charles. Sometimes I think perhaps I ought to tell you."

"All right, tell me anything you want to, *cher*. But not now, not before we can get out of this blasted heat. Are you sure that you want to go up Chartres, that you wouldn't prefer to go straight home?"

"No, no, I want to see the old place."

It was as Charles had feared; the sight of his grandfather's house was depressing to Paul—indeed, it would have been depressing to almost anyone who had known it in its days of grandeur. It had now changed hands several times and the corner lot had been sold off separately. Two nondescript buildings stood on the site of Le Carpentier's jungle and Aloïse Merle's formal garden; light and air were entirely shut off from all the uptown side of the fine old mansion. Its paint was peeling, one of its shutters was askew, a pane was missing from an upper window and grass was growing up between the paving stones of the banquette in front of it. Paul kept shaking his head as he stood looking at it. Charles gently took his arm.

"Come, Paul, let's go home. It's too hot for us to keep standing out here in the sun."

"Yes, I suppose it is."

He suffered himself to be led away. He would have been glad of Charles' company a little longer and, as they went along, kept asking him if he remembered this and that. But, mindful that his friend had spoken of un-finished work, Paul forbore inviting him to come in for a little visit when they reached 89 Royal Street; it would not be considerate to delay Charles under these circumstances. Moreover, still another reason prompted his fore-bearance: he really wanted very much to be alone, to take that refreshing bath, to get into that cool shrouded bed.

His room, arranged in exact accordance with his erstwhile tastes and wishes, had remained unchanged for many years; now, suddenly, it dis-pleased him. Why that open chessboard, its men set up in readiness for a game, a chair drawn up to the center table at which it stood? From force of habit, he had left it there, never using it, never intending to use it. With a quick movement of impatience, he walked over to it and upset it. The chessboard tilted with the table, fell to the floor and collapsed. The chess-men scattered in every direction. Briefly Paul stood looking at them. Then he shrugged his shoulders and, without making any effort to restore the order he had disrupted, began to take off his clothes. It was only a matter of min-utes before he was luxuriating in his refreshing bath.

REQUIEM

THE FUNERAL OF PAUL MORPHY

The remains of the marvelous genius laid in the ancestral tomb in St. Louis Cemetery—contemporary comment on his chess career.

The obsequies of Paul Morphy were very simple and very quiet. His relations and his devoted friends were around him. The news of his death had been as sudden as his demise, and the notice of the funeral so short that his admirers could not prepare the elegant tribute they would have done. But it was neither the wish of Morphy nor his family that the ceremonies should have been grander than they were. He had abjured the chess world long ago and he desired no recognition as the famed champion of the world, after he had surrendered the title unchallenged by his retirement. Morphy desired to be known only as a man and a Christian, and those with whom he was intimate knew that even in his years of eccentricity he was still a knight of courtesy and a man of heart. It was the funeral of the man and not of the great chess player.

Father Mignot officiated at the house and the grave. The body was exposed at Morphy's modest residence, 89 Royal Street. Numerous floral offerings betokened the affection in which he was held. At five o'clock the coffin was carried down by Edward Morphy, Edmund Morphy, Léonce Percy, Henry Percy, Edgar Hincks and Charles de Maurian, his lifelong companion and former adversary over the chessboard. The hearse, followed by a few carriages, drove to the old St. Louis cemetery. The tomb of the Morphys' was opened and Paul's body placed beside that of his father, a well-known figure in the history of Louisiana.

The Daily Picayune. Saturday morning, July 12th, 1884.

AUTHOR'S NOTE

"Quel livre biographie à ecrire pour un Louisianais, pour un Créole! Pour un Créole surtout, car Paul Morphy était un des nôtres."

The above statement, quoted from an article written by a lifelong friend of the Morphy family, Placide Canonge, which appeared in the New Orleans *l'Abeille* at the time of Paul's death, expresses a sentiment which I have long held myself: that a full-sized biography of Paul Morphy should be written and that its author should be a Creole. The book by Philip W. Sergeant, entitled *Morphy Gleanings*, is excellent as far as it goes, but it is confined to the highlights; and the one by Frederick Edge, entitled *The Triumphs of Paul Morphy*, is devoted entirely to his hero's exploits at the chess table in England and France during 1858 and 1859 and to his social successes during the same period. His niece, Regina Morphy-Voitier, has presented *The Life of Paul Morphy: In the Vieux Carré of New Orleans and Abroad* movingly and accurately, but she has confined herself to a pamphlet. Brief sketches of his life, with records of his most famous games, appear of course in every book relating to the history or theory of chess; and *The Torch on the Hill: The Centenary Story of Spring Hill College* by Michael Kenney devotes an entire chapter and various incidental references to the scholastic career of its most famous graduate. He has also been the subject of many learned analyses, of chapter length or more, written from the psychological rather than the biographical or scholastic angle. Contemporary newspapers devoted columns to his achievements in New Orleans, New York, Boston, Havana, London and Paris; and shortly after his death his mother's close associate, Léona Queyrouze, wrote a long résumé of his rise and fall under the title of *Premier et Dernier Jours de Paul Morphy*, which was duly translated and offered to various periodicals, none of which was sufficiently perceptive to use it. A few family letters—very few, alas!— together with some from his great friend, Charles de Maurian, have escaped destruction. But to the best of my knowledge, a full-length biography has never been written.

Though this is lamentable, it is also understandable. Paul Morphy lived forty-seven years; his triumphs were crowded into a twelve-year period, beginning when he was only ten years old and ending shortly after he had reached his majority. To write, factually, about this part of his life would be a delight to any biographer; to cover the remainder of it, sympathetically yet accurately, would not only tax his powers to the utmost, but inevitably give him the feeling that the latter part of his book had been anti-climatic.

Besides, if he were a Creole, his natural reserve in regard to family mis-
fortunes—a quality even more inherent among Orleanians than among most
people who share their other attributes of sensitivity and refinement—would
make this task difficult, if not actually repulsive.

Nevertheless, the fame of Paul Morphy should not be permitted to die.
The logical answer to the question, "How can this be prevented, in the
absence of a definitive biography?" seems to be, "Through a thoughtful and
comprehensive novel, the work of a writer who will make use of all known
facts about the protagonist, and who, when straying into the field of fiction,
will try to correlate the real with the imaginary in such a way that the
connection between the two will seem not only possible but plausible." For
example: we know that Paul Morphy went abroad for the second time in
1862 and that he did not return until 1865. We know the route he took,
even the names of the ships he took. We do not know what he actually
did while he was there, as in the case of his previous sojourn; but we do
know that he had previously been to Richmond, that Benjamin, Beauregard and Slidell were all family friends and that Benjamin had married one
of his cousins. The occupation assigned to him during this period seemed
not only logical but inescapable to me, when I decided to undertake the
creation of the type of novel I have tried to describe. We also know that,
before leaving Paris in 1865, Paul Morphy suffered some sort of a severe
shock which resulted in a nervous breakdown. We have no idea what it
was; again, imagination must enter the picture, but imagination properly
controlled.

In only one instance have I deliberately departed from the known truth,
and that after giving the matter careful and prayerful thought and taking
counsel with advisers whose judgment I respect: this is in regard to Paul
Morphy's love affair. The reason he was refused for a husband by the great
love of his life is a matter of well-authenticated record and this reason is
voiced by my imaginary heroine. *It is the only thing about her that is real.*
I believe I know who the object of his affection actually was; at all events, I
know the family, in which she may have been one of several sisters or
cousins, descendants of whom are still living. I could see no useful purpose
in violating Creole reserve by making factual use of this episode, since it
was possible to achieve equally satisfactory results by doing so fictitiously.

Aside from Charmian Sheppard and her family, the only imaginary
characters in the book—except for a few incidental ones who are mentioned
only once or twice—are the Marquis d'Ambres, the Prince de Lixin, the
gouvernante in the latter's establishment, and the Countess de Bonamour.
The beautiful house described as the *hotel particulier* of the Marquis
d'Ambres is now actually the residence of Maitre Tenger, one of the leading lawyers of Paris, and his family. The earlier part of its history, as given

in the novel is authentic; the latter part has been changed with his permission, and it is also with his permission that it is so fully described. I am indebted to my French publisher, Sven Nielsen, for my introduction to this house and its owner; and I am also indebted to M. Nielsen and several members of his staff, especially M. Georges Roditi, for help in authenticating various details of the Paris scene between 1858 and 1865, not only through correspondence, but also through drawings, photographs and books.

In listing others who have given me invaluable assistance, I hardly know where to begin or end, since so many have been not only so generous with their help, but have shown such perception of my needs and such genuine interest in trying to meet these. Since however, I must start somewhere, I will do so with Harold Leisure, co-owner and manager with his wife of the Plantation Book Shop in New Orleans. It has long been my habit to let the Leisures know my requirements for source material, of which they always have a large and varied supply among their old books; and one day Mr. Leisure appeared in my patio with two volumes for me among those in the little cart which he trundles about the Quarter in serving his customers. "You have said you needed more information about John Slidell than you had in your own library or could find elsewhere," he said rather diffidently. "You might discover a paragraph here and there which would interest you. I will leave the books with you and you can look them over. If you decide you want them, that will be fine by me. If you decide you do not, that will be all right, too."

One of the books was *John Slidell* by Louis Martin Sears, the other, *John Slidell*, by Beckles Willson. I found the first to be a good general biography, but the second a veritable treasure trove, as far as Slidell's activities while serving as Confederate Commissioner in Paris was concerned. I do not know whether I should be more grateful to Mr. Leisure, for bringing this book to my attention or to G. P. Putnam's Sons who have taken over the firm of Minton, Balch and Company, which originally published it, for permission to quote freely from it. Without it, I never would have known much that happened abroad during the War Between the States, especially in regard to naval operations, for this phase of Confederate activities has been curiously overlooked, to a very great degree, by biographers, historians and novelists alike. With the Willson book as a guide and the basis, I have been able to carry my investigations much further afield.

Next on my list I think should come Miss Muna Lee, Chief of the North and West Coast Section of the Public Affairs Staff of the Bureau of Inter-American Affairs in the Department of State. It was she who first acquainted me with the activities in Havana of John Benjamin Belt, with which I had hitherto been unfamiliar. It was also she who called my attention to the fact that Henri Vignaud, who is mentioned in the Willson book only briefly and incidentally, himself played an important role on the Paris scene. Both Slidell and Vignaud remained in Paris after the war; but though Slidell's activities came to an end with the Confederacy—and with his destruction of all papers relating to the work of the hundred secret service agents whom he employed!—Vignaud's subsequent career was distinguished along other lines. In 1869 he was appointed to a secretaryship in the Roumanian Legation at Paris and in 1872 he served as translator for the United States in the presentation of the Alabama claims for the Geneva arbitration. In 1875, he was appointed Second Secretary for the United States Legation in Paris, being promoted to First Secretary in 1885. He acted as umpire in the arbitration of 1905 of French claims against Haiti. After thirty-four years of service with the Paris mission, he resigned in 1909, at the age of 78, but was appointed honorary counselor. The French government promoted him to the rank of Grand Officer in the Legion of Honor and Tulane University conferred upon him the degree of LL.D.

Of equal importance and scope has been the assistance given me by Mario Mamalakis, an Associate Professor at the University of Southwestern Louisiana. It was she who unearthed the letter from Beluche, lieutenant to the notorious Lafitte, from the archives of the university, with its significant reference to Le Carpentier. The discovery of the letter in question enabled me to create a situation with which I would otherwise have been incapable of dealing. This is only one of the many items of major importance which Miss Mamalakis made available to me; in addition, she has helped authenticate various points, about which, without her assistance, I should have been left in doubt.

Samuel Wilson, Jr., the eminent architect, who is also an authority on almost everything pertaining to the history of New Orleans, past and present, disagrees with all Morphy's biographers—at least all whose books I have read and my survey has been thorough—and also with all Le Carpentier and Morphy family papers I have seen regarding Paul Morphy's birthplace. However, Mr. Wilson has leniently agreed that, for fictional purposes, I was justified in using the generally accepted opinion in regard to this, and has been most co-operative in loaning me drawings and notes taken from his files. Moreover, it was he who discovered and made available to me the Diego Morphy Commission, the Deed of Sale for the Le Carpentier property on Bourbon Street and the Inventory of Alonzo Morphy's will, which I have used on flyleaves.

Frederick J. Way, Jr., of Sewickley, Pennsylvania, Editor of *The Inland River Record*, and Leonard Huber of New Orleans are both authorities on travel by inland waterways, past and present; both have written valuable books on the subject and both are in possession of fine collections of drawings, documents, etc., relating to this; in addition, Mr. Huber is an authority on practically all phases of the Federal Occupation of New Orleans during the War Between the States and has freely put this material at my disposal. Both these gentlemen have been helpful to me in many ways. The drawing of the *Diana* and the *Baltic,* used on the flyleaf preceding Chapter 18 was made possible through the co-operation of Mr. Way; the reproduction of the Federal Order for Confiscation of Property which precedes Chapter 31 through the co-operation of Mr. Huber.

I would have said beforehand that I could not possibly write a novel that had any part of the War Between the States as its mise en scène without the wise counsel and generous co-operation of that peerless historian, Douglas Southall Freeman. However, Clifford Dowdey and Hamilton Basso, whose talents as novelists are equaled by their talents as historians; Dr. T. Harry Williams of Louisiana State University, who has written the definitive life of Beauregard which is lacking in the case of Morphy; and Hudson Strode, whose trilogy on Jefferson Davis has put him in the foremost ranks of biographical and historical chroniclers, have all come so valiantly to my rescue that Freeman himself would have applauded them.

I am also indebted to Eleanor Carroll Brunner for helpful editorial advice and encouragement to make the most of the French ships, to Luis Bolin, Press Counselor of the Spanish Embassy, for help with Spanish and Cuban reference material, and to the Reverend Patrick Donnelly, S.J., a former President of Spring Hill College, and now President of Loyola University in New Orleans, for help with reference material in connection with the former. To Sidney L. Villere and J. Henry Blache of New Orleans and Armand Beauregard of St. Louis and R. T. Beauregard of Houston for genealogical assistance. To Elizabeth Doyle of Wheeling College, the Reverend Vincent Liberto, O.M.I., Harnett T. Kane, John St. Paul, Jr., and Thomas Buckley of New Orleans, Henry W. Keyes of Boston, Mrs. E. B. Peebles of Mobile and Miss Peggy Slade of London for help with various historical details. To Señora Berta Becerra, Director of the Sociedad Economica de Amigos del Pais of Havana, for help in assembling articles appearing in the Cuban press at the time of Paul Morphy's various visits to that city; to John Hall Jacobs, Director of the New Orleans Public Library and Libby Buchanan, one of his able assistants; and Mrs. Rosa M. Oliver, Librarian of the Louisiana State Museum Library; and Robert J. Zeitz, Assistant Librarian at Spring Hill College for general help with research.

All the members of my domestic staff, both in New Orleans and Newbury, deserve their tribute of praise because of their tolerance with irregular meals, conflicting directions, or lack of any, and—I am afraid—occasional shortness of temper during the long grind of creation and especially during that "last hard mile" before meeting a deadline; among these are Edith Hill,

Leona Pfister and Myrle Welch. As for my secretaries, Geraldine Bullock and Veronica Hornblower, it is no exaggeration to say that the long grind would have resulted in complete collapse, and that the last hard mile never would have been covered on contract time, without their loyal, efficient and devoted co-operation.—FPK.

The Oxbow
Newbury, Vermont

Bibliography

Paul Morphy and the Golden Age of Chess by William Ewart Napier. Edited
    by I. A. Horowitz (David McKay Company, Inc.)

Morphy's Match Games: Being a full and accurate account of his most Astound-
    ing Successes Abroad, defeating, in almost every instance, the Chess
    Celebrities of Europe. Edited, with copious and valuable notes, by Charles
    Henry Stanley (Robert M. De Witt, Publisher)

Morphy's Games of Chess compiled by Philip W. Sergeant (G. Bell & Sons Ltd.)

Morphy Gleanings by Philip W. Sergeant (David McKay Company, Inc.)

The Exploits and Triumphs in Europe of Paul Morphy by Paul Morphy's Late
    Secretary (D. Appleton & Company)

Life of Paul Morphy in the Vieux Carré of New Orleans and Abroad by Mrs.
    Regina Morphy-Voitier (Privately printed)

"First and Last Days of Paul Morphy" by Léona Queyrouze. (Unpublished
    manuscript)

Paul Morphy: Sein Leben und Schaffen by Dr. Max Lange. (Verlag von Veit
    & Comp. Leipzig)

The Chess Reader: The Royal Game in World Literature compiled by Jerome
    Salzmann (Greenberg: Publisher)

The Human Side of Chess: The Story of the World Champions: their Tri-
    umphs and their Illusions, their Achievements and their Failures by Fred
    Reinfeld. (Faber and Faber Ltd.)

Chess Secrets I Learned from the Masters by Edward Lasker (David McKay
    Company, Inc.)

The Adventure of Chess by Edward Lasker (Doubleday & Company, Inc.)

The Book of the First American Chess Congress by Daniel Willard Fiske,
    M.A. (Rudd & Carleton)

The Chess Monthly, Volume III, 1859, edited by Paul Morphy & Daniel W.
    Fiske (Wm. C. Miller)

Duelling in Old New Orleans by Stuart O. Landry (Harmanson)

Gentlemen, Swords and Pistols by Harnett T. Kane (William Morrow & Co.)

The Golden Age of the New Orleans Theater by John S. Kendall (Louisiana
    State University Press)

Fabulous New Orleans by Lyle Saxon (Appleton Century)

The Ursulines in New Orleans, 1727–1925. Anonymous. (P. J. Kenedy &
    Sons)

New Orleans: The Glamour Period 1800–1840 by Albert E. Fossier, M.A.,
    M.D. (Pelican Press)

New Orleans: Its Old Houses, Shops and Public Buildings by Nathaniel Cort-
    landt Curtis (J. B. Lippincott Co.)

New Orleans: The Place and the People by Grace King (The Macmillan Co.)

New Orleans Holiday by Eleanor Early (Rinehart & Co.)

Queen New Orleans: City by the River by Harnett T. Kane (William Morrow
    & Co.)

The Romantic New Orleanians by Robert Tallant (Dutton)

Voodoo in New Orleans by Robert Tallant (The Macmillan Co.)

It's an Old New Orleans Custom by Louisa Robinson (Vanguard Press)

New Orleans by Laughlin & Cohn (Houghton Mifflin Co.)

The Mistick Krewe by Perry Young (Carnival Press, New Orleans)

Crayon Reproductions of Léon J. Frémaux's New Orleans Characters and Additional Sketches by Léon H. Grandjean. (Produced by Alfred F. Bayhi, New Orleans, 1949)

Old Creole Families by Grace King (The Macmillan Co.)

The Creole Aristocracy by M. H. Herrin (Exposition Press)

Old Plantation Homes and Family Trees by Herman Seebold (Pelican Press)

Plantation Parade by Harnett T. Kane (William Morrow & Co.)

Deep Delta Country by Harnett T. Kane (Duell, Sloan & Pearce)

Louisiana Gallery by Philip Kappel (G. P. Putnam's Sons)

Louisiana: A Guide to the State Compiled by Workers of the Writers' Program of the Work Projects Administration in the State of Louisiana (Hastings House)

Brave Mardi Gras by W. Adolphe Roberts (The Bobbs-Merrill Co.)

Royal Street by W. Adolphe Roberts (The Bobbs-Merrill Co.)

Beloved by Viña Delmar (Harcourt, Brace & Co.)

Steamboat Gothic by Frances Parkinson Keyes (Julian Messner, Inc.)

John Slidell and the Confederates in Paris (1862–65) by Beckles Willson (G. P. Putnam's Sons)

John Slidell by Louis Martin Sears (Duke University Press)

Lee's Lieutenants by Douglas Southall Freeman (Charles Scribner's Sons)

Beauregard the Great Creole by Hamilton Basso (Charles Scribner's Sons)

P. G. T. Beauregard, Napoleon in Gray by T. Harry Williams (Louisiana State University Press)

Jefferson Davis: Confederate President by Hudson Strode (Harcourt, Brace & Co.)

Dictionary of American Biography Edited by Dumas Malone, Volume XIX (Charles Scribner's Sons)

Secret Missions of the Civil War by Philip Van Doren Stern (Rand McNally & Co.)

General Butler in New Orleans by James Parton (Tichnor & Fields, Boston, 1866)

New Orleans Under General Butler by Howard Palmer Johnson, quoted in Volume 24, No. 2, April 1941 of the Louisiana *Historical Quarterly*

Butler Correspondence (I. 569–570) Butler to Stanton. New Orleans, June 10, 1862. From the Louisiana *Historical Quarterly*, Vol. 24.

Battles and Leaders of the Civil War, edited by Roy F. Nichols (4 vols.), 1957. (Thomas Yoseloff, Inc.)

The Torch on the Hill: Centenary Story of Spring Hill College by Michael Kenney, S. J., Ph.D., Litt.D. (The America Press)

Spring Hill College 1830–1905 (Press of Commercial Printing Company)

Spring Hill Alumnus News Letter, January, 1951.

New Orleans Daily Crescent, January 28, 1861.

The Times-Picayune New Orleans States Magazine, February 27, 1949.

Times Democrat, July 11, 1884.

The Daily Picayune, July 12, 1884.

Mobile Register, June 1, 1955.

Boston Evening Transcript, June 1, 1859.

Prensa de la Habana, October 18, 25 and 26, 1862; February 16, 1864.

Diario de la Marina, October 18, 19, November 1, 1862.

El Siglo, October 16 and 27, 1862; February 16, 1864.

Gaceta de la Habana, October 16, 1862.

El Tiempo, February 18, 1864.

Passenger Liners of the Western Ocean—A Record of the North Atlantic Steam and Motor Passenger Vessels from 1838 to the Present Day by Commander (S) C. R. Vernon Gibbs Royal Navy (Retired) (Staples Press Ltd.)

A Second Visit to the United States of North America, Volume II, by Sir Charles Lyell, F. R. S. (John Murray, Albemarle St., London, 1855)

The Story of the Nations: Modern Spain (1788–1898) by Martin A. S. Hume (G. P. Putnam's Sons)

Spain—A Short History of Its Politics, Literature, and Art from Earliest Times to the Present by Henry Dwight Sedgwick (Little, Brown and Company)

Essays in Applied Psychoanalysis by Ernest Jones, M.D., F.R.C.P. (The Hogarth Press Ltd., London)

La Princesse Mathilde by Marguerite Castillon du Perron (Amiot-Dumont, Paris)

Le Grand Siècle de Paris by André Castelot (Amiot-Dumont, Paris)

En Remontant Les Grands Boulevards by Jacques Castelnau (Le Livre Contemporain)

Etudes de l'Homme Physique et Moral, Considere dans ses Difference Ages by J. A. Perreau, Professeur suppl. au college de France, du droit de la nature et des gens (l'Imprimerie des Annales d'Agriculture)

Private letters of and to Charles de Maurian, Telcide Le Carpentier Morphy, etc. Archives, St. Louis Cathedral, New Orleans